Review Comments about *Beyond the 1*

"This book is about love, acceptance, and endurance. A great sequel!!"

Reviewed by Philip Zozzaro *San Francisco Review of Books*

"Li Bo's newest work is as compelling (if not more so) as his first, and will be enjoyed by lovers of both history and fiction." J. Chandler, Amazon reader review

Review comments about *Tienkuo: The Heavenly Kingdom* (vol. 1 of Li Bo's Sino-American Tales)

"I'm having a blast reading Tien Kuo. It is fascinating and well written." Ray Lum, former Asian Bibliographer and Librarian for Western Languages at Harvard-Yenching Library

"Exciting Book...I like it very much. The characters are believable and the cultural details about customs accurate." Dr. Alice Murong Pu Lin, author of Grandmother Had No Name

"I enjoyed the novel immensely–it's a fun and exciting read." John Rapp, Beloit College

"A rare treat. An engaging and historically accurate way to introduce young adults to a myriad of topics about China, including family, Confucianism, class differences, women's roles etc." Mel Horowitz, Former President, U.S. China People's Friendship Association.

"I was swept away with the compelling and engaging story. I was captivated with this adventure from beginning to end. To add to my delight, I came away realizing that I had been given insight into an historical event, so not only was I richly entertained, but I was cleverly educated as well." Donald Samson author of *Dragon Boy* & *The Dragon of Two Hearts*

"Masterfully interweaving history, culture, and characters, *TIENKUO* takes readers on a fascinating journey through 19th century China. *TIENKUO* gives us a delicious taste of a little known time and place and makes history come to life." Edward Tick Author of *The Practice of Dream Healing*

*Tienkuo: the Heavenly Kingdom* is a coming-of-age tale ensnared in history. The second Opium war & the nineteenth century Chinese Civil War are the backdrop for many of the goings-on in this story. The characters are well drawn and their travails are engaging. The adventure converges with the drama and burgeoning love story. A book offering great promise for its sequel. "A" all the way!

Reviewed By: Philip Zozzaro, *San Francisco Review of Books*

# CHAPTER 1
# TIANJIN, CHINA, 1870

Jason Brandt was exhausted. He'd been looking down at his semiconscious and extraordinarily beautiful Chinese wife for hours. And she certainly was beautiful despite the bandages that covered the deep gash on the right side of her head, a blow from one of the Tianjin rioters who'd killed so many more in the attack on the Sisters of Mercy orphanage.

Jason knew his wife, Black Jade, was terribly lucky. She'd lived, carried away from the massacre by one of the attackers, a member of the local gentry who recognized her as the wife of the Western reporter who'd interviewed his father a week before. Jason, only in Tianjin for a short while researching a story for his paper understood he would never know why Black Jade had been spared. He only knew that the young man had furtively carried her away knowing she was merely a guest as her husband had been at his father's own home.

What he did appreciate was that after days of sitting at her bedside in their temporary lodgings watching various physicians—Chinese and Western—come and go, she'd only minutes before momentarily regained consciousness. Then with a weakened and parched throat, she'd asked about little William and his big sister Mei-ling. Then, after a few sips of water, she'd fallen back asleep again. Still, there was more than that. She'd said she wanted to go home, to Shanghai, then just before sleep fully claimed her, she'd corrected herself.

"Back to Shanghai...yes, I'd like that...or maybe even to America. William is half American and he should know your country as well."

Incredibly relieved she was on the mend, that he had not lost her again; Jason sat thinking about her words. Did she really mean she wanted to leave China? Was she suggesting the family travel to America, a land even Jason, who'd been born there, had no memory of?

As he thought about her words, and what they would mean, he continued to stare down at her, taking pleasure with each of her now-less-labored breaths. Would she even remember the comment when she awoke. As he watched her, he felt as well the power of her suggestion and how easily it had pushed him back to that long night so many years before when, as a sixteen-year-old, he'd struck out in the middle of the night from his father Reverend Brandt's home. He still remembered that night as if it had been yesterday, remembering how convinced he was—as convinced as only a sixteen-year-old can be—that unless he fled his father's home, the aging missionary would send him home to America, away from Hong Kong and the only life he'd ever known.

So much had happened since that night, and once begun the memories flooded back, memories of his work with the Sino-foreign contingents who occupied Guangzhou during the Second Opium War. And of course of his friendship with Wu, the failed Confucian exam scholar who'd become his companion as they traveled into the interior of China searching for the famed Taiping Kingdom. Then actually arriving at the Heavenly Kingdom of Great Peace, that famous community based at Nanjing, led by the Taiping Wang, a man who astoundingly claimed to be the little brother of Jesus Christ.

Still, what he recalled most was the night he and Wu had come upon the unconscious Black Jade, unconscious as now, lying alongside a river having apparently failed in an effort to kill herself. Jason did not remember if he had fallen in love with her that evening or perhaps somewhat later. All he knew, was that thoughts of her soon invaded his consciousness, never to leave him literally from that night to the present, now in the midsummer of 1870. Had it really been twelve years since he'd fled his father's home, twelve years in which he'd become a professional journalist, husband, and father? It felt as if it had all gone by so quickly, their eventual marriage and building a life for themselves in Shanghai. Now she was asking, or it seemed perhaps, to give everything up and travel to America.

Still he sat there and wondered to himself if they would argue about it. Would she insist on their leaving China? Jason wondered as well if he genuinely opposed the idea. Certainly as a sixteen-year-old he'd argued with his father that China and not America was his home - that he absolutely refused to return, as his father had insisted - to the United States to go to college, someplace in Ohio he vaguely remembered. Of course, that was when he was a teenager. The more he thought of it, the more he speculated that perhaps it might be doable. He might not know the Boston area, but surely, some of his writings had become known in the United States. Certainly, there was enough interest in the China trade and his father was still alive. In fact, the older man had written often enough for Jason to know his father had even passed around copies of Jason's newspaper pieces to his friends in Boston.

For a moment, Black Jade distracted him. She'd suddenly moved, shifting her weight, but as she did so, he noticed with pleasure that her movements were those of a sleeper and not the unconscious and deathly ill woman he'd sat alongside for days. No, clearly life was returning to normal. At least as normal as it could be in the rented and drab quarters they'd occupied since decamping from their Shanghai home so many weeks before. In the background, he could even hear Zhu lao T'ai t'ai playing with the children somewhere not too far off. He'd doubted they were actually outside. Since the attack against the orphanage, there was still too much tension in the city. Besides Old Zhu, her Shanghai prejudices ever so often on display had made it clear she did not trust the local Chinese. Yes, life was indeed returning to normal.

Contemplating the situation, his eyes darted around the room, turning from the sleeping Black Jade to the bedside table and the package he'd received from his father. How many days had it been? He recalled opening it, but that was just before he'd left for Beijing and, of course, the riot he'd encountered as he rode back into Tianjin. How many days before had that been? Jason did not remember. Now curious he walked over to the half-opened package, picked it up, and returned to his seat beside his sleeping wife. It was a book—that much he'd remembered, but now he studied it.

*The Innocents Abroad*
Or
*The New Pilgrims Progress*
BEING SOME ACCOUNT OF THE STEAMSHIP QUAKER CITY'S PLEASURE EXCURSION TO EUROPE AND THE HOLY LAND; WITH DESCRIP-

TIONS OF COUNTRIES, NATIONS, INCIDENTS, AND ADVENTURES, AS THEY APPEARED TO THE AUTHOR
WITH TWO HUNDRED AND THIRTY-FOUR ILLUSTRATIONS
By Mark Twain,
(Samuel L. Clemens)
Hartford, Conn.:
American Publishing Company

Then putting the book aside, he picked up the letter from his father that he'd only glanced at a fortnight earlier when it had arrived just as he'd departed for his business in the capital.

Dear Son:

I hope this letter finds you well. Thank you very much for the photographs you sent of your family. The children seem healthy, and your wife is as beautiful as I remember your mother to have been. There is little to report here. I've left Boston for less expensive lodgings near your mother's relatives in Salem. As expected, I have not been able to find a permanent posting with a local congregation. On the other hand, I have been earning my keep giving talks and raising money for Christian missionary work in China. You would be amused. Here in Massachusetts, I am thought to be quite the expert on China, and the missionary officials seem satisfied with the money I am bringing in to help their cause. Enough for now. I am still reasonably healthy and one day hope to see you again, perhaps in China, perhaps here in the Boston area.

P.S. I am enclosing a copy of a book by a Mr. Clemens, a newspaper reporter like yourself who has made something of a name for himself as a writer. The man is not particularly popular among my own colleagues, but perhaps his efforts might inspire your own. I do not know. I gave up giving you advice long ago.

Sincerely,

Your Father Reverend Abraham Brandt

Carefully folding the letter and putting it in one of the last pages of the book, Jason turned back to the nicely printed volume his father had sent and turned to the opening paragraph and read the following:

THIS book is a record of a pleasure trip. If it were a record of a solemn scientific expedition, it would have about it that gravity, that profundity, and that impressive incomprehensibility which are so proper to works of that kind, and withal so attractive. Yet notwithstanding it is only a record of a picnic, it has a purpose, which is to suggest to the reader how he would be likely to see Europe and the East if he looked at them with his own eyes instead of the eyes of those who traveled in those countries before him. I make small pretense of showing anyone how he ought to look at objects of interest beyond the sea—other books do that, and therefore, even if I were competent to do it, there is no need.

I offer no apologies for any departures from the usual style of travel-writing that may be charged against me—for I think I have seen with impartial eyes, and I am sure I have written at least honestly, whether wisely or not.

Then after glancing over at Black Jade to assure himself she was still sleeping comfortably, he began to read.

Hours later, he'd made considerable headway into Twain—no, that was some sort of pen name—into Mr. Clemens' efforts, to introduce his fellow countrymen to Europe and parts of the

Holy Land, an exceedingly different view of Jerusalem than he remembered so well from all his father's sermons when he was young. Different and quite amusing, but there was something that bothered him as well about the book.

He thought for a while and realized it was the author's warning that the book would be no way a "record of a solemn scientific expedition" but something more of a "picnic." Earnest journalist that Jason was, he found himself wondering if there were only those two choices, to be incredibly pompous, full of the gravity and profundity that Mr. Clemens contrasted his own more irreverent style with. Could not one do both, entertain and teach? Jason wondered. Wasn't it important to produce material that would catch and keep a reader's interest even as one learned more? The topic was, after all, of profound importance. Wouldn't it be desirable if more Americans understood Europe and the Holy Land better? He asked himself.

More to the point, Jason realized that he was sitting there in his temporary lodging in Tianjin precisely because the gap in understanding between the Westerners and the local Chinese had been so enormous as to produce the massacre that had almost taken his beloved Black Jade from him. Could someone have helped reduce the confusion between the powerful Westerners and the Chinese before it would explode again? After all, those Chinese who had destroyed the orphanage and massacred the foreign priests and nuns did so thinking the orphanage rather than helping the local children was somehow a macabre institution dedicated not only to kidnapping and murdering local children but using their body parts for their bizarre religious rituals.

Staring at the book, Jason wondered if, inspired by Mr. Clemens's writings, he should try to emulate and yet also expand on Clemens's approach, to produce more than the journalistic articles he'd long published in the *North China Daily News*, more ambitious works that could improve Sino-Western relations and, of course, improve his own ability to support his family. Turning back to the book, two thoughts passed fleetingly through his mind—that he wanted to finish the book, especially those Middle Eastern sections that seemed to so curiously parallel his childhood memories of his father's Holy Land imagery, and perhaps meet Mr. Clemens himself one day. He had, after all, mentioned that he was, like Jason, a working journalist. But before he took up the book again, a quiet voice beckoned him.

"Husband," she said, her eyes open as she started to pull herself to a sitting position. "Bring the children in?" Then she added, "Husband, I think you should try to speak to them in English more, to them and to me as well."

Jason bolted from his chair, his back hurting from too many hours sitting, and went toward the door.

"Wait. There is one more thing…before you go. Bring me the hairbrush, on the chest."

# CHAPTER 2

# VISIT FROM AN OLD FRIEND

The next several days went by in a whirlwind as Jason, more and more comfortable that Black Jade was on the mend, went into the streets to gather enough material to write something more in depth for his editor at the *North China Daily News*. He knew there would be significant interest in the story and, from Jason's perspective, the explosion of suspicion and stupidity that had led to the destruction of the Sisters of Mercy orphanage. His articles would certainly not be the first word of the massacre to reach Shanghai. He'd been too distracted dealing with Black Jade's wounds to write something up immediately. But he knew he was in the best position to write something meaningful, something of the sort his employers at the *North China Daily News* and its readers had come to expect from Jason.

Nevertheless, this time Jason found himself planning the writing in a more complicated fashion. First, he would write the more immediate newspaper pieces that Barlow was already demanding - did he even know Black Jade had almost died in the assault? Then he would write a longer, more expansive magazine piece with more background for those American readers who knew less of China and probably had more eclectic interests than the hard-bitten, profit-minded businessmen and missionaries who made up the bulk of the China-coast newspaper subscribers.

At least, Jason thought to himself, he was lucky to have the contacts that he needed. He had already sold several such articles to the famous *Harper's Magazine* and to a few other lesser-known periodicals in recent years. But this time, his goals were even more ambitious, a plan to eventually produce a much larger work, something like that but more ambitious than Clemens's *Innocents Abroad*, which he'd devoured so eagerly especially so as he'd not only enjoyed the work but had begun imagining himself producing something similar. And it would have to be popular as well if the plan he and Black Jade had been discussing in the evenings were ever to come about. A return to America, not just a return, but a return with enough of a reputation as a writer to support themselves reasonably well.

Unfortunately, Black Jade had not been able to contribute much to his efforts. She certainly remembered well enough the first moments of the attack, the fear in the eyes of the missionaries who'd only just been discussing the increasing tensions as more and more local Chinese became convinced that the sisters were paying kidnappers to bring children to the orphanage, children who ever so often died soon after. The last images she remembered clearly were of a breathless young nun who'd run up to the Sister Superior while Black Jade was visiting, crying out that some sort of shooting had occurred. After that, Black Jade's memory failed. Jason had to assume the horrific blow she'd received to her head had occurred soon after.

Jason spent the next several days trying to find someone who could explain what had actually set off the riot though it was never quite clear. The only thing that was certain was that at some point a local French consular official had gotten involved and managed to kill a minor Chinese official before all hell broke loose.

What was certain was that by the time it was over more than sixty people, European, mostly French, and a large number of Chinese converts were dead. A few others, Westerners, unlucky as Jason had been to ride into town as the riot was in process were also attacked. In fact, three Russians, assumed by the local Chinese to be French, were also attacked, unlike Jason; they had been unable to save themselves.

Once his articles were dispatched to Shanghai to satisfy Barlow, who'd taken to sending him notes almost daily demanding them, Jason turned back again to his family's needs. By early July, Black Jade was well enough to travel and so off they went with their maid Old Zhu, six-year-old Mei-ling, and little William, now almost a year and a half old, back to Shanghai and the home they had built for themselves only a few years ago. Once settled in life resumed its usual pace as if they had never left Shanghai. Black Jade's recovery continued smoothly, though for months she continued to have occasional dizzy spells while Jason resumed his reporting for the newspaper. If there was anything that broke the usual pace, it was a stern lecture by Barlow one afternoon after they had begun talking about future assignments.

"I know you have heard this before, but I am again getting an earful about you every time I enter my club. Constant harping about how sympathetic you are to the Chinese. Especially in that piece you did on Tianjin. One fellow even insisted I fire you for justifying a massacre." Barlow spit again into the office spittoon, which, as always, was conveniently located near his big editor's desk.

"Well, I hardly justified it. But it did seem reasonable to explain how the sisters rewarding the worst sort of street trash to bring the children they thought were abandoned to the orphanage might lead to kidnappings."

"Still don't know why you defend the killers," Barlow bellowed. "They murdered all those people, didn't they? And I have heard, did a lot more to them, than you reported."

Jason did not say anything. He'd never thought it necessary to go into detail on just how gruesome the murders had been.

"So, what are you saying? My efforts to explain why the massacre happened just anger our subscribers?"

"Angers of course, but they still want to know what happened. They keep buying the papers, so I am not complaining and neither are the owners. Besides, the dead were French and Russian, neither too popular at my club. Now, if you ever try to justify the murder of Anglos—English or American…well, that would be something different."

Jason said nothing, knowing that no matter what Barlow threatened, Jason was his best writer and the only reporter with the language skills and contacts necessary to do the sort of writing Barlow wanted for the paper.

"But enough of that; I should not have brought it up. We have to finish planning your next writing assignments." With that, he glanced down at his desk, consulted a sheet of paper, and began suggesting more story ideas.

Jason sat half listening and half thinking about his larger plans, plans he had not yet revealed of becoming more than a journalist but a professional writer and departing for the United States. Thus far, he'd said nothing to Barlow. There would be time enough for that discussion. Forty-five minutes later he was again in the streets returning home. For a moment, he thought of buying wine, for they had a special guest coming that night. Then on reflection, he thought better of it. Prosper Giquel—his former Chinese language student from their earliest days in the Guangzhou occupation and now the illustrious director of a Chinese shipyard at Fuzhou—was coming to dinner. If there was anything certain in the universe, Jason thought it was that Prosper would bring the champagne.

An hour later, he was just finishing up preparing their rooms for the arrival of his old friend. In truth Old Zhu had done most of the cleaning and cooking, but Black Jade was more than willing to assign him additional tasks as he came through the door. At moments like those, he wondered if he'd spent too much time telling her how much less servant-master like the relationship was between the Western couples and their Chinese counterparts. Or at least how much he thought they might be. Finally, all was ready, and while they had a few minutes, he began to tell her about his meeting with Barlow and of the frustrations that usually went with them. However, there was no time, as his old friend Prosper noisily arrived at the door carrying a load of packages, while Old Zhu trailed behind him, eyeing with the suspicious look she always reserved for the enthusiastic Frenchman.

"*Bonjour, bonjour, monsieur, madame, une fois de plus, qing zuo xia*. Sit down, sit down, for I've an armful of packages for us to explore." Jason smiled broadly, remembering how important Giquel thought it to maintain the special pleasures of life. For a second he had a flash of the billiard table Prosper had somehow managed to lug around with his soldiers during his leadership of the Sino-French Ever Triumphant Army of the Taiping years. But that reflection was only a glimpse, as Mei-ling and William ran into the room smiling; they knew Giquel always had presents.

"Uncle Prosper!" they yelled in unison, the almost-two-year-old William doing everything he could to push himself past his big sister. "What have you brought us?"

"Brought you? *Mon Dieu, mes enfants*, why should I bring you something?"

The children were having nothing of it.

"What have you brought us?" they continued, not having any of Giquel's teasing. Jason glanced up at Black Jade, knowing both were a bit embarrassed at their ever-so-greedy children; it was a behavior neither Jason nor Black Jade remembered from their own youth.

"Well, wait, perhaps I have something." Giquel sat down, dropping his packages on the table.

"Ah hah," the children shouted, "we knew you'd have something!" Even Mei-ling, who was usually considerably more shy than her little brother.

"Why yes, there seems to be something in here," Giquel mumbled to himself as he rummaged through the packages. "First - we shall start with the littlest—we can't always follow Chinese customs of seniority, can we? A small trinket for my fateful friend Monsieur William."

With a flourish, he pulled out an extraordinarily lovely but somewhat miniaturized telescope that, while looking professionally made, was exactly the right size for William's small fingers. The boy squealed with delight as he ran off with it to peer out the window into the street below.

Then turning to Mei-ling, the sweetly smiling six-year-old, Giquel pulled out a stunningly beautiful doll and placed it into the eager fingers of the young girl, whose broad grin showed that Prosper had made another hit. And the gifts kept coming; Giquel's packages seemed endless. For Black Jade he'd brought a beautiful dress he'd purchased in Saigon during one of his most recent visits, and hardly surprisingly as Black Jade held it up, it looked like it would fit perfectly. Giquel was like that, Jason thought to himself with some envy. Maybe he should have been born French. They certainly knew about such things.

"And for my old language teacher, something I am especially proud of. My brand-new Franco-Chinese technical dictionary, which I have just published and which proved invaluable at the workshops of the dockyard. I offer it with great pride."

"It's so kind of you to bring such gifts," said Black Jade, who already knew Giquel from their wedding and subsequent visits, "but were they not expensive—too expensive?" For she had noticed, just as Jason had, that neither gift—the doll nor the telescope—was of the sort one could find at the local shops.

"Yes, in a way that's true but not as you think, my old friends. You see, there are advantages and disadvantages"—at the last word, Giquel's ebullience seemed to fade for a second, and then recovering—"to have an entire workshop of carpenters and optic experts at your disposal when it comes to having such things prepared."

Of course, Jason thought to himself, the dockyard at Fuzhou that Giquel directed, the effort to build all those Western-style ships, would probably require scores of experts in such manufacture. Still, Jason knew his old friend and former Chinese language student had spent a pretty penny having them prepared.

"Well, we thank you sincerely and hope the pleasure of giving is as generous for you as for the children," Black Jade said, taking his hand for a moment, as she had begun to become comfortable doing with Jason's friends.

"Wait, I think we have more here." And with that, a large pastry box was pulled to the center space and Giquel carefully untied the strings that held the package together. "Voilà!" he exclaimed, opening the boxes to reveal the most extraordinary pastries Jason had ever seen.

"Oh my God, where did you get such things in Shanghai"? Jason exclaimed, his mouth already eager for a taste.

"Why, in the most famous pastry shop in Shanghai, of course—Old Jacque's in the French quarter. It is far away better than any of its competitors," he explained with pride.

"I did not even know there was a French pastry shop. Wait, I remember what you taught me…a *patisserie* in Shanghai?"

"And you call yourself a reporter. *Mon Dieu*, your education is still singularly lacking. And, Madame, you yourself come from a culture that knows something of cooking…well, perhaps a bit more than something, almost as refined a nation of chefs as my own. How can you allow your husband to know so little of fine food?" With that, Black Jade simply began to laugh, looking from her husband, now unmasked as a country bumpkin of the American sort to his enthusiastic friend.

"These are for later, after champagne, for I am determined to have a wonderful evening visiting with old friends." With that Giquel, who had clearly noticed the children turning away from their gifts, their nostrils awakened by the package he'd just opened, were starting to look back, quickly he closed the package again.

"First we must have champagne," Giquel announced, turning to another of his packages. Jason watched his old friend closely. How long had they known each other? More than ten years. Had it really been ten years since they'd met in those first days after Guangzhou had been stormed? More than ten years since he and Giquel were both assigned to the Sino-European police units the Western allies had established and had decided to exchange language lessons, Chinese for Giquel and French for Jason. And fair trade it had been. Though, in truth, Jason thought to himself, Giquel had gotten the better deal of it. His Chinese had become, over the years, more and more fluent, and if he did not speak with quite the skill that Jason and Black Jade did, his late start with the language had hardly mattered. Only a slight hint of a French accent could be heard if one listened closely. Jason, on the other hand, while a lot better in French than he'd once been, was still very limited in his abilities.

"And the disadvantages?" Black Jade asked, for she had obviously been thinking less about Giquel's language skills than what he'd actually said.

"Madame, you are as good a listener as you are beautiful! But now is not the moment, maybe later. Now is the moment for champagne. Old Zhu, can you find us some glasses? Please," he said, turning to the servant who'd been watching silently in the background. With that she scurried off to the pantry.

Hours later, after they'd devoured the duck Zhu and Black Jade had prepared, drank far too much wine—for Giquel had naturally brought several bottles and the children had been sent off to bed—the three of them sat in the small parlor simply enjoying each other's company.

"So," Giquel began, "tell me of your plans. You did hint at some news."

"Mr. Giquel," Black Jade began hesitantly, "we have exciting news."

"E-x-c-i-ting news? Madame, you have been learning English I see. Excellent! It is not nearly as beautiful as French, my own native tongue, or Chinese of course, but it is irritatingly useful at times. See, a proud Frenchman admits it. And the rest of the news, for I sense your studying English is part of something larger."

"It is," she began, "but first I would like..." She was clearly searching for the right words and then, putting her lessons aside, switched back to Chinese. "We want to know," she said, glancing over to Jason, "what you meant by 'disadvantages.' We both know you too well not to see that something is wrong."

With that, Giquel sighed. "Of course, we've dined, spent time with your lovely children, stuffed ourselves with Old Jacques's best pastries, and it's time for my story of woe. Besides, I have begun to wonder lately if it's not Jason's fault anyway!" he said, smiling directly at his reporter friend.

"What! My fault? I barely see you these days; you've been so busy at the dockyard. What could I have done?" Jason exclaimed.

"It is indeed a long and discouraging story but happily one that is nearing resolution." Giquel, taking another sip, then began his tale. "When you saw me last, the dockyard project was going very well indeed. We managed to hire everyone we needed, really everyone we needed in Europe, to teach the Chinese how to build a Western-style shipyard and the beginnings of a new Western-style navy. And my relationship with Shen Baozhen, the mandarin assigned to oversee my leadership"— for some reason Prosper seemed to especially focus on the word "oversee"—"has been wonderful."

The couple sat quietly, waiting for Giquel to continue.

"No, the real problem has, I am afraid to say, been with my fellow countrymen. Indeed, most of them have been excellent to work with despite a few, shall we say, unusual aspects of their employment. For example, they have accepted grudgingly my insistence that they aren't immune to Chinese law as most Westerners are."

"You're joking," Jason interrupted. "They aren't immune, don't have extraterritorially, and they accept that?" Jason asked, amazed that the treaty demands that had been so much a part of the settlement of the Opium Wars did not apply to the dockyard workers.

"Well, 'accepted' is probably not the right word. I have explained since the beginning that while we have not renounced our rights as Frenchmen, they did not arrive at their own risk. The Chinese government hired them, they accepted the position, and they are responsible to me and ultimately their Chinese employers."

"And that worked; they accepted that?"

"Well, let it suffice to say, they wanted the work; the salaries are, I think, generous, and their passage was paid. That has not been the main problem. About two years ago, the French relocated their Ningbo consulate — a consulate directed by a man who has never liked me at Fuzhou, I believe, with the express purpose of making my life miserable."

"Is that how he thinks of his position?" Black Jade asked, pouring each of the men another glass of the after-dinner wine they'd opened a few minutes ago.

"*Bien Sur,*" Giquel said, standing up and increasingly agitated as he started to pace the room. "No, not really. He thinks he is merely protecting the French workers by overseeing their efforts at the dockyard. But that is not his right. Our workers are employees of the Chinese, brought here at Chinese expense. It really is none of his business to interfere, and interfere he's been doing constantly for the last two years."

"Was there something specific that happened? I don't remember seeing you so upset before."

"Well, yes, and the whole story is stupid. There was some bad blood between two of the French employees...an issue linked to something that happened in France long before they arrived at the shipyard. In any case, I..." He hesitated. "We eventually had to fire one of them and the man then sued me. He wants me to pay his expenses for his trip home and damages, almost seven thousand dollars. And that bastard, the consul, is supporting him."

"Seven thousand dollars!" Jason and Black Jade looked at each other, startled. It was an enormous sum of money; they both knew it would devastate Giquel's personal finances. His salary at the dockyard was generous but nothing in that range.

"So what is happening now? Are you going to have to pay it? Does the consul have that much power?"

"Well, he should not have any power with our employees. Shen Baozhen and I both agree on that, but the French authorities have, shall we say, disagreed. Worse, both the local French tribunal and the appellate court at Saigon ruled against me, insisting I compensate the man!" With that, Giquel sat down again, taking yet another deep sip of his wine, his momentary agitation over.

"Do you have any recourse, any hope?" Jason asked.

"The most logical argument failed completely. I tried to get the court to recognize that I might be the European director, but that Shen, my Chinese colleague, is ultimately responsible for all the decisions. And that's hardly merely a legal argument. It's true. We work well together, but Shen still has the last word. It has always been that way. It is, after all, a Chinese dockyard. Shen was even kind enough to send letters explaining that all dockyard decisions were ultimately his, not mine, and that I should not be personally held responsible for firing the man."

"Did it help?"

"Not really; we were ultimately arguing that the French establishment had no authority in the dockyard. Something they would hardly take kindly to. In a sense it was about French influence at the dockyard more than my role. I do, however, have hope. I am making progress arguing to my government that our country needs the work the dockyard offers our countrymen. Besides, and this was the coup de grace, I have been telling everyone I could that if things get worse, the Chinese will terminate France's links to the dockyard and invite the English to take over!" With that last comment, a hint of pleasure finally spread across Giquel's face again.

"I bet they loved that!" Jason commented.

"Well, the consular officials were not terribly impressed. But I am not without resources, especially among my colleagues in the French navy, and they are finally starting to rally around me. My hope now is for the financial finding against me to be reduced significantly, and the consular officials told to interest themselves elsewhere."

"Is that likely to happen?" Black Jade asked eagerly, caught up in the tale.

"I am beginning to think that the trial of the last two years will eventually be resolved satisfactorily."

"But?" she asked. "So how does all this become my husband's fault?"

"A good question, Madame. And one I have been thinking about for quite some time. Yes, indeed it really is, at base, Jason's fault. You see, the way I have come to think of the situation is like this: Jason was the first person with whom I ever seriously discussed the Chinese. We spent a lot of time in Guangzhou, not just studying Chinese, and he was, Madame, a wonderful language teacher but also my original guide to all thing Chinese. He taught me to not only to understand your language but also to appreciate and respect your people."

"Yes, all right, and where is the fault in that?" Jason asked, still confused.

"*Mon Dieu*, isn't it obvious? You polluted my mind. You made me appreciate the Chinese. I don't look down on them; I consider many Chinese good friends, insist at the dockyard, against all practice along this entire coast that my European employees treat their Chinese workers and students as respected colleagues. Of course, I am constantly treated with suspicion. And it is all your fault!" With that, Giquel raised his glass in mock salute.

"But enough of all that...We must continue our celebration. Talk of mutual friends and their fates. Have you heard anything from our mutual friend Gordon? Did you know they are calling him Chinese Gordon now? Those English do love their heroes!"

Jason thought for a second about the stern English officer who had, as Prosper had, led a Sino-Western army against the Taipings.

"Well, I would hardly call him a friend. I only interviewed him a few times. Most of what I know of him comes from you actually. So they call him Chinese Gordon now? I had not heard that."

"*Bien sur* 'Chinese Gordon,' though one wonders if anyone who calls him that back in England ever had the chance to hear him try to speak Chinese. He really was something to listen to." Giquel laughed. "But I have had a letter from him just recently. He tells me his work in central Europe is nearing completion, and he thinks he might soon take up a position with the military in Egypt."

"What's he like?" Black Jade asked. "I have heard of him, at least I think I have. What is he famous for?"

"Well, if you listen to the English, it is for destroying the Taiping Heavenly Kingdom all by himself."

Jason, watching his wife closely, said, "I know what you're thinking, but I think you would like him. He is as interested in religion, especially Christianity, as you are."

"Perhaps," she said, clearly distracted by something.

"But we have not gotten to your news." Giquel finally changed the subject again.

For the rest of the evening, the couple told Giquel of their hopes to depart soon for America.

"And how long will you stay there? Do you mean a visit or permanently?"

"Well, certainly a lot longer than a visit, but for how long we really don't know."

"And you say you will be staying in Salem. With Frederick Ward's family?"

Of course, Jason had completely forgotten that Frederick Townsend Ward, Gordon's predecessor with the Ever Victorious Army, had been from Salem. In fact, he'd even mentioned it one evening when Jason visited him in the months before he was killed in battle. What was it Ward had said of the place? Now Jason really wanted to remember.

But the evening was growing late. They were all exhausted, and sometime before midnight Jason and Black Jade saw their old friend to the door as each promised to stay in close touch. With that Giquel was off into the night.

# CHAPTER 3

# LEAVING FOR GOLD MOUNTAIN

The next several months were busy indeed. His most immediate task aside from feeding his editor, Barlow, a regular supply of articles for the *North China Daily News*, was to prepare the book he'd come to think of as his *China Tales*, a series of memoirs and vignettes of his experiences along the China coast over the years. Writing the book had taken months, but his carefully preserved newspaper clippings, going back for years, especially since his stay in the Taiping capital, helped him enormously, and by late 1871, the manuscript was ready for publication through the professional efforts of the staff of the paper and Barlow's personal support. Jason was especially grateful that the newspaper owners had been willing to support the book's publication without his paying for the printing costs. Fortunately, the royalties they had agreed upon certainly seemed fair to him.

Once the book was published, he eagerly took up the volume and showed it off at home to Black Jade, who'd contributed enormously as she'd once done for his series on Taiping women, and then to the children, neither of whom seemed especially impressed. Once that was accomplished, he set about with the next part of his plan: composing the letter that had been ruminating through his mind since that first night in Tianjin as he had waited for Black Jade to regain consciousness. The plan he had formulated as he read through Mr. Clemens's *Innocents Abroad*. In anticipation he'd already learned where Mr. Twain was living, apparently in Buffalo, New York, where he worked as an editor, writer, and investor in a newspaper called the *Buffalo Express*.

Samuel Clemens a.k.a. Mark Twain
Care of the *Buffalo Express*
Buffalo, New York

Dear Mr. Clemens:
It is as a fellow journalist and even more important as a great admirer of your work that I write to you today. My employer, James Barlow of the *North China Daily News* here in Shanghai, tells me he has had some dealings with you in the past and that it would be acceptable to write to you directly. I hope that is not a problem. A man of your accomplishments must receive a great deal of correspondence from strangers.

As I said, I am a great admirer of your work and so much of an enthusiast of your book *Innocents Abroad* that in my own humble way I have attempted to write something that includes that combination of information and entertainment that you so cultivated in your wonderful work on Europe and the Holy Land. My own work, entitled *China Tales*, was recently published here in Shanghai and thus far has had a modest success (Well, he was hardly going to tell him it had been out for an hour.)

My own thought, though, is that the book's true audience and the one I wrote for is not those Western residents of the China coast but Americans at home (my family hails from Salem and Boston) and thought you might be the best person to inquire about arranging the book's further publication in the States.

Please let me say as well, if this is too much of an imposition, I deeply apologize in advance and simply hope you find my small effort of some interest. I should add that I really would love your advice, but if that is not possible, I will certainly understand. As it happens, my family is leaving China shortly for a somewhat-extended stay in New England and will, I assume, be able to more directly peruse this matter myself if that becomes necessary.

For now, let me simply finish by saying whatever your disposition toward my *China Tales,* I have learned enormously from your efforts.

Sincerely

Jason Brandt

This day, April 1872

Then, before he lost his nerve, he slipped out long enough to have the letter, and the newly minted book sent off by postal service.

Over the next few days, Jason thought a lot about how long it would take the package to find Clemens, how long it might be before the author took up the package to seriously examine it, and whether he'd actually write Jason back. But as the weeks passed, Jason was too busy to think further on the matter. There was too much else to do.

He and Black Jade had to decide whether they would rent or sell their home; whether they would ask Old Zhu to accompany them, for she really had become an important part of their family; and when they might officially begin their journey to America. There was as well the question of just how they would proceed. They often talked late in the evening after the children were in bed, with Jason's daily writing done and Black Jade's language studies completed, for she had thrown herself into learning English with the same determination she usually took on such tasks.

The most important decisions, of course, were decided after considerable discussion. Neither had any idea when they might return. They could hardly look after their home from the other side of the planet, and both were deeply aware that they had no idea how long it would take to start earning money again in the United States. Jason had heard his father talk far too often of his frustrations to take the idea of finding easy employment for granted. No, they would need as much money as they could possibly raise. And there were the expenses of the trip itself. There were, after all, five of them—all of whom would require some sort of train and boat tickets, not forgetting food and lodging along the way. And it was most certainly five tickets, because once asked, Zhu had made it quite clear that she had no family to speak of, with her husband and son long dead and that she was eager to see the West. In her own way, she was as curious and open-minded as her mistress, another reason why the two women—Black Jade and Zhu—got along so well.

However, the last decision was more of a pleasure. The question was of just how they would return. There were two possible ways to travel from Shanghai to New England. One could take a ship from Shanghai to Singapore. Then through the newly opened Suez Canal, which allowed passage from the Indian Ocean to the Mediterranean that Giquel had told him about so eagerly, and then on to Europe and finally the American East Coast, his final destination. There was as well another way, travel by ship from Shanghai all the way across the Pacific to San Francisco—and then by train across America.

For Black Jade and Jason, it was an easy decision. They had both heard of San Francisco since they were children and wanted to see it for themselves. From there they could take the train across America. If they were to introduce their children to the United States and, of course, Jason himself, who had no memories of his babyhood in Massachusetts, that was clearly the best way. And so it was planned—from Shanghai across the Pacific and then San Francisco for a time, eventually taking the newly completed transcontinental railroad to the American East Coast.

In the last weeks, though, two events that would have lasting repercussions occurred, and both arrived through the post. Returning one evening Jason spotted a thick envelope waiting for him. He eagerly snapped it up, glancing only quickly at the return address. "New York." Had Clemens finally written? But then looking more closely, the letter, to his surprise, came not from Buffalo where Clemens lived but from an address in New York City and from a name he did not recognize—a Mr. Russell Sage.

He sat down on a chair, for the house remained quiet. Clearly, no one—the children, Black Jade, or Zhu—was home, so he slowly opened the letter. As he opened it, to his surprise a bank draft dropped down.

My Dear Mr. Brandt:

I trust this letter from a stranger finds you healthy. Nevertheless, the solicitations of a stranger cannot be very valuable to you anyway, so I shall get to my point. I am a businessman. My wife has brought your writings, articles in periodicals she enjoys reading to my attention. Frankly, sir, I have no ear for such adventures, and tales of curiosities found in other lands leave me entirely disinterested. However, I am interested in business and, of late, especially railroad investments here in the United States and perhaps elsewhere. Thus, the reason for my letter. From perusing your articles, you seem to be a knowledgeable man, as aware of Chinese culture as its industry. I noted, for example, considerable interest in your articles about the Chinese effort to import Western shipbuilding techniques and want your opinion on whether it would be worthwhile to invest in similar enterprises, especially railroads in China. What I require from you, sir, if you are willing to take up my commission, is a detailed report on the present state or lack of it of Chinese railroad development. Moreover, I am willing to pay for it.

Enclosed you will find a sum my advisers tell me is a reasonable amount, given the task I have requested. If you are agreeable, I look forward to your report at your earliest convenience.

The rest of the letter finished with a detailed explanation of how Mr. Sage wanted his money returned if the task proved impossible or Jason was not willing to take up the challenge of preparing the report. Curiously, Jason thought to himself, the instructions on returning the funds were somewhat longer than the actual research assignment.

Then turning back to the draft, he thought about the proposal. It would add to his burdens, but the money was reasonably generous...well, perhaps somewhat less than the work required but not unsubstantial, and more importantly Mr. Sage seemed like a person of substance. Jason had read just enough about New York City to know that the address sounded expensive. Having a contact in America, after all he'd not even heard from Clemens yet, and with the author, Jason had been the one asking favors. No, Jason quickly decided he'd take up the task. Between the contacts he had and those Prosper could supply, he was sure he could do the assignment fairly easily.

Within a few weeks, the report was sent off to New York City with a follow-up letter, mentioning that he'd be in the United States in a few months and that he was traveling with his family across the Pacific and then via train from San Francisco to Boston in case Mr. Sage had any additional questions that needed answering.

The last few weeks dragged on interminably. Jason, Black Jade, the children, and even Zhu were totally distracted as they thought about their imminent departure. They already had their tickets ready to go sitting above the fireplace, five tickets for the American steamer from Shanghai to San Francisco departing on November 11, 1872. But finally, when the waiting had become practically unbearable, the long-awaited letter arrived, this time correctly addressed from Buffalo and the offices of *Buffalo Express.*

My Dear Jason:

I hope this letter finds you still in Shanghai, for I am eager to be in contact. First, let me say, perhaps too boldly, that I hope I can call you by your Christian name, though I hope I do not presume too much, after all we are no doubt both scoundrels, are not all reporters as such, and should dispense with formalities.

I am delighted that you overcame your hesitancy to write me. Indeed, yours was not as you supposed the work of a stranger but of someone whose writings I have long been familiar. We reporters do, after all, have to keep up with the competition. Your book *China Tales,* though, was completely unknown to me. I dove into it as a pig might a pile of newly poured mash. Delightfully, it was worth it. What a fascinating work, and if my own *Innocents* in some way inspired it, I am especially pleased! Pleased as pudding as they say. However, I have never been quite sure what that odd phrase actually means. But, to the point, you're a professional writer and will want financials.

As you may have guessed, I am indeed a reporter and more formally an author as they say. Nevertheless, my interests in the profession go far beyond it. I find all aspects of the business—from the writing and promotion to the actual sales and printing—fascinating. If I might be so bold as to suggest. I myself would love to help facilitate the further publication of your book. What I have in mind is to offer the work in a subscription form...If they want it, they will pay for it in advance and we won't have to pay for printing until the book's future readers have coughed up the cash in advance. This is a method I have long found useful. I am enclosing a contract that I hope you will find reasonable. Please return it as soon as possible, as the interest in China here in the states continues apace, and I believe once available, the book will attract many readers.

I note that you are planning to come to America. Excellent. It might allow you to do some additional promotion of the work in person. If per chance, your voyage takes you through San Francisco, and I hope it will—in fact, I only just recently returned from living there for several years. For now, I will certainly send copies of any additional correspondence to the offices of the *North China Daily News*, and yes, I do remember Barlow; do give him my greetings. I will, however, also send copies to the offices of the *San Francisco Examiner,* a relatively new journal I have many friends at. If you do end up in San Francisco, I hope you will stop off there to see if any correspondence has arrived. I will also tell my friends there to receive you in a fashion befitting a visiting journalist. Which, of course, may merely mean they might try to get your roaring drunk!

Sincerely
Samuel Clemens
September 15, 1872

Jason sat stunned. The letter, it was more than he could possibly have imagined. It had arrived at the newspaper offices instead of at his home. Perhaps, Jason thought, Clemens assumed they would at least know where he was if he'd already left Shanghai. Grabbing the letter, he left the offices as quickly as possible. Almost sprinting to a horse cab to get home and share the letter with Black Jade. Everything was coming together, even better than they had hoped.

Finally, the long-anticipated day arrived, November 11, 1872. All their trunks were ready to go, and the family set off through the crowded streets toward the harbor and the magnificent ship that awaited the moment of its departure, first for Yokohama and then on to San Francisco. Once at the ship, their entire party boarded easily and established themselves in their quarters—Zhu and the children in one stateroom, and Jason and Black Jade in the other. There were only a few hours more before departure, and as planned, Jason took his leave to visit the offices of the newspaper one more time to say his good-byes.

"Now, both of you be careful. The railing looks safe enough, but either of you could slip through, so you are not to go on to the deck without each of you holding one of the adult's hands." Both children appeared disappointed.

"Don't worry my husband. We've plenty to unpack and arrange if we are to be in these rooms as we cross the great ocean. We can take our stroll on deck after you get back. But don't be long. I don't want to be waiting and wondering if you are going to make it back in time as the ship starts to depart," she warned sternly, yet with the smile he loved so dearly.

With that, Jason set off, though as he walked through the streets, he felt a very strange sensation, a sense that he was being followed; though every time he looked back, there did not seem to be anyone there. It was probably his imagination, he thought to himself. His imagination just playing trick with him. Without problems, he made it to the newspaper offices and said his good-byes, and received with satisfaction Barlow's promise to rehire him if and when he returned. Jason was grateful. Barlow had never been completely happy with his warm feelings for the Chinese, but he'd been supportive of his writings and was always a fair employer.

As Jason left the office and started off on foot toward the harbor, he once again had the sense of someone watching him closely. Then spotting the man, he began to walk more carefully. The fellow, a Chinese in cheap rags, was obviously watching him. But this was Shanghai and foreigners were not at all unfamiliar. Was the fellow perhaps from the interior and Jason a novelty not seen before? But that did not explain why he would have so obviously waited outside the offices of the newspaper. There were, after all, enough other foreigners in the streets that Jason should not have been an object of any specific interest.

And then as the fellow started to walk directly toward him, Jason realized his walk was familiar. Could it be! My God!

"Jason, it is you, isn't it?" his dear friend Wu asked him as he approached.

"What do you mean 'is it me?'! Is it you! You're supposed to be dead. Oh my God!" Jason hugged him, attracting no small amount of attention from those passing by. For seeing a reasonably well-dressed Westerner hug a Chinese in rags in the streets of Shanghai was hardly a common sight. Wu, clearly uncomfortable, gently disentangled.

"I don't understand. I thought you died at Huzhou...stayed there as the imperials retook the city and Black Jade and I slipped away."

"You are right; I almost died. I had been expecting to die, but I guess your arrival roused me from my lethargy...and yes, I know you are thinking it. So no, it's not a problem; the foreign drug is out of my system, but it took a long time." As he said it, Jason realized that while his old friend appeared terribly thin, he also seemed relatively healthy. The opium addiction that had almost destroyed him had obviously left his body.

"But I can't believe I am seeing you now at this moment. Black Jade and I are leaving Shanghai right now. I was on my way to the harbor to rejoin them on the ship. But I want to know what happened to you."

"It is indeed a long story, but if our fate does not allow the telling today, you will hear it one day I am certain. For now, though, my old friend, I have come to ask a favor. I am tired of hiding in the interior, tired of having no family, no chance to find a wife, no chance to carry on my family name. I need to start rebuilding my life again. I came here hoping you could help."

Jason's mind was racing as fast as it could. He had to get to the ship; they'd already talked too long, and he knew the departure hour was getting close.

"I have an idea," he said, pulling his reporter's notepad out from his satchel and writing furiously. Then a few moments later, as the passerbyers lost interest in the two men's conversation, he finished up his letter. Then dipping his hand back again into the satchel, he withdrew a wad of cash and handed it to his friend.

"Now, get yourself to Fuzhou. Just outside of the town is a Western-style shipyard. Take this letter to the director; his name is Prosper Giquel. He will give you a job and a place to stay. I am certain of it. We will catch up when we see each other again."

With that he hugged his skinny friend again, not caring who saw, and took off at a run for the harbor. There would be time to make the ship's departure, but he was pretty sure Black Jade would not be pleased with the tardiness of his arrival.

# CHAPTER 4
# A VOYAGE ACROSS THE SEA

R unning as quickly as he could, though he did not think he was significantly later than he'd initially planned, Jason arrived at the wharf and ran up the gangplank to the ship's deck. As he did so, he spotted Black Jade standing at the rail, not angry but obviously concerned.

"Sorry I am late, but something extraordinary has happened," he said breathlessly.

"What, what happened? Has someone been hurt?" she asked, concerned and curious.

"Quite the opposite, but I will tell you in the detail the story deserves after we depart. I don't want to ruin memories of our leaving. Let's go gather the children and bring them on deck. I think the ship will pull away quite soon. Then we'll be able to talk more."

With that, the two parents went below the decks, walking down the first flight of stairs and seeking the cabins so recently assigned them. It took a few more minutes than anticipated, since neither Black Jade nor Jason quite remembered where the cabins were. There would, though, be time to learn the ship's layout better during the long voyage, they both joked.

A few minutes later, though, the children were gathered up. Old Zhu was herself wrapped in her warmest clothing, for she had already decided that being at sea was likely to be very unhealthy, and up they went back on deck. For the next half an hour, they watched closely as the crew scurried about releasing various ropes and slowly pushing off. Then the ship started downriver toward the mouth of the Yangtze River Delta and the enormous ocean that lay beyond it. For a time, as they waited for the river travel to become an ocean voyage, Jason and his family slowly walked the decks of the ship, weaving their way through the other passengers who were doing the same thing and watching the ship's crew at their work. Some passengers, though, had obviously done the trip before and were already setting themselves up in the deck chairs reading or napping.

Sooner, though, than Jason expected, the ship began to emerge from the river's mouth and into the broader and choppier ocean that lay beyond. Then just as he was starting to reflect on how he would gather his family and return them below so he could share with Black Jade his astonishing encounter near the newspaper offices, a great boom, a cannon roar, broke the air, startling Jason as only those who have been in battle can be startled. Looking around he saw nothing, and then with his family in tow, they walked across the deck to the other side, the side facing toward the south, to find a most curious site.

A smaller ship, not as big as theirs but clearly a vessel capable of long-distance travel, was approaching them at considerable speed, its sails fully employed and black smoke pouring out the ship's chimney. Gently, for little William was not thrilled with his gesture, Jason took the telescope from his small son's hands and held it to his eye. Amazingly an officer of the ship—he might even have been the captain—was waving his arms wildly in their direction, a whistle in his mouth repeatedly blowing it so loudly that the sounds even made it across the distance between the two ships. As everyone watched, for the site had attracted not a few of the other passengers, the smaller ship approached, and then lowering a small boat to the sea, several seamen started to row toward them. Sitting among them, Jason spied three seated figures, two men and a woman. Late passengers, he wondered to himself. And he thought he had cut it close.

Within minutes, while the larger ships kept their distance, the smaller boat approached Jason's. As he'd guessed, the three passengers climbed carefully up the rope ladder that had been lowered to the boat. With that the seamen again pulled off and started to row back to their smaller vessel. A moment later, still at something of a distance, Jason and his family watched the three passengers consult with an officer and then follow him below the deck. Perhaps, Jason thought, they already had tickets. Who were they, this curious troop of voyagers, who had come so close to missing their passage across the Pacific? Who could know?

The only thing Jason noticed was that the two men both looked European, perhaps English. It was hard to tell, given the distance and the number of others also trying to watch the same scene. One fellow, the taller one, appeared rather like one of those English gentlemen Jason had seen hanging around Barlow's club on the few occasions when his editor had invited him, while the other was more casually dressed. As for the woman, that was even less clear. Even at a distance, Jason could see she was neither English nor French. On the other hand, she was not Chinese either. Her features were not that clear under the shawl she wore, but that much was obvious. Jason, turning to his right, glanced at Black Jade. She was obviously noticing the same thing, then turning to directly face him.

"Come, let's take the children downstairs. I believe you have something to tell me."

"Right, yes, I'd almost forgotten, though how I can scarcely imagine. Yes, let's take the kids downstairs, settle them in with Old Zhu, and then come back up here."

With that, they set off, though not as Jason had imagined. For at that very moment, Old Zhu, apparently taken by seasickness, threw up over the railing, and then first little William and followed by Mei-ling, reacting no doubt to their governess's illness, did the same. For a moment, Jason felt himself starting to get sick as well, and in the corner of his eye, he noted Black Jade in similar distress. The two remaining adults managing to keep their internal turmoil in check, quickly gathered up their children, and took them and their excessively green governess below the deck to their cabins.

It was almost an hour later before he and Black Jade made it back to the upper deck, their sense of queasiness somewhat at bay.

"They say one gets over seasickness fairly soon," Jason commented as the sea breezes washed over them.

"I certainly hope so, my husband. But you have held me in suspense too long. Now what happened to make you almost miss the boat?"

"Well, I was hardly as late as that couple we saw board at sea!" Jason proclaimed, smiling.

"What happened?" she repeated.

"Take this deck chair and sit down. You are not going to believe this. As I walked toward the paper's offices, I had a sense that someone was following me. Then I forgot about it as I went in. Barlow and I talked a bit, perhaps a bit too long, and then anxious to get back, I left the office walking briskly. Then the same thing happened, and then to my astonishment, a very gaunt, ragged Wu, our friend...you know our dear, long-dead friend, stopped me."

"What, Wu!" She was stunned. "Wu, alive...how can it be? He refused to come with us that horrible day as we left Huzhou. That much I do remember, something about his fate requiring him to die in the city. And his..." She hesitated.

"Well, I really don't know, but he appeared penniless, incredibly ragged, but he claimed to have beaten the opium addiction that had so destroyed him when we saw him last."

"So, tell me more. What did he tell you? Where has he been all these years?"

"That's just it; there was no time. He'd found me, looking for help. Said something about being ready to rebuild a life for himself again...but there was no time. I could already hear the ship; at least some ship ringing its whistle's announcing its departure."

"So what did you do?"

"The only thing I thought possible. I grabbed a handful of cash from my satchel, wrote a quick note to Prosper, asking him to give Wu work, and sent him off to Fuzhou to find the dockyard. It was the only plan I could come up with on such short notice. Besides, I am certain Prosper will treat him well. And that way we can at least stay in touch. I wish I could tell you more. But for now that is the whole story."

"Wu, still alive..." His wife just took in the information— their long-dead friend and traveling companion alive! Jason could tell his wife was taking it in slowly, a great many thoughts flowing over her as she stared out to the sea.

# CHAPTER 5

# A VISIT TO JAPAN

Over the next few days as the steamer sailed from Shanghai to Yokohama, their true starting-off point across the Pacific, Jason, Black Jade, and Old Zhu were busy trying to create a sense of routine for the two children. Clearly, eight-year-old Mei-ling and little William—would need a fixed schedule if the trip first across the ocean and eventually across America itself were to be accomplished successfully.

Mornings were spent eating in the two cabins they had reserved, with food the steward brought them. None of them found the breakfast completely satisfying given its lack of the Chinese elements they were all so accustomed to. At least the toast was tasty enough to keep everyone reasonably satisfied, and the hard-boiled eggs were popular.

After breakfast, everyone took a quick and vigorous walk around the deck and then returned to their cabins where lessons began. Some arithmetic, of course, but for the duration of the voyage, Jason and Black Jade decided language lessons; specifically English lessons would get the biggest effort. Jason was naturally assigned head teacher, though Black Jade had advanced enough that she too was starting to be able to help the children as well. Even Old Zhu, sitting in the background listening, began to mumble to herself some of the phrases they were all repeating aloud from one of the many English grammars Jason had packed for the trip. It was a rigorous schedule, but both parents were convinced that the success of their stay, for however long it lasted, depended in large measure on how well each of them could understand and communicate their thoughts to those around them.

One unexpected bonus was the presence of another family, an American missionary couple originally from the Philadelphia area, who were traveling from Shanghai to Japan to take up a new post there. Jason had not known the family in Shanghai, but the adults spent time chatting in the evening as they traveled, and the two children of the couple, two twin boys around five, eagerly played with William and Mei-ling in the evenings. Both Black Jade and Jason sincerely wished the couple had planned to stay on board across the Pacific, but that was not to be. It would have made the voyage, particularly for the children, ever so much more pleasant.

As the ship approached Yokohama, Jason felt a sense of regret. He knew their time was so limited and his interest in Japan great. He had, after all, heard about the land of the rising sun, as it was so often called, all his life. He had been interested in how much progress the country had made in importing the sort of Western technical and engineering skills his friend Giquel was helping transfer to China. From what he'd heard from Prosper and so many others, Japan's new leaders, for there had been some sort of revolution that returned power to their emperor from an apparently usurping figure known as the Shogun, were much more committed to Westernization than China's leaders.

Unfortunately, there would be no time to really explore or write something. He and Black Jade had discussed the issue at length. Their funds were limited, their goal to learn about America. Time spent in Japan would, at least on this trip, delay that effort and perhaps waste the money that they might sorely need in only a few months. Besides, neither one of them had any interest in disembarking for an extended stay after having just left Shanghai several days before. They did not find the idea attractive and knew it would be a disaster for the now-successful routine they had established for the children.

They were, though, eager to explore Yokohama for as many hours as they could while the ship was in port. Thus at dawn the entire family plus Old Zhu stood at the railing eager with the first light to explore the city before the ship set sail again later that day for the long voyage across the Pacific. They were not alone though. Another couple, the very correct English gentleman and the woman Jason and Black Jade now felt certain was from India, stood nearby apparently just as anxious to get to the shore. There was no time, though, for introductions, for almost as soon as the two parties arrived on the deck, a Japanese official with a few words of English directed them to the waiting boats that would take them ashore. Jason's party gathered in one, while the other couple went ashore in the other. Even though Jason was anxious to get to the shore, he did notice Black Jade watching not the wharf but the dark-skinned woman in the other boat. To his surprise, following Black Jade's gaze, he noted the Indian woman—and she was most certainly Indian despite tailored English clothing—was staring back. Clearly, Jason thought to himself, the two women were as curious about each other as they were about seeing Japan.

Ten minutes later they were ashore surrounded by a group of naked-to-the-waist porters, obviously anxious, as Jason thought to fill their rice bowls by conveying the new arrivals somewhere. Within seconds, the English gentleman, who had arrived first perhaps because his boat had been more lightly filled, was off. He seemed a determined fellow off to accomplish, who knew what? But there was no chance to speculate, as a decision had to be made; the porters were insistent on a destination.

"I thought we planned everything," Jason began, turning to his wife, trying to talk to her above the din of the various porters' demands. "I mean we don't really have a plan, do we...? Shall we just wander about?"

"It seems reasonable, and the children need the exercise," his wife added.

There was only one problem. How to tell the porters their assistance was not needed? Jason tried English; a few understood to a limited extent, but the porters were having nothing of it. Certainly, the new arrivals, five individuals in total, would bring in a good number of coins. The anxious fellows insisted that they must need to go somewhere. Then having an idea, Jason tried writing a few Chinese characters on his palm, characters that indicated they did not need any of the curious conveniences that were apparently waiting there for a direction or a location to seek out. His effort to write the characters failed, though he'd seen the Japanese in Shanghai use the method to great effect. The Japanese and Chinese languages were certainly different, but the two nations used enough of the same characters that they could often effectively communicate without conversation. At least in theory, for none of the Japanese porters could recognize the characters. Indeed, Jason thought, they were probably all illiterate.

His attempt to communicate was frustrating, and for Jason a relatively new experience. For most of his life, he'd been able to communicate well in the two most common languages along the China coast, English and Chinese. In fact, the closest he even remembered to the sense of frustration he was now feeling was in those earliest weeks with the Chinese Taiping rebels some of whom had spoken a dialect of Chinese quite different from what he'd learned as a child in Hong Kong.

Eventually, they managed to convince the porters that their services were not needed, at least for the moment. The funniest part, though, was when Old Zhu, protective of her family, barked at several of the fellows, telling them to keep away from the children, indeed, they had attracted considerable curiosity. Though none would have understood a word of Zhu's Shanghai insults, they obviously got the message and backed off. Within minutes the group was finally alone on the wharves, save two jinrikisha drivers following them at a discrete distance, obviously hoping the family would change its mind.

With a bit of calm, the family strolled about.

"I suppose it's not all that different from the Shanghai wharves." Black Jade sighed, a bit disappointed, for after the several days on the ship, in large measure closeted with the children, she was very eager to see something new.

"Well, those little wagons, what are they called? Right, jinrikishas are certainly interesting and probably very useful. I have seen pictures of them, but the chance to ride in them is certainly exciting."

"Look!" William yelled out, pointing not at the rickshaws or the people—people from all over the world, Chinese, Japanese, and European, who strolled near them. Following his son's eyes, Jason spied an actual European-style clown walking near them, holding a large advertising placard. The sign amazingly was in English—in fact, an English relatively easy to read, that all of them save little William and Old Zhu could read.

"A-c-r-o-b-a-t-i-c J-a-p-a-n-i-s-e troupe..." Mei-ling began to read hesitantly, and then Black Jade continued triumphantly.

"Honorable William Batulcar, Proprietor, Last representations, prior to their departure to the United States."

"It is what you call a circus?" she asked, turning to her husband, and then with confirmation told the children in Chinese.

"Can we go?" they cried out in unison.

"Well, I don't see why not, but look—at the bottom. It won't be for hours, not till one in the afternoon. Still, if everyone behaves, I think there will be time before the boat gets ready to depart. Yes, let's plan to see the performance later today."

Satisfied they'd gotten their father's approval, the family turned and started to walk more deeply into the port city. Initially the mostly Western-style buildings built of rough stone and brick were little different from the sort common in Shanghai. What Jason found interesting, though, was the number of relatively well-dressed Japanese, who wore clothing that seemed partially Western and partially Japanese. And while some of the men wore the tight and knotted hairstyles so common to the Japanese warrior class—the *bushi* he thought they were called—others sported very obviously Western-style haircuts.

"Look." Black Jade nudged him as they walked. A group of Japanese women were walking nearby, draped out in their traditional kimonos, their faces powdered very nearly white, and holding parasols, perhaps to protect them from the sunlight. Gesturing subtly, Black Jade pointed to her lips and then the women. Looking closer Jason saw what she had pointed out, for the women had covered their lips with some sort of deep-red coloring that only covered the very tips of their lips, a very curious and yet attractive decoration.

After at least an hour strolling in the harbor area, Black Jade suggested they hire the two enterprising jinrikisha drivers, for neither man had ever lost sight of them, and bargain for a block of time during which they would be shown the sites of the city. It took a bit of negotiation, but within minutes, the family had procured two jinrikishas, and piling everyone in, off they went—Jason and Black Jade in one, and the children on Zhu's lap in the other.

For another hour or two, they wandered the city, alighting when they cared to as the jinrikisha drivers waited patiently and then off again to explore more. They all found the city, with its divisions between the Western quarters and the native Japanese areas, both familiar and in some ways quite different. It was subtle, but it did seem apparent the Japanese were taking on the Western styles more readily than one usually saw in Shanghai with its greater cultural gap between Chinese and Western residents.

The activity that won the most acclaim from the little group was the many Japanese they found in one open space flying an enormous range of elaborately shaped and decorated kites. The crowd was indeed impressive, men, women, and children. Especially fetching were the young Japanese girls running full tilt pulling their kites behind them as tiny babies were wrapped tightly on their backs.

"Can we get kites?" the children enthusiastically begged.

"Of course," Black Jade said, turning to her husband, expecting him to follow through. It did not turn out to be terribly difficult. The kite sellers were readily available, and language was hardly a problem. As they say, Jason thought to himself, one can buy something in any language one wants. It only took a few coins and some counting on fingers—much easier than the more difficult negotiations with the rickshaw drivers—and two beautiful kites were acquired. Jason, amused, thought Old Zhu looked even more excited than the children.

An hour later, all of them were exhausted with the running necessary to keep the kites flying, for none of them had much experience. They entered a small teahouse for lunch. Once inside they were ushered into a small dining room where, to the children's delight, they were directed to sit on mats in front of the little table that centered the room. They quickly sat down with ease. It was clear, though, that Old Zhu, exhausted from running with the kite, for her enthusiasm had not waned at all, found sitting on the floor a bit too much and winced as her older knees tried to find a comfortable sitting space.

The food was a big hit. If it was not Chinese, it was a great deal closer than what was available on the American steamer. The bowls of steaming soba noodles were very popular, and the rice and various steamed vegetables were eaten enthusiastically. After lunch they all piled into the jinrikishas again and returned to the wharves where they had originally seen the advertising for the circus performance. Their timing could not have been better. Five tickets were quickly procured. It would be a bit tight, for the time to depart was growing close, but Jason was sure they had time to see the performance.

Within minutes, he and his wife nodded to each other as they watched the children's faces light up with enthusiasm and wonder as the show started. All began with an explosion of music from a Japanese orchestra. Quite a crowd had gathered—Japanese and Europeans—many with children arrayed themselves along rows of long narrow benches, ready for whatever delights the circus would offer. The acrobats began their performance with wondrous displays of acrobatic feats, often accompanied by the blowing of elaborate smoke figurines issuing forth from their mouths. Mei-ling was especially taken by an artist who juggled with lighted candles and another who threw an incredible number of plates into the air while spinning others on the tops of very thin sticks that he held in one hand. After a time, the acrobats and jugglers slowly finished their routines and others took their places with their own well-practiced wonders.

Then something more elaborate began to form. A large number of the acrobats returned to the wooden stage and began to form among themselves an enormously elaborate human pyramid, at the top of which more juggling was taking place—at least was until suddenly something seemed wrong. They were starting to topple. A quick glance at the bottom revealed the problem. One of the performers was struggling to pull away, yelling in both English and French as the entire audience sat shocked. A second later the fellow freed himself and bolted as his colleagues crashed to the floor with a variety of oaths from languages familiar around the world—a veritable Tower of Babel of swear words! What was most amazing, though, was that the fellow ran directly into the audience.

*"Mon Dieu, Mon Dieu!* Ah my master! My master!" the fellow shouted, throwing himself at the feet of a couple at the other end of the long bench Jason and family had chosen.

"Look, it's them!" Black Jade yelled into his ear over the roar of the crowd. "The couple from our ship."

She was right, Jason realized with a start. Yes, the English gentleman and his Indian companion were having an excited reunion. Well, the Frenchman and the woman in any case seemed excited. Then jumping up they departed immediately, though not before Jason saw them accosted by someone from the circus. Jason was too far away to hear the conversation, but it was obvious the fellow, perhaps the manager of the troupe, was very angry. Then abruptly the English gentleman thrust a handful of bank notes at the man and departed, his Indian companion and the apparently reunited French servant trailing behind him.

Once things calmed down, Jason realized it was time for them to depart. Gathering his little troupe, they exited the performance hall and headed back to the ship. Once on board they returned to their cabins. There was no sign of the three travelers they'd begun to develop so much curiosity about.

# CHAPTER 6

# NEW FRIENDS

That evening after the children and Old Zhu had eaten, Black Jade and Jason ventured upstairs to the first-class dining room. The food was the same as the porters brought to their two cabins each day, but the space in the wooden steamer ship's passenger compartments was extraordinarily cramped, and they wanted a calmer evening for once. It was not the first time they had eaten upstairs. But in their earlier excursions into the dining space, they'd been accompanied by the charming missionary couple, who traveled with them on board ship from Shanghai to Yokohama.

Now the experience would be different, for the two of them could hardly fill an entire dining table, and they knew they would be seated with strangers. At the entrance, a very solicitous maître d' greeted them, and they were efficiently directed to a table where two other couples were just seating themselves.

Once introductions were made, Jason and Black Jade sat down. Everyone was certainly polite enough, but Jason also sensed an ever-so-slight look of disapproval from one of the American women, a brunet of around fifty-five who slipped her husband a subtle glance of irritation as they sat down. He did

not immediately focus on the problem, though for another issue took up his thoughts. Neither American couple knew much
of China. Indeed, they were actually returning from India and
had only boarded the America-bound steamer in Yokohama.
That mattered, Jason thought, somewhat insecurely, because
had they known China and its famous *North China Daily News*,
they would likely to be familiar with his writing—something
that always made it easier to develop a rapport with unknown
Americans.

Jason knew he was probably overly sensitive, but the fact
that he looked and sounded like an American—indeed he
even had something of the New-England accent he'd heard in
his parents' home as a child, and yet knew so little about the
United States—always unnerved him somewhat when meeting
his supposed "countrymen." Indeed, that was a major element
in the family's voyage to America.

His thoughts were interrupted, though, by a slight kick
from his wife. While he'd been wondering about his own reception, Black Jade had tried with her limited but steadily improving English to engage the two couples. They were being
polite enough and even condescendingly complimented her
for not speaking the sort of Chinese pidgin English so common throughout Asia. Nevertheless, though, the meal passed
very quietly and the two couples left, led by the middle-aged
brunet, sooner than one would have guessed. In fact, they departed before the dessert waiter, who arrived a few moments
later, even had a chance to offer those at the now-diminished
table cake and coffee.

"Do you want something?" Jason asked his wife.

"No, let's go."

"But I was thinking of having coffee..."

"Let's go," she snapped, and off she went toward the salon
door and toward the stairwell that led below decks.

He had to run to catch up with her. "Are you OK?"

"Are you saying you did not see what was happening? You did not notice the look on the face of that woman as we— no, I—sat down. You would have thought a ragged coolie had plopped down next to her."

Jason tried to calm her down, to tell her they were just a rude couple, perhaps people whose experience in India had tainted them. It was certainly true the English treated the Indians around them as inferior dogs, to say the least. She was having none of it. She stomped down the stairs and, ignoring him, went into the children's cabin alone, closing the door behind her noisily. Jason took the hint as he kept going on alone toward the cramped compartment he and his wife shared.

The next day was tense as Jason tried to convince Black Jade that they should try the dining room again. He did everything he could to reassure her that while their dinner companions of the previous evening were certainly rude, the missionary couple they'd spent so much time with on the voyage from Shanghai to Yokohama were also Americans. They had been as charming and accepting as a couple could be. It took a bit of convincing, but she eventually relented. Thus, at the appointed dinner hour, the two of them stood apprehensively at the door to the dining salon. As they came in, they easily spotted the previous evening's grand dame glancing at them and then pointedly turning away. Jason felt Black Jade tense at his side.

Then a second later, the ever-so-solicitous ship steward rushed up to them, this time even more polite than the previous evening—suspiciously so.

"Good evening. We have a fine table ready for you!" he explained, almost as if he feared an incident. At that, he turned beckoning them to follow him. Black Jade almost imperceptibly groaned next to him. But in the next second, he heard her emit an impossibly quiet sigh of relief, for at the other side of the dining salon opposite them, another couple was also being seated. It was the English gentleman and his Indian companion. Black Jade even quickened her pace as she followed the steward and allowed him to pull the chair back for her.

"Good evening!" the tall Englishman greeted them as he stood up. "Phileas Fogg of London. And if you know it, of the Reform Club. May I present my traveling companion Ms. Aouda of her Majesty's India."

"Jason Brandt, mostly of Shanghai I think, and my wife Black Jade," Jason said, putting his hand out as the English gentleman took it up with a very precise handshake—neither too much nor too little pressure. The two women smiled at each other as they all seated themselves around the table.

"You are from India?" Black Jade asked enthusiastically. "May I ask from where?" she said politely, though Jason wondered whether she had a sense of the geography of the country he understood to be as huge as China.

"My family is originally from Bombay, " she said in very well-bred English. Neither Jason nor Black Jade had a clue where Bombay was, but at least the dinner had begun better than the previous evening.

With that, a waiter arrived to take their dinner orders. Generally, that went well, though there seemed a somewhat-long private conversation between Mr. Fogg and the waiter regarding the former's apparently precise meal requirements. Accomplishing that, the waiter left and Mr. Fogg turned back to his dinner companions.

"Mr. Brandt, where precisely are you traveling?" With that Jason explained that while they were planning to stay in San Francisco for a few weeks, they would soon after depart for Boston. Somewhat nervously, he added as they had not procured tickets in advance because the specifics of how they would travel or where they might visit along the way had not yet been determined.

"Well," Fogg jumped in. If enthusiasm might not be the best word, it was certainly a clear and perhaps professional interest. "You have a great many decisions to make."

Fogg, who seemed to possess the combined knowledge of an international shipper, railroad scheduler, and travel agent, laid out in precise detail what choices they would have to travel east from San Francisco. His knowledge was extraordinarily detailed. Jason listened with fascination, wishing he had a pen to write it all down. Indeed, there would be many choices to make once they were ready to move on from San Francisco.

To his side, as Fogg spoke of everything from train schedules to Pullman car accommodations, Black Jade and Ms. Aouda were engaged in a lively discussion of the food available to passengers, and Jason heard his wife tell her dinner partner all about the children as well.

As he sat there taking in the travel tips Fogg offered, Jason wondered if it would be appropriate to inquire about the incident at the circus. And where was the fellow? Apparently Fogg's French servant, he wondered. And had there not been yet another fellow with them when they originally boarded the ship in that dramatic fashion off the coast of China?

As the dinner ended, Fogg appeared to be finished with his travel suggestions and rather abruptly stood up. "Mr. Brandt, do you play whist?"

"Excuse me, whist?"

"It's a card game Mr. Fogg is very fond of," Aouda offered hesitantly.

"No, I am afraid I don't know."

"Pity," said Fogg as he bid them adieu and, nodding to the two women, walked off.

Jason and Black Jade looked at each other, perplexed. "It's no problem," Aouda offered. "Mr. Fogg has already found a group of men who gather in the salon after dinner to play whist with him. He is quite devoted to the game. I should add that he rarely invites others to play with him. He must have been impressed with you," she added warmly.

"Well, shall we stroll the deck?" Jason asked the two women.

"Another time," his wife said, smiling to him and taking her new friend's arm. "We ladies are going for our own stroll." With that the two women, arm in arm, walked off. "Don't forget to check on the children before you turn in," Black Jade called out to him as she left the dining room.

Jason sat there abandoned. A moment later the waiter returned. With nothing else to do, Jason helped himself to more coffee and a second slice of chocolate cake. It was delicious. Yes, the cake was delicious, and he realized with a start that being alone was a novelty as well. Normally, he spent a lot of time alone as he traveled through China reporting for the paper, but in the last few weeks as they had prepared for the departure and then begun the trip, he had found himself constantly with his family, everyone including the children, Old Zhu, and Black Jade. Even being alone with Black Jade had lately been rare, and then only late at night as they both fell asleep exhausted.

But now, sitting there in the dining room watching a few late arrivals finishing their dinners, he quite enjoyed it. In fact, he almost wished he'd taken up smoking; it seemed the right moment for such an indulgence. After accepting the steward's offer of a nightcap, he took up the glass and walked out on to the railing. It was a beautiful night. There was just enough moonlight to illuminate the very calm waters that spread out alongside the ship. The only thing one might have asked for was a bit less sound from the ship's huge steam-driven paddle wheels, but even *they* seemed to be making less noise than usual as the ship glided along.

As he slowly walked along the railing, he saw through an open port the salon Aouda had mentioned, full of cigar and pipe-smoking men. There among them sat his dinner partner Fogg, staring intently at the cards he held closely in his hands. For a moment, Jason thought of entering but then stopped. The entire atmosphere of the salon reminded him too much of Barlow, his editor's club. Jason had never been comfortable there, and this would probably be no different. He moved on. There were a few small clumps of people standing at the rails talking among themselves. For a moment, his eye caught two young lovers holding hands and ever so discretely kissing.

As he walked to the other side of the deck, there were even fewer passengers at the railing, and the moon's light seemed to illuminate the walkway less well. Standing there simply taking in the waves that lapped mildly against the ship's side, he realized that two men were standing at something of a distance from him, and their voices sounded strained. There was some sort of tension between them. But he could hear almost nothing, save a few words and phrases "bank robbery" and "Absurd! My master is an honest man!"

What could that be about? Jason wondered to himself. Then a moment later, the shorter of the two stomped off. As he passed Jason, the reporter realized it was the Frenchman from the circus—Fogg's manservant. Then a moment later, the second fellow, himself walking without a word, started to walk the other way, but as he turned the light from the moon suddenly illuminated his face. In a flash Jason recognized where he knew the man from. It was the second fellow, the other man who had boarded their ship with Fogg and Aouda so dramatically as they departed Shanghai. What could that be about? he wondered.

For the next ten minutes or so, he was alone on the deck until...

"Whoa there," the voice and breath were both close, as a rather inebriated man, a fellow of perhaps fifty, almost slammed into Jason as he tried to walk along the deck. Jason, fearing the fellow would pitch himself overboard by accident, grabbed the man, helping to right him.

"Well, thank you, young man. Guess I had a bit too much of the ship's fine stores of brandy," he said sheepishly.

"No problem, but you might want to stand here for a moment until you get your bearing," Jason suggested.

"Probably a good idea. So, young fellow, where are you from?"

"My family is from the Boston area. We are going there now," he added.

"Lovely place Boston...been there a few times myself. My own people hail from Baltimore. Looking forward to getting home, I am. Had a bit of business in the Orient, but I've had enough of that. You're on your way there now you say?"

"We plan on stopping in San Francisco for a few weeks, but yes, then on to Boston."

"San Francisco, eh." The fellow looked concerned. "Oh, it will be nice enough to be back on Yankee soil I should think. But if I were you, I would just move on. San Francisco is a dirty place, not a place a Bostonian like yourself would likely to take up an affection for."

"Why do you say that?" Jason asked, taking another sip of his drink and eyeing the man suspiciously, for he had an idea of what was coming.

"Too damn many heathen Asiatics, of course. Filthy people, opium dens, basically just men living in their Chinatown. It's not a place a God-fearing Christian would want to visit except for—well, between us—you know, a bit of fun."

"Do you know the San Francisco Chinatown well?" Jason asked, finding himself sobering up a lot faster than he expected. Maybe it was the ocean winds that were dropping a bit in temperature, he thought to himself.

"No, can't say I've been there myself, but those Asiatics bring with them enough diseases and crime; it's hard not to hear about their presence. Oh, I suppose the Japanese are OK. They seem, from what I saw in Yokohama, to have some appreciation of civilization, but not the Chinese. My God, man, have you ever been to Hong Kong or Shanghai? And those in San Francisco are no better."

With that he pulled an expensive watch from his waist pocket and consulted it with some difficulty by the moonlight. "Well, good evening to you, and take my advice. If you want to see San Francisco, take a day or so. You might like the Cliff House and then get yourself on a train east. You will be a lot happier."

A moment later Jason was alone again with his thoughts. What had he gotten his family into? The previous evening's encounter at dinner had been unpleasant enough, but how Americans might receive his family—his partly American, partly Chinese family—was not something they'd spent a lot of time thinking about. In Shanghai, they'd been well known, with Jason's writings relatively popular. But in America...How would the reception be—the reception for the ethnically Chinese Black Jade and Mei-ling? And what of William who so clearly looked partially American and partly Chinese? He took another, this time significantly larger, slug of the drink.

Finally, he started for his cabin, and with not an insignificant amount of effort, he found it. The small space was empty. Black Jade was apparently still gone, still talking somewhere with her new friend. He fell asleep on the bed without taking off his clothes.

"Wake up." She was insistent, insistent even for Black Jade who'd never had much problem speaking her mind. "Wake up, I have heard the most amazing story."

As he pulled himself to a sitting position, she handed him a glass of water from the water canister and plopped herself down cross-legged on the bed.

"I've had the most amazing conversation with Aouda," she started out enthusiastically. "They are in a race, a race around the world!" she said excitedly.

"A race? Around the world?" Jason said, coming fully awake and wiping the sleep from his eyes. "Against whom?"

"Against time. It's amazing. Not against a person but against time itself. Mr. Fogg bet people in his London club—he even mentioned it…the…what was it…? The 'reform club'—that he could go around the world in eighty days."

"You're kidding." He was now fully awake. "Why?"

"Well, that was less clear. Aouda says it is some sort of bet, thousands of pounds riding on it. As she tells it, the bet started during some sort of whist game. The card game he invited you to play. The men were arguing whether it was really possible to go around the world in eighty days. There had been an article saying that modern transportation would now allow such a thing. And Fogg took up a bet that he could do it."

"I guess that explains why he knows ship and train schedules so well," Jason commented, reflecting on this new information. "Where does she fit in? Are they married?"

"No, not married, though Aouda is very fond of him—certainly more than either of them know. That is an even more astounding part of the story. She met him in India. Mr. Fogg and that French servant, you know the one we saw at the circus, rescued her from certain death."

"What do you mean?"

"She'd been married to a much-older man who'd died, and she told me the custom was that widows should follow their husbands in death."

"Makes sense to me," he quipped, though his midnight attempt at humor only earned him a punch on the arm.

"Be serious; it's true. Her dead husband's family was going to burn her to death on his funeral pyre when Passepartout—that's his name—and Fogg showed up and carried her off."

"That is quite a story. So what happened next?" he asked, eager to hear more.

"Well, she was supposed to travel only as far as Hong Kong with him, but the one relative she had there had departed long before. So now she simply travels with him on the race around the planet."

"To travel around the world in eighty days to win a bet. His saving a damsel in distress. You had quite an evening's worth of fine stories. So what do you think of her as a person?"

"She is a fine companion, a good friend. I only wish I could get to know her better before she moves on. They are immediately boarding a train as soon as the ship arrives in San Francisco. But what of you, my husband, after we ladies deserted you? How did your evening go?"

"Actually rather nicely. I had some brandy, stood at the rail for a bit, and then came back." He thought for a fleeting second about telling her about the fellow from Baltimore but dropped the idea. There was no point.

"Did you check on the children?"

"Ah, I think I forgot…" he said sheepishly.

A moment later she was out the door. By the time she returned a few moments later, he was already falling asleep. Black Jade changed into her sleeping clothes and fell down asleep alongside him.

# CHAPTER 7
# GOLD MOUNTAIN

The next few days were uneventful. True there were some rough seas, but no threatening storm delayed the ship. In fact, the only contribution the somewhat-more-turbulent waters made was to see their seasickness return, particularly the children and Old Zhu. But even that turned out well, for Aouda, who'd apparently become even more used to turbulent waters during ocean storms before she'd boarded the ship bound for America, spent her time having the ship's kitchen prepare light vegetable broth and sitting with Black Jade and the others in their cabin. With that many individuals, two children and three adults, crammed in. The space had become impossibly crowded. Indeed, Jason could only stand at the door and peer in from time to time. Still, none of the company seemed worse for wear, and the storms calmed themselves soon enough.

As for Jason, he spent time wandering the deck and sitting alone in the dining salon between meals, planning future news articles. From time to time, he passed the other salon, the one that had so clearly turned into a gentlemen's club, and spied Fogg contentedly playing whist. The man seemed quite calm.

Not the sort of demeanor one would expect from a fellow racing around the world, with thousands of pounds sterling at risk. But then, Jason thought, there was not a lot to do while the ship still steamed along hundreds of miles off the coast of San Francisco anyway.

Meals were usually taken either with the children or more formally with Fogg and Aouda. Jason found he rather liked Fogg, at least found him interesting, but he really did not get to know much more about the man than he'd learned during that first dinner. Fogg was clearly content in his ways and aside from a very slight concern that the ship was steaming toward San Francisco at a reasonable rate did not seem to have a care in the world. His only vice, as far as Jason could see, was his constant affection for whist, his daily card game. Indeed, he clearly spent most of his waking hours thinking either about his last or next chance to indulge.

As for Aouda, she was quite different, and the friendship she and Black Jade developed was very genuine. The two women spent an enormous amount of time together. From what he could gather, they were mostly talking about the lives of Asian women. Black Jade was—he knew, especially from their effort years before to write about the lives of the women of the Taiping Heavenly Kingdom—quite interested in the subject. Apparently, it seemed Aouda, with both her Indian and English upbringing, was just as drawn to the topic.

The evening before their arrival, though, the two women seemed more tense. Jason knew they were quietly saying their good-byes, promising to stay in touch. And that last evening on board was the right time to do so, for Fogg had made it clear they would be leaving San Francisco on the first train east.

The next morning, only a few minutes before dawn, Jason awoke, and nudging Black Jade awake, he quietly beckoned her to get dressed and follow him. A few minutes later, they were on deck where several of their fellow passengers had also gathered—for there, with a hint of fog over it, lay the open harbor, and rising alongside it were buildings that snaked their way up the hills.

"So that is Gold Mountain?" she said quietly, using the term for America so common among the Chinese.

"So I am told. You know as much as I do," her husband responded, squeezing her hand.

San Francisco lay before them.


For the rest of the morning, as the ship docked and preparations were made for disembarkation, Jason and Black Jade gathered up their little brood. Jason himself was distracted going through the many documents, their marriage certificate from the American consulate in Shanghai, birth records, medical records, affidavits his father had sent certifying that Jason himself had been born in Massachusetts, and so forth. He did not anticipate a problem, but one never knew.

After a time, all their goods were packed, and Jason was about to call for a porter to help them carry their belongings ashore when the crisis struck.

Little William's telescope, the one presented by Uncle Prosper (for that is what the children called Giquel), was missing. For twenty frantic moments, they searched the entire compartment and then started to slide their hands into the bags that had until then been so neatly packed. Nothing! Meanwhile the tension level began to rise, especially as William by then started to cry while big-sister Mei-ling made frantic efforts to calm her little brother.

"The other cabin!" Old Zhu suddenly blurted out. With that there was a mad dash to the door, as if one could even try to move that quickly in the tiny space. Jason made it through first and strode out.

Five tense minutes later, the crisis was resolved. The child-sized telescope, so skillfully manufactured at the Fuzhou Dockyard Giquel directed, was found. It had rolled under one of the beds and caught itself near the back. All was again well in the world.

Within minutes a ship's porter helped them carry everything to the deck. It was almost deserted, for most of the first-class passengers had already departed. With hardly a problem, the entire family passed through customs and other formalities. There are advantages to a first-class ticket, Jason thought to himself. However, as the family stood there—for the carriages that had earlier so eagerly awaited the first-class passengers seemed to have already left—they began to look around. It was their first moments on the land in almost a month, and they found it almost difficult to stand.

After a time as their equilibrium returned and the sea legs (developed from the necessity of rebalancing on the ship's constantly shifting decks) were left behind, they found themselves for want of immediate transport options, really taking in where they were. The sensations that especially filled them were the smells and the temperature, for the morning's fog and the relatively chilly air enveloped them, drawing all their attention at least until another spectacle began.

Only a few yards away, pouring from the ship's steerage cabin, hundreds of third-class passengers were coming down the gangplank carrying meager parcels in their arms, looking—how could one describe it?—terrified and exhilarated at the same time. Jason knew there had been many poorer Chinese workers on the lower decks of the ship, of course, but the steamer's construction had been designed to limit the contact as much as possible between those paying for first-class transportation and the rest.

As his entire family watched, the laborers had their parcels very roughly searched by some of the same customs personal who had only just treated Jason's family with such courtesy a few moments before. A great deal of yelling, in English and in Chinese, filled the air. But unlike either the customs agents or the debarking laborers, Jason and Black Jade could understand everything being said, the insulting comments in both English and Chinese, as the two national groups encountered each other a few steps from the ship. The Chinese was, after all, easy to understand, because it was largely the familiar dialect of the Guangdong province Jason and Black Jade had spoken all their lives. And Black Jade's English comprehension had expanded impressively after weeks of constantly listening to Aouda's precise English Indian School girl speech.

"What are they doing, Mommy?" Mei-ling asked, obviously upset by the treatment the poorer Chinese were receiving.

"I think they are looking for opium, darling," Black Jade said quietly. "You have heard Mommy and Daddy talk about how terrible that drug is, how it destroyed the lives of so many of our friends."

But it was obvious Black Jade was upset as well. She'd certainly seen Chinese laborers treated roughly in China, but somehow here, here in Gold Mountain, it was, she somehow imagined, supposed to be different.

As the men passed through the customs gauntlet, they were loudly organized on the other side by local Chinese; men who appeared somehow official were organizing them by where they had come from. Perhaps local Chinese community officials, Jason wondered.

Then, a smaller group, about a dozen young Chinese girls, descended from the ship. As they walked onshore, crowds of men started to shout obscene curses at them while others simply laughed at the women. In truth few were really old enough to be called women. They were then being roughly examined by the customs officials and handed over to several older Chinese women dressed completely in black who quickly pushed the newest arrivals toward a waiting wagon.

"Sir, will you be needing a carriage?" the voice near his ear caught Jason's attention.

"A carriage, sir, to take you to your hotel?"

"Ah, yes, yes, of course," Jason said, handing the man the address of the hotel Fogg had recommended. The man certainly had been a wealth of travel information.

With that the entire family followed the fellow to a carriage large enough to carry everyone and their trunks. Once they were all settled in, the driver gave the horses a subtle nudge and they were off, everyone sitting quietly, even little William for a change simply watching San Francisco go past them. Jason was as fascinated as everyone else but also discretely aware of Black Jade glancing at him from time to time. She was clearly torn, by the sights of the city and the spectacle she'd just watched.

For the next few minutes, they traveled briskly through the streets, watching the sights and listening to the horses' hooves clatter against the wood-covered streets that seemed very well designed.

"Daddy, look." William nudged his arm. "What are those?" the boy asked, pointing at the little windmills that arose from so many of the buildings.

"I don't know, maybe something for pumping water into the buildings?" Jason guessed, though not really sure himself. But he had little time to study the curious devices, for they all arrived soon enough at the hotel Fogg had recommended.

"Good morning, Mr. Brandt. We have been expecting you," said the cheery desk clerk.

"You were expecting us?"

"Why yes, an English gentleman and his charming companion stopped by a few minutes ago to tell us of your arrival. They were quite solicitous, concerned that as you were traveling with children, you would want your rooms immediately available. We were quite delighted to oblige. Frankly, we don't have that many young guests here in San Francisco. How many rooms will you be needing and for how long?"

My goodness, Fogg really is the soul of efficiency, Jason thought as he requested the two adjacent rooms they had been requesting since the trip began—one room for himself and Black Jade, and the other for Old Zhu and the children. The arrangement had worked well for the long weeks on board the ship, and he now hoped it would continue to be so successful as they traveled toward Boston. For how long though, that had been less certain. He knew the real goal of the trip to understand America had only begun that morning. How long would they stay specifically in San Francisco? He and Black Jade would have to discuss that after they'd had more of a sense of the city. For the moment, he indicated a minimum stay of one week to get them started.

Within minutes, the rooms were ready—thanks to Fogg's advance warning. Jason and family found themselves setting up their rooms; they were not terribly large, for Jason could hardly afford two spacious quarters on his limited savings. Compared, though, to the cramped spaces available on the steamer, the entire family felt like they had become monarchs in this new land.

An hour later, after a brisk walk, both within the hotel and a quick energetic hike in the area directly around the hotel, Jason's brood returned to the lodging house for a charming lunch in the dining room Then the entire family returned to their rooms to relax, everyone except Jason, for he and Black

Jade had decided that upon arrival, Jason would set out to see if there were any letters that awaited them.

By midafternoon Jason left the hotel with the intention of finding both the local post office and eventually the offices of the *Examiner*, the newspaper Twain had written him about. Neither proved difficult to find. At the post office, he was somewhat disappointed not to find a letter from Giquel, who had known the family would be passing through San Francisco. Perhaps it had taken Wu more time than Jason had guessed to get to Fuzhou and the offices of his old French friend. Still the more he thought about it, the more he realized there probably had not been time for a letter from Giquel to have been waiting for him in California's ever-so-charming gateway. And "charming" was exactly the word that came to mind, for Jason had already started to develop a fondness for the city.

If no letter from Prosper Giquel awaited him at the post office, he was nevertheless not disappointed. The wealthy financier Russell Sage had written him another of his somewhat-terse and quickly-to-the-point notes. The New Yorker had been delighted with Jason's report on the potentials of Chinese railroads and wished to talk more. The financier invited Jason and his entire family to stop in New York City on their way to Boston. Sage made it quite clear he was willing to facilitate the request by subsidizing their New York hotel bill and lodging during the stay as well as a small additional sum. Again, the sum, not generous but reasonable.

For the moment, Sage only asked for an approximate date for their arrival if the arrangement met Jason's approval. The only thing that was somewhat surprising was that the ever-to-the-point Sage had mentioned in the last paragraph that his wife, apparently her name was Olivia, was interested in meeting Black Jade, having developed a sense of her from Jason's writings. Knowing that Sage was offering more cash for his thoughts on China helped relieve the private burden Jason had been feeling over the previous weeks, as money flowed only outwardly from the wallet he'd carefully hidden around his waist.

Once he left the post office, it was only a short while before he, now on foot, found his way to the offices of one of the two newspapers that served the city. As he walked into the *Examiner*'s office, the smells of the place, old coffee, printers' ink, and the filth of offices that generally held few women all rushed through his senses. For a moment, he thought he was back at the *North China Daily News* as he waited. He gave his name to the young man who apparently served as the receptionist and ad writer. For a few more minutes, Jason listened carefully as the fellow carefully took down a customer's ad. Apparently, a carriage with two horses that were going to be advertised in the next edition.

Finally, it was his turn.

"Yes, Mr. Brandt. Welcome. We've thought you might arrive soon. Mr. Clemens has already written, and you've got quite a little reception waiting you. Let me take you to the editorial offices. A few seconds later, Jason was ushered through a door that exited to the left of the reception area and into a room of men, all sitting around with cigars and their feet up on the furniture. There were at least two bottles of brandy sitting half open.

"Gentlemen," the clerk said enthusiastically, "our guest, straight from China, has arrived. Let me present Mr. Jason Brandt."

With that the entire small company of middle-aged men jumped to their feet to greet him.

# CHAPTER 8

# TOURING SAN FRANCISCO

Over the next few minutes, Jason could not have been more grateful to Mr. Clemens. He had obviously written enough about Jason to warrant his warm greetings from his fellow journalists who were as relaxed as men of their sort can be after the paper, and the *Examiner* an afternoon paper, had been sent off to the printers. The timing of Jason's arrival could not have been better chosen. He was offered wine, beer, a slice of apple pie, chewing tobacco, cigars, really anything from the array of goodies the journalists had scattered around the room.

"Jason, I know you have just met a lot of people—scoundrels all, as Sam likes to say—but let me offer you my special greetings, for I've been assigned to be your guide here in San Francisco by our mutual friend."

The idea that Mark Twain had given these men reason to think he actually knew the well-known writer gave Jason pause for reflection and pleasure.

"First, of course, let me introduce myself. My name is Charles Nordhoff, and Sam, knowing of my interest in those new to California, asked me to show you around our fair city."

Nordhoff, who appeared to have a slight Germanic accent, wore glasses and sported a neatly groomed beard that covered much of his chin while leaving the cheeks clean-shaven.

"Well, that is too kind, sir. I simply could not presume to ask such a favor from a stranger," Jason offered, somewhat uncomfortable.

"Nonsense, Sam asked me, and more importantly, he knew my showing you the sights would be as helpful to me as you." With that, the fellow started digging into his satchel for something. A few seconds later, he pulled a book from the bag, and then opening the book, he withdrew an envelope neatly stored within to keep it from being crinkled.

"First your letter from Samuel. He sent it to me, assuming I would be in the best position to find you." Jason was handed a relatively thick envelope that was clearly sent by Twain. Then after studying the envelope for a second, he looked back at Nordhoff, who was standing there with something else to present.

"And now with the enthusiasm only another writer can understand. I would like to offer you a copy of my new book literally just off the presses. Indeed, the reason Sam knew I'd be the best sort of guide you can have." With that, he handed Jason his book while the others looked on smiling.

"Right, Jason, now you can find out what a foreigner, an East-Coast Yankee and a Prussian to boot thinks of our California," one of the other reporters said laughingly, though Jason could tell Nordhoff was somewhat sensitive about the teasing.

*California for Health, Pleasure, and Residence: A Book for Travelers and Residents*

By Charles Nordhoff

Author of *Cape Cod and All Along the Shore*

Studying the book and glancing at its comprehensive table of contents and beautiful lithographs, as Nordhoff stood by smiling like a new parent, Jason slowly took in the work. As a writer, he was envious. As a new tourist in San Francisco, he wanted to immediately curl up somewhere and read the book.

"Mr. Nordhoff, this is truly remarkable, and it just came out you say? It looks wonderfully useful. I am deeply grateful. I am sure my family can use it. We arrived, as you heard, only just this morning and were planning to set out tomorrow with our children to start exploring the city."

"You have children; that is even better. We don't see that many children in California. I am very eager to see how my book serves their needs, for, as you can see, this is not my first excursion as a travel writer. Indeed, I am pleased to say my Cape Cod book has been very well received, and I expect to write another travel book as soon as I see how this California book does with the public.

"No, please understand. Even if Sam, an old dear friend and fellow scribbler, had not asked me to show you around, your agreeing to do so would be a favor to me personally. I am eager to understand better what visitors really need."

"Well, if you put it that way, then let me enthusiastically agree. Even a moment's perusal already tells me I can learn a great deal from your work, about California, and as a writer. So when do we start?"

"Well, as it happens, I am free for most of the next week. How about tomorrow morning? Can I pick you up at your hotel? Oh, I should ask, how many in your party?" Nordhoff asked enthusiastically.

"Five of us—my wife, our two children, William and Mei-ling, and the children's governess known as Old Zhu."

"A Chinese governess..." Nordhoff hesitated for a moment. "Right, of course Sam said your wife was Chinese. Well, that makes it even better. I have never shown a Chinese around the city. As I am sure you have already seen our city includes a great many citizens of—what do they call it?—'The Middle Kingdom,' I think. But frankly not that many likely to go touring. Yes, that will make it even better," he said, clearly savoring the idea.

"Do you like early starts? I know that is hard with children, but I know a wonderful place that serves excellent breakfasts, offers fantastic views and a very, very special treat for the children you will read about in the book."

"I think we can manage that," Jason said gratefully.

"Shall we say eight in the morning then? I will arrive with a carriage just near the front door of the hotel."

"I really can't thank you enough, and again, everyone, I cannot tell you how honored I am that you offer a fellow newspaperman such a warm reception. I think, though, that I must leave now. I abandoned my family at the hotel and they are probably wondering what has happened to me since I left to make my rounds." With that he left, patting his pocket to make sure that the precious letters, from Russell Sage and from Twain, were carefully secured within.

He'd walked to the offices of the *Examiner*. He wasn't, after all, traveling with the children or Black Jade, who could not walk terribly far despite the fact that her feet had never been as tiny or painful as her Chinese sisters, with their more successfully bound feet. No, he thought to himself. No use taking on the extra expense, since he was alone and San Francisco was interesting enough to study as he walked. But first, he stopped and, finding a spot to sit for a moment, slowly opened the letter from Mark Twain.

> My Dear Jason:
> If you are reading this, I am assuming you have made it to the *Examiner* offices and that my friends there have received you well. But do keep your head and

wallet about you. And don't let them talk you into contributing something about China without promising a fair fee in advance. I am assuming you have also met Charles, another one of our competitors for the public's reading dollars, but don't hold that against him. He has done some fine work. I hope you don't mind I encouraged him to serve as your tour guide. If you are as determined as I expect you are to learn about your home country, he will be far and away your best guide.

Thank you for sending back the contract so promptly. I am absolutely delighted you found the contract satisfactory and look forward to a mutually advantageous relationship.

Samuel Clemens

PS, About *China Tales*. Organizing the second printing is going very well indeed. I hope you don't mind, but I wrote a modest forward to the piece (Mind! Jason almost yelled to himself. Mind! Are you kidding?) that I modestly assume will help sell subscription sales—and they have already begun to arrive based on some advance advertising I've done.

I am guessing you won't arrive here until after the first of the year and as you probably have no idea what New England winters are like—forget every impression you may have already arrived at in what folks here think of as tropical California, obviously folks who have never been in San Francisco itself. But, I digress...

By early spring you will have arrived in New England, settled in somewhere, and we can start scheduling some public talks. Interest in all things Chinese is at a height, and I believe you will be in great demand as both a writer and speaker.

I don't know what path you have chosen to head east, but whether those plans include passing near Hartford, Connecticut—for I have just taken up residence here—or more directly to Boston, I look forward to receiving you here as my guest when the time is ripe. And if you do end up in Boston first, don't be concerned. Hartford is quite close and transportation easily arranged. Once you have an idea of your more immediate plans, please write or telegraph me at the following location.

Sincerely

Samuel Clemens a.k.a. Mark Twain

Wow, Jason thought to himself. Things could not be working out any better. Standing up, he looked around the street for another moment or so, studying the buildings. Pulling up his coat a bit tighter around him, for the city seemed awfully chilly, he hailed a cab. Money problems seemed to be increasingly manageable, and he was anxious to get back to the hotel.

The combination of San Francisco's impressive wooden slatted streets and the convenient horse taxis made the travel easy despite the steep hills that reminded him in so many ways of the hills on Hong Kong's Victoria Island. Once at the hotel, he paid the driver and went in. To his surprise and pleasure, Black Jade, Old Zhu, and the children were sitting in the lobby. Even more positively little William was eagerly showing off his telescope to two other little boys, who were taking great pleasure looking through it.

"You are back, my husband," Black Jade said, spotting him. "Do you have good news?"

"Good and interesting news, better than we could have hoped. But let's talk later. Has everyone had their supper?" for it was already starting to get dark outside. For a moment Jason reflected to himself what a long day it had been. Had it really started with them standing at the rail, staring at San Francisco as the ship glided toward the port?

"Everyone has eaten except me. I was waiting for you to return," she said.

"Excellent, let's get everyone upstairs and settled down. Then we'll come down ourselves in a bit, unless you are terribly hungry. The reporters at the *Examiner* stuffed me with a lot of apple pie and such."

"No problem; I can wait." With that the entire family started off toward their rooms—little William a bit reluctantly, for he was enjoying his new friends. Mei-ling, though, seemed eager to go upstairs. Sitting quietly with Old Zhu and her mother had no doubt not been nearly as entertaining for her as for her little brother.

An hour later, everyone was settled in their rooms, which, after weeks of cramped quarters on the ship, still amazed them all. Promising the children they would return to say good-night in a bit, Jason and Black Jade left for dinner.

A few minutes later, the couple sat downstairs in the dining room, looking over the menu and listening to the waiter describe the possible meals available to them. After choosing and watching the fellow retreat to the kitchen, Black Jade turned to Jason.

"I know we are in America, that this whole trip is about learning about America, but if you don't get me to Chinatown fast for a real meal, you are going to have a very angry wife to deal with," she said, laughing.

"What, you think I love this stuff? I may have grown up with my mom's Western cooking, but you and I know I much prefer Chinese food. Sometimes I think that was the main reason I ran away from my father's home when he tried to send me back here for college."

"So when can we go, tomorrow morning?" she asked eagerly.

"Well, that's just it; I want to tell you about my day, and it includes breakfast plans. First though to business, the part that helps pay for this dinner you plan to dislike so much," he teased. With that he pulled out the two letters, the one from the business-man Russell Sage and the other from Mark Twain. Explaining first Sage's offer and then Twain's, he was extraordinarily excit-ed to tell her all the details, for Black Jade's first thoughts were always about keeping the family financially solvent.

"So we will meet this very rich businessman? Can we see his house? That I would especially like to do."

"I don't know about that, but it's certainly more than a busi-ness invitation." He pointed at the last paragraph. "He says his wife is anxious to meet you."

"So I am supposed to meet the wife of the great business-man, and in this country businessmen are very important, are they not?" she asked tentatively. He nodded. She sat quietly, wondering if she were concerned about clothing.

"Well, then that seems excellent. It should be very helpful knowing him. Who you know cannot be less helpful here in America than it is in China. What did Twain, or Clemens—goodness, what am I supposed to call him...say?"

"Actually I don't know; I guess we will find that out eventu-ally. But here is what is important. He got the contract and has started the process of reprinting the book here in America. And this is the best part. He himself wrote some sort of pref-ace. That is an incredible honor!"

"That is good, that he wrote something in your book you have not seen?" she asked curiously.

"Oh, I doubt it's anything I would be uncomfortable with. What matters is that he is a lot better known than I am, and his name sells books. He even said they were starting to get ad-vance orders for the book, and it's not even printed yet." Jason quickly went over the rest of the letter, telling her of the chance to give public talks in part to sell the books. "The best part is that we have this very generous writer publisher committed to the books' sales, because part of the profits is his as well."

"My husband, I could not be more pleased." At that the waiter arrived with their dinners, neatly lit the table's oil lamp, for it had begun to be much darker in the dining room, and poured each of them more wine.

Black Jade looked down, contemplating the huge slab of beef and the large baked potatoes that sat alongside it quite smartly and then turning to Jason again.

"So tomorrow can we have breakfast in Chinatown?"

Jason laughed. My darling, I would love to do that. But that is the other part of what I needed to tell you." As they ate he pulled out the book he'd brought with him to the dining room, showed it to her and explained about Nordhoff. She looked interested but disappointed as well.

"So tomorrow after he shows us the sites, can we have lunch in Chinatown?"

"Darling, I absolutely promise you…in the next twenty-four hours, I will get you to the nicest place I can find in Chinatown to eat. And I say that knowing that, I think we might even be able to afford it."

# CHAPTER 9

# MORE SAN FRANCISCO ADVENTURES

Hours later, the two of them lay in bed together, unable to sleep. So much had happened in the less than twenty-four hours since they'd arrived in San Francisco.

"You know," Jason said, turning to his wife, "you never told me what you did while I was gone."

"It was not nearly as interesting as your afternoon," his wife said, rolling toward him. "We mostly stayed in the rooms, un-packed for a while—who knows how long we will be here? I managed to ask the desk people about having laundry done. It was sort of odd. If I understood the clerk, he made a joke about never having had a Chinese woman ask him to have laundry done. But he took the clothing and said it would be available later today."

"Well, that sounds sort of successful. Your English is getting better and better every day. I think it helped a lot that you spent so much time with Aouda on the ship."

"At least I did not have to keep reminding her to speak English to me. Sometimes you drive me crazy, husband, con-stantly speaking in Chinese. I saw how much easier your life was in China knowing the language. I want to have the same advantage here," she said, that steely look in her eye he'd known for so long coming to the surface.

"Anything else to report?" he asked, though in truth he was finally getting sleepy and the bedding was a lot more comfortable than on the steamer.

"Not a lot. We looked around the hotel some. There was one thing. We encountered a Chinese maid, a young woman from some village near Guangzhou I'd never heard of, and tried to talk to her."

"Tried?" he asked, his curiosity aroused, for while they'd both seen a great many Chinese in the streets, he certainly had not yet had the occasion to talk to one of the city's many Chinese residents.

"She seemed very nervous about talking to us, concerned, I guess, that her supervisor or someone else would come by... she did talk a bit."

"What did she say about living here instead of at home?"

"The only thing that was clear was that it is a very complicated story, lots more money here, in some ways a lot better life; apparently a few years ago, it was even better," she added.

"And now?" he asked, sitting up in bed, ready to hear as much as his wife could tell him.

"Certainly better, though not as good as it was before they finished the big railroad when there was an enormous amount of work. But, yes, much better than at home...but in some ways a lot worse. The Americans seem very unhappy with their presence...calling them all sorts of vile names."

"What sort, about what?" he asked, for he knew if his plan here in America was going to be successful, he was going to have to know as much about Chinese in America as the Chinese in China.

"There really was not much more. As we spoke an American woman, the sort you said might be Irish on the ship, came by, maybe the head cleaning lady, and the conversation abruptly broke up. Sort of had to anyway; William was pulling at my dress. He badly wanted to go to the lobby."

"Interesting. What did Old Zhu think?" he asked, for he had found the family's governess often very acute in her comments about people.

"That was another unexpected part at least for Zhu. She could barely understand a word the woman said. You and I know the dialects of both southern and northern China. We grew up in the south, speak the same language most of the people here do. I don't think Old Zhu had been more than twenty li from Shanghai before she got on the steamer with us."

"That is going to be frustrating for her," he commented after a second.

"More than frustrating, I know she has been trying to pick up English phrases herself. She is not stupid. She knows she needs to be able to communicate, but I don't think she realized; not sure I'd thought about it, but practically all the Chinese here so far speak the language of the south. You heard them at the harbor this morning. Zhu knew she would not be able to speak to the whites. But not to be able to communicate with the Chinese upset her more than she said, I think."

"You are right; that had never even occurred to me. Well, she is part of the family. We will have to be careful," he said, though not exactly sure what that meant.

"What about the kids?" Jason asked, lying back down on the bed, starting to feel as sleepy as he had earlier.

"Well, that is the really irritating part. They are picking up the language much faster than I am, especially William. Did you hear him jabbering away with those kids in the lobby?"

Jason nodded, though his eyes were starting to close as he fell into a deep sleep.

Black Jade lay awake for a time, staring up at the ceiling. Gold Mountain was starting to be a lot more complicated than she had expected, even for a Chinese woman married to a successful American.

⊷⊶

"Wake up, my husband." Black Jade was pushing against his shoulder. "It's time to get up. You said we needed to be downstairs by eight."

Slowly Jason pulled himself awake and, rubbing his eyes, stared at his wife. She had obviously done her toilet, seeing the wet towel hanging from the rack near her, and started for the door.

"I am going to get everyone else up. So get dressed yourself. I will see you in a minute."

Slowly Jason pulled himself from the bed. It was incredibly more comfortable than the one on the steamer, and he started toward the washbasin. A few minutes later, he was ready and standing at the door to the next room, watching his family and Old Zhu preparing themselves.

Within thirty minutes, everyone was ready, and the entire crew marched down the stairs and toward the lobby entrance. They were on time. There standing at the door was Nordhoff, with a carriage large enough for all of them waiting. The driver looked sleepy but ready to go as well.

"Mr. Nordhoff, let me present my family. This is my wife Black Jade, my children Mei-ling and William, and Old Zhu, our children's governess."

"Well, I am delighted to meet everyone. This is indeed a pleasure."

Black Jade stepped forward and boldly took his hand to shake it.

"Mr. Nordhoff," she started out, choosing her words carefully. Jason could tell her English had clearly been influenced by Aouda's English boarding-school education.

"My family and I are deeply honored that you have offered to show us the sites of San Francisco."

Nordhoff beamed with surprised pleasure while Jason wondered what he had been expecting, pidgin English?

"Madame, the pleasure is all mine. I love San Francisco, and the opportunity to show her off to visitors is a great pleasure indeed. I hope your husband has shown you my modest guidebook on the subject."

"He did indeed. It is truly the work of a great scholar."

"Well, I am not sure it is the work of a scholar, but thank you. And, Madame, this being your first full day in America, may I inquire, do you have an American name? For I am afraid many here will mangle your Chinese name beyond your wildest imagination."

"Of course," she said.

"What, you have an English name?" Jason asked his wife, surprised.

"Indeed I do. The old English missionary lady you hired to tutor us in English while you were traveling for the newspaper gave us one, Mei-ling and myself."

"I had no idea," Jason said, laughing.

"It did not seem important till just now."

Nordhoff was clearly amused, and watching his charges, he cut in, "And, my lady, can we have the pleasure of knowing it?" He bowed.

"Of course, let me first present my daughter Norma," she said, indicating Mei-ling at her side. "And of course, my son William; I guess that won't be a problem here in America."

"I am quite sure. And you, Madame?" Nordhoff asked while Jason looked on, shocked.

"I am known as Nellie; I guess Mrs. Nellie Brandt."

Jason just looked at her. "Nellie…my wife's name is Nellie?"

"Yes, I am Nellie Brandt."

"Well. Nellie Brandt," Nordhoff began as the two parents stared at each other. "Let us begin. What do you all know about San Francisco?"

Suddenly Mei-ling, now Norma, raised her hand as high as she could. The entire company turned to her.

"Yes, my lovely Norma, what have you heard?" their guide asked with genuine warmth.

Speaking slowly but with very clear English, Mei-ling said, "Everyone is rich in Gold Mountain."

"Rich, rich, yes, of course. Well, little one, you are certainly right. There are a lot of rich people and a great many others who came here hoping to be rich. Anything else?"

"What I know, Mr. Nordhoff, is that a great many Chinese left my country when I was young to come to America, to come to as my daughter said Gold Mountain to get rich. And many came back with lots of cash. Some built very nice homes for their families, and others sent money home. We heard many stories about Gold…about, San Francisco and California."

"Much of that is true, at least what I know of myself from the United States. Many Chinese came here in the years of the Gold Rush…but that was more than twenty-five years ago. Back in '49 and then more recently, as the railroads were being built. Your countrymen found a great deal of work. It is more complicated than that. But enough of that for now. It's time to begin our tour."

With that, he turned to the driver to steady the horses while the entire family climbed aboard.

"To the Cliff House, sir," Nordhoff cried out, for the streets were already getting louder with traffic, and the sounds of horse hooves against the wooden boards louder still.

A short while later, they arrived at the path leading to the Cliff House, an extraordinary structure mounted on the top of a cliff directly facing west. While they could have chosen to sit on the veranda, the group decided to sit inside, looking out one of the windows onto the Pacific.

"If any of you are feeling homesick, I can assure you that if you look in that direction there"—he indicated, pointing with his arm and extended finger—"a few thousands of miles in that direction, you will first come upon Japan, which I assume you have seen on the way here and then beyond that Shanghai."

They all looked outward while Jason wondered if everyone else was feeling both the excitement and ambivalence he felt. Once breakfast was served, Nordhoff stood up dramatically. "And now we depart for our most precious special treat and especially so for you two. Little William and Norma."

Both children beamed excitedly.

"Now follow me down to the rocks below." Excited, they followed a path down toward the water's edge. As they approached the rocky shoreline, the sound of the ocean waves splashing against the coastline initially caught their attention, and then another sound raised itself, the sound of a honking of sorts, and then suddenly, perhaps startled by their approach, an enormous creature arose, something like a seal but much larger, its mouth open roaring at them.

Jason grabbed his entire family to hold them back.

"Oh my God," he hollered above the sound of the crashing water and even louder honking sounds, for now an echo of honking had emerged from an enormous tribe of sea creatures that stood or slept near the largest."

"What is it?" Jason yelled to Nordhoff, who stood there smiling happily.

"It's a sea lion. You have seen seals I presume."

"Well, yes, but nothing like this!"

"Let me have that," Mei-ling suddenly yelled. Looking down at his children, Jason saw Mei-ling grabbing at her brother's arm, for his little satchel had as always included the telescope. The little boy was happily staring into it at the incredible creatures. For a moment Jason felt like copying his daughter and snatching at the telescope himself.

"We will all take turns," Black Jade said loudly over the din. And so they stood, perhaps for half an hour. Nordhoff himself wandered the beach area, looking at shells, as the entire Brandt family took turns looking through the telescope at the entire brood, and without it those closest to them. They were in awe, and the sensations, from the cold wind whipping around them to the sight of these magnificent creatures, were almost overwhelming.

"When you said a treat for the children, you were surely understating the situation," Jason said as Nordhoff slowly approached them.

"And are we ready for our next adventure?" he asked, obviously delighted. The giant sea lions had been the hit he expected.

"Can we stay longer?" Mei-ling asked. "Just a bit longer?"

"Of course," Black Jade said, "but we can't stay too long. We have only just begun our explorations."

A bit later the entire troop walked slowly back to the carriage, where the driver still awaited them, wrapped both in a coat and a thick blanket.

Pointing to the man as they approached, Nordhoff commented quietly, "So look at the fellow there. He is trying to persuade you that sunny California is not nearly so sunny as they say.

But in truth, you are all getting the wrong impression. Once you get away from the city itself, California can be very pleasant— one of the only tropical places Americans have within their territory. But you would not know it to be so in San Francisco in December. So now, how about something totally different?"

The Brandts looked at each other. "Yes, you are the guide," Jason said, speaking for his little brood.

"Excellent, what I have in mind now is special even for me. Something quite new; not even the San Francisco people know it as you will…at least not yet."

"Coachman, would you be so kind as to take us to the bottom of Clay Street?"

"Certainly, sir." The coachman then added, for it was the first time he'd said a word to them, "And, sir, I think I know where you are going…and I am curious as well." With that, the driver nudged the horses with considerably more enthusiasm than he'd previously used.

A while later they were at the bottom of Clay Street. At first nothing looked unusual, but then Nordhoff jumped from the carriage and called out to a man standing in a top hat, "Andrew, our guests have arrived." For a moment, Nordhoff conferred with the man and then walked him over to the little group.

"My friends, I want to present to you Andrew Hallidie, whom I believe will be as famous as any in America, and quite soon I think." Hallidie looked pleased with the praise of the journalist.

"My friend Mr. Hallidie is just now doing final testing on his most amazing transportation machine." With that Nordhoff gestured across the street, where a curious contraption only a few seconds before obscured by a large horse-driven carriage, was now revealed before them.

There before them was the strangest machine any of them had ever seen. It was a carriage of sorts, but then little William yelled out the question that was in all their minds.

"Where are the horses, Daddy?"

"Where are the horses indeed," Jason mumbled, for there in front of them stood a low-riding carriage that seemed to fit perhaps ten passengers. "Clay Str. Hill R.R. Co." proclaimed the sign along the roof and a large number "10" on the front.

"Where are the horses indeed...in fact, where is the engine?" Jason asked, turning to the two men who beamed alongside him.

"That is the wonder of it," Hallidie said. "We call it a cable car. It is pulled along by cables under the street," he said, pointing at them beneath the carriage. "And you are lucky indeed to know my friend Charles. Half of San Francisco is begging for a ride, but it's not yet finished. Too many technical problems to open it up yet. It works wonderfully but isn't as reliable as it needs to be for the public yet. But enough of that. We are still testing it, and Charles prevailed on me to let your family sit on our little cable car during one of its test runs. Can't have it running empty all the time. That is not a test. No, let's see how it feels to a family." With that he gestured and all of them climbed aboard, arranging themselves in the several rows. Nordhoff himself and Hallidie stood in the open area behind the row of seats.

The last thing Jason noticed as the cable car abruptly lurched forward with a start was the terror in Old Zhu's eyes and the driver of their carriage, for Jason had a clear view of him standing wide-eyed and mouth open staring at them.

For the next few minutes, the car was pulled by the unseen cable loudly up the hill along the rails that Jason now realized ran up to the top of the street. It was an incredible experience, and he was only partially aware of those crowds on the streets watching them, some with amazement (perhaps people who'd never seen the device before) and some standing at the door of shops laughing somewhat among themselves.

Three quarters of the way of the hill, there was a loud clanging sound and the cable car jerked to a stop.

Nordhoff and Hallidie jumped out and helped the family to the street.

"No problem; that's why we are not yet open to the public. Cable keeps getting locked up under the street. But no worry. We will get it fixed. I am hoping to have the line completely running by this summer."

"It is truly amazing. Is this common in America?" Black Jade asked.

"No, madam, not common at all. I believe it to be the first ever. But once I get it working properly, I'd like to see it all over the city...and maybe beyond."

"Mr. Hallidie, of that I have no concern. What you have shown us is extraordinary...I look forward to seeing your device spread across not just America but China as well," Jason said graciously.

"China..." Now there's a thought, Hallidie said to himself.

With that, Nordhoff directed the group down the hill back toward the carriage below.

"Mr. Nordhoff, can we now have you as our guest at lunch. I am told San Francisco has many wonderful Chinese restaurants."

"Madame, let me first off thank you for the invitation, but I am afraid I have to run. Can we start out again tomorrow morning at the same time?"

"That would be wonderful. So, you are sure you won't join us for the lunch then? Can I at least pay for this morning's carriage?" Jason asked.

"Of course, but I have a better idea. Let me give the driver the name of a well-known Chinese restaurant. Let him take you there. Then pay the driver. Once you have eaten, you won't have any problem finding another carriage to take you back to the hotel." With that Nordhoff bowed to Jason's family and, after conferring with the driver for a moment, strode off. "Until tomorrow morning." He waved back at them and was off.

A short while later, the carriage turned on to a relatively broad street and pulled to a halt in front of a large obviously Chinese restaurant, which advertised itself in signs both in English and Chinese. As the group entered and mounted the stairs, for the restaurant clearly occupied the entire second floor of the building, Old Zhu let out a yelp of joy as the smells of the restaurant entered their nostrils. The group had not eaten Chinese food since Shanghai, and their enthusiasm was obvious as they entered the dining room and were greeted by a very well-dressed maître d'.

"How many in your party?" he asked Jason as he emerged from the stairwell well behind his children.

For the next twenty minutes, complete disorder reigned as each of them, even Old Zhu, individually chose dishes offered them by the several young attendants, who roamed the room offering food from small carts. The entire family ate ravenously, as if they had not eaten in days, though they had all had a Western-style breakfast only a few hours before.

After a time, his hunger for Chinese food quenched, Jason began to look around as the rest of his family chatted and consumed more and more of the very well-prepared dishes. More relaxed he studied the decor with its elaborate wooden carvings and festive, red Chinese decorations. This was clearly not a working-class establishment. In fact, as he studied the other customers, he realized that this was the first time he'd seen very obviously middle-class and richer Chinese in San Francisco. Certainly, there had been a lot of laborers, but these people were of a very different sort. And here and there in the room, the groups of diners included not just separate groups of Chinese or Westerners but a few tables, like his own, included mixed groups of both Anglos and Chinese. Here was yet another aspect of America's Chinese world he'd not seen before.

Once the entire family had completely stuffed themselves—and "stuffed" was most certainly the right word for it—Jason asked for the bill and paid it. A few minutes later, it was a very happy family indeed that climbed aboard another carriage and headed back to the hotel.

# CHAPTER 10

# THE GREAT TREES

Over the next few days, their mornings were spent touring with Nordhoff and in the afternoons taking his suggestions for further outings. Especially popular with the children was a trip to Woodward's Gardens, an enormous mansion on Mission Street, that housed a huge array of animals, museums, and most exciting of all, an incredible row of enormous glass fish tanks that was just opened allowing the public to view what had largely been invisible to them, the life of fish below the water. Like the cable car before it, Jason had never seen anything of the sort. America, he kept telling his family, had a great many wonders for them to discover.

Nordhoff, aware that they had already purchased their train tickets to move on east, kept hinting that there was something really special, something the public knew nothing about that he was saving for last.

"You will want to bring a variety of clothing, for our excursion will see us through a range of climates," he hinted mysteriously.

"So, Mr. Nordhoff, you have already been too kind. What is this place you have in mind? And I hope you have not taken too much trouble in the planning," Black Jade responded.

"Actually this is especially for me. Everything we have seen so far is written up in my travel book, everything except perhaps for the cable car and the new fish tanks at Woodward's, for they were only being planned when I was writing. But I now have an idea for yet another California volume and have heard of a very special place, near and yet far from here, that the public should know about as well."

"What can you tell us about it?" Jason asked, his curiosity aroused.

"Not much. I have never been there. I only heard about it a few weeks ago. We will all be tourists this time. And I certainly hope it will be something special, since you are leaving our fair city so soon. So why don't we plan on meeting tomorrow morning at the same time? But bring somewhat-warmer clothing, for a boat ride this time, maybe extra sweaters." At that, he left as Jason and his family set off for their dinner, dinner at the same Chinese restaurant they had discovered their second day in San Francisco and had then made a tradition in the several days since.

"Let's walk a bit," Black Jade said as they descended to the street after their meal. "I'd like to get some air."

A few minutes later, the family had entered one of the small Chinese shops and Black Jade was holding a small but sturdy black walking stick up for Jason's inspection.

"I don't think I have walked as much since we were teenagers, trying to find the Heavenly Kingdom. My feet may not be as unnatural as they might have been, but it is still hard to walk this much on them. What do you think of this one?" she said, handing him the cane.

Jason eyed it carefully. "Don't you think it is a bit heavy?"

"Yes, it is. It is heavier than the others there. But I rather like how sturdy it is. Do you think it's well made?"

Jason studied the walking stick more closely, rested his weight against it, and even swirled it a bit in the air, a difficult feat in the tight spaces of the curio shop. As he did so, he saw the look of disapproval in the face of the older Chinese man sitting near the door.

"Yes, if you want something this solid, I think it will do quite well." With that, he paid for the stick and the entire family walked out the door. The last thing Jason noticed was Old Zhu giving the store employee a dirty look. She'd obviously seen his anger when Jason swung the walking stick and was giving no ground.

"So should I find a cab now?"

"No, now it's time for me to test my new walking aide. Let's just pick a direction and walk till we need to hail a cab"—she gestured with the walking stick. Happily, Jason noted it was at least downward rather than upward, always a real possibility in this city of hills. Within minutes, they were well beyond the borders of Chinatown, for the restaurant itself had been near the periphery—perhaps, Jason had wondered to himself, to entice those Americans nervous about entering any more deeply into the Chinese section's distinctively foreign atmosphere. As they walked, the commotion in the streets became louder as they suddenly came upon a procession of Americans demonstrating and carrying placards high above their heads. Given how narrow the sidewalks were, the family had difficulty stepping back away from the crowd to a somewhat-more secure spot they could watch from. It took only a second to understand what was going on.

"We want no slaves or Aristocrats."

"The Coolie Labor System Leaves Us No Alternative - Starvation or Disgrace."

"No, to Chinese Strikebreakers."

"Mark the man who would crush us to the level of the Mongolian Slave—We All Vote."

And the last "Women's Rights and No More Chinese Chambermaids."

Jason's reporter's instincts aroused. He grabbed for the notepad in his bag and started to write down the statements on the placards verbatim. Then looking up and seeing the look on Black Jade's face, he put the pencil down. Even Old Zhu appeared distressed. One did not have to be literate to understand, and several of the signs carried drawing that could not be misinterpreted.

As they stood there, a young boy, no more than ten, sped through the street passing out flyers to everyone willing to take one. As he ran by, even before he had a chance to offer one, Jason put out his hand. Holding it up he saw it was an announcement of sorts of an upcoming public lecture by a Catholic priest named James Bouchard.

"Chinaman or White Man, Which?"

The talk was being advertised as something that would discuss the employment of Chinese who were, according to the flyer, not deserving the name of human. Jason stuffed the sheet in his pocket after glancing a second more at the list of adjectives assigned the Chinese from "vicious" to "corrupt." He turned to see Black Jade staring over his shoulder. She'd clearly been trying to read it herself.

"Let's go," he said abruptly. "The crowd is moving off. Let's find a carriage and get back to the hotel. A half an hour later, they were there, again treated with great kindness. Apparently, a Chinese family's money still earned respect, he thought to himself. The family spoke little as they prepared for bed. Even the children were unusually quiet. That evening as he and Black Jade discussed the impending departure, for they planned to leave in only a few days for Chicago, the next leg of their trip, she turned to him.

"Is this trip turning out as you imagined? I know it was my idea, but even I am beginning to wonder."

"It would be funny if it was not so serious," he began. "We had the idea of seeing America after you almost died because of suspicions and ignorance about Westerners in China… and now in America…we find this hatred of Chinese, or at least in some quarters hatred of Chinese. Sometimes it feels like we have found the mirror image of Shanghai here in San Francisco, another city divided by tensions and ambiguities between our two peoples."

"Do you remember the night when Prosper told us he was being sued basically because he treated the Chinese well?"

"How can one forget? But I am not convinced either of us really knows what is going on here. If there is anything I learned as a reporter, it was not to jump to conclusions. It is too easy to be embarrassed after a mistake ends up in print."

"Perhaps, my husband, we should decide not to draw an opinion until we've been here for six months," she suggested hesitantly.

"I like that. For now, maybe we should simply conclude that America may be a lot younger than China, but it is perhaps just as complicated. Let's just enjoy the next couple of days we have here in San Francisco. I am sure Chicago will be as different from San Francisco as Guangzhou is from Beijing."

"And how do you know that, my husband?"

"I have no idea, in fact. Please don't tell anyone, but I know Chicago is on the way to New York, but I have not a clue where it is."

"You are such a good American," his wife said. "But I bet you could travel between Shanghai and Nanjing with your eyes closed."

"OK, OK. That is why we are here. And, yes, I do remember this was your idea. So let's go to sleep. I love the beds here, and

I am afraid the train sleeper cars will be no better than those on the steamer and with maybe less space!"

"Well, are you at least excited about tomorrow? It is our last day with Charles, and he has built up tomorrow's secret so much, I doubt I will be able to sleep. It's all the children talked about while I put them to bed." But when she looked down, her husband was already snoring.

When they arrived on the sidewalk the next morning, Nordhoff was there, beaming with a large cap flung over his shoulders and a picnic basket he'd obviously prepared in advance.

"Welcome, everyone, to our special day. Now hop into the carriage. A small boat is awaiting us at the pier." A quick drive through the streets had them back at the water, though not at the same spot they'd arrived at the previous week. Nordhoff directed them up the small gangplank and saw to it that everyone was arranged around the benches of the small launch. Once each of them was settled in the small ship apparently operated by a small steam engine set out into the harbor. There seemed to be only a few sailors on board what was probably a fishing boat of sorts. Nordhoff seemed to know the captain well, and after a quick set of introductions, the captain resumed his duties while the small tourist party watched the water and the spectacular views of San Francisco that rose up from the sea.

After a short while, it became obvious that the boat was crossing the harbor entrance northward and then, after turning out into the Pacific slightly, was moving north along the shoreline. After what seemed no more than forty minutes, it became clear that the captain was looking for a particular spot along the coast. Rounding another corner of the rough boulder-strewn shoreline, they sighted an especially pointed rock that looked almost like an arrowhead reaching for the sky. Just beyond it lay an open cove and a delightfully sandy beach.

"We are getting close now," Nordhoff said. "Madame, I see you have brought your walking stick. That will be helpful." With that he directed everyone to the boat's opposite, where an even smaller boat had been pulled along. Within minutes the small party had been ferried to the sand and Jason and his entire family stood there, enjoying the beautiful beach.

"Now don't get comfortable. We are not there yet." Nordhoff started off at a walking pace up the beach toward the trees. Everyone followed him…In fact, little William, who had taken quite a shine to Nordhoff, ran alongside him and at times just ahead. Black Jade, Jason, and Old Zhu brought up the rear. It was cold but surprisingly less so than along the coast within San Francisco itself.

When Nordhoff reached the tree line, he turned to allow his little group to gather around him.

"Ho there, Nate, your timing is perfect. We have just arrived." The young fellow, about twenty, walked up to the standing group. "My Friends," Nordhoff began again. "This is Nate Brown. He is really our guide today. He knows the place, and we don't want to get lost. There are no trails in here, and our captain expects us back and alive on the beach in a few hours."

"So where exactly are we?" Jason asked.

"This area is called Marin County. Basically we are just across the bay from San Francisco in an area that has seen an enormous amount of logging over the last few years. This section is particularly hard to get to and its trees less altered by man's saws. But I have never been here either. Only heard about it by accident, and only with great difficulty was I able to contact Nate here who knows the land well. So, Nate, what can you tell us?"

Nate was clearly not the public speaker that Nordhoff was.

"Well, gents and ladies…it's sort of hard to describe. I myself only know it because my usual work is as a logger. But my family's home is nearby, and I know the place. Let's see...well, it's called Redwood Canyon, but it don't know the saws at all... ah. shucks how about I just shows you." With that, he started off into the tree line, with the entire group following closely.

At first, nothing seemed particularly different, but as they walked, the terrain changed dramatically. It began to darken as the size of the trees grew taller and taller, so tall that less and less light made it to the ground. Soon the sound of oohs and ahhs began to be emitted from the throats of everyone in the group, for none of them—save Nordhoff who'd seen and written of the Giant Sequoias of Yosemite in his book—had ever seen anything like these giant cathedral-like trees. And the smell, an incredible almost sweet smell, permeated the entire area. It was like nothing from this world.

"Mr. Nordhoff," Black Jade began. "You have outdone yourself. This is the most extraordinary place I have ever seen. And you say the public does not know of it...does not have the chance to experience it?"

"Not that I have ever heard, but mark my words, the public will eventually come to know it well. I imagine that someday, its natural beauty will be appreciated and even preserved. I have already heard of talk of doing so. For now, though its protection, is that it's so difficult to reach."

As the adults looked on, the children were staring wide eyed straight up at the largely obscured sky and walking with their hands rubbing against the enormous trunks that seemed to require an entire company to latch arms around it; they were so large. For the next hour, they simply wandered among the trees, for the place seemed as restful as anyone could possibly imagine. After a time Nordhoff unwrapped his picnic basket and unveiled a variety of goods, from fried chicken to cookies. With a flourish he opened the last package—a large carefully sealed, light wooden bowl of Chinese fried rice.

"You shouldn't have," Black Jade said, taking his hand as she had done the first day. "Our family will always be grateful, and if we can ever receive you as a guest, perhaps in Massachusetts or in Shanghai, it will be our greatest honor to do so." And then looking up at the trees, she said out loud, though to no one in particular, "This place gives me the feeling the Catholic sisters used to talk of when they spoke of God."

For the next half an hour, the small group ate their picnic among the trees while their guide Nate sat at something of a distance, playing what looked like a mouth harp. It could not have been more pleasant.

"Mr. Nordhoff," Black Jade began again as the children and Old Zhu walked nearby, inspecting the ground fauna, digging their fingers through the rotting pieces of bark of older trees that had fallen long before. "There is something I need to ask you." She quickly described the political demonstration they had seen the day before and said bluntly, "Can you tell us what Americans really think of we Chinese?"

Nordhoff nodded. "I have thought since we first met that our few days together would include that conversation at some point. I don't really know what to tell you. Here in America there are a great many Americans and as many opinions of the Chinese as there are Chinese themselves. And most of the opinions are completely contradictory. We hear the Chinese are hardworking and honest, that they are lazy thieves, that they spend all their money on opium and take jobs from white men. The list goes on and on."

"But is there no common theme to any of it, any way of making sense of the attitudes?" Jason, ever the reporter, asked.

"There are certain commonalities one can discern. Certainly the better off; those who want to employ Chinese for lower wages think upon them very positively, and those richer merchants who are hoping to expand the trade with China itself seem reasonably positive. When there was plenty of work, during the Gold Rush, or before the railroad work was largely complete, things were better. But when people fear for their livelihood, their sense of fair play goes out the window."

"So is it just about immigration itself, not specifically the Chinese?" Black Jade asked. "Simply about people working for less money?"

"In part," Nordhoff said, clearly thinking about it himself. "Actually sometimes what folks think of the Chinese is linked to what they think of the Irish. For a lot of folks, the Irish are much more hated. But maybe that's more true back east."

"Are you yourself not an immigrant, Mr. Nordhoff?" Black Jade asked quietly.

"You are most perceptive, Madame. I arrived here myself as a teenager from the Germanies, from Prussia to be exact. But most Americans don't seem to harbor many prejudices in that direction. Against blacks, especially in the South, against Irish back east, Chinese here in the West, and I supposed Jews pretty much everywhere. I don't know what to tell you. The situation is also changing quickly. I really don't know what it will be like in a few years." And then turning to Jason, he said, "If you are really planning to write and speak about China here in America, you are going to have a very 'interesting' time of it."

"I guess so. But first I feel like I need to simply understand America better, and I now fully appreciate why Mr. Clemens suggested we spend time together. I have learned an enormous amount from you. And as my wife said, we will be grateful for the rest of our lives."

With that, Nordhoff gave a little bow and walked over to see what the children were looking at. Two hours later, they were back in San Francisco for a last evening. This time their dinner included Nordhoff who later, after another fine meal at their

adopted restaurant in Chinatown, departed with a good number of handshakes and hugs from the children. Apparently,
Nordhoff himself was leaving the next day for a meeting in San
Jose, a city apparently a day or so to the south? Jason was not
sure.

# CHAPTER 11

# CHINATOWN

From long habit, Black Jade and Jason woke early the next morning. But there really were no plans other than to pack for the next day's train ride east.

"So how shall we spend the day, maybe our last in San Francisco, for I can't imagine when we might return?" he asked his wife, who lay beside him half-asleep.

"I have been thinking that it's time to explore a bit as adults. The children and Old Zhu can stay in the hotel, and you and I should try to learn more about Chinatown. We really have not learned much in our excursions there. Mostly the Chinatown the Americans tour with such nervousness during the day, always staying on the biggest and most open streets."

"It sounds worthwhile to me. So then, after breakfast and packing, we should set out."

With that, the two lay back in bed, resting a while longer before pulling themselves up and starting their morning routine. Within a few hours, the bags were largely filled, save what they would need for their one last evening in the hotel. Once that was accomplished, Jason and Black Jade set out on their own.

It was nearing noon before they arrived at the center of Chinatown and began to slowly walk through the streets, taking in the sites, exploring some of the goods in the shops more slowly and methodically than they had ever been able to with the children.

"Here, look down this alley. Do you see that doorway further down? It looks like some sort of teahouse," Black Jade said, gesturing into the alley ever so much narrower than the street they were walking on. "Let's get some tea and lunch."

As they walked in the darkened room became quiet, and the customers, all Chinese men who sat drinking tea and eating from small bowls of noodles, looked up to study the new arrivals. Nothing seemed out of order. From the back came the familiar smell of opium.

A middle-aged Chinese approached them. "Perhaps you are lost?" he said hesitantly in fairly good English.

"No, we'd like to rest here for a moment," Black Jade said, with that commanding tone Jason had heard so often. She'd used the Cantonese dialect of her youth rather than the northern dialects she'd become accustomed to in recent years.

"Please bring us tea and a bowl of noodles."

As they sat down, Jason saw the entire room tense even more so than it had when they first walked in. Lost tourists were apparently not that rare even in a shop that deep into an alley. However, once they sat down, at least two of the customers got up and abruptly left. For the next few minutes, Black Jade and Jason sat in silence, waiting for the noodle bowls.

"*Lo Fan!* White man, you should leave, leave right now."

Jason looked up, unsure in the darkness where the voice had even come from. A moment later though, it was obvious as a young Chinese, maybe seventeen, his pigtail silhouetted in the shadowy room, approached the table aggressively.

"You should leave right now, leave with your Chinese whore who never should have brought you here!" He spit out the words in relatively good English. Jason jumped up abruptly, spewing forth a slew of fluent Cantonese insults ready to defend his wife.

"Wait, stop," the voice yelled out from further back in the restaurant. As Jason and the teenager stood there, not quite head to head but close to blows, the older Chinese slowly approached the table. He clearly had authority here. The owner, Jason thought for a second as the man approached.

"Little Translator, Jason, is it truly you here in Gold Mountain?"

"Merchant Xu, Xu Pakwah...I can't believe I am seeing you here!" Jason said in his fluent Cantonese, the fluency of which was already gaining remark from the small groups of men who sat nearby listening intently.

"Sit down, young one." He gestured to Jason. "You will always be welcome in my tea shop." Then turning to the still-obviously angry teenager, he said, "Now go sit down. This man is not like the others. He knows China better than you do!"

"But, Merchant Xu...he could get us arrested. The white police don't care what we do, but with him here..."

"I said 'sit down.' Jason and"—he eyed Black Jade who was standing quietly—"are my guests. Leave if you don't like it."

With that the young man, even more enraged, stomped out of the shop without a word. Merchant Xu watched him for a moment, obviously disappointed. "He is not a bad fellow, the son of an old friend, but the whites have been vicious lately. But that is another matter. Please sit." With that, he called to the back and changed their orders. "Bring bowls of the best duck soup for our guests and my finest rice wine."

Then he sat down himself. Jason, watching the other customers, could tell the owner's behavior was very unusual. After a time, the rest of the customers returned to their noodle bowls or at least pretended to interest themselves in eating, though it was obvious Jason and Black Jade still held the bulk of their attention.

"Merchant Xu, let me present my wife Black Jade."

She nodded to him.

"And where are you from, young woman?"

"My home is a few days north of Guangzhou."

"How is it known?" Xu asked. "Perhaps I know it."

"It is very small." It was obvious she was evading his question, but Xu did not seem to mind.

"And you are married?"

Jason nodded.

"Children?"

"Two," Black Jade responded. "A girl and a boy."

"Ah, a golden family," the older man mumbled to himself, and then turning to Jason, he said, "And you here? Do you have any idea how many times your father came to me after you disappeared that day after we last spoke? He kept asking me what I might have seen. At least he did so until he finally found out you had gone with the Western soldiers to Guangzhou."

"I am sorry if I caused problems for you," Jason said, feeling the years fall away as he sat across from Xu, the merchant he had spent so much of his childhood buying vegetables from to fill his mother's dinner plates.

"But you, Merchant Xu, here? When did you leave Hong Kong? How long have you been in America?" he asked with considerable interest.

The old man thought for a while. "Hard to say. It was years ago, maybe a couple of years after you left. I had the idea I could make a real fortune in America. I'd certainly done well enough selling food to the white settlers in Hong Kong. Coming here seemed like a way to improve my standing even more. So when did I leave, not sure; I was there long enough to hear that you had arrived in Guangzhou, then later that you had run off again, and much later that you were writing newspaper stories. Your father continued as a customer, and we spoke often." And then, Xu began to remember something.

"Did you really travel all the way to Nanjing, all the way to the Heavenly Kingdom?"

Jason looked at his wife and then nodded.

"Wait..." He seemed to be remembering something else now. "Did I not hear that you had actually met the Heavenly King? Yes, that's it...your father Reverend Brandt told me that."

At that there was a slight murmur in the room, for the failed Cantonese civil-exam student who had challenged the entire Qing dynasty claiming he was the little brother of Jesus the Western God was indeed famous. Again Jason nodded and then said, "It was a long time ago, but, yes, I did get to see him in an audience once with Reverend Roberts, a colleague of my father."

"And you, did you find your dreams fulfilled in Gold Mountain?" Jason tried not to be distracted by Xu's interest in his own story. Besides, he could tell Black Jade sitting next to him, her leg slightly touching him, would not be pleased with a conversation about the long-gone Taiping Kingdom.

"Did I find Gold Mountain? Did I find my dream?" Xu said to no one in particular. "At first, it was wonderful. The Americans needed our labor, and many came here enthusiastically. Some even as early as the Gold Rush years and then to build their great railroad across the country."

With that one of the other men, a fellow about thirty, swung around and joined their group. "It really was Gold Mountain. I came here years ago, worked for a time, sent money home, even returned for a year and came back again. Those were good years," he said enthusiastically, pushing his pigtail back that had been hanging in front of him. With that opening the entire room simply moved over to the table Xu, Black Jade, and

Jason occupied. For the next two hours, the two visitors were told story after story, different for each individual about coming to America.

"But why has it gotten so bad now?" Jason asked.

"Now it is very bad," one of the men began. "They constantly accuse us of being filthy coolies, of having been captured like the black Africans and sold here as slaves. That may be true for some Chinese but not those here in America. We came just as most of them did, as immigrants hoping to make money for our families. We are accused of taking the white men's jobs, spreading disease."

The descriptions and tales of woe went on and on, with several of them contributing one story or example after the other.

"And is there no work now?" Black Jade asked.

The men looked at her. Even here in San Francisco women were expected to be less bold than she traditionally was. But they were a long way from home, and even here deep in Chinatown, some traditions were falling away.

"If there were no work, we would all leave. Most of us planned to stay no longer than it was necessary to earn our fortunes," responded the original fellow who had joined the conversation uninvited.

"There is still plenty of work," another chimed in. "Many here hire us even as they claim to despise us. Have you heard of the white leader Stanford? I think that's what they call him. He constantly attacks us and just the same hires us in large numbers. Attacks us as a politician, hires us as business owner."

"Perhaps we should return to the hotel," Black Jade whispered to Jason. "I am concerned about the children."

Within a few minutes, their deep appreciation to Merchant Xu expressed, the two of them left the cafe. It took a moment for their eyes to adjust even to the dim light of the alley and even longer when they found themselves in the wider, more sunlit street.

"What do you think?" Jason asked her.

"I thought we had an agreement not to draw any conclusions till we knew more. But it was certainly interesting."

"I could not believe our luck...that Xu was there, someone from China I actually knew well."

"Luck, I don't think that was it at all. It was our fate to meet him and have him help us understand Gold Mountain," she said with considerable certainty as they walked on.

Within moments, as they walked, they heard loud swearing, swearing in Cantonese and English. Turning a corner and peering down yet another alley, they saw a fight going on. Two young American men were beating a Chinese, beating him severely with their fists, pummeling him to the ground.

Jason, without thinking, ran into the alley, and grabbing one of the men, he struck him solidly on the jaw, knocking him down. But then, the other kicked Jason's knee, and he himself fell, the other man kicking wildly at him. Jason covered his face with his hands, trying to protect himself, until the loud crack of solid wood hitting human flesh rang out. With that, the blows against Jason stopped and the men, all four of them, looked up to see Black Jade swinging the walking stick with great effect, against one white and then the other. The two whites jumped up, gave Jason and the Chinese an aggressive look, and ran off.

"I knew there was a reason I thought this walking stick would be helpful," she said without emotion. At that Jason and his wife both realized the young Chinese victim who was himself slowly getting up was the very same fellow who'd ordered them from Xu's tea shop. With a glance of disgust, the Chinese spit on the ground and, without a word of thanks, turned and walked away from them.

"Can you walk, my husband?"

"Yes, I am fine. He really only tripped me."

"Then let us return to the hotel and see the children. And finish packing, for I am anxious to see Chicago." With that and a bit of a swagger, she exited the alley. Jason could only look on with wonder, impressed as he had been that day he'd first seen her lying next to that river in southern China so many years before.

# CHAPTER 12
# ACROSS AMERICA BY TRAIN

The next twenty-four hours flew by as they made final preparations to depart for Chicago. Meanwhile Jason composed telegrams for his father and Mr. Sage to give them an idea when he would arrive. From what he'd learned from Nordhoff, the trip would take seven days if they were to go straight through, an idea that Jason, the father of two small children, found abhorrent. So instead, adding the two days they had planned for Chicago, he was in a fairly good position to tell both of them when he might arrive—first in New York and then eventually in Boston. He also took care to give them both the name of the hotel Nordhoff had suggested they stay at in Chicago during the break in the trip.

Finally, they were off again, ready to leave San Francisco behind and start the next part of the trip, several days by train. Jason's money, while draining enthusiastically from his money purse, was still holding out reasonably well and allowed him to purchase, if not the most expensive accommodations—at least what seemed likely to be reasonably comfortable. Happily, he reminded himself, hotel expenses would soon be decreasing. Mr. Sage had promised to put them up in New York City and they would, soon enough, be staying with his father. The reverend had already written that while his small cottage was not very spacious, he was reasonably confident it would accommodate them all until Jason's family had a chance to find their own lodgings.

The New York tickets, several hundreds of dollars' worth of them, had already been purchased, so Jason, always concerned about his cash flow, was feeling reasonably confident. On the other hand, he was already composing articles in his mind that he might send back to Barlow at the *North China Daily News* and reflecting on how his knowledge of China might be helpful to the rich investor he would soon be meeting.

At last they, all five of them, boarded the train and, once inside, began working their way through the carriage to their assigned seats. It was quite crowded, hopefully filled, Jason thought, not only with the passengers themselves but also with those well-wishers who were there to see them off. To Jason's pleasure, he noticed several other children coming on board with their parents as well. If they were indeed passengers and assigned to the same carriage, it would be a great relief, he thought to himself. Little William and Mei-ling—should he think of her as "Norma," Jason mused to himself—were handling the stress of travel wonderfully well. Old Zhu was also incredibly good at distracting them with activities, especially paper cutting. But they were still children, and the limits of their patience was, at times, very near the surface.

Eventually, as the train whistled and the conductor ordered everyone off who were not themselves passengers, Jason turned to his wife sitting next to him. Quietly, he took her hand as she whispered into his ear.

"Your leg, my husband. Is the blow from that dreadful man any better?" she asked sweetly.

Jason was surprised she had even noticed, as he'd been trying to hide the slightly painful limp he had developed since the previous day's scuffle in the alley in Chinatown.

"It's OK...still to be honest, I am awfully relieved we are not about to undertake another of Charles's excursions. There is no way my leg could handle an excursion among those Sequoia trees, despite how beautiful they were. Besides, I bet it hurts a lot less than the fellows you wacked with your walking stick!"

"Well then, I guess you are lucky; we have only to sit here for a few days and watch America go by," his wife said, smiling with pleasure.

At that the train lurched forward and began to move while several passengers gave a hoop of excitement. Looking more closely at the passengers who surrounded him, he noticed with interest that among the passengers was an older American woman, perhaps around seventy, clearly traveling with a Chinese maidservant. While he studied the younger woman, Jason noticed that she too was quietly looking at his own family, though making a show of not doing so.

Looking back at his children, he realized with surprise that Black Jade had dressed them especially well. In much nicer clothing than they had worn on the ship or even in the streets of San Francisco. Thinking about it he realized with a start that she had decided to use the family's clearly middle-class status to give the children some additional prestige, which might lessen whatever demerit their Asian appearance might earn them.

Studying his children more objectively, he began to wonder how different their reception in America would really be once they settled in. Mei-ling was, of course, his stepdaughter and completely Chinese, though he never thought of her that way. He was, after all, there at the moment of her birth. On the other hand, little William's face showed a more ambiguous Eurasian tone, which sometimes appeared more European and sometimes more Asian. Turning toward his wife as she herself gazed out the windows watching the outskirts of San Francisco role by, Jason wondered what his wife was really thinking about America and the future despite their oath to forsake opinions for a time.

A few hours later as the train proceeded toward Sacramento, the entire train came to a dramatic halt as the conductor walked through, advising everyone that they needed to descend to the station platform for dinner. And they were politely told to be quick about it, for the train engineer did not want to lose time at the very beginning of the trip. They quickly called to the children, for both of them had spent the last few hours at the end of the carriage playing with the other children, who happily had ended up settling in their car as well.

Next to him Black Jade carefully put her Bible back into her handbag. She'd been reading it with considerable enthusiasm, not just for its spiritual insights but as a tool to improve her English. In fact, their travel conversations were frequently about words she did not understand. She was certainly diligent enough in her religious studies, Jason thought to himself. And she was certainly committed to the topic significantly more than he was. Impressively she'd finished the Old Testament on the steamer ship from Shanghai and as they had arrived in San Francisco, begun the new. A new testament for a new continent, he thought to himself but said nothing. For Jason religion, while interesting, was more an intellectual concern. People were often interested in religion, and Jason as a reporter was interested in what motivated them. But his curiosity went no further than that.

During dinner, which to Jason's pleasure cost only a dollar each, another of the passengers spoke loudly of plans he had heard to have dining cars placed on some of the trains so that passengers would not have to disembark for every meal and the train move more expeditiously. Had he been traveling alone, Jason thought, that might be a fine improvement, but traveling as he was with his entire family, he was glad for the break in the routine. The children always seemed to appreciate the novelty.

As they walked back toward the train, Jason spied Old Zhu walking not with them but closer to the young Chinese maidservant, with whom she had apparently tried to start a conversation. Just in front of them walked the older woman; the Chinese woman's employer who had a mild look of annoyance on her face. Once back in the car, employer and servant went back to their own seats while Jason's brood settled themselves in among their books and the children's toys. Occupying a place of honor was the doll Giquel had given Mei-ling so long before. True it was starting to look a bit worse for wear, the doll's dress in need of a cleaning, but the smile on its face and pretty eyes glowed as attractively as ever, and Mei-ling rarely let it out of her sight.

"Who is the young woman?" Black Jade asked, leaning over to Old Zhu. "Could you understand her?"

"We only spoke for a moment," Zhu began, "but she's from along the coast and has traveled a lot among many of our people, and yes, we did speak a bit. Her story is like many, at least from what I could catch in snatches. I don't think her mistress liked us talking, especially as she had no idea what we were saying." With that she turned to the children and, resuming her own duties, began to help them organize their things.

As the evening drew on, and the train started climbing, Jason was pleased they had the extra clothing Nordhoff had mentioned they would need. San Francisco's cold and drizzly environment had given way to a steady cold as the train traveled eastward and started to climb. Jason was also impressed as he noted how efficiently the train car itself was heated by what seemed to be water pipes sunk into the floor of the carriage. The fact that the room had the sense of a parlor about it, with ample room for him to write, was especially appreciated. It was the first time since he'd left the steamer that he'd had a real opportunity to reflect on what he'd seen thus far and make notes for himself on future articles. One long-term project Barlow had suggested to him, about the possibility of future American trade investments in China, dovetailed nicely with the consulting work he hoped to do with Sage. But still, his ever-deepening sense of the suspicion Americans, at least on the West Coast held for Chinese, troubled him significantly. It really was not something he'd had a good sense of when he first put his family, his Chinese family, on that ship in Shanghai bound for America.

At around eight in the evening by Jason's watch, the porter arrived and, in an extraordinarily impressive fashion, began to transform their carriage into a sleeping area. With remarkable efficiency the chairs, sofa, and tables were manipulated and transformed into sleeping births as the family, indeed a considerable percentage of the passengers, looked on in awe. It was a sight to behold. A few minutes later, a set of clean sheets and bedding were laid out, and the family's sleeping space prepared and as comfortable looking as they'd enjoyed at home.

Gathering up the children, Jason, Black Jade, and Old Zhu settled them in, and after a time they themselves changed into their sleeping clothing and turned in. As Jason lay there, he found the gentle motion of the relatively slow-moving train calming and fell asleep quite easily. Just before he did so, though, he noticed Black Jade already in a deep sleep. It was rare that she fell asleep before him, and for that he was grateful. He knew that despite her self-confidence, a feature that had both served her well and ill over her life, she had a tendency to worry a lot. That, he sometimes thought was one of the reasons she was so interested in religion. It did, he so often noticed, have the ability to calm even the most nervous of personalities.

The next morning, as Jason woke early, he saw most of the passengers still asleep around them and the porters silently laying fresh water and towels for the early risers to employ. Very quietly for fear of waking his party, Jason dressed and used the facilities to prepare himself for the day. Then finding a relatively calm place to stand, he stared out the window watching the increasingly mountainous territory roll by and the patches of snow that dotted the ground. After a time, the carriage began to get noisier as more and more voices were raised from the partially obscured sleeping areas and the occasional early riser, like Jason himself, began to emerge.

After a time, the porter announced an upcoming breakfast stop, and everyone who was not yet ready finished up quickly. Within half an hour, the train pulled to a halt and everyone stepped down into the invigorating and cold air that greeted them harshly after they stepped from the toasty carriages.

"Whoa!" Jason yelled out, grabbing the children's hands and running ahead of the crowd toward the waiting dining room that stood just alongside the tracks. Behind him, he could hear Black Jade and Old Zhu discussing energetically in the Shanghai dialect just why they had set off to travel in such a cold environment. It certainly was nothing like the regions of coastal and southern China they knew. As for Jason himself, he'd seen snow often enough during some of his trips to Beijing not to be very impressed.

As they entered, the always-attentive train porters reminded everyone that while they had no intention of leaving anyone behind, eating with efficiency was a priority, for the train would be pulling out of the station relatively soon. With that advice, Jason's crew ate their fill and returned to the carriage. To their pleasure the train's efficient staff had completely transformed the carriage once again. Where beds had once stood, the previous day's comfortable array of tables, sofa, and writing table was ready for them.

"I think we can forgo our English lessons, don't you think?" Black Jade commented, pointing down the car at five-year-old William and his big sister standing in a circle of other children. The two children were jabbering away in English and apparently without any problems understanding at all.

"I think I am getting jealous," Black Jade said, smiling. "I work so hard at my language lessons and they pick it up while playing!" With that, she took up her Bible, dictionary, and writing paper with earnest and went back to her own lessons. Jason watched her study for a while, thinking about her improving English skills. He himself spoke the sort of American Massachusetts English he'd learned in his father's home in Hong Kong. Black Jade, though, sounded different, for the English she was increasingly employing, especially when others were around them, had been deeply influenced by the British tutor he'd hired, and new friend Aouda's English boarding-school upbringing and vocabulary she was picking up from the King James Bible. In truth Black Jade had an almost aristocratic tone to her speech. Jason had no idea if that would be helpful or not, but it certainly seemed to surprise some of those they'd encountered along the way who clearly expected her to speak the Chinese pidgin English so common along the coast of China and to some extent in California as well.

Looking up Jason noticed five-year-old William surrounded by a group of very eager boys who seemed especially intense. Getting up he walked over to the group and realized that William had brought his telescope out and was letting some of the boys use it to look out the windows. But boys being boys, there was tension as well, as some refused to pass it over once they got it into their hands.

"OK, boys," Jason said, as several of the boys' parents watched him. "We need a timekeeper. Norma"—quite deliberately, he used her English name—"would you do the honors? Five minutes a boy," he said, handing her the watch he always carried in his pocket.

Mei-ling literally leaped with glee as she took the watch and with it an air of authority.

"Five minutes each. And, William, you have had enough time with it already. Pass it to...what is your name?" she asked another boy who was perhaps six.

"David," he said, excited for having been chosen to use the telescope next.

"OK, William, give David the telescope now and Norma will time it." With that William reluctantly handed it over.

"I want it next," yet another boy chimed in. Meanwhile a young brown-haired girl raised her hand shyly.

As Jason looked on, his eight-year-old daughter began to organize the sharing.

"Let's see," she said, putting her fingers to her lips. "Let's go boy, girl, boy, girl and add a game. OK." She thought for a second. "Who can guess what number I am thinking about...a number between one and ten?" At that several children started to yell out numbers while Mei-ling held Jason's watch with pride and little David stared out the window with obvious pleasure.

As Jason started back toward his seat, one of the parents tapped his shoulder, a young laughing fellow of perhaps twenty-five.

"Say there, that isn't fair. When do the adults get to use that thing? I'd like to peek through it myself."

"I'll see what I can do. I may have some influence with the timekeeper," Jason offered as he walked down the aisle of the train. As he walked he spotted Black Jade and Old Zhu beaming.

# CHAPTER 13

# MORE TRAIN ADVENTURES

By afternoon, now a full day, after boarding, a regular routine had set in, partially facilitated by the necessity of leaving the train to eat. Almost everyone in the hustle and bustle of departing for meals was pulled from the smaller family group that surrounded each of them and their traveling companions with whom they had boarded the train. New friendships were formed even among the most unlikely groups and not much slower than the children had done.

By midafternoon, the older woman, who'd been traveling with her maidservant, was now chatting enthusiastically with both the servant and Old Zhu, asking them questions and teaching along with her maidservant, their new friend, a number of English words. To Black Jade's delight, even at the distance they were from the trio, it was obvious that Old Zhu was slowly trying out the few English words she had so far picked up.

As for Jason and Black Jade, for a time his wife made a major and successful effort to take up a conversation with the mother of one of the boys who was playing with William. Meanwhile Jason spoke at length with one of the porters about life on the trains. It was, Jason thought, a fascinating lifestyle, and the specifics helpful if he were to be able to converse intelligently with Mr. Sage. Jason still knew very little about the man, though he had asked Nordhoff what he knew. Not all that much was known, except that he was some sort of investor, had at one point been a politician in upstate New York, and was particularly involved with the development of railroads.

On the afternoon of their third day of travel as both children lay napping nearby, Jason gazed out the window through his son's telescope at the vast expanse of the American plains that spread out before him; he again admired how well made the device was. Small, for Giquel's staff had known it would be held by a small boy. It had all the sophistication of an optical device designed for the naval fleet his friend Giquel was building for the Chinese emperor.

Thinking of Giquel naturally brought his mind to his old friend Wu, whom he had sent off to Fuzhou looking for work. Surely, by now, Jason thought Wu would have arrived and begun whatever work Giquel offered him, for Jason was sure his old friend would have honored his request to employ Jason's Chinese friend. Then, remembering he'd told Giquel that he would most certainly check at the post office in Boston, he hoped his old friend would have a letter waiting for him.

"Let me see your notebook," Black Jade asked, raising herself from the slightly napping position she'd taken sometime before.

"Are you planning to write something or sketch?" he asked, for Black Jade often demonstrated the keen eye of an artist.

"Why do you ask?"

"I was just wondering what you needed, pen or pencil," he responded.

"Certainly pencil, for I expect a lot of mistakes. I am going to try to write a letter to Aouda. Are you not curious about what happened? Did they win their bet? Did they make it around the world in eighty days?"

"Right." He'd almost forgotten, though in truth he'd spent a lot less time talking with Fogg than she had with Aouda.

"There was a lot of money riding on it, right?"

"An enormous amount, though Aouda did not know how much. Mr. Fogg never talked about financial matters in front of her. But she knew he was willing to spend incredible amounts to stay on schedule. So give me a pencil. I have Fogg's address, and once this is complete, we can mail it in Chicago."

"Wow!" Suddenly William jumped up and grabbed the telescope. "Indians!" he yelled.

All heads turned toward Jason's son as he excitedly looked out the window. Just outside, riding along on very swift ponies, were several native Americans, attempting to keep up with the train. Surprisingly, given the weather, they rode shirtless and had bird feathers clearly coming out of their dark-brown hair. William watched them excitedly for a time, as did the rest of the children and a good percentage of the adults.

After that excitement had passed, Jason found himself reflecting on how different the people around him were from those first days in San Francisco. There in California he had seen an enormous number of Chinese, but as they traveled East, the number of Chinese he saw through the train windows or in the many small towns they'd passed seemed fewer and fewer. And the terrain, it was so different as well. California had been full of mountains, rolling hills, and those impossible-to-forget giant trees. But as they got closer and closer to Chicago, the land was impressively flat.

Finally, and it really seemed like that after traveling for so many days, the conductor came through the train, announcing that they'd be in Chicago in about an hour.

"Maybe we should start gathering up our goods," Black Jade said. "The children's things are all over the compartment."

"Did you finish your letter?"

"No, but there is time. I want to make it as perfect as it can be, and then after you go over it, I'll copy it again. I have not forgotten how much trouble a bit of carelessness caused our friend Wu. Do you think Prosper will write anything about him?"

"I am hoping to get a letter in Boston. There will certainly have been time enough for Wu to make it to Fuzhou and for Giquel to get a letter to me in Boston. At least I hope so."

For the next few minutes, the family packed up the materials, books, notepads, games, and so forth, that they had strewn about them and then sat patiently, watching the rest of the passengers doing the same. After a bit, the train entered the outskirts of Chicago and was soon pulling into the station there.

"Here we go again," Jason said as he grabbed William's hand and Black Jade took Mei-ling's.

As they entered the depot and then exited, Jason was aware of several different sensations. That it was a lot colder than on the well-heated train, that the smell of water was clear. Certainly the enormous Lake Michigan he'd read about could not be far, and more surprisingly the smell of burned material. It had been more than a year since the great fire, but the clear and distinct smell of smoke still lingered very obviously.

"Can you take us to the Palmer House?" Jason asked the first coachman he spied.

"My horses, sir, are old, but I am afraid they don't trot that slow," responded the fellow while rubbing his fingers together for warmth.

"Excuse me?"

"The Palmer House, sir, it burned down in the fire, supposed to have been quite a fine place I've heard tell. Didn't have time to see it myself. It burned down only a fortnight after they built it."

"Yes, I'd heard that, but I was told by a friend it had been rebuilt," Jason said. "Now at something of a loss?"

"Still doing so, sir, but it's not nearly done. I reckon your friend had no idea how ambitious their plans were for the new hotel. I can take you to another fine place, same block—probably just as nice."

"Well." Jason looked at Black Jade, who nodded. "OK, let's go. Thank you."

"Shall we go the long way, sir, and let you see a bit of the city on the way? It's not much more cost."

"Yes, please do," Black Jade said in as crisp English as Jason had ever heard her express.

"Yes, ma'am," the fellow cried enthusiastically while eyeing her with a surprised look.

As the carriage moved through the streets, Jason was especially aware of how different Chicago looked from San Francisco, the much wider streets laid out on an entirely flat surface. Moreover, the clothing seemed more formal than in San Francisco.

"Look around." Black Jade nudged him. "In San Francisco there were so many Chinese. Have you seen anyone from China yet?"

Jason shook his head.

"Look!" Mei-ling cried, for the carriage driver had turned a corner and revealed an enormous body of water just ahead of them.

"Would you and your family like to have a look, sir?"

"Absolutely." With that, almost everyone alighted and walked toward the waterfront, though Jason noticed that Old Zhu sat comfortably in the carriage. He wondered if she were tired but suspected as well that she did not intend to let all the family's possessions sit in some stranger's carriage while her employers wandered along the shoreline.

Looking out over the enormous expanse of Lake Michigan, Jason was amazed. He'd never seen a lake this size. Certainly, Xi Hu near Hangzhou was impressive but nothing like this. On the other hand, he thought to himself, it wasn't an ocean either. Certainly, there was nothing of the energy that lapped along the coast of the Pacific like those waves that had slammed into the rocks below the Cliff House in San Francisco. Within a few minutes, the family was back in the carriage and off again, though this time, as the carriage moved away from the fresher air near the waterfront, new smells filled their nostrils.

"Can you smell it, ma'am?" the driver asked the beautiful and apparently sophisticated Chinese woman in his carriage.

"Not really. What is that smell? It's unfamiliar," she responded.

"Burnt wood and fresh timbers. Look yonder down the street. You heard of our fire, burned down a good chunk of the city. They say some Irish lady's cow started it. Damn shame… lots of dead…huge numbers of buildings lost…"

As the carriage rounded another street, they were shocked to see an entire row of burned-out buildings. Whether they had once been private homes or businesses was not at all clear. Further down the street, the sound of hammering roused above the din of the noise the horse hooves were making. It was clear a huge building boom was going on with an enormous number of different construction sites all working near each other. The entire family sat in awe, looking at the giant piles of stone, as if parts of the streets had become quarries, and the incredible piles of wood and lumber being shaped before them. Clearly, Chicago was being rebuilt from the ground up.

As they continued down the street, an enormous structure started to rise up ahead of them. At the base, it looked like an old European-style castle with turrets, but what made it different was that rising from the center was a much higher tower that seemed to rise into the sky.

"What is it?" Jason asked, deeply impressed by the structure.

"May look like an old European castle, but it's actually part of the city's water system…over a hundred feet high. What's really impressive was that it was one of the few buildings around here to survive, sir," said the coachman, clearly proud of his city.

The carriage stopped again as everyone just stared up into the sky at the building's extraordinarily ornate stonework.

"You know I knew absolutely nothing about Chicago when I started this trip. We are on the way to Boston," Jason told the man. "I am very pleased we decided to stop. Thank you for suggesting this diversion."

"Delighted…We Chicago types are proud of our city. I came here with my parents when I was a lad from somewhere in New Hampshire, but I hardly remember,"

Then a few minutes later, the driver yelled, "Over there up yonder. You see that enormous construction site? That's where you were fixing to check in…no idea when that will be the new Palmer House."

As they passed the site, the driver pointed again. "It's over there, so just down the street a piece…another hotel that I am sure will fit your needs."

"Yes, I see it. Thank you. How much do I owe you?"

"Two bits will be fine, sir. But before you get down, I don't just pick people up at the trains. I am a bit of an amateur tour guide myself. People often hire me to show them around the stockyards. Do you know about that, sir?"

"No, I don't think…no, wait." Jason remembered Nordhoff had spoken of some sort of giant stockyard in Chicago. "Yes, I have heard of them. Are they worth seeing?"

"Absolutely, sir. I have shown folks from all over the world and they are always impressed. Your little ones will be especially interested I suspect. If you like, sir, I could pick you and your folks up in the morning and have ourselves a tour. Not very expensive. What do you say?"

"Yes, we would like that very much," Black Jade answered before Jason could even turn to her.

"Good, I think you won't regret it. So what do you say... maybe around nine?"

"We'd like that," she said as she directed the children to the sidewalk in front of the hotel the driver had stopped at. Within a few minutes, Jason and his entire family had settled into two adjacent rooms they had rented. Only this time an interior door allowed them to link the rooms more into a suite that was especially convenient for Old Zhu and the family.

Then as the family explored the hotel, Jason left for the main post office, hoping to see if letters had arrived for him. Finding the building turned out to be quite easy, for the ability to always orient himself vis-à-vis the lake made the search and directions he occasionally asked for quite helpful.

Once at the post office, he secured two letters—one from Twain and another from Mr. Sage, who welcomed him on his progress moving toward the East Coast and promised that his assistant Abraham Broad would be waiting at New York's Grand Central Depot to receive them when they arrived at the appointed time a few days hence. Mr. Sage wanted only confirmation that they were still moving along on the same schedule Jason had previously mentioned. Again Sage reiterated that his wife, Olivia, wanted to meet Mrs. Brandt, as she was especially interested in women's issues in Asia and was hoping to learn a great deal from their guests.

Turning to the letter from Mark Twain, Jason was equally pleased. Twain wrote, as he usually did, in an especially amusing fashion about some of the trials in getting Jason's *China Tales* in print, some hassle with the covers and that sort of thing—details that would have been boring if anyone other than Twain had taken them on. Again, the letter suggested a visit to Hartford either as they traveled toward Boston or soon after that.

As Jason stood up from the bench along the waterfront to continue his walk back toward the hotel, he almost wished they were leaving immediately instead of exploring Chicago for another day. While he walked, he tried to recall what Nordhoff had said about the stockyards. Jason's memory was vague. Still the more he thought about it, the more he became curious. A city of animals. What an image!

As he entered the hotel, one less-positive thought struck him. Given what he had seen thus far the chances of finding a Chinese restaurant for his family to dine in that evening seemed very unlikely indeed. Chicago was an impressive place, but in matters Chinese, it was clearly not San Francisco. As he started up the stairs, he paused for a second and then, remembering the room numbers, picked up his pace as he headed toward the rooms they had rented for the night.

# CHAPTER 14

# CHICAGO

As they exited the hotel the next morning, the driver hailed them from across the street.

"Ho, there; good morning, folks. I see you have your warmest clothes. Definitely not California. Chicago can get pretty cold this time of year. But I don't think it will get too bad. And the animals at the stockyard will be more awake, so the trip will be even better."

As they climbed aboard and arranged themselves for the day's excursion, the coachman continued with his introduction.

"There are two ways to get to the city of animals as some call it, by train and carriage. The train is a bit faster, but most folks prefer carriage. I figure it's because most of the tourists I show around have just gotten off a long train ride! So just relax for a spell and I'll start talking when we get closer." With that, the man turned and began to concentrate on the traffic, for there were a good many carriages in the street and maneuvering around them and their horse teams could be tricky. For next hour or so, they moved slowly through the streets as Jason's family enjoyed the variety of views Chicago offered up.

"OK, folks, we're getting close. What you are going to see is a wonder that you will remember forever. I've not traveled much myself, but the folks I have shown the stockyards too—and they have come from across the world, even from Japan or China I think. Not sure, and Europeans always tell me they've never seen the likes."

As the carriage proceeded, Jason began to hear a distinct and increasingly loud roar of some sort, but it was hard to really distinguish the sound.

"You hear that? That is the sound of tens of thousands of cattle, sheep, and hogs, all nicely penned up in their own little city. What you've got here is a giant stockyard, used to be a swamp that the railroad folks put together to link up the western cattle herds to the meat markets of the East."

As he spoke the carriage moved closer and closer to the facility. An enormous city of animal pens rose before them; it seemed to go on forever with pens, processing plants and a host of other buildings whose purpose were unclear.

"Can't say so myself, but I have heard tell from some of the other tourists that the animals here are more comfortable than the people living in some of those tenements in New York City," the fellow said as Jason and his family stared out in wonder at the enormous facility.

"We've even got a hotel, that's got private bathrooms if you believe that and lots of housing for the couple of hundred men working here—even a school for their children. Ain't nothing like it in the world. I bet once you folks get to Boston, you will think about this place every time you bite into a steak!" he explained enthusiastically, for the man had proven quite a Chicago booster.

"Look yonder, the place is growing incredibly; they say millions are being spent to keep expanding. They plan more facilities even for tourists. In a bit we'll be seeing some of the strangest animals you'll ever see…Last time I was here they had a two-legged sheep and a six-legged hog."

"Oh!" both kids explained. "Can we see that now?"

"Just down the road apiece. Can't guarantee what they will have today, but I suspect it will be special," the driver promised as Jason nodded and Black Jade whispered to Old Zhu what he'd said.

Hours later, exhausted after their three-hour tour, the carriage started back toward downtown Chicago. The entire crew slept, save Jason who'd climbed up to sit with the driver.

"I really want to thank you. We were incredibly lucky to have you pick us up. We have gained as much of a sense of Chicago as we could possibly do so in a very short time."

"How long will you be here for, sir?"

"We are off again tomorrow morning. Frankly I am beginning to wish we could stay and explore more, but we've been traveling since Shanghai, and my family is ready to settle in again," Jason commented.

"Shanghai. Now that's a city I'd like to see some time."

"Well, here's my card. If you ever get there and I'm back, I will see to it that you have yourself a fine tour," Jason said, handing the man his card and shaking his hand.

"I might just take you up on that, sir."

After that, the two rode along in silence for the rest of the way into the city. Then as their coachman guide was paid and the family stepped off the carriage, Black Jade whispered into his ear.

"Oh, I can't wait. Steak and potatoes again." She sighed.

"I promise you we will find some place in Boston to buy ingredients to make something eatable," he whispered back.

By midday the next day, they were already settling into the train car again, and their railroad routine easily reestablished. After all the time it had taken to travel by rail from San Francisco to Chicago, the much-shorter trip to New York seemed as nothing. In fact, most of the trip was accomplished while the family slept. Late the next morning, after a quick breakfast, the conductor came through announcing the train's imminent arrival at the New York City's famous Grand Central Depot. As they gathered all their worldly goods together, Black Jade turned to her husband.

"Tell me again, what is supposed to happen now?"

"It's not as clear as I'd like. Mr. Sage said he was going to have someone named Abraham Broad meet us, an assistant I guess, and he, I assume, will take us to the hotel they've reserved for us. Beyond that, I have not a clue. I suppose we'll meet the Sages somewhat later. Why? Are you concerned about something?"

"Well, what I have learned about this country so far is that scholars don't matter. What matters are businessmen. Mr. Sage, you saw those comments about him in the magazine we bought in Chicago, is a very important man. If you can somehow be helpful to him, serve as a long-term adviser on China, it could make our lives a lot easier."

"I thought you were proud of how much money my writings brought in?"

"I am proud, but this is the same sort of knowledge, and for a man who has a lot more money than any of your editors will ever pay you."

"It's hard to argue with that. So, how's this? I will do everything I can not to make the man angry…and you do your usual beautiful woman from the Orient routine. How's that?"

"Sounds good. Wait, I think we are slowing down."

And slowing down they were. Within minutes Jason's family, with Old Zhu holding fast little William's hand, slowly moved down the platform toward Grand Central Depot's open reception hall. The room was enormous, with a huge crowds of women dressed in long dresses and, like the men and even the children, all wore hats. The ceiling was incredibly high and the crowd in a sort of frenzy as people rushed by the family either running toward or from the trains.

Jason just stood there frozen, his family looking at him as if he knew what they were supposed to do next. Happily, as he tried to orient himself, his thoughts were interrupted.

"Mr. Brandt, Mr. Brandt!" a young man yelled as he approached them. "Welcome to New York. I am Abraham Broad, Mr. Sage's assistant. I hope your trip was not too demanding?"

"It was very comfortable," Jason responded, incredibly relieved that he would not have to try to navigate New York City alone.

"Here let me take your bags, ma'am. Let's first gather up your trunks and get you all settled in for a moment before we talk. With that the young man gathered up the trunk tickets Jason was holding and walked off, leaving the family standing there hoping they were in the hands of someone who knew New York's enormous metropolis a lot better than they did. Within minutes Broad returned with a porter and all their trunks nicely balanced on a hand cart.

"Mr. Brandt, can we two talk for a moment?" he asked, suggesting a direction toward a quieter part of the hall. Jason nodded and followed him.

"Mr. Brandt, the situation has changed somewhat. Mr. and Mrs. Sage have been waiting enthusiastically for your arrival. Had even planned a nice dinner at their home, but a telegram arrived this morning from Troy. It's a much smaller city, a few hours north of here. Apparently, the headmistress of a school there that Mrs. Sage attended and with whom she has remained very close has taken ill. And as the older lady is very advanced in years, the Sages felt it important to travel north immediately and invited you to accompany them. Mr. Sage told me to assure you that you are very welcome to travel with him. Indeed he said you two would have more time to talk this way than he had originally anticipated. And he said to assure you it is just as easy to get to Boston, maybe even a bit faster from Troy than from New York City."

"You sure it won't be a problem for Mr. Sage or Mrs. Sage?"

"No. Quite the contrary. I can assure you they were both quite interested in having you travel north. Mrs. Sage even said that if Mrs. Willard, I guess that is the lady's name, was feeling better than the reports we've received she would very much want to meet your wife. Indeed Mrs. Sage herself told me meeting your family would probably do a world of good for her old teacher. Let me add privately and please don't quote me. Mr. Sage is being loyal to his wife's wishes, but I know personally that Mr. Sage has not in recent years been very comfortable in Troy and would love the distraction of interesting guests."

"Well, I don't know how interesting Mr. Sage will find us, but let me ask my wife. I doubt it will be a problem. So what happens now?" Jason asked.

"Mr. Sage has his own Pullman rail car; it's actually only a few hundred yards from here. If you are open to going north, I will just take you over there, get your family settled in, and I believe Mr. and Mrs. Sage will be along in about an hour. At least that was the plan when I left there a while ago."

Once Jason explained the situation to Black Jade she readily agreed. Besides, she told him, she really did not have the energy to take on a city the size of New York after such a long trek. Troy sounded much easier. There would be she added plenty of time to see New York City while they were here.

Ten minutes later the family was settled into Sage's Pullman car. It was certainly fancier than they'd traveled in across the country but not that much different, and the furniture looked as if it had not been reupholstered for some time. Jason's most immediate challenge was to get the children out of the swivel chair that was bolted to the floor in front of a well-worn roll-top desk.

"I thought he was supposed to be rich," Black Jade whispered in his ear once they were beyond Broad's hearing.

"I don't know any more than you do."

A second later Broad walked up again. "Good. It looks like everyone is settled. I am still guessing that the Sages won't arrive for a while, so if you want to explore Grand Central Depot for a time, it should not be a problem. It is a fascinating place. Just make sure you know how to get back to this Pullman car. How about if we, say,"—he consulted his watch—"all return by eleven?"

Jason nodded, shook Broad's hand, and then a few minutes after the young man had departed, he himself left the car and walked with his family back into the station's grand hall. For a few minutes, the entire family walked slowly through the structure infinitely more relaxed than the crowds that rushed around them.

After a time, Black Jade raised her arm and asked somewhat more loudly than usual, for the depot was quite noisy, "Who are those people?"

Jason followed her arm and spotted a group of men wearing dark clothing, long beards, and hats. "No idea," Jason commented.

"They're Jews, people who killed our Lord," a man standing nearby answered casually. "Not the sort you would want to know better," he said before walking off.

"Jews..." Black Jade said. "The same people written about in the Bible?" she asked, for if Black Jade was anything, she was an excellent student of the Bible. It had, after all, served as her principle tool to learn English.

"I guess so," her husband commented, unable to offer any additional confirmation, for he knew as little as she did about modern-day Jews.

"Daddy, look!" Mei-ling yelled out.

And there, perhaps a hundred and fifty feet from them, strode a small group of travelers, travelers who looked a lot more familiar than the very foreign-looking Jews they had just seen. For just across the hall, accompanied by several adult Chinese men, was a small contingent of Chinese adolescents, perhaps around thirteen, walking through the station in very traditional Chinese-student gowns.

"Who are they, Daddy?"

"I have no idea," Jason said, disappointing his daughter as thoroughly as he had his wife. But before he even had a chance to search his memory for who the Chinese children might be, Broad's voice hailed them again.

"Mr. and Mrs. Brandt, there you are. Perfect, let me present Mr. and Mrs. Russell Sage."

# CHAPTER 15

# WITH MR. AND MRS. SAGE

"Mr. Brandt, Mrs. Brandt. Welcome to New York City, and let me first say that we are delighted that you have chosen to join us on our trip north," Russell Sage bellowed out over the noise of the crowd rushing around the two couples. For all the world, Jason thought, he looked like the sea captain who had ferried them across the Pacific. Steel-blue eyes very animated and clothing while not expensive that he wore well.

"Let me present my wife Olivia, who I should add first introduced me to your writings." Sage had a powerful determined air about him that made him seem even taller than he actually was.

"Thank you as well. And this is my wife Black Jade," Jason started.

"Or if you like, Nellie," she said in her most polished English. "For that is the name my English-language teacher gave me."

"Delighted." Sage put out his hand that Black Jade eagerly took into her own.

"Mrs. Brandt," Sage's wife said, stepping forward. "And your children, they are beautiful," she said, crouching down to the children's level to greet them.

"And what is your name?"

"William, ma'am," the young boy said. "And you?" Mrs. Sage said, turning to Mei-ling.

"My name is..." She hesitated and looked at her mother. "Norma."

"Well, Master William and Miss Norma, I am very pleased to meet you. That is a wonderful doll you have there, Norma."

"My wife is a former school mistress," Mr. Sage said quietly into Jason's ear.

Suddenly Broad spoke, again loudly, above the din. "We should probably move back toward the Pullman car; it's almost twelve thirty. I believe the train is scheduled to leave soon."

Sage turned back toward his young assistant. "Now, Abraham, do you really think the engineer will leave me standing here in the station?"

"I suppose not, sir," the young man said, laughing.

"But you are right, young Mr. Broad. A contract has been struck with the passengers. They put down good money to go to Troy and to go now. So let's not delay them."

Within minutes, the entire party was back in Sage's Pullman carriage and getting themselves settled in. Old Zhu and the children, at one end, were playing games that their governess always carried with her, while the adults arranged themselves in the pleasantly stuffed chairs at the other end.

"Abraham, are you not forgetting something?" Sage asked sternly.

"Oh yes, sir, I didn't forget; it's here somewhere in my coat pockets." For the next few seconds, Broad fumbled through his jacket looking for something, while Sage stood there, obviously mildly irritated.

"Got it, sir, and I am sorry, the rush of the morning. Sometimes it's hard to be as organized as one might like," the assistant said as he pulled a sheet of paper out of the inner pocket of his jacket.

Sage listened but clearly had doubts about how difficult it was to become organized. Taking the paper, he studied it for a moment with serious attention and then, putting it into his coat pocket, looked up.

"The morning's stock figures. If there is anything you should know right off about me, it is that I live for information, particularly the economic kind."

"So now you've learned the most important thing to know about my husband," Mrs. Sage said, laughing. "Please call me Olivia. Olivia Slocum Sage is my full Christian name."

"Do tell us about your trip so far, all the way from Shanghai. I would love to hear of your adventures. When I was a girl, my father traveled a lot. I missed him dearly but loved to hear his stories when he got back."

"Excuse me, Olivia, if I could I would like to say something first," Sage said, clearly with something important on his mind.

"Mr. Brandt, you are our guests over the next day or so, and of course, I am anxious to talk to you about China's industrial goals. However, I have had some bad experiences with newspaper reporters; all politicians, and former politicians as I am, have had bad experiences. Can I ask your assurance that anything I might say will never end up in any of your writings?"

"Absolutely, sir. You have that assurance."

"Good. Now that that is settled," Mrs. Sage cut in. "Now do tell us about your journey. I dare say all the way from Shanghai to, well, now Troy though I suppose, I will know as much about the last leg of the voyage as you two!" she said enthusiastically.

"It really is quite a tale and includes a great many adventures," Black Jade began. "We started out—I don't think I even remember exactly how many weeks ago in Shanghai on a boat to Yokohama, Japan..."

As she spoke, Jason watched his wife closely. The tale was well told—the mention of their meeting the couple that was racing around the world especially well appreciated, as apparently both Mr. Sage and Olivia had read something about the bet in the newspapers. What struck him most was that it was obvious Black Jade had been planning the tale, perhaps hoping it would be useful in getting to know new people, and her words flowed as smoothly as they possibly could.

Jason also noticed that she was even working hard to make her language sound as crisp and as aristocratic a tone of English as her teacher and Aouda had spoken it. The two Sages listened attentively, though from time to time Sage cut in to ask specific questions about time tables and accommodations. Clearly, his professional interest in travel and especially railroads added a different dimension to his appreciation of the tale.

"Then, of course, we arrived here this morning and you know the rest."

For a second Jason thought of asking Sage about the troop of young Chinese students he had seen in Grand Central and then thought better of it. It would not due to be asking Sage about China while he was trying to find a way to make his own knowledge useful to the man.

"If I might ask Mrs. Sage," Black Jade started.

"Do call me Olivia."

Black Jade started again. "Olivia, Mr. Broad told us your former teacher was ill. Perhaps you know that in my country, a teacher is an extraordinarily revered person. Indeed, we have a saying that 'A teacher for a day is like a father for a lifetime.'"

"Nellie, we Americans do not have such a saying; sadly teachers here are not that respected. However, Mrs. Willard is exactly such a person. She has spent her entire life helping to educate young women, to educate them when many said women should not have an education. And Emma, for that is her Christian name, made sure that her charges would not only be educated but able to support themselves even if they did not have a man to depend on. Oh, I do hope she is feeling better than we have heard and that you can meet her," Olivia said, clearly in awe of her former teacher.

"Mrs. Sage, Olivia, for me that is very interesting. I don't really know your country, but I have known many Westerners in Shanghai and, of course, traveled across your country for weeks. From my perspective, Western women seem so much more free than the women of my country. It's hard to imagine they have needed such champions?"

"I don't pretend to know much about the Orient, much about China. I was hoping to learn a great deal from you," Olivia said while Jason, sitting quietly, noticed Mr. Sage very surreptitiously eyeing Black Jade's feet.

"But," Olivia went on, "I can assure you that while it might be less obvious than in your country, we Western women remain very much under the thumb of our menfolk as well. Of course, some of those men folk are much kinder than others," she said, turning to her husband. Sage laughed and said nothing.

"Speaking of Mrs. Willard, let me add one minor observation. She is, as Olivia says, a dedicated teacher, has been all her life. But as one who grew up quite poor and had a chance to make something of myself in Troy, a block away from her famous Troy Female Seminary I might add, and yes, my dear, with all due affection for the old lady...what is she, seventy or so now? Has a bit of the aristocratic queen in her as well." Sage turned to his wife, carefully observing if his slightly negative comment about her hero was received without too much rancor. When Olivia said nothing, he went on.

"My earliest memory of her is maybe around 1824, not sure exactly, but I was a bit under ten and the famous General Lafayette showed up in Troy to visit Mrs. Willard's female seminary. There was a huge crowd in the park in front of the Presbyterian Church, next door to the seminary and a giant sign, I can read it from memory to this day..." Sage closed his eyes as if reading an internal memo and recited.

"America, commands her Daughters to welcome their Deliverer, General Lafayette."

"And all the Troy Seminary students were decked out there as the General arrived by canal boat. Troy, I should mention, is right alongside the Hudson River. It was an incredible sight. The old General and the school's head mistress, a couple of aristocrats meeting there on the steps of the seminar."

"What did they say?" Black Jade asked, getting into the story.

"Not sure what they said, but I remember distinctly that the students were all beauties, indeed ended up marrying a couple of seminary students myself." He glanced over to his wife, unsure perhaps if that particularly aside had been appropriate. "In any case the students sang some sort of song about Lafayette being a hero and all. It was quite a day...never forgotten it since that moment."

"My husband jokes a bit, of course, but it is true. If you are lucky enough to meet her, and I do hope she will be feeling well enough, you will find she is, in fact has always had, something of an aristocratic tone to her manner. But frankly, I think she needed that to accomplish her goals. The school has always been called a seminary rather than a college. Mrs. Willard understood, and especially so decades ago that there was too much resistance to call a girl's school a college. Too many men thought women should not have such degrees. Mrs. Willard understood that but then went on to offer a curriculum that was every bit as demanding if not more than what a male would find at a college. I myself still have terrors when I think of my own final exams...all of which had to be presented publicly, mind you."

"China, as you probably know, is a country that has a tremendous respect for educated people," Jason commented, "perhaps not so much for girls but certainly for education itself. Have you heard about the famous Chinese civil service exams?"

"Only slightly, but I would love to learn more. I spent most of my life as a teacher, and am very interested."

For the next hour or so, Jason and Black Jade told the two New Yorkers all about the Chinese exam system, which because of their friendship with Wu, they knew far more about than most outside of the Chinese literary classes. After a time, the conversation drifted toward religion, and both women became even more lively as they discussed their mutual interest in the Bible. As they spoke it was obvious that Mrs. Sage was increasingly impressed with "Nellie's" knowledge of the good book. She should know the book well enough, Jason thought to himself, as she had been copying it line for line since she'd first conceived of the idea of moving the family to America for a time.

"Why don't we move forward and allow the ladies to chat?" Sage said quietly to Jason. "For myself, I don't have much interest in the topic. So tell me, had you ever been on a railroad before arriving in San Francisco? Are there none in China yet?" he asked, his professional interest aroused.

"Certainly none that I know of; I have heard talk of laying a line sometime but not yet. Steamships yes; in fact, I have a good friend who has been involved in building an entire fleet for the Chinese at Fuzhou," Jason added.

"So how was that arranged? I'd very much like to hear about that, and besides I think we have a bit of time before lunch is served."

For the next half hour, Jason told Sage about the Fuzhou dockyard and for a time about the arsenal that had been built at Jiangnan just outside of Shanghai to introduce the production of Western-style ordnance.

"Wait," he blurted out to no one in particular.

"What?" Sage asked, his curiosity aroused.

"Oh, sorry, I just remembered something I have been thinking about."

Just then a young woman Jason had not seen before, a very pale-looking woman whom Jason guessed was Irish, announced that lunch was ready. With that, everyone rose and moved to the very formal dining area that occupied one section of the expansive private Pullman car.

"Excellent," Sage said, "I ordered chicken sandwiches for the adults, bread butter and jam for the children…and Jason, I hope you like German beer, because I have a fine stash over there in that cabinet. You will find a nice selection of Sarsaparilla in there as well."

"This is very pleasant," Black Jade said, delicately biting into one of the sandwiches.

"Yes, and so much less of a distraction than hanging around a restaurant waiting for service, don't you think, dear?" the enormously wealthy railroad tycoon asked his wife.

"Of course, dear, and you are too well known in Troy to eat in peace anyway. Excellent idea," Olivia said, though for a second Jason thought he saw a very subtle smile on her face as she bit into her own chicken sandwich. The entire group ate quietly, even the children whom Old Zhu was watching like a hawk lest they disturb the tranquility of the moment. They ate in silence until a moment later Broad arrived and whispered something into Sage's ear.

"It looks like we will be arriving soon," Sage said, turning to his wife and guests. "Abraham, that last station we stopped at. I assume you did not forget."

"Absolutely not, sir; here you are. Right off the telegraph wires." He handed Sage the sheet. The man studied it for a second and then without a word scribbled a note on the paper and handed it back to his assistant. "Be sure to telegraph this in once we get to Troy." As Sage put in what Jason assumed to be a stock purchase, the train abruptly pulled to a halt in Troy's train station.

"So what do you all think? I propose we have the baggage sent over to the Troy Hotel and we just walk over to the seminary. It's not very far."

At that Olivia finally spoke up. "Russell, I am sure we ladies will want to freshen up a bit at the hotel and then I think it best if I walk over alone first and find how Emma is feeling. We have no idea yet if she can even receive visitors."

"I suppose you're right, Olivia. Besides that, will give Jason and I chance to talk a bit more about China's future industrial goals," he said, happy her suggestion allowed him to get back to business. "So you will go over and talk to the family and come back for us."

"Yes, I think that will work well." With that, the group climbed into the carriage Mr. Broad had hailed and headed off toward the hotel.

# CHAPTER 16

# THE TROY FEMALE SEMINARY

Forty-five minutes later, Jason found himself sitting in one of the large easy chairs in the lobby of the Troy Hotel. Everyone was checked in. Black Jade and the rest of his family were upstairs settling in for what Jason thought might be a two-night stay. Russell Sage sat just opposite him, looking at yet another note about stock prices his assistant had arrived with a moment before.

"Jason," Russell Sage began, finally looking up and speaking more seriously. "I have been joking about my wife pointing out your newspaper articles and that magazine story about you a while back. That is true, I did not know about you. But I had been looking for someone like you for a long time." Sage paused, clearly distracted by something for a second and, then taking a pad out of his pocket, he scribbled a note to himself.

Then going on, "You are going to hear a lot of things about me; some of them kind, some of them, unfortunately, around here, perhaps not so kind, and a lot of it will be lies. What you should know about me, though, is that I don't indulge in a lot of the pleasures many men with my wealth do. I am rather tight, in fact. But you will hear enough about that, I am sure." Russell Sage laughed as if he rather enjoyed his reputation as the cheapest money mogul in New York.

"What is true about me, though, is that I am fascinated by business, fascinated with simply making money and seeing that that money grows into industries that will help America get stronger. I assume you know I was earlier in life the congressman from this area?"

Jason nodded, for his knowledge of the famous Mr. Sage had grown as they traveled across the country.

"What I care about is making America stronger and in the good old-fashioned Yankee way, with making a profit on that growth for myself. As America grows, so grows the world, and the opportunity for investment even beyond our shores. I have spent years building railroads and playing my part in helping to see those trains make it all the way to California. Now it is the time to think even bigger."

Jason listened closely, having, of course, a good idea where the conversation was going.

"The way I see it China is the next big challenge. I keep hearing talk of their emperor's efforts to industrialize. I'd like to be part of that. I'd like a chance to invest there as well. That is where you come in. I have done a lot more research than you might imagine, really digging into your career."

Sage eyed him, clearly wondering if Jason would be bothered by such an investigation. The younger man said nothing. "What I have learned is that you have better contacts and know more about China than almost any American I have ever come in contact with. And you are obviously an especially observant writer to boot. That is why I first wrote you." At that, Sage paused as Black Jade descended down the staircase and his own wife Olivia walked into the lobby from the street.

Sage stood up. "Jason, we can talk later. So, Mrs. Sage, what have you learned during your visit to Troy's famous Female Seminary? How is the old gal?"

"I talked to her son and her caretaker. They were right to encourage our visit. She really does seem to be failing," Olivia said, wiping a tear from her cheek with a handkerchief. "I think it is important that we walk over right now."

"But, Mrs. Sage—"

"Olivia."

"Olivia, can we burst in on your old teacher? Is it respectful for Jason and I to visit at such a time?" Black Jade asked.

"That is just it; as you will see in a moment, Emma Willard is not like most people. She is delighted that you and your husband arrived, eager to meet both of you. She is a women of extraordinary curiosity and anxious to welcome you, especially you."

"Well, if you are certain…" Black Jade hesitated.

"More than certain, and her nephew William assured me that such a visit might even help her rally. As I left she was already insisting that they help her from the bed and into a big chair she loves to sit in to receive visitors."

"So we are off," Sage said, already starting for the door. He was obviously already bored by too much speculation. "Olivia, are you coming, dear?"

With that, the three of them started off as quickly as they could, despite Black Jade's relatively slow gate to catch up with the famous New York banker. Within a few minutes, they had arrived at the Troy Female Seminary Willard had founded generations before and entered the small private quarters Willard occupied on the first floor.

"Olivia, Russell, Mr. and Mrs. Brandt, do come in!" yelled a much louder stronger though aged voice than they had expected. As they entered an older woman with very strong, high cheekbones and a white bonnet on her head sat in a large arm-chair, wearing a full black silk dress beckoning them deeper into the room. It was clearly a study, though Jason spied a partially closed bedroom door over to one side.

"Come in, come in...sit down...Bill, get us three more chairs." The woman they'd been told was on her deathbed had suddenly become the ringmaster of a circus.

"So, Russell, you still making money hand over fist?" she said cheerily.

"Absolutely, ma'am," Sage said, laughing.

"Well, you keep at it. Mark my words, Russell. I predict all that money will do a world of good one day."

"Yes, ma'am," Sage said, obviously amused.

"Mr. and Mrs. Brandt, let me welcome you to the Troy Female Seminary. I am so pleased Olivia and Russell, that's Mr. Sage"—and then turning back to Sage—"Or are you still going by Congressman Sage?"

"Just Mr. Sage, though in truth I am partial to 'the Sage of Troy,' as folks used to call me a while back."

"Right you are...but you will always be Russell to me." Then turning to Jason and Black Jade, "I've known Russell since he was a lad, working at his brother's store."

Sage sat quietly, listening with amusement. "So, Emma, I see you are in good health." He laughed.

"Nonsense, I won't see the spring."

"What do you mean, Emma? You will live to be a hundred I am sure," Olivia offered tentatively.

"Rubbish," the old lady said. "My ticker is getting more and more erratic all the time. Look here!" With that, Mrs. Willard pulled out a pad out from under the blanket that covered her legs. "I've been keeping a record for a week, irregular heartbeats, weakening respiration. I have even made a graph. If it wasn't my own heart, I think I might even try to write an article on it." She laughed, though it was obvious to everyone in the room her energy was flagging and she knew it. Off to the side, her nephew was watching closely.

For a time, Mrs. Willard, who'd clearly traveled a lot, asked her guests about their journey from Shanghai by ship and the subsequent train trip across the country. But even as she asked, Jason had a sense that she had something else in mind. Suddenly she changed the subject.

"Well, gentlemen, now is time for the ladies to chat a bit. Russell, have you shown Jason around our wonderful Troy?" And then to Jason, "I know you have already seen San Francisco and Chicago, but Troy has its own special wonders. Russell, I think you should give Mr. Brandt a tour."

"Yes, ma'am," Sage answered enthusiastically. "So, dear," he said, turning to Olivia, "why don't we meet you in a while in front of the First Presbyterian?" Olivia nodded and Jason got up, and taking Emma Willard's hand, he shook it. For an old lady in her eighties, it was still a surprisingly strong handshake. A moment later he and Sage emerged into the very late-afternoon cold of Troy. Once outside, Broad walked up and quietly handed Sage his stock figures again. Sage read them and put the sheet into his pocket.

"So let's walk for a spell. Over here on the right, that's the church I mentioned." As they walked through a small park surrounded by an iron railing, Jason studied a large Greek Revival building with enormous Doric columns.

"We should look inside later. It is quite impressive. It was built when I was a lad." Sage was quiet for a moment, as if he were wondering what was appropriate to say. "Married my first wife in there, seems like a lifetime ago. She died a few years ago," Sage said, clearly distracted by the thought.

"And Olivia. Where were you two married?" Jason asked.

"Just across the river...In fact, let's walk over there. I want you to see it properly." Sage set off at a good clip toward the Hudson River that ran only a few hundred yards distant from them. As he walked, Jason found his demeanor changing. He'd been friendly enough all day, but now Sage seemed to be relaxing in the fashion people often took on with strangers. As they crossed the street closest to the water, appropriately named River Street, Sage gestured.

"Down there, like Mrs. Willard said, I started out working in my brother's store. Paid me four dollars a month...bit later. I bought my first plots of land, over there just opposite the store."

A hundred feet later, they were at the river's edge, looking at both the water itself and the many patches of ice that floated on the surface. Jason pulled his coat closer to him, but Sage did not even seem to notice the cold winter wind that was hitting them.

"Look down yonder. You see that Iron Bridge down there. It's called the Congress Street Bridge. It was just built. Second largest highway bridge in the country and we are all quite proud of it." They both studied the bridge for a time as Sage pointed out various features only a professional investor would be aware of. Then after a time, he spoke again.

"Do you ride much, Jason?"

"Not in the last couple of months, but yes. It would be very hard to be a newspaperman in China without riding well." Though as he responded what he really remembered was the time, how many years had it been, since he'd found himself wounded and flung over the saddlebags of a horse like a sack of rice? But now was not the time to tell Sage about his time with China's infamous Heavenly Kingdom of Great Peace.

"When I was young," Sage said, gesturing out across the Hudson, "I used to make money ferrying horses from Troy down the river to New York City. It was a great experience—my own ship, being the captain, taking no nonsense, infinitely more satisfying than arguing with fools in congress."

"When did you serve in congress, sir?" Jason asked.

"Congress..." Sage's thoughts were clearly much more with the river and his captaining of boatloads of horses. "Congress, oh that...that was years ago; you were probably just a kid. But let's move on. There is much more to show you." Sage was clearly getting into showing off his boyhood home to his guest from Shanghai.

As they walked, Jason realized with a start that Broad was walking at some distance behind them, occasionally turning people away who apparently wanted to talk to Sage. A few looked quite irritated. Not at Broad but at Sage himself. The businessman seemed completely oblivious, and Broad was obviously well practiced in running interference for his employer. As they arrived back at the First Presbyterian Church, the beautiful church with the enormous columns Sage had shown him, neither woman was in sight.

"I guess we keep walking." Sage laughed. "So, let's see, let's go down the opposite way. I will show you where Troy's best citizens live. Even lived there myself for years.

"Do you know much about the civil war, Jason?"

"Which one, sir?" Jason asked hesitantly.

"Right you are. I forget there was one in China about the same time as the one here...No, I meant the American Civil War."

"Just what I read in the papers. Not much more than that."

"Troy had its own unique part in it. Not just in sending men, but right here in Troy we built a completely iron ship, christened her the *Monitor* that fought it out in the civil war; some even claim it had a decisive role in winning the naval battle for the north. Built right here in Troy."

At the mention of iron ships, Jason's attention was aroused. He'd spent so many long hours listening to Prosper talk about ship designs that he knew his friend would want to hear all about the ship.

"It was an impressive vessel, built very quickly in a few months with armor plating all over it. Most impressively, most of the ship was below the waterline, making it even more effective as a fighting ship. Fought it out with a confederate iron clad called the *Virginia*, I believe. A major naval engagement it was - between the union and confederate forces around 1862."

"Right, I have read about that...and the *Monitor* was built right here. Right here in Troy? I thought the other ship was called something else...the *Merrimack* or something?"

"You remember correctly...most folks remember it that way. The confederate ship was renamed the *Virginia* when the rebels reworked her. But yes, it had once been the US *Merrimack*. You have a good memory. I wish I knew as much about the Chinese Civil War. I have seen your writings but how much were you directly involved."

"A lot more than I sometimes wish. Not really as a soldier, but reporters tend to get pulled into the thick of the fighting far too often," Jason added as they walked into a larger, more open residential area with a park in the middle.

"This is what we call Washington Square." For the next few minutes as it finally began to darken, Sage spoke to him of the wealthy families, his former neighbors until he had decamped for New York City a few years before. Once they had navigated the square, they started back toward the Troy Female Seminary. Both men walked quietly, with Broad still a few yards behind them watching attentively but just distant enough to be unable to listen to their conversation. After a time, Sage spoke again.

"Jason, what I have in mind is twofold. I want you to feel free to accept either offer. As you have seen, I am a man of business, many businesses over my lifetime but in recent years mostly as a railroad investor." Sage paused for a moment and then said, "I don't like to waste money; you should see what some men with my means use their money for. Huge homes along the Hudson, enormous yachts. I am just not interested. I spend money to make money, and I want to engage you as a long-term adviser/consultant on China's railroad potential."

Jason listened carefully, wondering what was coming.

"What I propose is that you prepare a report every two months on what you have heard on anything, even remotely related to the topic—decision making in China, tensions between our two governments that might it make harder to invest, specific plans to develop railroads—anything that would be helpful. I know China doesn't have any railroads yet, but I am certain it will at some point. I want to be part of that. Do you think you can do that? I should not think it would be all that much of a diversion from your regular work. Just much more focused in your reports to me."

"Yes, I think I could. In fact, frankly I am as interested in learning about China's industrial future as you are in investing in it."

"Good, now this is what I am offering. You will write me regular reports. I will pay you quarterly." Sage mentioned a reasonable fee somewhat higher than he'd already been paid for the first report. "And, Jason, I consider this a long-term project. Nothing is going to happen immediately and don't think I expect it to. Is that acceptable?"

"Yes, I think it is, sir."

"Now there is other thing. Olivia has taken quite a shine to your family and suggested another business arrangement between us while we were all preparing to visit old Mrs. Willard. Olivia proposed that instead of paying you directly, I take at least three quarters of each payment and invest it for you. She is quite proud of my financial skills. Naturally, I would take a small percentage of the earnings," he added parenthetically. "But I feel confident the money will grow and eventually provide you with a nice supplemental income. For the money to grow, of course, you would need not to access the principal for a while, say two years at minimum. I can't guarantee anything, of course. But I have an excellent record and my wife knows it. So what do you think?"

Jason was stunned. He'd expected the small additional revenue stream from writing Sage the reports he needed, but this additional business arrangement was quite unexpected. He'd grown up the son of a Hong Kong missionary, that is with no funds, managed to carve out a reasonable income from his writings but had little more than what he'd put aside from the sale of their house for their travel expenses. He thought for a second of requesting the time to ask Black Jade what she thought but was certain he knew already.

"I think your offer is a generous one, and I accept, both as to the reports and your kind offer to help me invest the funds," the younger man said, turning to shake Sage's hand.

"Excellent, then let's figure I will deposit some funds in advance as soon as I get back to New York City. But now we should be getting back." Then pulling out his watch and holding it nearer one of the street lights, he said, "We've been gone more than ninety minutes."

# CHAPTER 17

# EMMA WILLARD

Mrs. Willard watched closely as the men left.

"Have a good walk, gentlemen," she said with a somewhat-strained voice as they departed. Then turning to her nephew, she said, "Bill, you too...now scoot. I will be fine. Olivia and I have known each other longer than you have been alive."

With that, the younger man, who'd been sitting quietly on the other side of the room, left. As he closed the door behind him, the laughter of several of the seminary students entered until as the girls walked past and the heavy door closed, it became quieter again.

"Olivia, darling. Could you put another piece of wood in the stove? That's a dear. Now both of you come and sit closer. Darling Olivia, you do look so well. I wish I had your warm skin tones at my age."

Olivia started to say something and then thought better of it. Her hero, the woman who had always awed her, was sitting before her obviously weakening, and she wanted to hear everything Emma had to say.

"You and Russell, the marriage, it is working out well?"

"Yes, ma'am, he is very kind to me. Sometimes it is hard. Russell has so many enemies, so many that hate him for making so much money, and so many that hate him for hardly spending any of it either. But to me he is very kind."

Mrs. Willard sighed. "That is very good to hear. Men can be a blessing or a curse for womenfolk, most often a bit of both. I suppose you remember what I told you about my second husband?"

"Yes, ma'am, I remember it very well. And how often you've told me that educating a young woman to be self-sufficient, to be able to support herself, is as important as helping her be a good wife and finding a faithful and responsible man."

"And I don't suppose it is any different in China?" Willard said, turning toward Black Jade.

Black Jade chose her words carefully. "Mrs. Willard, in truth I am overwhelmed. Women here seem so much freer. Yet I am learning that the challenges of women are not all that different anywhere. I cannot imagine a school like this for girls in China. Olivia told me all about it as we came up by train. It is truly astounding what you have accomplished."

"Teaching is the Lord's work and raising young women to be self-sufficient an especially important part of that work," Willard said as Olivia nodded. "But take my hand and let me ask questions for a bit. I have spent my life in study"—she gestured around the room at the enormous and well-filled bookshelves— "and there on that shelf there, works I myself have written on topics from the circulation of the blood to American history. But I know so little about China, and to have such a refined Christian woman, Olivia tells me you know the good book well."

And then for a moment, the older woman became distracted. "I even studied Hebrew and Greek to know it better"—then she regained her train of thought—"to have you here to educate me. It is a great opportunity. So tell us of your upbringing, of your sisters in China."

For the next forty minutes, Black Jade told her of growing up in China of her inability to have children with her first husband. When she began she had every intention of holding back most of the story, of offering much more general information, but there was something about the power of Emma Willard's eyes and bearing. Black Jade thought for a second that the woman reminded her of what she'd heard about the Empress Dowager Cixi in Beijing.

Willard's interest and concentration was intense, and Black Jade could see her fingers moving under the shawl on her lap as if her hands were anxious to take notes.

"And, Nellie, I know this is considered especially private, but I am an old lady and don't have any time left to hold back my interest. What of foot-binding? We ladies in the West hear about it so often but know nothing."

For a second Black Jade paused. It was not a subject she often spoke about, but with Willard it felt different. She told her of her own experiences, of the criticisms she'd received for not having had them properly bound as a child, of the pain then and years later when still as a young woman she'd stopped binding them.

Olivia and Willard listened quietly with few questions.

"And today, it is still a common practice, is it not?" Willard asked.

Black Jade nodded.

"When are you returning to China, Mrs. Brandt?" Olivia questioned.

"I really don't know. My husband is an American who knows nothing about this country, and we have a son who is half-American. That is why we came. So we could all better understand your country. But how long we will stay? We don't know at all. We sold our house in Shanghai, assuming this would not be a quick visit, but how long, no idea. We have not yet even finished our journey here and won't until we get to Boston and Jason's American family."

"When you do go back to China, I want you to consider something very carefully. We were put on this world to serve a purpose. You did not even arrive at my doorstep by accident. God is much more directive than that. When you go back, I want you to strongly consider opening a school for the education of young Chinese girls. And a real education, not just to be good wives but to be able to support themselves, if something goes wrong in their marriages. Will you consider that, my dear Nellie?"

"Yes, ma'am, I absolutely will."

"And, Olivia, are you listening carefully? You know we have had this conversation before. God has—after all your challenges, after all the travails, your father's business failures brought you—given you a kind husband with enormous wealth. These things don't happen by accident. When Nellie returns to China and starts her school—and mark my words, the words of a dying old woman—that is what is going to happen. You, Olivia, are going to help her financially to accomplish that goal. Maybe we will even see a Shanghai Female Seminary one day. Are you agreed, Olivia?"

"Of course, Emma, but don't think I did not know you would have this in mind the moment I brought Nellie in," she said, laughing. Willard might have once been her teacher and later her employer, but the two women—one middle aged, one much older—had known each other for decades.

"Now, take my hands, both of you. I hope I see you both again one day soon. But in truth, I doubt it. I want to remember this moment for as long as I can."

With that the old lady seemed to fall back into her chair, exhausted. Olivia carefully removed her hand and laid the older woman's on her lap as Black Jade did the same. Olivia held her finger to her lips and indicated the direction of the door. As they left they spotted Mrs. Willard's nephew sitting anxiously on a bench in the seminary hallway.

"She is asleep now," Olivia said quietly.

"Mrs. Sage, I cannot tell you how much I appreciate your coming up for a visit. It meant a world to her, and when she heard you were bringing a special friend, she revived so much I thought it was a decade ago." The nephew really did seem very grateful.

A few moments later, they exited the seminary and, turning left to the Presbyterian Church, found their husbands sitting on its wide steps between two of the tall white columns, though how white they were was less obvious in the dim lighting. But still as Jason looked at his wife, he realized she and Olivia were holding hands as they walked toward the two men. Black Jade had a look in her eyes like nothing he had ever seen.

Suddenly from out of the darkness, Broad arrived and handed the two women additional scarves, for it had gotten considerably colder. At that the two couples started walking the short distance to the Troy Hotel, walking in silence, each of them caught up in their own thoughts.

As they approached the hotel, Sage turned to Jason.

"So shall we have a light supper before we head upstairs?"

Olivia, though, answered before Jason could. "Russell, I know you love our beloved American train system and everything wonderful Mr. Pullman has accomplished in making them so comfortable. But Jason's family has not slept in a real bed, a bed not moving along on rails for days. I think they will want to eat in their rooms and retire early."

Sage though was undeterred. "Then a glass of wine before you two go up. I am sure everyone is up for that."

Jason looked at Black Jade, who nodded. A moment later they were sitting around a table.

"Russell, are you certain this won't look questionable, two married ladies in the hotel's lounge drinking?"

"Mrs. Sage, folks in this town have known us both for decades; they are not going to start revising their opinions for good or ill at this late date. Olivia, shall I assume white wine?"

Olivia glanced at Black Jade, who nodded.

"Barkeeper, two white wines for the ladies, and two whiskeys for my colleague and myself," Sage called out without asking Jason. The professional Wall Street tycoon was returning in full force.

"So, Jason, what are your plans next?"

"We are still heading toward Boston, but we are most likely going to visit another writer, a fellow who has been helping me and lives in Hartford, Connecticut, which I believe on the way." As he spoke Jason realized he was not at all sure where Hartford was vis-à-vis Troy and Boston.

"Not exactly, but not that far off either. You won't have any problem going from Troy to Hartford and then on to Boston... Andrew," Sage called out. His assistant had parked himself nearby at the bar.

"Yes, Mr. Sage."

"Before you turn in, I want you to gather all the train information the Brandts will need to travel from Troy to Hartford and then on to Boston. Can you do that?"

"Of course, sir," said Broad, taking a full swig of his small glass and exiting the hotel.

"So who is the writer? Someone I might know? Something tells me he is not a financial analyst. Those writers I do know."

"His name is Clemens, but he goes by the name Mark Twain," Jason said, wondering what the reaction would be. Would a man like Sage know of someone like Clemens?

"Clemens. Clemens…Mark Twain you say…can't say…"

"Of course you do, Russell," Olivia said, cutting in. "Just last year I forced you to put down your business correspondence for at least twenty minutes while I read you that wonderful story about that jumping frog somewhere in California."

"Oh that fellow! Wait, I think I do know, but he's a regular writer…Isn't he also a newspaperman…used to write for the California papers for a time…and"—Sage thought for a second— "for some paper in Buffalo?"

"Yes, that is exactly him, and I have long admired his work. Especially a book called *Innocents Abroad*, about a bunch of Americans trying to find their way around Europe and the Holy Land."

"I know that book," Olivia burst out. "I've not read it, though." At that she pulled a small notebook from her purse and wrote down the name carefully. Olivia had not been Emma Willard's student for nothing.

"Sounds like an interesting fellow. So you know him?"

"We have been in correspondence. I think I can say with pleasure that I know you better than I know him. But we've been invited to his home in Hartford for a visit on our way to Boston."

"You will have to write both of us about that when you can. Nellie, you still have the address I gave you earlier? We do get so many letters from people asking for something of Russell. We have two addresses—one public and one much more private we give only to a very few people."

"I have it right here very carefully protected," Black Jade said, tapping her own purse.

"Well, Mr. and Mrs. Brandt, please tell your children we loved traveling with them this morning and that we are sorry we won't be able to say good-bye in the morning. Olivia and I have to return on the first train south. We've a social engagement to attend tomorrow evening." With that, Sage stood up as did his wife.

"It has been a delight to meet both of you. And, Mr. Sage, I will start on that project we spoke of as soon as I am settled in."

"No rush; it's as I said a long-term project."

"Nellie, Jason, I really do hope your settling in, in Massachusetts goes well and that we hear from both of you again soon."

"And, Olivia, don't forget you have Jason's father's address as well. I too want to keep up with you. And thank you for your kind words about the children. We are very proud of them ourselves."

With that Sage walked off, Olivia just behind. As she disappeared up the stairs, Olivia turned once more back to the couple and waved an especially warm good-bye to her new Chinese friend.

# CHAPTER 18
# FORMING A NEW PLAN

Later that night as they lay next to each other in bed, Jason asked her more about her conversation.

"It is much like I've already told you. We talked about women in China, about her proposal that I start a school to educate young women to be self-sufficient in China as she did here in America."

"I should think there would be a tremendous amount of resistance at home about that, about educating young women to be able to support themselves?" Jason asked, thinking about the implications of such an effort.

"From what I learned, it was greatly resisted here in America when she first started about fifty years ago." And she persisted. "I don't think Chinese girls deserve less," Black Jade responded with certainty.

"And what of her suggestion that you take on that challenge yourself?"

"I had never even thought about it, never even considered such work. The more I think about it, and Mrs. Willard is an extraordinary woman, it really seems like the right thing to do. Besides, you travel so much in your work. Of course, neither of us even knows when we will get back to China. For now, though, I like the idea and it inspires me to learn even more to prepare myself."

"Anything else, I am really curious. I can't tell you how disappointed I was when she threw me and Mr. Sage out."

"I can tell you she was not just planning out my long-term future. I told you we talked about the Bible. They are both very religious women, religious but also, especially Willard, religious in a scholarly fashion. She's incredibly anxious to learn, to learn about practically everything. Did I tell you she'd published on a range of subjects from blood circulation to American history? And she insisted that when we do go home, we should go by way of Europe, which she knows well. But more importantly, according to Mrs. Willard, we must go through the Holy Land. She had a great interest in Jerusalem and encouraged both of us, Olivia herself and our family, to visit it."

Jason listened carefully. "Well, I guess we already came here across the Pacific and then by train since San Francisco. I don't see why we can't return the other way. Fogg made it sound easy enough, and Prosper has told me so much about traveling that way that I can even picture it myself. Did you ever hear him talk about the Suez Canal he is so proud of? I think he even met the Frenchman who directed the project once."

"Of course, he loves that the French beat the British at something." Black Jade laughed.

"Yes," Jason said, thinking more seriously about Willard's suggestion. "I don't see a problem with the idea. Let's figure out a way to pass through Jerusalem on the way home. I need to look at a map first, though. I am not exactly sure about the geography. And I can think of a bonus. We might even impress my father, the very serious-minded reverend with the idea that we are interested in the Holy Land," he said, laughing quietly and then, "Oh wait, I think I solved another of our mysteries."

"What?" she said, her curiosity aroused.

"Do you remember Yung Wing? I think we both met him at a reception in Shanghai a year or so ago."

"That very Americanized Chinese from Hong Kong? Didn't he have a degree from some famous American college?" she said, vaguely remembering the man.

"Exactly, Yale I think. In any case, before we left Shanghai, I heard that Li Hongzhang had agreed to have him lead a group of Chinese students to the United States for an American education, some sort of technical and military education. It must have been approved and that's who we saw arriving in New York City."

"So you have your first story to write about. I bet Barlow will be anxiously waiting to hear about how it's going."

"Of course, as usual you are already ahead of me... I think that is why I married you. Yes, of course you are right. Maybe I could even write something up for readers here in America. But first I suppose I have to find out where they are studying and how far it is from Boston or Salem...or wherever we will be living."

"What I remember most about Yung Wing was something that he said about forgetting his Chinese by the time he got home. Didn't he say something about spending months trying to relearn the language?"

"I'd forgotten that. Yes...you're right. He must have been gone a very long time."

"While we are on that topic," Black Jade said as she put her hand on her husband's arm, "when do we move on? I am anxious to finally settle, and the children need a real routine again."

"I was thinking that we would get tickets tomorrow. I think Broad will have left some sort of information with the clerk downstairs. So let's plan to explore Troy a bit and then move on the next morning. We could spend one day at Twain - Clemens or whatever and then move on to Boston the next day. I am not sure of the distances or schedules, but that is, I think, reasonable."

"I like the plan, especially about getting to Boston and your father's home. I really liked Olivia, but I am getting tired of traveling nonstop and meeting new people constantly. Besides speaking English still gives me a headache if I do it too long."

"You could have fooled me. You are beginning to sound like you have spoken the language all your life," he said, kissing her good night.

⇒╫⇐

The next day was spent wandering around Troy, seeing some of the damage from the recent fire that had destroyed many of the inner city buildings. For Troy, like Chicago had, had its own recent fire disaster and for a while learning about the Erie Canal that passed so close by from a local fellow Sage's assistant, Alexander Broad, had engaged to walk them about a bit. Later, in the early evening, while Black Jade and Old Zhu put the children to bed, Jason sat in the Troy Hotel's lounge reading the local paper, the *Troy Daily Whig*, looking for international stories. If he was to earn his living writing articles, especially on China-related topics, it was important that average readers in midsize towns like Troy be interested. What he found, though, was discouraging.

The *Daily Whig* certainly had a reasonable amount of international news, mixed in with a more complete coverage of national and New York State developments and a daily dose of advertisements for piano lessons, iron fittings, horses, and medical treatments. Unfortunately, the vast majority of the foreign material was about developments in Europe. Jason searched in vain for something on the Orient and finally noticed a single small notice about a local store selling goods from Japan. That

167

was it. Finding the ad and just that single ad put him into a momentary depression about their future. He'd been feeling so good. Mr. Sage's offer, while not all that substantial financially, had given him somewhat more confidence that they'd be able to support themselves in America for a time and hopefully put aside enough money for the expensive trip home as well.

However, staring down at the little ad for Japanese curios undid that confidence. And the next day, what would it bring? Jason asked himself, meeting Clemens the writer he'd put so many hopes on. It had, after all, been Twain's enthusiasm that had in part inspired Jason's decision to upend much of Black Jade's and his well-established life in Shanghai, for who knew what in Massachusetts? He finally took another sip of his drink and went upstairs, almost certain he would be unable to sleep. Happily, that was not the case. He fell into a very deep sleep the moment his head hit the pillow.

The departure went well the next morning with only one surprise, which was not at all unanticipated. Sage had paid only for the first night of their stay in Troy. The expense was not significant, but it did add to Jason's sense that the famous Mr. Russell Sage was indeed a very curious fellow. He decided not to mention it to Black Jade. Their trip to Troy had turned out to be perhaps more meaningful for Black Jade than Jason himself. The newspaper reporter had, after all, merely met another reader interested in is reporting, albeit a considerably wealthier one. But Black Jade had been inspired by her meeting with Emma Willard in a way Jason had only just begun to appreciate.

By late in the day, the family found themselves pulling into the Hartford train station and a few moments later being hailed by a young man Mr. Clemens had sent out to pick them up. Within minutes, after first checking the larger of their trunks with the train station's left luggage service, there was, after all, no reason to take the bulk of them to the Twain household; they were off. Old Zhu and the children chatted amiably about the views of Hartford that passed by them while Black Jade and Jason sat quietly. Both knew how important the success of their visit to the writer's home would be for their future plans and were quite nervous, though nothing was said between them.

# CHAPTER 19

# HARTFORD AND THE TWAIN FAMILY

"Jason, you may have just made the worst decision of your life!" the dashing writer said to his visitor as he prepared yet another round of billiards for the two men in the upstairs room, which Twain clearly used both for entertainment and writing. His words startled his somewhat-younger visitor from China, for Jason was several years younger than Clemens. Until that moment everything had been going so well. He'd even managed to keep up with Clemens's billiard game, thanks to his years of friendship with Giquel, for Jason's friend Prosper was rarely far away from one.

In fact, since they had arrived earlier that afternoon, Sam—for it was Sam, Samuel Clemens/Mark Twain had told him to call him—had greeted him as a professional colleague and fellow world traveler. And his wife Livia, a relatively quiet and apparently physically frail young woman, had made everyone feel at home, a feat especially easy given the fact that the Twains had a very young daughter, whom William and Mei-ling/Norma had taken to with almost as much enthusiasm as Twain's cats.

Professionally it could not have been better either, for Twain had presented him with a very professionally bound volume of *China Tales* and even better an impressive royalty check from the advance sales. And Jason had not even begun the public talks promoting the book they had eagerly discussed, while Livia showed Black Jade and Old Zhu around their home in Hartford's most fashionable neighborhood.

"So why do you say that? So far my plans seem to be working out. I've arrived within a day or so of my father's home in Massachusetts with some money left in my pocket. And that royalty check for *China Tales* really does offer hope that English-language readers, not just in China but here, will appreciate my writings on China," Jason responded tentatively, for Sam's opinion had become more and more important, as he had learned more about the writer over the course of the afternoon. Twain had clearly grown up with little money somewhere out in the Midwest; Jason was not sure where, but the man was now renting a lovely home in a fashionable neighborhood in Hartford. Obviously considerably more people than Jason's father, Reverend Brandt, had bought a copy of *Innocents Abroad*.

Twain took a deep puff of his cigar, put the billiard stick down, and leaned against the table, the game clearly over. "Oh, I definitely think there will be interest in your work. Your writing is especially readable; you are a fine observer of humanity, especially of course of the Chinese variety... sure I think you should throw in a bit more humor, but that's just the old storyteller in me offering a bit of unrequested advice."

Jason listened with intense energy, for Twain was more than a fine writer. His spoken words were as impressive as his written and as thoughtful. In fact, Jason had only come to understand during the early dinner that the Clemens household staff had prepared for their guests, that the man was as impressive as a speaker, as a writer. Just listening to him had given Jason pause. Did one have to be as eloquent as Clemens to be successful as a public speaker promoting his books? he wondered.

"Well, I can say it only took me a few minutes to realize I will never be the humorist or public speaker you are."

"Oh, you will do fine. Just start slow. Maybe find a few kind audiences near Salem that will greet you, as the returning son, all those members of your family you've never met near Boston and Salem. Just start slow and everything will work out. Besides your topic itself will bring them in. There is certainly plenty of interest in China these days. And your take on China is unique."

Then going on Clemens got more serious. "Folks always tell writers to write about what they know; sure it's a generalization, and most generalizations are stupid, including this one. Your strength at least, as I have seen it as a reader while I was preparing the preface, is that you do stay close to your roots. It impressed me deeply and even encouraged me a bit in my own work."

"I am very flattered," Jason responded, feeling an enormous sense of pride. "But how so?"

"Precisely, because you've stayed close to your roots. Sometimes I forget that. A lot of this life style comes from my writings, and my wife's family. And as I said, while we ate supper, we are building a much nicer home in the neighborhood, because *Innocents Abroad* was so successful, sold over a hundred thousand copies. Hell, I'd have made even more if I controlled the royalty structure better, but that is a tale for another time. The public loved *Innocents Abroad*, but I was less pleased because the gimmick was being an outsider, the naïve American tourist on the travel circuit." Pausing, Clemens took up a billiard cue and casually chalked it without taking a shot and then after a moment began again.

"It worked well and brought in a lot of money I am delighted to say, but it was not really me. Since then I've been working to write more about what I really know, the American west, and growing up along the Mississippi. It may not have the gimmick I used in *Innocents Abroad* going for it, but I think it can be better work. Reading *China Tales* reinforced that sense of keeping one's writings close to home."

"But I am still waiting, Sam. So why was this trip the worst decision of my life?"

"No, hold on there. I said 'maybe.'" Clemens paused as he took another puff off his cigar and Jason stroked the cat that had just arrived demanding attention.

"Right now this country actually needs a man like you here," Twain said in his eloquent but very clear Southern drawl. "I mean it, something mean is happening in the country, and when a fellow as cynical as I am sees a new level of *mean*, it says something. Jason, a few years ago, Americans tolerated Chinese immigrants, hired them by the thousands to do everything from washing clothes and with the Irish playing a huge role in building the railroads. Now far more Americans have a very negative attitude about the Chinese even as some like me see them as a very amiable people who work incredibly hard. Perhaps that's part of the problem; their work ethic intimidates folks, and it's getting uglier, especially as the economy weakens. Mark my words, if the economy gets any worse, if folks can't find jobs, the anger against the Chinese will grow. And that anger is moving from the West Coast; you must have seen it in San Francisco as you passed through, toward the east."

Jason nodded. "So are you saying my family is in danger? That my wife"—he hesitated—"Nellie is in danger?"

"No, she is probably fine. You are the one in possible danger."

"Me? I look and sound like a native. In fact, my New England accent is more obvious than yours."

"Well, that is most certainly true." Clemens laughed. "It makes me wonder what your parents sounded like; that's not it. The issue is that your heart and sympathies are with the Chinese, and don't deny it; I've read your book and met your charming wife. So, that's the rub. You are going to very quickly become the fluent speaker of New England-style English who in public will end up, you think, explaining; many in the public will call it defending, what a lot of people are increasingly calling a 'heathen race.' Some folks, even those idiots in congress, and I can assure you most are idiots, I worked there for a spell, are calling for some sort of immigration ban." Clemens paused for another puff and to clear his throat.

"And in the middle of all this, Jason Brandt, excellent writer, fluent English and Chinese speaker, is going to start a lecture series that speaks very positively of Chinese civilization." Then after another puff, "I have seen this before, and mark my words, history does not repeat itself like some phony sages claim, but it rhymes all the time. And one of those rhymes might run over you."

"That is a lot to digest. You really think it will get that bad?" Jason said, deeply startled.

"I have made a good life for myself judging folks, finding humor in truth and stupidity, and yes, I think the real challenges of this trip were hardly moving your charming family thousands of miles across the Pacific and then by rail across the continent in our fancy new train system. The real challenge will begin the first time you open your mouth in a public forum and start talking about China."

For the first time, Jason picked up the whiskey glass Sam had handed him as they entered the billiard room. He'd completely forgotten it had been there while they played and talked.

"It's true; I've already developed something of a sense of what you are warning me about." Jason went on to tell his new friend about that afternoon on their own in San Francisco's Chinatown without Twain's friend Nordhoff.

Twain listened attentively to the tale and the drama of its ending as Black Jade used her cane to such good effect.

"That's just it. You have the ability to enter both worlds, the Chinese and the American, to really understand both. I can think of only one person like you and his role is limited because he's Chinese. But you are a Boston man through and through at least on the surface, and that will attract attention."

"Are you talking about Yung Wing, the Chinese who graduated from Yale?"

"Exactly, do you know him?" Clemens asked.

"I have met him, not here but in Shanghai, and we have a lot of mutual acquaintances. By the way, I am glad he came up. Do you know where he is? I believe he is leading some sort of Chinese Educational Mission."

"Yes, from the papers and a friend whom I believe knows him. Actually, he is closer than you might have guessed. The group has settled here in Connecticut."

The news deeply pleased Jason, for if, as Black Jade had said, his first article would end up being about the educational mission, having them nearby would be terribly helpful. He did not want to leave on an extended trip right after the family settled in.

Clemens interrupted his thoughts.

"Jason, maybe I spoke too dramatically. It is sort of an occupational hazard. I think things will turn out wonderfully. What matters is that the public has China on the mind, and any writer such as yourself, any writer fixing to eat regularly, can only consider that a blessing. I only wish I could be around to advice you a bit as you get started."

For the next few minutes, Sam told Jason about the family's impending departure for England and some of their plans while there. Listening to Clemens, who clearly had a more sophisticated sense of England than his narrator of *Innocents Abroad*, reminded Jason of the conversations about returning to China through Europe when the time came. After a time, talk of Europe faded and the two men walked back into the parlor where their families were gathered.

# CHAPTER 20

# GOOD ADVICE FROM SAM CLEMENS

J ason woke the next morning with a start. It was the day he'd long dreaded, the day when he would finally see his father again. The father whose home he'd run away from in Hong Kong and later refused to leave Guangzhou for. Despite all his letters over the years, the two men, father and son, had not been in the same room together since Jason was a teenager. But that encounter was hours away. Feeling around in the bed, he realized with a start that Black Jade was not there. Quickly getting up and rinsing a bit with the nightstand's water and towels that Clemens servants had so conveniently laid out, he went downstairs.

"And you call yourself a newspaperman!" Sam yelled out as he neared the room. "I swear you only had that one whiskey I poured you after supper and you sleep the whole morning away!"

"Good morning, Daddy," William and Mei-ling called out as he entered the crowded kitchen where the children squatted on the floor. Jason's daughter was holding the Clemens's' baby girl on her lap, while William played with the cat. At the long table, Old Zhu was practicing her very limited English while teaching Livy, Sam's wife, how to cut paper figures.

"No lady turn hand this way," Old Zhu said, excited with the chance to teach someone her favorite pastime. They had obviously been at it for a while, since at least three projects lay on the table…two of them done with Old Zhu's skills and a third more amateurish one cut by Old Zhu's clearly earnest student Mrs. Clemens. The rest of the table was covered with architectural drawings, obviously plans for the new home the family was building nearby.

"Husband, Mr. Clemens has been telling us about the Holy Land?"

"The Holy Land, how did that come up?" Jason asked as he took the cup of coffee Clemens's cook handed him.

"I was telling Livy about Mrs. Willard. She is quite well known." At that Livy, who was about the same age as Black Jade, though ironically considerably more shy and reticent than his own wife, turned. So much for cultural stereotypes, Jason thought to himself.

"You see, Jason, I studied at Thurston's female seminary and the Elmira female college. Both schools had teachers who studied at the Troy Female Seminary. I've never met Emma Willard but almost think I have, for many of my teachers spoke of her so often. I am indeed very jealous that Nellie was able to spend time with her. She sounds like an incredibly admirable woman," Livy said quietly, for she seemed, even as she spoke and manipulated the scissors as she'd been shown, to be in some sort of pain. For a second Jason realized Black Jade was watching closely as well.

"Oh, OK. I've got it. You told them about how you're are planning our return home before we have even arrived. And, of course, about Mrs. Willard's insistence that you visit the Holy Land during our return."

"It does seem like a remarkable opportunity, whenever we get around to going home. And Mr. Twain, I mean Clemens... oh dear, I keep getting confused."

"I assure you, ma'am"—Sam laughed—"you are not the only one!"

Black Jade pushed on. "Mr. Clemens has been telling me all sorts of things about the trip. It does not sound that hard to break our trip home to see Jerusalem. It is not all that far from the Suez Canal. Look here, under the house plans and you must see those as well, yes, here...look at this map. We can certainly do it."

"Jason, if there is one thing I have already learned about your beautiful and strong-minded wife, she is most likely to get her way when she wants it. And I might add her interest in religion is going to be very helpful to you in your work," Twain offered, laughing.

"Why would that be?"

"Because, young man...and I've got at least half-a-dozen years on you, so I can be honest here. Your writings show a bit of healthy skepticism about religion," Sam explained.

"And that's bad?"

"Absolutely, this is a God-fearing country. Your audiences on China will be full of future and former missionaries and missionary poseurs. You can't anger them with your cynicism. We need to sell some of those books we have had so nicely printed and bound. Believe me, I know that. Hell, I've got writings I don't plan to publish until I am so dead it won't even hurt if some fool decides to burn me at the stake. No, in this country, it can be a lot easier if one is as enthusiastic as our wives are about the Bible's teachings. My advice to you is to make sure

Nellie's at your talks and jumps in when the audience starts pushing you about faith. She will be a great distraction."

The entire room, save the children, burst out laughing, and then that one last laugh after Black Jade quickly translated for Old Zhu, whose English skills were not yet up to such advice.

"So this is your big day, seeing your father after so many years."

"Oh, it's that obvious. Yes, it's true I am nervous, but I thought I was hiding it pretty well."

"Jason, my husband earns his living observing people. It can, at times, be a bit unnerving. And while it might seem like he talks a lot." She looked over at her husband, who was obviously deeply in love with her. "While he's talking his real self is watching people very closely. I think that is why his writings can be so meaningful for people," Livia offered.

"My advice to you about seeing your father...and remember, once you leave here by train after lunch, it will only be a few hours to Boston. Just don't have any expectations, neither positive nor negative. I am sure he must be a good man. He certainly raised a fine son. OK, you ran away, but I admire that sort of thing anyway - makes a wonderful story...And your father is going to meet his wonderful daughter-in-law and grandchildren. I should think he will be much more interested in them than you. So you are probably off the hook."

Jason nodded while noticing how closely Black Jade was listening. Her sense of the importance of family and especially one's father-in-law was, of course, particularly high given her background.

"But enough of that. What say we walk you over and show you where the new house will be? Livy and I are hoping that both of you will be here to enjoy it when we finally get it fully built."

"Sam, Jason needs some breakfast first and then we can all walk over there. It will be nice to have the exercise before the train ride," Livy said.

Hours later, after a train ride shorter than Jason would have liked despite more weeks of travel than he cared to remember, the train pulled into Boston's impressive train station. As it did so, Jason felt Black Jade's hand on his arm gently rubbing it. Ten minutes later after gathering up their goods and hiring a porter, they entered the station's great hall. If Jason's family had not been so distinctive, neither man might not have recognized the other, for the older man had aged enormously and Jason had become a man.

"Hello, son," Reverend Brandt said, recognizing his son before the younger man had spotted him.

# CHAPTER 21

# BOSTON

"So what are your immediate plans?" Reverend Brandt asked his son as they sat in the Parker House's restaurant. It was the first serious conversation they'd managed since the somewhat-awkward greeting and introduction at the station two hours before. After that, their time had been taken up with traveling to the hotel, for the older man had rented, at Jason's request, three rooms to cover the party, and with getting the children settled in with a meal in the room. Both children were exhausted, and Old Zhu was telling them ghost stories as the three adults left for a more private meal.

As the men spoke, Black Jade sat quietly, listening and trying to reconcile the older missionary, whom Jason had spoken of so often over the years, with the man in front of her. She sensed that both men were uncomfortable after so many years and the changing circumstances of their relationship. When they had last seen each other, Jason was a teenager, a boy who'd run away from home after his Hong Kong-based missionary father had tried to force him to return to America for college. Now the two men sat there, casually eating their seafood meals, oysters, and crab cakes they'd both ordered while trying to establish a new relationship.

"My immediate plans are, of course, completely tied to your efforts. You sent Sam's, Mark Twain's, *Innocents Abroad*. The book, of course, inspired me to write *China Tales*," for he'd already proudly given his father one of the new American printed copies. "Now I am hoping to promote the book and start reporting again. It's all a little vague, but that's the plan. And I would not have gotten this far if you had not sent that book."

A slight smile crossed the older man's lips, pleased that his runaway son-turned-man had cared enough to credit him with the effort.

"The first place you will need, of course, is a place to stay once we go north tomorrow."

"I thought we were staying with you."

"I thought that at first as well. The more I thought about it, I realized the place I managed to rent in Salem is too small for your family. But we got lucky, one of your mother's older cousins had a house in Rockport she wanted to rent and we got an excellent price. It's quite close and on the coast which I think both of you will especially like. The most practical part is that from there you can easily come back here to Boston, either by boat or train. Even better, the property has a small separate building that you can use to write in. I still remember how hard it was to write my sermons in Hong Kong with only one small child, you, running around."

"Is it very expensive?" Jason asked nervously. "We have savings, and the book has earned some money, but I am not really bringing in any real income yet."

"That's the beauty of it. The owner, you should call her cousin Gertrude, was close to your mother when they were young. She inherited the place a while back and jumped at the chance to rent it, more as a gesture of affection for your mother than to earn money. The rent is very low and besides, in honor of your return I paid the first three months anyway. If you don't like it, you can always move. The only real obligation is to visit Cousin Gertrude as soon as possible to thank her."

"That should not be a problem," Black Jade finally said. "Family is very important. Jason should visit all of his relatives even if he doesn't know them at all."

Reverend Brandt nodded as she spoke but did not respond directly to her. His gesture confirmed the impression both Jason and Black Jade had already anticipated. The older former missionary might be trying to hide his feelings, but he was clearly ambivalent about his new daughter-in-law, a sentiment they'd long expected from the tone of some of his letters.

"Perhaps you should not have told him you were my third husband?" Black Jade had teased him long ago when they had both realized that Jason's letters to his father in the years before their marriage had probably spoken just a bit too much about his friendship with the intriguing Chinese woman he'd met traveling toward the Heavenly Kingdom.

"So what's the plan now, do you want to explore Boston a bit and then go north?"

"Father-in-law, Jason has told me often of how beautiful you have said Boston's harbor is. We want to see that early in the morning. And we need to go to the post office for we are hoping for several letters. But after that, can we travel north to that home you spoke of in…"

"Rockport."

"Yes, that home in Rockport. We have been traveling for a very long time, and settling in is what we need now. Besides, Boston is very close, is it not? I believe we can easily see it when we can appreciate it more."

"Jason, I think your wife's absolutely right. So let's plan an early breakfast, a walk over to the harbor, the post office, and then simply go north. If we get an early start, we can be there by nightfall. It is not that far, and there are plenty of transport options."

"Sounds like a plan. So how about we meet tomorrow at eight here in the dining room? I will bring everyone down and we can get started. Can I pick up the check?" Jason said.

The older man nodded, stood up, tipped his hat to his son and daughter-in-law, and left the dining room. The couple sat there for a time and then left themselves. As they started up the stairs to their second-floor room, Jason spotted his father. The older man had not gone to bed, rather his son saw him at a distance sitting in the hotel bar drinking a small glass of something alone. He quietly pointed him out to his wife. "That's not the man I remember, drinking hard liquor."

"It was a long time ago. He was a missionary then, and you were a child. How well did you really know him?"

"I thought I did, but maybe I don't. I suppose no one knows him in Boston anyway, so he might feel freer to drink hard liquor. Besides that, what did you think?" he asked, anxious to assure himself that his father had not insulted his wife with his somewhat-distant behavior.

"I think it's going to be a lot of work, but I can manage it. Besides I have no choice."

"Why don't you have a choice?" he said, smiling.

"Well, Mr. Expert on China, did you know that a father-in-law can in Confucian tradition force a divorce even if the couple loves each other?"

"Not sure I did; I guess it never came up before. So I guess it's good for me that you intend to charm the old gentleman."

"Yes, indeed. In fact, you are lucky in lots of ways." She laughed as they approached their room, which was separated only by a closed door to the one that housed Old Zhu and the children.

"Welcome to Boston, my wife."

"Welcome home, my husband," she said as they entered their room.


The next morning with Black Jade's ever-so-handy cane in her hand, the family set off toward the harbor Jason had heard so much about. His father had told him since he was a child that it was every bit as beautiful as the Hong Kong harbor he'd grown up alongside. This was his chance, though even before they arrived he'd made up his mind to be terribly impressed regardless of what anyone else thought. For Black Jade it was less of an issue. She'd never seen Hong Kong's harbor, and Shanghai's waterfront along the river was not all that impressive anyway. Certainly, Boston would be able to compete well.

"You know, son, I spent most of your childhood telling you how beautiful Boston's harbor was, mostly because I wanted to encourage you to go home at some point. But put that aside, and I know you have already seen San Francisco, so you have a lot more perspective. I do think you will find it very attractive despite my buildup over the years." With that, the older man led them around a corner as each saw the harbor for themselves.

"It really is impressive, Father," Jason said, ironically more impressed than he'd expected. For the next half an hour, as the group struggled against the cold wind that was coming off the winter waters, they studied the enormous numbers of ships that filled the harbor.

"Had enough?" his father finally asked.

"Not really," Black Jade said, "but it is awfully cold, and I want to keep the children healthy. Thank you for bringing us."

"OK then, let's go to the post office and get your mail, then gather up our things at the hotel and head for the train station. I do though have one more treat in mind before we leave Boston."

"What's that, Grandpa?" William asked loudly over the roaring wind.

"You will see a bit later, my little man. You have all braved the wind quite enough. Let's get ourselves a cab to go to the post office. Within twenty minutes, Jason and Black Jade were descending the steps to the street again with a small precious package of letters. Quite expected were the letters for Jason, one from his editor Barlow back in Shanghai, hopefully an assignment, Jason thought to himself, and the long-awaited letter from Giquel. At last, they both thought as he showed the envelope from Giquel's Fuzhou dockyard to his wife. Finally, they both hoped they would have news of their long-lost friend Wu.

More surprising, though, were the two letters for Black Jade or Nellie Brandt as they were addressed—one from Aouda, not totally unexpected, but another from Olivia Sage, whom they had only just met a few days before.

Fingering the letters, Black Jade said, "Let's wait till we are back in the room so we can read them without distraction." Jason nodded. Her suggestion made sense, though he was a bit disappointed. However, the family was still sitting in the none-too-warm horse carriage, and here was not the place to read the letters with the concentration they deserved. Ten minutes later, they were back at the Parker House. While Reverend Brandt, Old Zhu, and the children went up the stairs to gather their goods, Black Jade and Jason headed for the parlor to seek out the overstuffed chairs and the chance to read their letters. The last thing Jason heard as his family disappeared up the stairs was his father's effort, with his never-very-impressive Cantonese, trying to talk with Old Zhu, whose Chinese linguistic skills had never gone past the Shanghai dialect.

Quietly the two opened their letters. Jason started with the most obvious business-oriented one from Barlow. No surprise there. Barlow, remembering Jason's offer to continue to write for the paper, had already sent off an assignment. He was to find the American Educational Mission Yung Wing was leading and report on how the effort had begun. No surprise there.

"Oh my!" Black Jade suddenly said aloud. "You have got to listen to this."

For the next few minutes, Black Jade read him Aouda's letter. They had made it around the world in time to win the bet but in an extraordinary turn of events they had not realized they had done so until just a few moments before the stroke of midnight. They'd apparently been confused by the international dateline. But all was saved. Fogg won his bet, his fortune saved, and most dramatically asked Aouda to marry him!"

"You could not have asked for a more dramatic tale," Jason said. "I mean if it had not happened, if I had not actually met them, I'd have thought it was some sort of fiction, a novel conjured up by someone like Sam."

"And there is more. She encourages us as well—I am beginning to think fate is guiding us to visit her in England on our return home."

"Well, I guess that has been settled. How we get home to Shanghai. Right now, I am more concerned about how we get to our temporary lodgings in Rockport. Father said we'd leave right after an early lunch and frankly I am nervous."

"You're nervous. You know perfectly well that I will end up spending more time there than you," his wife responded with her usual strong-minded tone. "But what of Giquel's letter?"

"I am not sure I should open it yet…it looks quite long, and I am concerned about getting to…what was it…can't seem to keep the name in my mind, Rockport before dark."

"I think you are right. Let's let Olivia and Prosper wait until we are on the train."

With that agreement the two went up the stairs to the rooms, which were by now relatively empty with the bags nicely packed. Old Zhu had done a fine job. As they entered, Jason could hear his father now trying to talk to Old Zhu in English, having apparently given up on Chinese.

# CHAPTER 22

# BOSTON

Within minutes they were on the way to the railroad train station where the senior Brandt explained he had already purchased tickets.

"Father, let me at least pay the expenses you are putting out. I am not a child anymore. I really do have my own funds," Jason said as his wife nodded her silent approval.

"Well, you will be needing those funds until you are more settled in. Besides, I figure I am ahead. Just think about how much money I saved *not* sending you home to college. And, of course, you were kind enough to return that money you 'borrowed' that night that we both probably want to forget."

The old man laughed, though Jason was not sure he was joking or perhaps making a private dig either about his son's lack of a college education or youthful departure with the funds his father had put aside for that effort. His father after all, had gone to a small Bible college before he left for China as a young man, new bride in tow, and had put aside for years the money to send his offspring to college as well.

Once the bags and trunks were left with the station's left luggage service, the group piled into another coach.

"And now my special treat," the reverend said enthusiastically. "Coachman, the Oyster House on Union Block, please."

"Eh, sir, that's a good choice, sir. The misses and I go there every Sunday we can."

"You are going to like this place," Jason's father said, turning to his son's family. "I think it is the place I missed most when we lived in Hong Kong. This restaurant is one of the oldest oyster houses in Boston, so old the last king of France, Louis Philippe, lived here when he was in exile during the French Revolution. When I was a boy, my father used to take me there just to watch old Daniel Webster stuff his face between drunken speeches denouncing his fellow politicians."

"Sounds like a very special place," Jason said, already starting to taste the promised lunch. "What's the best thing there?"

"Well, it is famous, of course, for its oysters. They've a beautiful round wooden oyster bar that's been there for at least fifty years. You will see it as we go in. My favorite lunch is the incredible plates of mussels and corn bread. I used to sit up nights in Hong Kong thinking about that, especially the corn bread."

A few minutes later, the couch pulled up to the restaurant and the family piled out. Within minutes, they were seated in two of the booths that sat just opposite the round oyster bar his father had spoken of and ordered their meals. While the children wanted neither the oysters nor the mussels, they loved the corn bread and chowder, and stuffed themselves without complaint. Old Zhu, in a fit of enthusiasm and, for a moment, embarrassment at her boldness, ordered a bit of everything save the clam chowder that she eyed very suspiciously.

"I am beginning to see why you like Boston so much. It has a very different feeling from either San Francisco or Chicago," Jason said.

"Or Troy, or Hartford. Of course, we did not actually see New York, just the inside of the train station," Black Jade added.

"Those cities have their charms; well, actually I've never been to Troy, Hartford, or Chicago, but I do know San Francisco and New York. Boston really is special, as I hope, you are coming to appreciate," the senior Mr. Brandt responded.

"So how hard will it be to visit Boston from Rockport?" Jason asked, genuinely falling under the spell of Massachusetts's showcase city.

"Not terribly hard, probably no more difficult than going from Hong Kong to Guangzhou. As I recall you managed that trip quite well as a boy," his father said, with an ironic smile on his face.

Two hours later, they were back in the train station looking for the carriage they had purchased seats for. Once the entire family was settled and as the reverend pulled out a book to read and Old Zhu played with the children, Jason and Black Jade pulled out the two letters they had not yet opened.

"Maybe you should start with Mrs. Sage. That is the most unexpected one, at least so soon," Jason said hesitantly.

Black Jade nodded and opened the envelope. As she did so, two different slips of neatly folded paper, on very different stationery, fell out. Black Jade put one aside and took up the other.

My Dear Nellie:

Though I very much enjoyed meeting you and look forward to further correspondence, I did not, in truth, expect to be writing you so soon. However, sad news has arrived from Troy in the time since we both left. Mrs. Willard died in her sleep the evening of our visit. I am told it was a gentle death, which I truly hope is true, for she was, as I am sure you understand, the heroine of my youth and my role model ever since. I know you did not spend much time with her, but I did feel a true bond had developed between the two of you even in that short time. And so I was not at all surprised by the note her family found on her nightstand. Though Mrs. Willard has passed, I am certain the administration will accede to what may have been her last wish.

Hoping all is well. Both Russell and I look forward to hearing from you and tales of how your effort to learn about America goes.

Olivia Slocum Sage

"What does it say?" Jason asked anxiously as Black Jade put the letter down.

"Emma Willard died." For a moment, Black Jade stared out the window, contemplating the New England countryside that passed by them as they traveled north out of Boston. It was obvious Jason could see that the death had deeply moved her. Then a moment later, she took up the second letter. The handwriting was delicate and difficult to read, an indication of a weakened hand.

Dear Miss Norma Brandt:

I am delighted to inform you that you have been granted admission to the Troy Female Seminary with a full scholarship. This scholarship includes both room and board, and will be available whenever your parents think you are ready to take it up. Congratulations.

Emma Willard

"Oh my God! And she did not even meet Mei-ling!" Black Jade said, handing the admission letter to her husband, who read it closely.

"What an amazing woman!" Jason said aloud.

"What is it, Daddy?" Mei-ling asked. "Something about me?"

"Darling," Black Jade said, "that very kind lady I talked about, the lady who ran the school to educate young women, has offered you admission and a scholarship when you are ready."

"Do I have to leave now?" the girl asked anxiously.

"Not at all, dear. The offer is very kind but would be for later, when you are older, and we don't really even know if we will be here that long. But it was a wonderful gesture from a very special person," Black Jade said, hugging her daughter.

"Who's the letter from?" Reverend Brant asked curiously.

"It's from an older woman who just died but who founded a school to educate young women in Troy, NY. Her name was Emma Willard."

"Willard, Emma Willard. I know that name. It comes up a lot in my talks."

"Your talks on missionary work in China?" Jason asked, his curiosity aroused. "Why would Emma Willard's name come up?"

"Folks around here are certainly interested in China and missionary work, but they are also very interested in arguing about women's rights. It comes up all the time. Men and women arguing about women's rights, women arguing among themselves about it, and Willard's name comes up often. She was some sort of radical about educating women, right?"

"I am sure some people saw her that way," Black Jade said quietly.

"Which brings me to another issue I wanted to talk to you about," the reverend said. "Jason, you said you wanted to start giving public talks, and to practice with a reasonably friendly audience. I have been thinking about that and I've even thought of a topic that might bring out an audience beyond your mom's kinfolk. What about a talk on Frederick Townsend Ward? I assume you knew him, right?"

Jason nodded. He'd not known well the famous son of Salem who'd gone off to lead an army against the Taipings. Ward after all, had, died only a few months after Jason began reporting on the Civil War from Shanghai. But, yes, he'd spoken to him several times.

"That might work. I could introduce myself and my family to the community, perhaps sell a few books and get some practice public speaking. Sam Clemens insisted that I practice with a friendly audience when we talked about promoting the book in Hartford," Jason added, warming to the idea.

"Clemens did, eh?" his father said, smiling. "Not surprised that he did."

"Is there something I should know about?" Jason asked warily.

"So he did not tell you?" His father laughed.

"Tell me what exactly?"

"Couple of years back, he gave a talk in Rockport itself. Several of us came over on a Sunday afternoon from Salem by coach to listen. Turned into a disaster. Everyone was all set for a funny talk. The guy's supposed to be a humorist or something, and no one thought he was funny at all. Those who invited him even wanted part of his fee back. Apparently, it got even nastier the next day when someone woke him too early. Town talked about nothing else for a week!"

"I am so glad you told me," Jason moaned.

"It's all right, darling. Maybe their expectations were too high. Mr. Twain certainly has quite a reputation to live up to," Black Jade said, finishing with a hopeful "At least you don't have that problem."

"Thank you so my much, darling wife."

The older man laughed loudly as he listened to his son and daughter-in-law talk. Then a moment later, he took up his book again. Jason for his part sat there feeling a sense of disaster looming in his chest. He was supposed to talk to an audience that thought Mark Twain was boring!

"What about Prosper's letter?" Black Jade nudged him.

"I completely forgot. Can you believe that! I've been waiting for months to hear from him." Quickly pulling out the envelope, he opened it and slipped out the relatively long letter.

> Chère Amie,
>
> If you are reading this letter, you have crossed the entire Pacific, traveled the great new railroad across America, and ended up in a city even we French know well, the splendid metropolis of Boston. I am told the seafood there is wonderful and the local beers well worth sipping. One day, I hope you can show me the city as I have long promised to show you Paris. For now, though, I have much to tell you.
>
> First, about your friend, Wu. What a curious fellow. He arrived here several weeks ago, and as you requested I offered him work and lodging. He has turned out to be a very hard worker, and as I have managed to establish that his Chinese writing skills are very impressive, I am even considering making him my Chinese secretary. If I hesitate at all, it is only because he seems so mysterious. He has confirmed that he knows you well, especially from our time together during the Guangzhou Occupation. Is this the same fellow who was teaching you to write Chinese even as you were teaching me to speak it? I vaguely remember you mentioning that once.
>
> Aside from that tidbit about Guangzhou, he says almost nothing personal. I've tried to ask him more about

your friendship, but he always changes the subject. I am really quite curious. He clearly has ties to the literati class, though when I asked, he said was not a degree holder but little else. And another thing, he hides it, but I have noticed that he does everything he can to avoid contact with my own superior Shen Baozhen, the mandarin official in charge of the dockyard. Is there something I should know? For now, I remain impressed with him and, as I said, will most likely have him serve in my own office as my Chinese secretary. Oh, and another thing, he has begun the study of both English and French. Well, perhaps English more than French; he is smart enough to know the former can be more helpful than the latter, but he seems committed to learning both.

For now, a few more items. First, I have had a letter from our mutual friend, George Gordon. They may soon stop calling him Chinese Gordon for a new name, perhaps Gordon of Arabia, since he seems so much more involved there these days. I'd written him of your return to America and effort to learn more about your own native land. You know how patriotic the old boy is… good, loyal subject of the queen as one might say. Well, he was very positive about your decision and asks that you take the opportunity to visit him when it becomes possible either in London, where he often is, or perhaps as you travel through the lands of our Arab friends on your return.

One more thing, I am sure you remember Yung Wing. As you probably know, Governor Li has dispatched him to America with a group of young students to learn about American military practices. If they are anywhere near you, could you check in on how they are doing? There is a very real likelihood that yet another educational mission will be dispatched under my own leadership soon, not though to America but to Europe. Anything you can learn of the American group's successes or failures would be a great help as we plan our own educational mission.

 Sincerely
 Your old Friend
 Prosper Giquel

As he read each page of the long letter, he passed it over to Black Jade, who studied it as closely as he had.

"I guess we still don't know what happened after we left Huzhou," she said, disappointed.

"Well, I suppose we can hardly expect him to tell Prosper or especially that Chinese official who he really is, that he was a high-ranking Taiping rebel," Jason whispered, though he was not sure why.

"Looks like we are getting close," the reverend said, standing up and peering out the window. "We will need to engage another carriage to get everyone to the house itself, but I think we should be there before nightfall," the older man added, looking up at the late afternoon sky.

An hour later as they walked through the small cottage in Rockport, his father turned to him. "Jason, I am going to take a carriage back to Salem, but I promise to return tomorrow afternoon to see how you are all doing. Another thing, check the cupboards. I put some supplies in there before I left for Boston so you should be all set for a bit."

"Thank you, Father. You have been more helpful than I could possibly have hoped."

At that Black Jade stepped forward and took the older man's hand. "You are truly a kind man, and knowing you helps me understand why Jason is such a good person."

At that the old man beamed and then, tipping his hat, left by the front door. Jason, Black Jade, Mei-ling, William, and Old Zhu were at last alone in their new home.

# CHAPTER 23

# ROCKPORT

As soon as the door closed, Black Jade and Old Zhu walked to the cupboard to see what might be available, for it was already dark outside and the family had not eaten since lunch at the oyster house in Boston. Looking over the limited groceries Reverend Brandt had brought earlier—coffee, tea, several tightly wrapped loaves of bread, a few tins of jam—the two women looked at each other and then Old Zhu burst out.

"Now?"

"Now!" her mistress said enthusiastically as the two women started to push aside the baggage and trunks, obviously looking for something. Suddenly Jason realized what was happening. There had always been one particularly heavy trunk among their goods, the one trunk that Black Jade had never required opening, which was good since it had been especially well sealed during the journey. With a knife Jason did not even know his wife had with her, the trunk was opened quickly and displayed before the family.

As its contents were revealed, a distinctly familiar series of aromas hit their nostrils. Admiring the carefully packed interior, Jason watched as the women drew out what seemed like an enormous amount of rice, dried mushrooms, and vegetables and box after box of spices. Within minutes as the supplies were added to the cupboard, and water put on to boil, the small home in Rockport, Massachusetts, started to smell like a restaurant in Shanghai.

While the women cooked, Jason and the children explored the cottage's few rooms and even ventured outside into the increasingly cold New England coastal air to look at the adjacent room his father had said would serve as a quiet writing space. It was not much but the small wooden stove near the writing table would certainly provide enough heat once lit to make the room a usable work space.

After they'd all eaten their fill, Jason turned to his wife.

"Do you want to take a walk outside for a few minutes? I think the moon is bright enough to see reasonably well," Jason asked.

Black Jade nodded and, after giving Old Zhu a few instructions about getting the children off to bed, grabbed her heaviest wrap and a hat she'd purchased in Chicago to protect her against the wind. A moment later, they were in the street.

"I wish I'd asked Father a bit more about this place, but I think the ocean is probably in that direction. The smell of salt is very distinct." A moment later, having asked a coachman who sat in his carriage half-asleep a block or so past their cottage, they were more certain. After walking a bit further, the sound of powerful ocean waves hitting against large rocks became even more distinctive. As they walked they looked as well as one could at the small homes that stood around them on what was clearly the primary road that led to the sea. One could hear the sounds of laughter and conversation coming from the buildings and the low glow of oil lamps, which pushed up against the curtained windows.

"Wait, I am not sure we should go much further." For as they had approached the sea, the buildings and the light they emitted diminished while the street got darker and darker. They were clearly at the end of some point. All around them from three sides, the ocean crashed into the rocks. The simple power, much more dramatic than anything they remembered from that morning below the Cliff House in San Francisco, overwhelmed them. The two sat there holding hands and simply listening.

"Are you nervous?" Jason asked.

"Not about the rocks, but yes, I am nervous. Until this moment we were traveling, staying as guests in hotels, or with people like the Twains. But now, this is it. When I first said we should do this, I am not sure what I was thinking. But now the reality of it is overwhelming."

Jason squeezed her hand. "Let's just take this one day at a time. Don't assume we will be here for six months or six years. Always knowing we can go home will make it a lot easier."

"So you don't feel at home? This is your country; you look like these people, sound like these people. Did you hear your father, your kin, your family, especially your mother's people live in Salem, and some even here in Rockport?"

"They may be my relatives, but I don't know them or this place. My home is in China, in Shanghai, with you. I am not going to change my mind on that."

Black Jade took his hand again and hugged him.

"There is one thing I have been thinking about," she said slowly, forming her thoughts.

"I have been remembering what Yung Wing said when we met him in Shanghai. He said he had almost forgotten his Chinese by the time he got home and had to spend months relearning it."

"I remember that," Jason said. "Why do you bring it up?"

"Right now Mei-ling and William both speak and understand Cantonese and the Shanghai dialect. And, of course, their English gets better every day, much faster than mine. That's not a problem now. What I am worried about is that I think they could both easily forget the languages of China just like Yung Wing did. Will you promise me that the three of us will both speak and expect responses from both of them in Chinese?" She asked with a concerned look on her face Jason could see despite the weak moonlight.

"Of course, though you know it's sort of ironic."

"Why ironic?" she asked.

"Well, you remember, those last couple of months in Shanghai, you were constantly insisting that I speak to you and the children in English, and now you want the opposite. Wife, it is very hard to please you!" he said, laughing. Jason's little joke got him punched in the arm as the two started back toward their new home, carefully watching for the various landmarks they had memorized as they'd left the cottage. Without problem they found their way back to their new home and entering quietly found everyone else sound asleep.

# CHAPTER 24

# SETTLING IN

By the late morning of the next day, as Old Zhu and the family worked to turn the cottage and adjacent writing space into a real home, they discovered the truth of his father's comments about how many relatives Jason had in the area. By nine the first visitors had arrived, individual women, a few families, all carrying various baked goods, from pies to cakes and even a few containers of roasted pork. The live lobster, though, offered by a fellow who claimed to be a second cousin of his deceased mother, earned the most credit from the children, especially so when he offered to teach the family how to look for clams in the sandy waters around Rockport.

If everyone was to be believed, Jason was apparently related to a third of the people from Salem to Rockport, and apparently at least half, the elder among them, claimed to have known Jason quite well as an infant before his missionary parents had set off for Hong Kong. Jason had absolutely no memory of these people. Still he began to think he must have been an incredibly cute baby to have left such an impression, though, as the visitors came and went, each staying for only a short visit. As they dropped off the welcome tokens, Jason began to realize that curiosity as much as family ties drove all those to their door. Certainly the arrival of the long-lost relative from China and indeed word of his arrival home with a Chinese family must have dominated the gossip for weeks in a place as relatively small as the Cape Ann area he now understood to be the name of the entire region around him.

What impressed Jason most was how gracious Black Jade was. The children might have been tiring of meeting so many new adults, and the novelty of so many cakes wore off after they'd eaten too many slices, but his wife maintained the most charming disposition imaginable. The strong-minded and frequently very opinionated wife he'd met so long ago was nowhere to be found. Each visitor was welcomed in an extraordinarily gentle way, with an obvious deference for the older and senior among them. She was working as hard as she possibly could to ease her family's way into the local community. One element of each conversation that especially intrigued him was the concentration she employed as she asked each person their name and their relationship to Jason's family. She was clearly memorizing the names and family lines of everyone who arrived. In fact, after a time, as new people arrived and others left, she herself was volunteering information on who was related to whom, by marriage, the siblings, and related cousins.

Jason was especially interested in how well she pretended to not even notice how many of them were taking every opportunity they could to peek at her feet. Anyone watching who did not know her would have thought she had no idea that the locals were intensely curious about the famous Chinese practice of foot-binding.

Finally, long after lunch the last of the visitors departed and Jason sat quietly with Black Jade, who was holding her head almost in pain.

"Are you all right?"

"I'm fine," she said, switching for the first time in hours back to Cantonese. "Between speaking English and trying to welcome everyone as best I could, I am exhausted."

"Well, I don't know how you did it. By late morning you seemed to know more about who was related to whom than the men did and even a few of the women."

"I may be here and married to you, but I am still Chinese. That is the Chinese way."

"I guess that particular skill did not come up much when we were in Shanghai, did it?" He laughed, but then someone new knocked at the door. Both of them looked at each other and groaned quietly as they went up.

When they opened the door, a redheaded middle-aged woman stood there holding a very large wrapped picture frame.

"Please come in," said Black Jade, as if she didn't have a care in the world greeting the new visitor with enormous warmth.

"Oh, please sit down. You must be exhausted from all the visitors. My name is Miriam. Jason's mom and I were very close friends as girls. But I can tell you all about that some other time. For now, you two should just rest, but I wanted to drop this off. We've a lot of retired sailors and painters around Rockport as you will learn soon enough. Sometimes they are the same people and I thought this would make your arrival easier." With that, Miriam started to unwrap the painting. After it was partially opened and everyone had gathered around, it was Old Zhu who first recognized the image, emitting a squeal of delight.

"Shanghai!"

For that was exactly it. Miriam had arrived with a painting of Shanghai's Bund as seen from the river by passing boats. The painter had clearly been to the city, perhaps even put paint to canvas there before the city. The entire family just stared in awe.

"This must have been very expensive," Black Jade said. "We can't accept such a gift," though it was obvious she had every intention of doing so as her fingers gently rubbed the outside frame in awe.

"Nonsense," Miriam said. "The painting is a symbol of my deep friendship with Jason's mom. No, please enjoy the painting. It will help you remember your home in China even as you get to know us folks in Rockport."

"Thank you very much," Black Jade said, obviously moved. "Can you stay and have tea with us?"

"I would love to, but I have to run. I am meeting one of my students' parents. The work of a teacher never stops they say. But I will be back."

"You're a teacher?" Black Jade said with genuine interest.

"Yes, going on seven years now, mostly since my husband died in the war. But more on that later when we can really talk and you have had a rest from meeting so many people."

With that Miriam pulled her wrap tightly around her and exited into the wintery wind.

The arrival of so many visitors over the morning had disrupted the family's effort to unpack and set up the house in a fashion that met their needs, but by midafternoon they had made considerable progress and Black Jade decided it was time for the entire family to get some exercise. Within minutes, everyone was outfitted in their warmest clothing and set out to walk along the same road that had led Jason and Black Jade to the ocean the previous evening.

"I can't believe how cold it is here," Black Jade said, pulling her shawl around here even more tightly. "I still remember how hard it was to get used to the winters in Nanjing and Shanghai compared to southern China and now this. How long will it last, when is spring?"

"You are asking me? Forget what those people were saying this morning. I grew up in the same climate you did. My father will be able to answer that question when he shows up. He did say he would come by today."

"Well, I have learned one thing. When Old Zhu and I made clothes for this trip, we tried to imagine how cold it would be. We were not even close. We need to start again immediately."

"Daddy, look!" Mei-ling yelled as the coast came into view. Within minutes the entire family stood looking out into the bay, at distant islands and the Atlantic itself. As always William's telescope was shared as each of them in turn looked out into the very rough waters that crashed on the rocks before them.

"I think we've had enough," Black Jade said. "I don't want to have the children out here any longer than we need to. You remember the Twains lost a child just last year perhaps to the cold?"

"Yes," Jason said, remembering one of the more moving moments during their visit as Sam's wife Livia had told them of the little boy who had died just the year before. "OK, let's start back, everyone."

William was a bit reluctant, but he soon turned away and started back with the family as well. As they walked, Jason realized that from the windows of some of the homes, people were watching them with considerably more suspicious eyes than those family members who had visited them that morning. He said nothing to Black Jade, though it certainly seemed altogether likely that she had seen the people as well.

Suddenly Black Jade veered away from the path Jason was certain led back to their rented home. "Where are you going?" he yelled over the wind's roar.

"Look there, a store, food, cloth, oil lamps." She was right. Just around one of the corners and across the street, a store stood with some of its offering clearly visible from the street. A minute later they were inside exploring what was available.

"Greetings, folks, how can I help?" the man who worked there called out as they entered. "Come in and get warm. I've a wood stove right here that will take the chill off."

"Thank you very much. We've just moved to Rockport..." Jason started.

"Yep, everyone around here knows all about you folks. You're the Reverend Brandt's long-lost son in China. The name is Patrick Haskins. What can I do for you? Something special you need?"

At that Jason turned to his wife.

"Yes, indeed," Black Jade said, stepping forward and taking Haskins's hand and shaking it. "Thank you very much. What we need most immediately is cloth, very thick cloth, to make warmer clothing for the children."

"No problem, ma'am. I guess it is a lot colder here than where you are from, I reckon."

"Yes, a lot colder," she said with a smile.

For the next few minutes, the shopkeeper showed Black Jade and Old Zhu a variety of materials while Mei-ling looked on closely and William tried to look back out into the street with his telescope. Jason meanwhile wandered the store until he spotted a newspaper, the *Gleaner*, a monthly on sale near the door. While the women studied the various materials, he read the paper to get a sense of what it covered. It was his first chance to see a local paper since the *Troy Daily Whig*. He'd been in New York too short a time and was too distracted in Boston. In fact, he still remembered his irritation at not remembering to buy a Boston paper until after their train had left the station traveling north.

"Anything else, ma'am?" Mr. Haskins asked, catching Jason's attention again. At that moment, Old Zhu whispered something in Black Jade's ear. A second later she nodded as Old Zhu stepped forward.

"Do you have rice, please?" she asked, somewhat nervously.

"A bit. Folks around here tend to eat bread and potatoes. But I do have one bag; you never know what people might ask for."

With that Haskins went into a storage area at the back of the store and a moment later returned with a medium-size burlap bag that had been clearly tied to keep the moisture out.

"Got a few pounds here. If you are going to be here for a spell, I can order it more regularly if you like."

"That would be very kind of you," Black Jade said.

"So how much do we owe you?" Jason asked after a moment.

Haskins walked over to the counter, surveyed the material the women had chosen, the rice, the newspaper, and few other items the family had added to the pile.

"Let's say two dollars. And figure in a week or so I should be able to have a more regular supply of rice for you. I can have it sent up from Boston. I am fairly sure it's grown further south where it's more popular with folks. But, it should not be hard to keep a regular supply. I know your family just got here, but you will find Rockport's growing faster each day, more railroad lines, telegraph links. We are not nearly as isolated as we once were. When I was a kid, we had to go over to Salem for everything," Haskins said with very clear pride in his city.

"Well, thank you, Mr. Haskins," Jason said. "I am sure we will see you often."

"Just call me Patrick; that's how I am known."

"Well then, thank you, Patrick," Black Jade said as the family girded themselves to go out into the cold again. The walk back to their new home only took a few minutes, but Jason could see that Old Zhu was quite pleased with herself. She had obviously realized that her job would require her to be able to go to the store and she'd successfully ask about rice in the language she still said sounded so funny.

"Wondered when you folks would return," his father said as they entered the cabin. The reverend was sitting in the cottage's most comfortable chair, reading a book. Greeting the older man, Jason noticed that he looked considerably more pale than he'd been the night before.

# CHAPTER 25

# FAMILY

"Father, when did you arrive?"

"Just a short while ago, son. So I see you have met Haskins. Did he treat you all right?" the older man said, starting to cough for a moment.

"Yes, he was quite welcoming. Is that a surprise?" Black Jade asked as she started to boil water for tea.

"Not at all," he replied, in a tone that did not seem very convincing. "You just never know with folks. So what did you buy?" he asked, changing the subject.

"Just a few supplies, mostly material to make warmer clothing for the children. Which reminds me. How come during all those years when you told me how wonderful New England was, you never mentioned how cold it gets in the winter!" the son asked as he extended his hands over the stove that, along with the fireplace, kept the room warm.

"Now there's a good question. You know in truth I think I sort of forgot about it myself. I was in Hong Kong for more than twenty years. Actually came as quite the surprise to me as well. I guess one just forgets."

"Well, thanks for that," Jason said, laughing. "It really would have been nice to have a bit of a warning."

"Jason forgets that Shanghai can get cold in the winter as well," Black Jade intervened. "Here, Father, take this tea; it's warm, and we brought it with us."

The older man sipped the tea slowly. "You know I'd forgotten how much I love this stuff. And speaking of that, I love the smell of the Chinese spices you've added to the room. It's sort of funny; when I was in Hong Kong, I used to dream of Boston food. Remember how we tried to have it made at home in Hong Kong?" Jason nodded as the old man went on. "And since I returned, I find myself thinking about Hong Kong dumplings all the time."

"Well then, you have arrived at the right time," Black Jade said, nodding toward Old Zhu, who stood at the stove preparing dinner while the children drew pictures in their notebooks on the floor.

Over the next forty-five minutes or so, as Old Zhu cooked, Jason and Black Jade told Reverend Brandt about their morning visitors. The older man was impressed, claiming even he did not know everyone they mentioned.

"Not surprised, though, that so many showed up. You two are quite the rarity here."

"What do you mean?" Jason asked.

"Well, I am sure you have noticed this is not San Francisco or even Boston. Most folks around here have been here for generations. What goes for 'foreign' usually means British, or Scotch, or even Irish, of course—though *they're* none too popular—and a few even more foreign types like the Spanish and Portuguese. But Chinese residents. That would be quite a novelty. Yep, not surprised they showed up in droves."

At that Old Zhu indicated that dinner was ready, and the family sat down to an impressive array of dishes, some of which she'd just made and others she'd been slow cooking for hours. After saying grace—as Jason noted, his father had not changed that much—the family dug in, with the reverend helping himself with extraordinary enthusiasm.

"Can't tell you how much I have missed this grub," he said after taking his full. "Can't even remember when I had dumplings like this last."

"But," Black Jade said, "you do go to Boston. Are there not Chinese restaurants there?"

"Frankly, daughter-in-law, never really thought to look. But I am pretty sure I have not seen one. There is a section of the city near the train tracks, by the old tidal flats, sort of an immigrant neighborhood, Irish, Jews that sort, and I think I have seen a few Chinese walking around there but no restaurant."

"Oh," Black Jade said as she turned to discipline William for kicking his sister under the table. Jason could tell she was also hiding her disappointment. A moment later, though, she turned back to the two men.

"And what about Miriam? I don't remember her family name, but she said she was a friend of Jason's mom when she was a girl. A redheaded woman older than Jason and I but younger than you," she asked the reverend tentatively.

"Miriam Parsons. Of course don't know her well. Grew up, of course, in Boston before I met Jason's mom, but yes, Anna, my wife, often spoke of their friendship. She came by, did she?"

"More than that." Jason jumped up to get their painting they'd not yet had a chance to hang.

"Now that is right nice! Guess your mom was right about Miriam. Anna often said Miriam always knew the right gesture to make with people. I think Jason's mom was even a bit jealous. Miriam's got a knack for understanding people, probably helps her as a teacher."

"Tell us about that. She mentioned it, but it was only in passing. She was not here very long," Black Jade said.

"Don't know a lot. I spend most of my time, of course, in Salem, but I think she works at the new school that just opened at Pigeon Hill. They've got several dozen kids who go there."

"Would that be a good place for our children?" Black Jade asked tentatively.

The old man thought for a second. There was clearly something on his mind he did not mention. "Not sure, but I am certain Miriam would have a better sense of it. Your kids homeschooled so far?"

"Yes," Jason said. "William's only just ready for school, but Mei-ling's been homeschooled. Mostly languages and some math, and Black Jade likes to read them the Bible; there is a lot of history in there of course."

"Son, I would definitely talk to Miriam, but you should also know Rockport's got a new lending library, mighty fine collection they managed to build with the money from, can you believe from public lectures and taxes on dogs? They are even building themselves their own library building. The collection is not as impressive as you will see when you get over to Salem, but it's not bad. And it's cheap. I heard it only costs about fifty cents a year to join."

"Well, we will definitely check that out. Considering the weather, it's best to have a specific goal in mind when going out. Speaking of that, when will it get warmer? Black Jade asked me, but I don't have a clue." Jason said.

His question aroused everyone's interest, even Old Zhu who had clearly understood the question as well.

"Hard to say; weather varies a lot. At least you've been lucky the last couple of days."

"Lucky!" Mei-ling burst out, her first comment of the evening.

"Absolutely, it's been something of a warm spell," the old man said and then seeing his absolutely crestfallen audience, "Well, sure it can get a lot colder around here. But that was not the question. It won't be that much longer, a few weeks. Come March it will start getting more comfortable."

"I guess that is good news," Jason said as he got up and held his hands over the stove again. There was clearly a draft somewhere that he decided to add to his list of things to do around the house.

"But that reminds me. Been thinking about the idea of a lecture. Even talked to a few folks. Spending an evening listening to a speaker is very popular around here. Real range of topics, from the Adirondacks, that's some mountains over in New York, to talks on the local prison. Some historical stuff even; I went to one where the fellow compared Napoleon and Bismarck. I assume you've heard of them to Washington and President Grant back when he was still a general."

"That would have been very interesting. But, Father, if I start giving talks on China, won't that hurt your efforts to support yourself and raising funds for missionary work?"

"A couple of issues there. First, I think we would mostly attract a different audience, but more to the point, I am getting tired of giving talks. One has to be on the road all the time; it really is a young man's work, and I should add a young woman's as well since we have also had some fine women speakers."

"Are you sure?"

"Yes, I am absolutely sure. My health is not what it was, and I can get by with the few Hebrew and Greek students I have and the rent from my parent's home in Boston. Don't really need much these days. I am not saying I won't be working for the missionary society and giving talks but not nearly as often. Just finding it harder and harder these days."

"What about the topic?"

"Just like we said. Something like 'Son of Salem, Frederick Townsend Ward of China: The Man I Knew' seems like a subject that would bring out the most folks. And if we do it on a Sunday afternoon, it will be easier for people to gather here in Rockport."

"Wouldn't we want to do it in Salem where he was from?"

"That makes some sense, but you are living here and the Salem folks will come anyway. It makes more sense to me to use the talk as a way for you to meet more of your neighbors. I don't know how long you will be here but for however long this could be helpful. So what do you want to charge?"

"Charge..." Jason thought for a second.

"It should be free," Black Jade said definitively as both men turned to her. "Free, because Jason is new at this, and it can be our gift to the community. We will worry about fees when you talk elsewhere. And besides, some of them might buy copies of *China Tales* anyway."

Both men looked at her, nodding. "I like that." Then, Jason said, turning to his father, "Do we have a date in mind?"

"I will check on that but am thinking of the middle of March, and I plan to have the honor of introducing you," the reverend said, starting to pick up his coat. "But for now I need to get going. One of the coachmen told me he was taking a group back to Salem about now, and going in a group saves a bit of cash."

"When will we see you again?" Black Jade asked.

"Not to worry. I will be around plenty. Have a lot of time on my hands these days." With that, he turned and started to open the door and then shut it. "Wait, completely forgot, went around to the post office this morning. Figured you'd have been telling folks you were ending up in Salem since you didn't know about this place. My hunch was right. You've got a letter from your illustrious friend Twain." With that, the reverend handed Jason the letter, tipped his hat to Black Jade, and was off into the cold.

Jason took the letter addressed to him at the Salem post office and slowly opened it.

Jason: I hope this letter finds you healthy and that your reunion with your father went well. Things here are at a frantic pace, but aren't they always. We are making progress on the new house even as we prepare to depart for a stay among our British cousins. For now, a couple of important pieces of information: first, I am sending with this letter all the particulars on my business agent, Mr. Mark Strong. Once you are ready, he will be able to help you plan your talks to promote the book. He will then ship you copies and can work with you on the agreements we worked out in the contract. It should not be difficult, but do recall that public speaking while it can offer great rewards also has its challenges.

I still remember the first time I gave a formal talk; it was in San Francisco and on, I think, the Sandwich Islands. Not sure now. I give so many talks. What I remember was that I arrived expecting an empty house, walked on stage to discover the hall was full, and completely panicked—stood there like a damn fool, until the Lord or some other deity took pity on me and granted me a voice again. Have not had a problem since. Don't forget what I told you. The most important thing is to start with a few friendly audiences, maybe folks from Salem itself or Gloucester; it is not far.

Also, you will find here the particulars on an old dear friend, Joseph Twitchell, a neighbor and pastor, though don't hold that against him. The man actually knows the meaning of both humor and toleration, rare among his professional colleagues. I wish you could have met him, but he was out of town when you and your charming family visited. What matters is that he is a Yale man and thus a classmate and acquaintance of Yung Wing, the Chinese fellow you asked me about. If you write Twitchell, he will most certainly be able to put you in touch with Yung Wing and his young charges. He is expecting to hear from you. Hoping all is well.

Sam

p.s., One more thing. Whatever you do, don't agree to speak in Rockport. There is not a funny bone in the entire town. Believe me; I know what I am talking about.

"Great!" Jason said, handing the note to Black Jade and pointing to the last sentence.

Listening to her break out laughing was not Jason's best memory of arriving in Rockport.

# CHAPTER 26

# A VISIT FROM A COLLEAGUE

The knock at the door startled him. It wasn't that he did not want to take a break, but the door of the small adjacent building where he'd spent much of the afternoon organizing his work was very close to his chair, and the sound pulled him from a moment of deep concentration. Still he thought for a second, he'd already made a lot of progress since he'd left the main house. Best of all, even before he'd retreated to the small work space, the home his father had rented for them provided, there had been a very pleasant surprise. Miriam, the redheaded middle-aged teacher, had stopped by again.

Apparently Miriam herself had had a surprise visitor the evening before. The father of one of her students stopped by the schoolhouse after the teaching day to ask if he thought the newly arrived Mrs. Brandt would be willing to take his son as a student of Chinese. The request itself, as Miriam had explained, was quite unusual. Certainly some of the locals wanted their children to learn Latin and, of course, French; indeed it was something of a rage, and Hebrew and Greek often attracted attention among those hoping to place their children with the clergy for a living. But Chinese, that had never come up. The family, though, had spent generations in the China trade. Indeed, they, according to Miriam, had even read Jason's articles in the *North China Daily News* and with the Brandt family's arrival had decided that it made sense to give one of their younger boys the opportunity to learn something of the language of the country their family members had been visiting from time to time for generations.

While Black Jade and Miriam discussed the idea and then went off onto other topics, Jason left for the small writing space he'd set up. It was to be his first opportunity not to prepare the space, making sure the heat worked well enough, blocking drafts or cleaning the small window so he could look out into the snowy landscape but to actually write. An hour later, his initial correspondence was accomplished. Sealed letters for Twain's business manager and friend Twitchell were ready to go, and he had begun putting together an outline for the piece he'd worked on periodically since the trip began. Jason had no idea if Barlow, obviously waiting for a report on Yung Wing's American Educational Mission, would be interested in a more personal narrative of returning to America after a lifetime spent in China. Still Jason thought that eventually someone might find it useable or at minimum it might prove the basis for one of the public lectures he was planning. Certainly, Sam had made it clear that if he could develop a reputation as an interesting speaker, he could bring in a fair amount of cash quite separately from his writings. Jason had even managed to start notes on the more immediate challenge of speaking on Frederick Townsend Ward, when he was interrupted.

"Mr. Brandt, good afternoon, sir. The name is Levi Cleaves. I'm the owner editor of the new advertising paper the *Rockport Gleaner.* Sorry to bother you. Just spoke with Miriam and Mrs. Brandt, and they said it would not be a problem."

"No, of course, it's not a problem. Let me find you a chair." With that Jason pulled the material he'd stored on the room's second chair, for he'd not expected visitors quite that soon, and gestured for the sandy haired fellow to sit down. "Let's put your chair over here a bit closer to the stove."

"No need for that," Cleaves said, pulling off the thick scarf that he'd wrapped around his neck. "I expect I am a lot more used to Cape Ann winters than you are."

"So how can I help?" Jason asked as he put water on for tea.

"Well, I expect my request won't be much of a surprise to a fellow like you. You see, I've started a paper; I hope you've had a chance to see it since you arrived."

Jason nodded and started to compliment the effort.

"Mr. Brandt, fact is, I only started it a couple of months ago, and it's so far just a monthly at that. I promised the locals, who've not had a paper, that it would be 'lively and local' and that I'd focus exclusively on local people and merchants. So far it's working out. Even managed to double the last issue, we had that much material."

"Congratulations. So how can I help?" Jason asked, remembering his first impressions of the paper. It had hardly been the *North China Daily News* or even the *Troy Daily Whig*, but it had given him, a new resident, a useful sense of the place.

"Well, sir, that's it. The arrival of your family is the most 'lively and local' story we've got. Folks want to know all about you, so I came by to interview you. You are sort of exotic and local all at the same time, and people are curious."

"Frankly, Mr. Cleaves, in the days since we got here, I thought we'd already met everyone. You would not believe the amount of cakes and cookies that have arrived. In fact"— jumping up Jason grabbed a tin off one of the shelves. He'd only filled it the day before with some of the welcoming food they'd received.

"I know you've met a lot," Cleaves went on after biting into one of the cookies. "Damn, that's good." Then turning back to Jason, he said, "But those are only the people who can claim real or at least a tenuous tie to your family. Rockport's a lot bigger than that. So as a favor to a fellow journalist, can I interview you?"

"Of course, though I will be honest with you. I have a lot more experience asking the questions than responding."

"No problem. So let's get started. First, can I get some particulars on your role as a newspaperman in China? I am sure my readers would find that fascinating and frankly so would I."

For the next forty minutes, Jason answered questions about his life in China, his work, his family—in short doing everything he could to help the man produce an interesting story, without undermining any of his own writing ideas or possible public-talk topics. And he made a special effort to avoid revealing anything he or perhaps Black Jade might be uncomfortable about. That included the specifics of his running away from home or Black Jade's role with the infamous Taiping rebels. They were very far away from China, but an instinct kept him from discussing such issues even in the heart of New England. After a time, Cleaves set his pen down.

"You've been terribly helpful, Mr. Brandt; you don't mind if I call you Jason, do you?" the somewhat-older man asked hesitantly.

"No, not at all."

"Well, there is one more thing I wanted to ask," Cleaves started off carefully.

Jason had not been a reporter for almost a decade without learning a few things. The man had left his most controversial question for last.

"Certainly, there is still a few minutes before I need to go back to join the ladies," Jason said, reflecting as hard as he could on what the man might have in mind.

"Have you heard of North Adams, Massachusetts? It's not far from the area you passed through going from Troy to Hartford."

"Can't say I have. Why?"

"Well, a while back, there was quite a scene there. As I understand it, granted I was not there, bit out of my area, but it was covered a lot by the papers, even some of the national ones. Apparently a local shoe manufacturer got tired of dealing with his workers, labor union stuff and all, and imported a bunch of Chinese from California as strikebreakers."

"Interesting," Jason said, leaning forward with genuine interest. "So what happened?"

"As I understand it, not a lot. A real ugly scene as they arrived. Big crowds, lots of taunts, insults to the Chinese workers as foreign strikebreakers, but not much more. I think things eventually calmed down, but it was quite the talk all over the region for a time. And you've not heard anything about this?"

"No, not really. Frankly, I have seen almost no Chinese since I got here. Of course, I heard about such tensions in San Francisco as I passed through but around here. No, I know nothing."

Cleaves looked a bit disappointed but pushed on. "Well, can you tell me your thoughts on the issue on the idea of importing cheaper Chinese labor from the far West for factories here in the East?"

So that was it, Jason thought to himself. The fellow wanted, either intentionally or not, to involve him in what was clearly a growing controversy across more of American than he'd realized. He poured himself a second cup of tea and offered his guest one.

"No thanks," Cleaves said, clearly disappointed that Jason had not immediately offered a usable quote. Putting the tea down, Jason took up another of the cookies and munched it slowly. He had enough knowledge of his own profession and sensitivity about the situation that he wanted plenty of time to think before responding.

"Mr. Cleaves, Levi, as I have explained, I grew up in China, became a writer there and spent most of the last several years wandering around China, writing about developments there mostly for a local audience of English speakers. My wife and I brought our family here to learn about America, and to continue my writing from a somewhat-different perspective. At this point, I really don't know enough about what happened at…"

"North Adams"

"Right, North Adams, to even begin to formulate an intelligent impression. You will have to forgive me if I beg off that sort of question until I have been here longer."

"Quite understandable, Jason," Cleaves offered, though it was obvious the man was disappointed. "Well, I had better take my leave. I have taken up too much of your time."

"No, not at all. I rather appreciated it, and it was great fun to be on the other side of the pen, as they say. Do come again."

With that the fellow left while Jason returned to his writing table and took up the sheet he'd already labeled "Questions for the Connecticut educational mission trip." At the bottom of the sheet, he left a space for more questions and then, drawing a line, added one more line:

After Connecticut, North Adams

Then pulling out the book of American maps he'd purchased as they had traveled across the country, he turned to one that covered the American Northeast. After finding Troy, New York, and Hartford, Connecticut, he carefully surveyed the area in between. There it was, in Western Massachusetts, near the New York border, North Adams. Now how would he get there? Then thinking for a moment of his dinner aboard ship with Fogg, he realized what he really needed now was someone with the knowledge of the regional means of transportation as impressive as Fogg's had been of traveling around the world. Looking up at the half-filled bookshelf above him, he thought that he was going to need that shelf soon, filled with every travel gazetteer and train and coach schedule he could possibly find if he was going to successfully accomplish his goals here in America.

Studying the largely empty bookshelf, he picked up one of the few volumes he'd acquired since the arrival in the United States: his new friend Nordhoff's book on California—there under Charles's name, author of *Cape Cod and All Along the Shore*. Jason may have only just arrived, but he'd already learned enough to know where Cape Cod was. Just southeast of Boston. Did another guide of that sort exist for the northern area? he wondered. Then after staring at the map for a few minutes, tracing with his fingers the spaces between Rockport and Boston, the western roads toward Hartford and Troy, he finally closed the volume, locked up his study, and braved the cold for the few seconds it required to return to the house.

# CHAPTER 27

# A WORKING JOURNALIST

The next week or so went better than Jason could possibly have hoped. Miriam proved to be a godsend. Not only did she make every effort to befriend Black Jade, but she also had a daughter about the same age as Mei-ling. After considerable consultation among the adults, it was decided that Mei-ling or "Norma", would start school as a student in Miriam's classroom, and each morning the widowed Miriam, her daughter Janette in tow, stopped by to pick up Norma on their way to the school where Miriam worked. In the afternoon Norma was dropped off again by Miriam and Janette as they left for their own nearby home.

Within a few days, yet another piece of the family's routine was added, as Miriam arrived with a boy about ten named Jack Driscoll, who'd been sent by his father to learn conversational Chinese from Black Jade. That effort turned out to be especially advantageous, as everyone, Old Zhu, little William, Mei-ling, and Black Jade, simply integrated Jack into the family's late-afternoon activities even as they taught him Chinese. Within days, reports were coming back that the boy's family was especially pleased with his progress.

"Do you think you are settled in enough for me to leave on my first reporting trip?" Jason asked late one evening as they lay in bed. "If I am to give that talk in a couple of weeks on Ward, I need time to go and return before that."

"My primary concern is starting to resolve itself, so perhaps now is the right time for you to go. How long do you think you will be gone?"

"Not sure right now. I've already gotten an invitation from Yung Wing. After he heard from Twain's friend Twitchell, he wrote me directly. Apparently they have the students scattered all over and only occasionally bring them back for group activities. I need to time my visit to when the bulk of the students are together."

"That certainly makes sense. The boys probably would not learn English if they lived near each other. I've been impressed with how well Jack is doing just hanging around our home in the afternoons with no one speaking English."

"I guess that is why they call it sink or swim. But you said your main concern. What did you mean?"

"Really the same thing we have been talking about since we got here. How the Americans would treat a Chinese family? When we were all together, with you standing there, it was less an issue. But I have been worried about the children, especially Mei-ling who is old enough now to go more formally to school like the other children here. What it would be like for her."

"And now?" her husband asked her.

"Well, God! Oh, I know you are more doubtful. But I think God did bring Miriam to us and even little Jack and Janette. Now I can send Mei-ling to school knowing that Miriam is not only the teacher there; she is looking out for her. She already has two friends her own age for companionship and protection."

"I see what you mean. And, of course, it really is an issue. That is, after all, why I added North Adams to this first trip."

"So when do you want to leave and for how long?" she asked.

"I thought I would leave the day after tomorrow and be gone for this first trip a little under a week. That should give me time for both the travel and interviews."

"Did you ever figure out how you would travel? In China you were usually on a horse. There are a lot more options here," Black Jade asked.

"Not really. At some point, I probably will use a horse, but it's still awfully cold, and I don't know the region at all. As I see it, the most obvious thing is to partly retrace our steps, back down to Boston, then train to Hartford. Then I am less sure but somehow from Hartford to North Adams and back. I guess I will figure out the rest as I travel. But it should not take a very long time, and between the railroads and horse carriages, it should be a lot faster than traveling in China."

"Do you think China will ever have railroads like the Americans do? And I think Aouda said India does."

"If I had the answer to that, I would be able to write my next report to Mr. Sage a lot sooner. But I don't see why not. In India, of course, outsiders are making the decisions. In China, I am less sure, but that is the whole point of the Yung Wing mission as I understand it, to introduce that sort of technology to China, and Prosper's already shown they are obviously interested in steamships."

"But steamships off the coast and railroads running through the countryside are very different things," Black Jade said, reflecting on Jason's comment.

"Yes, of course you are right. But I will have a better sense of this after I talk to Yung Wing. So it's agreed I leave the day after tomorrow? You think you will be OK alone and all?"

"We won't be alone anyway. Miriam's very close. Your father can be here in a few hours. No, everything will be fine. Go earn us some more money, husband."

"All right, wife, I will try to do that." He started to go to sleep when she put her arm on his shoulder.

"Speaking of your father, have you really looked at him lately?"

"What do you mean?"

"I don't think he is well."

"Has he said anything to you?"

"No, but I don't think he would. Men, Chinese men, American men, tend to act as if nothing is wrong unless their leg falls off."

"Well, should I ask him?"

"No, but let's watch him more closely, and be more insistent on his staying here instead of returning to Salem when the weather is too cold."

"OK, and thanks for saying something. My mind has been so much on the writing and planning this first reporting trip that I think I have been oblivious."

...

"So how is your father, the esteemed Reverend Brandt?" Yung Wing asked him late that evening as he sat in the man's parlor a few days later. It had been a very long two-day trip begun early in Rockport as he set out for Boston and then the second train toward Hartford, Connecticut. It was Jason's first trip alone in months, and he found it almost a novelty to be able to sit quietly, without worrying about whether William or Mei-ling were behaving or if Black Jade and Old Zhu had everything they needed. All in all, the day had gone quite pleasantly. He'd written up more questions and read again several times the invitations from both Yung Wing and the shoe factory's owner. And for pleasure he'd managed to get a copy of *Roughing It*, Sam's new book about his adventures out West as a young man. Given that Jason himself had just traveled through the area and for the moment was infinitely more interested in the United States than in the areas from Europe and the Near East Clemens had written about in *Innocents Abroad*; he found the book even more delightful. But still it had been a tiring trip, and he'd only just arrived in Hartford an hour or so before.

"My father is well, sir," Jason said, not wanting to bring up Black Jade's concerns. "In fact, he is living not far from here. In Salem, Massachusetts, where he retired from his pulpit in Hong Kong. Did you know him well in China?"

"Well, no, but I occasionally saw him in Hong Kong. Will you give him my warmest greetings?"

"Of course. And thank you for inviting me to visit the educational mission. I had only the vaguest idea it had been approved. Didn't you mention the effort to convince Prince Gong when we spoke last year at that reception in Shanghai?" Jason asked, trying to establish some sort of rapport. After all, while he and Yung Wing had much in common in an inverted sort of way—one, the Chinese deeply immersed in American culture, indeed the man's Chinese seemed to almost include an American tone to it, and the other, Jason, an American raised in China. Still their paths had infrequently crossed, and Yung Wing was significantly older.

"I might have; it was all very vague at that point. What I do remember was meeting your wonderfully charming wife. If I might ask, and perhaps I have been in America too long to suppress my real thoughts, but isn't your wife an unusually outspoken woman for a Chinese, and beautiful as well?"

"No need to be concerned about your memory. You most certainly do remember Black Jade. While she can control it, she is about the most outspoken woman, not just Chinese I have ever met."

"And is she doing well?"

"Very well, and her strong personality and I might add self-discipline has allowed her to fully commit herself to learning English. In fact, she has become quite proficient. I hope you can see her one day soon," Jason added. He'd arrived exhausted, but his energy revived by the meal and especially the chocolate cake Yung Wing had offered gave him the energy to begin a more serious conversation. Yung Wing no doubt sensed that, and reaching over to the small table near him, he removed a book. To Jason's surprise it was his own *China Tales.*

"Jason, I want you to know that when Reverend Twitchell told me of your letter, I was delighted that you were here. And especially so when the good reverend got me a copy of your book. Apparently he and Mr. Mark Twain are good friends. I have been reading it ever since with deep enthusiasm regarding your visit."

"Well, I am honored. It was a small gesture on my part to help people understand the Celestial Empire."

"That's just it," Yung Wing said, switching to English, which he seemed even more comfortable with to Jason's surprise. "Neither country understands the other well. I have done what I could to introduce America to my native land, and your efforts have literally done the opposite. I don't think there is another Westerner who understands China as you do, and without the usual Western tendency to condemn everything one encounters."

"That is very kind, but surely there are others, some missionaries and diplomats—Mr. Hart, Mr. Lay, Mr. Parkes of course," Jason ventured.

"Perhaps. Their language skills are impressive, but they have always had an agenda, and certainly they don't have the public forum you have had in the *North China Daily News* and now this fine book. In fact, the only Westerner I have ever met who had a similar sense of understanding without being judgmental is the Frenchman, Prosper Giquel. Do you know him?"

"Indeed I do. We have been friends since I was a teenager."

"Somehow that does not surprise me at all," Yung Wing said, savoring another bite of the chocolate cake that sat on the table near the men. "But, Jason, I need to ask you a few questions before we formally start your interview."

"Of course. What is it?"

"Jason, I am very willing to cooperate with your effort to write about our educational mission. Indeed, I hope you write for audiences both at home and here in America."

Jason nodded, for he had already mapped out both his ideas for China-coast newspaper articles and a larger piece for one of the American journals like *Harper's* or perhaps the *Century*.

"The fact is it would be a fine thing if an article, one hopefully sympathetic to our mission, which I believe yours likely to be, appeared. And most importantly one written by someone who really understands our efforts more than most journalists do. So I am delighted to be of help, and when the boys return late tomorrow, you can interview them as much as you like. I am sure they will have improved their English in the weeks since they started staying in the private homes we are boarding them in, but that won't be an issue for you. You speak more Chinese dialects than they do."

"I cannot tell you how much I appreciate your cooperation. But you mentioned another issue of concern."

"Well, it is a bit awkward, but I would like to ask a favor of you, something you can't write about in the papers," Yung Wing asked.

"Of course, that is not a problem at all. Anything you specifically tell me that you don't want shared I will be willing to honor. But how can I help you?"

"It's complicated, but I am sure you know that there are plenty of influential people at home from Prince Gong to Zeng Guofan and Li Hongzhang who support these efforts to transfer Western technology and science to China; they support the Jiangnan arsenal outside of Shanghai and your friend Giquel's shipbuilding effort at Fuzhou."

Jason nodded, having written of such projects for years.

"But," the older man went on, "there are many others, sometimes people very influential with the Empress Dowager Cixi who are very much opposed, believing that the Western ways are too foreign or that the foreigners would never allow China to obtain technology that would actually allow her to protect herself from the superior Western military ordnance."

Jason continued to listen closely. Certainly he was familiar with the arguments; indeed he and Prosper had often spoken of them. But how was that an issue here? he wondered, waiting for Yung Wing to get specific.

"The problem for us is that those more negative attitudes played a role in organizing our own educational mission. I have been saddled with a minor-level mandarin named Ch'en Lanpin, who appreciates nothing of what we are trying to accomplish and was sent to simply make sure the students remain appropriately Chinese."

"How can I help with that?" Jason asked, intrigued.

"Ch'en and I don't get along at all. He has no appreciation of what we are doing here. No understanding of America. He does not know any Americans and cannot communicate at all. He is quite isolated with only his mission to keep the boys Chinese on his mind."

"And talking with me would accomplish what?"

"Frankly, I think a conversation with you, indeed an interview with someone like you, with whom he can communicate easily, could be very helpful. You are less foreign, yet so obviously an American even as you know China so well. From my perspective such a conversation would be very useful. But, of course, you cannot publish anything about this aspect of your visit."

"Well, I am certainly willing to try, and of course I do need to interview him as well if he has such an important role in the mission's success. Do you know that he will agree?"

"It has not come up before. The journalists who have come around have mostly talked exclusively to me. The boys are only just starting to learn English, and Ch'en of course can't communicate with them at all. But, yes, I do think he might cooperate with you. You have written a sympathetic and knowledgeable book on China. In his mind that makes you almost a scholar, so I think he will be cooperative."

"Can you give me an example of the sort of problems that have come up so far? I know it has not been very long, but what has been an issue?"

"There is one obvious thing. We have made sure the boys can't congregate together by paying various local households to take them in. That has been wonderful for their English-language skills, but Ch'en has insisted they remain wearing the traditional garb of a Chinese student even here in America, which makes it harder for them to become part of their communities. Something that is vital in my personal experience. Frankly the outfit makes them look in the eyes of American boys like girls, and it's impossible for them to play sports. And if it is not the clothing that is in the way, then it's their pigtails, which the Western boys love to grab."

"And Ch'en won't relent on this issue?"

"Not so far. It's the sort of problem we are having. It might sound trivial, but it is getting in the way of making the effort a success. I can't imagine what it would have been like for me as a boy here decades ago if I had been forced to keep wearing clothing so different from the other boys."

"I will certainly talk to him, try to get his perspective and if possible perhaps bring this up, but as if I had heard nothing from you. I think I can be a pretty good actor when I need to."

Yung Wing smiled. "That is all I ask. So that is settled. What else can I tell you about our effort here in New England?"

For the next hour, Yung Wing offered as full an explanation as he could of their plans to eventually bring over a hundred young Chinese to study in the secondary schools of America. Then to have them go to various colleges as Yung Wing had done at Yale and other institutions from Rensselaer Polytechnic Institute to the Massachusetts Institute of Technology culminating in their entrance into the American military and naval academies. It was an astoundingly ambitious project and one that was surely costing the Imperial government a great deal of money Jason imagined.

After a time, Yung Wing abruptly changed the subject. "But I have talked too long. You must be exhausted from having traveled so long from, where was it? Salem?"

"Rockport."

"Well then, Rockport. There will be plenty of time to talk tomorrow and, of course, prepare for the students' arrival. I expect they will be arriving in the late afternoon. I will try to schedule an interview sometime after that with Ch'en. For now, let me have my servant take you to the room we have prepared for you." With that, both men stood up and Jason followed the young Chinese domestic who had arrived suddenly to direct him to his room.

Before he went to sleep, despite his exhaustion, the young writer forced himself to write up his notes as carefully as possible. It would be too easy to forget the smaller details if he did not make notes immediately after the conversation. And then, completely spent, Jason's head crashed against the pillow. Within seconds he was in a deep but satisfied sleep.

# CHAPTER 28

# TENSIONS WITHIN THE EDUCATIONAL MISSION

"Do you mind if I ask you something a bit more personal?" Jason asked Yung Wing the next morning as they were finishing the breakfast of pancakes, eggs, and bacon Yung Wing's cook had provided them.

"Of course, if it will help you understand what we are trying to accomplish here."

"Did you experience the sort of anti-Chinese sentiment I am starting to find common here in America when you were here as a boy?"

"An excellent question, and no, it was a very different time. Now understand I left China for America decades ago, before the California Gold Rush, long before the building of the transcontinental railroads, both of which brought a lot of Chinese to America."

"Why did that matter?" Jason asked, though guessing he already understood the answer.

"After the Gold Rush and the transcontinental railroad construction era was over, America was left with lots of Chinese and few jobs. It was in that context that people started to agitate, especially on the West Coast against cheaper Chinese, as they say it, 'coolie' labor. In fact, ironically some of the loudest voices today are from the Irish, whom the American establishment dislikes almost as much as the Chinese." Jason nodded, remembering what Charles Nordhoff had told him in San Francisco.

"Have you ever heard of Denis Kearney?" Yung Wing asked him suddenly.

"I don't think so. Who is he?"

"One of the sort I mentioned an Irish immigrant from California who has been especially linked to attacks against Chinese laborers. If you don't know the name now, I suspect you will soon enough." With that Jason wrote the name down and underlined it.

"In fact," Yung Wing went on, "without telling him about yourself, I would try to interview him. I think it would help your work."

"Thanks. I appreciate that suggestion a lot. Did I mention that after I leave here, I am going over to North Adams where they had some sort of incident a while back?"

"No, you didn't, but I'd like to hear about what you learn at some point."

"Absolutely. I do want to stay in touch. Not just for this article. It really seems we have a lot more in common than I understood in Shanghai," Jason said, looking at his pocket watch. "Do you think we have a bit more time before the students start returning? I would awfully much like to learn more about your background if there is time."

Yung Wing looked up at the clock on the mantle. "Yes, I think there is plenty of time. I should not think any of the boys will show up till after lunch."

"What about Ch'en Lan-pin?" Jason asked, wondering where the other leader of the mission was, for he'd not seen him at all since arriving the previous evening.

"Oh, I don't think that is much of a problem. He does not much approve of me and likes my Western furnishings and household even less. I don't think he will show up until the bulk of the boys have arrived late in the day. So, what can I tell you about myself that you don't already know?"

"What I would really like to know is more about your early life in China, about how you ended up here as a student at Yale."

The reference to Yale clearly pleased Yung Wing, something Jason had already noticed. The fellow was terribly proud of having graduated from the prestigious American university.

"Well, there is not a lot to tell, but I suppose I can give you an idea." With that he called for more coffee for the two men. Jason accepted the new cup, though in truth he would have much preferred tea.

"I was born not far from where you grew up in Hong Kong, on one of the islands near Macau. My parents had the idea that while my brothers should earn a Confucian degree, it might be useful given the number of foreigners around if I could study with them."

"Was it a religious issue, were they interested in Christianity or something like that?" Jason asked, his curiosity aroused.

"Well, frankly they didn't talk about it with me. I was a child, perhaps around six by the Western standards, not someone a Chinese family would have consulted about their future with. But, no, I have guessed it was more of a practical decision, and it did work out. My limited knowledge of English as a child really did help after my father died. Eventually I ended up in the Morrison school that relocated to Hong Kong where I occasionally saw your father also."

"So how did you end up coming here? Did you come alone?"

"No, not alone but not at all like what we are trying to accomplish now. One of my teachers, Mr. Brown, decided that he needed to return home and convinced the school, and interestingly the editor of the Hong Kong paper, the *China Mail*, to finance me to come here. The idea was that we would study for only two years and then return. The deal was sweetened for our parents with an offer to give them financial help while we were gone."

"And your mother agreed?" Jason asked. "I can imagine that was quite a controversial decision."

"It still is to today, but, yes, she did agree finally. We left in 1847; you must have just been a boy then in Hong Kong, right?"

Jason nodded, not wanting to interrupt the story.

"So anyway, it was an incredible trip, my first, all the way from Hong Kong to New York. It took almost a hundred days to get across and a lot more tedious than what you just did. It was not possible in those days to simply cross the Pacific and take the transcontinental train." Yung Wing stopped for a moment and stroked his moustache as he perhaps drifted deeper into his memories.

"So you were alone with Mr. Brown?" Jason asked finally.

"Alone, no, not at all. There were three young Chinese boys. But I ended up having the longest stay in America."

"What happened to the rest?"

"One got sick and went home and another, today a distinguished physician, ended up leaving America for Scotland to study medicine before going home."

"So how did you end up at Yale?"

"Well, that is an entirely different story. We did not have the funding to stay for college, and what money was available required that one promise to become a missionary in China."

"Why was that a problem? You are a believer, are you not?" Jason asked, getting even more curious.

"As an individual, absolutely. But frankly I was not inclined to become a missionary and had an idea that I wanted a wider range of ways I might serve China than that. It was a difficult decision, but it seemed to work out. Indeed, I doubt I would be here today leading this educational effort if I had taken that choice."

"So how did you manage to get through college?"

"Well, financially, I did end up with some outside funding and a wide range of jobs, worked at one of the Yale eating clubs, at a library, and other efforts. Academically, I managed it as well—though higher math almost did me in I must tell you honestly!" Yung Wing laughed to himself as he explained. "But I pulled it off, graduated in the Yale Class of 1854, the first Chinese to ever accomplish such a thing." Yung Wing beamed.

"So then what happened?"

"Well, the first thing I had to do after returning was to re-learn Chinese; I'd not been with anyone who spoke Chinese for years..."

"Yes, Black Jade and I both remembered you telling us that when we met in Shanghai."

"So once I felt more comfortable, I ended up working a wide range of different jobs, with Mr. Parkes, with the customs service; even tried to become an attorney in Hong Kong for a time, but the local Anglos stopped that. Figured I'd have too much of an advantage being able to speak both languages," Yung Wing explained, obviously pained by the memory and then going on.

"But I always had the idea of bringing a group of young Chinese here to America to have them gain the advantages of Western education and then to go home and help China. And finally, after all those years, we are here actually doing it!"

"It really does seem extraordinary," Jason commented. "You know there is one thing I have been wondering about. You mentioned you're not being able to come here originally by train because the Americans had not yet built the transcontinental system. Do you think China will ever try to build railroads? Black Jade and I talked about that a lot as we rode across America."

"Well, that is quite another question. New factories, new guns and artillery, and your friend Prosper Giquel's naval projects but railroads...quite another issue."

"Why would railroads be so different?"

"Now that's a much more complicated issue, and frankly we don't have that much more time. I need to prepare for the students' arrival. How about this? You make your preparations to interview them as you like later today after the formal program while I talk to Ch'en about your interview with him. And say tomorrow morning before you leave for North Adams we can have breakfast and I will tell you what I understand about that particularly complicated challenge, the celestial kingdom and railroads."

"OK," Jason said, getting up from the table. "I look forward to your insights. And thank you again for your time. You have been incredibly helpful and generous."

"It's a great pleasure. I am delighted you visited."

With that, Jason left and went back up the stairs to the small bed-and-sitting room he'd been assigned to the evening before.

# CHAPTER 29

# THE STUDENTS

"Free yourself from resentment and anger to show respect for your body and life," the leader intoned while the boys repeated. "Put a stop to false accusations in order to protect the good and honest," he added, a moment later dramatically writing out the seven characters that represented each phrase. "Make the most of schools and academies in order to honor the way of scholars," with each phrase carefully enunciated by Ch'en Lan-pin, the Confucian scholar officially responsible for the Chinese part of their education. The boys then skillfully wrote out the characters on the white sheets that lay before each of them in their traditional silken gowns.

Jason, sitting quietly in the back of the room, had done everything he could since the students started to arrive to make himself as invisible as possible. If the boys had any curiosity about him, they certainly did not show it. Yung Wing for his part made no attempt to introduce Jason to the boys as they arrived—sometimes alone, sometimes in groups—to the large home that was serving as the primary place for the students' regular Chinese studies efforts.

The home itself, not terribly far from Yung Wing's, was, to Jason's eyes, quite a shock. He already understood from Yung Wing that the mission's co-director Ch'en Lan-pin had none of his Yale-educated colleague's enthusiasm for American culture. In fact, Jason had hoped to discuss the man he was about to interview more, but that was not possible.

But as he and Yung Wing had walked the short distance between the residences, he could see that Yung Wing was clearly distracted. Something serious was on his mind. The fellow who had been so conversational only hours earlier now remained deep in thought as Jason wondered what the next stage in his study of the educational mission would bring.

Once at the door, a servant received them, and from the first instant, Jason was astonished. As they left the Hartford street behind them, Jason felt they were entering the home of a high mandarin official back in China. Nothing, not even the smells or the decorations—nothing save the building's core floor plan reminded him of any building he'd yet seen in the United States. Jason was not sure how he'd done it, but Ch'en, who from a distance had with the mildest of head nods, acknowledged his arrival, created a small island of Chinese civilization in the middle of Connecticut. Once their coats were taken, Yung Wing silently directed Jason to a relatively large parlor, where the lessons were expected to begin shortly. Finding a chair near the back, Jason set himself up so that he could subtly take notes while sipping from a small cup of tea a servant had brought for him. Once comfortably in place, Jason sat as inconspicuously as he possibly could.

For the next several minutes, as they waited to begin the formal Recitation of the Emperor Kangxi's Sacred Edicts, Jason had watched the two co-directors, each in their turn, examine the boys individually. Yung Wing greeted them quietly in English, clearly gauging how well their study of the language was progressing. Meanwhile Ch'en, only a few feet away, though the distance felt greater, checked their robes and inquired about whether they had carried out the required Chinese lessons each day even as they struggled with the American curriculum with its focus on everything from Greek to Mathematics.

Eventually, though, the initial greetings over, the students carefully arranged themselves in the chairs that had been set out for the lessons. One or two of the boys stole quick glances at the American sitting at the back. Jason could tell they were wondering about him and made a subtle effort to nod, recognizing their curiosity. One boy, perhaps a fellow who was taking on American ways faster than the others, even gave him a teeth-filled smile back in return. None of the other boys made any such effort, and within minutes, the recitation and rituals associated with the Sacred Edicts had begun.

"Be moderate and economical in order to avoid wasting away your livelihood. Give weight to kinship in order to promote harmony and peace." As Jason listened he realized that while he had certainly heard the famous principles of behavior, the famous Kangxi emperor (for a second Jason tried to remember the man's dates) had supposedly written as a young man. But now he felt he was listening to them for the first time, actually appreciating the wisdom they contained. In fact, he found himself recognizing how, in so many ways while they were certainly Confucian enough, they also represented values of human interaction, not all that different from the Ten Commandments his father had drilled into him as a child. "Put a stop to false accusations in order to protect the good and the honest." How different was that, Jason thought, from not bearing false witness against your neighbor he'd heard all his life!

Up till that moment, Jason realized he'd never really appreciated the common-sense humanity they represented, for, after all, the sacred edicts had always in his mind represented something very different—his friend Wu's youthful downfall in the weeks before they'd met on the wharves of Hong Kong. For a second his mind drifted, and he wondered, as the lessons went on, about how soon, if ever, he'd be reunited with his long-lost friend. That Wu was obviously well in Fuzhou, working for his friend, was a source of relief for Jason, but he still wanted to see his boyhood companion once again.

Suddenly a bronze bell sounded quietly and the lessons ended as the boys rose and stretched their arms and legs and, like boys everywhere, walked as quickly as they could toward the parlors doors.

As Jason watched them, a servant tapped Jason quietly.

"I am told you speak Chinese," he whispered quietly. Jason nodded. The fellow looked relieved.

"Excellent, His Honor Ch'en Lan-pin has asked me to inform you that the students are having some light refreshments in the next room. They have been told to return here in a few minutes to meet with you. After that His Excellency invites you to visit with him in his study. For now, can I get you something to eat before the students return?"

Jason nodded his appreciation and turned back to his notes. There would be only a few minutes in which to collect his thoughts before the group interview began.

"Have you been told who I am?" Jason asked in his most polite Cantonese. At that, several boys' mouths opened up in surprise. They had certainly met many reporters since they arrived but none who addressed them in the language of the celestial kingdom.

One boy tentatively raised his hand and began in the hesitant English he'd been developing since their arrival.

"We...we are...no were told you are a"—he hesitated—"reporter."

"You don't have to prove to me you are learning English," Jason interrupted, laughing. "I am from Hong Kong, near Guangzhou, like so many of you are," for he had already realized that the students were overwhelmingly from southern China.

At that another boy raised his hand, a gesture he'd probably learned here in Connecticut, Jason thought.

"Can we first ask who you are?" the boy asked with considerably more self-confidence than Jason had seen demonstrated by any of the other boys while the educational mission's staff was in the room.

"Of course, but may I first ask your name?"

"My name is Tong Shao-yi."

"Well, Mr. Tong, my name is Jason Brandt. Like you, I grew up in southern China. And like you, I just arrived from China, in our case from Shanghai, and I am living a few days' travel from here with my family."

"Do you have children?" Tong asked. He was clearly the boldest of the students.

"Yes, I have a wife, who is also from southern China, and two children."

"Your wife is Chinese?" one of the other boys burst out.

"Yes, and she is very beautiful. I have a girl eight years old and a son almost four."

The boys turned and looked at each other in amazement. This reporter was very different from the ones they had encountered as they traveled across America and settled in.

"Why do you speak our language so well? Are you a missionary?" another asked.

"A good question. No. I am not a missionary. But my father was a missionary for many years in Hong Kong. So I grew up speaking Chinese as much as English."

The boys listened attentively. At least the strange reporter's story was beginning to make sense to them.

"So does anyone have any other questions of me?"

One boy, smaller than the rest, slowly raised his hand.

"Yes."

"Have you ever been to Beijing and seen the Emperor or the Empress Dowager?"

"Well, I am afraid I have not seen them. But I have been to Beijing several times and even talked to very important officials."

The little boy looked a bit disappointed but not too much.

"So any other questions? You fellows have done a fine job interviewing me. Maybe you should all become newspapermen when you grow older. So it's my turn if you don't mind."

Turning to Tong, the boy who had begun the conversation, he said, "So, Mr. Tong, where are you from? Can you tell me something about your family and how you ended up here in America?"

Tong was clearly pleased that he'd been called upon first.

# CHAPTER 30

# ADJUSTING TO AMERICA

For the next few minutes, the boys, whose average age Jason thought about twelve, introduced themselves, each saying something about their families and the host American families they lived with in the area.

"And your families in China were willing to let you travel so far without a problem?" he asked after the introductions concluded.

"No, it was very hard," one of the boys blurted out. "My *Ye-Ye*, my grandfather, said the foreigners would eat us!"

Several of the boys laughed, but another added, "It's true, I heard that a lot, that the foreigners paid criminals to steal babies to eat them."

"Yes, I heard that too. It happened up north somewhere, but then they all got killed. Have you heard about that, mister?"

"Yes, in fact, I was there, in Tianjin, when it all happened. If your families believed that, why did they send you?"

"My father said it was nonsense. Besides he knew Master Yung's family, and he'd come to America and was now an important person, an official mandarin of the emperor."

As the boys spoke, it became increasingly obvious that most of the boys had some sort of link to Yung Wing or Yung at least was well known among their families to be considered a successful example of what could be accomplished with a Western education. None of what the boys explained surprised him. His friend Prosper Giquel had often spoken of how difficult it could be to recruit students for Western educations. If it wasn't the fear that the Western Christians might actually use the children in their sacred rituals, it was the more common concern that a Western education could not possibly hope to bring the same rewards a more traditional Confucian education offered.

"OK. So now that you are here, what do you think? Don't worry about offending me. This is my first time in America as well." With that, the students again turned to look at each other. This American really was different.

"They smile all the time and show their teeth," one boy, a bit taller than the others, suggested.

"And they kiss! The lady I stay with kisses me every night before she sends me to bed. I hate that."

"Squeezing the cheeks is worse," another boy, sitting to the side near the bookshelves, offered. "That's a lot worse."

"No, it's not," several piped in. For the next few minutes, the boys argued among themselves about the relative merits or lack of having one's cheeks kissed or squeezed by the locals whose homes they were staying in, while Jason sat listening, quietly laughing to himself.

"Anything else?" he finally asked, though the argument did not seem anywhere near resolution.

"Cheese!" one yelled.

"Right, cheese!" At that there was general agreement. To a boy they hated cheese. Jason was not surprised. From a Chinese perspective, the stuff really did seem quite awful.

"So what is the best part of being here?" Jason finally asked.

"The railroads," one called out from the back of the room. Several nodded in agreement.

"And all the running and playing," the first boy he'd met, Tong, asserted himself once again. "One thing I have noticed is that Americans value physical activities far more than people do at home. They like it when a boy can run fast and jump high. That is what has really surprised me, that they value that as much as learning. Sometimes I think more."

"That's very insightful, Shao-yi," Jason commented. "It is good that you can observe people that closely."

"Do the rest of you agree with Mr. Tong that the Americans especially like physical activities?"

At that all the boys nodded in agreement.

"Do you all take part in sports?"

"Yes, sort of," Tong said, "but sometimes it is very hard."

"Why?"

"The boys tease us about our clothing, call us girls, because our robes look to them a little bit like girls' dresses."

"And they pull our pigtails and make us fall!" the taller boy threw in with obvious frustration.

"Does that happen to all of you?" the reporter asked. To a boy they all agreed. For the next few minutes, Jason heard all about the frustrations of trying to attend American primary schools wearing the clothing of a traditional Chinese student. It was, as Yung Wing suggested, becoming a major problem.

"Well, you boys have been wonderfully helpful. I think lots of people in China and America will be pleased to hear how well you are all doing. Is there anything else I should ask you about?"

With that Tong once again began, but first he stood up, obviously hoping to emphasis his point.

"Mr. Brandt from Hong Kong and Shanghai. There is something we would like to ask."

"Yes. Go ahead."

Tong turned back toward the door, assuring himself that it was indeed shut. "Could you talk to His Excellency Ch'en about our clothing and queues which they call pigtails here? It we could dress as Americans and wear our hair like them, it would make our lives a lot easier. We all think His Excellency Yung understands, but we can see the two don't agree on this."

"Or anything else," another boy said even more quietly just to Jason's left.

"Boys, I have never even spoken to His Excellency Ch'en, but when I do, I promise to keep your issue in mind. That is all I can offer. Is that acceptable?"

Tong, so obviously a boy with leadership potential, surveyed the room and then turned back to Jason. "Thank you. We do appreciate your understanding."

With that, Jason stood up. As he did so, the rest of the room followed suit, each stretching their legs from the session. The noise was apparently loud enough for the servants to fling open the doors and the boys summoned. As the students left the room, the same servant who had spoken to Jason earlier walked up to him.

"His Excellency Ch'en Lan-pin has invited you to meet in his study at three about ten minutes from now. When you are ready, please return here and I can show you the way."

"Thank you very much, so ten minutes from now." With that, Jason left the parlor and used his time standing in the street breathing the fresh air. His assumption had long been that interviewing the more traditional Confucian scholar would be the most challenging.

Fifteen minutes later Jason found himself in Ch'en's beautifully furnished study. The room was exquisite with beautiful lacquered furniture of the sort one could easily find in the homes of upper-class Chinese at home. For several moments the two sipped the freshly brewed tea the servant had brought them while each man surreptitiously sized up the other.

"Well, Mr. Brandt, I have not spoken to many Western reporters, but I am told they always ask what we Chinese think of America. If you don't mind, I would like to ask you the same thing. As I understand it, I have actually been in America longer than you."

The question surprised Jason but also helped him to relax. Ch'en was quite different than he had imagined.

"You have been informed correctly, your Excellency. I arrived from Shanghai only a short while after you did, and indeed had the same experience as you did traveling across America by the new transcontinental railroad system."

"And what have been your thoughts?" Ch'en asked with penetrating eyes. This man was clearly not the narrow Confucian ideologue he'd expected.

"In truth, what has stood out most was my impression of the technology. In San Francisco, I had a chance to ride on a horseless vehicle that was being prepared as part of a system of public transport."

"Yes, the cable car, you rode in it?" Ch'en's eyes showed a hint of jealousy.

"Yes, my friend knew the builder, and they let us sit on it, as it was being tested."

"Did they explain how it worked?" Ch'en's interest was clearly aroused.

"Yes, a bit, I am not an engineer, but they did tell me. The way it worked was with a series of underground cables…" For the next few minutes, Jason tried to recall everything Nordhoff's friend had explained while Ch'en listened with intense interest.

"What else has impressed you?" the interviewee continued his role as the interviewer.

"Well, the railroads of course." Ch'en nodded in agreement. "And I suppose how diverse the country is. In my work, I have traveled a great deal in China, all along the coast, and in my youth walked a great deal in the interior. But America is much more diverse physically and in terms of its people, and that has surprised me a great deal."

The mandarin official continued to listen carefully. Clearly he was as interested in his guest as Jason was interested in hearing his story.

"But I go on too much," Jason finally said. "I am taking up too much of Your Excellency's time."

"No, not at all. Mr. Brandt, let me explain, and please do not tell Yung Wing what I say here. But frankly I have been here for months now, traveling across this country, living first in Springfield and now in Hartford and yet I can speak to very few people save the embassy staff. Yung Wing, for all his faults, can at least talk to everyone, and sometimes I am a bit jealous. So your visit is as much a treat for me as helpful for you. Do you mind if I ask you a few more questions about things I have wondered about?"

"Not at all, sir. Indeed, I am honored."

For the next thirty minutes, Ch'en went over one question after another, about Western behavior, clothing, politics, and, most of all, their technology. Interestingly Jason realized with a start that he was working from a notepad he had sitting at his side next to the tea glass.

At last, the official seemed with a stroke on his sheet to have finished and turning back to Jason.

"Now, Mr. Brandt, it is I who have taken up too much of your time. I am completely at your disposal. What questions can I answer for you?"

# CHAPTER 31

# STAYING CHINESE

"My questions, Your Excellency," Jason started off carefully, "are probably not that different from those the other Western reporters ask. What do you hope to accomplish with this block of students and, of course, those scheduled to arrive in future years?"

With that the mandarin official began a list of the scientific, engineering, and military skills it was expected the boys would acquire during their years in the United States. As he spoke, Jason began to understand that while the broad outlines of the plan were exactly as Yung Wing had outlined, the two men seemed to focus on rather different aspects of the educational mission, the first to formally educate Chinese students in the American style. It took a bit, but Jason soon understood that while Yung Wing had enthusiastically outlined the plans to have the boys go from their early schooling through high school and then attend universities ultimately graduating from the American military academies, Ch'en spoke enthusiastically of the challenges of maintaining their students' Chinese educational training with all of America's challenges.

"Your Excellency, there is something I do not understand. I truly hope I do not offend, but you seem to focus on the boys' Chinese education. But isn't that less important here in America? They are, after all, here to gain an American education," Jason asked, not at all sure if the question would seem insulting and yet it had to be asked.

"Mr. Brandt, I am not at all offended. Your question hits at the heart of our entire mission, something in truth my colleague Yung Wing has never fully appreciated, and why, to be blunt, I am ultimately in charge of this effort, not him."

Jason nodded, impressed with how straightforward Ch'en was being.

"There you see; I make my own point. Rather than the more polite approach of the celestial kingdom, even I am obviously influenced by Americans' bolder way of speaking." The mandarin laughed almost aloud and then went on. "Mr. Brandt, how much do you really know about Yung Wing?"

"Not a lot. I asked him about himself last night when I interviewed him. And I met him once in Shanghai. But only the barest outlines."

"And you did not meet him in the rebel capital at Nanjing?" Ch'en asked Jason, watching his reaction closely.

Jason was dumbfounded. This conversation was going in a very different direction than he had anticipated.

"Nanjing, no, I did not even know he was there. I certainly never met him when I was there. When was he there?"

"I think it was before you arrived. But that is another matter. What you need to understand is that I am in charge because while Zeng Guofan and the court absolutely understood that they needed Yung Wing's American cultural and linguistic skills; indeed he was sent here as a purchasing agent for weapons long before the plan for the educational mission began, but that Yung Wing could not lead the mission because his background makes it difficult for him to truly appreciate one of the most important goals of the mission."

"And what is that, sir?" Jason asked, absolutely intrigued.

"To learn enough of American science, technology, and military skills to contribute to the safety and health of China while still retaining enough Chinese cultural and educational knowledge and behavior to exert that influence back home."

Jason nodded, slowly trying to reconcile Ch'en's vision with what he'd learned from Yung Wing.

Ch'en continued with an absolutely earnest look in his eyes. He had quite obviously thought a great deal about the issue. "Yung Wing is not as I assume you understand a Confucian scholar. Indeed, he has never passed even the lowest rung of the civil service exams. When he went home after Yale, he was almost completely Americanized. He could neither find a proper place for himself, nor could he even establish himself as a lawyer among the Westerners in Hong Kong. There he was, as he may have told you, seen as a threat, to the local Anglo lawyers with his Chinese skills and face. But among the personnel of the Celestial Empire, he is seen as ignorant of the most important issues of our tradition. He simply does not have the Confucian knowledge or credentials to be taken seriously by the influential administrators in China. And the effort he made in Nanjing to offer his services to the rebel king, I guess he did not tell you about that, did he?"

"No." Jason nodded. "I really don't know anything about that aspect of his life. But if Yung Wing has so many questionable elements to his career and is so obviously Americanized, why did His Excellency Zeng Guofan employ him for this mission?"

"Because his skills and ties to America make him absolutely essential for this mission; but his enthusiasm for, let me say it bluntly, all aspects of American cultural tradition however questionable makes it difficult for him to understand that if our boys return to China as Westernized as he is, they will be useless to the Celestial Empire. Thus my role to ensure they gain the advantages of a Western technical education without becoming so Americanized that they will be unable to function as equals with those who matter at home."

With that, Ch'en picked up the hookah that had earlier sat idle and took a long draft on the fumes that slowly seeped from it as they talked. As he did so, Jason sat reflecting on Ch'en's explanation.

After a time Ch'en put down the pipe. "You seem caught in thought. Does my explanation of what we are trying to accomplish here surprise you that much?"

"No, I suppose not, Your Excellency. In fact, it makes complete sense. I was just thinking…" Jason's words trailed off into thought.

"Just thinking about what?" the mandarin asked, taking a sip of tea from the beautifully blue ceramic cup.

"It is, of course, absolutely true what you say. Though I had not quite appreciated how the Confucian literati would really think of Yung Wing even as they honor him with this important mission. And I suppose on a personal note, your comments made me reflect on how people might really see me with all my own Chinese ways despite what I look and sound like."

"And you are a writer, significantly more free to be yourself than Yung Wing is as an official of the Celestial Empire," Ch'en said. "But even as I want you to understand what is really going on here, I ask that you be relatively vague in your writings about the actual challenge. I explain to you what is happening with the hope that it can smooth the way toward ultimate success if more people understand our goals and challenges. But not to insult Yung Wing or make our relationship any more difficult than it already is."

"I absolutely understand, Your Excellency, and will do everything I can to be as accurate in my reporting as I can without complicating your life. For I truly appreciate how honest you have been. And now, I am certain I have taken up too much of your time." With that Jason began to rise.

"Wait, Jason—may I call you that? See, I have even taken up the more informal ways of the Americans, but I do have one more question. Can you tell me what impressions you have of your conversation with the boys themselves? My servants tell me the conversation sounded quite lively even if they could not hear what was being said."

The boys... Jason thought to himself, feeling guilty. He had completely forgotten their request and then recovered.

"There was something, Your Excellency. For the most part, all seems to be going as expected. They are learning English, getting used to their American families, but there seemed to be a problem with their attire," Jason said, watching the mandarin carefully.

"Yes," Ch'en said, without revealing his thoughts.

"The impression I got was that the Chinese robes make the boys more objects of humiliation than companions. Apparently they are seen as girls, a great insult to them and something that makes it harder for them to meet American boys and truly improve their language skills. And, apparently, as we both understand, Americans appreciate far more than at home games of physical competition. Their queues are apparently used as tools against them—holding them back from competing successfully." There, he'd said it.

Ch'en took another draft on the pipe. "This has, of course, come up before between Yung Wing and myself. One of the boys even dared ask me about it. I had thought that the clothing and queue would create something of a barrier, the very barrier I spoke of to retain their Chinese appearance and have resisted any suggestion that they dress as Americans. Indeed, though a problem as the boys see it, perhaps an advantage later as they eventually return home. But you really think wearing Chinese clothing can impede their Western learning efforts?"

"I do not know, Your Excellency. I can only tell you that the boys themselves seriously believe their silken robes do."

Ch'en sat there in deep thought for a time. "Well, I will reconsider the issue. Perhaps it is true the balance between the need to have the students gain a Western education without becoming Westerners requires some compromises."

"And the queue, Your Excellency, the boys say the Americans use it as a handle to trip them in physical games."

"That, Mr. Brandt, is not something we can negotiate. The imperial officials might not care that much about our boys wearing Western clothing, but to have them cut off their pigtails, the very symbol of the Qing dynasty, that is impossible. There is simply no way I could explain that to my own superiors. But I have no doubt the boys can figure out a way to make the pigtail not fly in the wind behind them as they run. They are, after all, quite clever young men. No, we can do nothing about the queue, but I think we might be able to resolve the less-sensitive issue of clothing." With that he went back to his tea, and Jason, realizing the interview was over, got up and, as politely as he could, left the room.

# CHAPTER 32

# WITH YUNG WING

"Let me add one more possible issue," Yung Wing added as the conversation seemed to be nearing its end. The two of them, Jason and Yung Wing, had spent the last hour having breakfast in the latter's very comfortable dining room, talking about the possibility of railroad development in China as they ate scrambled eggs and toast expertly toasted over the nearby kitchen fireplace by one of Yung Wing's servants. Just up and to the left of the open fireplace, the built-in oven emitted the wonderful smell of some sort of stew Jason imagined was already being prepared for lunch. As he smelled the concoction, mostly Western with a slight hint of Chinese spices enticed his nostrils and reminded him somewhat discouragingly that he would be long gone, on his way to North Adams, before lunch was served.

"And let me reiterate that I mention this with the understanding that you won't write about this issue. Indeed, I don't even know if it is really going to happen. But frankly I feel, perhaps foolishly, a kinship with you, given the sort of mirror image connections we both have to China and America."

Jason nodded, knowing full well that the two men, the older Yung Wing and he, shared a very unique perspective. Each of them, Yung Wing the Americanized Chinese and Jason the Sinofied New Englander, was linked as few others are.

They had already spent most of the last hour discussing how different the introduction of railroads would be to efforts like that of Jason's friend Prosper Giquel to transfer Western steamship development to China. The ships so obviously operated off the coast, beyond the ability to impact on the lives of the Chinese people. They laid out no iron rails that could both disrupt the land's *fêng shui* nor demand right away across private lands. But trains were quite another matter. Their potential to disrupt life was infinitely greater than merely building Western-style ships.

"But let me at least tell you what I have heard, or at least heard before I left Shanghai last spring. It was well known among the Westerners that the mandarins looked upon the idea of railroad building with infinitely less enthusiasm than shipbuilding. I gathered that winning the support from both the local officials, the court, and all those whose lives would be disrupted by a railroad would be impossibly difficult. That seemed quite well understood, but just before I left, I heard a rumor that some of the Western officials based in Shanghai were trying to secretly develop such a project without the knowledge of the mandarins."

"I don't understand," Jason asked, puzzled. "How could one build a railroad in secret? It does not make sense. And why would they want to do that anyway? Would it not be stopped as soon as the project was discovered?"

"Most likely," the older Chinese began. "But I think the idea was to begin the project as if it was simply another effort to lay out a regular road and then eventually build up enough momentum that the project could not be stopped later."

"Would that work?" Jason asked.

"I don't know. What I do know is that whatever the mandarins, even the most conservative of them, think of Western culture, they seem fascinated with railroads. Even my colleague Ch'en is fascinated with them. I am certain that that is the only thing he looked at with approval here in America as we traveled east."

"I noticed that myself when we spoke."

"When you spoke, of course...My goodness, I had completely forgotten. I have been so busy with the boys' visit. We owe you a huge debt of gratitude!"

"You do, me, why?"

"Why, my young friend, word came this morning that His Excellency has offered the boys a compromise. They are to keep their queues and deal with the teasing from the American children in whatever way they can. But, and this is what matters, they have been given permission to wear American clothing when they return to their host families. You did it!"

"I am delighted to hear that. Did he give a reason?"

"No, but it's obvious. You convinced him. I don't know what you said, but it worked. The boys will be forever in your debt." Yung Wing beamed with pleasure.

"Well, then my visit has been a complete success. I was able to help you. And you and your colleague have given me wonderful material for an in-depth story about the American Educational Mission from China. A fine trade. And I look forward to staying in touch while we are both here and, of course, when we get home."

"Yes, I too hope our friendship will only grow over the years. And now, what are your plans?"

Jason glanced at his pocket watch, confirmed its time with the large clock in the room, and then turned back toward his host. "I leave in about a half hour. A coach is picking me up to go to the port, and from there I set out again, this time, as you know, for North Adams, Massachusetts."

"How long will it take you to get there, especially in this weather? I am sure you are starting to wish you had waited till spring. This is hardly the Hong Kong weather we both know so well."

Jason nodded. "You are probably right. In fact, I have been thinking I should use the winter months for longer writing projects. But there was nothing to be done about this first effort. The stories needed to be written, and I wanted to know how easy it would be to travel in New England at this time of year. But as to how long it will take, I really am not sure. Going from Chicago to Boston by train seemed straightforward. Trying to go now from Hartford to North Adams is less clear, but I suppose I will know in a day or so. The first leg, once I leave here, is to travel north up the river and then start westward, as I understand it in the direction of New York State. Though only to you would I admit how unsure I am of the geography here. Frankly I would be much more comfortable trying to find my way from Shanghai to Hangzhou," Jason said smiling, amused at how hard Yung Wing laughed, clearly remembering perhaps mirror-image experiences he had once had in China. But then the fellow turned more serious.

"Jason, let me just take this last opportunity to thank you again for your interest in our small efforts to help China toward the future and to take my leave. I am afraid that I am needed at Ch'en's residence shortly."

With that the older man stood up, tightened his belt, and left the room. Jason was left there sipping a bit more, happily of the tea that had been offered that morning while contemplating his departure for North Adams and the very different situation he expected to find there.

Twenty minutes later, as Jason was exiting Yung Wing's residence and about to enter the coach he'd requested to take him to the river port, a breathless young Chinese servant, the same fellow he'd met the day before at Ch'en's, ran up to him, almost slipping in his haste in the icy streets, calling out to get his attention.

"Mr. Brandt!" he called out in Cantonese. "Mr. Brandt, one moment, please. His Excellency has sent you something." Jason, standing there with his coachman watching him, waited as the fellow covered the last few yards that separated them.

A moment later Jason sat in the coach, his bag next to him and a beautifully wrapped package on his lap. He knew it would take him a while to get to the port, where his journey northwest toward North Adams was scheduled to begin, and slowly unwrapped the package. The paper was much like one could easily find in any store in Hartford, but once opened the box inside was entirely different. Within a lovely green wooden box, beautifully encased in a cloth covering ornate decorations lay a beautiful set of tools for calligraphy: two brushes, a lovely stone surface to grind inks, and even a tiny spoon to facilitate mixing the inks before their application. There was even a lovely three-pronged brush stand to avoid soiling one's workstation. As he studied the box, a short note dropped out, and in elaborate Chinese strokes, Ch'en had written the following:

> Brandt, friend of China
> Even as you have come to America to learn of your heritage, it is important that you not forget the skills of your adopted home. May these brushes inspire you to continue your writings not only in English but in Chinese as well.
> Ch'en

I guess I have become another of His Excellency's Sino-American boys, Jason thought to himself as he very carefully rewrapped the package and placed it deeply into his traveling satchel. Then, thinking about the visit and all he learned, he watched the still-snow-filled streets of Hartford pass until somewhat later he found himself at the port ready to begin his first leg toward the very different environment he expected in North Adams.

# CHAPTER 33
# NORTH ADAMS

Two hours later Jason sat shivering in the small passenger seating area located on the top deck of the Connecticut River steamer he'd boarded an hour earlier. He was not sure but he thought he might be colder than he ever remembered. It was not just that the small coal stove seemed phenomenally incapable of heating the space it was assigned, but at least two of the windows were broken, blocked only partially by what looked like a very poorly fastened calfskin drape that let in tremendous blasts of cold air off the river. He'd imagined he would be able to use the time to prepare for North Adams, to read through the notes he'd taken over the last few months about the tensions there between the locals and the Chinese strikebreakers the local factory owner had imported from San Francisco. Nevertheless, all he could think about was the cold. How stupid. He'd kept chastising himself for thinking he could do a reporting trip in the mid-winter in New England. It had all seemed to make sense as he'd sat in the toasty office he'd set up next to the home they'd rented in Rockport. But now the decision seemed an act of madness. He'd be more likely to freeze to death than gather the material he needed to write his first major newspaper pieces on Sino-American relations.

No, the more he thought about it, the more he wished he'd stayed in Rockport, prepared his upcoming talk on Frederick Townsend Ward, and waited out better weather. However, it was too late for all that. The only thing left to him was to try to stay warm and hope the train ride west, away as it would be from the cold winds coming off the Connecticut River, might be a bit more comfortable. Happily, that turned out to be the case, and within a few hours, he was sitting comfortably within the Boston train as it steamed west while he looked over his notes. If the train cabin was not as comfortable, or new as those he and his family had ridden only a few months before as they crossed the country, it was still a major improvement from the incredibly drafty boat he just disembarked from. On his lap sat his copy of *Hub to the Hudson* by Washington Gladden that he had managed to pick up at the station after leaving the steamer and waiting for the train. If it was not the sort of amusing travelogue he'd become familiar with from Sam Clemens's writing or his own feeble efforts to copy the great master, it was still readable enough. At minimum, it helped pass the time as he sped westward toward North Adams, and what he imagined would be another piece in his tale of the Chinese in America, similar and yet he assumed probably quite different from what he'd seen among the official educational mission.

"Going all the way to Troy, are you?" The voice was loud and, Jason thought, hinted a bit of whiskey.

"Excuse me." He looked up, confused. Troy was not where his thoughts had been.

"Troy, NY," the man continued, tipping his bowler hat as he leaned across the train aisle and extended his somewhat-fleshy hand. "Just thought you looked like you were on a long trip," he said, nodding at the relatively large satchel at Jason's feet.

"No, well, actually I was just in Troy a short while ago. Now I am going to North Adams."

"That's probably best. This time of the year, it can be treacherous you know."

"No, I don't really. Why is that? The train seems comfortable enough."

"Not from around here, are you?" the man said, eyeing Jason more closely. "I can tell a Boston accent when I hear one. Suppose you're like a lot of those city types, know Boston and New York, don't get out West much, right?"

Jason looked at him for a moment, wondering what he should say, that his ignorance went a lot further than an unfamiliar section of Western Massachusetts, but it did not matter. The man did not seem to even notice his hesitation.

"Name's, Smith, Barnaby Smith, an engineer by trade," he said. "Mind if I move over?" he said loudly while looking askance at an older woman in a long dress and hat who was clearly glaring at him as if she found his loud voice, necessary given the noise of the train, an unacceptable distraction.

"No. Of course not," Jason said as he moved a few of his things to make space for the fellow. "So what brings an engineer out this way, Mr. Smith?" Jason asked, carefully putting *Hub to the Hudson* back and pulling up the cord that held the satchel closed.

"The great tunnel of course," the fellow said, "been consulting on it for more than two years now, and it's finally getting close. They say the first complete borehole might be ready by Thanksgiving."

"Tunnel?" Jason asked and then before Smith had a chance to register complete surprise, "Yes, of course. I am sorry, I'd quite forgotten." Jason was doing everything he could to dredge up what he'd read and now realized heard discussed in Troy.

"So you are working on that tunnel through the mountains to bring the trains down from the hill to the Hudson River."

"Absolutely," Smith said with pride, though it seemed clear as well that his mind was racing, trying to figure out how someone with an accent like Jason's could have been so unfamiliar with a tunnel project that had been going on for most of the young man's life. Nevertheless, his pride left his curiosity in the dust.

"Yes, not just me. My dad, an engineer in his own right, worked on it. Used to come here myself as a lad to see the work with him. Really wish he were still alive to see the progress we have made. They say it will be the longest tunnel in the Western hemisphere when it's done."

"That really is incredible. Oh, I should explain; my parents were from Boston, but I grew up quite far away."

"Now that makes sense, seems hardly possible for someone from Massachusetts not to know of the tunnel given how much money and how much bickering the effort has brought. My dad used to say the politics were even trickier than the drilling."

"And you say it will be finished this year?" Jason asked, now more interested as he began to wonder if the effort would make it easier for he and Black Jade to take up Emma Willard's offer to let Mei-ling study at the Female Seminary.

"Well, not quite that ready. There's hope that the original borehole would be complete before the end of the year. But it will be quite some time before it's ready for a train to travel through. Hell, it could be a few more years. But that's just the finishing; digging the original line is the really impressive part. I can tell you I'm proud to have been part of it!"

"So how do people get to Troy now?" Jason asked with growing curiosity.

"That's just it. The train stops and they all pile onto stage coaches…Young folks today are often not even that familiar with them and off they go heading down the hill. But this time of the year, with that slope, one slip and well, it would not be pretty—not for the passengers, not for the horses," he said with a flourish. "So what's your business in North Adams?"

"Well, I am a reporter, working on a story," Jason said, a bit unsure how the fellow would react. He'd learned in a fairly long career both in China and more recently in America that people often had very strong feelings about reporters and not always positive ones.

"Reporter, eh, has something happened? Some Frenchman punch out a Chinaman again? Used to be a time when I'd meet a reporter every time I took this train."

"Not that I know of…but why so many reporters?" Jason asked, his words out of his mouth before he realized. "Wait, because of the Chinese strikebreakers at the shoe factory. Were you there when they first arrived?" he asked enthusiastically, his hand slowly moving toward his satchel where his notebook lay.

"That I was, quite a day. One of the most amazing scenes I'd ever seen, thousands of people all standing around the train station waiting for a bunch of Chinese workers to arrive…some of them liquored up…talking rough…talking like they were going to start something."

"Mr. Smith, would you mind if I asked you to tell me more about that day? It would help a lot for my own work, and…" Jason hesitated. "Do you mind if I take notes?" For a second, Jason worried the fellow would clam up. Lots of people did when a conversation with a reporter became more formal, but it was obvious that would not be a problem.

"Not at all, sir. Always looking for a chance to impress the Mrs. It's Smith, none of that Smyth stuff for my people—really plain folks from Springfield."

Jason made an especially obvious effort to write down his traveling companion's full name and hometown. Over the years, he'd learned that people really appreciated that. The effort could open doors.

"So, you were there as they arrived. What was it like? What sort of people were there?"

"Let me see. Well, there was Mr. Calvin Sampson himself of course, the owner who'd come up with the scheme in the first place, you know, to break the St. Crispin Union folks by bringing in Chinese laborers. He'd sent his business agent all the way across the country to hire a bunch of them to work in his shoe factory. So Sampson was there, and with, if I remember it properly, a group of security guards he'd brought with him for the occasion."

"So people were expecting trouble? There was that much anger against the idea of employing Chinese laborers?" Jason asked, taking notes as quickly as he could without interrupting Smith's story too much.

"More complicated than that actually. You sort of need to know something about North Adams; it's not like the Boston area. Not a bunch of wealthy old families. Places like North Adams are mostly old-stock Yankee Protestants—plain folk really and those with money earned it themselves. They tend to be very skeptical about Catholics and labor agitators, so for them the Chinese were an unknown, but a lot of the immigrant shoe-factory workers, Catholics, often Frenchies from up north were none too popular either."

Jason stopped for a moment, reflecting on what he'd just heard. As with Hartford, the story was clearly more complicated than he'd initially understood.

"So the long-time locals, they were not against bringing in Chinese workers from California?" he asked, thinking of perhaps the contrast with what he'd seen in parts of California.

"Not sure I would say that, probably more curious than any-thing else, but it really was a huge crowd...St. Crispin Union types, laid-off shoe-factory workers, families out in their Sunday go-to meeting clothing to see something different."

"So what happened when the Chinese arrived?" Jason fi-nally asked, after making a few more notes.

"Well, that was the really funny part," Smith said with a smile. "Absolutely nothing, Chinese arrived, got off the train and started walking toward the barracks Sampson had pre-pared, and people just stared. The Chinamen's clothing was just so different; even the Crispins just stared. It...it was more like men from the moon had arrived than a bunch of strike-breakers. The only real pushing I saw was folks pushing each other to get a better look."

"So there was no violence?"

"Not sure. Maybe I heard something about a few rocks thrown and some drunks yelling curses, but from what I saw did not look like any of the Chinamen understood a word any-way. Kind of hard to insult people who can't understand you. No, maybe a few incidents, but the crowd was huge, and I saw no real violence. Come to think of it, must have been a lot of your newspaper colleagues disappointed that day."

"Why would that be?" Jason asked, though pretty sure of the answer.

"Well, a good riot makes better—what do your people call it?—'copy.' Not at all that much to write. Bunch of Chinamen arrived in North Adams, walked from the station to their fu-ture barracks...people stared..."

For a moment, Jason just sat there thinking. That the Chinese workers' foreign clothing had protected them from attack really struck him as fascinating. In Hartford, similar robes had made it harder for the boys to fit in, while in North Adams they had pro-vided a shield of sorts from attack. Then remembering Smith's comment about disappointed reporters, he said, "I guess you're probably right. So what happened then?"

"Can't really say. I had to leave for the tunnel, didn't hear much after that except—from time to time about a few incidents, between the locals and the Chinese but really not all that much. So you're here to write more about it?"

"Yes, but more about how it has gone since then. I have an appointment with Mr. Sampson tomorrow at around noon. Do you know him?"

"Know him by sight, not to talk to, but he is pretty well known by anyone who passes through North Adams—self-made man, really typical old New England stock if you know what I mean."

"I think so," Jason said, though the only real image he had of such people was his father, and the reverend certainly was not the sort of self-made businessman industrialist Calvin Sampson apparently was.

For the next hour or so, the two chatted about North Adams, and to Jason's pleasure Smith confirmed that the place he'd made his reservation for, the Wilson House, would be especially convenient for his goals.

"I really think you will like it. I usually stay there when I am in town, though I do have a cousin who sometimes puts me up as well. First class, really fancy but not that expensive, easy walking distance from the train station, bunch of different rooms, even a billiard room."

"Can you tell me how far it is from the telegraph office?"

"That's the beauty of the place; post and telegraph's in the building. You can get most of your work done right in the building, excepting when you are at the factory itself." At that, Smith stood up and walked to the window.

"Looks like we are getting there...You can see the place for yourself soon enough. I would start gathering your belongings...and every sweater and coat you have...looks frigid as hell out there."

"Really was excellent to meet you, Mr. Brandt. Here take my card. If there is anything else I can help with, do not hesitate to ask. Usually get my messages at the Wilson House...I'd be honored to show you around the tunnel if you have time before you leave."

"Thank you. That is very kind. I may just call upon your hospitality," Jason said as he gathered up the last of those possessions he'd spread out on the seat alongside him. Within minutes the train pulled to a stop and Jason found himself walking into the enormous Wilson House, which at first glance certainly did live up to his traveling companion's description.

# CHAPTER 34

# NORTH ADAMS

Check-in at what seemed the especially efficient Wilson House in North Adams could not have gone more smoothly despite the effort by the desk clerk to engage him in a conversation Jason was too tired to take part in. Still, he mumbled his way through a few pleasantries and then set off following the bellboy to his room. Once there he gave the fellow a dime, locked the door behind him, and collapsed on the bed without even taking more than his boots off. He was exhausted, so exhausted that even the nagging hunger in his stomach or his by-now filthy clothing from all the soot that swirled around both the steamer and train bothered him not in the least. All he cared about was rest. There would be plenty of time to prepare for his afternoon interviews in the morning. Within seconds of closing his eyes, he was in a deep sleep.

Two hours later though, he awoke. His belt was cutting into his waist, and he'd had enough rest to keep him for a while. Getting up he looked out the window onto the street. It was late in the day, maybe around 4:30 p.m., and though the sun was still fairly bright, he doubted there would be much more daylight. The sun set quite early at this time of the year, he thought to himself as he explored the room a bit, his eyes moving over the washbasin and the lovely pitcher that sat next to it. After washing, changing his shirt, and making a stab at shaving, though he'd never had much of a beard to shave, he quickly left the room, descended the staircase, and exited the hotel, hoping to see more of the town before nightfall.

As he walked, the impressions he'd gotten from Smith on the train seemed to come to life. North Adams was different from the other New England towns he'd seen thus far. It had none of the gentility and smell of old money Boston, or the salt-impregnated air of a fishing village like Rockport. Not that he'd had all that much chance in the winter to even walk around the small town he and his family had settled in. No, it had been far too cold in the months since their arrival to explore much.

Nevertheless, North Adams was different as well. Its growth was obviously quite recent, a town of new factories, apparently of the self-made Yankee industrialists Smith had spoken of and immigrants. As he walked, Jason tried to guess where Sampson's factory might be. But asking proved problematic. There were few people on the streets; it was, after all, getting late and colder by the minute. The few people he saw were not Rockport types. Indeed, he passed several men along the street who seemed to be speaking French, though it did not sound much like the French his friend Prosper Giquel had taught him in China. No, this was, he imagined, the French of the people of Canada. Quebec, he thought, that section directly north was called, but he was not sure. Further down the street, he passed another group of men, clearly Americans, though of the lower classes—men whose clothing looked more like miners, filthy as could be though without the dark black coal dust common to such men. Jason wondered if they were workers from the great tunnel, looking for a tavern after a day spent deep below the surface. After a half an hour or so, the cold became unbearable and Jason headed back toward the Wilson House to warm up. Ten minutes later, for he'd picked up his pace greatly as he shivered with cold, Jason entered the wonderfully warm lobby of the hotel.

For the next few minutes, Jason sat in one of the overstuffed chairs in the lobby, waiting for the cold to pass from his body. After a moment or so, he began to study the relatively full room and to admire the woodwork. North Adams had nothing to apologize for. Whoever had built the Wilson House had taken great pains to make it as comfortable as any establishment in New England. What especially stood out was how wide a clientele the place seemed to serve. Around him, as he sat, walked all manner of visitors. Many were quite well dressed, while others still in work clothes moved among them. Clearly, the building's inner rooms varied enough to attract a diverse clientele. After a time, as he felt warmer, he got up and began to explore. Down one corridor to the right, he found what looked like a working-class bar of sorts. As he entered, it was clear that the better-off hotel guests had other locations more to their liking, for none of them sat either at the tables nor at the bar. Curious, Jason went in and took a seat.

"Can I bring you something?" a young woman with a strong Irish accent appeared as if from nowhere.

"Is there a list of food I can look at?" he asked, finally remembering how long it had been since he'd eaten.

"No, not likely, maybe in one of the other parlors, but here we're more simple. We've mutton stew, bread and fixing. Can I bring you a plate?"

"That will be fine."

"And to drink, shall you have a beer?"

"Yes, I think I'd like that. Thank you."

With that, the young woman was off.

"So you are the new reporter," a voice from behind him beckoned with a strong French accent.

"Excuse me?" Jason said, turning around behind him.

"*Oui*, the new reporter, *n'est pas*. North Adams is not so large that the arrival of a newcomer is not noticed. And Monsieur Smith loves to chat to any and all, as you no doubt learned on the train."

"Well then, I guess you have spotted well. Yes, the name's Jason Brandt, and you?" Jason asked, fully turning his chair in the direction of the fellow, a dark-haired man in a worker's cap who sat with several friends at a larger table just behind him.

"Please join us; *mes amis* and I were just about to eat as well."

"Thank you. That is very kind of you," Jason said, glancing around to see if the waitress had noticed he was moving his seat.

"So, you're here to tell more lies about the Crispins, are you?" the fellow said, bringing on a laugh from his three friends beside him.

"Why would you think that?" Jason asked, excited at his luck. Reporting for this trip was turning out to be easier than he had expected.

"Monsieur, if you are here writing about us, you have surely already read all sorts of articles—*morceau de merde*, we call them about the evil unions—and our attack on the Chinese strike-breakers? It's been the news ever since our Chinese 'friends' arrived a while back."

"Well, I have certainly seen some of those articles, but I wanted to see for myself. Sometimes I see things a bit differently than other reporters," Jason said, wishing he'd responded otherwise. His "different" perspective might not be helpful here. Happily, the fellow did not ask the obvious follow-up or at least did not get a chance, for Jason cut in with his own question.

"So the stories about the tensions between the Crispin Union men and the Chinese are not true?"

"Not as true as many here think. I can tell you that. Lots of folks around here want to turn it into a race-hatred thing. You know, monsieur, we hate the Chinese while everyone else hates the Irish." He laughed as he said it, winking at his comrade to his right.

"You just watch that Frenchy," the man said, "or me and my brother here from Dublin will deal with you and your type!" But he smiled as he spoke; the men were obviously friends.

"Your supper, sir." The waitress had arrived with Jason's pint and the stew.

"Thank you, ma'am; that smells wonderful. Excuse me, gentlemen, but I don't remember when I've eaten last."

"Take your time, have your fill. We're not going anywhere... not much to do in this town at night anyway."

At that Jason looked out the window and realized the sun had finally set outside. Then after several bites of the bread dipped in stew, and an effort to quench his thirst with the pint, Jason turned back to his new acquaintances. Wiping his mouth with the cloth napkin, he looked up again at his impromptu dinner companions.

"So there is no race hatred in any of this?" Jason asked.

At that the larger of the two Irishmen laughed. "Oh, there's certainly some who feel that way, don't you know? But that's not at the heart of it." His two companions both nodded in agreement.

"So what is it then?" he asked, wishing he could get to his notebook; the men would probably not mind, but he knew his stomach would. He had to keep eating even as they spoke.

"It is the same old thing, the working man trying to make a decent living and them's that got the power and money trying to stop him. It's always the same story."

Jason nodded, wondering if he should ask more questions or let the man just continue; often that was the best technique, and in this case it worked as the fellow, seeking to fill the vacuum, as Jason remained silent, began again.

"We used to have it good around here. Lots of work in the shoe factories; some of us made five or six bucks a day, even early on three dollars for many...and that even from Old Mr. Sampson the owner. You know of him?"

Jason nodded, though did not think it prudent to say he had an interview scheduled with him the next day.

"So what went wrong?"

"What went wrong was Sampson got greedy, wanted to pay us less, didn't care how skilled we were, and he hated the Union—you know about the Crispins, right?"

Jason nodded, not wanting to stop the man's train of thought.

"Well, the Knights of St. Crispin were the best thing that ever happened to the working man. There's thousands of us working together to try to protect the little guy. Hell, we've even got a women's division, but the owners, frankly everyone with any money, hated us. They can't abide by the lower classes doing a bit better."

"Amen," said his French colleague, who'd given the floor to his Irish friend.

"So where do the Chinese fit in?" Jason asked, already knowing the story but wanting to hear how these men saw it.

"Well, we fought Samson, union tried to protect us with a strike. Can't make shoes without workers you know. And we did everything we could to make sure Sampson could not replace us with strikebreakers. Fact is we were fairly successful until Sampson got what the ruling classes probably thought was his 'great idea.' Sent one of his foreman, Mr. Chase, all the way to San Francisco. You can do it all the way by train now you know."

Jason nodded, remembering well how that might be possible.

"Went direct to San Francisco in California and hired a whole bunch of Chinamen, signed 'em up as contract laborers, way cheaper than us, and brought the whole lot of them across the country to break our strike...and we think to break all the union efforts."

"And what happened?" Jason asked bluntly.

"Sorry to say, it mostly worked. Did not take old Sampson long to get the men, really boys actually up to speed, and sooner than we expected, they were producing a good line of shoes. Hate to admit it though."

The smaller of the two Irishmen, the one who'd thus far sat quietly, suddenly spoke with a burst of energy. "The working man never gets a break!" while slamming his knife into the wooden table. Several of the other patrons in the restaurant looked up momentarily and then went back to their own conversations.

"So what did you and your colleagues think of the Chinese after that?"

At that the French Canadian began again. "You see, monsieur, some of us hated them, told all sorts of stories about them and their filthy habits, but a lot of us, especially me and some of my friends, knew they were not all that different from us. The locals look down on my people, immigrants from up north, us trying to make a living, but we understood the Chinese were no different. Just another bunch of foreigners the owners were willing to use when they were needed just like us."

"Did the majority think that, that the Chinese were not the enemy?"

"I would not go that far," the larger Irish man said and then after a huge gulp of his beer, "Fact is some of us liked the fact that the newcomers were even more different than us foreign

Irish and French Catholics. When everyone looks down on you, it's not half bad to have someone else to despise."

"Yes, I suppose you're right. So have you ever actually spoken to any of the Chinese laborers?"

"You see a few around from time to time, but mostly they stay among themselves in the barracks Sampson built for them. And I don't think more than a few can communicate in English anyway. It makes it hard to compare thoughts."

"So there has been no communication?"

"That's not completely true. I think some of the Crispin leadership made an effort, word got out that the Chinese themselves were none too happy, and they were approached about joining the union."

"Interesting! And what happened?"

"Not much that I know of...they really are different. Don't know anything about unions, and a buddy of mine claimed the only thing they really want is to finish up their contracts. Three years they signed up for and return home to China. Frankly, it's not hard to understand. They say China's so cheap the fellows can earn enough money here to set themselves up nicely at home for life."

"Well, I am not sure about that," Jason said.

"You know China, mister?"

"A bit, but more to the point that it would make it harder to unionize the Chinese workers under the circumstances, I should think. Did anything ever come of the effort?"

"Not that I know. All we hear are rumors, but Old Sampson was happy enough. The union was thumped, the Chinese were making shoes he could sell, and he even recruited another bunch after a while."

For the next hour, as his three companions got more and more drunk, Jason tried to milk his beer, after a time his second beer, and learn as much as he could about the work of the factories. None of the men had ever found another full-time job, but they all seemed to be getting by with odd jobs here and there. At least they had enough cash for beer. Eventually realizing his three friends were not going anywhere, he excused himself and returned to his room, anxious to write down everything he could of the conversation and wishing he'd not had that second glass.

# CHAPTER 35

# AT THE NORTH ADAMS
# SHOE FACTORY

"Mr. Brandt, I presume?" Jason looked up at the man standing next to his table. He'd come downstairs only a few minutes before and ordered breakfast, eggs, toast, and strips of bacon that he had already half-finished while sipping coffee and reading the local paper. It was a lot like those he'd seen in other small towns in the United States. Not all that different from his own *North China Daily News*. Indeed, the layout seemed particularly familiar on that score, though the actual content was not the same. Here the readership was not Western businessmen come to seek their fortunes along the China coast but farmers, manufacturers, and those working on the tunnel. Still practical men with very different interests than those his father, Reverend Brandt, had always shown.

His father, in fact, was on his mind at the moment, because the deep cold had continued and Jason was wondering how the aging minister was taking it. He may have grown up not that far from North Adams, but decades in Hong Kong had certainly changed what his father was accustomed to weather-wise.

Pushing those thoughts from his head, he turned to the fellow politely standing opposite him.

"Sir."

"You are Jason Brandt, the reporter, are you not? North Adams is not so large as to be unable to spot a newcomer." Jason looked at the man and studied his nicely trimmed beard and thick eyebrows, thinking he'd just heard the same line the evening before and then.

"Yes, of course. I am sorry. I was caught up in my own thoughts. Please sit down. How can I help you?"

"Frankly, it's the opposite. I have come, I think, to help you. Name is George Chase. I work for Mr. Sampson, whom, I believe, you have an appointment with this afternoon."

"Yes, just after lunch. Why, is there a problem?" Jason asked, worried. He really needed to talk to Sampson if his articles were to be the success he hoped.

"Probably not, but I did want to talk to you this morning. There is a bit of concern on Mr. Sampson's part."

"Really? Can you explain? I have been looking forward to meeting him this afternoon. Has something come up?"

Mr. Chase studied Jason closely, perhaps wondering what he should say and then after some hesitation, he said, "Probably not. Well, let me order some coffee and we can talk. He turned to the waitress, who'd been watching them, and pointed to Jason's cup. A few seconds later, once Chase had his own coffee, he began again.

"This is a small town, Mr. Brandt," he began as Jason wondered to himself how many more times he would hear that. Hell, he thought to himself, it was a lot bigger than Rockport as far as he knew.

"In any case, Mr. Sampson's heard about your activities last evening, carousing with some of the same men fired last year. Frankly he's concerned that you've come here to write something, attacking him for hiring the Chinese instead of white men."

Jason laughed and then realizing that might be misunderstood, he said, "I am sorry, but if you knew more about me, you'd understand why I laugh. No, I can assure you I am the last person to question his hiring Chinese workers."

"That's what I told Calvin—excuse me, Mr. Sampson—this morning. Besides I reminded him of the letter from Mr. Sage, who speaks quite highly of you."

"Mr. Sampson knows Mr. Sage? They've spoken of me?"

"Of course, and we are not so far from Troy not to have heard of the American who arrived at the Troy Female Seminary with his Chinese wife and children. And yes, Mr. Sampson's been somewhat in contact with the congressman—we still call him that, for years. Fact is as soon as you wrote, we realized you were the same fellow we'd heard had wandered around Troy with Mr. Sage a while back. So Mr. Sampson wrote Sage and he vouched for you. To be blunt, Mr. Sampson is a busy man not all that taken by reporters. He only agreed to talk to you because of Sage."

"But last night caused a problem?"

"Well, it did cause Mr. Sampson pause, but I convinced him you were just doing your story. That no good reporter would only talk to him. That you had to talk to the Crispins, that it was part of your job."

"And that worked?"

"Absolutely. Sampson is many things to many people, but they would all agree on one thing: he is a hardworking man who believes everyone should follow his example. And after we discussed it a bit, he understood why you spent the evening with those men."

"Well then, I look forward to our conversation this afternoon. It is still scheduled for one, correct?"

"Yes, one. So I will be seeing you then, a bit later." Chase started to get up.

"Mr. Chase, you are absolutely right that I need to talk to everyone who can help me understand, and that includes you. Would you mind staying a bit longer and giving me your perspective? I mean if Mr. Sampson would not mind?"

Chase hesitated for a second. "You want to talk to me?"

"Am I right that you were the person who actually went to California to recruit the men?"

"Yes, at Mr. Sampson's orders, of course."

"Well then, I would love to talk to you if you don't mind."

"I suppose I could, doubt Mr. Sampson would mind. Waitress, can you bring a bit more coffee?" Then turning back to Jason, "If you don't mind, I can give you some background, but I'd rather not be quoted about anything that might contradict something Mr. Sampson might tell you. Does that work for you?"

"I should think that would be fine. So to get started, can you give me some background on the entire affair? You are a foreman for Mr. Sampson, are you not? Been for a long time, right?"

"Yes, that's right, but there is probably not a lot to tell you that you don't already know. Been a lot in the papers already."

Jason nodded but said nothing, and Chase continued. "There was a lot going on back then. The shoe industry was growing a lot. We had lots of orders, plenty of work, and a good-sized labor force of French Canadians, Scotsman and Irish. Mr. Sampson was happy and confident about the future, confident enough to build a new building and buy all the latest equipment.

"So what went wrong?"

"What went wrong was the Crispins...showed up, started organizing the men, making demands Mr. Samson found unreasonable, all sorts of issues about money mostly...and we were paying them a fair day's wage as it was…around three for some, up to six for others. But they could not be satisfied. And then they went on strike. Everything stopped. You've got to understand how powerful the Knights of St. Crispin were a few years ago."

"I think I have a sense of that…How did Mr. Sampson react?"

"Much like the rest of the owners. He was angry about the money, but angry as well that his own workers, people he'd hired, were telling him how to run his business. Frankly pretty much a standoff, Mr. Sampson against the Crispins and his workers…wasn't at all clear to me how it would all turn out."

"So you were not all that confident about your own future?"

"Not at all. Mr. Sampson couldn't make shoes without workers, and I could not supervise an empty factory. Told the wife we might have to move on…We have family closer to Boston and even wrote asking if we could visit them for a stay."

"Sounds frightening," Jason commented, thinking about the huge chance he and his own family were taking relocating themselves for however long in Rockport.

"It was indeed. Then one day Mr. Sampson called me into his office and handed me a newspaper as I sat down. It was all about the new railroad opening up to the West…and another article was on all the Chinese workers who were without work, because the line was finished. That's the thing about Calvin."

For a second Chase paused, clearly thinking he'd been too informal in front of a stranger, then going on, "He's always thinking, always trying to learn enough to improve his business, keeping up with the times, a bit like building that new factory, which he did about the same time. So anyway, he sent me off to California to hire contract Chinese laborers in San Francisco. Now that was a great experience, all the way there on my own and then back with seventy-five young Chinamen. Wait, you just did that yourself, didn't you?"

He nodded. "I did indeed, though the line was even newer when you did it. Not sure how different it was."

"Well, still you have a sense of it. Frankly, except for some of the Chinese here, especially Charlie Sing, you're the first person I've met I can really discuss the trip with. Love to tell my wife about it…but it's hard to get her to Albany let alone San Francisco." Chase stopped, clearly savoring the memory of his crossing the country by train.

"So who is Charlie Sing?" Jason asked, though he'd figured that out already.

"Sing, you'll probably meet later this afternoon. I met him in San Francisco, older than the rest of the Chinese, already knew a fair amount of English when I met him. He's the Chinese foreman."

"Is he the only one who speaks English?"

"Not anymore. Some of the others are learning fairly fast. They were still very young when they got here. You know how young folks are with languages."

Jason nodded. "But you say they have not all learned English by now?"

"Well, that's just it. Most of the time they are with each other, working in the factory, living in the barracks Mr. Sampson set up for them. There's a few have ventured out more, been received into the local homes, by some of the more charity-minded locals, gone to church with them on Sundays plus dinner afterward. But not all of them. That's really no more than a half dozen at most."

"So most are still quite isolated?" Jason questioned, trying to get a better sense of the situation.

"That is probably true, but I'd ask Charlie, Charlie Sing, when you meet him. He'd have a better sense of that than I do." With that Chase pulled his watch out of his pocket and, consulting it, added, "Mr. Brandt, can I call you Jason?" Jason nodded. "Well, I have to run, several errands to do for Mr. Sampson and the wife, not sure I know which one I am less enthused to disappoint, and I have to be back at the factory when you arrive. Mr. Sampson wants me there, especially after the interview to show you around the factory. So if you don't mind, I will take my leave now. If you have any other questions, we can talk during the tour."

With that the two men stood up, shook hands, and Chase walked off briskly toward the door of the breakfast room. A moment later, Jason saw him through the window of the Wilson House pulling his coat up around his collar and heading off against the wind.

# CHAPTER 36

# AT THE SHOE FACTORY

"So how well do you know Russell Sage?" Sampson asked him. They had hardly been together more than a few seconds when Sampson began to vigorously question him. If anything, Calvin Sampson reminded Jason of Mr. Sage, except he told himself he'd seen Sage in unusual circumstances, the last-minute train ride with the wives to Troy, while Calvin Sampson was sitting in his very comfortable office at work as official as the man probably ever was.

"Not terribly well. We did, though, spend a fair amount of time together; in Troy, it was a bit unusual. The family received word, just as my family and I were arriving in New York for an appointment, that an old teacher, a mentor really of Mrs. Sage, was quite ill in Troy."

"That would be Mrs. Willard of course. She was quite well known in these parts, began her work, I believe, educating young women in Massachusetts, not New York. My wife often—" Then he stopped himself, for Sampson was clearly not a man who enjoyed being distracted from the task at hand, and he said, "So you interviewed Sage as you would interview me?"

"Actually not, sir. Our relationship is of a different nature," Jason said, not at all comfortable that Sampson had taken over his interview.

"So what is it then? If you are half the reporter I am told you are, and yes, I do my homework, you knew I'd want to know."

"Well, it's of a private nature, but I can tell you this. Mr. Sage is, as you well know, an investor; he's interested in China, and I have been helping him understand investment possibilities there."

"Right, heard something about that…By the way, you sound like you're from Boston. But grew up in Hong Kong, right? So you speak the language of the Chinese I have working for me?" It was obvious Sampson's mind was racing, trying to think through the implications of a reporter who could actually speak to the men in their own tongue.

"Well, it is a bit more complicated than that. And frankly I have not met any of your Chinese workers yet, but yes, I probably can."

With that, Sampson turned to Chase, who'd been sitting quietly in the third chair closer to the fire warming his hands. "Hear that Charles, ten minutes with our men and this fellow, will know them better than you did after crossing the country with them!"

"I doubt that, sir," Jason piped in, but Sampson ignored him for a moment, and then turned back.

"Well, you have convinced me, agent of Russell Sage, reporter from China. I guess, you really are something different from those who've been here before. So what can I tell you? Ask away."

"Sometimes it's best to just be blunt. Why did you hire the Chinese to replace the locals? I have heard all sorts of stories and reasons, but I want to hear it from you."

"Hear that Charles, this young fellow might have been raised in China, but he still thinks like a New England Yankee, old stock shows."

Chase nodded affirmatively and went back to heating his hands over the fire.

"Asked me straightforward; well, you get a straight answer. I did not need the locals. Actually, they are not really locals anyway. But the point is I did not need the Crispin men anymore. Just did not make good business sense."

"And why not?" Jason asked, having expected any number of answers other than the one he got.

"Look, Mr. Brandt, I assume you've done some homework on me, but I need to give you some background on who I am. I came up the hard scrabble way. Worked on a farm, sold shoes from a wagon for my cousin, finally got my own store and then started manufacturing shoes myself. I have spent my entire life building up this business, doing everything I could to follow the trends, new shoe styles, new ways to make them, to market them. And finally I made the biggest plunge, built myself a new factory, latest technology, to make shoes more efficiently. It was a very proud day indeed when the new facility was up and running for the first time—really one of my proudest moments."

"So what happened?" Jason asked when it was clear Sampson had run dry for the moment.

"What happened was that the Crispins started pushing me for higher wages, pushing my workers, some of them I'd known for years, to make demands on me, threats to strike, to stop the work if I did not cave in. They wanted to make me, the man who'd built the factory into some sort of lackey for their trade union. That was not how I grew up, worked my own keister off for every man who gave me a chance. And when I had my own chance, I went for it. That's the world I know. But it was more than that…the Crispins really had the timing all off."

"What do you mean, the timing?"

"Fact is the Crispins were pushing for more money and security when I did not need them as much. I hired them when I needed their skills, shoe-making skills. But times change and I'd just put every fancy modern machine I could find in that new factory, mortgaged myself up to my eyebrows, hoping to make the shoes more efficiently. Make 'em cheaper, makes it easier to sell them, and with production up, I was in a position to be that much more successful—just basic business."

"So," Jason began to understand, "you did not require trained shoe workers any more, the primary Crispin bargaining chip was hollow."

"Exactly right, young man. They wanted guarantees that I would not cut down the work, that I'd keep paying them wages for skills I did not need anymore. Didn't make a whit of sense to me. Why'd I buy all that new equipment for, if not to save money and build production." And these were—mind you— machines simple enough that it did not take a journeyman shoe maker to operate them."

"So it was not a battle between you and the union's as some have said?"

"Well, it was certainly a battle, and most men of my kind don't abide by unions, that's true. But it's not like I am against a bit of rebellion, against taking on the authorities. Hell, my granddaddy was part of Shay's rebellion—so the Sampsons have a streak of rebel in them. But this was business. I am not a charity, don't mind giving to charity, but I am not one. The men were making demands I did not need to meet."

"So I sent Charley here to San Francisco to hire some contract laborers. And it worked, even with the new barracks the train tickets, food and all; they are still a lot less expensive and no one's complaining about the quality of the shoes going out the door either."

With that, Sampson sat back in his office chair clearly pleased with his explanation.

"The way you put it, it really is hard to argue with the logic," Jason said, absorbing the story.

"And from what I hear, most of the Chinese have been happy. Mr. Sing my Chinese foreman told me the other day that several were already making plans to go home with their savings. Has not cost them much to live here, I provide for most of their needs and they can just save. But I suspect with your background you will know more about that by this afternoon."

With that Sampson turned to look at a young woman, perhaps about twenty who had entered the office quietly during the last part of the conversation. Mr. Sampson, "I have those papers you asked about."

Sampson took the papers and glanced at Chase who standing up spoke for the first time."

"Well, Mr. Brandt, I think Mr. Sampson has answered most of your questions and between Mr. Sing and myself we should be able to handle the rest.

At that Sampson turned again to Jason and extended his hand. "Thank you for coming, Mr. Brandt, and please give my regards to Mr. Sage when you see him again."

"I will, sir, and thank you for your time."

At that Sampson turned back to the secretary and started to look more closely at the stack of documents she had brought him while Jason and Chase exited the office.

As he exited, he realized he must have been very preoccupied before the interview with thoughts about how it might go, because he suddenly noticed a horrific smell he'd not earlier been aware of.

"That's from some of the tanning fluids," Chase said casually as he saw Jason pulling out his handkerchief. "You're really better off taking it in. The worst of it will go away as your body adjusts. Don't hardly notice it myself these days, not really unless some out-of-town relatives stay at the house and mention it. We sort of live with it."

"If you say so," Jason said, putting the handkerchief back in his coat pocket and taking in a whiff. "So where are we off to now?"

"We are starting off at the main production facility. I want to give you a tour and Charlie Sing is there waiting to meet you."

"Excellent. I really appreciate your taking the time."

"Not a problem, or at least I hope it won't be. You never know with you reporter types till the story comes out," Chase said matter-of-factly.

"Mr. Chase, I hope I have already convinced you and Mr. Sampson that I am not here to do a hatchet job on anyone?" Chase nodded, but Jason did not think he looked very convinced.

"It's over here, Mr. Brandt, in this door. You can easily smell the tanning room, but I don't think we need to dwell there. Here is the heart of our little establishment, the assembly room." Chase opened a large double door and gestured his guest in. As they entered a few of the workers glanced up, but most concentrated on their efforts.

"Over there you can see the strips of cured leather, and look yonder there over near the wall crates of soles…Charlie Sing, our guest is here." Chase raised his voice to get the attention of a man several years younger than Jason. Mid-twenties, Jason thought to himself, who was walking toward him. As he walked, Jason thought for a second of Yung Wing. Charley Sing, as Chase called him, was in work clothing, very different from how Yung Wing dressed, but there was something very Americanized about him, something in the way that he carried himself that seemed less Chinese than American.

"Mr. Chase, how can I help?" Sing responded as soon as he was close enough to be easily heard above the factory floor's din.

"Charley, this is Jason Brandt, the reporter I told you about. He's come to do another story on our little enterprise. Mr. Sampson thought you might be able to help."

"I will help in any way I can, Mr. Chase."

"Excellent, so if you could, just walk Mr. Brandt through how we run things here and tell him a bit about your countrymen as well."

"Absolutely. Mr. Brandt, could you follow me?"

For the next several minutes, the young Chinese foreman explained to Jason with considerable expertise and obvious enthusiasm about the work, how the shoes were assembled and the different jobs the various laborers carried out. It was all very formal, with Charles Chase following behind mostly listening and occasionally adding tidbits of information to the tour until one of the workers, one of the few other white men in the large assembly hall, approached Chase, looking anxious.

"Are you who I think you are?" Sing quietly asked Jason as he steered him a bit away from Chase and the fellow who seemed to be heatedly telling him something.

"Not sure. Who do you think I am?"

"When young man in China, in Guangzhou, call it Canton here, before I left from Hong Kong, I heard about an American who had walked among the foreign soldiers but grew up among us Chinese. A lot of stories and then later, in San Francisco, when I look for things to practice English reading, I find old copies *North China Daily News*. You wrote them, didn't you? And you the same person I hear about in Guangzhou before that?"

"Guilty as charged. Yes, that's me...but I live here now. I am honored that you remember my work."

"What I remember you only writer who understand us Chinese."

"Perhaps. I can certainly tell you that my editors brought that up a lot, and it was not always a compliment."

Sing looked puzzled for a second and then laughed. "Oh yes, that be problem sometimes."

"So what is your real name?" Jason asked Sing in Cantonese.

"Oh right, I guess you know it's not Charley Sing; it's Chung—"

But before he'd even finished his response, the sound in the room suddenly changed. Loud voices in Cantonese and English broke out, angry swearing, and for a second as Jason glanced around, he saw something being thrown across the room and, at the last second, Charles Chase diving for the floor as the wooden shoe last hit Jason squarely in the forehead.

# CHAPTER 37
# A SEVERE HEADACHE

The first thing Jason heard was whispered conversations at something of a distance from him. Spoken too quietly to hear properly, but he thought he heard the phrase, "starting to wake up." For a second he wondered whom they might be talking about...and then he remembered. What had happened? The last thing he recalled was talking to Chase and Charlie Sing and then...loud yelling...what happened after that?

He thought of opening his eyes, but there was still too much pain in his head, and the light, he could see even through his mostly closed eyes that very bright light was streaming in through the window almost directly at him. Indeed, he thought a curtain had been raised a second before.

"Mr. Brandt...Mr. Brandt, can you hear me?" Her voice was sweet and caring as Jason slowly opened his eyes, squinting at the light.

"Charles, pull the curtain down. Our guest does not need that much light right now."

Over to the side, now pulling on the blinds, Jason spotted Charles Chase following his wife's instructions. They were in a small bedroom, though Jason had no idea how he'd come to be in the room.

"Mr. Brandt, you were hit by a wooden shoe last thrown across the room. Those things are very solid, and I am afraid one hit you. Frankly, we are all mortified that a guest to our small community was treated so badly."

"That's all right, ma'am," Jason said. "I have suffered much worse assaults in the past, I can assure you. So what happened?" he asked as he raised his arm to his forehead, only to feel a piece of gauze and bandages attached.

"Well," Chase said as his wife turned to him to respond. "Well, it is a bit embarrassing. We really have not had many problems, but something came up between two workers—one Chinese, one Irish—and well, I guess somebody got a bit heated and threw the wooden shoe last. Suppose it's my fault you got hit. I saw the thing coming and ducked. Sorry about that."

"No hard feelings, Mr. Chase. Such things happen. How long have I been here? I assume this is your home."

"Yes, as soon as we saw what had happened, and it really was only a few hours ago, we carried you here. The doctor's already come and gone. Said we were to let you get some rest and you'd be fine."

"I cannot thank you enough for your kindness," Jason said, already feeling the pain in his head lessening as the bright light from the window had been removed.

"It was the least we could do. I can assure you Mr. Sampson is mortified that such a thing happened on his property to a guest."

"Please tell Mr. Sampson that there is nothing to be concerned about; really I already feel better already. If you don't mind, I'll rest a bit more and go back to the Wilson Hotel."

"We'd really like you to have supper with us," Mrs. Chase said. "We don't get a lot of visitors and certainly not folks we've accidently done injury to."

"Mrs. Chase, I could not be more grateful, but I really must be going. I have a lot of notes to write up on my visit."

"Hopefully not a lot about the flying shoe last, I pray."

"Not to worry; it sounds like a very minor skirmish, and my only problem was not to duck as fast as you. But thank you very much for the invitation."

"There is something else, Mr. Brandt."

"Yes?"

"We were not the only ones mortified that you were injured. Charley Sing's been sitting on the porch all afternoon. He is very anxious to talk to you and I think apologize for himself and his people."

"Again, not necessary."

"Perhaps not, but as I said he's been sitting on the porch for a couple of hours. Do you mind if I send him up? He really is very anxious to speak to you."

"Of course! Let me wash up a bit and then send him up."

---

Ten minutes later a quiet knock at the door attracted Jason's attention. He'd already taken the time to wash, and was sitting in a small chair sipping a glass of tea Mrs. Chase had brought him a moment before. The throbbing pain in his head had subsided, and for the most part, he felt relatively well again. "Come in," he called out.

As Jason turned to the door, Charlie Sing stepped in hesitantly.

"I hope you are feeling better, Mr. Brandt; my countrymen were humiliated that you were hurt. That sort of thing rarely happens, just a moment of anger but to have so distinguished a guest hurt. Well, I don't know what to say."

"It's really fine, I can assure you. I feel much better, almost good as new, and I have certainly experienced worse, I can tell you that."

Sing looked at him closely and then, glancing at the door as if he was wondering if one of the Chases would enter again, switched into Cantonese.

"That would be during your time with the long hairs, the Taipings, right?"

"So you have read my work. Well, yes," Jason began, switching himself to the dialect of South China he knew so well after a childhood in Hong Kong and Guangzhou.

"So you really lived among those of the Heavenly Kingdom, actually met the Tien Wang?"

"Yes, I suppose I did, though not personally; there were a great many people there as well."

"And your wife, Mr. Chase, says you arrived in America with a Chinese wife."

For some reason, Jason hesitated, a habit from his years in Shanghai. That Black Jade had lived among the Taipings, once been the wife of a Taiping Wang, was not something he advertised in Shanghai. Did it matter here in North Adams? he wondered. However, before he had a chance to answer, Sing or he supposed Chung, as he was probably known among the Chinese, had moved on. The man was clearly distracted by his enthusiasm for meeting the well-known writer Jason had become to those who followed events in China.

"There is another story I have heard as well, but I hope it is not impertinent for one such as myself to ask." He seemed more hesitant than before, and again glanced nervously toward the door." Watching the man Jason wondered if he actually thought it would matter if one of the Chases entered. They were, after all, speaking Cantonese.

"I told you earlier, before the accident, that I'd heard about a young man like yourself in Guangzhou, a young man who worked with the foreign soldiers but who was kind to the locals. And then later that I read your writings in the *North China Daily News.*"

Jason listened to him carefully. Despite the head injury, he remembered very clearly Sing/Chung telling him that. What more could there be? he wondered.

"I have also heard another story about that young man, the one some call the white friend of the Chinese, about how he freed a shipload of coolies imprisoned on a ship in the middle of the river, that he crawled aboard and saved many of my countryman...and that"—Sing hesitated—"that something unfortunate happened that night as well, that one of the foreign devils died during the rescue."

Jason sat stunned. He had not thought about that night for a very long time. How could this man, sitting here in North Adams, Massachusetts, know about that night? he thought to himself, breathing very slowly, trying not to reveal his surprise. It was one thing to be cautious about Black Jade's Taiping background, but he was sitting here in America, the killer of a white foreigner in China, a man who might well have been an American with family nearby. It was the first time in all those years Jason had thought beyond the horror of the night he'd freed Wu to the man he'd killed to save his friend.

"I am so sorry. It was wrong of me to ask. This one made an error. I am sure it was someone else. I need to apologize again," Sing said, obviously noticing Jason's discomfort.

"*Mei you wen-ti*, it's not a problem...many things happened in my youth some of which I regret deeply, some I am proud of. But let's talk of it no more."

"Of course, Mr. Brandt, and I have erred again. For I came here to invite you to the Chinese barracks. My countrymen would like to receive you as a guest, to apologize and to have the honor of sharing our meager dinner with you. Is that possible? Do you feel well enough or would you prefer to stay here and visit tomorrow? Mrs. Chase said you might be staying the night."

"You know I would like that? And this evening, right now is excellent. In fact, it would be my honor. So what sort of dinner are you able to prepare among yourselves here in North Adams?" Jason asked warming to the idea of the offer. He could meet the men, do some interviews this evening and with luck be back on the train by tomorrow afternoon. He was already getting anxious to return to his family in Rockport, maybe with luck he might even make it back by tomorrow night or at the latest the next morning.

"You know the reputation of Guangdong people, we are known as the greatest cooks in China, and even here with so few genuine Chinese ingredients we have been able to produce food more editable than the potatoes and big chunks of meat the Americans are so happy with."

"Well, in that case, I am doubly looking forward to taking you up on your kind offer. Let me just gather my things and give my regards to Mr. and Mrs. Chase and we can be off."

# CHAPTER 38

# A SPECIAL GUEST

Although the distance was not far, Mr. Chase, after making a genuine effort to convince Jason to spend the night, insisted that at minimum a carriage be called to take Jason the few blocks to the Chinese barracks. Given the cold, and now very dark starless night, he gladly accepted the offer and set off with Sing in the carriage. Within minutes, they were at the building and alighting from the carriage, entered the large facility that apparently housed the more than one hundred Chinese workers employed by Calvin Sampson.

As he entered, Jason saw scores of men, young mostly in their early twenties standing eagerly in somewhat disordered rows all straining to see him. It was not quite the reception he'd expected. They clearly had been waiting for him and Jason suddenly realized Sing had obviously sent someone ahead to tell them their invitation had been accepted. As he looked around the room, the first time he'd been in the presence of so many Chinese since he'd left San Francisco's Chinatown his nose took in the smell of Chinese spices. If it was not as authentic as what Black Jade and Old Zhu had managed from their magical trunk in Rockville, it was a fair facsimile.

"Mr. Brandt, please sit here in the place of honor, we've prepared for you. Our food is humble but we are eager to share with you. And"—he lowered his voice a bit—"I have taken the liberty of telling my colleagues *some* things about you, and they are honored. You, of course, know how much scholars are honored among us."

"Well, I am hardly a scholar, merely a scribbler for newspapers and such. Nevertheless, the pleasure is all mine. I am deeply honored by you and your countrymen's kindness." It was the first words Jason had uttered aloud in the room and the reaction was electric. Those nearer leaned forward eagerly, their mouths showing real surprise. Jason thought he heard people whispering around the room, confirming to each other that he really did speak with the native tongue of a man from Hong Kong.

"I am sorry they are making such a fuss. I don't want you to feel like an exhibit in a Western zoo, but my countrymen have very little experience with foreigners who can speak our tongue. And never someone with your skills. If I close my eyes I would not even know you are not one of us. And you know more than the dialects of the south I believe?"

"After my youth in Hong Kong I traveled north and until recently had a home in Shanghai. In truth, until I arrived in San Francisco I had not spoken the Cantonese of my youth for a long time. I've become fairly comfortable in the dialects of the north."

"And your wife, for we would be equally honored to meet her one day."

"She too is from the south, but has also learned northern dialects and like yourself has become a very proficient speaker of English."

"You are too kind. My English is very bad merely enough to help Mr. Chase and Sampson communicate with their workers."

"So not everyone here knows English. It's been a while that you have been here, has it not?"

"For some, yes; for others, no. Another group arrived from San Francisco fairly recently. Nevertheless, the fact is that we work and live among our countrymen. Only a few have developed friendships beyond this room."

As they spoke, Jason watched the faces of the young men around him who were following the conversation with extraordinary attentiveness and at regular intervals passing on what was being said to those too far from the table where Jason sat to hear properly.

"Ah, our food arrives," Sing announced enthusiastically. At that Jason saw a huge cooking pot being passed around full of steaming noodles that were ladled into the bowls of those around him. The smell was impressive indeed. Somehow his hosts had gathered enough Chinese like ingredients to produce a recognizable bowl of noodles and hot sauce. They even had chopsticks, a beautiful pair of which he was handed by one of the men serving as a waiter. Further down the table an enormous tea pot was being passed around to fill the cups of the waiting diners.

After he had eaten for a time, Jason turned to Sing again. "So tell me how you came to be here in North Adams serving as the Chinese foreman."

"There is not a lot to tell. The story is like a lot of others. I grew up in the south as you know, eventually signed a contract with the foreigners to come to America to work on the railroad."

"So you yourself worked the rail lines?"

"Yes, but only for a short time. The work was ended very soon after I arrived. But I could hardly go home. I'd originally hoped to earn enough to return home to my family a rich man but I had not earned nearly enough."

"So what happened then?"

"Like so many I spent time near San Francisco, a town called San Jose, working in a laundry. That's where I became more proficient in English talking to the customers. The owner was very old, terrible at English and he needed my help because even then I was fairly good with the language."

"Where does Chase enter the story?"

"After a time, I left San Jose and returned to San Francisco. My English had gotten good enough that I hoped to find work in one of the fancy Chinese restaurants in the city that catered to Americans. You have seen such places no doubt."

Jason nodded, remembering fondly his time in San Francisco's Chinatown. "Go on."

"Well, I was actually in just such a restaurant hoping to find work when Mr. Chase walked in. He happened to talk to me first, telling me what he was looking for and well…that conversation turned into this job. It took a while to gather the men together but a few weeks later we were off riding on the train tracks I'd been working on not that long before."

"Is your story much like the rest?"

"No, most are a lot younger than I am. They arrived much more recently. They did not even know the railroad work was ending. They were sort of stranded and easy to recruit. No one had any idea how far North Adams was, in truth, I had no idea and Mr. Chase was offering room and board, a three-year job and a ticket back to San Francisco when it was over. It was not difficult to find those willing to sign the contracts."

"I should not think so," Jason said, reflecting on the story, and then turning to one of the other Chinese, a young fellow perhaps no more than twenty who was listening attentively.

"And you, my friend. What can you tell me about your experience here?"

"Mr. Sing is correct," he began somewhat hesitantly while he nervously toyed with his queue. "They told us in the village that if one went to Gold Mountain, you would return a rich man. And the next village over from mine did have such a man. He'd returned only a few years before and purchased a fine home and two concubines!"

Jason smiled, having heard such stories and more importantly such hopes many times before. "So how did you come to be here?"

"It's much the same for everyone. I walked from my village toward the city and eventually found coolie contract merchants who brought me to San Francisco but when we got here there was no work. Those who had arranged the trip were very angry. Soon though I heard about Mr. Sing and Mr. Chase and found them in an office they'd taken in Chinatown. A few weeks later, I was here with everyone else."

"Was it hard to arrive and see so many angry faces upon your arrival?"

"No, not really, we did not care and here, unlike in San Francisco the Americans seemed more curious than angry. We Chinese think that in this part of the country they dislike the Irishman more than us."

"So no real problems?"

"Mostly just ignorance, a few of my countrymen where insulted when the local boys tried to sell us rats to eat. But I thought it was just boyish pranks."

"So have you met any local people, made friends?"

"In my case, yes, there is a local family that invited several of us to attend Sunday church and supper with them. At first a lot of us went but most stopped. Their customs are just too strange. But I have continued and found the family very pleasant."

"But you are more unusual?" Jason asked as several other young men seemed to answer for their friend.

"I think that is true. Most of us just want to finish our contracts, take the money we have earned and go back to China to start new lives."

Jason sat thinking for a moment and then turned back to Sing. "Would that be true for most of the men here?"

"Pretty much. In fact, I expect most will leave as soon as the contract term is up."

"What about you?"

"Me, no, Charlie Sing likes America and has nothing to return to in China. No. I plan to save my money and try to open a business."

"Do you think Mr. Sampson will hire more Chinese when this group leaves?"

"That I don't know. On one hand, he is satisfied with the work we do and hates the white men's unions. But I also know some people pressure him to hire locals. I don't think he has decided yet."

With that, Jason spent another hour or so walking the room, gathering a few more of the worker's individual stories and then taking his leave found a carriage to take him back to the hotel. He was anxious to leave for Rockport as early as possible in the morning.

# CHAPTER 39

# ROCKPORT AGAIN

Jason left his room at dawn and, after a quick breakfast in the hotel, eagerly set off for the train station and what he hoped would be a quick return first to Boston and then north toward Rockport. His first reporting trip, because of the last-minute extension to North Adams, had been significantly longer than he would have liked, and he was anxious to return to the family's new home. Happily, the route was far less convoluted, because he was not making the diversion through Hartford and the train comfortable enough to get some work done as they traveled.

Trying to write in a moving stage coach had been impossible but in a train, something could actually be accomplished. As he traveled, he found himself wondering how long it would be before his friends in China would have such conveniences and then amusing himself, he suddenly realized that if he had the answer to that question, he'd be ready to write another report to Mr. Sage, the financer.

Then, looking down at his copy of Gladden's *Hub to the Hudson*, which covered the route of the train, he wondered if his writing career would ever see him producing something similar for future Chinese train travelers. For the next few minutes, he imagined himself doing a volume on travel between Shanghai and Beijing, a book that would include the more useful material writers like Gladden had included in his more formal guide-book, combined with the type of amusing commentary Sam had at the core of his *Innocents Abroad*. Would the two approaches meld well? More importantly, he reflected for a time as he stared out the window, would people pay for such a book?

Overall, as the train traveled somewhat nosily along, he felt especially gratified. Between the two very different stops, Hartford with its official Chinese educational mission and the very different story in North Adams, he felt certain he had very usable material. Even more exciting as he peered out the window was the realization that the first hints of the end of winter were slowly emerging. That alone was enough to cheer his spirits as he sat there impatiently wishing the train would move faster. He was terribly anxious to get home.

It took the rest of the day and an overnight in Boston before he finally started the trek north toward Salem and Rockport. By late afternoon, he was anxiously approaching his rented home, having taken a coach from Salem. As he rode, it felt as if he'd been gone for ages, though it had not really been that long. More exciting was that the last days of February had produced relatively pleasant weather, and he was enjoying the view in ways he'd not appreciated before.

He almost ran the last few blocks to the small rented house and opened the door expecting to see everyone there—Black Jade, the children, Old Zhu, maybe even the local boy who was studying Chinese with the family. The room, though, was completely deserted. Not a soul, though they could not have gone far. The fire was still burning and something was cooking in the pot hanging above the flames. He put his things down and walked outside again. Where could they be? he wondered.

For a moment he stood there without a clue. It was late in the afternoon, not all that long before sundown…he speculated and then with a hunch he started toward the shoreline up Bearskin, the little spit of land that stuck out into the sea. As he walked he took in the smell of the fishing boats that stood around him and within minutes, he reached the end.

His guess was correct. There they were; initially he spotted the children jumping among the rocks, rocks he distinctively remembered telling them not to play on, and then a second later, the three women—Black Jade, Old Zhu, and it looked to be Miriam. Old Zhu seemed to be wading in the water, perhaps looking for clams, while Black Jade and Miriam were standing next to something he did not initially recognize.

"Hello there!" he called out. "I see you've taken up painting."

Black Jade whirled around at the sound of his voice and then, carefully stepping across the very unevenly piled rocks, started toward him enthusiastically. When she actually ended up standing in front of him, of course she stopped short. Jason had long known she was not going to hug him in public, but that thought quickly faded as the two children, Mei-ling and William, arrived and embraced him with considerable strength that he could feel even through the thick winter clothing Black Jade had wrapped them in. Off to the side, Old Zhu watched carefully with an approving look in her eyes.

"Come, I want you to see what Miriam is teaching me," Black Jade said gently, taking his hand and leading him back to what Jason now realized were quite obviously painting easels.

"Welcome back, Mr. Brandt," Miriam offered with a warm smile.

"Pleased to be back Miriam." He waved back as he took in all the subtle brushstrokes Black Jade had applied to her canvas.

"Miriam tells me that this is the perfect spot to learn to paint. She is teaching me the Western style that she herself has studied. See that point over there to the right...I am trying to capture how it rises out of the ocean waves."

Jason studied the painting closely. It was just begun, but the hint of rocks and crashing waves was evident along the lower portion of the canvas.

"This is very impressive. I had no idea you wanted to learn to paint!" he exclaimed, looking back and forth between the canvas, the rocks and the ocean scene she was trying to capture.

"Neither did I, but Miriam has been painting for a long time and offered to teach me. But this is very simple of course, only my third day, really only since the weather improved a bit."

"And all this time, I thought you were just pining away for me...for me to get home like a dutiful husband," Jason said, laughing.

"Pining away, yes, absolutely, and learning to paint. A proper compromise, I should think."

"As always you are right, my wife."

"And so, tell us, all of us, how was your trip? Was it successful? Will Barlow like the material you gathered? I want to hear all about it."

"Oh, you certainly will," he said as he watched Black Jade and Miriam start to gather up the painting supplies as Old Zhu rounded up the children. The sun was setting, and the ocean's breeze was becoming especially cold again. Within ten minutes, the entire family arrived at their small rented cottage where Old Zhu's cooking emitted the most wonderful flavors from the cooking pot above the fireplace.

# CHAPTER 40

# PREPARING FOR THE LECTURE CIRCUIT

"I really could use a drink," Jason said as he dropped for the first time in days into the one chair he found particularly comfortable in the house his father had located for them.

To his surprise, Miriam, Black Jade, and even Old Zhu, whose English was apparently improving, all giggled at the same time.

"He doesn't know?" Miriam asked, smiling at Black Jade.

"I did not know till my father-in-law told me a few days ago."

"Don't know what?" Jason asked, looking around the room, really wishing he could have something to drink. The evening in North Adams had reminded him how good a glass of beer or whiskey could be at the right moment.

"Well, Jason," Miriam began, "it all started with a lady named Hannah Jumper and her hatchet. I guess that particular story did not make it all the way to Hong Kong."

"I guess not," Jason said, exhausted, as he listened to Miriam and casually watched Old Zhu struggle with the unfamiliar cooking space and dishes. For a second he wondered why the women had not packed a proper cooking wok and then realized the weight was probably prohibitive for such a long journey.

"But," he went on, "I am guessing the end of this story means that a weary traveler is not going to have a drink in my own home."

"No, Jason," his family's new redheaded teacher friend told him, laughing. "When I was a young lass, old Hanna and a bunch of her friends went around and destroyed all the liquor stores in Rockport. Seems the ladies, and my mom was one of them, were sick of you menfolk getting drunk all the time. Towns been dry ever since. It is quite the story. I have even seen the hatchet myself at one of my mom's friends' houses, but that's too many details for now. Welcome home. Your family's been anxious for your return."

At that Black Jade jumped up and walked Miriam and their little language student to the door. They spoke for a moment outside. Then Black Jade returned and, closing the door behind her, finally gave Jason the hug he'd been looking forward to since he'd arrived. Within minutes the entire family was sitting at the table eating as Old Zhu sat in the corner cutting the paper shapes she so enjoyed.

Over the next several days, Jason spent each day after the children were packed off to school writing up his trip to Hartford and North Adams, while Old Zhu and Black Jade busied themselves in the main house. Late afternoons were spent more and more frequently at the waterfront as Black Jade practiced her painting. She seemed especially interested in catching the light as the sun was setting over the coast. Jason, usually exhausted from his stuffy and to an extent cramped day in his writer's shed, enjoyed that part of the afternoon, which he generally spent sitting on one of the large granite boulders strewn across the area. That the weather was improving steadily as the early days of March arrived only made the time even more pleasant.

Within a week, his extended essay for Barlow was ready, copied, and sent off in multiple copies to his editor in Shanghai, and he began to think about how the material might be incorporated into a larger writing project when his father abruptly walked into the cottage one evening carrying a satchel.

"Good, I've caught you at home!"

"Where else would we be, Father?" Jason asked, looking closely at the old man, whose limp seemed a bit worse.

Black Jade for her part leaped out of her chair, took the reverend's satchel, and even more quickly placed a cup of hot tea into his hands as she ordered Jason to remove himself from the family's most comfortable seat.

"Where would you be? Well, rumor has it that the Mrs. is becoming quite the painter, thought you might still be out at Bearskin point."

"Father, you have heard about my painting? It is really a very humble effort," Black Jade said, sitting herself in a chair opposite her father-in-law.

"Humble or not, and from what I know of you, daughter in law, if you have taken it up, it's probably a serious effort." She smiled sweetly.

"The neighbors know all about it. Hell, I first heard about it from the woman who washes my clothes in Salem last week."

Both Jason and Black Jade looked at each other in amazement.

"What, you thought this was Boston, that no one would know your business? And it's not Shanghai either. People around here know everybody else's business."

"*Ye-ye*, what did you get us?" William yelled out, though it was obvious his older sister was just as curious. "What is in the bag? Something for us?"

"You two won't find out until I get a proper hug," the old man said, extending his arms to his grandchildren. Only William was really his own blood, but the reverend had extended his love to both of the children without reservation, Jason reflected with a satisfied sense. Though he also found himself wishing his father had been as affectionate when he was growing up in Hong Kong.

Once the children were satisfied with the taffy their grandfather had brought for them, the family settled down to talk. From his satchel, the reverend took out yet another package, this one carefully wrapped in oilskin.

"While you have been busy gallivanting around Connecticut and Massachusetts, I have made progress as well. What do you think?"

With that, the older man dramatically unfolded the oilskin and revealed very professionally printed flyers about Jason's upcoming talk.

A Salem Man in China
Frederick Townsend Ward,
The Man I Knew and the Struggle He Fought
By Jason Brandt
Of the *North China Daily News* and Rockport's Newest Resident
Thursday, March 20th, Rockport Lecture Hall
7:30 Free and Open to the Public

"Very well done, Father!" Black Jade proclaimed, taking one of the flyers into her hand and showing it to the children. Even Old Zhu studied the nicely designed flyer closely, though Jason was sure she did not have a clue about the Western lettering.

"So we already have a date even! Yes, and you only have a couple of weeks to get ready. Can you do it, son?"

"I guess I will have to, though I wish Sam had not told me about his first talk in California; he apparently froze up completely.

"You don't want to use him as your model anyway. Folks around here still talk about his lecture right here in Rockport a few years back…and it's not kindly. But don't worry, you are going to do just fine. More important though, have you requested those extra copies of *China Tales?* We will need you to sell some books. Your beautiful wife was right; this first effort should be free, a gift to your new neighbors…but it won't hurt if we can sell some books as well."

"I think so, at least the last I heard from Sam's agent, they were being sent, and that was before I even left for Hartford. We should be good to go."

"Well then, as your father and the man who will introduce you, I look forward to your talk. I never met Ward, but I have heard about him for years, and I am anxious to hear what you have to say."

"You had better be, since I am going to practice on everyone in this room right up to the evening of the talk!"

And with that, he raised a glass in a mock salute. "And we'd even toast this new enterprise with something worthwhile if you had not dropped us in the middle of the driest part of the land," Jason said, laughing.

"Oh right, sorry about that," his father said as the entire family laughed, even little William who quite obviously had no idea what was so funny.

# CHAPTER 41

# A PUBLIC SPEAKER

"I am not going out there." Jason knew he sounded like a fool, but only Black Jade could hear him whispering as he stared through the slightly parted curtains. The audience was huge. Indeed, it was far larger than he had expected for his debut lecture on Ward, a man he felt he should have known far better if he was to pull off this talk in front of no doubt the man's blood kin and perhaps scores of people who had known him before he left Salem to seek his fortune.

"You should be honored, my husband. That so many people have come so far to hear you speak. They say they even added an extra coach so many wanted to come from Salem."

"Yes, just wonderful…Well, at least we are not charging them, so they can't complain too much if I am terrible."

"But look to the back; it looks like Miriam is selling a lot of books, so this will help our purse as well. Renting the hall was not inexpensive."

Jason had forgotten that their new friend Miriam had volunteered to sell Jason's *China Tales*, copies of which had only arrived the evening before. Moreover, for the first time, as he focused through the slightly parted curtain, he had a sudden appreciation of his own father's speaking skills.

It had been years since he had heard the elder Brandt speak in public and then only in a language the older man spoke poorly to Chinese converts who'd never seemed all that interested. Now Reverend Brandt was in his element, speaking in his native tongue to an audience that was very excited to be in the rented hall for the afternoon. Maybe, Jason thought ruefully, he should have been the warm-up act for his father.

Then studying his father closer, he noticed the elderly reverend was starting to look nervously at the stage's side entrance. Clearly his father, after warming up the audience, was about to more formally introduce his son and wanted confirmation Jason was ready. Knowing he had little choice, Jason parted the curtain a bit more, enough so his father could see his face. The older man glanced toward him and then, looking relieved, turned back to the crowd and began a more formal introduction of his son, the well-known writer whom he was so proud of. For a second, as Jason stepped out on to the stage, he realized he had never heard his father say anything of that sort, that he was proud of him. It gave him the confidence he needed to walk to the center stage, shake the reverend's hand more firmly than ever before, and turn to the audience.

"First let me thank everyone here for the honor of your attendance. I sincerely hope I can live up to your expectations. My talk this evening of course is on Frederick Townsend Ward's career in China. I emphasize that because of course many of you here knew him far earlier and better, knew him long before he headed off to China."

With that, he glanced down to the first row that had, at Black Jade's suggestion, been reserved for the late Mr. Ward's kin who had arrived in large numbers. Some might have had doubts about the younger Frederick, but it was always nice to have a famous relative.

By the time he'd finished his preliminary comments, Jason had relaxed and even managed a passing thought that he'd avoided his friend Sam Clemens's original panic attack at his own first public talk. In that sense, he was already ahead of Mark Twain, an encouraging thought.

Within minutes Jason had covered the basic background he knew his audience needed to understand Ward's career, particulars about the Confucian Manchu government, the Taipings, the merchant community and of course Ward's own role fighting to defend Shanghai against the rebels with the rag tag band of mercenaries he'd put together. Over the previous weeks, Jason had worked hard to remember as much as he could of their actual conversations. As best he could remember, he'd spoken to Ward at least three times and had dinner with him once. Jason had mined what he could of those conversations to make his prepared remarks as interesting as possible. When he finished talking perhaps forty minutes later, he'd earned a solid round of applause and then asked for questions.

Over the next twenty minutes or so several men, one after another asked questions about the actual fighting, weapons and such which allowed them as well to ensure that everyone present understood they themselves were veterans of America's own civil war. Other men asked about the Western merchant treaty port community along the China coast and more general questions about the trade. It was obvious several were considering becoming more involved including the family of the young boy Black Jade was tutoring and who was sitting with his parents beaming with pleasure.

Then, after what Jason thought was his reasonably successful maiden lecture was drawing to conclusion, an older woman stood up near the side, balancing herself on a rough brown cane. That was something of a surprise in itself, because to that point no woman had uttered a word.

"Mr. Brandt, I am sure folks here are looking forward to the pies and sweet meats many of us have brought for the reception later. But if you don't mind, I do have one more little, so to speak, question." As she spoke, Jason glanced to the back of the room where many had already begun to gather and chat quietly.

"Not at all, ma'am, ask away."

"Well, Freddie was my nephew, and when he died his family was sent a package of things and among them was this." She stopped talking for a moment and started rummaging through a bag that stood at her feet. After a moment, she'd successfully retrieved whatever it was and held it high above her head so everyone could see.

To Jason's surprise, she was holding a single shoe, a tiny golden lotus shoe. He glanced over to Black Jade, who'd leaned forward in her own chair to see what was being displayed. As she did so, he saw that Old Zhu was whispering intensely into her ear, waiting for a translation of the question she'd suddenly become very interested in.

"When I first saw this thing," the older gray-haired New England woman started, "I assumed it was a child's shoe, but some of the menfolk who've been to China tell me that's wrong. It's for a grown woman, yet a shoe no grown woman could possibly fit in. Can you tell me about this 'foot-binding,' as I am told it's called?"

Jason was stunned, though he was not all that sure why. Still, foot binding was not a topic he'd expected to discuss or one the Chinese comfortably spoke about among themselves. As he thought about his response, he noticed a slight movement and noticed that both Black Jade and Old Zhu were subtly pulling their feet under the chairs beneath them.

"Well, ma'am, I am hardly an expert on that subject. It's not something most menfolk, and certainly not Western men like myself, know all that much about." He was stalling. Why should he be surprised by the question? He had himself wondered often about the custom.

"Well, young man, you must be in a position to know something of the practice. Your father tells us you have spent almost your entire life living with the Chinese. Surely a young fellow like yourself did not spend all his time among the menfolk." Her comment got a laugh and the attention of the group that had already left their seats and gathered around the food table in the back.

"Well, that is true, ma'am. I can tell you what I know. That contrary to what one often hears, not all women in China have bound feet. The Taipings about whom I have been speaking did not bind their daughters' feet, though I am not sure if that was part of their belief system or the fact that the Hakkas, a local Chinese group found in the south, never bound their daughters' feet either. And they made up the majority of the early followers of the Taiping Wang."

"But, young Mr. Brandt," she continued. Jason was beginning to get an idea of where Ward's own strong personality had sprung. "Why do the Chinese bind their daughters' feet? It looks painful and must make walking more difficult."

"Yes, I believe that is true," Jason began, glancing at his wife who was busily translating for Old Zhu even as she glanced back at Jason intensely.

"Frankly I don't know a lot about how the binding is originally accomplished, but I can tell you that there is opposition to the practice. I have even heard that some of the Manchu emperors opposed the practice and that among them it is rarer than with the Chinese."

"And the reason for the practice itself?" She was not going to be deterred, and her voice quite loud for a woman even a New England matron was attracting even more listeners.

"Well, I guess"—again he glanced subtly, he hoped, toward Black Jade—"I am told that a long time ago, it became the thought that it made women more attractive to the menfolk."

That comment aroused considerable controversy, and at least half the audience turned to their neighbors to discuss the propositions that binding the foot could be considered comparable to other forms of female beauty.

For a moment, Jason thought the moment had passed and that he should just thank everyone and try for one of the dessert items himself, but his questioner was having none of it.

"Mr. Brandt, you have given us a wonderful talk, and we have all appreciated it, but it is quite obvious I've hit upon a topic your wife might be better able to address. Can you invite her to the stage? I am sure we would all love to meet her. My young cousin Miriam tells me her English is wonderful." Was everyone in this region related? Jason wondered to himself before turning to Black Jade, who was looking very uncomfortable. This development was not anything any of them had expected.

Suddenly from his side, his father appeared, and passing him the old man walked up to Black Jade, whispered in her ear for a moment, and then taking her hand led her to the stage.

She stood there for a moment, looking very nervous and then with that determined look he had seen so often she turned to the audience.

"Let me first offer my apologies for my English. I am a very poor student of your language and unsure if you will be able to understand me."

"No problem," several people in the front row yelled out.

"Well then," she began hesitantly and then picking up speed, "Soon after I came to America, I met a teacher who told me that women in America should speak their minds, that they should let their voices be heard. Perhaps you know her. She died recently, but she was a great lady, a teacher called Emma Willard."

"Of course!" the older woman who had begun the conversation shouted out enthusiastically. "Mrs. Willard was known even here."

"Well, Mrs. Willard impressed me greatly. We have a saying in China that a teacher for a day is like a parent for a lifetime. I only had one day with Ms. Willard as we traveled through Troy and visited her school for young women. But. it was a great opportunity for me. And to her memory, for we are told she died earlier this winter, I am comfortable giving my thoughts on foot-binding, as you call it here.

"Let me just say, don't believe anything you hear from men, any man. I think foot-binding was invented by Chinese men to control Chinese women." Black Jade's bluntness surprised everyone in the audience, including Jason himself.

Taking a deep breath, Black Jade then dived into the topic. She spoke for at least twenty minutes about how the process was carried out during a young girl's youth by the older women of the family, about the pain and the belief constantly expressed that it would help find a suitable husband. Jason realized that the crowd at the back of the room had disappeared as she talked, as everyone returned to their seats, initially to keep munching on the desserts. But then even that soon stopped, as the crowd became completely silent listening to Black Jade's explanation and of the stories she told of how she'd heard of young women dying of festering infections during the process.

At no point did she speak personally, but Jason could tell she knew her listeners were trying secretively to look at her own feet as she spoke and, among those close enough, to see Old Zhu's feet as well.

As for the family's long-time servant, it was obvious that Old Zhu had understood just enough of the conversation to be extremely uncomfortable.

After a few more minutes, Black Jade seemed exhausted, and Jason, who stood near the side of the stage, watched his father step forward and gently touch Black Jade on the arm for a second before turning to the audience.

"That's it for now, folks. Let me and my family thank everyone for coming. It has been a wonderful afternoon. We expect to be able to offer more such talks in the future. Don't forget the food in the back, and of course, Miriam's still got more copies of *China Tales* for sale as well. Again thank you for coming."

With that, the old man turned back to his family. "You two did a wonderful job, but I suspect you will want to go now."

"Yes, thank you, Father. I am exhausted." Black Jade really did look spent. Jason took his wife's hand and left the hall, Old Zhu and the children just behind as they walked the few blocks in the still-cold air toward their rented home. Within minutes, they were inside enjoying the warmth of the still-burning embers in the fireplace.

# CHAPTER 42

# A NEW TEAM FORMED

"I don't know what to say my husband. I ruined your talk," Black Jade blurted out as soon as they were seated with two cups of warm tea in their hands, for the weather had turned much colder during the lecture and their short walk home.

"Not at all. As soon as you began speaking, I became your rapt audience and could not get enough of your thoughts. No, you were wonderful! I am surprised we did not think of working together from the beginning."

"Are you sure, my husband? It was not a problem? Your father whispered that I should go up to the stage, that it would help greatly."

"And he was absolutely right. My father knows these people and audiences a lot better than either of us do. No, I think we were better as a team than I could ever have been alone."

At that moment, the door opened and his father, who'd lagged behind a bit chatting, entered, more animated than Jason had ever seen before. So much so that he wondered if his father was still carrying that small flask his son knew he frequently had hidden in his coat pocket.

"My children, you were both excellent! A perfect complement to each other. I am surprised that we did not anticipate that at first."

"You are sure, Father?" Black Jade asked, jumping up to put another warm cup of tea into her father-in-law's cold, reddened hands.

"Absolutely. I stood around with the crowd. Wait, I gathered some cakes for everyone..."

With that, the two children who'd been playing in the corner jumped up and surrounded him, taking several dessert items each as their grandfather kept talking.

"It was obvious the combination worked perfectly. The men liked Jason's political talk, his discussion of the war, and the trade, but the women were fascinated by Black Jade's contributions. Women's rights are quite the topic these days. How often can one hear a frank Chinese woman talk in English about such topics? Never! And I might add in such excellent English!"

Black Jade beamed. She had worked hard on her English, worked at it since long before they had departed China, and though she said nothing, her father-in-law's praise was deeply appreciated.

For the next hour or so, the adults sat discussing how best to promote the lecture series they had in mind. His father was full of ideas, especially on using the many contacts he'd made among various New England congregations, raising money for the church's efforts in China. Moreover, he reminded them, almost every town had some sort of lecture venue that could be used, either freestanding or rented out by the churches.

While his father talked, Jason noticed that the older man's energy was waning faster than usual. Certainly having come over that morning from Salem had been demanding. And the talk itself draining, for his father had been active at every moment of the effort, from introducing his son to helping Miriam sell the books. As Jason looked closer, he saw that his father was starting to look older than he'd ever seen him.

"But, Father, enough excitement for the day," Black Jade said. "Old Zhu has prepared a sleeping space for you here, right in front of the warmth of the fire."

For a moment Jason thought his father might protest, claim he wanted to return to Salem on the last carriage. Then it became clear he too knew he needed to stay the night. That he was simply too old and the weather too demanding to return to the small home he himself rented in Salem, using income from the rental that arrived monthly from the home his family owned in Boston.

Once that was settled, the family began to settle in for the evening, waiting to eat a supper Old Zhu had been busily making while the children played and the adults dreamed of the possibilities of a new and more lucrative speaking tour.

"I have been thinking," the senior Brandt said just after dinner and as he started preparing himself for a night's sleep. "Folks in Boston, especially around Harvard College, would probably be interested in such a talk. We might even be able to advertise it in that newspaper the students just founded. Advertising rates will probably be cheap. Heard the administration was upset the students even began such an effort. My cousin sent me a copy. I think it's called the *Magenta* or something. I will bring one over next time I come by. It's at my cottage."

The *Magenta*, Jason thought to himself. So the Harvard students had started a newspaper. Good for them! One heard enough good things about Harvard students that Jason guessed they would have the talent to make it a worthwhile effort. And the idea of speaking at Harvard certainly sounded attractive.

He might have grown up in Hong Kong but even he'd heard of that famous American university and, despite his several trips to Boston, had still not made it across the Charles River to see Harvard. Yes, he thought to himself, having he and Black Jade give a talk on campus might be a good idea indeed.

# CHAPTER 43

# HARVARD

Jason wondered if he'd ever been that young a reporter. Then he reminded himself that they were not real reporters, at least not yet. No, they were a couple of nervous Harvard College undergraduates.

"We really can't tell you how much we appreciate your giving us so much of your valuable time," the youngest of the two, a fellow from Connecticut, blurted out.

"Not at all. I am impressed. I did not even know Harvard had a student newspaper, and I tend to take note of such things."

The two looked at each other and laughed.

"You were right about that, sir, at least until just recently. Our newspaper, we call it the *Magenta*, at least for now, was only just founded. Our first issue did not appear until a few months ago, last January."

"The twenty-fourth," his colleague offered enthusiastically.

"Right...and I can tell you the administration was none too happy about it."

"Why?" Jason asked, his own enthusiasm aroused, curious about the paper, which he'd already been given a copy of as the young men had arrived at his father's family's home just across the Charles from Cambridge.

There was, after all, plenty of time before this evening's talk. Black Jade and the rest of the family were all upstairs with his father after a long walk along the Charles River.

In fact, the entire family had only just returned to the house, which luckily was available. He knew his father was not happy about losing the rent due to his tenant's departure, but it made Jason's family's stay easier. After all, Rockport was too far north to have been a convenient base from which to take up the many speaking engagements that had poured in from the smaller towns around Boston since their first talk in late March.

There certainly had been plenty of invitations, for word of the new and unique public lecture team had spread fast. Still, the funds they'd earned thus far would not have gone far if they'd had to pay for lodging closer to the city as well. So much so that that Jason, well aware of how helpful his grandparents' inheritance had been for his father, had offered to pay the reverend rent, but the old man would have none of it. No family member, the retired clergyman had insisted, was going to pay rent. Besides, the building, his father reminded him, would after all be his own inheritance one day.

"So what made you decide to cover tonight's lecture?" Jason asked, turning his thoughts back to the eager young undergraduates who sat just opposite him in the house's front parlor. The furnishings were not to Jason's taste. A bit too elegant, he thought to himself, but taking on his more usual role as interviewer was certainly comfortable enough.

"Well, sir, my aunt's an old friend of Mrs. Pennington, the widow who invited you and your wife to give a talk. Her husband used to teach at Harvard College. Quite the radical for an older lady she is."

"Why do you say that?"

"David, I think you have probably said too much. You should let Mr. Brandt draw his own conclusions. They will meet soon enough. Your talk's at three, is it not, sir?" the somewhat older of the two students asked, putting his hand gently on his enthusiastic friend's shoulder.

"Yes, three. I have found that three on a Sunday afternoon attracts the best crowd. Well then, if that is not a good subject, can you tell me how you yourself became interested in a topic on China?" Jason asked. "Is your family in the trade?"

"Not at all, sir," the young man David said. "My family lives in Hartford, and there is an entire school, at least some sort of community of Chinese living there—have you heard about them, sir?"

Jason nodded, waiting for the young man to go on.

"In truth, sir, I don't know much. They arrived after I moved here to attend the university, but my younger brother says they are a bunch of young Chinese fellows not much younger than we are, and living with local families. My little brother's been telling me all about them. That sort of piqued my interest in China. And so when I heard you and the missus were going to speak, we set up this interview, and of course, we'll be attending the lecture as well."

"Well, thank you. I appreciate your helping me get a sense of your visit. So are there additional questions I can answer?" Jason said, taking sip of the tea Old Zhu had silently brought into the room for him and his two guests.

They talked for a while and then Black Jade appeared at the door of the parlor, subtlety trying to get his attention.

"Excuse me," Jason said, getting up and walking into the hallway with his wife, who was standing there alone looking anxious.

"Is there something wrong?"

"Probably not, but your father says he is not coming."

"Why is that a problem? He has heard us giving the same talk for weeks. I am sure he is just sick of us."

"Perhaps, my husband. But we both know he was looking forward to this talk—to hearing his children welcomed at the illustrious Harvard College."

"So what did he say?"

"Just that he was more tired than he expected, that the walk along the Charles was a bit much for him and that he wanted to rest."

"I suppose we should just take him at his word. There will be other opportunities for him to feel such pride. Remember that note from Yung Wing about Yale wanting to invite us? He can go there with us when the date is settled."

"I am sure you are right, but I want Old Zhu to stay here with him. She is not comfortable anyway. You know how tense she gets when the audience asks questions about women that she thinks are inappropriate."

"I thought she did not understand half of what was said?"

"She doesn't, but she always insists I go over everything they asked and how I responded afterward."

"Really, how come I did not know that?" Jason asked, surprised.

"Isn't it obvious? She does not think you should be exposed to such female issues either."

"OK...I guess that is reasonable." Jason laughed. "So it is agreed. Old Zhu stays here with him. Fine...so," he said, pulling his watch from his pocket, "we should probably go. If she is staying here, the children might as well, don't you think?"

"That is already resolved. Mrs. Browning's children, from next store, showed up while you were in the parlor. Both of ours went over to their home for the afternoon. We don't need to pick them up until after we get back."

"OK, let's get going then."

"Well, that was a very illuminating lecture," began the older woman, Mrs. Pennington, who had invited them. "I am sure both the menfolk and the ladies appreciated the doubly insightful presentation you have given us. I know I was very interested in what Mrs. Brandt said about the lives of Chinese women, especially about secondary wives, and my husband tells me Mr. Brandt's comments about the trade and recent war were fascinating." There was a general murmur of agreement as she spoke.

There was as well, though, something about her tone that told Jason that more was coming true, their dual presentation, was not all that different from the talk they had given three days before in Framingham even if the beautiful decorations in the Cambridge church's lecture hall, were considerably more attractive than any room they had heretofore spoken in. He was not soon disappointed.

"But what my friends and I would really like to know is what the Mrs. Brandt thinks of the life of women here in the United States. We are not allowed to even attend the very college, Harvard that so many of our husbands, fathers, and brothers attended. Can you comment on that, Mrs. Brandt?"

Jason turned to his wife to whom the question was addressed. She had become enormously more confident since that first talk in Rockport almost six weeks before. But now he noticed a hesitancy he'd not seen recently. Indeed, it quite surprised him. During the last two weeks, Black Jade had become quite blunt on the role of women in China, often denouncing Confucian family practices he'd had no idea she felt so strongly about. In fact, he often wondered if she were speaking more from personal experience or from what she had learned among the iconoclastic Taipings.

"Mrs. Pennington, first let me say," she began, choosing her words very carefully and expressing herself with that slightly

English tone she'd picked up from her friend Aouda on the Pacific voyage and that she still retained.

"Let me say how honored we are that your community in Cambridge, alongside a university so well-known I'd heard of it even in Shanghai, invited us to speak. We hope to learn as much as we teach during our visit. Nevertheless, let me also be honest with you. I only arrived in your country a few months ago, and much of the time has been spent waiting for the weather to improve, so I have not really learned very much yet."

"But surely you have gathered some impressions. I am told you arrived some six months ago."

"Well, that is certainly true, though it is very little and no doubt full of mistaken impressions. I can tell you that the situation here is very different from China. That from my perspective the women here seem enormously more equal to men than I am used to. Yes, I understand women are not equal in the way some speak of it. Nevertheless, for an outsider, it is much more confusing.

"But I learned a lot in the few hours I had with Mrs. Emma Willard at the Troy Female Seminary, the woman I spoke of earlier and perhaps even more, because of our greater time together from her former student Olivia Slocum Sage, the wife of the famous financier. And what I learned was that the issue is not whether men and women have different rights in America or in my own homeland but whether those rights are equal in themselves."

With that it was obvious Black Jade's stand had pleased Mrs. Pennington, who looked entirely satisfied. Their hostess then turned to survey the audience for any last-minute questioners. As she did so, Jason noticed that Old Zhu had entered the hall, looking quite exhausted and breathless.

For a moment he wondered how she had even found the hall; they'd not given her the address, and her English was still so limited. Then suddenly Jason realized something was wrong. Something very serious must have forced their Chinese servant to set out apparently alone across a city she knew nothing about, without enough language to even navigate!

Even as he stood up, he saw that Black Jade, from her vantage point, had seen Old Zhu enter even sooner than he had. She immediately left the stage and walked to the older woman, who was in truth more his wife's companion than servant. The two began a rapid-fire conversation in the Shanghai dialect Jason was too far away to hear. A second later though, she returned to his side.

"We have to leave. I'm going outside to find a carriage. Please give our thanks and meet me outside in five minutes."

"But what has happened? Is one of the children…"

"No, it's your father, but I am not sure what. Just say goodbye to the audience and meet me outside."

# CHAPTER 44

# FATHER

Minutes later, he exited the church after having made his quick good-byes. He'd stayed just long enough to be polite, without having to tell people something urgent required his attendance at home. He had no idea what the problem was and thought explanations might delay him further.

"Hurry," Black Jade said as he climbed into the horse cab she had only just managed to flag down. Old Zhu was already inside.

"So what do we know?"

"Your father's fallen into a very deep sleep," Black Jade said quietly.

"What does that mean? What exactly did you see?" he asked Old Zhu, switching to the Shanghai dialect the older woman had grown up with.

For the next few minutes, Old Zhu explained that when she'd brought the reverend lunch, she noticed that he was sleeping very deeply, not even rousing when she'd accidentally dropped the platter near his bed.

"So he was breathing when you left?"

She nodded, looking tearful. Then after a moment, she explained that she'd stopped to inform Mrs. Browning before she'd set off to find them. The neighbor then promised to look in on the reverend before sending Old Zhu off with a flyer she'd had about the upcoming talk just across the river.

The distance from Boston to Cambridge had seemed short enough only a couple of hours before, but now, as they found themselves waiting at the river for another ferry to arrive, Jason began to wonder how serious the situation was with his father. For a moment, he distracted himself, trying to remember what he'd heard of the recent legislative discussion of building a bridge across the river between Boston and Cambridge. The issue had come up in the context of a general conversation about railroad development in the United States. However, all Jason could remember was that the idea was more speculation than plan. No agreement had been arrived at and certainly nothing that would speed their way back to his father's home just across the Charles.

When they finally arrived, the couple found Dr. Myrick, a physician who lived a few blocks away, just exiting the building. A few seconds later and they would have altogether missed him.

"Dr. Myrick, Jason Brandt. We met a few weeks ago, when my son had the flu," Jason blurted out as he ran to meet the man.

"Ah yes, Mr. Brandt. Well, I assume you know why I was summoned, sir?"

"Well, only in part, Doctor. I was told my father was ill..."

"Then I hate to be the one to have to inform you, but I am afraid the gentleman is gone, looks to have passed in his sleep—a very gentle way to go I must say. And I am sorry for your loss." The doctor stood there in the street, clearly trying to look sympathetic while wishing to be off.

Jason stood there stunned, not knowing what to say. "But surely, Doctor, he was not that old. What could have happened? Can you tell me anything more?"

"I really can't, son. Sometimes the Lord just takes people in the Lord's good time, and from what I know of your father, knew him a bit, he certainly lived a full life. Serving the Lord in China and all. Mr. Brandt, you should probably go to your family. I can see your wife there at the steps. Mrs. Browning told me your children were still at her home and know nothing. You will want to be dealing with that. In a day or so, stop by my office and we can talk more if you like."

With that, the older man touched Jason's shoulder a bit and then walked off hurriedly toward his own home, the sounds of his footsteps quickly blending in with the sounds of horse hooves, which surrounded them.

Jason slowly walked back toward the house, realizing that Doctor Myrick was right. Black Jade, who had entered their home as Jason had gone off to catch up with the physician, had obviously gone to the older man's room and then quickly returned downstairs. The look on her face confirmed the doctor's report.

"Come inside, my husband," Black Jade said as she gently took his hand and led him into the building.

# CHAPTER 45

# MAKING NEW PLANS

He sat reflecting on the porch as scores of horse carts went by and the rays of New England's emerging spring warmed his face. It was hard to imagine, Jason thought, that it had been almost two weeks since his father died. It seemed like he'd only just arrived, just begun the effort to develop an adult relationship with his father a few weeks before. Though in truth, Jason thought to himself, it had actually been months since they had arrived in the dead of winter. And he was now, only months out from Shanghai, sitting not in a rented home in Rockport but, for the moment at least, in the home he'd just inherited on the riverfront just opposite Cambridge on the Charles.

From within the house, he could hear the sounds of the children talking with Old Zhu and realized he'd not quite noticed before that English was more and more often becoming their language of choice. Old Zhu was obviously struggling with the new challenge. The children had been brought up to speak both English and Chinese, especially the dialect of Shanghai, of course, but now after so many months in the

United States, Jason could see that their language habits were already changing.

Still, he thought to himself, it was probably understandable and positive. Good for the children and even for Old Zhu, who needed to learn as much English as she could if she were to function here in Massachusetts. She had told him so herself after what was apparently the trauma of trying to find the auditorium they had been speaking at when the reverend died.

Jason listened for a few more minutes to the conversation and vaguely wondered where Black Jade was, for her voice was not among those. She could be within the house. But then he realized he was only stalling. His father's burial had been a demanding effort, and the number of visitors who'd stopped by was impressive. Jason had had no idea how well thought of his father was, but now those tasks were complete. Even the lawyer had come and gone, and the paperwork was already being drawn up to give him the title to the house, which Jason was beginning to understand was worth considerably more than even his father had led him to believe.

Thus, the question he and Black Jade had been quietly discussing the previous evening returned. What should they do next? Return to Rockport? Rent the home for income? Sell it for an investment and eventual return to China? Settle down here in Boston? None of these issues had even been in his thoughts a few weeks before, and now decisions had to be made.

The previous evening, after the final estimates had come in from the lawyer who had agreed to help with any potential sale, he and Black Jade had talked for hours. Neither had any intention of returning to China immediately, but neither did they have any interest in remaining permanently in the United States. At some point, they would be returning home, but when that might be was not at all clear. Deciding what to do with the house was linked to that decision.

"But how can you even consider selling a home your father and his family owned?" she'd asked him several times the previous evening.

"But," he'd tried to explain, "I have no memory of this building and from what I know, even my father lived here for only a few years in his childhood. So that should not be an issue if we decide to sell it."

His wife looked doubtful. She came from a society with a lot deeper roots in land than anything even Jason could really understand. If he had any real link to a plot of land, it was the home they had had built and then just sold in Shanghai. Indeed, even as they had traveled across the Pacific and overland on the transcontinental railroad, Jason had often fantasized about buying back the property when they returned. No, in his mind, Shanghai, where he'd built his adult life, was his home—not Boston or even Hong Kong where he'd spent his childhood.

But that was not the issue at hand. Staring for a few moments more at the horse traffic and the sailing boats just beyond on the Charles River, Jason got up and went into the home and up the stairs.

"So, my husband, have you decided?" Black Jade asked him as he entered the room.

"I think so. At least at the moment, it seems best to stay in Rockport, to sell this place and invest the money for our return. I don't know how long it will be, but I would love to let the money grow into a sum we can use to rebuild in Shanghai or even buy the old house back. What do you think?"

"Do you think Mr. Sage would help you invest the money if we did sell this house?" she asked, always the more practical of the two.

"I don't know why not; he already makes suggestions for my earnings from the railroad reports. Why don't I write and tell him what we are thinking of doing?" Then looking more closely, he realized she was dressing for an outing. "So where are you going?"

"Do you remember Mrs. Pennington from the talk last month?"

"How could I forget? That is probably along with our first, the one lecture I will never forget, especially waiting for that ferry on the way back here after Old Zhu found us."

"Well, she has invited me to a meeting of some of her lady friends to discuss women's rights."

"That sounds interesting. Can I go? It might give me some ideas for more articles."

Black Jade smiled, crossed the small room, and gave him a warm peck on his lips. "No. This meeting I am told is just for the ladies." With that, she picked up her parasol, for the early spring's sunlight could be quite powerful, and walked down the stairs, leaving Jason quite alone and feeling lonely.

Then with Black Jade gone and the children nowhere about, Jason entered the downstairs study he'd been using partly as an office and took out a pen. Within a few minutes, he'd written three letters—one to Mr. Sage, reporting on the most recent Chinese railroad-intelligence information Prosper had send him, coupled with the material he'd gathered earlier from a few other China-coast-based friends he'd queried soon after they had settled in the United States. All in all, he thought it was a reasonable update on what he had initially submitted and hoped Mr. Sage would be pleased. In the months since he'd arrived, he'd had a much-better chance to follow the well-known financier's activities in the local papers, especially so since they had had ready access to the Boston newspapers.

At the end of his report and in a more informal section, he'd written of his father's death and the decision to sell the home. And, of course, the question that had prompted him to spend the afternoon on the report in the first place—the question of how such monies might be invested if the house went for the amount he'd been told it might bring.

That task finished he wrote Sam a letter, describing his impressions after more than a dozen public talks and he and Black Jade's evolution into a dual presentation. He knew Sam already knew, because the older writer had written him a hasty note just weeks ago, asking how it was going and reporting that an audience member at one of his own recent talks had mentioned he'd seen the two speakers recently who'd been lecturing on China and liked it.

The man had forgotten the couple's name, but Clemens, of course, realized immediately whom he'd been talking about. That letter had arrived only a day or so after the reverend died and Jason had waited until then to write back, about the lectures and, of course, his father. Jason knew Sam would be interested in the progress of the talks and more than a little disappointed that he'd never met Jason's father. Sam or Mark Twain as the public knew him, was a student of the human personality and had already heard enough from Jason that he'd indicated an interest in meeting the older man. Now, of course, that would never happen.

The third letter was to the lawyer who had offered to help sell the house. The attorney had been quite certain that the home, well located as it was, would easily sell and at a good price. In fact, he had already told Jason that he knew of several potential buyers with the cash available to buy the home outright. Jason explained he and his wife had decided to take the man up on his offer and asked for the effort to begin and a bit of advice on how much time they might have to gather the more personal private possessions from the house before any potential sale.

Clearly, the small house they were renting in Rockport could not hold any more furnishings, and given their long-term desire to return to China, there was little point transporting such bulky items across the oceans. Still Jason thought perhaps some of the home's furnishings could be stored until he and Black Jade made a final decision.

His letters written, folded and prepared for posting, Jason returned to the porch to watch the traffic pass in front of the house. The views here were very different from what he had grown up watching in Hong Kong and Shanghai; indeed Boston was very different from Rockport as well, and the sights had fascinated him ever since they had first arrived. Besides, Jason thought to himself, he might not have this fine view much longer.

The following weeks went by quickly. The early spring turned into full-blown summer, and work on the house progressed well. He'd found a place to store items they would make decisions on later, and several potential buyers had already looked over the property. Meanwhile Black Jade, and on occasion even Old Zhu, had been spending more and more time being received as guests in many of the homes of relatively prominent Boston and Cambridge matrons. Apparently, Jason gathered, though he was almost never invited that the chance to chat with the two women from China, particularly one who had become so fluent in English, was very popular these days.

Jason himself was busy enough. His writing kept him quite occupied, and both children had mastered English well enough that they were easily able to fit in with the local children despite their unusual background and appearance. There were, after all, few Chinese girls like Mei-ling in Boston and even fewer children with the mixed heritage William carried with him.

That the children had encountered few problems was an enormous relief to him since arriving in Boston. Rockport had been smaller, and their role in the community had already been established when they had arrived, and the friendship with Miriam was enormously helpful. Nevertheless, Boston was something quite different, and Jason had worried, worried as much as Black Jade, though he'd never quite admitted it to her. But they had both been wrong. At least among the children directly near the house, Mei-ling and William had found friends who accepted their differences readily. He also knew, of course, that Chinese were still a rarity in the Eastern United States. Thus far, at least as far as Jason knew, the East Coast had not experienced the levels of anti-Chinese sentiment they'd seen and heard about in California. Still he sometimes wondered if it would always go as smoothly.

# CHAPTER 46

# A WARNING FROM A FRIEND

The lawyer Mr. Shane had been right. Within weeks buyers had been found, buyers well off enough to purchase the house with cash. Meanwhile he and Black Jade were awaiting a check from the new owner's bank and starting to plan their return to Rockport. Things really did seem to be going smoothly, Jason thought to himself as he sat in the unusually comfortable wicker chair he'd positioned on the porch, casually watching the slow-meandering way the local postman moved down the street toward the house.

It had become something of a ritual for him of late—spending his days writing in the parlor and then sitting on the porch awaiting the mail. There was almost always something interesting in the pile the fellow, Jason thought his name was Andrew, dropped off.

Jason especially liked getting feedback from readers, from those who occasionally wrote from China and more often lately Americans who had seen his more and more frequent pieces in East Coast newspapers. From China usually came the more positive comments, sometimes from readers who claimed to have met him at some point in Hong Kong or Shanghai. However, the letters from the United States were quite different. More often than not, they were more negative, and those from the West Coast particularly so.

Overall, while he seemed to have developed something of a following for his usual topic, China and things Chinese, most of those who actually wrote, seemed to feel obligated to correct his supposedly obvious pro-Chinese biases. Some even claimed to have spent a few weeks in China or working alongside Chinese in America and wanted Jason to understand the true, usually sinister nature of the people from the Middle Kingdom. Some days the mail was so heavy that Jason found himself creating three piles, one for those from China, usually positive, and those from the American West Coast, with their vicious certainty. The East Coast letters genuinely from Boston or New York tended to be less easy to categorize. Once that was done, he'd often pull some of the best or at least most interesting to share with Black Jade, though he never showed her those that included threats.

But today was different. He'd been very anxious about the mail lately. He knew he was about to have the money from the house, and Russell Sage who usually was so prompt in correspondence had been quiet lately. That in Jason's experience was somewhat unusual. Jason's last report had been sent off weeks before. Yet he'd heard nothing from Sage, either about his update on Chinese railroad development activities or the request for advice on investing the house money.

It seemed like forever but finally, Andrew showed up—at least Jason thought it was Andrew. They had chatted far too many times to ask him again what his name was.

"So, Young Mr. Brandt, I hear you and the misses will be going back to Rockport soon, or will it be China again what with the house money?" the fellow asked brightly as he dug into his satchel. "Got quite a pile for you…I must say you writers create a lot of work for us postal delivery fellows, not that I am complaining, mind you. It's important to have work."

Jason laughed but said nothing as a larger-than-usual pile of mail was handed to him and the man walked off toward Jason's neighbor. There was just enough wind, he could not remember if Boston was windier than Hong Kong or Shanghai, to avoid opening the letters on the porch. Gathering up the glass he'd had sitting next to him, Jason returned to the parlor. The house was very quiet around him. As he went in, he glanced at one of the envelopes, particularly fine paper addressed to Black Jade but curiously without a return address. Probably another tea invitation, he thought to himself as he laid it on the table near the door. He was fairly certain she would be back soon.

Ten minutes later, he'd sorted but not opened the letters. As usual, many appeared from readers, though there was at least one that looked to be from his editor, Mr. Barlow in Shanghai—probably another article request. Casually Jason put it aside. The note he'd been hoping from the bank about the cash for the house was not there yet, but then he'd been told it would be later in the week anyway. Nor was there anything from Prosper or Sam, both of whose return address on a letter always improved his mood enormously.

However, Jason spied at least one letter he'd been looking for—a note from Russell Sage, finally! Jason had been particularly interested in hearing from the famous entrepreneur with whom Jason and Black Jade had so accidentally developed, if not a friendship at least something of a relationship. And the money Sage paid him for gathering information on Chinese railroad development came in handy even if Sage had convinced him to allow the man to invest part of it for him. Eagerly, Jason sliced open the envelope with a letter opener. The note was relatively short. Sage did not waste anything least of all words. The older man was quite pleased with the report, informing Jason he had shown it around to a few of his investment partners who had shown equal interest. The note ended with a mention of the money invested and a small check.

There was nothing else. Indeed, the note was shorter than Sage usually wrote, and to his disappointment, Jason found himself wondering if Sage had forgotten the primary question he'd been asked. How the significantly more money that was coming his way should be invested?

It had been Jason's hope that the older and very experienced Sage would offer him advice. Jason was sure that however well his writings did, especially his books over the years, the money from the house would most certainly be the only real money ever likely to come his way. He wanted to invest it properly. Besides, neither he nor Black Jade had given up the idea of returning to China one day, perhaps even buying back the home they had once loved so much. That Jason knew, considering how much Shanghai was growing would require considerably more than he'd sold it for.

An hour later, his disappointment forgotten, he'd gone through the mail, had lunch with the children, listened to tales of their day, and chatted casually with Old Zhu about her efforts to improve her language. She was certainly better than she'd been when they'd arrived in Rockport, even after those months traveling, but not much. As far as Jason could tell, her understanding was better than her ability to actually produce English. Of course, they rarely used anything other than the Shanghai dialect when they were together. Besides, it offered a chance to expose the children more frequently to Chinese, which they were increasingly less interested in than the English they used every day in the streets and with the tutor Jason had hired to work with them since they'd been withdrawn from school in Rockport.

Around four, Black Jade, to Jason's pleasure, returned from her tea. She looked tired but still as always extraordinarily beautiful, as beautiful, he thought as that day eons before when he'd first seen her half drown alongside the river in southern China, as beautiful as when he'd first seen her with his friend Wu—whom he suddenly remembered. It was another reason he was discouraged by the lack of a letter from his friend Prosper Giquel. Wu was working for him at the dockyard in Fuzhou, and Jason had been hoping for an update from him as well, which usually arrived alongside Giquel's messages.

"Husband," his wife said, turning her full attention on him. "And your day, I trust you wrote enough to keep us eating for another month?" she said, laughing. Ever the practical one, he thought to himself, offering her a light hug…She rarely wanted more if the children were near. "Where is the mail? Did I get something from Aouda? She owes me a letter. I don't want to forget about her before we have a chance to see her again in London."

"You're still convinced that we should go home via Europe?" he asked, already knowing that while he had often contemplated returning as they had arrived, across the continent, maybe seeing more of the American West as they traveled, Black Jade was already planning a quite different return.

"Absolutely, and I have even more ideas. Some I even discussed with friends at tea today. Besides, didn't you tell me your friend Prosper was likely to return to Paris soon? I am not going home without seeing London and Paris. The ladies at lunch said that it would be more expensive to return that way, but we really should do it anyway."

For a moment he could tell she wanted to add something else; clearly another idea, altogether different, was forming in her mind, but he knew her well enough to know that she would not share it until she was more certain. Then, her thoughts turning elsewhere, "What is this?" she asked, picking up the clearly unmarked expensive envelope he'd put aside for her.

"No idea. It came with the mail today, certainly someone with the cash to buy expensive paper but forgetful enough not to bother with a return address."

As he spoke, she slit open the envelope with the silver letter opener that was always left on the small table near the door.

Jason watched her reading it closely and then quizzically, sitting down obviously rereading what from Jason's vantage point looked to be quite short. There was clearly something there that puzzled her.

"Husband, we need to talk. Where are the children?"

"I think they are both next door. What's going on...what's in that letter?" She handed it to her husband and gestured for him to sit in the chair opposite.

My Dear Friend:

I am sorry to be writing in such an awkward fashion. Your husband has, as you may know, written my husband about a financial matter. For reasons you might guess, he has asked me to respond to you in this manner. He knows I care about you and your beautiful family, and of course, we all have hopes that you will one day accomplish your dreams for the young girls of your native land.

For now, though, it has been suggested that the money that is coming your way should not be placed in a bank but be better placed in a strong box in the form of gold coins.

Hoping this is helpful and that we all weather well the challenges of the future.

Your Devoted Friend,

O

He read it, and then, like his wife, reread it more slowly.

"Olivia?" he asked, knowing the answer already.

"Olivia," his wife confirmed. "She knows something, or of course, Mr. Sage knows something...When do you expect the money to arrive from the new owner?"

Jason thought for a second. "I think I was told later this week," knowing what she was thinking.

"Tomorrow morning go to the bank, check to see if the draft has arrived, and buy the gold."

He nodded. "So what can be happening..." he started to speculate as his reporter's brain began to stir.

"Don't even think it," she blurted out. "Mr. Sage knows a great deal about the finances of this country, but even he could be wrong. Right now, we need to protect our family. Do we have a—what did she say?—don't recognize the word, 'strong box'?"

"It is like a locked box...but I am not sure. I might have seen something in the attic when we were working up there."

"I think you should check now," she said. "And, my husband, I am serious this is not something for you to look for a story in. We need to keep this to ourselves, Olivia, or rather Mr. Sage knows something and is trying to protect us. We need to respect that."

"You are right. Well, let me go up to the attic," he said as he started out the room and then noticed the book she had put down near the letter...

"What is the book?" he asked curiously.

"Just something; this afternoon's host lent me. I will show you later. Now go look for that strong box and I will see if Old Zhu needs any help with dinner. We can talk more about this tonight after the children are in bed."

# CHAPTER 47

# NEW PLANS

"Why are you and Mommy so quiet lately?" Mei-ling asked him as they were sitting down at the table to have dinner one evening later that summer. Jason looked closely at his nine-year-old daughter, really stepdaughter, though he almost never thought of her that way.

"Quiet? What makes you say that? I don't think we have been quiet," glancing over at his wife who was putting down the book she was reading and moving to the table.

"But you have been, for months, both of you. Are you missing *yeye?*"

"Grandpa!" little William yelled out suddenly. "Grandpa!" His yell startled Jason. He did not realize William was even listening. The boy had himself only just entered the room, but his translation was not surprising. The youngest of the family, he had been the most enthusiastic about exclusively using English. Indeed while Mei-ling's English—thanks to everyone's hard work in Shanghai before they left home and the months since—was even more impressive than her mother's efforts, little William was far and away the star of the family. Sometimes

357

Jason thought William sounded more like a natural-born American than he did. In fact, he was sure of it.

"Well," he began, turning back toward his daughter, the daughter who was increasingly becoming as beautiful as her mother. "I do miss him. I did not see him after he came home, but when we followed last winter, it did give me a chance to be with him more."

His daughter seemed satisfied and turned toward Old Zhu, who was offering her something to eat. A moment later, their old servant and his daughter were chatting away in the Shanghai dialect as if they never left. Indeed, sometimes they spoke so quickly even, he who had learned the northern dialect much later had at times difficulties following them.

"Are you still reading that book, Mommy? Is that also making you sad?" Willie asked, turning to his mother as he took a portion of the mashed potatoes. It had not been easy, but Old Zhu was getting quite good at producing some of the local cuisine. She'd even told Jason one day that she was thinking of trying the famous clam chowder, though she'd admitted the smell of milk made her somewhat sick.

"Well, little one, it is a sad story but also very interesting."

"Tell us about it," Mei-ling asked. "It looks like you are almost done."

"It is about this country, or at least parts of it. Not so much around here but a story of slavery in the southern part of America."

Jason had not read it, but *Uncle Tom's Cabin* was certainly famous enough. Indeed, he'd been planning to read it once his wife finished it.

"Well, perhaps I should read it to you one day, perhaps at night, but I want to finish it before deciding. It is a very sad story so far."

Both children looked disappointed. He knew they were both interested in hearing stories about America. Black Jade's tales from China had long satisfied them well enough. Nevertheless, he also knew they were increasingly immersed in their lives here in America and wanted to fit in more with the friends they had already made in Rockport and more recently in Boston.

But Jason knew as well that it was not just the famous Mrs. Stowe's story that had made their household tense of late. Both of them had been busy emptying the house in anticipation of their return to Rockport coming up within days, and that sense of dread that had descended on them weeks before with the arrival of the letter from Olivia Slokum Sage. Indeed, only the day before, the ever-cautious Olivia had written yet another letter, again discreetly asking if they had obtained the strong box, she'd written of previously.

Something was up. Clearly Mrs. Sage knew, at least enough from her husband, to try to protect her friends, and Jason was grateful. He'd promised Black Jade not to investigate, to put aside his reporter's curiosity for the moment and just take advantage of their fortunate link to the very well connected Mr. Sage. Still, Jason sometimes wished he could ask Sam Clemens what he thought. Sam was as interested in financial matters as literary. Happily, though, Sam had already departed for England and there would be no temptation to discuss it in person, a temptation Jason knew would be difficult to resist had they actually accepted one of Sam's frequent invitations to visit Hartford again.

Thinking again about that visit, Jason picked up Sam's most recent letter. It had spoken not only of his enthusiasm for another European adventure but also of the progress on the new house he and Livia were building...and, Jason realized, excitement about their new neighbor—for Sam had written that the well-known writer Mrs. Stowe lived right next door. Mrs. Stowe, Jason suddenly realized—he'd not focused on that casual reference earlier. Putting down his fork for a moment, he reached over to the book that sat next to Black Jade.

"Mrs. Stowe, Harriet Beecher Stowe. I just realized something. Sam's moving next door to the author."

"The famous Mark Twain lives next door to her?" Black Jade asked enthusiastically.

"This is one of those moments when I am reminded that I might look American but grew up in China."

"What do you mean, husband?"

"I mean Sam simply assumed I knew what he meant; now I do. Sam, or Mark Twain, is not the famous writer on his new block; it is his new neighbor Mrs. Stowe. That is what he meant to tell me."

"So we could meet her? I would very much like to do that."

"When Sam gets back from England, it should not be a problem; he has been anxious to have us see the new house. You know how excited they were about the floor plans when we visited. I should think there would be something a lot more real when we can visit next."

With that the family resumed their dinner, and Black Jade switched back into the Shanghai dialect while questioning little Willie about his day. She was increasingly determined to reinforce the language with the children, particularly her youngest son. Both of them, Jason and Black Jade, were more familiar with the dialects of the south but had determined that their future lay in the north, and besides Old Zhu was always there to lend a hand if there were problems.

As for Jason himself, half his mind was on watching his family talk and the other wondering about where his next story for the Shanghai paper would come from.

# CHAPTER 48

# THE COLLAPSE

He did not have a long time to wait for the next story. The morning had begun calmly enough. Well, perhaps not that calm, as Black Jade and Old Zhu moved like a flash around the house, supervising the final packing of the wagon team they had engaged to take their things, along with some of his mother's family's possessions, back to Rockport. It was not that much, but Jason had already arranged to have some of it stored in Salem as the family continued on to their rented cottage. Quietly Jason thought to himself, with the gold he'd secretly packed in among some of the trunks and his own saddlebags, for he had planned to ride alongside the wagon team on the horse he'd engaged, the family could certainly afford a bit more.

By noon, little Will and Mei-ling had said their good-byes and they'd even been given a fine send-off by several of the local ladies who'd been kind enough to offer his family, and especially Black Jade, the hospitality of their homes. Overall, though the send-off was hardly that emotional, Rockport was not that far from Boston, and everyone expected them to return often despite the move. To himself Jason thought about how future good-byes might be different when he and his family eventually made the decision to return to Shanghai. But that moment, he was sure, was quite some time off.

When the last good-byes were said, and the keys now officially in the hands of the house's new owners, Jason settled down on his ride, listening to his family's several conversations within the carriage's interior. The day was quiet enough that the children's voices, considerably louder than either Black Jade's or Old Zhu's, rang out, both in English and the Shanghai dialect, from the rented carriage's interior. Suddenly he heard what sounded like a gunshot ring out over the usual roadside din.

"Did you hear that?" Jason asked, pulling the horse up parallel to the carriage's driver.

"Did, sir," the fellow said, with an accent Jason thought sounded as if the man had just stepped off the boat from Dublin. "Was it a gunshot? Can't say I have heard that many at home, and I missed your civil war here?"

"Well, that is two of us, but I have been around war enough to know it was almost certainly a pistol fired somewhere nearby."

With that, and no further gunfire, Jason let his horse fall back a bit, as it was easier to look within the carriage. For a second his eyes met Black Jade's, who was looking at him questioningly. He shrugged, raising his hands openly, gesturing he knew nothing more, and turned back to the road. Crossing the Charles had taken much of the morning, but now the road north toward Salem was relatively open, and they were making good time.

Nevertheless, Jason thought, as he watched the homes and a few businesses that lined the road, that something did seem different. As the minutes wore on, he began to notice more and more men leaving the buildings and standing in the streets among themselves, talking intensely. Clearly, something was going on, though Jason had no idea what to think until they passed one group of men, relatively successful businessmen from the look of their clothing, talking louder. Jason could not really hear what they were saying, but one name did stand out, something like Cooke. At least that is what he thought he heard.

"Husband!" Black Jade yelled from the carriage, her arm extended to attract his attention. "I think we should find an inn for lunch soon."

"I will start watching for something suitable. It should not be hard," he said as he pulled alongside the carriage driver.

"Heard the Madame, sir. There is a place just ahead. We can let the horses rest, get fed, and have ourselves a nice meal. Owned by a feller from Belfast, came here when the potato crop went bad, known him for years."

"That sounds fine...lead on," Jason said, himself hungry and hoping that they might be able to get some news as well. Roadside inns were usually full of travelers with the news of the day.

⚓

The crash of glass startled all of them as they opened the door to the inn. Black Jade instantly pulled little Willie who'd run ahead of them back, while Old Zhu did the same thing with his sister.

"No problem," the red-faced fellow in his mid-fifties called out as he stood there in a cooking gown, pulling the door open wider and gesturing them in. "Sean, is that you back there?"

"It certainly is, Shamus," their driver called out from behind Jason, "brought you a fine family that needs a meal."

Jason stepped forward and walked into the building, studying the room and, in his peripheral vision, his wife's eyes; she was clearly waiting for a sign from him to proceed.

A second later, he gestured everyone into the inn's eating space, a relatively large room crowded with travelers, mostly men and a few families near the rear.

"I tell you that is impossible," one fellow to their right yelled out above the din of the room. Indeed, he seemed very agitated. Near his feet, a cleaning lady was cleaning up. Jason guessed it was the origin of the breaking glass they'd heard as they entered.

"Don't pay no mind to them...a couple of local businessmen who often argue during their lunch. Folks around here are used to them. Actually nice fellows if you get to know them. So can I show the family to a table?" the Irish owner offered, looking more closely now at Jason's party, one that was considerably different than most of the locals who visited.

"Yes, if you please," Black Jade said, disarming the man. A beautiful woman regardless of her background always had powers Jason could hardly even begin to appreciate. And it worked here as well.

"Excellent, ma'am. So where are you folks from?" the innkeeper asked.

"Just now from Boston, returning to Rockport," Black Jade said in her ever-improving English. Indeed his wife had already begun to focus her considerable language skills on learning the French she'd begun in Shanghai.

"Rockport, eh?" the fellow said. It was obvious he had expected a different answer from the Chinese woman standing in front of him. Nevertheless, he said no more, quietly showing them to their seats and explaining the foods available.

"I tell you that is absurd!" the voice rang out above the din, yet another outburst from the table the owner had mentioned a moment before.

"I just read it in the paper this morning, the general, I mean the president, just dined at Cooke's place a few days ago."

"Grant? The man's a fool!" his colleague yelled back. "He might have known something of war but finances nothing... and I tell you it does not matter what the papers say. My nephew works with the telegraph company. The lines have been ablaze all morning...Cooke's company went down."

"Mommy, can I have some of that cake for dessert?" little Will asked, pointing toward the bar.

"Perhaps, but be quiet for a moment," Black Jade said, silencing their younger son as her eyes darted back and forth across the room, straining to hear the conversation across the space and back toward Jason. Then he realized what she was actually looking at, not him but the saddlebags he'd brought into the inn with him.

She knew what they contained. Most of their gold-coin stash, and then leaning over, she whispered in Jason's ear, "Are they talking about the same banker Mr. Sage spoke of on the way to Troy?"

"I think so. Can this be what Olivia was trying to warn us about?" he whispered.

"You folks decide what you want?" the owner asked as he walked up to them again. "Saw your little ones eyeing the cake...wife just made it this morning."

"The lamb, potatoes, and chowder seem fine...and we will decide on the cake later. Thank you," Jason said. "But about those men..."

"Don't pay them any mind; they're almost finished anyway."

"No, it's not a problem. I was just wondering if you knew what they are carrying on so much about."

"Not really. I have been working all morning...something about a big banking firm failing...That Cooke guy I think... they's been several folks in here all morning talking of it. Not sure what it means...Takes a while for real news to make it up here from the city."

"Would you like a beer with your lunch...? Got lemonade as well."

Jason glanced at Black Jade and then back. "I'd like a beer, and could we also have a large pitcher of lemonade?"

"Coming right up..."

A moment later, the two men, still arguing, left the inn, and the room became somewhat quieter. Indeed, within minutes, most of those dining finished up and Jason and his little group had most of the room to themselves. Behind the bar, the owner sat chatting with his countryman, their driver Sean, in words Jason had no understanding of.

"I think we should leave. I don't know what is happening. But I would rather be in Rockport than here. I feel exposed like this with everything we have on that carriage," she whispered in Cantonese, the language they'd begun their relationship with. It surprised him. She was so gifted with languages, even more so than he was, that he almost never knew what was going to come out of her mouth. But that she chose the language of both their childhoods gave him a sense of her level of discomfort.

"What about the cake?"

"Have them wrap up several pieces. We can have them as a snack later. Do you think we can make it to Rockport by tonight?"

"It's too far, but I think we could make Salem and just take rooms till tomorrow morning. It does not get dark for quite a few hours. I'll ask the driver; he might be able to go longer. He'd be ready to hire the carriage out sooner that way."

"Then do it, husband. I have a very bad feeling. I want to be home, or at least as much at home as we can be here."

They had pushed their luck against the darkening sky and the man Sean's resistance to traveling as the day grew into evening, but there was still a small amount of twilight left as they pulled into the inn they'd eaten at a few times when visiting Salem.

While Old Zhu and Black Jade retired to their rooms with the children, ordering food to be served there later, Sean left the building to attend to his horse team and Jason, after seeing his family safely upstairs and the bags with them, went out into the streets hoping to find more news. He'd agreed to meet Black Jade later in the hotel parlor and was not at all surprised to find her there upon his return looking anxious even as she continued to read the book he thought was a French grammar on her lap.

"What did you find out?" she asked him in English as soon as she saw him approaching.

"It's what we thought. The famous financier, banker railroad investor J. Cooke's bank seems to have failed. I heard it in a tavern down the street. The staff from the telegraph office next door was in there. Apparently several other banks in Philadelphia had closed their doors as well."

"So Mr. Sage knew?" she asked, again in Cantonese.

"I think we can assume that," Jason said, continuing the conversation as she had begun it. "And I assume he'd wanted to warn us but could not take a chance and so devised that scheme with his wife."

"What does it mean to us?"

"I really don't know. I suppose it's good we don't have any money in those banks, but the ones around here were open today. I did ask that...but what happens next, I have no idea."

"Let's leave at first light. I want to be back in Rockport while this thing works itself out." Then she added, "Do you think Mr. Sage was hurt financially. Olivia had been hoping she could convince him to help sponsor the school for young ladies we were talking about in Shanghai."

"I have no idea…but if Sage was aware enough to help protect our assets, I should think he did the same for his own."

"You are probably right…at least I hope so. I would like to think all the time I have put into learning Western languages has been put to good use in plans for the school; maybe we could name it after Mrs. Willard even or perhaps Olivia's husband, Mr. Sage."

"It is going to be a while before we know if the seminary, I think of it as your future Shanghai Female Seminary, is going to happen. But from what I know of Mr. Sage, I am pretty sure he would not want anyone to think he was generous enough to fund such a socially useful enterprise."

It was the first smile he'd seen on his wife's face since early morning, and he was glad of it.

# CHAPTER 49

# SALEM

Jason woke at dawn, for a moment unsure where he was. The unfamiliar room did not help get him oriented. After a second as his brain cleared, he remembered he was in the hotel in Salem, Black Jade alongside him still sleeping soundly and the adjourning door, apparently left somewhat ajar partly open to the room where Old Zhu and the children slept. If he listened closely, he could even hear the quiet snores of their devoted family servant.

Studying his wife, it was apparent she was in a very deep sleep, unlikely to wake anytime soon. As quietly as he could, hoping not to wake her, he slipped from the bed, closed the door to the next room, and slowly dressed. There was just enough light coming in from the lowered drapes to dress and carry his boots out the door. Then in the sofa chairs that sat just opposite their second-floor room, he put on his boots and descended the stairs. Though the family had eaten there once with his father the previous winter, he had no memory of the hotel's floor plan, and it took a while to find the breakfast room.

As he entered there was only one other customer, a middle-aged man intently reading a newspaper at the other side of the room.

"Morning, sir," the voice rang out just behind him. "Coffee?"

"Yes, thank you."

"And will you be having breakfast, sir," the young waiter, obviously yet another new arrival from Ireland, asked him.

"No thank you. My family is upstairs. I think I will wait till they are ready to eat."

"That will be fine, sir. Saw your family as they came in last night…sort of dark, but I helped Sean set up the horses for the night. Fine fellow Sean."

"Well, he certainly seems to know a lot of people. That much I have seen." Jason laughed.

"Us Irish tend to know each other…bit safer, don't you know…and it's always good to talk of home sometimes. Aren't you the departed Reverend Brandt's son?"

"Yes, he was my father."

"Nice fellow, sometimes a bit stiff but still good man. Sorry about your loss."

"I appreciate that."

"Actually, I only recognized you because I went to that talk you and the misses gave last spring. Traveled all the way over to Rockport to listen."

"Well, I am flattered; do you have a special interest in China?"

"Not really, only went because of that other guy, heard he was really interesting a while back, but that was before I got here."

"Other guy…Not sure what you mean."

"You know that Chinaman who spoke a couple of years ago. It was just before I got here, but some of my buddies said it was interesting. So when I heard you were talking on the same topic, I went over there."

"And I hope our little presentation did not disappoint."

"Not at all. China sounds really different. Ireland is different from America, but China sounds way different, like to see the place one day. They say what with the new railroad and steam passenger ships, it is a lot easier, don't even have to walk like that Italian guy."

"Marco Polo?"

"Right, that guy…had a cousin once who'd read his book… talked about that guy's visit to China a lot. So is it true. It's a lot easier to visit?"

"Well, it is not cheap, but the trip these days is a lot faster, and the canal's open in Egypt, so it is easier in both directions."

"That Suez thing, right?"

"Yes, and with the railroad finished…you can do it either way these days. You should see China…but if you don't mind, can you tell me more about that Chinese speaker who lectured here?"

"Don't know much. Like I said, I missed his talk…my friends told me about it. Said it was really interesting. Chinese guy but with great English. Seemed to know a lot about America also… lots of good stories…"

"Do you remember his name?" Jason asked, realizing that his father had also mentioned the fellow, though he was not sure his father had seen the talk either. The elder Brandt had often traveled outside of Salem.

"No idea…Something Chinese I suppose, only thing else I remember was one of my buddies said the talk was fascinating, the guy quite impressive a speaker but sort of full of himself if you get my meaning."

"I think I do. Anything else? I am quite curious."

"Sorry...it was a while back, and as I said, I was not there myself. More coffee?"

"Yes, thanks," Jason said as the fellow walked off, leaving Jason to try to dredge up his father's comment. Then he remembered a question one of the people in the Rockport talk had asked. It had been prefaced by a comment about something she heard from another speaker. At the time, Jason had assumed she'd been referring to the usual sort of talk returning missionaries often gave, the sort his father had often given. Now as he played back that evening...it had after all been his first public talk and his mind less relaxed than it might otherwise have been. But yes, she'd mentioned the speaker was himself Chinese? Now there was perhaps another story.

For the next few minutes, Jason sat there trying to figure out how he could trace the fellow down until he was distracted by the slamming down of a coffee cup across the room. It was the businessman still reading his paper with a furious energy, an energy that reminded Jason of the previous day's news. What was happening? he wondered to himself. Then his mind flashed back to the saddlebags. If things were going to get ugly, those bags might be the only thing between him and his family starving.

Then after a moment, he remembered another reason Black Jade probably wanted to get home. He knew, though he did not think she wanted him to know, that she had buried a stash of the money that had been left from selling their home in Shanghai in the floor of the cottage.

# CHAPTER 50
# A SURPRISE VISITOR

Years later when Jason reflected back on that particular New England fall, his mind always seem to link the world of isolated Rockport closing in around itself as storms both financial and climatic bore in on them. In retrospect, despite his father's death, the summer of 1873 had seemed a relatively positive time. The family had smoothly made the transition to the United States, begun their careers as public speakers, gained the not-insignificant inheritance from his father, and started to make friends. And all that had been complemented by their pleasure at seeing New England's beauty in the early spring and summer months. Indeed, by the first of September, despite Mrs. Sage's obscure warning, life did seem to be going well for the Brandt family. And little Willie and Mei-ling had themselves made enough friends to help them forget to some extent those they left behind. But then everything had changed.

"Was there mail today?" Black Jade asked Jason as they sat together on the Rockport granite shoreline rocks, watching the children and Old Zhu look for clams.

"Yes, but not what you were hoping for. We have to be realistic. How are people going to have the energy to organize a public entertainment, and that is what we are, while their menfolk are losing their jobs, and the women can't even make pin money from sewing."

"So are we too, to live on what we have saved?" Black Jade asked. She had always been more concerned about financial security than he was.

"Well, we are a lot better off than most, and thanks to Mr. Sage and your friendship with his wife."

"But even she is worried; you saw that last letter. Olivia still hopes we can start that female seminary when we get back. But even she said funding is less sure than it might have been."

"Well, we're not ready to go back yet anyway, are we?"

"No, I have still too much to learn. My English is still very weak. Moreover, I want to improve my French. I wish Prosper had taught me more. Even Old Zhu thinks we would attract more students if we could offer the daughters of the Chinese merchants of Shanghai that language as well."

"And your future painting classes, my wife, are you not planning to master that as well, the Western painting style before we return?"

"It would be helpful." She smiled, putting her fingers to his lips.

"Look, they have done well. See how Billy's arm droops carrying that bucket. We will dine nicely tonight and without buying food. You know, you really don't have to worry so much; we have enough money for now."

"I will stop worrying when you start bringing in money again. For now, enjoy your clams!"

With that, he got up, ran through the rock-covered sand, and took the obviously heavy bucket from his youngest child.

⊷ ⊶

Weeks later the situation had not changed much, but a routine had set in. Jason working on various story ideas, the kids back under their friend Miriam's tutelage at the Rockport schoolhouse, and during the late afternoons, before the cold New England wind set in, Jason would sit on the rocks, watching Black Jade with her easel trying to capture the beauty of Rockport. At least the situation did not change much until one day in the late fall.

"Curious guest you have there," one of the locals commented as Black Jade and Jason walked back toward their rented cottage.

"Excuse me?" Jason said, but a gust of wind drowned him out and the fellow moved on without even noticing Jason's response. A minute later, they had their answer.

"You really should train your servants to be more polite," rang out a voice just as they turned the corner.

"Here I am a fellow countryman and your Shanghai T'ai t'ai servant makes me sit out here in the cold waiting for your return. I am sure the master would have something to say about that!"

Jason stood there dumbfounded. There on his small porch was a twenty-something Chinese man in full mandarin garb whittling on a piece of wood. From behind him, he saw Old Zhu crack the door with a hard look and then a welcoming glance.

"Can I assume I am addressing the famous writer Jason Brandt, though I doubt I could have guessed wrong?"

Jason did not know what to say. The man's English was wonderfully developed and his clothing so surprising, he could for the moment only stare.

"And you are?" Black Jade asked, using an officious tone he thought she'd picked up more from their shipboard companion Fogg than his Indian companion and her friend Aouda.

"Who am I? Now that is a question worthy of the Sage. What would you say if I told you I was a missionary from China to enlighten the heathens?"

"A missionary? Right...So what denomination are you?" Jason said, laughing as he realized the very fellow he'd wanted to meet had shown up on his doorstep.

"Well, it's not official yet, but I have been thinking I might announce my presence to the Americans as the first Confucian Missionary to Gold Mountain, sort of returning the favor your father offered in China. Am I right, that your father was a missionary among the Guangdong people?"

"My father is dead, but, yes, he was a missionary, but a Confucian missionary, now that is an interesting idea," Jason said, his mind spinning over the possibilities.

"Who are you really?" Black Jade asked him pointedly in Cantonese.

When he hesitated, she switched to the language of Shanghai and then with a linguistic talent that always amazed Jason into the dialect of Nanjing, which he clearly did understand better.

"As you have guessed, I am not from the South. My people are from Shandong. And my name"—he stood up straighter, clearly getting a better sense of how formable Jason's wife could be—"and my name is Wong Chin Foo."

"And you are not a Confucian missionary to America," Black Jade said definitively. "There is no such thing."

"True, but maybe there could be..." He was starting to get defensive and then reversing himself, "But wait, like your husband I am a journalist, at least trying to be one." With that, he dug into his satchel and proudly presented a piece on the Chinese of Cuba; it was in manuscript form. He handed it to Jason. "I am hoping you would look it over."

Jason stared down at the document with curiosity. "And you are also a public speaker on Chinese topics, are you not?"—though why he even bothered to get the confirmation, Jason was unsure.

"Exactly, so you have heard of me?" he said, switching back into English. "And your children, a boy and a girl, are beautiful," though he had had only a passing glimpse of the children who had run past him into the cottage.

"Yes, thank you. We have indeed heard of your talks. I was hoping to meet you one day. We are just sitting down for dinner; we have clams and plenty."

"Thank you very much. I have not eaten today. The opportunities to earn my living speaking have lessened as I am sure you already know."

With that Jason beckoned him into their small cottage, while sensing the angry stares of not one but both of the women, Black Jade and Old Zhu, he shared his life with. Neither woman was nearly as curious and at least twice as suspicious of their guest as Jason was.

⇥⇤

"So why do you think I should write an article about you?" Jason asked as the dinner slowly ended. For most of it, Jason's family and their visitor had exchanged stories of their arrival in America. Wong, not unlike Yung Wing whom Wong apparently knew of, had been brought to America by missionaries. He had even returned to China for a time and only just returned to the United States.

"You should write an article about me because it would be good for both of us," his guest said matter-of-factly, pulling out a wad of tobacco and pulling off a portion to chew.

His combination of Chinese and American habits intrigued Jason. To the far side of the room Jason watched in his peripheral vision Old Zhu and Black Jade putting the children to bed and whispering quickly among themselves. He wondered for a second if they were trying to exclude him or their guest from understanding them. It had already been established that his knowledge of the Shanghai dialect was minimal.

"I am serious. I know what you write about, have read most of your articles, even many of those you wrote before you left China. In short, I am exactly the sort of curiosity you often investigate in your stories."

"OK, granted, you are right. But why are you doing me a favor? Why do you want it done?"

"Isn't it obvious? I earn my living giving talks. Rather as you and your beautiful wife do."

Again, form the corner of his vision, Jason spotted Black Jade; she was not flattered.

"And the more publicity I can win, the easier it is for me to schedule talks, fill my purse, and keep my stomach full. That is not why I came here. I came because you are not using your talent and position properly."

"I am not using my talents properly?" Jason asked, startled by the rebuke. "And how is that?"

"That is a much bigger issue and why I really came to see you. Nevertheless, let us talk more in the morning. For now, let me simply thank you and your family for being so gracious. I will put my sleeping mat, if that is acceptable, near your fire and rest."

Black Jade had already reluctantly invited him to stay, though she had contradicted Jason's offer that the guest sleep in his writing studio in the next building. As far as Jason could tell, the young man was lucky. Had Old Zhu been making the decisions Jason was sure Mr. Wong would have spent the night shivering on the rocks that over looked Rockport's little spit out into the sea.

# CHAPTER 51

# A NEW CHALLENGE

"You are trying to make trouble for my family!" Black Jade burst out with irritation. They had spent most of the morning after the children were sent off to school listening to Wong's frustration with America.

"Not at all, what I am saying is that the Americans are ignoring their own basic documents, their own declaration that all men are created equal by treating Chinese differently, keeping us from voting, from becoming citizens. They fought to free the black people and treat us as if we are not human! You can do something about that!"

"How could I have such a role or want one?" Jason asked. "I am merely a journalist far from home."

"You are far more than that. You may think you are from China, but your white face and writings give you a power and influence I can never have. And you know important people, that writer Twain you mentioned last night."

"So what is it you think my family should be doing?" Black Jade asked, warming slightly even as Old Zhu working silently in the background clearly was not.

"Your family knows China, and people will listen to your husband. He should do more than write about Chinese students and laborers. Hartford and North Adams—yes, I have read all your writings. You should be helping Americans understand the Chinese, to know we are as human as the Irish and blacks whom they so often despise but consider as men. Men who do not eat rats for lunch. And now, that it is even more important than ever."

"Why now?" Jason asked, not completely against Wong's proposal but unsure where it might lead.

"Because the whites are even more unhappy with the Chinese now that there are fewer jobs. They allowed us to build their railroads, us and the Irish, but now that's finished, and there is no work and the anger against our presence is growing. In the west, you have been there recently I believe, they hate us even more."

"We passed through California on the way here, and yes, we did see what you speak of, especially in California."

"So what exactly do you want from us?" Black Jade pointedly asked, again her defenses about her family raised considerably.

"For now only that you inform yourselves more on what is happening here. I can give you names of people you should interview; men like Mr. Hoar and Mr. Sumner...interview them and then just write about the larger story of Chinese in America. I ask only that you take a larger view than you have been."

"What you say makes sense. If not whether I should take a more public role but simply on writing more on the larger question of how the Chinese are treated here in America, the bigger story but somewhat like I wrote about those Chinese boys in North Adams."

"Yes, exactly. And then there are the ladies," he said, looking directly at Black Jade. "I hesitated to mention it before the children left, but look at this." From his satchel, the young man pulled out another pile of papers, this time a carefully folded newspaper, and handed it not to Jason but to Black Jade while he himself went to warm his hands over the fire Old Zhu had just stirred back to life.

Jason leaned over to read over his wife's shoulder. It was a page from the *San Francisco Chronicle* talking about the rescue of a number of Chinese women who had been brought to the city to serve as prostitutes.

"You were involved with this?" Black Jade asked, warming to their guest a bit more. For a second, her attitude reminded him of how slowly she had finally taken to their friend Wu so long before in China.

"There, see my name is listed there," He leaned over pointing his finger at part of the article. "And I wrote the original letter that was smuggled out and got Mr. Gibson involved."

After reading the piece slowly, and a least twice, Black Jade glanced up at Old Zhu who was watching intently and then handed the note to Jason who read it again before handing it back to Wong. The young man very carefully folded it and replaced it in his satchel.

"Well, Mr. Wong, I think..." Jason started glancing at his wife who clearly approved, "why don't we spend the morning in my writing study. I will interview you and hopefully we can help each other, a newspaper story for me and something that will help win you a few more speaking engagements."

"But not near here!" Black Jade burst out. "My family needs to eat, and we earn money the same way."

"Yes, I promise to start looking for engagements far away."

"Will you go back West?'

"No, that is not possible right now. But that is a story for our formal interview."

Hours later. After Wong had eaten an early supper with them and departed, Jason returned from writing up his notes of the interview.

"What do you think my husband?"

"His story is amazing; I am anxious to write the article itself. Turns out he can't return to San Francisco because the Tong brothel owners blame him for the loss of their girls, and he has a price on his head in China."

"What! In China? Why?"

"Well, he claims he tried to start a rebellion against the emperor."

"Some sort of late Taiping?"

"It was all a bit vague but he clearly cannot go back."

"Where does he go now?"

"I don't know, back toward New York I think and then maybe Washington D.C. He seems interested in learning more about the efforts to exclude Chinese from becoming American citizens. I know he wants to become one. He was clear about that. He reminded me a bit of that supervisor in North Adams, the one who said he had decided to build a life in America. In any case, he has enough money to get started."

"And how do you know how much money he has?'

"He told me, and I saw inside his purse when I lent him more."

"You lent him money!"

"I sort of had to. I am sure he will pay us back. But his business agent stole all the money he had made over the last few months. He barely made it to us, assuming we would help."

With that, she turned away and walked out the door briskly mumbling something about looking to see if the children were returning home. It was obvious his wife was not pleased, even before he looked across the room at Old Zhu who was pretending not to be listening.

If the next day or so was a bit chillier than usual in the house, the cold winds that swept over Rockport as the fall edged toward winter was only part of the problem. Black Jade was still unhappy with her husband's loan of cash to their visitor. Happily, though the afternoon mail resolved most of the tensions.

"Is there anything from Aouda or Olivia? No, but there is some interesting stuff, Barlow liked the last piece I sent home about the problems with railroad stocks, says his investor readers where very interested in the economic news here and I have even got another check." He held it up, knowing it would relieve her frequent worry about their family's finances." And a note from Wong Chin Foo. He must have mailed it right after he left."

"And what did our new 'friend' the Qing bandit, tong enemy, and Confucian missionary to America have to say?"

Jason had still not figured out what she really thought of the man. On one hand, she did admire him to an extent. She appreciated his efforts on behalf of the Chinese women he'd help escape the brothels in San Francisco and after all, as a former Taiping herself, it was hard to challenge the man for his opposition to the Manchus. Jason knew his wife was ambivalent, while her companion and servant Old Zhu had no such qualms. For her, Wong was simply trouble.

"It is a list of politicians mostly from the New England, a lot of old style abolitionists who are against those who would exclude Chinese from immigrating and denying those already here citizenship. And then another even longer list, mostly of fellows from the West committed to doing so."

"And what does he want of you?

"Just to consider interviewing them, maybe going to Washington, or at least starting here with some of those who are local and there are several. But there is also something even more interesting."

"So you tease me! What is there?"

"What you were hoping for, an invitation to visit Sam and Livia for Christmas at the new house in Hartford."

"For Christmas…and will his neighbor be there, Mrs. Stowe? I really want to meet her."

"Sam knows that and it says right here he already invited his famous neighbor and she knows of your interest in her book."

"When is Christmas, how much time do we have to pre-pare," Her eyes were already scouring the room her thoughts on packing.

# CHAPTER 52

# AT THE TWAINS

"So George, you old Scoundrel, I know you have an opinion on what our young guest has been saying. Spit it out man." Twain, beckoned with his cigar even as Livia his wife appeared somewhat disapproving.

Jason's family had arrived by coach a bit more than an hour before, and were only just finishing up dinner in the downstairs dining room with at least half a dozen other guests.

"I mean it, the pile of cigar ashes dropping dramatically into a nearby ash tray. Can't say I remember anything ever holding old George's tongue" Twain gestured dramatically toward his Negro servant. "So what do you think of Jason's talk of how Americans treat our Chinese guests here in, what do they call it Gold Mountain?"

"Well, Mr. Twain" George began "can't says as I find it all that bad that the white folks have found people they likes less than my people." For a while I thought the Irish might have a crack at that, but no, it looks like the China folks have won the derby."

"That's George for you," Twain said laughing, he always sees the practical side of any issue." And you Mrs. Stowe, you have never been reticent to offer your opinions on how poorly otherwise God-fearing folks treat others.

At Twain's question, Jason felt Black Jade sit up next to him. She had been acutely aware that Mrs. Stowe was among the guests but the older woman, had arrived during the dinner from her own home only a few yards away and had sat quietly during most of the meal as the men, mostly writers and other local celebrities spoke.

Mrs. Stowe laughed a heartier laugh than Jason would have expected from her appearance.

"No, Samuel, you know well enough I have too often had my say about man's inhumanity to man."

"Mrs. Stowe certainly has, at least according to our late lamented president!" Twain jumped in. "Jason, do you know what President Lincoln said to our guest when they met before that scoundrel Booth killed him?"

"No, I guess not?" Jason said, catching a glimpse of the children running up and down the magnificent staircase.

"You really have been living in China. Sometimes a fellow can forget that listening to you. You sound so Boston," Twain added.

"He sounds just as native in my own tongue," Black Jade piped in, "but what did Mr. Lincoln say to Mrs. Stowe?"

"Go ahead Harriet tell them the story." Twain said with a flourish as Kate the Irish maid ran over with an ashtray barely catching the wad of glowing embers.

"No Samuel, you go ahead and tell the story."

"But I was not there" Cried the famous writer and orator.

"All the better for the telling of it" Stowe laughed.

"Well, if you put it that way, Folks say Honest Abe leaned in on our guest and said, "So you're the little lady who started the whole war! Now that is influence for you. What more can an author want!"

Jason looked at the older woman more closely. "And what did you say, Madame?"

"Well, at the time it was a rather funny evening. But the truth is, my little tale about Uncle Tom's Cabin created a lot of pain before people came to understand some of its truths about humanity and proper Christian thinking."

"So Jason, tell us more about your Chinese visitor, this Wong fellow—a Confucian missionary to America. I love it! The man's got gall, I will say that for him. He should be a writer."

"Actually he told me he hoped one day to open a newspaper for the Chinese here in America."

"But if you don't mind," Jason said helping himself to more brandy as Mrs. Stowe, Black Jade and Livy gathered themselves up to leave the dining area they had all been sitting in.

"Excellent..." Twain mumbled as the ladies departed, "now we can get down to some serious drinking...Cigar?"

"Sure." Jason took the Cuban Twain handed him and lit up. The powerful aroma quickly adding to the aroma Twain's own stogie was putting out.

"What do you think of his pushing me to become more of an advocate for the Chinese here? Wong seemed convinced they needed more of a champion and that I was the right person."

"What do I think, can't claim to be a real friend if he pushes such a role on you!" Twain roared, make you some sort of a mixed duck, half politician half abolitionist somewhere between an idiot and a preacher. You're a writer man, that is your role and there's no greater role, amusing folks and making them think."

"So I should just ignore what is happening. Even I can see the hatred of the Chinese that has built up out West and arrives here with greater strength each day louder with each notice of another firm failing." Jason responded with a commitment that surprised even him.

"Not at all; he let me fill your glass again; loves the ladies, but they tend to have either too much preacher or jezebel in them, and," lowering his voice somewhat, "around here it is the former that prevails." With that Twain pulled Jason's glass from him and handed him another, larger one.

"Mr. Twain, you don't want to be drinking that much..." George said still sitting on his perch near the wall piped in without much conviction.

"Right George, much obliged but this is the Christmas season. I may not be much of a spiritual man, but I think I understand the true meaning of the holiday, it's a free for all, to enjoy a bit of living. But you're right George it is good to be a bit prudent, just keep a watch out for the ladies return for me will you.

"Absolutely" mumbled the older gentleman who'd dozed quietly in an arm chair most of the evening stirring only long enough to pour himself another drink from time to time.

Twain, casting an amused smile in the direction of the retired old professor, then turned back to Jason. "What I am saying man is, be who you are, a writer. Nevertheless, your Chinese friend is right; you should take up the larger picture. Such things should be said..."

"In fact, though I would not wish this on a dog, and remember I am a cat man myself, I think you should go down to Washington and start talking to some of the scoundrels down there. Help you get an idea of the lay of the land, and assuming you will still be here for the election you will be better able to write about that if you've spoken to some of those free loaders before their lies get too outrageous."

With that, Twain erupted into a coughing spell so loud his wife glanced into the room to see if the writer was in distress. A second later, assuring herself nothing was substantially amiss,

Livia returned to the more civilized gathering she had prepared for the ladies in the next room.

"Can that Sage fellow help you with that? Make you some connections?"

"Russell Sage, I had not really thought of it."

"Well, you got to. The man's got money and used to be a congressman himself as I recall. Now there is an unusual combination, man with the brains to earn money who's willing to waste his time with those scoundrels in Washington."

"It does make sense."

"Makes all the sense in the world, write about what's going on, but keep folks laughing, they learn best that way, always been my approach, and it seems to work."

"But..." Jason said, glancing through the archway and toward the small atrium where the women had gathered. The distance between the two groups was no more than thirty feet, and he wondered if they could be heard. "Mrs. Stowe was much blunter." He tried to speak more softly. "I have read enough of her work to see she used a hammer to tell her stories."

"And you have not seen much since old *Uncle Tom* have you, she took quite a beating, she won't talk about it but people used to send her slave body parts so angry they were with her stirring up stuff."

"Body parts!"

This time Twain leaned forward and spoke quietly. She has not written a lick about race in years. Though she has been encouraging me to take up the subject and I have a mind to."

With that, Twain gestured to George who had been listening closely then holding up his glass and pointing toward Jason's. "I think we can let the old Professor sleep through this round" he whispered.

# CHAPTER 53

# HARRIET BEECHER STOWE

"So your husband is of the Hebrew race?" Black Jade asked in her most precise English.

Mrs. Stowe appeared startled and then laughed. "Goodness, no, my dear girl. Why do you ask?"

"But..." Black Jade began. Jason could tell his wife was taken aback. She was already nervous enough about finally meeting her hero in person, the woman who a generation before had written *Uncle Tom's Cabin*, the book Black Jade had been slowly absorbing for months. The invitation for lunch had been waiting for them when they had awoken that morning at Sam's beautiful home only a few yards away.

"But do you not call him Rabbi? Is that not a term for the spiritual leaders of the Hebrews, or have I misunderstood?'

The older woman laughed yet another hearty laugh as she looked across the room at her husband, who was himself smiling heartily as he brought sweet cakes in from the kitchen. The home was very different from Twain's; nothing like the almost European elegance of her more flamboyant neighbor's home, but quite comfortable in itself.

"You are right and wrong, my dear. I very much call my dear husband my little Rabbi, but only because of his great interest in the Hebrew people. He is a retired professor of religious studies and unlike many so-called Christian friends does have a strong respect and interest in our Lord's people."

"And are there many Hebrews here in America?" Black Jade asked. "We saw some as we passed through New York City when we arrived."

Mr. Stowe, his curiosity aroused by his guest's questions, sat down in the armchair nearest her.

"There are not many here in Hartford, but there are more in New York City, as you say.'

"And do they have the same problems as my people and the African people here?" she asked.

"Sometimes, yes, that is true," the retired professor responded.

"But are they not white? Do they not look the same as other people here?"

"Well, perhaps, but the issue among the Hebrews is not that they look all that different, though sometimes their clothing makes them stand apart. But their religion—they are not Christian. I am afraid many of my fellow citizens have enough problems with folks not being the right sort of Christians."

"You mean the Irish, Irish Catholics?" Jason asked as the old man nodded.

As they spoke Jason could hear the sound of Will and Mei-ling playing just near the window with Twain's little one. For a moment he wondered if they were bundled warm enough and then realized Olivia, Old Zhu, and Black Jade would have seen to that long before.

"Yes, the Irish, and the French Canadians, for many of my countryman. Catholics are already beyond the pale, and Jews still carry the stigma of those who believe they killed our Lord." The professor started off as if beginning a lecture.

"But all that is poppycock," Mrs. Stowe piped in. "Only the ignorant believe such tales. The Romans crucified our Lord, and folks have blamed the Jews ever since. People just like to hate people."

"So the Hebrews do have the same problems as Africans and Chinese here in America?" Black Jade asked again.

The older professor glanced at his wife waiting for a response.

"Go ahead, this is more your subject than mine."

"Well, to answer your question, the Hebrews, or Israelites, or Jews, if you will—they are known by many names—do have problems here in America but not like those of your people. Americans tend to be God-fearing people deeply devoted to their understanding of who has God's ear. But most of the time, they are more focused on race, as African and Chinese people understand so well."

"And you, Mrs. Stowe...Mr. Clemens said last night you no longer write about the black people?" she asked.

"Yes, I heard Sam say that. He thinks because I am so much older, I'd miss his whispered comment. But on that the famous Mr. Twain is largely right."

Jason watched, saying nothing. Black Jade's role speaking alongside him in public over the last few months had given her even more confidence. And of course she had never been as soft spoken as the other Chinese women he'd known in his life.

"And may I ask why? If it is not rude? Living with my husband, and getting to know Mr. Twain, has given me an even greater sense of the importance of writers, even more than when I was among my own people. And we respect scholars greatly."

Mrs. Stowe and her husband looked very closely at the beautiful Chinese woman sitting just opposite them in their front parlor. It was obvious they had never encountered a woman like Black Jade. There were after all so few Chinese women in America and certainly none with her bearing and language skills.

"Sam's only partly right, but I have not strayed nearly as far from my early path as it might sound." Mrs. Stowe said. "I am a deeply Christian woman who came by my abolitionist passion from that perspective. I may have moved from my writings about our African brethren, but I am still writing about how people treat people, simply more about the ladies these days— about our rights as women. Indeed, when I began my career I only had my pen. Mr. Stowe had to read my writings aloud in public. What you have been doing—and Sam told me all about it before you arrived, that you and your husband speak together in public—was simply impossible."

"So your work is much like that of the late Mrs. Willard?" Black Jade asked.

"Yes, and that reminds me, you knew her, right?"

"We met her as we traveled East, for a few hours in Troy just before she died," Jason piped in.

"Mrs. Willard was greatly admired in this house. Indeed, my own sister established a school here along lines similar to those of Mrs. Willard."

"A school for young woman, here?" Black Jade asked enthusiastically.

"Yes, indeed, but let me ask you a question. Your interest in the Hebrews is unusual among your people, is it not?"

"Unusual? Yes, perhaps, but my interest is more than that. When I was a younger woman, I often heard about Hebrews and Christians, about the Western God's life and death."

"From missionaries?" Mrs. Stowe's husband, the retired professor, asked as he filled everyone's teacup anew.

"Missionaries and—perhaps you have heard of them?—the Taipings, the people some call the Heavenly Kingdom."

At that, Jason sat up straighter. That Black Jade had once been the wife of a Taiping Wang, married to one of those who had challenged in the name of the Western God, the throne of the Chinese emperor, was not something they often brought up with other people. Not in China, not in America. It was, he thought, a sign of how much she admired Mrs. Stowe.

Mrs. Stowe looked hesitantly at her husband, who after a second put down the silver tea service he was carrying.

"Yes, we know something of them, Christian and not. The leader claimed to have a new revelation from God about himself and Christ the Lord, right?"

"Yes," Black Jade said.

"We did not hear much, only that it was something similar to our Mormons here. And that is the origins of your interest?"

"That and what I learned from a very kind Catholic sister in Tianjin," Black Jade said quietly.

This was quite a morning, Jason thought to himself, with his wife speaking not only of the Taipings with the Stowes but also of that day in Tianjin where she had barely survived the slaughter of the French nuns.

"If I might ask, are you a Christian, Mrs. Brandt?"

"I don't know. I know that I am very interested in Christianity, and I have even thought my husband and family might return to our home through what people here call the Holy Land as we travel." At that, she glanced a bit nervously toward Jason.

Jason smiled. He had long known that was why she really wanted to travel east instead of back across America as they had come. She'd spoken often of wanting to visit Aouda in London, of learning more French in France, but Jason had long suspected her real interest was focused considerably further east than Europe.

"Mr. Twain would be a fine source on that topic," the older Professor said enthusiastically. "He has traveled in the East, you know, as has Livia's brother."

"And did you know Mrs. Willard yourself?" Black Jade asked, quite obviously changing the subject. The idea of visiting Jerusalem had been ruminating in her mind for some months, but Jason knew she was not quite ready to discuss it further. After all, it was a plan perhaps for some years later.

"Ah, Mrs. Willard...I did not know her, but my sister was a great admirer and did visit her, especially in the years she was planning her own school. And we heard a lot about Mrs. Willard's Troy Female Seminary."

"Wait, I just forgot..." Mr. Stowe jumped up. "I forgot to tell you, Sam came by when I was in the kitchen. He asked that you delay your return to Massachusetts by a day."

"Why? Did he say the reason? We'd not wanted to overstay our welcome," Jason said.

"Oh, that's nothing." Mrs. Stowe laughed. "The Clemens run their home—some call it the castle—like a writer's boarding house. One Californian fellow stayed for weeks."

"But did he say why he needed us to stay longer?" Jason asked.

"Something about a meeting he'd set up tied to your conversation last night. He's asked a few friends over for conversation tomorrow evening."

Jason looked over to Black Jade, who was nodding.

"Then I guess we stay a few days longer," he replied.

"Good!" Mrs. Stowe said enthusiastically. "Now tell me more of your plans to set up a school for young ladies in Shanghai. I have heard only the briefest remarks about it. Sit next to me, dear, and tell me all about it. Your husband can help bring in some of the wood from the shed. We, I am afraid, don't have quite the number of servants that Sam has managed to hire."

# CHAPTER 54

# A CONVERSATION

"Damn it! Where did I put my matches!" Twain burst out. "I hate it when Katy comes in here…That woman cares far too much about dust for my taste!" With that, the writer started digging among the piles of books that were strewn across the billiard table. Finally, in frustration he turned to his older guest, "Governor—"

"Of course, Sam, here's a light."

"Fine, now that that's settled, Governor Hawley—ex-Governor I suppose, so we don't have to be too polite—was kind enough to join me, and I expect the good preacher Twitchell will arrive shortly."

It was a small group that had gathered in the upstairs billiards' room, Mrs. Stowe's husband, their host Sam, and the former governor and current newspaper publisher Joseph Rosell Hawley.

"Joe, much appreciate you're stopping by. Jason and his wife Black Jade are my guests as you know, speakers on the Chinese issue and of course Jason's a journalist, so we all know what sort that makes him."

Jason laughed knowing how much Twain liked to pontificate on the low morals of his fellow writers."

"Of course, Brandt, I know young Jason's work well, seen several of your pieces, think my papers even run some of them. Delighted to meet you! So how can I be of service?"

"Appreciate that Joe, I asked you and Twitchell to come by, Jason's been urged to take a more public role defending the Chinese here. Thought you and the preacher could give him a bit more understanding on that."

"Well, tell me more...are we talking about politics?"

"No, not that!" Black Jade said, surprising herself with her outburst. My husband is not a politician."

"Wise decision," Harley said, winking at Jason as he addressed her, "but tell me more."

"Well," Jason began, "we met a young Chinese man, came by our home in Rockport, claimed the Chinese were being treated worse every day, that I should take a lead in defending them because I am white and yet know China and the Chinese well. That only I was in a position to do right by those Chinese who live here."

"Am I late?" Another older male walked in the room.

"Not at all, come on in," Twain yelled out from his perch by the wall.

"Black Jade, Jason, this fellow's a preacher, but don't be nervous; he's one of the good ones."

"Thanks, Sam."

"No I mean it, and Twitchell fought the good fight, for black folks, at Gettysburg and knows the Chinese well, speaking of, were you able to bring your Chinese friend, that Yung Wing fellow?"

"Seems he is out of town, took me a while to find out. But Mr. Brandt am I right that you are already acquainted with our Chinese colleague here in Hartford?'

"Yes, indeed, and I am sorry I did not say something before. Yung Wing had already written me that he would be traveling during my visit. My wife had wanted to see him again."

At that, the reverend took Black Jade's hand and shook it enthusiastically.

"So, Twain began again, we were just discussing that some Chinese fellow has been pushing Jason to take a bigger hand in Chinese affairs, more than a reporter I guess, that's the charge right."

"So it seems, but more to the point I cannot even consider the issue unless I understand more of what is happening here. My wife and I have not been here much more than a year and frankly still have only the vaguest sense of the country."

"Another wise decision," Harley said and then after taking a large sip of his host's brandy, "Jason, Mrs. Brandt, the thing about this country is that there are a whole lot of folks here who don't really believe in it."

"Excuse me?" Jason asked, confused.

"Thing is folks here claim to believe in two things, our Declaration of Independence, our republic and to be Christians but reject both every chance they get."

"Well said." Twain applauded as he leaned over and grabbed the bottle himself.

"Sam here's the devil's cheerleader, but sometimes he's right. What you need to understand folks is that hanging around Hartford, what we locals call Nook Farm can give you the wrong impression. Mr. Stowe, there"—he gestured toward the retired professor, who appeared to be nodding off again just as he had the previous evening—"Mr. Stowe's wife—you have met her I assume?"

Both Jason and Black Jade nodded listening attentively.

"…helped set off our little fight…You are sitting in the heart of the abolitionist world, even if we are a bit long in the tooth these days."

"Excuse me?" Black Jade said.

"Sorry ma'am, your English is so impressive I forget, I suppose if I don't look at you I could easily forget you're not from here…what I mean is that New England folks at least a lot of us really do believe in the ideas this country was founded on. Just like they wrote in the Declaration of Independence that all folks are created equal."

"And most Americans don't?" Jason asked arousing a loud humph from Twain who took another deep pull on his cigar and then blew a huge ring across the room that seemed to completely cover the billiard table."

"Well, Harley went on…if you asked them they might say yes but the folks out west hate the Chinese and Johnny Reb, my excuses to Mr. Twain, our most illustrious local ex-confederate, but our southern neighbors, the former confederate rebels, hate the blacks. Can't really accept they lost the war."

"But they did lose the war and was it not about the black people?" Black Jade asked tentatively.

"In part, yes, they failed mostly in forming their own country. Honest Abe, excuse me, President Lincoln fought to keep the country together…So the rebels now accept that they can't have their own country, but they still insist on running the south as they always did."

"So what does that mean to the blacks in the south?" Jason asked wishing he was comfortable taking out a notepad.

"For now not too much, President Grant is still trying to protect them a bit…but that may not last. The rebels, former rebels I suppose are just trying to find another way to control the south, to totally run it as if it were a separate country, a country mostly of the southern white elite."

"Which…" Twain said starting to pace energetically across the room "is why the next election is so important."

"Your president, Grant, he was a general in the war, was he not?" Black Jade asked.

"The greatest among them. Yes, and he's done what he could to help the blacks build a new life since emancipation." Harley said as Twain interrupted him.

"That is the core of the thing, folks down south think that if they can get the right man in the White House, someone who will just let them run things as they want down south, run out all the republicans—the democrats can just have it their way, almost another confederacy reborn…that's their dream…And none of our northern republicans will do a damn thing to stop them." At that Twain sat down, coughing a bit, enough to catch the attention of George his servant who stuck his head in as he passed the door.

"Is that likely?" Jason asked. "Likely that after all those dead, all those who died in the Civil War, the north would allow the south to simply run things completely as they like, to ignore black people's rights?"

"Unfortunately, quite possibly so. People up north especially in New England are just tired of the fight, they have moved on, their precious union was saved and they have other things on their mind. But the election will matter. Sam's right, we get a southern democrat in the White House and they will most likely let the south do whatever they want as long as they claim to still be part of the Union," the former governor offered as he poured some sort of fluid from a flask into the coffee George had brought in earlier.

"And if a Republican, a man from Lincoln's party wins that won't happen?" Jason asked…

"Now that is hard to say, true most republicans have a bit of abolitionist blood in them…but that was a long time ago…

and a lot of dead bodies ago, most just don't have the stomach for more fighting. Folks sometimes say victory goes to the most committed and these days it's Johnny Reb I am afraid."

"And what of my people?" Black Jade asked quietly sipping the glass of tea George had brought her a few minutes earlier.

"Well, that's another subject, different and yet the same." The former governor sighed.

"How so?" Jason asked.

"One thing you have got to know about this country folks, only two things really matter and it's not ancient titles as in Europe or from what I have heard learning among your people."

"Then what matters here in America?" she asked leaning forward listening intensely.

"Money and the Vote. It is really that simple. Moneyed people run the country but those with the vote can at least try to protect what they have."

"And blacks have the vote right?" Jason asked.

"They do for now" Twain said waving his cigar again but "not for long, at least not in the south."

"Sam's right?" Harley went on. "They were given the vote, at least the right to vote but down south they are doing everything they can to take it back, not just the vote but any influence southern white republican's might have…and they are the only ones who might protect the southern black vote."

"And Chinese?" Jason questioned.

"That is where it gets more complicated. Have you heard of Senator Sumner?"

Jason turned to Back Jade who clearly did not recognize the name either.

"It was a while back, the battle over black folks right to vote. Senator Sumner—you should meet him when you can—has tried to get laws written to allow anyone, white or black, Chinese or whatever, to be able to vote. The way Sumner saw it, anything else was a rejection of the Declaration of Independence, that 'we hold these truths to be self-evident that all men are created equal...' and so forth."

Taking the cigar, Twain handed him and lighting up, despite the somewhat disapproving look earned from Black Jade, Jason asked, "I take it that did not happen?"

"No. Some Western senator, Stewart or something, stopped it. So in theory blacks have the right to vote but often can't, and Chinese are not supposed to have it at all."

"And why is that so important, the vote?" Black Jade asked.

"Like I said, ma'am, money runs this country, but votes do count. Politicians are afraid of people with the vote because they need them at election time, voting for them—or at least not for the other guy."

"And if they have the vote, they can at least try to fight back... to protect what they have and without it they are powerless?"

"Pretty much sums it up, ma'am."

"So the blacks in theory can vote but usually can't and the Chinese just can't...OK...and many white people just assume they are inferior because they look somewhat different...So how is their situation different?" Jason asked, intrigued.

"Pour me another Sam...and the reverend looks thirsty too." Their host poured a glass full for Harley and a more modest amount for the reverend. Over against the wall, Stowe was snoring again.

"There the situation is different folks. Southern whites need black labor for their fields. Their entire economy needs them. They have accepted that they can't hold them as slaves these days so they have done what they see as the next best thing. Control them as poor indebted laborers...ends up being the next best thing.

"And Chinese?" Jason asked...standing up and leaning against the wall.

"Now that is the difference…out West, when they were building the railroad folks in the West needed Chinese labor but now the trains been built, the economy's gone bust…Westerners just see the coolie laborers as competition, cheap competition and without the vote the Chinese can't defend themselves."

To Jason's surprise, his wife let Mr. Twain pour a tiny sip of brandy into her tea glass and then after sipping deeply. "And religion does not matter? Does not their Christianity make them think differently? There are certainly plenty of Christians in China who treat the Chinese well, plenty of missionaries who treat and run schools. And"—she paused for a second—"even orphanages."

At that Twitchell stepped forward from the deep chair he'd been sitting in.

"Mrs. Brandt I would deeply love to be able to tell you that it matters. But in truth not all that much…folks may grow up with the Lord's teachings with a sense of Christian charity but most of the time they are quick to hate anything different and the Blacks and Chinese seem mighty different, especially to people who have not known any personally."

"So, gentlemen, I ask you in full honesty do you think my husband should be more prominent in defending my people here in America?"

Twain and Harley both looked to Twitchell, the spiritual leader among them.

"That ma'am is really a moral question, perhaps one the reverend is best suited to address."

Twitchell looked at his friends "I am not against speaking my mind but I would like to hear what our dear Professor Stowe thinks. At that, all eyes turned to the older man who had been leaning up against the wall awake again and listening.

"Reverend, you put me into an awkward position and I think you know it…" he began slowly. "My family really my wife's of course took a very strong stand against the treatment of blacks before the great war, and is today very sympathetic to women's rights and probably those of the Chinese as well. It is the Christian thing to do."

Jason looked at Twitchell, unsure what the reverend had apparently provoked and he apparently intentionally.

"But I think most of us here, at least the locals among us, know that my brother in law, Harriet's brother has been strongly concerned about the importance of bringing our southern brothers back into the fold despite their many faults."

"So, sir," Harley piped in. "I am well aware of the eminent Mr. Beecher's recent comments, do you and your wife share them, that we have no obligation as Americans or Christians to uphold the equality of all people under God?"

"No, of course we do not, I am just saying it is at times more complicated than that.

"And you yourself, Reverend Twitchell?" Black Jade asked. "What do you a man of the cloth say?"

"Ma'am, I have no ambivalence on that score. I think each of us should do what we can to support our fellow man. But, Sam, you are unusually quiet, a rare moment for you. Are you not going to advice your colleague as well?"

"Of course, I still think he should take a larger role, hell that is why I asked everyone here. but as a journalist, as a writer, as a truth teller...and in this case, a bit of truth, some denunciation of hypocrisy serves both the author's morals, assuming he has any, and I don't recommend them in general and his purse. No ma'am to answer your question I think both of you should do what you can to serve both yourselves and your fellows from China. Just do it well, and maybe best in print, it's also a bit safer I find."

At that, Twain, poured another round of liqueur and again to Jason's surprise Black Jade let him almost fill her tea glass.

# CHAPTER 55

# NO CHINESE

As he sat there waiting for California's infamous anti-Chinese rabble rouser Denis Kearney to arrive in the rented hall near Boston's port, Jason sat studying the crowd, mostly working men, many speaking an Irish brogue Jason was, in the many months since arriving in Boston, becoming more and more familiar with. And there closer to the front, conspicuous both in his mandarin garb and the number of empty seats around him sat Wong waiting quietly for Kearney's public address to begin.

While Jason stared across the room, studying the crowd and seeing the small empty circle around Wong he wondered why he had not sat down next to his new acquaintance. After all, Wong himself had written to tell him of his intention to publically confront Kearney. He was even, Wong had written considering challenging the man to a duel. But no, Jason had whispered as they had arrived, coincidently at the same moment earlier, that it was best that he retain the distance of a professional journalist which Wong seemed to accept though, Jason thought with a hint of disappointment.

Nevertheless, there was more than that. Jason found himself also thinking back to the letter he'd received from Yung Wing, regretting his absence that evening some months before with Sam, the former Connecticut governor Harley and his friend Reverend Twitchell. From the letter, it has been obvious that Yung Wing's presence would have most certainly changed the tone of the conversation.

Since for reasons not yet clear, Kearney appeared to be late Jason reached into his pocket and took out the letter Yung Wing had sent him just after he had departed Hartford.

> To My Dear Colleague Jason Brandt:
> I hope this letter finds you well. Once again, my heart is in distress. I have only just learned more about you & your families visit to Hartford. Moreover, I remain saddened that I was not able to meet your entire family. Perhaps another day. There is, though, another reason for my regret as well. Reverend Twitchell, another fine person whose acquaintance I have come to appreciate, has informed me of the nature of your conversation and enquiries in Hartford. In truth, I would indeed have very much enjoyed taking part and offering a few of my own thoughts on the subject.
> First, let me say that the general discussion of your taking a more active role, at least as far as your writing goes to help your countrymen understand the celestial kingdom better, is certainly a worthy thought. But as far as I understand it, the individual who first encouraged you in this endeavor...the Shandong man known as Wong, I am afraid, I can only offer my considerable concern about the man's motives.

Yung Wing had gone on to enumerate a great many concerns, both political and moral, about Wong that he felt Jason should be aware of. Meanwhile, as the crowd kept growing and the general noise in the room grew louder, Jason skimmed the rest of the letter even as he watched the seated Wong across the crowded room.

"You here, not surprise. I see you have recovered well, Mr. Brandt!"

Jason looked up in startled surprise, "Charley Sing! What are you doing here? Should you not be in North Adams? Here sit next to me," Jason gestured pulling his coat off the adjacent seat.

"Yes, Thank You. Sitting next to you in this crowd might be a bit safer." Charley said switching into Cantonese.

"Yes, I guess you are probably right," Jason whispered back in the language of their youth in Hong Kong. He could already see some of the other members of the audience, some of whom had been staring daggers at Wong in the front row now turning their attention to the new arrival.

"But what are you doing here Charlie? Did Mr. Sampson dismiss you?"

"No…no she, not, no he not" Charley said, switching back to English as he looked at those around him becoming ever more suspicious. "Mr. Sampson give me more responsible work…he sends me Boston hire six more workers to replace those who went home."

"So you were not planning to come here today?"

No, but local Chinese, not San Francisco, Boston have small Chinese community, heard about this talk… this hate Chinese Irish man and that other fellow too," he gestured toward Wong who was still sitting quietly staring at the still empty podium.

"Wong, do you know him?" Jason asked.

"Not know him but few Chinese here can. He knows no Cantonese; they say he looks down on us as much as the Irish do."

"But he claims to speak for the Chinese, to wish to protect their rights?" Jason asked again in Cantonese as the conversation became more political. And he did not give a damn what the men around him thought, several of whom were starting to appear potentially aggressive as they sipped what appeared to be whiskey from a small flask.

"It could be what you say" Charlie Sing responded...but I only hear he thinks himself very superior...several men from villages near my own told me that just this morning."

"So why are you here now?

"Because I want to make my home in America...and this hate Chinese Irishman and this strange fellow Wong...make it easier or harder for me. So I hear about this talk and come... but," Sing went on as he glanced around, "still good see a friend face."

Jason laughed almost aloud just as the crowd's energy turned up dramatically. Denis Kearney had arrived. From the back of the hall, the ruddy faced Irishman strode quickly forward almost jumped on the stage and yelled out, "The Chinese must go!"

Kearney's voice was louder than Jason expected. His slick-backed black hair peaked with a few hairs that reached for the ceiling as the man began his talk, telling his audience that he had only arrived the evening before by train.

"I am telling you my friends, that the Chinese may not be the threat they are in the West but they most certainly will become so. Only now some of them are already taking the jobs of white men, and Crispin members over in North Adams...at the shoe factory we've all heard of.

"Yeah," the crowd yelled, as one especially drunk fellow roared Kearney's own slogan back at him—"the Chinese must go."

At the mention of North Adams, Jason gave Charlie Sing a glance, but his new acquaintance was watching not Kearney but Wong, who still sat alone in the front row.

"I tell you, the Chinese—heathens every one of them—are good for nothing but women's work. Rat-eating parasites the owners want to use against us God-fearing workers." With that, Kearney dramatically threw off his jacket and began firing up the crowd while the bulk of the audience enthusiastically took up his call, interrupting Kearney with an ever more frequent and angrier, "The Chinese must go!"

As Jason listened to the rhythm of the talk, he began to notice large signs being slowly lowered from the balconies: "NO CHINESE CHEAP LABOR IN THE US," they read.

Then, almost as quickly as Kearney had begun a few moments before the mood changed as Wong, dressed in his full mandarin garb slowly rose to his feet. The act itself seemed to startle the audience which quieted almost as soon as he did it.

"Who Are You to Denounce the Chinese! "Wong bellowed out in English less accented than Kearney's own. "Yes, You, look at me, you who just traveled all the way from California on a train built with Chinese labor. We are men just as you are!

Kearney looked for a second startled while Jason wondered how often he encountered challenges from Chinese in his audience. And then recovering himself.

"You heathen! You have a lot of nerve invading these premises!" he shouted...go back to rat-eating China and be damned."

"Are you afraid to stand up to a real man?" The diminutive Wong bellowed out in a voice that swept the auditorium, though Jason thought he also noticed him surveying the room to gage how his audience was reacting and even steal a glance in Jason's direction and then to the opposite side of the hall.

It was only then that Jason noticed a block of men, obviously reporters standing near the wall. Clearly, Jason was not the only reporter Wong had notified in advance.

"Afraid of a Chinaman. Rubbish!" Kearney yelled out. "But I have no time to let you distract me from my work here...distract me from helping my fellows see you, you people for what you are, a tool of the owners to keep the working man down. Get out!"

With that, Kearney turned to his side and gave a knowing glance to several large men who'd entered the hall with him. Within seconds, rough hands had been placed on Wong and the fellow pushed toward the door while the crowd roared.

Jason felt Charley's hand touch his shoulder. "I think we should leave as well."

Jason nodded. He had certainly seen enough for one morning. As the two of them rose, Jason could feel the angry stares of those around them, most directed toward Charley but almost as many toward himself, the Chinaman's obvious companion. Within seconds, they were out the door and for a moment standing in the fresh Boston air when the sounds of a commotion reached their ears from the alley that ran alongside the building.

Without thinking the two of them ran to the alley where the sounds of fighting had begun. Rounding the corner, they saw Wong, with a piece of timber holding off four burley men intent on beating him. For a few seconds the enraged Wong was clearly holding his own until one of the fellows, with a lucky grab caught his pigtail and jerked him to the ground.

"Shit" Jason heard himself mumble as Charlie whispered "Aiyee" to himself, a second later, neither of them really considering their actions had run in and joined the mêlée. Jason wielding the piece of pine board Wong had just dropped while Charlie, pulling something from his pocket and wrapping his fist around it started pummeling the fellow standing over Wong kicking him. The two clearly had the element of surprise on their side, at least for a few seconds and they were able to push the men back far enough for Wong to spring to his feet kicking one red headed fellow right in the knee, a blow that caused him to yell loudly.

"Back up...Wong, we are with you?" Jason yelled as the three of them faced the four men who slowly advanced on them the advantage of surprise now spent. Then from the stage door, two more men entered the alley hate in their eyes, hands holding, not boards but what looked like pipefittings.

"Damned Irish Scum!" the voice could not have been louder as suddenly from behind him Jason heard a loud Boston accent, one that sounded vaguely familiar. Then the sounds of police whistles.

Pushing past him waving a cane was a middle-aged man dressed as if for church swinging a cane furiously while directing two local police officers toward the alley.

Seeing the police, the several men, at least one of them limping turned and ran while the older man grabbed Jason's arm.

"Young Mr. Brandt, are you all right? I think those Irish scum won't be bothering you again." Jason turned to see a man he recognized as one of his father's missionary friends, a man Jason knew who had himself worked in Hong Kong for a time greeting him, while patting one of the officers on the shoulder.

"Fine job Fellows. You make the force proud. I will most certainly put in a good word for you to his honor."

"Not necessary, sir. Don't like troublemakers, any sort, and those Irish bring far too much of it." The fellow responded though Jason thought he was studying as well the two disheveled Chinese standing nearby. With that, the older fellow set off again and Jason turned to his two Chinese companions, who still stood as he did, just a bit into the alley as the street traffic past them a few yards away.

"So shall we have a beer?" he asked in English, knowing Wong knew no Cantonese and Sing none of the northern dialects. But as he asked, he realized Wong was gazing past him to a group of men, the same fellows Jason had spotted as reporters inside the hall.

"Thank you for your help, Jason, and for yours, my countryman," Wong said, turning to Sing who had been watching him closely. But beer, perhaps another time, I should speak with those gentlemen." With that he walked off to meet the approaching reporters who gathered around him asking questions."

"Should you not be among them, the reporters?" Charlie Sing asked him in Cantonese.

"I think I've had enough reporting for today...and I still want that beer. You interested?"

"No like beer, taste no good...and around here bars no like Chinaman anyway...better I go now. But very good see you again, Mr. Brandt. I saw what I want see today."

"Which was what exactly?" Jason asked his reporter's instinct kicking in.

"I see Irish hate Chinese man and," he hesitated, "and this Northern Chinese man...say he speaks for Chinese."

"Yes, Wong—what did you think of him?"

"Troublemaker, I think...maybe wrong...but what he says important." With that, Charlie Sing set off at a determined pace himself leaving Jason standing alone at the entrance to the alley, his heart still beating quickly from the excitement of a few moments before. The afternoon's events had given him that much more to think about as he continued toward Washington, his next stop on his effort to learn more about the politics of the Chinese presence in America.

But, that trip was not for a few days, for now he headed back to the Parker House, his only place to stay in Boston now that the house had been sold and its comfortable lobby bar where he hoped to write up his thoughts on the afternoon, and finally have that beer even if it would be enjoyed alone.

# CHAPTER 56

# WASHINGTON CITY

"This has got to be some sort of joke!" the burly senator exclaimed with a tone somewhere between irritation and laughter.

"Excuse me, Senator. I am not sure I understand," Jason said, bewildered. This was not turning out to be a good day. He had barely managed to avoid getting completely soaked as he traversed streets from the Willard Hotel Sam had recommended. Washington's roadways had turned out to be not only especially full but very chaotic as the horse traffic rushed down its rain sodden streets and now this, his first appointment with the famous Senator Stewart from Nevada, turning into a disaster.

"Son, are you sure Clemens—what is it he is calling himself these days, Twain?"

"Yes..." Jason managed.

"Whatever. Are you sure he is a friend of yours?"

"Well, I thought so. If I might—why do you ask, Senator?"

"Because I fired the man. He was my secretary, you know that...don't you?"

Jason thought for a moment. "I am not really sure. He just said I should talk to you, that you were important to my work and that he knew you."

"Well, that he does, but you would have been better just sending the note from Mr. Sage. Now he is a fellow a man can respect, was a congressman himself, though before my time... knows politics and how to make money. Odd that you know both of them."

"I suppose so. So Sam worked for you?"

"Absolutely. His limited success came later, though I doubt it will last. The man is a lunatic...I had him corresponding with folks back in my district. He would go out of his way to insult them, funny stuff, I admit. But that is not the point."

Despite himself, Jason started to laugh. "Yes, that does make sense, and I suppose Sam telling me to use his name to get an interview with you is probably Sam's idea of another joke. He has not changed that much."

"But I really would like to talk with you. My interest, as I am sure your secretary explained, is regarding the position of the Chinese here in America. I am told you are an expert on the subject."

"Well, that is certainly true. If I do say so myself, the Chinese owe me a favor, protected them when some of my more naïve colleagues almost got the lot of them lynched."

"You refer to Senator..."

"Sumner of course, the old fool and others...Have you spoken to him yet?"

"No, I had wanted to begin with you."

"Right you were. Problem with men like Sumner; they know nothing of the Chinese. It's all abstract to them and, if I might add, beneath the surface...just protecting their friends."

"I am not sure I understand you, sir."

"Look, son, it's only those of us from out West who understand the situation. There's hardly any Chinese east of the Mississippi. New England folks think this whole Chinese thing is just an extension of the abolition fight, about equality and other such stuff."

"And it is not?"

"Only on the surface. Hell, I am sure I know far more Chinamen than my aging New England abolitionist colleagues. And I am more the friend of the Chinese than those around here who take credit for supporting them."

As Senator Stewart spoke, Jason glanced around the room, thinking of how ornate the wood-filled office was and the capital itself, more impressive than any building he'd ever seen. Of course, he reminded himself, he'd only stood at the entrance to Beijing's Forbidden City. While here in the more open environment of Washington, he'd been able to walk into the capital without hindrance to make the appointment the day before with the senator's secretary. Then looking more closely at Stewart, he tried to remember again what information he had managed to learn about the man in the few days since he'd taken up residence at the Willard Hotel.

"How long have you been here in Washington, young man?" Steward asked him.

"Really only a few days...not much more time than to see some of the buildings. I visited the patent office I'd heard..." Jason's voice trailed off, stopping himself from mentioning it was Sam who had insisted he visit it.

"Far more interesting than that stone-faced chimney they're building to old General Washington" had been his exact words. And indeed Sam was right; the Washington Monument would probably be impressive if ever finished, but from what Jason had seen earlier that morning, it certainly did not appear like much yet.

"Look, son, it's not an issue. Say just remembered, your friend Twain loved the place. The man loves contraptions... obviously, he told you to visit it. My secretary told me you were staying at the Willard, good place to stay; full of reporters, especially across the street in the bars...I'd spend some time listening to those fellows. They'll give you a good education indeed to the ways of this town."

"Which are primarily what, sir?" Jason asked, taking a chance on interrupting the senator.

"Money and votes. Ain't no more than that. You want to learn about the Chinese—well, they don't really matter, at least not where I am from, not out West. They don't have the vote, saw to that myself, and since out West-most folks won't hire them, there is not any money to be made in their labor either."

"Not sure I understand, surely some might want to employ them out West, would they not? They certainly work hard and are cheap to employ," Jason asked, holding his pen just above his pad, waiting eagerly for the senator's response.

"Look, not really sure why I am talking to you. You are not a voter anywhere near my district, not at least as far as my secretary could ascertain. Do any of the newspapers in my district print your material?"

"Actually I don't know, perhaps but am not sure. But certainly, sir, the issues are larger than that. America's relationship with China, plenty of American businessmen have interests there; indeed that is, in fact, how I even know Mr. Sage."

"There is truth to that my reporter friend. But most senators like myself have more immediate concerns, keeping the voters happy back home and winning the money to do so... and doing that means keeping men, working men like the Irish happy. And they don't want to compete with the Chinaman."

"And they, the Irish can vote but the Chinese cannot as I understand it" Jason asked somewhat cautiously bringing up the primary reason he wanted to interview Stewart, the man's role in denying the Chinese the right to vote.

"So what is your interest in all this Chinaman stuff anyway? Your accent's New England -- this side of the Mississippi folks don't spend a lot of time thinking of such things. Doubt you would even be able sell an article on the subject."

As the senator from Nevada spoke Jason realized with some satisfaction that his decision to ask Twain and Sage to avoid mentioning his background in their letters of introduction had been correct, it might have complicated matters.

"Frankly I do find some interest, particularly those interested in the China trade, lots of folks in New England have ties to China and such," Jason said vaguely. "But you mention something I am quite interested in...Your role in the suffrage vote. I am told that ensured the Chinese would not be included when the blacks were allowed to vote."

"Absolutely, I am quite proud of that...situation was not at all like some folks around here think."

"Not sure what you mean, Senator?"

"Excuse me, I don't have a lot of time...but let me be clear about a few things. Some of my republican colleagues, and we are all of the party of Lincoln will tell you the issue of the Chinese was no different from that of the former black slaves. But that is completely wrong."

"Look, Jason, can I call you that?" the senator began and then without waiting, continued. "Your average black man's situation is completely different. America needs their labor...especially the former Johnny Rebs...and speaking as a politician the blacks want to be here...make their home here and are willing to vote Republican. That holds sway around here in these corridors."

"And the Chinese situation is different?"

"Completely, first of all not only were they not born here like the blacks but they came as contract laborers, men whose only interest is to go home...talk to any of them, they all want to make some money and go back to their villages and be big men...rich from what they call Gold Mountain. Did you know they call this place Gold Mountain?"

Jason nodded without saying anything as the senator went on.

"So if we had included Chinamen in the voting laws for the blacks, we'd not have added any long term voters and the Irish would have attacked them."

"Excuse me?"

"Son, from New England things look very different, hardly any Chinese in the Northeast, hardly any blacks for that matter. My voters and I mean the Irish workers out west do not want to go back to the Emerald Islands; they want to build families and show up at the polling booth when I need them. And they don't want to compete with cheap Chinese labor. Can't be done...bunch of Chinamen living together, hardly any wives...They can work for almost nothing and the Irish cannot compete...That in a nutshell is what it's about son. It's not skin color, it's about money and politics...and don't let those New England politicians tell you any different. Give the Chinese the vote, and they'd be slaughtered to a man out west. Hell I probably stopped a massacre...I could tell you..."

"Senator."

At that, the senator's young aide, the fellow Jason had made the appointment with the day before, appeared at the door.

"Yes, Andrew."

"Your next appointment is due and then there is a vote scheduled on the floor just after that..."

With that, Senator Stewart stood up shook Jason's hand and headed for the door, then stopping for a second as Jason gathered up his writing material.

"And once more, remember the money, votes and money. There are plenty of folks, folks who don't like the working man who'd love to have even more Chinese scabs here. Ask your abolitionist New England friends about who their friends are." With that, the senator rushed through the door as his secretary Andrew politely waited for Jason to finish gathering his things.

# CHAPTER 57

# SENATOR SUMNER

"Mr. Brandt, Mr. Brandt!"

Jason, walking the long halls looking for Senator Sumner's offices barely heard the call so distracted was he by the crowds of men standing in the halls smoking cigars and laughing. He'd just been here the day before when he'd visited Steward and Sumner's offices hoping to arrange interviews with their secretaries but now, with the halls far more crowded than when he'd visited much earlier the day before everything looked different.

"I am glad I spotted you. I sent a boy off to the Willard this morning but was told you'd already left."

"True, I left early for a walk, my first time here in Washington City."

"And what do you think, how does it compare to the Chinese Capital?"

"Very different...Jason began...realizing that Sumner's secretary, George, he thought that was his name knew more about him than he'd conveyed in their short conversation the day before."

"It's George, is it not?" Jason asked. "Is there a problem with this afternoon's appointment with the senator?"

"No, not at all. Well, there has been a change. Actually the senator is not here today." Then seeing the look of disappointment, he quickly added, "But I think you will be more than pleased with the change."

His curiosity aroused, Jason turned to the young man, perhaps in his mid-twenties, really only a few years younger than Jason himself.

"So, now you have me intrigued. So I will still have a chance to interview the senator?"

"Yes, of course, but…well, let's walk a bit. What have you seen of Washington City so far?"

"Actually not much, the patent office, tried to walk around this morning before my interview with Senator Stewart but between the rain and the mud spewing up from the omnibuses…it was not very successful," Jason said pointing down to his boots now covered in dried mud.

"So you saw Senator Steward this morning?" George asked as he walked Jason out the majestic doors of the capital and out on to the steps. Unlike earlier that morning, they were greeted with what appeared to be a wonderful spring morning.

"Beautiful isn't it?" George asked as the two of them gazed out over the grassy areas that sprung up between Washington's stately government buildings. In the distance the monument, still not nearly complete had a few working men standing around it, perhaps discussing the next stages of either construction or financing.

"Are you from here?" Jason asked.

"From here, hardly, most of those who work for the senators and congressmen come from their home districts. I am from Cambridge; my parents have known the senator for ages. But I have lived here for three years now."

"So, George, you obviously have something you want to tell me."

"Well, first of all, let me apologize. When you came by yesterday, I had no idea who you were…but when I spoke to the senator later, he was very familiar with you."

"You showed him the letters of introduction from Mr. Sage and Mr. Twain…" As he mentioned Twain, his voice trailed off, remembering Stewart's reaction.

"Never got the chance, Senator Sumner had heard of you… you and your father, even said something about knowing your grandparents. Boston society can be a lot smaller than it looks to outsiders. And he knew your writings."

"That certainly sounds helpful…so when is the appointment?" Jason asked. He'd not planned to spent more than a week on the entire trip and though he knew the weather in Rockport was starting to become more pleasant, he worried frequently about how Black Jade and the children were doing.

"That is just it, there's no appointment, you have been invited to dine with the senator at his residence this evening…I am assuming that won't be a problem."

"No not at all, though I admit to being somewhat surprised, the politicians here seem very busy, frankly, to receive such an invitation though I certainly appreciate it. I guess though I am just surprised the famous Senator Sumner has time to dine with a mere journalist."

"Mr. Brandt, Jason, if I might. How much do you really know about the senator?"

"Well, I know he was very involved with the abolitionist movement, that he fought with Senator Stewart over the question of enfranchising the Chinese as were the blacks…but actually not that much more. As you have probably learned, I grew up in Hong Kong, spent much of my adult life living in

Shanghai...No I suppose I really don't know that much about the senator. Is that a problem?"

"A problem...no but perhaps you should know a bit more. How about this, take a few hours to explore Washington City more. I will meet you in the Willard Lobby at six. The senator dines at seven. I can walk you over and we can talk on the way. Does that seem reasonable?'

More than reasonable. And will there be other guests? That can be a bit awkward if I start asking questions like a reporter which is of course why I am here."

"Not at all, and no there will be no other guests. You will have the senator's full attention. So the Willard Lobby then... at six."

With that George tipped his hat and walked off leaving Jason standing half way between the Capital and the White House, standing there alone wondering why Senator Sumner had made such a gesture.

⚊⊹ ⊹⚊

"So Senator Stewart said nothing about Senator Sumner?" George asked after they left the lobby a few hours later walking in the early evening toward the senator's residence."

"No, not really, I mean I have surmised that they are on different sides on occasion, different backgrounds...but are they not from the same party both Republicans?"

"Yes...sort of" George responded tentatively saying no more.

"Well, I am not sure what you might be wondering about but as I said Senator Stewart said nothing, indeed I really only had a few minutes with him."

With that, George seemed satisfied. The two men walked on, each caught up in their own thoughts. Occasionally George would quietly point out some interesting building or the occasional notable who walked by them. But until they had walked further away from the government buildings, toward the more private residences the man remained largely silent until he burst out, as if he'd come to a decision.

"Senator Sumner is a great man. I want you to know that."

"I am afraid I don't understand why are you concerned I might think otherwise?"

"This is Washington, people talk, especially those journalists that inhabit the taverns across the street from the Willard."

"I can assure you I've not encountered any of them. I only arrived the day before yesterday from Boston.

"Well, then let me simply say that I am concerned you might get the wrong impression this evening."

"Why would that be?"

"Frankly, the senator is getting on in years, perhaps his best days are behind him and he can at times show more frustration than his accomplishments suggest. He was as you may have heard very influential in the struggle against slavery, an expert on foreign policy...Practically single handily kept the English from helping the south in the war."

"George, you obviously care for and respect the senator deeply. If you are comfortable doing so just tell me what is on your mind?"

"Perhaps you are right, let me explain, the senator is often alone these days. He never had a personality that easily made friends but at least his influence kept many coming to his doors. But even that influence has faded as President Grant's support has diminished."

"I guess what I am saying is the senator is vulnerable. He has few visitors and at times can be quite bitter, I am nervous, that you a writer with ties to Massachusetts might get the wrong impression and write of such things. There I have said it."

Sumner's assistant looked as if a huge burden had been lifted from his shoulders.

"George, I am not here for any sort of character assassination, indeed my topic has little to do with the senator accept in so much as he can help me understand the Chinese question. I don't believe you have anything to be concerned about."

As Jason finished George stopped abruptly in front of an attractive brownstone that featured not only a fine hedge but elaborate iron grating leading to the front door.

"We have arrived," He announced, his voice considerably more relaxed than previously.

A moment later, after they'd rung the bell the door sprung open widely and Jason found himself being ushered into a parlor by a fellow who reminded him somewhat of Mark Twain's butler."

"Come in, sir. The senator is waiting for you in the parlor… here let me take your umbrella…Washington City can be so wet this time of the year."

"Thank you," Jason said, handing the man the umbrella and light coat he'd brought with him from Boston, which this early in the spring had still been relatively chilly when he'd left Boston for the train ride south.

"Welcome Young Mr. Brandt." The voice boomed out even before the large but somewhat bent man, Jason imagined him well over six feet, walked slowly toward them holding a cane has he approached.

"I trust this dinner invitation is more to your liking than a formal interview in my office."

"Absolutely, Senator, it is an honor. I have only been here a few days and already have a sense of how busy folks can be in this town. Thank you again."

"Nonsense, most folks around here like to look busier than they are. Been here myself for decades, and I can tell you there's plenty of free time...besides, I'm not that busy myself these days."

"Well, regardless, sir. It is an honor. If I might your secretary, Mr. Carry mentioned you knew my family."

"That I did, more knew of them then knew them...but when I was a young man, I met your grandmother a few times. She was a beauty, made quite an impression on me. So later, I sort of followed the family's fate, remember when her daughter married your father and his work as a preacher in Hong Kong certainly added to the notoriety of the family.

"I had no idea. So you met my grandmother. I barely remember by mother, her daughter who'd died when I was a youngster."

But there's more, when you started writing in China, I realized almost at once who you were...Mr. Carry, George will tell you, spent my life in studying foreign policy...mostly Europe but China too...lots of New England and especially Massachusetts men have businesses there. But you already know all that."

At that the older man turned and beckoned Jason into the room he'd emerged from, a room, part parlor part library that housed an enormous collection of books, a small warming fire in one corner and a great many expensive looking brands of brandy and cigars."

"Here can I offer you something, young man? Or do the families of Hong Kong Missionaries not indulge?" the elder man asked, suppressing a laugh and then turning to his aide.

"George...you can go now. Mr. Brandt and I are settled in and Martha will be serving in a bit. Thank you. Now go find some mischief to get into—I promise I won't tell your parents."

With considerable reluctance, the senator's secretary gathered up his hat and left. It was obvious from where Jason sat sipping the brandy the senator had poured that the fellow would have preferred to stay. His protective nature was not hidden, but the man had spoken and George took his leave.

"Don't pay George any mind," the senator said, after he heard the front door shut. "His father's an old dear friend…but he worries about me. Sometimes I think he sent his son down here to keep me out of trouble!"

Jason said nothing…just listening trying to get a sense of the man. He'd spent years as a journalist, but Sumner seemed of a very different order than most of the men he'd interviewed over the years.

"So, Mr. Brandt, first let me show you something." The older man sprung up again from his chair he'd only sat in a few moments before and, grabbing his cane, went to the far side of the beautifully furnished room and pulled a volume that immediately looked familiar to Jason even at some distance.

"Your father sent this to me…Did not know the man, but over the years he'd written me, at the request of a mutual friend, his impressions of Hong Kong."

"My father wrote you reports?" Jason asked, astounded. "I had no idea."

"Yes, indeed…we had quite a number of mutual friends… Boston is a lot smaller than you might imagine. I had asked through one of them and your father indulged me…knew I was the head of the foreign relations committee…"

"I really had no idea…In truth, Senator, sometimes I feel like I have learned more about my father since he died than when he was alive."

"Son, I am more than twice your age. I can assure you it is often like that…for the good and for the bad. People can be quite a surprise…even folks one thinks one knows well. Politicians learn that fast…at least if they are successful."

"So, Mr. Reporter, what do you know of me? George tells me you met with Senator Stewart this morning. Did my name come up?"

"A bit, but not much...The senator gave me only a few minutes...I guess around here not being a constituent or someone who at least writes for local papers back home does not earn one a lot of time."

"Right you are about that. So, why did you want to talk to me...the China question I am told."

"Yes, I have heard you were very involved in the battle over whether the Chinese gained the vote?"

"And that's it...not curious about the caning...Sometimes I think that is the only reason anyone will have heard of me a hundred years from now."

"Excuse me?" Jason asked, looking unsure. "The caning?"

At that, the senator's eyes widened as he looked much more closely at Jason than he had previously.

"This is going to prove a more interesting evening than I had imagined. You really don't know?"

Jason was starting to feel uncomfortable, found an imbecile by the man he'd hoped to interview.

"So it's true, what I have heard...and I have heard about those talks you and your wife have been giving back home. You seem so New England, sound it too."

"Well, it is true my..."

"Nothing to be uncomfortable with, son...just interesting. You are too young to really remember...and you have spent your life in China, have you not...only arrived in Boston just recently?"

"Yes, sir, grew up in Hong Kong, wandered China for a long time before settling in Shanghai."

"During their own civil war. Much like our own, I imagine."

"Yes, that's true…but if I might…what caning were you referring to, sir?"

"There is plenty of time for that story. Here have another brandy; we have a few minutes before Martha will announce dinner, and I want to hear all about you, how you fared after you left your father's home, and yes, I know all about that too!"

With that, Jason took another sip and started to explain what happened the evening his father had insisted he leave Hong Kong for college in America. The evening was turning out to be completely different than he'd expected or could possibly have imagined. As he spoke he had the feeling the senator had all the time in the world, and a level of curiosity and sophistication to indulge in a series of very specific questions he barraged Jason with, following the path literally until he and Black Jade had made the decision to relocate to America for a time.

# CHAPTER 58

# DINNER

"And how different are the educated Chinese from the workers we meet here?" the senator asked, after they had eaten the plate of oysters Martha, the senator's housekeeper, had presented them.

"Not sure exactly what you mean, sir, quite different I suppose."

"Perhaps I should be more clear, as I understand it you speak the language quite well and have known men not only of the upper classes but the sort of workers we see here?"

"Well, yes, I grew up with the type of men who most often are the sort who end up here in America, especially the West Coast, most are from the southernmost province near Hong Kong. But in my adult years have learned something of the northern dialects."

"And your work has allowed you interaction with those men of substance, the leaders of the Middle Kingdom?"

I have certainly known some of them, interviewed many, some I have met on my own…and others, a colleague, a French naval engineer friend who works for the Chinese has introduced me to."

"A Frenchman who works for the Chinese government?" Sumner asked with interest.

"Yes, quite so, names Prosper Giquel, speaks English and Chinese and is helping them construct a navy near the port of Fuzhou."

"And this Frenchman has no problem working with the Chinese?"

"Not that I know of...Why do you ask?"

"It is a long story but perhaps worth telling." The older man said as he rose, limped obviously toward the small bar in the room and filled his glass with more bourbon.

"Martha...where is the rest of dinner?" he roared.

"Coming, sir, the older maid bellowed with a strong Irish accent from some hidden part of the house.

Sumner harrumphed and then returned to his seat.

"When I was young I visited Paris..." His eyes misted up for a moment, perhaps as he remembered his lost youth. "I noted with some surprise how easily educated blacks mixed with polite French society. Mind you, I was not from the south... but still, watching their interactions, I realized, probably had not given it a thought before that, that what separated men was not birth, not color, but simple breeding, education, and culture."

"I suppose that is true. Certainly, that is what I have seen in China as well. Foreigners and even the Chinese elite look down on their uneducated classes as if they were a breed apart when only their different upbringing really sets them apart."

"Which is precisely why I asked you about the Chinese elite?"

"Well, then I would have to say it is the same there. The elite are not all that much different than those here in America, if perhaps a bit more formal.

"And yet they know nothing of Christianity?" the senator asked.

"Well, some of course do, those who have contact with the missionaries and the recent rebellion was somewhat linked with Christian ideas...but yes, that is mostly correct. They have their own idea of morality not all that different from what people here value...at least in terms of behavior."

"From that Confucius fellow?"

"Yes." Jason responded wondering where the conversation was going.

But then Martha arrived with the meal, lamb and potatoes with a small soup...clam chowder to the side and the two men began eating in quiet."

"There is something that remains unclear to me, Senator... something I keep asking everyone I talk to."

The senator put down his spoon and looked up.

"Yes?"

"Why would America give blacks the vote and not the Chinese? Certainly, their humanity is no different and as we have both agreed, only a lack of education makes some of them seem inferior to those likely to be bigoted anyway.

"Well, that is the thing, isn't it...but to me..." the senator said, applying a napkin carefully to his lips and then taking another generous sip of the bourbon he'd fetched from the counter.

"More?" he offered.

"No, sir, thank you, though."

"Yes, of course, men like me think this issue is neither about the Chinese nor the blacks but who we Americans ourselves are...a nation born of the Declaration of Independence but as well a declaration of the equality of humanity...I have always tried to live up to that. It drove my fight against slavery and more recently the struggle over the Chinese."

"But you were successful over slavery...but not with the Chinese. How are they different, sir?"

"You flatter me to say I was successful. True, I always considered the war to be about slavery but I was deeply in the minority, even among my fellow republicans.

"Was not President Lincoln a republican and an abolitionist though, Senator?"

"If old Abe were here now, I think he would blanch at your suggestion. No, our martyred president…a man I truly admired, was absolutely against slavery against spreading slavery…fought to end it with all his strength…but at base, his greater priority was the country itself…keeping the union together preferably without slaves of course."

"But the war did end slavery and eventually the blacks gained the vote but not the Chinese."

"Understand, had not fought a civil war? Carried off a generation of the nation's finest young men to then simply allow the defeated south to keep their black slaves. And if they had not been later granted the vote they'd still be vulnerable to the loss of freedom. Even now, our southern brethren wish to turn the clock back, to get their former slaves under their thumb as much as possible. Reverse the results of the war in my opinion."

And the Chinese?"

"The Chinese situation could not be more different…at base, as I am sure some have told you…America needs black labor. It does not need Chinese labor, at least, many working men, especially the Irish don't want to compete with them… and they have the votes."

"I have heard that before…from many sources…despite the charges and all the attacks about rat eating. This is about jobs and votes.

"Most things are," the senator said, taking up his spoon again. "You will want to hold back some appetite, Martha makes the best apple pie in these parts."

"So it is not about race at all, Senator."

"More on the surface than reality...people use the language of hate, of race of religion...not a proper Christian, not a Christian at all..."

"You refer to the Irish Catholics or the Hebrews."

"Yes, and of course not white...black, or at least dark skinned like the Mexicans or the Chinese...but the thing is...what really moves people is money...that is the issue that defines everything...does this group or that, advance my wealth...and black labor slave or cheap black labor is necessary to parts of America."

"As were the Chinese when the railroad was being built?"

"Exactly, but that was then. Now the railroad is done, and the crash of '73...you were here for that?"

"Yes, it happened just after we arrived."

"Well, the crash put too many out of work...too many folks needing a job and who now see the Chinese as cheap labor... they cannot compete with."

"Are there not those who would wish to employ them? The wealthy industrial types perhaps?"

"Absolutely, plenty of men, men of my party, perhaps former party have links to those who would employ them. Cheap labors a great boon to those with the money to employ others."

"But not you, Senator?"

"I am as interested in commerce as the next man...and as a senator very concerned about Massachusetts doing well. But for me...the thing begins and ends with the republic...with the Declaration of Independence...with the call for the equality of humanity...and the schools to actually make them equal."

"Your ideas certainly seem worthy...and such ideas have no following?"

Sumner stopped, looked at the young reporter, half his age who sat opposite him at the dining table/"

"Let's get some air, walk off this dinner. Martha, my over-coat" the older man bellowed.

A moment later, Martha appeared a pie in hand. "But no dessert, Senator?"

"Not now…perhaps you can give our young guest a slice to leave with. I need some air."

⊷⊶

Minutes later, Jason walking slowly stood alongside the sena-tor as the older man, leaning heavily on his cane strode down the front steps of his residence…The streets were dark but the moon bright enough above made it easy enough to navigate Washington's wide streets.

After a block or so Jason realized they were being fol-lowed and for a moment felt concerned until he realized it was George, the senator's secretary who had discretely reappeared.

After a few moments of silence, the two of them stood with-in a few hundred yards of the White House.

"Have you visited our illustrious executive mansion young man?" the senator asked, turning to face Jason.

"No, I did not know that was possible…but you must know it well. What is it like?"

"I once knew it well…President Lincoln valued my advice and I was often there helping to give him council."

"And President Grant?"

Once again, Sumner looked at Jason as if he'd just landed from mars…a look even in the somewhat dim moonlight Jason could see.

Reflecting quietly to himself Sumner gazed at the building for a time saying nothing. After a time, he spoke. "I am afraid the current occupant of the White House has no interest in my advice...indeed, I did what I could to deny him the honor of a second term."

"But I thought Grant was as dedicated as you to defeating the south, ending slavery."

"Grant is a soldier...whose only qualification, which President Lincoln in his desperation appreciated, was his willingness to sacrifice our brave union men in bloodbaths."

"Which won the war, did they not?"

"Eventually, but I was not among those who lionized General Grant."

"And as president?"

As president he has proven himself still the soldier, expecting his orders to be followed by senators as once colonels did."

"Oh, I can see how that might be a problem."

"More for me perhaps than the general turned president," Sumner said, turning away from the building. "But that is a tale you should hear from others. Suffice to say, the man you see before you no longer has the authority he once held. Indeed, there are days when I have no idea what I am doing at my office...and your concern for the Chinese...I would be very surprised if their situation did not get greatly worse over the next few years. I might have been their champion a few years ago, but I am exhausted, and those who agree with me tend to have other more pressing issues on their minds."

At that, the old man winced a bit...touched his hand to his chest and then grabbing onto a nearby rail held it for a moment while George, who'd continued to follow them at a reasonable distance came running up.

"Senator...stop...just rest a moment here, I will call for a horse cart."

"You will do no such thing...just let me rest a moment and then we will walk back. I need the air."

Ten minutes later the three men arrived at the door. As George and the senator entered, Martha handed Jason a neatly wrapped package. As he turned to go Jason heard the senator's voice, now stronger ring out once again.

"Mr. Brandt…"

"Yes, Senator?"

"When I am next in Boston, perhaps we should dine again."

"I would like that, sir."

With that, the senator entered and George, looking deeply relieved, tipped his hat as Jason set off down the street.

# CHAPTER 59

# WITH COLLEAGUES

"And who might you be?"

The voice startled Jason from his concentration, concentration he'd dearly wished to maintain as he wrote up his notes in the long hall of the Willard's lobby, a spot whose lighting was significantly better than that available in the small room he'd taken upstairs. It had been an especially long day, begun with that early morning walk before his meeting with Senator Stewart. He was exhausted.

"Excuse me?" Jason said rubbing his eyes and taking a sip of the coffee one of the ubiquitous waiters had been willing to fetch him even as those others around him sat sipping what appeared to be rum filled nightcaps."

"My friends and I, fellow journalists all, have been wondering. Sort of an occupational hazard I'd say. Saw you come in the other day…walk out this afternoon with Sumner's man and now writing up notes…You some sort of reporter?"

Jason surveyed the three men standing before him. They appeared to be a bit in their cups but not aggressive, rising he extended his hand.

"My name is Jason Brandt, most recently of Boston and yes, you have found me out. I am as some might say another scribbler, a fellow who writes to earn my supper."

"Planning to stay long?" the older of the three men asked, though he could not have been more than forty.

"Actually not, but is there some reason you ask? Here, sit down; I would love to chat."

"So you're not aiming to join us reporters...covering Washington City...government and all? They's already an awful lot of us here competing for interviews...tidbits from those the public is interested in...and not enough newspapers willing to pay for material as it is. So who do you write for?"

"Well, let me assure you on that score...and what you say about competition to keep one's belly full...I think I passed at least five veterans of the war, most of them lacking arms or legs begging in the streets as I returned here just now."

"So who do you write for?" the fellow asked again, clearly not at all interested in the many former soldiers begging in the streets.

"The *North China Daily News*...that is at least who I usually write for—had a regular position there until recently."

"Never heard of it," the fellow commented as he turned to his fellows. "A Chinaman's paper?"

Jason laughed. "Well, I suppose some Chinese read it." As he spoke, he wondered how his friend, Wu's English was coming along. "But no, the readers are Westerners, mostly Americans and Brits who live in Shanghai, in China, businessmen in the trade."

As he explained it became obvious, his new colleague's demeanor had changed. He was not unwanted competition. Maybe Sumner and Stewart for that matter were right, at base, jobs and the money to survive were almost always at the core of any issue.

"So, gentlemen, be assured you have no extra competition. I will be off in the morning and my articles unlikely to compete with your own. Now, will you join me for a drink? I have been sipping coffee but a brandy would be more to my tastes.

"Just came from one of the taverns across the street, cheaper over there."

One of the younger men suggested hesitating.

"As my guest," Jason said putting down a few coins on the small table. It seemed a worthwhile expense and besides he'd dined for free.

"Well, fellows, I think we can accommodate a fellow journalist. Thanks, Mr.... Grant?"

"Brandt," Jason said, laughing, "not to be confused with the president."

"Right, you are the fellow," he said, taking off his cap as his two friends dragged two nearby chairs over to where Jason was sitting. The youngest of them, a fellow no more than in his early twenties, eagerly caught the attention of one of the waiters and ordered a round of drinks.

"OK, not the president's namesake. But speaking of such things, why were you walking with Sumner's man?"

"Why? Sumner had invited me to dinner and he was showing me the way."

As he spoke Jason was unsure if he should mention what he took as the senator's special invitation, but the reaction was not what he expected.

"Sumner...dinner with Sumner...why would you want to talk to that old fool?"

The youngest of them burst out, "Nobody cares what Sumner thinks."

"But I was under the impression Sumner was one of the most senior senators, deeply respected."

"That was a long time ago." The older of the reporters said, perhaps a bit too loudly. "Back in the war years when Honest Abe was in the White House, yes, certainly but not for a long time. Even lost his post in the senate."

"He is not a senator anymore?" Jason asked in astonishment.

"Sure he is a senator, but not a powerful one. He and the president hate each other. Opposed the president's reelection you know, not even a republican anymore I am told."

It was all coming together now Jason thought for himself, all the time Sumner had for entertaining. His quiet bitterness and certainty that the situation would get worse for the Chinese.

"So Sumner's influence is completely spent?"

"Dead as a door nail." The third reporter, a fellow who'd said nothing till that moment blurted out.

"So why'd you want to talk to him?"

"It is as I said, I write on issues of interest to those in the China trade. It's my understanding, he was very much for the Chinese gaining the votes as black men have done."

"Suppose so, the oldest of the three said "It is not something one speaks about here much."

"I was under the impression it was a very much discussed issue, the role of the Chinese."

"In the far West, yes absolutely, but here, no not much, hardly any Chinese around. When folks want to get themselves riled up they mostly talk about all the Irish flooding in…taking honest American jobs away."

"There was that thing in Western Massachusetts, that shoe-factory thing, right?" one of the reporters said, clearly working to dredge up an old memory.

"Yes I do know about that…but not more of an issue."

"Not here but the San Francisco papers certainly care a lot."

"So Sumner's a spent force here?" Jason asked.

"These days most folks only heard of him because of the caning, of course."

"Wait, the senator mentioned that...but I did not know what he meant."

"Didn't know, well, that must have surprised the old man... it's probably the most famous—"

"And painful!" his young colleague burst out.

"Most famous AND painful thing ever happened to him."

"Sorry, I really don't know," Jason said feeling a touch of the same embarrassment he'd felt earlier in the evening."

"Well, it was a long time ago, before your time...and If you really spent years in China...your family tradesmen or missionaries—that sort?"

"Father was a preacher in Hong Kong."

"Right, well, you would not have heard of it."

"So, what happened?"

Stroking his chin, as if trying to drudge up memories from years before the oldest of the reporters finally explained after a moment's hesitation.

"Must have been the mid-fifties. Several years before Fort Sumter, before the war...not sure what year...be that as it may... Your Mr. Sumner hails, as he does, from Massachusetts, hot bed of liberals and abolitionists...gave some sort of speech against slavery, attacking the institution...and I guess more personally those senators who supported it."

"And another senator attacked him?"

"Not quite...relative of the fellow, a congressman came over from the other chamber, attacked him a couple of days later... beat him near to death...right there on the senate floor."

"And what happened? Did no one rise to defend the senator?"

"Not sure about what happened exactly then. Sumner was out cold. Think it took months maybe years for him to recover...

but there was some other guy, another northern congressman who called out his attacker...can't remember their names.

"Burlington?" one of the younger companions hazarded a guess.

"No, not that, but you are close...right, Burlingame—Congressman Burlingame—challenged the man...what was his full name...can't recall. In any case, Burlingame challenged him to a dual...but the guy found some excuse not to take him up."

"Burlingame...Anson Burlingame?" Jason asked.

"Yes, that's it. You know the fellow?"

"Well, no, actually, he is dead. Died a while back in Russia, I think. But I certainly know of him, negotiated the treaty between China and America."

"Did he? So he became an ambassador?"

"If we are talking about the same man. Yes, I guess, must have left congress and become a diplomat."

"President Lincoln appointed him after he lost his last election." The voice startled them all as the waiter offered the needed information and the plate of oysters that Jason's new friends had apparently ordered.

An hour later, after retiring somewhat tipsy to his room, Jason sat reflecting on what he'd learned. Of Sumner's failed role with the laws governing Chinese in America and his "acquaintance"...must of have actually been friends...with Anson Burlingame whose treaty with China, that some now claimed was too friendly to China and now regularly challenged by the growing anti-Chinese crowd in the west. It was an interesting angle that Jason realized he should develop not only in his writings for the *North China Daily News,* but in his next report to Mr. Sage. Indeed, the financial importance of his relationship with Sage seemed to grow in his mind every time he had walked by another of the destitute Civil War veterans he'd kept passing in the streets of Washington City all day.

# CHAPTER 60

# A NEW PLAN

He'd known something was up for weeks. True, Black Jade had not acted all that differently since his return from Washington. Nevertheless, it was also true that they'd not talked privately all that much lately given how much time he'd spent in the adjacent writing space next to the rented home in Rockport they were living in again. Black Jade had herself seemed busy as well. Each morning after sending the children off to school, she'd worked with Old Zhu to plan the day's meals and then set off to the harbor to practice her painting. However, he'd suspected she was bored as well.

"Husband." She turned to him one evening as they sat along the harbor listening to the waves hit the rocks and taking the local fragrances deeply into their nostrils, on the one hand of the salty aroma of sea water and on the other the buttery smell of lobsters cooking in a nearby shack.

"So what is on your mind?"

"How important is it that we remain here in Rockport?"

"I never really thought about it. I mean we came here because my father lived in Salem and he found this place for us. Do you miss Boston; do you want to go back there?"

"No, not there but Miriam, Old Zhu and I have been talking—"

"The three of you? I had no idea Old Zhu's English had advanced that far."

"You wouldn't. You travel constantly and only talk to her in Chinese."

"OK, agreed. Then about what, about moving?"

"Yes."

"Where?"

"It is time for Mei-ling to go to higher school, and Miriam says that school in Troy, Mrs. Willard's school is best…that having a chance to have Mei-ling there for free is too good an opportunity to miss."

"So you want to move to Troy—want all of us to move to Troy?"

"Yes, and Miriam says there is a boy's academy nearby in a place called Albany…very close…not sure how close…but very near, maybe a few hours' carriage ride. Rockport is pretty but too small. We could live there, see the children often, and travel more."

"You mean give more talks together?"

"That and perhaps travel with you when you do your reporting."

As he looked at her closely, it was clear she was unsure how he would react to her proposal. Nevertheless, the more he thought about it the more it made sense.

"I never thought about that but we really don't have any real ties to this area. Troy certainly has good rail lines to New York and the Hudson River ferries are just as convenient. And you coming along would be a lot more fun. But Old Zhu, what about her?"

"She would stay at whatever place we took in Troy, near Mrs. Willard's school and could even go to Albany if Willie had a problem while we travel. What do you think?"

"There could be one problem though," she said hesitantly.

"What?"

"The more time I spend in this country, the more I see some people are uncomfortable that we are married, that Willie is white and Chinese."

"Why is that a problem?"

"Would people talk to you about Chinese issues if they knew I was your wife?"

"On that there is no issue. If they don't like it, they can be damned," he said with a level of conviction that clearly pleased her.

"Then it is settled we move?"

"Sure, why not…We should make the move soon. You don't want to be doing that after the weather turns bad."

"Good," she said simply and then turned. "It is time for supper."

⟐

The following weeks went by quickly as plans were made first to make a preliminary trip to Troy to find a place to live and then to initiate the efforts to enroll the children in their respective schools, the Troy Female Seminary and what he now knew to be the Albany Boys' Academy in Albany.

Especially helpful was a long letter from Olivia Sage who'd, Jason learned, been informed of the plans to move long before he had. Olivia had written a detailed letter discussing the various locations in Troy they should consider renting and even a more specific list of available rentals she'd heard about from her friends who still lived there.

Given how extensive the list was and how long it had probably taken to gather the material, Jason found himself wondering if Black Jade had written to Olivia the moment he'd walked out the door for his last reporting trip. Nevertheless, he said nothing; he'd already begun to feel guilty for leaving her in Rockport for such long periods. Certainly, Black Jade may have grown up in a small village in southern China but she had spent her adult years not only in the Taiping capital of Nanjing but more recently in Shanghai. Troy might not be quite as lively as either of those two cities but it was a far more interesting place than Rockport he agreed.

By the early summer the move was accomplished an effort made that much easier given how many of their family's belongings had been stored after leaving the Boston home. The cottage in Rockport had been far too small to hold much of what they had taken from the family home.

Now, as Jason stood on First Street in Troy, no more than a few hundred yards from the Female Seminary, and just around the corner from the high Greek facade of the church whose steps he'd sat on with Mr. Sage when they'd first arrived he felt quite satisfied. The children would be starting school soon; the place they'd rented on First Street, if smaller than his now sold family home in Boston was a lot more spacious than the Rockport cottage. Moreover, it had become obvious that the steamship lines and rail connections to New York were far more convenient. And if it was no longer possible to walk to the beach in the evenings, at least the Troy house offered easy access to the Hudson River that both of them found relaxing enough to walk along in the evenings.

But most important was the shear energy of Troy which if somewhat subdued that cold week in January when they had first visited was now in full bloom with the shops on River and Congress streets filled with shoppers each afternoon. If he could have done something about the number of bars or people who talked in the streets to the wee hours, it would have been perfect. Rockport, aside from the sound of crashing waves had been a lot quieter. Nevertheless, he reminded himself there were always tradeoffs with every decision.

As for Old Zhu, the situation could not have been better. Not only was she now more able to converse with the many Irish maids who sat together in the parks on Sunday afternoons, she was introduced one afternoon to a young woman from Hong Kong whose husband had just established a Chinese laundry nearby. True, they did not share the same Chinese dialect but Old Zhu had picked up some Cantonese listening to Jason and Black Jade over the years and with the newly acquired English language skills both possessed the two had been able to communicate well enough. Apparently, Old Zhu's new friend's husband's brother had initially set up a laundry in Albany. Then, the two had then gone in together in an effort to establish a second site in Troy which had only just opened.

That very evening, Black Jade with Jason and the children in tow carried all the laundry they could gather to the newly opened shop for an excuse to meet the owners and help them get their business started.

As they sat having the tea which as anticipated had immediately been offered Jason could see how pleased Black Jade was. The first Chinese woman she'd spoken with save Old Zhu since they left San Francisco and amazingly one whose dialect she had no problem understanding. Indeed, it was quite late before the family, the children already asleep, as the carriage took them back to First Street, arrived at their rented lodgings.

"What is bothering you?" he asked an hour or so after they had gone to bed and then suddenly realized after initially falling asleep that she'd lain awake alongside him unable to end her day. Sitting up he finally got up and in his nightshirt lit the gas lamp.

"Just tell me."

"Go to sleep, it is nothing."

"I am not going to sleep till you tell me what you are so upset about." he said slipping into the Cantonese of their youth. These days they usually spoke in English, initially at her insistence so she could practice—than as the months and then years piled up simply out of habit. The children after all were becoming quite resistant to speaking Chinese and Old Zhu herself was getting relatively good, he'd come to understand in English as well. Nevertheless, there were times when Cantonese seemed to be the right thing to use.

"Husband, you said nothing, not to the family not to me since we returned home. Surely you can do something; people listen to you."

"Do what?" he asked having no clue what she was talking about.

"Do you not know?"

"Know what?"

"About elder brother's wife?" she insisted incredulously.

"I have no idea what you are talking about...what wife, whose wife?"

His wife stared at him at first as if he were an idiot, and then more reflectively as if she were trying to understand something.'

"He said nothing to you?"

"I guess not...about what...his wife...his wife was there."

"No not his wife...elder brother's wife..."

"You mean the brother in Albany."

"Yes, of course...what did you men talk about when you smoked those cigarettes on the porch?"

"I don't know. He told me about how he and his brother set up the laundry in Albany, some of the problems they had getting started...hard to attract customers who were not accustomed as in California to take their laundry to Chinese for cleaning.

"That is all?"

"I think so…what is going on?"

"His wife only talks about one thing…her sister in law… stuck in China…the husband has the money to send for her… to make their family whole again. But the Hong Kong officials won't let her…don't want any more Chinese women coming to America…say they are all bad women."

"You, we did not have any problem."

"That was a long time ago…and you are…" she said switching back to English, "a white American with money. They barely looked at me…and besides she said things are getting worse. America might not even let me in soon."

"So she wants me to help?"

"She did not say that…but I told her you were an important writer that you wrote about such things…that maybe you could. That you talk to powerful men in Washington City.

"You give me more credit than I deserve. The only man who talked to me at length only did so because he'd lost any influence and was bored." Again, he felt like everyone, first Wong and now his own wife were expecting more of him than he could deliver.

"Well, I could at least try to write about the issue…maybe send off a few letters…it might help.

"Letters, completely forgot…a pile came from Salem today…from Olivia, from Aouda in England. Letters from Mr. Sage, Barlow and even one from Prosper."

"All that…at once?"

"Miriam must have saved a pile up until she was sure we were settled in and that the package would arrive safely. Do not be mad at her…or me. I put them aside when Old Zhu told me about the new Chinese neighbors."

"So where are they, this treasure of correspondence?"

"Down stairs near the back door. I was holding them when Old Zhu walked in."

If Jason had been sleepy earlier that possibility was now completely vanished as he picked up one of the oil lamps burning on the bedroom table and descended as quietly as he could down stairs to the kitchen.

A few minutes later, he went through the pile. It was indeed an abundance of riches, a letter each from Sage and Barlow and within the envelope from Prosper yet another, one from his old Friend Wu.

Since the letter from Wu was the most special, he took it up first.

> Old Friend:
> I write hoping that all is well for your family for Black Jade and your children. One-day wish to know them. Perhaps one day soon. Reason why I write...first hope you keep up your Chinese...English getting better, Prosper also teaching me French but hard to write. Continue in Chinese.

The rest of the letter was in Chinese which Jason had only a bit of trouble reading though he did make a note to himself to practice more...if he lost his ability to read the many characters he'd studied for so long it would be a real problem when they returned home. But more to the point, was Wu's explanation that Prosper, as his more immediate work was finishing up at the dockyard was increasingly talking of following Yung Wing's American Educational trip with one of his own...and that he'd offered Wu the position of Chinese secretary to the mission, at least an informal position.

The last part was a bit vague, why Wu's new position had to be informal but that mattered little considering the primary reason for the letter. Wu believed that it would not be long before Giquel departed with a group of students for Paris and had offered to bring him along to Europe. What he wanted to know was when Jason and his family would be passing through Paris since the family's long term plans to return to Shanghai through Europe were already well known among his friends.

Wu's question provoked in Jason the same set of questions he and Black Jade had been asking themselves constantly since they had arrived. When would it be time to go back? Nevertheless, the answer of course was linked to Black Jade's new conviction that she had to be ready to start the girl's school in Shanghai upon their return and the planning for that effort was, they both knew, arduous. There was not only the money to be raised but Black Jade's own expectation that she needed to serve both as the principal of the school and one of its teachers, at this point teacher of both English and perhaps French and painting. His wife was, if he knew anything about her, a long-term planner and of course, part of the reason the family found themselves in Troy was its proximity to the city's major educational institutions, the Female Seminary and the nearby engineering school a few blocks away.

Indeed, Black Jade's planning was becoming more and more obvious. Especially so when he reflected on the fact that Olivia Sage had through correspondence introduced his wife to Emma Willard's younger sister Almira, an accomplished educator in her own right who, while quite old was said to be visiting Troy soon and, he'd been told, been hoping to meet Black Jade. Which of course brought him to the reality of how much the Sage family continued to be his own family's benefactor, largely through Olivia rather than Russell of course, he thought to himself as he picked up first Sage and then Barlow's letters.

After he finished reading the two letters, he looked up to see the early light coming in through the front window of their first street rented home. Unfortunately, the buildings opposite blocked his view of the river, his one regret about the place that had thus far worked out so well for his small family.

The letters were surprisingly similar. Of course, neither Barlow of the *North China Daily News* nor Mr. Sage had ever met, but both their letters were full of inquiries about the growing effort to bar the Chinese, initially women and then men from entering the United States. Both men, linked as they were to the business communities in China and US respectively, were primarily concerned that such a move would negate the Burlingame Treaty and more importantly hurt the trade so many had worked hard to nurture.

Barlow, his editor, for his part wanted more information on what was going on, news his readers were regularly calling for as they made their plans along the China coast. Sage though was much more specific. Although he asked for his usual update on industrial developments in China, that Jason knew Prosper's letter still unread would probably be helpful with. But more to the point the former congressman had much more immediate news.

Apparently, Congress was planning to hold hearings on the Chinese question in San Francisco and Sage gently suggested Jason should not only go but testify on behalf of the Chinese. It was not exactly an order, Jason hardly worked for Mr. Sage but it was quite emphatic and was accompanied by a promise to pay his expenses, expense for the entire family if need be for him to go.

The offer of a fully paid trip to California and back was quite unexpected. Indeed he'd heard nothing of the planned hearings in San Francisco, but he assumed Sage would have better sources within Congress than he had. The more he thought about it, the more it made sense. He could write about the hearings for the *North China Daily News*, strengthen his relationship with the Sage family who had become important to his future and take on a role he'd been considering since the moment Wong had arrived on his doorstep long before in Rockport.

Moreover, he realized with satisfaction, it would please his wife as well given the very conversation they'd had only a short while earlier. He was half tempted to go back upstairs and wake her, finally deciding to wait. Now completely awake he slipped on his day clothing, boots and left the house to walk along the river. How soon he wondered to himself would it be before he and Black Jade, for the children would obviously stay here in school, be boarding one of those ships to make connections in New York for San Francisco.

A few minutes later, staring out over the Hudson River, he realized Sage had not specifically said when those hearings were scheduled and the letter from the businessman had of course been delayed. A few minutes later, he found himself at the telegraph office waiting for it to open so he could wire Sage asking about when the hearings were actually set. He'd not agree till he'd spoken to Black Jade, but they needed the dates before any decisions could be made.

As he waited, he remembered the unopened letter from Prosper Giquel in his pocket and eagerly opened it. To his surprise, it began in French the language he'd studied with as Giquel as his teacher years before. Indeed, it had been in exchange for Jason's own Chinese lessons with which Giquel had accomplished far more than Jason ever did with French. Still, he knew enough to read the letter slowly, increasingly able as he proceeded to translate the material in his own mind into English. After the usual greetings, it became obvious why Giquel had written in French a language far less likely to be known along the China coast then English.

So, my old friend…you seem to have neglected a few minor details about our good friend…Giquel had written obviously not mentioning of whom he was writing. I managed I pride myself a bit on my detective skills to learn a bit more…intelligent, a quick study as you originally wrote. But, I had no idea of the fellow's revolutionary record. Mon Dieu, you have sent me a Jacobin in the clothing of the Sage - but do not fear, your secret and his is safe- a fine fellow who has become more and more helpful.

Well, the cat was out of the bag as they say…Giquel had realized that Jason had sent a former rebel, former senior Taiping figure to him without warning. Although so many years after the end of the rebellion, Jason had no idea how much the Manchu government still cared about finding such people. Nevertheless, he had no interest in finding out. His close friend was, he was certain, still doing what he could to disguise his role in the rebellion and Jason's own wife had a connection he'd preferred not to advertise. They were, after all planning to return home one day.

At least, Jason noticed with some relief that Prosper was obviously impressed with Wu and not angry about not being informed of his background, which could at best have been awkward.

After that, Giquel had gone on to tell of progress at the Fuzhou Dockyard, his plans for sending an educational mission to Europe and a bit of teasing that the Americans were making it less likely to do business in China, as word arrived of the efforts to exclude them…From Prosper's perspective, America's enthusiasm for turning its back on China could only help his beloved France.

The fact that Giquel, as well as Barlow and even Sage had largely written of the same issues convinced Jason all the more of the necessity of going to San Francisco for the hearings and he waited impatiently for the telegram office to open all the while wishing he'd left a note for Black Jade.

# CHAPTER 61

# ON THE CHINESE QUESTION

"Mr. Brandt, are you not simply an agent of former Congressman Sage and his business friends, people who merely want access to the cheap labor Chinese offer any employer?'

The question startled him. In fact, almost everything about the last two weeks had been hard to comprehend. After all, the last minute request from Sage to attend the hearings at the notoriously tightfisted financier's expense and then the realization that he and Black Jade had less than two weeks to get Old Zhu and the children settled into their respective schools in Troy and Albany. Then after hurriedly accomplishing that, almost immediately heading south on the Troy ferry in a last minute dash to take the same train they had taken only a few years before toward San Francisco. And now after a failed effort to get both himself and his wife signed on as potential witnesses, he'd found himself sitting opposite the panel of politicians, congressman and senators, most of whom were glaring at him.

"Mr. Brandt," the congressman said, leaning forward his thick hands resting on the mahogany table that separated the congressman from the witnesses. "Did you not hear the question?"

"Hear the question, of course, Congressman, but I don't understand your question. I am here as a reporter for the *North China Daily News*, a paper based in Shanghai whose readers are very interested in these hearings."

"Mr. Brandt, are you not a good deal more than that. Reporters chase stories not become part of them. Are you not sitting here before this panel as a witness?"

"Well, of course, but merely because it has been suggested, in fact, requested that I do so because of my personal background. I grew up in China, indeed for most of my adult life have lived and worked there...and it has been thought that I might be able to offer information needed by your commission."

Then just as the congressman opened his mouth to respond with what appeared likely to be another aggressive volley, the committee chairman interrupted him with an inquiry about how much time he needed to talk to the witnesses. Jason, who had almost immediately felt on the defense since sitting down in what otherwise might have been a very comfortable high backed chair, had at least a chance to look around the room and what he saw sincerely surprised him.

Black Jade, was being escorted into the hearing room by Charles Crocker the railroad tycoon who'd served as a witness the previous day, testifying about what he reported as his very successful experience working with Chinese laborers on the great effort to build the transcontinental railroad. Somehow, Black Jade had met Crocker himself, and the businessman had decided to escort her back to the hearing room.

As he tried to catch her eye his attention was again drawn to the front of the room as the committee chair, having apparently finished with his congressional colleague addressed him directly.

"Mr. Brandt...Please indulge me if you will," the older and impressively whiskered committee chair began. "Some of us are really quite uncertain why you're here, while others have insisted you have something to contribute. So let me ask you a few questions to clarify matters. Am I correct that this is only your second visit to California, and your experiences here have been limited to less than ten days in total?"

"Yes, but..."

"Excuse me, Mr. Brandt, but indulge me...and is it not also true that almost all of your experience in America—and yes, the committee understands you were raised in China—has been on the American East Coast, where the Chinese question has hardly arisen?"

"Yes, Mr. Chairman." Jason said recognizing there was probably no point in attempting to do more than simply respond.

"Which, Mr. Brandt, is why several of us really are quite uncertain what you have to contribute."

"Excuse me, Mr. Chairman." A loud voice from well down the panel suddenly attracted the attention of almost everyone in the room. It was one of the senators, whom Jason recognized from the previous day, a fellow who had questioned the railroad man with a reasonably positive attitude, drawing from him a testimony that spoke very well of how industrious, reliable, and cooperative his Chinese railroad workers had turned out to be.

Just for a second Jason thought he saw a hint of irritation in the chairman's eyes as he turned to his colleague "Yes, Senator, is there something you wish to contribute...?"

"Not so much to contribute, Mr. Chairman, but merely to expand on your line of inquiry...if you might allow that?"

The chairman, running his fingers thoughtfully through his whiskers with enough energy that Jason thought he saw a chunk of moustache wax drop off, swiveled to his side looking for a response from the congressman he had initially interrupted.

With a relatively generous wave of the hand, the fellow made clear he had no objection.

"Well then, Senator, it looks like you have the floor."

"Thank you, Mr. Chair, and to my distinguished colleague."

"Let me put it to you this way, Mr. Brandt," the senator said, his voice remaining a timber louder than he really needed in the room, clearly a fellow who was used to addressing large crowds, Jason thought to himself. "I am told you were in the hearing room yesterday for several hours listening to a range of those who supported some sort of ban on Chinese labor and those who argued, quite convincingly, that the Chinese had contributed mightily to the impressive and relatively quick development of the West Coast over the last decade."

"Yes, Senator," Jason said, not sure if he should interrupt.

"Well, then what do you think you can contribute, not as a reporter writing about these events, but as someone with considerable experience in China, experience I only learned about this morning from my staff." At that, the senator raised his somewhat-pudgy hand in the air and waved a copy of a book, Jason recognized as his own *China Tales*, in the direction of his congressional colleagues.

Then senator passed the volume to the congressman to his left and turning to Jason again indicated he expected him to address the committee.

"Well, you are certainly correct, Senator, that as my wife and I sat listening to the hearing yesterday..." For a momentary second, Jason saw the senator become uncomfortable at the mention of Black Jade but only for that quick flash as Jason went on turning to his impressions of the hearings.

"Well, to make a long story short, I heard a great many people speak of how industrious the Chinese are. But as well, strong opinions that suggested allowing more into the country would be a disaster, a disaster that stemming in some opinions from their uncivilized nature, their inability to assimilate enough to become true Americans as some other foreign groups have. And as a more practical matter, the fact that living together as they do as bachelors they can work for far lower wages than white men, mostly Irish workers need to support their families.'

"That does seem to sum it up well, your reporter's skills allow a reasonably objective summary," the senator cut in, turning to his colleagues. "And your own background, does that give you any different perspective on the dilemma we find ourselves arguing here?"

Jason eyed the senator closely studying his clothing, noticing for the first time that he seemed better dressed than many of his colleagues, a politician perhaps with stronger ties than some to the moneyed classes he thought for a second, an observation that possibly explained something of the politics Jason assumed were part of the backstory of the hearings. Then, taking a deep breath he tried to project his voice with some of the same strength the senator demonstrated with such ease.

"Well, sir, it is true as has been mentioned, in many ways I am an outsider to these issues, with little knowledge of the role of the Chinese here in California but perhaps the experience I have had growing up and living in China does offer that 'different' perspective you asked about."

"I really do not see how this witness can contribute. His own words indict him," another congressman suddenly blurted out but was then correctly reprimanded by the chair who seemed to be making an effort to accommodate the entire committee.

"Go ahead, son," the senator said, capturing the room's attention.

"Thank you, Senator. Well, first, sir, let me state the obvious, most of the Chinese who come here are from the area near the British Colony of Hong Kong where I grew up. That matters because I speak with fluency their native tongue, indeed I have met Chinamen here who knew or knew of me at home. So perhaps I am more in a position to speak for them because many have spoken to me in their native tongue of their goals and aspirations."

"And what have you learned from such men?"

"In truth, Senator and the other members of the committee. What we have heard here is in part true. Many, perhaps most of the Chinese workers, have no intention of staying. For the Chinese, family is especially important as are their home villages. If they travel here, it is often simply because they hope to make enough money to return home from as has been said "Gold Mountain" with far more money than they could possibly earn back in China. But that is certainly not true of all of them indeed."

"So you do not anticipate most staying here?" the senator asked with a clear sense that Jason had offered a perspective he found helpful.

"Largely true, though I have also seen how easily Chinese can assimilate to American culture, learn the language well and begin the effort to build new lives as so many others have done over the generations."

"Are you suggesting that Chinese can become Americans, can fit in as well or, I might add, only a bit tongue-in-cheek as others from the Germans to the Irish have?"

"If you put it that way, Senator, perhaps that is true. However, there is another issue I believe is worth discussing. There seemed a sense yesterday that California might soon be swamped with Chinese. Personally I do not see that happening."

"Why not if they can make so much more money here than in China?" another congressman asked, throwing his own inquiry into the ring with a tone that only hinted of animosity.

"Well, sir, I am sorry I did not catch if you were a congressman or a senator."

"Congressman, but go ahead. Why don't you see that happening?"

"Just as America was torn apart by a civil war a decade ago, in the early 1860s..." Suddenly Jason realized he did not really know when the American Civil War had occurred and quickly moved on. "China was itself convulsed by a struggle that was much larger and lasted far longer."

"And why does that matter?"

"Because, sir, a lifetime in China convinced me that the Chinese are so tied to their families and home villages that they would only leave if they really had to, and that Civil War, so disruptive, has been over for more than a decade; the China I know is slowly recovering, indeed starting to industrialize. The number of jobs, particularly along the coasts, are growing...my point, sir, is that I believe that the numbers who feel they need to leave China to seek their fortunes is diminishing, thus making those who arrive here likely to go down rather than up in the future."

"If I might, Mr. Chairman, this is all very enlightening...but this is California, not China, and the fact is that our working white men cannot work for the absurdly low wages the Chinese accept."

"Well, Mr. Brandt, my distinguished colleague has a point. What can you say to that?"

"Well, it is true that young Chinese men, living together speaking little English can pool their resources and offer their labor at wages the whites, the Irish for example with their families cannot. But..."

"Exactly my point Mr. Brandt, even you admit the Chinese undermine the white working man!" the same congressman exclaimed.

"Excuse me," the apparently more senior senator intervened again. "There is another matter that I am told has not been discussed here that you might be able to offer an opinion on."

"If I can, Senator."

"Indeed I hope so, I am told you have special knowledge of Chinese industrialization efforts, efforts that could result in that enormous society purchasing industrial goods made here in America by American working men. Is that so?"

"Well, it is true that the government of China, especially some of the great officials along the coast are attempting to industrialize. Indeed, while initially purchasing some ships made here in America they have started their own industrial facilities that have made significant purchases of the equipment necessary to found such establishments."

For the next few minutes, Jason offered the same sort of information he had gathered frequently from Giquel and Yung Wing that had been so often at the core of his reports to Russell Sage. For a moment he wondered if the financier would be pleased with his sharing such information, it could after all prove financially helpful one day but then, remembering that he was only here at Sage's initial encouragement, assumed the investor would not mind. Feeling more confident, he went on at length of his knowledge of how much France was gaining from the links to the Fuzhou dockyard, which might one day also complement American business. Prosper had only recently asked him to learn more about Troy's famous engineering school Rensselaer Polytechnic Institute which Yung Wing was as well asking about and brought to mind the various conversations he'd had with Yung Wing, the previous year at his new friend's wedding in Hartford.

"Excuse me but you are talking of manufactures that come from back east, not here in California. We are not concerning ourselves with such issues." The congressman said who had, since he'd begun testifying, been obviously committed to limiting the impact of Jason's contributions.

Ever the conciliator, the committee's chair stepped in again. "Thank you, sir. Your point is well taken. We are venturing past the topics of our mandate but—"

"But, Mr. Brandt, you were about to add some additional issue...what was that?"

"Thank you, Senator. I think this is an important issue, as I have said living together without families the Chinese men can work for less than the Irish can for example...but that is not likely to be their first choice. There are few Chinese women here...were there more I expect the Chinese would have as settled and somewhat more expensive life styles as the Irish, and once the greater language burden is overcome, which I have seen accomplished. Why my—"

"Yes...that is a very good point," the senator bellowed out, cutting him off again. It was clear the senator, however supportive of Jason's perspective, did not want mention of Black Jade in public, and Jason was increasingly aware of why. Indeed, for a second he caught his wife's glance in his peripheral vision, which confirmed she had drawn the same conclusion.

"Well, Mr. Brandt," the chairman's voice drew his attention again. "I think we have heard enough of your opinions. Thank you very much for your time, and give my regards to Mr. Sage when you speak to him next. I have been told he speaks very highly of you."

"Thank you, sir." At that, Jason realized that another witness had already been positioned to take his place as Jason hurriedly gathered his paper and pens to leave the witness chair.

# CHAPTER 62

# BACK TO TROY

Gathering his papers and trying to leave the witness table turned out to be more difficult than it looked. Behind him, the next witnesses were settling in at the table as the committeemen had begun another polite argument about something… Jason was not certain. Ahead of him, he saw that Black Jade had already left the chamber and wondered if she would be waiting outside for him as he managed to quietly work his way through the crowd of intense on-lookers who were eagerly chatting about the hearings. Several of them nodded to Jason as he passed them, a few even suggesting with their eyes that they had appreciated his efforts, but it was obvious as well, that most had not. Indeed, he felt a sense of real antagonism projected in his direction by more than a few.

Eventually though he'd managed to find a path through the increasingly loud and crowded room to make his way from the chamber that opened out into a large and well-lighted hallway. There standing at a distance stood Black Jade looking extremely tense standing alongside but not speaking to a fellow Jason recognized as some sort of assistant to Charles Crocker the railroad magnate. The man himself though was nowhere to be seen; clearly, he had left his assistant to attend to Black Jade until Jason arrived.

"There you are sir, the tall, bearded fellow gestured in a friendly fashion. Mr. Crocker sends his regrets, had another matter to attend to but he asked me to convey his appreciation for your efforts and that of your wife."

"Thank you, I am sorry Mr. Crocker had to leave, I would love to talk to him further? Is he going to be around over the next few days?"

With that question, Jason realized he'd erred somehow. Black Jade's eyes had flashed a sign of disapproval though he was not sure why."

"Frankly, I don't know Mr. Crocker's Schedule? I could ask if you like?"

"Perhaps, but let me get back to you? I don't want to bother him; I am sure he is quite busy?" As he spoke he could see his comments earned his wife's approval."

"Well, I will be off then, Mr. Crocker will be needing me to catch up with him." Then turning to Black Jade. "It was a delight meeting you ma'am and I hope you are feeling better now? Can I suggest that hallway it leads to an exit less often used near the side of the building."

With that, the fellow left at a brisk pace while Jason turned to his wife with a questioning look.

"Not now...Hotel now!" She said turning toward the hall that led to the building exit. Jason, found himself hurrying to keep up with her. Obviously, something had happened and he was not going to hear until they were back at the hotel. Within minutes they were outside and Black Jade, still steaming over something gestured for him to find a horse carriage taxi for the ride back to the hotel.

"What happened?" he asked in Cantonese as soon as they were seated?"

"Not now..." she said, glancing up at the carriage driver, perhaps forgetting they were speaking a tongue the man could not possibly understand. Then thinking for a moment further she turned to him.

"What time does the train station close?"

"I have no idea. Why?"

"You should go there...see when the next train leaves for New York?"

"But we already have tickets, for next week. I thought you wanted to see more of San Francisco before we left?"

"I miss the children," she said turning away from him.

"Are you going to tell me what happened or not?"

"Only if you promise to see if we can take an earlier train?" She said, that look of determination he had seen so often before. When she took on that face, he knew there was no getting around her. The people in that hearing room might have found the Chinese docile but Jason's experience was quite different.

"OK...right after we get back to the hotel I'll go out and check...the train was not all that filled on the way here. I doubt it will be a problem."

"Good" she said turning to stare at one of the larger buildings as they passed it. There was a flock of birds sitting along one of the window ledges and he watched her study them.

"There was a crowd near the door..." she began hesitantly. The usual signs...the Chinese must get out...mean pictures...

"Of course I saw them too as we arrived...and when we were here last time."

"Yes," she said, "but after you went inside, more people arrived. And they seemed to know who I was. Several ugly women and an old man had a big banner saying 'NO RACE MIXING,' and they were practically sticking it in my face."

"I am so sorry. What did you do?"

"*Do*, no idea. This is not my country. I just stood there wishing I was home."

"Back in Troy…yes…miss it and the kids."

"Back in Troy…" she said out loud, sounding unsure. "Maybe, but I really think Shanghai."

"Oh, right. Yes, I understand that even better. But how did you come to be with Crocker and his man?"

"That man, Mr. Crocker, he came up with his aide, shooed them away from me, and walked me into the committee room."

"Right, yes, I saw you coming in. It was so crowded that I was happy you had even made it in. They really should have let you testify with me."

"The people here don't want to hear the Chinese spoken of as people. There would have been no interest," she said with resignation and then turned away from him again, pretending to study the city's street life but obviously in deep thought.

⊷ ⊶

Over the next few days, Jason was glad he'd carried with him a lot of reading material and several notepads because his wife spent most of the time on the train sitting in silence. He knew she was thinking about the timing of their return to Shanghai. She'd told him that much but it was obvious she was uncertain of her feelings. Black Jade though had been happy enough when he initially returned to their hotel room with word that he'd managed to exchange the tickets for a train leaving the next day. Once that was accomplished, she'd sent him out to the telegraph office with a short message she wanted to send to Olivia about visiting as they passed through New York on the return trip to Troy.

"So, are you going to tell me what you're thinking?" He finally asked a few days into the trip after the train departed

Chicago. A few years earlier the couple had lingered in that growing Midwestern metropolis, even visited the enormous stockyards but this time Black Jade had no interest in tourism and Jason, who'd traveled considerably more around the United States than his wife had since their arrival was even less interested.

"No, not yet. I don't really know what to say…just that I think we are moving too slow. By the time we get home we won't even know Shanghai, the children will be too Americanized to fit in at home."

She was certainly right about that Jason thought. Little Willie barely remembered China and was less and less willing to use Chinese even when his parents pressed him. Moreover, he did not look all that Chinese anyway. As he grew older the little boy's features were as much New England as Chinese. Indeed, Jason sometimes thought he looked more like some of the darker Mediterranean peoples one often encountered in Boston. His sister of course was obviously Chinese, but her mannerisms and clothing tastes were becoming more and more American as well.

"Are you saying you want to go home now?"

"No, not now but perhaps sooner than I used to think. Americans don't like Chinese any more than Chinese like Americans." She said with a certainty that reminded him of the outspoken young woman who had so charmed him more than a decade before.

With that, she turned back to her copybook that he now noticed was full of French phrases. Indeed, Jason knew his wife, with her uncanny ability to pick up languages had throughout most of the trip been working on French with as much energy as she had earlier attacked English. It was obvious he thought to himself more evidence that they would be starting that trip home soon enough and that perhaps he should start trying to learn all those words in French, Prosper had taught him so long before in Guangzhou.

Then turning back to his own work he took up his writing pad and returned to the piece he'd prepared on the congressional hearings. There was no question that the editors at the *North China Daily News*, dependent on a readership that relied on decent relations between the United States and China would be very interested in the controversy raging in California about the presence of the Chinese workers.

After a few minutes his wife, while not looking up from her copybook, put her hand on his squeezing it for a moment. At least that part of their lives was still fine he thought to himself studying her while trying not to be too obvious. She was still as beautiful as always and the slight aging she'd experienced in recent years made her only more attractive to him.

—≼‡ ‡≽—

"Mr. and Mrs. Brandt I presume?" The conductor's voice startled them both. They had fallen asleep in their chairs, each with their writing books on their laps. It took a second for Jason to focus on the fellow who was standing in the aisle with the late afternoon sun streaming in directly behind him.

"Sorry, sir, I did not realize you were asleep. I can come back later."

"No, that is not a problem," Jason said, standing up as Black Jade rubbed her eyes behind him. "What can I do for you?"

"That's not it, sir. We just received a telegram for you, actually for your wife."

At that, Jason could tell Black Jade was fully awake.

"A telegram, delivered on a train, such good service," Jason said as he took the envelope.

"Yes indeed," the man said. "Actually though the service is not usually that good but the sender seems to have some influence with the owners. In any case, can you sign for it?"

"Of course," Jason said, taking up the man's pen.

"Thank you, sir. Incidentally we will be stopping soon for dinner," the fellow commented as he started down the aisle as many of the other passengers looked on studying the travelers who had rated a personal telegram delivery.

"Let me have that; it must be from Olivia." Of that, Jason was sure; only the wife of the great railroad magnate was likely to have the influence to have the telegraph not only locate the couple but also arrange personal delivery.

He watched as Black Jade carefully read the telegram with a smile.

"Well?"

"Mr. Sage is gone on another business trip, but Olivia will host both of us the day after we arrive in New York."

"I take it Olivia has something to do with your future plans?" he asked tentatively, for she'd still shared so little of what she was really thinking.

"I hope so," his wife said and then silently went back to her French copybook.

⊶ ⊷

It took Jason a while to realize how different she seemed. Olivia, who'd become somewhere between a big sister and mentor for his wife, was talking a mile a minute, showing them around the home. At the same time giving the servants last-minute orders for lunch to be taken on the small deck behind their fifth avenue home, while introducing them to her mother, who sat it in a side room contentedly knitting.

There was something about her, somewhere between a classroom teacher, with the full voice of someone familiar with speaking in public, and an aristocratic lady of the sort he'd met from time to time in Boston that caught his attention, but it was more than that. Suddenly he realized what was different. While Black Jade had spent a good deal of time with Emma Willard, her family members and Olivia during their first visit to Troy. Jason had only seen Olivia in the presence of the powerful, commanding Mr. Sage himself, whose presence seemed to diminish everyone else. Now Sage was gone. Off, he thought Olivia had mentioned, somewhere in Delaware on railroad business and Olivia was fully in charge.

"No, sit you two. You must be exhausted from the train ride. When did you get in? I think Mr. Sage told me the Western train usually arrives in the early afternoon."

"Usually, Mrs. Sage—"

"Now, Black Jade, remember I told you to call me Olivia. First names among friends is always best."

"Yes, as you wish," Jason heard his wife say, without actually addressing the older woman who was at least a decade older than her by her first name.

"We are tired, though not simply from the trip...from sitting so long across your huge country."

"Of course, then we shall stay standing a bit longer. You, I assume, took a cab here I am sure."

Jason nodded. It really had not been that far, but Jason knew his wife was never fond of walking anywhere, not with feet that were still somewhat deformed by their early binding, which however incomplete had left her less able to walk comfortably and certainly not in the hot summer sun that she religiously avoided anyway.

In a flash Mrs. Sage turned, leaving her startled servant, a young woman whom Jason guessed was from Ireland, standing there with a tray of lemonade in a lurch as her mistress set off.

"Then you must at least see a bit more of the house."

Over the next few minutes, Olivia, as Jason was trying to think of her, marched them through the house, pointing out as they went the many maps of Mr. Sage's holdings and another series of charts that seemed to indicate that he also owned tenement houses somewhere in the city on streets he had vaguely heard of.

"Wait, down this hall, Jason, you and Black Jade will probably find these things interesting. It is Russell's collection of Indian memorabilia. He has quite a collection. You must have seen Indians along your route at times."

"Well, we heard a lot about them, especially after word came about the fate of General Custer. Somewhere in the Indian lands."

"Yes, everyone has heard quite enough about the unfortunately departed General Custer though I can tell you in confidence that many who knew him won't be all that saddened, he was thought quite the egomaniac."

"What do you think will happen now Mrs. Sage?" Jason asked his reporter's curiosity starting to emerge?"

"No idea though Mr. Gould, one of my husband's railroad partners said in my presence that this would only open up the Indian lands more quickly as a result."

Jason started to ask another question when he felt his wife, who'd been holding his arm squeeze it a bit harder than necessary. Clearly he'd forgotten why they'd come to their illustrious acquaintance's home.

"But perhaps we could return to the covered deck and enjoy the cooling drinks you had prepared," Black Jade said with as charming a tone as he knew her capable of mustering.

"Yes indeed, enough of the house tour, down we go."

For the next hour, Jason sat quietly as Black Jade and Olivia talked. At first, they spoke of Mrs. Willard, how much Olivia had admired the woman, her commitment to women's education, and more immediately simply as the lifelong mentor of her earlier years.

Black Jade of course had only met Mrs. Willard once for no more than perhaps an hour but the formable woman, the founder of the Troy Female Academy, accomplished writer and world traveler had profoundly impressed her as no one in her life ever had.

Then as the conversation became more personal Black Jade spoke of their experiences in San Francisco and the increasing urgency about the plan hatched years before with Mrs. Willard that cold afternoon almost four years before to found a Shanghai Female Seminary upon her return to China.

"My dear, I can understand how you feel seeing people looking down so often at you and your family…and I agree from what I myself know the situation is likely to get worse before it improves. Nevertheless, you cannot let people's disapproval make you change your own plans."

"But—" Black Jade started.

"Young lady, don't let these surroundings fool you. I too know something of what you speak."

"You, Mrs. Sage…but you are a great lady."

"A great lady perhaps to someone like yourself, even perhaps your husband, who has spent more time in China than among America's better families. Nevertheless, I can assure you the real elites that surround us in this expensive neighborhood think of us as the upstarts: Russell, the hated upstart from Troy and his former teacher—worse yet, former governess—wife masquerading as blue bloods. I tell you this in confidence. Russell has a reputation for thinking only of business, but in truth, it is only with business that he feels really comfortable around the older moneyed elite of this city, who we both know speak behind our backs of our humble origins."

"I had no idea...there is so much I don't understand about this country but that sense of who matters and who does not is familiar to me...but do you think the idea of starting a school in Shanghai is now a bad idea?"

"Of course not, my dear. I am as committed at this moment as when we hatched the idea with dear Mrs. Willard, but I am considerably older than you...and in the matter of schools and teaching far more experienced."

"Yes of course, Mrs. Sa...Olivia that is why I asked to visit to gain the advantage of your insight."

"Running a school requires several essential characteristics, deep commitment and strong character that it was clear you possessed long before you arrived in Troy but that is not enough."

Jason watched as Black Jade nodded in deference, she was listening deeply taking in every word carefully.

"Operating a school demands far more. It requires a very experienced teaching staff with a wide range of skills essential for a young women's practical education and the ability to raise money. Forgive me my young beautiful friend from the far away empire of the Chinese, but as I understand it, neither you nor your husband has any experience in these areas."

Jason and Black Jade looked at each other and then back to Olivia.

"Yes, you are right. But does that mean the thing can't be done?"

"Of course not, there are simply more tasks to accomplish. Your daughter is already enrolled at the seminary, is that not true?"

"Yes, she started a few months ago."

"Then this is what I propose, and I truly think this can be accomplished, I do after all have more than a little influence among those running the school these days. Mrs. Wilcox was one of my students when I taught there and all administrators, especially ones operating schools that are having financial problems are very attentive to those thought to be in a position to donate funds.

"So what is your plan?" Black Jade asked looking even more serious if that was possible."

"Actually I have had this idea in mind ever since we spoke of your moving to Troy and enrolling your daughter. I propose you enroll yourself, they do have older students there from time to time...enroll in an accelerated program which I am certain you can quickly master...especially so, given how well you have accomplished English so far."

"Thank you," Black Jade said modestly.

"But there is more than that; I think that after not very long we could arrange to have you become a teacher there."

"A teacher...of what? What do I have to offer?"

"Chinese, of course, I know you have experience teaching Chinese in Rockport and the seminary attracts some young women expecting to marry missionaries. It would work wonderfully. But for now, you would yourself take a more traditional course, French...you are still studying French and planning to go to Paris on your way home are you not?"

"Yes, *bien sûr*," Black Jade said with a smile.

Excellent...well for now, the larger plans should remain our secret. Just return to Troy, see your wonderful children and enroll yourself. That will not be a problem. Meanwhile, I will start scheming on how we will get you hired as a Chinese language teacher and perhaps better in a position to learn more about fund raising."

"Thank you so much Olivia" Black Jade had a smile on her face she'd rarely exhibited over the years.

"Nonsense, Emma put this plan in place, I am merely her devoted assistant. Now tell me about your beautiful daughter, how she is doing at the seminary and that charming little boy, little William."

For the next hour, the conversation turned to an intense discussion of the children, their lives in America and of Olivia's many opinions on child raising. The woman really was a force of nature Jason realized surprised that he'd not noticed it as much during their earlier visit.

# CHAPTER 63

# A SURPRISE MEETING

"I t should only be a few more minutes, Mr. Brandt."

"Thank you, I quite understand he must be very busy."

"Well, that is, of course, true, but I know for a fact he is interested in speaking with you, there is simply the press of so much other business these days. Can I get you something?"

"No, that is not necessary. I am quite comfortable as is," Jason said. Indeed, he was feeling relatively relaxed though he'd hardly felt that way two hours before when the message had arrived at the hotel with the invitation. As a matter of fact, he'd been extraordinarily stressed out for months, more exhausted than he remembered ever being in his life as a journalist. Moreover, Black Jade had hardly been any less pressured.

The fact of the matter was, Jason thought to himself, in the months since he and his wife had returned to Troy from San Francisco their growing responsibilities had pushed them both to their limits. Black Jade for the first time in her life had thrown herself not into self-study but a routine of leaving every morning with Mei-ling for the short walk to the Female Seminary for an extraordinarily full day of French and English composition lessons, plus painting class. And to her husband's surprise, mathematics which she had also decided would be important for her plans as well. All the while attempting to be supportive of little Mei-ling who was growing taller each day and in some cases sitting alongside her mother in classes.

Evenings were spent with the two, mother and daughter studying alongside each other while Old Zhu scurried about preparing food and keeping the household running properly.

As for Jason, he'd only had a few opportunities to spend any real time with his wife and daughter, and even less with his younger son Will who'd enrolled in the Albany Academy hours away by both boat and carriage. No for Jason that fall turned out to be one of the biggest professional challenges of his life, a challenge which had begun the moment he'd returned to Troy to find a pile of letters from his editors in Shanghai who wanted him to cover not only the Chinese question but the American elections. Apparently the electoral battle to succeed General Grant, which had by the early fall become a contest between Rutherford Hays of Ohio and Samuel Tilden of New York was of enormous interest among many of the paper's American subscribers and his editors had decided to use Jason's presence to keep their readers happy.

The problem of course, that Jason could not share with his Shanghai based editors, several of whom bore names he did not even recognize, was that while his recent dispatches had spoken in length of congressional issues, quoted congressmen and senators he really knew nothing of how the US government operated and especially how an election campaign was waged.

"But you don't have a choice." Black Jade had insisted when he spoke of his uncertainty, his strong sense that he could hardly master the intricacies of the American electoral process in time to follow the campaign intelligently.

"I understand what you are saying but you must keep up your ties to those in Shanghai, especially at the paper, we will be home soon enough and those relationships must be maintained." She said with a sense of certainty he knew her conclusion warranted. In fact, he realized that his link to the paper would only diminish over time as even more new editors came and went. No, she was right, for now his only option was to feed the Shanghai editors articles that would satisfy them and their readers.

But knowing he had no option only added to the pressures that fall as Jason spent most of the time traveling, attending rallies, interviewing politicians and above all sitting up late at night with his fellow journalists trying to learn as much as he could from them about how the system worked. True his fellow reporters were never willing to share anything publishable. But of the basic outlines, the republican's enthusiasm for waving the bloody shirt against the democrats, most of whom had at one time been Johnny Rebs was easy enough to absorb while many of the southern democrats hoped to regain control of the south, or at least force the republicans to let them reassert white control over their region seemed obvious enough. However, who was for and against immigration, drinking, fighting over monetary policy or their hatred of Catholics made covering the election at times a nightmare. Still, as the weeks went on, Jason felt he was making progress and his reporting more authoritative and confident.

Indeed, by the first week of November he'd finally thought he'd survived the ordeal, produced enough acceptable material to feed the hungry mouths he'd come to think of in the place of his editors. More importantly, he was looking forward to getting home to Troy and resting up - spending more time with his family during the holiday season when the seminary closed down but alas that was not to be.

When word came down after Election Day that the election had become uncertain, Jason like so many around him was shocked. Part of him of course was delighted. Like any journalist, the idea of an important story gaining another lease on life, or at least a few more weeks of material to please one's editors was not necessarily a bad thing, but for Jason the uncertain election brought new problems. This was unchartered territory for everyone involved, even his new reporter colleagues at the Willard, said a stalemated election rarely happened, and it would only be those with the best long time sources, few of which Jason had, that would be in a position to understand how the election battle, which was apparently moving into an entirely new arena would play out. Nevertheless, lacking a choice, he set out only taking time to telegraph Troy that he'd be delayed before returning home. Doing so made him feel a bit guilty, Black Jade had begun to take more seriously the family's preparations for the Christmas holidays but he knew she would have agreed it was necessary even insisted. As always, her sense of the importance of keeping open his links to Shanghai's reading community, even at a distance really mattered. Indeed, she'd even gone as far as to search out details about at least two of the Shanghai editors and sent the one married editor a gift for his wife whom, Black Jade somehow found out was from Albany.

No, learning everything he could about the back room discussions between the democrats and the republicans, between Hay's men and Tilden's, between the courts that were more involved and the new election commission that had been put into place to facilitate adjudicating the contested election, had been a nightmare. Still, as Jason sat there he wondered if the rumors were true that a decision was likely to be announced at any minute.

Indeed if the summons had not come a few hours before, Jason was sure he'd right now be out in the streets trying to find someone with an inside scoop on what was going on. Would it be Tilden, who initially seemed to have had a lock on the presidency or another term for the republicans in the form of Hayes. But that effort had never occurred forgotten by the sudden and whispered conversation about an invitation that was to remain secret, that would allow no formal interviewing or publishable information. Such a strange request, but how could one possibly refuse Jason thought to himself as he once again studied the long hallway that even at this late hour seemed to have so many young men scurrying around the corridors of the building which despite its importance had always struck Jason as being awfully small.

"Mr. Brandt?" Another young fellow, one whose approach Jason had not noticed beckoned him.

"Yes,"

"The President can see you now."

# CHAPTER 64

# PRESIDENT GRANT

The office was smaller than he'd imagined though quickly enough Jason realized he'd been shepherded into a small space that was obviously not where the great issues of the day were decided. Still the room was large enough for several chairs.

"Welcome to the White House," the older man, the president himself, said, offering a warm and firm handshake. "Have you been here before?"

"No, sir. Well, I have walked outside of the building often enough, but to be invited in, to meet you, sir, is an honor."

"And, son, have you been informed of the rules of our little conversation?" Grant asked. Before answering the man, Jason studied him closely. He was smaller than Jason had imagined. Surely, he'd seen him before, from time to time riding in a carriage in Washington City but always at a considerable distance. Now the man stood before him, looking older and more stout than in the wartime pictures Jason had seen so often. Heightwise the man was no taller than Jason, though clearly in his late fifties wearing a double breasted suit that fit snugly around his solid frame."

"Yes, I do understand, that this was a private conversation not to be written about but—"

"Excellent, then do sit down. This is my son Jessie and my aide Schuyler. They will be sitting with us as well."

Jason nodded, now even more curious…Why would the president want his teenage son here…What sort of meeting was this?

"So, Mr. Brandt," Grant's aide began as the president himself and his son took chairs at the furthest distance possible in the small sitting room. "Tell us something of your background. You have developed something of a reputation among many of our acquaintances, but we'd like to hear more from you personally."

"Of course, well, you have heard the larger details. I was born in Hong Kong, my father was a missionary, grew up speaking the local dialect, eventually ended up serving in the British occupation forces that held the city of Guangzhou, people here call it Canton."

"As a soldier?" Grant asked quietly from his perch near the window.

"No, sir, not really. It was late 1858; I was hardly more than a boy." Just how he'd come to be with the troops seemed best left aside, not with the president's young son listening in. It would not perhaps do to announce how he'd run away from home rather than return to the United States and college. "What I did, for the most part, sir, after the initial battle, I was to serve as a translator, initially for the troops, French and British, and then with those who policed the city during the occupation."

"That must have been fascinating," the young man, Jason understood to be named Jessie, said aloud with enthusiasm.

"Actually it was."

"And then, we've heard you ended up with the rebels?" Grant's aide asked tentatively.

"Yes…though that was much later. I traveled overland with two friends and spent a fair amount of time in Nanjing, the capital of the Taiping Kingdom. It was there that I really began my career as a newspaper writer."

"And we are told you know the other Chinese dialects, not those just from the south?"

"Yes, that is true, at least the most dominant of the northern dialects, though the Chinese have many, and there are some I have no understanding of, but yes, if that is your question, I have little problem communicating in any parts of the country I have seen thus far."

"And of the great men of China, do you know many?"

"Well, I have met many of them, even interviewed them from time to time, especially during the war years when many were less exulted than they are now. And of course, many used my presence to ask me about the Westerners."

"So how do the Chinese view you, as a foreigner or not?"

"I am a foreigner, but I suppose an unusual one, especially for those from the south where I speak with a native accent, but even in the north, where I have lived for years, I am well known I suppose."

"Well, Mr. Brandt, please indulge us a bit more if you don't mind."

"It is not a problem at all, sir. I remain honored to be invited here."

At that Grant himself leaned forward. "So during the war, did you see much of the fighting itself?"

"Yes, I was not a soldier, of course, but as a reporter I often traveled with the troops, watched the fighting, occasionally was forced to defend myself."

With that Grant looked even more interested and began a series of questions about the nature of the fighting between the rebels and the Imperial Forces and on what role the foreigners, like General Gordon and Ward, both of whom Grant was clearly familiar with, had played.

As he spoke Jason had the feeling that while the president was interested from a professional perspective on the nature of warfare during the Chinese Civil War, something else was also going on that he did not understand.

Eventually, though, some secret signal was passed between his hosts, and it became obvious that the audience was over. The president stood up and shook Jason's hand again. "Thank you, Mr. Brandt. The conversation was a delight and a lovely distraction at a time when I have surely needed such a diversion." With that, Mr. Schuyler escorted Jason from the room.

"Well, that was interesting," Jason said aloud even as in his peripheral vision he noticed the energy in the White House halls had grown greatly while he'd been inside.

"Yes, the president was interested in your tales, and young Jessie was entranced. So...you are probably wondering what that was all about...why in the middle of the battle over the next president the current one would decide to take the time to invite someone like yourself to visit."

"I can hardly deny that the question did come to mind."

"So it's time for an explanation. The president has decided that once out of office he and his wife and youngest son Jessie will depart for Europe. But there is a possibly, at this point very vague that he might go much further...that he might decide to visit the orient, spend some time in, what do they call it the Middle Kingdom and if that occurs, he'd like someone with him to help him understand the experience."

"As a translator—"

"That and much more, someone there quietly in the background who would serve as an advisor, someone who could help him get far more out of the trip. You would be free to send reports back of course and if you cared write up the entire trip in book form."

"Wow that is a lot to absorb. Do you need my agreement now? My family is as I mentioned based in Troy, my wife and children studying at schools in New York."

"No not at all, the entire trip has not even been planned. The general might not even go to China and we would only expect you to meet us there, perhaps in Hong Kong as he arrived. So what do you think?"

"I really had no idea that the meeting had such a goal...my first thought is that it would be an extraordinary experience. And you don't have another reporter the president would prefer working with?"

"Actually we do, a fellow from the *New York Herald*, John Russell Young...he will be traveling with us for the entire trip. However, he is an American through and through. Knows nothing of Asia. Your role would be unique. So what do you say?"

"I need to talk to my wife but I find the idea intriguing. Let's just say I am interested and will contact you after I have spoken with my family."

"That seems good enough for now. I am delighted. I have been with the president for a long time and it was clear he was comfortable with you. So," the fellow said as they approached the exit, "we will be looking forward to hearing from you." With that, the man walked away leaving Jason at the White House door as crowds suddenly started arriving and voices began yelling.

"It's Hayes..."

"No. It can't be...that's theft!"

Something had happened, the election decided...had it happened while they were inside. Within minutes, the meeting receded in Jason's mind as he ran back to the hotel hoping his colleagues could tell him if it was true, if Hayes had been chosen while holding to himself as promised the story of his very strange interview at the White House.

# CHAPTER 65

# AN UNEXPECTED OPPORTUNITY

"You told the emperor...I mean the president you needed to ask your wife?" she blurted out they sat near their rented First street row house in Troy.

"Of course, this means I would be gone for months; it seemed the right thing to say that I would ask you first."

"This is indeed a strange country," Black Jade said more to herself than to Jason.

"OK, perhaps it is. Nevertheless, what do you think? Should I go with him? I thought you wanted to go home soon."

"Yes, but I am not ready yet. No, you should go. It is a great opportunity. You could renew ties in Shanghai. We have been gone too long. And maybe even see if it would be possible to buy our old home back and then rent it till we get there."

"I suppose, so you and the children would be all right, I could be gone for months, though it is not even certain this trip will happen anyway."

"We will be fine, the children have made friends and the school faculty and even the Willards, they are not running the school anymore have been wonderful and Old Zhu has even settled in. And there is something else, something I have not told you about..."

"What?" Jason asked his curiosity aroused as he studied his wife, whom he now realized had become even more Americanized since they had arrived in Troy. True she was wearing mostly American clothing but now it was even her mannerisms, the way she moved her body that seemed more American.

For a moment, they were both distracted with the sounds of the children's voices rising from the floor below. Little Willie was home for the weekend from the Albany Academy to see his father and had apparently done something to irritate his older sister. But what Jason noticed most as his wife walked to the stairs and listened more closely was that the children were yelling at each other in English, indeed Willie sounded almost native.

"I would let them be, they can settle their problems themselves," he said to his wife as she paused at the head of the stairs.

"It is not that; I just don't want them to hear us talking."

"So what is the big mystery?"

"Not so much a mystery but we have not talked much about my role at the school, it has become more complicated."

"Your studies are not going well?"

"No that is not it...everything is fine, I know how to study, I certainly watched enough young men memorize material at home and five years of constant English study has made me quite comfortable. If we were home and I were a man I would think I could even become a Confucian scholar, now would that not shock our friend Wu!"

"I suppose it would but then, if everything is going fine what is the issue? Is Mrs. Sage's idea about having you teach Chinese not working out?"

"Actually that goes well also. I don't know if Olivia had anything to do with it but Mrs. Wilcox did approach me a few days ago and asked if I were interested."

"Then that is wonderful, you'd gain the teaching experience you wanted and learn more of the seminary as a faculty member than as a student. So what is the problem?"

"That is just it...the longer I am here at the school and with the Willards, they are retired but live on Second Street and have often asked me to tea knowing you were traveling. In any case, they have told me far more about the female seminary and a lot of it is not very good."

"What do you mean? The place is famous. Old Mrs. Willard is still a legend around here. When I mention where we live, where you and Mei-ling are studying people always know the place, it is about the most famous thing in Troy."

"I thought so too, but things seem to have changed. The school is having problems, they even stopped letting students board here. Despite Emma Willard's promise before she died, Mei-ling could not have even studied here if we had not moved here. "

"So what is the problem?"

"I am not really sure, they used to draw a lot of students from the South but the war stopped that and now, I have been told there are other newer schools and even some colleges for young women that are closer to big cities like New York and Boston and have better facilities. Almost the entire faculty is worried that the school might have to close."

"Wow I had no idea. So does that make your becoming a teacher impossible?"

"Not necessarily...they have an idea that they could attract young women hoping to marry missionaries, young women like your mother once was."

"So there is the chance you could spend your time if I go home for a bit actually teaching here, that sounds positive."

"Yes, I think so but all this is enough reason for you to go."

"Why?"

"Mrs. Wilcox has told me every so often, and the Willard's even more how important it is not only to be able to attract students but wealthy benefactors, there is one such person they often mention, a man named Mr. Gurley who cares enough to be supportive and help out with finances."

"What about Olivia, surely Mrs. Sage can help also."

"Olivia cares enough but the money is not really hers to give away. It is Mr. Sage's and he is not the most generous of men as you have seen."

"He has certainly been helpful to us."

"And that is true, and over time he and Olivia may help the school even more."

"But what does any of that have to do with my going to China with Grant, why do you think that will help?"

"Mr. Grant, do we call him that now that he is not president anymore?"

"No idea but what is the connection?"

"Being here has convinced me that we cannot start the school without a lot of money from rich supporters and being around Grant, being in his inner circle even for a short time would make meeting such people easier?" she said with certainty.

His wife was nothing if she was not a long term planner and when she set her mind to a thing it was almost always the right course and done well. In fact, he thought to himself she had not really changed all that much since the night he'd found her half drowned alongside that river in south China more than a decade before.

"So it is settled, if Grant decides to go to China I will be available."

"And now you can take me for a walk along the river and tell me about the election."

━┽ ┾━

For the following fifteen minutes they walked slowly along the river as Black Jade maneuvered as well as she could on her frequently uncomfortable feet.

"That makes no sense." She blurted out, the people here, the Americans are so certain their system, this democracy is better than letting heaven decide who rules. And they let a man who did not win the people's vote become president?"

"Well, it is more complicated than that but you are mostly correct."

"So what is it I don't understand?" She insisted. "It seems simple enough; they only pretend to believe in people voting for their leaders themselves. So you tell me Mr. American why this Hayes fellow is moving into the White House instead of Mr. Tilden?"

"Why do you always assume I understand this place any better than you do."

"Because you look like them!" She blurted out as she sat down on a bench they'd come upon overlooking the Hudson River.

"OK, I cannot deny that…from what I can see it is always the same thing, it is about who has power and who doesn't. Those who voted for Hayes hate the southerners; still think of them as Johnny Reb traitors. So he won but mostly because they have this Electoral College thing. It lets the smaller states and in this case the southern states have more power than their numbers allow."

"Why does that matter? People here say Mr. Tilden won the election."

"It seemed like that a first, at least he probably won the most votes but not enough electors from the states…several in the south were uncertain."

"But Mr. Willard says those in the south are democrats. So why didn't they fight for Mr. Tilden?"

"From what I could understand, they care less about Tilden than getting the northern troops out of the south. They want to control the south, the black's labor again."

"But they lost the war, it is as if the ex-Taiping's were still important in China."

His wife's mention of the Taipings surprised him. She almost never mentioned the formerly powerful group that had once challenged the Beijing based Manchu government for control, a group Black Jade as the widow of one of their major military commanders had once had an important role within.

"I see what you are saying but unlike the Taipings, the southerners have something to bargain with. The Republicans needed those electoral votes. And while I am not sure what exactly happened they seem to have traded their support of Hayes for his willingness to end northern domination of the south."

"So the whites could retake control of the blacks?"

"It does seem that way?"

"And President Grant? He fought them in the war. Sent troops to protect the black people…you know I practice my English on the Troy papers every day…He does not care that Hayes has made such an agreement?"

"I have no idea. I should not think he would support such a move. But he said nothing when I talked to him…in fact he acted as if the election battle was not happening while I was there. Did I tell you it seemed to have finally been resolved while I was talking to him?"

Black Jade turned away from him and studied for a time a barge that was passing on its way south toward New York City and then turning back.

"Well, my husband let us hope Mr. Grant contacts you soon and that the trip can be accomplished quickly and then we can go home. If the blacks have lost their freedoms again can there be any justice for the Chinese."

Jason said nothing but knew she was probably right. The two of them continued to study the river traffic in silence.

# CHAPTER 66

# HONG KONG AGAIN

His father was wrong, Jason thought to himself. Hong Kong's harbor was more beautiful than Boston's, and it smelled better as well, Jason assured himself as they entered the harbor after weeks at sea. Just watching the skyline, Victoria Island on his left and Kowloon to his right, brought back extraordinary memories, which his deep-long breaths pulling in the brisk air made only more real to him.

How long had it been since he'd been in Hong Kong? He thought to himself. Almost a decade since he'd left Shanghai, but Hong Kong, when had he been here last? He tried to remember. Sure, his reporter's work had brought him back a few times in the late 1860s, but Jason was not even sure how often. Most of the time, he'd spent reporting far further north along the shore and returning not to his boyhood home but Shanghai, where he and Black Jade had built a new life after the Civil War.

Leaning over the rail, he watched the enormous range of Chinese junks and Western ships glide through the waters, with Victoria's peak filling in the background. He could not have been more anxious to disembark and more ambivalent about the family's decision so many years before to relocate to America. It was supposed to be temporary, at least that was the original plan, and now as he could view the wharves more clearly, watch the porters carrying their wares, he began slowly to smell less the ocean breezes than the cooking pots along the shore. Suddenly he knew they'd stayed too long in America. This was home and he would insist as soon as he'd done his business with the former president that he, Black Jade, and the children even more definitively start planning for their return home.

Hours later, after checking into a hotel in Kowloon, one he did not even remember from earlier visits, he'd taken a brisk walk down Nathan Street, exploring various alleys, just taking in the sites he'd once known intimately until, eventually, he found himself sitting on the hotel's veranda overlooking the street. With just a bit of effort, the site allowed a view of the harbor as well. The only negative aspect of the day's walk was when he'd tried to find his father's home. The building seemed gone, a much larger warehouse built on the site that disoriented Jason for a time. There was now nothing to do until Grant arrived, as he understood it some three days hence.

For the next two days, he wandered the city spending each afternoon relaxing on the hotel's veranda reflecting on his return until on the evening of the third day, his reflections were interrupted.

"Brandt, my good man, I had heard you'd returned." Jason looked to find Robert Hart, the inspector of customs, hailing him as he approached holding a cup of tea. "Didn't even know you followed the custom of the Queen's People."

Looking down at his cup, Jason laughed. "Yes, I guess you are right...but frankly I had not even realized it was teatime. But, Robert, it is good to see you. What brings you to Hong Kong? I thought you were settled further along the coast."

"Probably the same reason you are. I assume you are here because General Grant, President Grant I suppose we should say…has arrived. Are you part of his party?"

"After a fashion. He has been doing some sort of around the world tour…Europe and more recently in India."

"Yes, indeed, just arrived myself from Singapore. Encountered him there. We spoke for a bit, about his plans for seeing China."

"And then, I suppose you know more of his plans than I do."

"So you are not back permanently. Where is your beautiful wife? I have heard her English is now better than my Chinese."

"Black Jade is still in New York, studying at a school founded by an American educator of women…Emma Willard."

"Emma Willard, I have heard of her, a writer of some note as well, right?"

"Yes. But, Robert, how long has it been…feels like a decade since I saw you last."

"No idea…did I not see you at some social affair in Shanghai a few years ago? When did you leave for America?"

"Late 1872."

"And you had never been there, in America before that, right?"

"Not as more than a baby, and yes, it has been quite an experience."

"I have read your dispatches, but you've not written much of your own experiences…living where?"

"Close to Boston and then more recently Troy, up the Hudson River from New York City."

"But, my good man, what role do you have with Grant's entourage?"

"Not exactly set. He asked me before he left, indeed, before he left the White House, to be a sort of private guide, an interpreter of sorts for him if he decided to come to China. I agreed and few months ago, I received a note saying he was leaving for the Orient and giving me an idea of when he would arrive here."

"Anyone else part of the correspondence?" Hart asked, taking another long sip of his tea and then adjusting the spoon and plate so it seemed to line up just so with his hand.

"Not that I know of, nothing very mysterious about it. But why do you ask?"

"I hesitate to bring it up, probably nothing, my good fellow, but the reason I'd heard you'd returned was that certain people in Shanghai have been making inquiries about you, about you and your wife...The effort came to my attention through mutual friends."

"Who? Why would anyone be asking such questions?"

"Well, that is less certain, the queries passed my desk from somewhat-vague sources, but I have an idea that it may have come from certain Japanese diplomats in Shanghai. At least that was the impression of the fellow who told me."

"Why would the Japanese care anything for me or Black Jade for that matter?"

"I have no idea, but that was why I was not surprised to see you this afternoon. I'd heard you would be traveling with Grant, and these curious inquiries were part of that information."

"Robert, you know far more than I do about such diplomatic matters. What do you think is going on?" The last part of his sentence was cut off by a shrill pack of sea gulls that swooped near the veranda fighting over a still-kicking fish one of them had apparently caught.

"Why...I don't know, not much for speculation...You know that, Jason, you interviewed me often enough in the old days."

Jason remained silent, hoping his reporter's trick would get more out of Hart; the Superintendent of Trade always knew more than he revealed.

"Well, let me indulge in a bit of speculation…just that speculation, of course."

Jason continued in his silence, slowly bringing the teacup to his lips.

"It may be that the news that you were planning to travel with the former president and your well-known sympathies, nothing wrong with that mind you, for the Celestial Kingdom might have created some level of concern."

"My views are well known, being a writer insures that but why would the Japanese care what I think of anything?"

"Things in Japan are quite different these days…they have taken on the sort of industrial projects our mutual friend Prosper has long been so involved in, and like England, my own beloved homeland, they have become more assertive, especially in some of the islands between Taiwan and the Japanese Southern Islands."

"I have heard something of that…but what has that to do with me?"

"Just speculation of course but perhaps they are concerned you might turn Mr. Grant's head against them, make him more sympathetic toward Beijing than Tokyo would prefer."

Jason paused for a second to reflect on Hart's speculation. "But Grant is out of office, why would that even matter these days."

"Well, my man, that is just it…Are Grant's days of power and influence over? Certainly many have speculated that he might be considering another run for the White House. He is still quite young and popular in many quarters…And who knows if this Hayes fellow will even run again.

"That makes sense, so do you think I have anything to be concerned about."

"Not if you don't have anything to hide. What can they do? But turning to a different topic, Jason, you're an excellent writer, I enjoyed your *China Tales* immensely and now you have had this other adventure...You should consider writing about your impressions of America...the inside outside perspective so to speak, if not Tocqueville than another *Innocents Abroad* approach."

Jason found himself only half listening to Hart's enthusiastic suggestion for another book project, his mind was on the earlier comment, about having something to hide. Could Black Jade really accomplish her dream of setting up a Shanghai Female Seminary along the lines of the one in Troy if her ties to the infamous Taipings, China's version of the Confederacy were well known?

"Well, my good fellow, it has been a delight to see you. It seems likely we will see each other again soon, if not in Shanghai in Beijing. I cannot imagine how many formal receptions we will both have to endure over the next several weeks."

With that both men rose, shook hands and Robert Hart set off in the direction of the hotel's rooms while Jason sat sipping more of his tea and reflecting on the conversation.

# CHAPTER 67

# GUANGZHOU

"I still find it difficult to believe."

"What can't you believe?" Jason asked Russell Young, the *New York Tribune* journalist who rode alongside him. At Jason's suggestion soon after they had met that morning, the two had secured horses and set out for Guangzhou while the former president was still being feted by the British Colony's Western merchant community.

"I can't believe that you grew up here among these people; you seem so New England to me, so Boston."

As the bearded fellow, who did not look all that different from President Grant himself, spoke, Jason wondered what he really meant. That Jason was too American, too civilized to have been brought up in China, or at least in Hong Kong? The two had gotten along well enough, since they'd been introduced by one of the many military officers who was traveling with Grant. Indeed, having been told that the former president would be occupied in Hong Kong for a few days before moving on to Guangzhou, where he hoped his journalist colleagues could meet him, Jason had suggested the excursion overland. It was the manner he'd spent much of his life traveling in China.

Young himself had readily agreed to accompany him, once it was clear that Jason represented no journalistic threat, that his writings were about America and China, while Russell planned to use much of the trip, indeed already had in the European and earlier oriental sections to mine the notoriously laconic former president's opinions on the Civil War, a topic his American publishers were sure be interested in.

As they rode on, Jason found himself nostalgically watching the peasants working the rice fields or from time to time approaching the two Westerners with goods to sell, from cloth to one entrepreneurial fellow who was convinced that what the two foreign barbarians really needed was the egg he carefully cradled in his hands.

For a time, when they had first set out, Russell had asked him a few questions about the curiosities of China that lay as a panorama around them while Jason explained what he could of what they were seeing, but the effort lasted only for a time. It was obvious Young had little sincere interest in the Chinese he saw around him.

"Frankly, I have spent enough time in California to find little of interest in the Chinese. Not surprised you took your family home."

For a second Jason thought of correcting him and then thought better of it. He had managed to lessen Russell's competitive concern that Grant had asked a second journalist along and there was no reason to antagonize the man. Grant spent an enormous amount of time surrounded by a large entourage and Jason had come to understand his time with the man would be limited and Young might be his only steady companion for the next month or so.

"So tell me about this paper, this English coast China paper you write for, are we likely to be able to visit it when we get to Shanghai?"

"Hopefully yes, I need to stop in, meet the newer, younger editors, seems to have a lot of turnover since I left."

"Makes sense, if the editors don't know one, it is not likely they will solicit articles." For the next hour or so Young told Jason of his own professional efforts to earn a living by his pen in New York. It was interesting enough, but not a distraction from Jason's constant curiosity about their impending arrival in Guangzhou. He'd been in Hong Kong a few times since his youth but Guangzhou as the Chinese called it, not since that night he'd left looking for his friend Wu and then from a city still occupied by the Anglo-French soldiers. Now though the Chinese were back in charge, indeed it would be President Grant's first visit to a real Chinese city, something Hong Kong, despite the very Chinese nature of parts of the city could hardly claim.

If plans went as hoped he and Young would arrive a full day ahead of Grant and get a sense of what plans had been put in place to welcome the ex-president, information that he knew Grant's party would find helpful when they arrived by boat a bit later.

<hr />

By the time they finally arrived in Guangzhou Jason found he really had had enough of Young. The man's vision was American through and through, his criticism of the slow pace of Chinese life was starting to wear on Jason and he was delighted to leave the man behind at a lodging house they'd found near the Western trading facilities across the river from the Walled City itself. They'd managed to secure two rooms and while Young was anxious to retire, Jason set out on a walking tour of the city he'd left behind so many years before. It was the first time he'd walked the streets since he'd earned his living as a translator for occupied Guangzhou's many police patrols. Within a few minutes, to his surprise he found himself taking a path through the city that largely paralleled one of his patrol routes of more than a decade before.

As he walked, he realized of course that Guangzhou was not Hong Kong. Its population still found the foreigners relatively foreign, at least more than their cousins in the British colony to the south. How had they changed Jason kept asking himself? In his earlier experience, Guangzhou had had a reputation for hating the foreigners, been itself conquered and humiliated by the foreign occupation of more than a decade before. Now, Jason kept wondering as he strolled the crowded cities within the walled city – how did they feel about foreigners? Certainly many eyes followed him and more than a few children ran up to him asking for sweets, indeed their numbers grew quickly as they realized that the strange foreigner spoke their language, not the few words of Cantonese some of the Westerners managed but as well as they did themselves. What was more interesting was that from time to time several of the merchants who stood at the doors of their shops stared at him not with curiosity but what seemed uncertain recognition. Could they possibly remember him as the young teenager who'd walked their streets with the soldiers so many years before? None of the adults though spoke to him directly and Jason did not stop to talk, his memories were of a much more antagonistic Cantonese population then he expected awaited the former president. Indeed, the fact that he walked alone brought back memories he'd not known he'd even still harbored. As night fell, bidding his youthful entourage good-bye he exited the city's walls and returned to his lodgings across the river, eventually collapsing into a fitful sleep filled with memories of the night he and his comrades had survived an all-out assault on the poorly fortified police stations.

# CHAPTER 68

# AN UNEXPECTED INVITATION

By the second evening of their arrival, Jason had begun to wonder if the plan to accompany the former president had been a wise decision. He'd hardly seen the man and then only at a distance as Grant had been led from one banquet to another, Chinese leadership having apparently demanded from the local governor that the man be greeted with full honors during his stay in Guangzhou. As for Jason himself though, it had been two days of standing around occasionally chatting with Russell or the occasional mandarin who ended up in is presence. That he could communicate, even answer their few questions about the needs of the American leader's entourage turned out to be helpful to an extent but Jason knew there were certainly others who could have served the same services without him leaving his family behind across the enormous Pacific.

Sure, the president's associates had paid his expenses and even a reasonably generous salary but that was hardly what he and Black Jade had envisioned from the trip, indeed as the hour grew late, though the humidity had not yet broken, Jason was feeling positively discouraged, discouraged at least until the quiet but determined knock at his door.

"Mr. Brandt, are you awake?" Jason did not recognize the voice at least not immediately until he opened the door and saw Jessie, Grant's younger son standing there.

"I hope I have not disturbed you, sir."

"Not at all Jessie, how can I be of service?"

"My Father, I mean the president is having problems sleeping and was wondering if you might join him for a nightcap, a bit of whiskey brought with us from Tennessee?"

"How could I refuse such an offer?" Jason said snatching up his hat and grateful that he'd not yet removed his boots for the night. They could be such a problem to pull on and off.

"Excellent, my father will be very pleased. Just follow me, sir. The president is lodged in a building just down the street."

...

"Mr. Brandt, can I call you Jason?" Grant asked as he entered the small sitting room.

"Of course, sir. How may I be of service?"

"No reason to stand on ceremony young man, just a couple of Americans in a faraway land having a drink. Here, take up a glass."

At that, Jason found the former head of the union armies, the man who'd defeated the Confederacy carefully filling his glass.

"Can't stand on ceremony, never could abide by it...and nothing in this trip has changed my mind...not the uppity English or the ever so "supposedly civilized" Parisians!" Grant laughed as he took a swing of the burning liquid.

"But Jason, young Mr. Brandt, you are not just another American having a drink with your countrymen are you."

"Well, sir, I suppose my background is a bit, as you well know...different."

"Exactly, which is why I asked you here. I want you to help me understand what I am seeing and hearing. The truth of the matter is I have learned a great deal more about the world since I left the White House than when I occupied that exalted position. But there is still so much I don't understand."

"Well, if you could be more specific, sir, I would be delighted to help."

"Learning more about my hosts would be a start. They are incredible hosts, offering the most gracious foods, some of which I have even liked and the most extraordinary compliments."

"Well, sir, that would certainly be true, there is nothing the Chinese love more than the opportunity for a fine banquet, and the arrival of a dignity of your rank would get the best such welcome they could muster."

"I have been told, the welcome I have received is far grander than high-ranking Europeans have received. Is that so?"

"I have not seen anything of the like in my time in China. The enormous crowds, the huge reception you have received is, in my experience, quite unprecedented."

"And why would that be do you think?"

"I have a couple of thoughts on that...and, of course, my experience of Guangzhou or Canton as the foreigners call it is of an occupied city that harbored great hatred of foreigners. First, of course, the Chinese are starting to get a sense of the differences between the Westerners. They tend to think we all look alike. But in the last few decades, the usually very insular mandarins—that is, the Confucian officials that are serving as your hosts, Manchu and Chinese alike—have started to appreciate that the French and the British are different; that even the Americans, who speak the same language as the British, are quite different."

"So what conclusions do they take from such observations?" Grant asked as he leaned forward and took in a deep breath on his cigar.

"Two things. First, they do understand that America, unique among the Western Powers they have encountered, has not played a significant role in the assaults against China. That matters and then, of course, there is the possibility that they might be able to use the differences among the Westerners to Chinese advantage."

"You are suggesting they think that I might be of service to them, as the former leader of a nation that has not made the usual demands the Europeans, and as I heard recently the Japanese have made of them?"

"And, sir, the possibility that, as some suppose, you might again win the White House as a future leader as well."

At that, Jason watched a glance pass between Grant and his son, just a glance and then nothing more as Grant changed the subject.

"So tell me more about the Chinese officials I have met. I have tried to discuss commerce with them, tried to discuss whether China would be introducing railroads, perhaps become a market for American manufactures and there has been no interest whatsoever. Indeed, they keep asking me about my family and then offering their condolences when I mention my granddaughter."

Jason laughed. "Well, sir, it is true the role of women in China is rather different from what we know in America. My wife—did you know she was Chinese, sir?"

Grant nodded.

"Well, my wife has very strong opinions about such matters, it is too bad she is not here to answer your questions.

"She is at the Troy Female Seminary is she not?" Grant asked.

"Yes, sir, taking a basic course there as is my daughter and my son is across the river at the Albany Academy. Indeed, when I left there was talk that my wife would begin teaching Chinese to those young ladies who anticipate marrying missionaries."

"She sounds like a very interesting woman. Perhaps my Julie should meet her one day, but tell me more about these Chinese officials, Manchu and Chinese. Have you known many? "

"Yes, in fact one of my closest friends studied for years to become one of them. They are, to say the least very different from those who live in America. We of course have men such as yourself, soldiers who sometimes become politicians who are often much respected and many men of business..."

"Like your friend Mr. Sage," Grant added.

"Yes, very much like Mr. Sage," Jason said, beginning to realize that Grant had clearly learned a great deal about him, probably long before that first meeting in the White House which now seemed long ago.

"The men you are meeting could not be more different, sir. They are reared almost from birth on the Confucian classics, even the Manchus here are deeply influenced by the teachings of the master, and Confucius, as we call him, was deeply interested in human relationships, about hierarchy and harmonious living within a society that is obviously very crowded, that could not survive without a very stringent set of behaviors to govern relationships among them."

"And what of progress, of the introduction of labor saving technologies, they don't seem to have much interest when I ask about such things." Grant said leaning forward and pouring Jason a bit more whiskey.

"Sir, you have seen the number of people in the streets and that is only the men, there is an equally large though more invisible population of women as well. In such a country labor saving devices are not all that attractive. Labor is cheap and social harmony not improved by technologies that put people out of work."

"It always comes down to that, doesn't it? If the Irish in America fear the Chinese make it harder for them to earn a living, technology in China threatens jobs as well here."

"Yes, sir, I suppose that is perhaps the best way to think about it. In every country, people's primary concern is making a living. There are other issues as well of course, railroads in America don't disrupt ancestral graves, and ours is a huge country with a small population relatively new. If railroad magnates proposed laying tracks through the graveyards of Boston, they would have a problem as well. That is one of the reasons the Chinese have been more open to the introduction of steam technology for ships than for railroads."

"That makes sense, so is there no chance that China will become more industrialized in the fashion of Europe or American?"

"To the contrary, sir. I think that to an extent that would be an incorrect assumption. Frankly, sir, when I was in the west, in San Francisco I had the opportunity to listen to a great deal of testimony that was presented to a committee that was investigating the question of stopping Chinese immigration to California."

As Grant nodded Jason suddenly felt stupid. The man would most certainly know more about the hearings than Jason himself did.

Seeing his hesitation, Grant raised his hand. "Do go on, Jason. I am quite interested in your thoughts on the question."

"Well, sir, those in California think they know the Chinese, but they only meet the least educated, the least sophisticated, young men who breaking much of Chinese tradition about responsibly to their families and home villages traveled to the west. They are an industrious group but very different from the elites you are meeting, men who have no need to travel abroad to seek their fortunes."

"And your point?" Grant asked, looking uncertain.

"Simply, sir, that the Chinese are people, just like the other races, they differ enormously among themselves, in their attitudes, education, interests. Nevertheless, on the issues, you are most curious about; your role here makes it unlikely that you would meet such people. The Chinese are introducing you to what they think of as the best of their society and if I might be so bold, military men or men of commerce of which China has many are not so considered."

To Jason's surprise, Grant laughed heartily. "Listen to that, son, snubbed in Europe as a man of no birth, common type who'd risen too high for his station, now we learn my military status carries no weigh either with our current hosts."

"The world is surely a curious place, Father," Jessie, who'd remained silent for the entire conversation, chimed in. "Don't forget, Father, the other issue you wanted to discuss."

"Of course not, son. Mr. Brandt, what do you think of a private stroll tomorrow morning, just a few of us in the streets at dawn so I can really see this city, on my feet rather than from one of those infernal sedan chairs trapped in the sea of silent faces that have greeted me so far?"

# CHAPTER 69

# AN EARLY-MORNING WALK

As the small group—Jason, the former president of the United States, U. S. Grant, his young son Jessie, and a military aide—all dressed in civilian clothing, exited the building at dawn and began walking toward the small bridge that separated the Guangzhou's western quarter from the old city, Jason was already exhausted. He'd spent a fitful night worried that he'd made a world-class mistake agreeing to lead Grant's small group into the city at dawn so Grant could get a real look at the life of the city. What, he worried quietly to himself, would happen if America's beloved former leader, the hero of the American Civil War, was attacked, or worse by Guangzhou's street toughs? Jason, after all, unlike his American colleagues, had no false impression of how docile the Chinese were. Nevertheless, of course, he chuckled to himself, the idea that Jason's warnings about street toughs could discourage a professional military man like Grant, veteran of countless battlefields, seemed almost funny in retrospect. The man was insistent and there was little Jason could do but agree. That was after all why he had been invited along Jason realized, to give the man a sense of China he'd never gain from his formal hosts.

"They really do get up early don't they?" Grant said quietly into his ear as they entered the city gates to see an enormous number of people already scurrying about, carrying evenly balanced poles of goods toward the venders' stalls, while others did Tai Qi.

"That they do. At this time of the year, dawn is easily the best part of the day—plenty of light and the heat of the day has not yet arrived."

"What are those exercises they do there, sir?" Young Jessie asked pointing to an open space full of people doing their morning exercises.

"It is called Tai Qi, a sort of exercise that combines physical movement, an almost dance-like movement with meditation."

"And does it actually help with one's health?" Grant asked stopping to watch them, not concerned that a few bystanders had themselves begun to watch the small group of foreigners as they themselves studied the exercise group.

"Well, they are outside in the fresh air, moving their bodies, doctors both here and in America say that is important."

"Have you ever done it, Jason?"

"Yes, not often. In some ways I really am the Westerner people take me for, but I have taken part a few times, in Hong Kong when I was a child and later as an adult in Shanghai."

"But not here, not in Guangzhou?"

"No, sir, the Guangzhou I knew around 1860 was very different in many ways."

"Father, those young people over there, are they talking about us?"

"Jason what do you think?"

"Let's stroll past them; it is the direction I was planning to go anyway."

"Then lead on," the former president said.

"OK," Jason said as the group passed closely by the men and then moved more directly into an open market where the sellers were laying out their goods for the day.

"No problem, they were just saying that we were probably part of the group that traveled with the barbarian...sorry that is what he said, with the Barbarian King."

"Anything else?"

"Well, that was mostly it."

"Jason, come on young man, what else did they say as we passed?"

"Well, sir, one of them was telling his comrades that he'd managed to get a bit closer to the foreign king and was thoroughly unimpressed, he said the fellow wore very common clothing."

At the description Grant began to laugh, "Well, he is right, compared to the finery of the mandarins or even some of my active duty military colleagues I don't think my attire would impress anyone. But do you think the fellow recognized me?"

"Frankly, sir, most Chinese think we all look alike and the idea that a foreign king, as they think of you would be wandering around the local market would not occur to him."

"Father, Captain Roberts, look here, it is like a wondrous zoo for fish!"

At that, Grant headed off toward his son who had discovered the row after rows of live seafood, fish, eels, turtles, etc. that were the staple of any seafood vending area in the country. For the next quarter hour Jason found himself translating for his colleagues as they asked questions of the many sellers in the market while Captain Roberts their only obvious security stood back somewhat at a distance watching the crowd.

An hour later the group sat in a teahouse taking in the sites while Jason informally translated the tale the teahouse's storyteller was proclaiming to the crowd, a tale of great love and loss from China's long past.

"Returning to our conversation of last night, am I likely to meet any Chinese leaders different from the sort I have met so far, different from these scholarly Confucian types?" Grant asked as he opened his collar somewhat, the day's heat was starting to rise.

"I doubt you will officially meet people other than Manchu or Chinese officials and they are steeped in Confucianism, but there is one man whom I believe is likely to be different, Governor Li, Li Hongzhang. I think you might have a lot in common, during the war he led many of Beijing's troops to victory."

"He is some sort of powerful official in the north right? Yes, I am told that he is important, that I am to travel to see him in Tianjin. Do you know that city Jason?"

"Yes. Yes, quite well in fact," Jason said. "I was there for quite some time around 1870," trying not to let his voice reveal the emotions the city brought back for him, he'd almost lost his wife there, indeed it was in Tianjin that the decision had initially been made to visit America. "During the war Governor Li led many of Beijing's troops against the Taiping rebels and in doing so came to appreciate Western military ordinance. In fact, he is behind a lot of the efforts the Chinese have accomplished in recent years to learn Western technology."

Grant's eyes showed recognition. "Is this Governor Li behind that Chinese educational mission in Hartford, Clemens has spoken of?"

"Yes, exactly, led in part by a Chinese fellow who graduated from Yale more than a decade ago. I have met him several times."

"A Chinaman graduated from Yale?" Grant asked in surprise.

"That is my understanding, brought there with a few others by missionaries."

Grant did not reply, he was clearly taking in this new information, about a breed of Chinese neither Confucian mandarin nor coolies.

"I think you would find him very interesting, sir. His name is Yung Wing."

"Indeed I would, perhaps when I return home. And this Li Hongzhang fellow, he is living even further north than Shanghai, in this Tianjin place, never heard of it."

"Tianjin, I think I have, sir," Captain Roberts, who'd been quiet for almost their entire stroll, suddenly spoke. "Is that the city where those Catholic nuns died...sounds like it, though I admit all Chinese cities sound almost the same to me."

"Yes," Jason said, without elaboration.

"Father, there is another group of men watching us just outside of the teahouse."

At that, the three older men turned casually without being obvious toward the direction the youngest among them had indicated. He was right, a group of young men, better off than many in the streets around them had gathered and were clearly watching them at a distance.

Studying them closely for a time Jason turned back toward the group. "They look to be part of the Confucian literati, probably still students studying for the exams."

"Should we be concerned?" the officer asked.

"I don't know but perhaps so, the literati are often among those most unhappy with the presence of foreigners. Coolies might see us as a source of income but not the Confucian scholars, we are in so many ways simply competition. Nevertheless, let us just stay here for a bit, perhaps they will depart. We still have time. I doubt anyone has even noticed your absence yet, sir."

With that Grant and his son turned their attention back to the teahouse, taking in the sites though Grant himself kept a subtle watch on the group. Roberts, for his part made no pretense at disinterest and watched the fellows closely.

"Your tea has become cold" the server said to Jason as he positioned himself between the group and those who watched them from outside. As he did so, Jason saw the fellow drop a note near Jason's teacup. "From one of the other gentlemen," he whispered quietly and withdrew.

"What is it?" asked Grant, who had obviously seen the gesture.

Casually taking up the note Jason unfolded it. A short note, written in very clear Chinese characters, "You should leave, it may not be safe."

"It's a warning, from someone who clearly knows something about me, written in Chinese warning us to leave, says it's not safe."

At that Grant's eyes narrowed, he glanced at his son and then his face took on quite another look, an expression Jason had not seen before."

"Captain Roberts, I assume you brought the satchel I asked about."

"Right here, sir. Within easy reach." With that, the man reached down and squeezed the soft canvas bag he'd been carrying all morning. In the effort, Jason realized his hand was revealing the outline of a weapon, some sort of pistol.

"Then we stand slowly, Jessie throw one of those piles of copper cash down they gave you yesterday and stand behind me as we walk." The tone of Grant's voice was quite different, infinitely steelier than Jason had heard before.

"Now Captain Roberts, if you would position yourself between those fellows and my son as we walk."

"But General."

"Captain, do as I say." Grant said and then methodically without a hint of concern he began to walk back whence they had come an hour before toward the river and city walls. The man clearly had a better sense of where they were than Jason would have guessed.

They had gotten no more than thirty feet down the street, when one of the students screamed "English pigs!" in Cantonese and threw something at them, some sort of projectile...a lance of some sort that whirled past them.

Roberts whirled around, dropped to his knee, and fired a round, which dropped the young man who'd hurled the lance.

"Over there, behind that cart!" Grant yelled pushing his son down and pulling his own gun out.

"WAIT, STOP!" Jason yelled out in Cantonese as loud as he could while running into the street positioning himself between the two groups.

"THESE MEN ARE AMERICANS, NOT ENGLISH. GUESTS OF THE GOVERNOR! HURTING THEM WILL BRING DISASTER DOWN UPON YOUR FAMILIES!"

His words and he knew the fluency of his Cantonese stopped the men in their tracks. Several had been advancing toward Grant's little group even as one had stayed behind to tend to their colleague whose leg was running with blood.

For a second Jason stood toe to toe with the men, less than ten feet in front of them and then with a silent signal they turned around, lifted up their colleague and ran off in the opposite direction, their friend's leg leaving a bloody track behind in the dirt.

"I guess that's over." Jason said as he turned around to find Grant and Roberts advancing behind him their guns drawn, the hard looks on their faces slowly disappearing.

"What did you tell them?"

"Just the truth, that you were not English, that you were the guests of the governor."

⟞⟝ ⟞⟝

Ten minutes later, as the small group entered the compound, Grant turned to Jason.

"Can't remember a better, more invigorating walk in years! I thank you, Jason."

"But, Mr. President, I hope this has not turned your thoughts about the Chinese? They were just a few young hot heads."

"On the contrary, they have grown in my estimation indeed. Docile, passive, mere cheap labor unable to fit into America... absurd stuff, not at all Jason, your Chinese compatriots have grown enormously in my mind...patriotic fellows ready to stand up for their country against the imperialistic English barbarians. I am indeed impressed."

Jason just nodded, not knowing what to say.

"But one more thing Jason" Grant said as he stood at the door of the lodging house where most of his party still slept.

"Not a word of this morning, not to my wife, not to Russell Young, he has quite enough to write about without our little excursion this morning."

With that, the former president gave a slight salute, gestured for Captain Roberts and his son to enter and then followed them leaving Jason dumbfounded in the street before he slowly turned and returned to his own lodging down the street.

There was still time to catch a bit more sleep before the rest of the group rose.

# CHAPTER 70

# NORTH CHINA

B y the time they reached Tianjin, Jason had lost all ambivalence about his decision to take up the former president's
offer. In the weeks since they left Guangzhou, first for Shanghai
then Tianjin, he had accomplished almost everything he and
Black Jade had planned. The editors at the *North China Daily
News* had greeted him like a returning hero and made clear
that the paper would have even more use of his services once
he and his family returned.

More exciting was learning that one of his former acquaintances, the fellow he and Black Jade had sold their home to
was open to selling it back. According to the fellow, a devout
Irishman who exported goods between Dublin and Shanghai,
his wife was convinced that their growing family would over the
next few years outgrow the residence. Indeed, the woman was
pregnant with their fourth child and would be, according to
her husband quite open to selling the home back if a reasonable profit could be earned. No immediate plans were made,
neither family had a specific schedule in mind, but Jason went
away feeling that much more confident that his family could
resume their previous life without great difficulty. Jason even

found himself studying a piece of open land, he'd never really noticed before, that stood within walking distance of the house, a parcel of land that Jason hoped might remain available a few years in the future when it might make a perfect location for the school Black Jade was hoping to start.

Even more encouraging was his growing relationship with and impression of the former president. Indeed, after that first walk with Grant, Jessie and Captain Roberts, that apparently no one other their small group was aware of, such dawn excursions began to be quite common. In Shanghai they took two more excursions without incident and Grant, especially as the visits to early morning teahouses became a favorite of the former president, continued to pepper Jason with questions about the Chinese.

"So Mr. Lincoln actually asked you to go to Ford's theatre with him?" Jason asked once as the small group sat in yet another teahouse on their first early morning outing in Tianjin, a city they had only arrived in the previous evening.

"Yes, but I declined, Julie had asked me to accompany her somewhere, don't even remember now what the errand was." Grant sighed. It was clearly a moment he often reflected on.

"If you'd been there, you could have stopped that Booth fellow; I am sure of it, Father," Young Jessie commented.

Grant turned to his son with a look that suggested they'd had that conversation many times before.

"Maybe, I doubt it. Who knows what might have happened… What's done is done."

"But if I might, sir," Jason, ever the inquisitive journalist pressed on "If you had somehow stopped the man, things might have been so different."

"Well, that fellow Johnson would never have gotten in, that's for sure" Jessie piped in.

"And you, sir, what do you think?" Jason asked hoping to hear more from the man himself.

"I suppose, we might have made more progress with the south, been in a different situation today if Lincoln had lived."

"Why, sir?"

"Maybe, the truth is that Lincoln had infinitely better political instincts than Johnson and better than I ever did. I still have never gotten over the fact that politicians don't just take orders from their leaders like any good soldier does."

Jason laughed and then went silent again hoping that Jessie would as well. At least he could always depend on Captain Roberts to remain silent. He never saw Grant as more than the famous civil war general, a man to be protected never as a mere companion.

"After the war," Grant began but then took in a puff of smoke followed by a bit more tea, "the real question was how to reintegrate the south into the larger nation, how to make them feel part of the United States again while ending their control over the lives of the south's blacks. It was an impossible task, Johnson only made it worse, forced himself into a fight with Congress trying to please the southerners really his own people too much…barely survived the impeachment."

"But you, sir, you certainly tried to carry on Lincoln's legacy once you were in office."

"Perhaps without his skills. In truth I have always thought I missed my last and greatest opportunity to successfully reunite America when I was not there that night at Ford's theatre."

Emboldened by the easy camaraderie that had developed between himself and the former president Jason decided to push on. "But surely, sir, there is still the possibility that you might regain the White House at some point. You are still very popular at home."

At the question, Grant looked at Jason and smiled. It was hardly the first time someone had speculated on the possibility that once the former war hero and president returned he would be in a position to compete for the presidency again in 1880.

"Jason, you have been listening to too much speculation, my time has passed." He laughed, "Now let's turn to the matter at hand; we've not had that much time to discuss this Li Hongzhang fellow. I am supposed to officially meet him in a few hours. Tell me everything you know about his background and those industrializing projects he's been involve in, about that arsenal you mentioned the other day, the student groups…really wish I'd been able to see that dockyard your French friend helped direct but my hosts were not having anything of that request."

For the next hour as the sun rose higher and the day warmed, Jason told Grant everything he could about Grant's next host. The president himself almost indifferent to the cultural treasures he'd been shown for weeks was finally looking forward to meeting the famous Chinese leader, the first said to be more interested in the development of China's future than in celebrating its illustrious past.

As he spoke, Jason watched Captain Roberts in the background. The man had become significantly calmer over the weeks as it had become obvious that the Chinese authorities knew exactly what was going on. Indeed, each morning, very quietly as they walked several Chinese fellows, well-built and obviously athletic had begun to appear near them everywhere they went. Jason had first noticed them in Shanghai and he now saw the same fellows appear at a distance in Tianjin. Indeed, Captain Roberts and he had discussed the men privately. It was obvious after their second appearance that the Chinese authorities had discretely dispatched the group to protect their illustrious guest without making it obvious they were doing so.

In fact, as far as Jason understood Grant himself had never noticed and Roberts and Jason had agreed between themselves not to say anything. The former president was having too much fun believing they were completely on their own.

⊷⊷

Thirty minutes later, having taken leave of the former president as they returned to their lodgings, Jason found himself feeling somewhat discouraged but in truth quite optimistic. Certainly, Grant had put off his question about whether the man was considering competing for the presidency when they returned. But that was to be expected. More encouraging was a more general impression that were Grant to return to office, the stranglehold the southern democrats had over the lives of their black neighbors might be lessened. Indeed, if Grant was hardly Senator Sumner, the man's sense of basic decency, growing knowledge of China, and obvious hope that China might become a market for American manufactures might after the 1880 election see the full weight of the presidency arrayed against the growing anti-Chinese sentiment. At least it seemed that way to Jason as he opened the door to his room only to be surprised by the difficulty he encountered in opening it. Someone had jammed something under the door, a large envelope that had been wedged under it making it difficult to swing back. Bending down to pick it up, Jason saw that the thick envelope, without any hint of its origins was addressed to him.

# CHAPTER 71

# A THREAT

Picking up the envelope Jason glanced behind him out into the corridor to see if anyone had seen him pick up the packet. There was an older woman sitting at the end of the hallway and at least one cleaning woman working in a nearby room but no one took any notice of his actions. Closing the door quietly he carried the envelope over to the bed and sat down.

It was addressed to him in large letters, letters made by someone who, it seemed, had learned late in life to create Western-style letters. Jason Brandt and nothing more. Opening it, a few documents fell out across the bed. Two of them seemed to have been fastened together, one in Chinese and another in English...

"I first knew the Chinese woman, wife to the Western writer Brandt in Nanjing, when she was the wife of the infamous Taiping commander..."

He was shocked; it seemed to be something of a witness statement, a testimony from someone from the Taiping years, and there were two copies one in Chinese and another in English. He sat there stunned, going back and forth between the documents comparing them as they line for line outlined details of

Black Jade's role among the Chinese insurgents. Then, having offered details that clearly proved the writer had been there, the author turned to their friend Wu and his even greater role. The document was very thorough, even including information about Wu's escape as Huzhou collapsed and his eventual arrival at Fuzhou.

Putting down the document Jason picked up the third document, one smaller and shorter. It simply read, "Turning Grant's head against Japan will help neither your friends nor the Chinese you defend so publicly."

Dropping the material on the bed Jason sat there reflecting on what he'd received. The other foot had dropped, Robert Hart, the superintendent of trade's warning had taken on more meaning. Someone, obviously the Japanese were monitoring his actions and had become concerned that at Jason's prompting the former, and perhaps future president would throw his influence behind China in the growing competition with Japan. But what could it be Jason thought and then remembering, those islands off the coast of Japan, what had Hart called them, his memory failed him. Nevertheless, that must be it. The Japanese were warning him off, threatening his wife and friend. This trip was turning into something quite different than he had imagined. Helping the influential American understand something more of the Chinese in America and China itself seemed a worthy enough cause but now he'd entered the arena of international intrigue he had not bargained for.

Jason spent the rest of the day alone, wandering Tianjin, as Grant was received by the famous Li Hongzhang. He could have tried to look up former colleagues as he'd done in Shanghai but wasn't in the mood. The last time he'd been in Tianjin, after the massacre and the days searching for his wife, trying to determine if she'd died alongside the Catholic nuns she'd been visiting the day of the massacre, had been among the most traumatic in his life, and he had no interest in anyone's company.

Sometime in the early afternoon, he found himself in front of the site of the former orphanage run by the French Sisters of Charity. Black Jade had enjoyed their company; indeed it was probably those sisters who'd especially nurtured her interest in Catholicism, and he was sure first spoke to her of Jerusalem, which he was increasingly expecting to see sooner rather than later. Nevertheless, he now had to worry about whether this apparent warning might complicate the family's plans further, the plan to return to Shanghai and found the school. Indeed, Jason had no idea whether the Chinese officials would even care that Black Jade had been the wife and then widow of a Taiping leader. And as for Wu, he was already in Paris with Giquel and the other educational students. Indeed, Jason thought it was not even clear, whatever the intentions of the letter writer, whether the individual had any real leverage against Jason and those he cared about.

⇒⊢ ⊣⇐

Hours later, it was more clear what was going on. Jessie, the president's son, sought him out excitedly talking of how well Grant and Li Hongzhang's first meeting had gone. The two men, in so many ways alike, had hit it off wonderfully, talking for hours not only of their parallel efforts to defeat insurgents but their interest in modern manufactures as well. Li had apparently spoken at length of his efforts to encourage transfers of Western technology from the West, from Europe and America to China, and even opened up to a limited extent regarding the resistance he'd met in some quarters toward such efforts.

"And what you'd be especially interested in was they even talked about you for quite a while," Jessie related enthusiastically.

"Me? Li Hongzhang knows who I am?" Jason asked incredulously.

"Absolutely, seems the governor has regularly had writings such as yours translated; he seemed very familiar with your articles and even knew something of your testimony to that congressional committee. Father told me later that Li was very different from every other mandarin he'd met, that he even said he hoped to visit America one day and was very open to the idea of China purchasing more American-made manufactures."

"That must have been quite a conversation. I am not surprised though. Governor Li has been behind most of the efforts; they call them self-strengthening here, to learn Western technology."

"And that is not all. Governor Li told Father that you should do more than guide our morning walks; he even knew about them!" the boy explained. "That Grant should bring you with him to meetings, especially in Beijing."

"So it has been decided that we move on to Beijing? I thought that was not decided."

"It has. They still need to work out the imperial audience though, Father says the Chinese don't want it...bunch of diplomatic issues I don't understand and Father does not care about...says the emperor is a child and such things can wait till he reaches his maturity."

"Well, if they can avoid an argument over whether the emperor meets Grant it solves a lot of problems. Do we know when we set off for Beijing? That is going to be a lot more complicated, it's quite far from the coast, not like the cities we have visited so far," Jason said, wondering if Grant's relatively large entourage would set off overland. That seemed unlikely, given the state of the roads only horses could easily traverse and the Western women, including Grant's wife Julie were not accustomed to such travel.

"That is not clear, they have not worked out how such a journey could be accomplished...probably by river boat I heard but that is not settled." With that, the young man gave his farewell and set off in the direction of his mother who was beckoning toward him down the long hallway that separated them.

# CHAPTER 72

# TOWARD BEIJING

Somewhat to his surprise, Jason was in complete sympathy with the former president who sat opposite him sipping whiskey and smoking a cigar. Grant was speaking in relatively low tones; one never knew who among the Chinese around them had any English, as he complained of the agonizingly slow pace of their travels since they had departed for Beijing that morning.

For Jason who had become accustomed to the growing American railroad system and who'd before that largely traveled by horseback within China's interior the circus like movement of their entourage, which filled several boats and more often than not was pulled along from the banks by sweating Chinese laborers, seemed almost painful.

"Can't believe I let the governor talk me into this." Grant was saying with irritation.

"I suppose he felt you needed to see the capital, perhaps that you might influence people there beyond what he himself can accomplish." Jason suggested.

Since Li Hongzhang had praised his work so profusely to the president, his status had risen somewhat. From being a largely invisible guide during the early-morning walks that everyone seemed to know about and pretend they didn't, he'd been more and more often invited to the formal activities. In some sense, it was a compliment, though he knew his journalist colleague Russell Young was hardly pleased with the evolution of Jason's role. Jason understood the man's frustration well enough. The fellow did not care a whit for China, what he wanted was more of Grant's war stories which he hoped to fill a travel memoir with one day. Grant himself though, years beyond his civil-war generalship and even his presidency was more interested in understanding the world around him, understanding for knowledge itself and Jason was beginning to fervently hope, because the man might one day win the White House again.

"But isn't Governor Li the real power in China? How could he not be with the emperor a mere child. Everyone says that, at least the Westerners I talk to. I even asked the governor if that was true!"

"You did!" Jason asked with surprise. It was not the sort of question he imagined someone directly asking a Confucian mandarin.

"Sure, sometimes there are real advantages to being me. And besides, he and I had become great buddies before we left Tianjin, hoping to have even more conversations before we leave…smartest fellow I have met here in China, a real leader, knows something of the world beyond China - has ideas for how China can progress more." Grant said reflecting on the conversation even as a fish jumped out of the river and dramatically landed at their feet flopping in apparent shock that he'd hit a wooden deck rather than returned to the river. Within seconds one of the Chinese boatman, had wacked the creature and walked off down the deck with his catch.

"So, Mr. President, if I might ask," Jason said, leaning in even closer, "what did he say?"

"Oh, just what you'd expect. Even I knew he would not answer. Just said he appreciated my compliments about his leadership and changed the subject. What else could he do? The translator was doing his job, and we were hardly alone. Frankly, I wish you'd been there. Li might have been more honest. He does have a positive impression of your work."

"I appreciate your saying that, but, sir, I doubt if the conversation would have been any different if I had been doing the translating."

"Maybe not, but when I meet this Prince fellow...forgot his name..."

"Gong."

"Right, Prince Gong. I want you there with me."

"It would be an honor, sir."

"So, Jason, tell me about this fellow. Not a Chinaman I am told."

"Right, like a few others you have met, he is a Manchu, brother of the last emperor, the one who died during the Second Opium War."

"What do you know about him? Is he the real big man?"

"Frankly, sir, I am not sure anyone knows that much and his actual role is quite uncertain."

"What do you mean? Shouldn't that be obvious, Right, I understand better than most that he who holds the title may not be in complete control, spent years coming to learn that in Washington City. But here...if Gong's not in control, if Governor Li is not in control, who is? The child emperor?"

Jason himself now surveyed the deck. The only one in a position to hear them was Grant's son Jessie and Captain Roberts. Even Russell Young had walked off bored with the talk of China and Grant's wife had retired much earlier. Satisfying himself that he could speak with relative safety, China was after all not a place that suffered loose gossip even among the relatively privileged Westerners who in growing numbers lived within the empire.

"Well, let me tell you what I think I know, really no more than a hodgepodge of Western rumors and what a few Chinese who trust me in Beijing have said over the years."

Now Grant leaned forward, wiped his brow and grew more attentive as even he seemed to recognize the sensitivity of the topic.

"You may have heard that there was some sort of coup when the last emperor died, several of those around him seem to have tried to assert their own authority, given of course the youth of the emperor to take power but Gong and the imperial wives, two of them somehow conspired to over throw them."

"Women over threw men in China! " Grant said leaning in even closer.

Having the former leader of the union armies, the ex-president of the United States hanging on his every word might have emboldened some individuals but Jason only felt uncomfortable.

"That is how I understand it, Gong seems to have been initially their partner and more recently, at least from what I heard when I was last here, some sort of rift has broken out between Gong and the Empress Dowager."

"I thought you said there were two of them?"

"Yes, two of course but that was early on. If the rumors I have heard are true, only one of them, the Empress Dowager Cixi, has any real power."

"So she is the real power, some sort of senior regent for the boy king...emperor? But I thought women had no real power, that they were simply a burden always under the control of their husbands." Grant asked clearly reviewing the cultural material he'd learned over the previous months.

"It is true that a woman as a daughter, as a wife has no authority but a woman as a parent even a mother is quite another thing. Confucian culture gives as you know great respect for parents, and filial piety, the respect for parents goes incredibly deep."

"So that is how she controls, from behind some sort of feminine silk screen? So where does this Gong fellow fit in? Li wanted me to see Beijing and visit with Gong. He clearly seemed to think it was important."

"I suppose that might give us something of a clue. Gong tends to be seen as supportive of importing Western technology, indeed he is the head of the office that is responsible for such things while Cixi is said to often side with the Confucian conservatives. Maybe Li thought your visit would give Gong some sort of chip in the national politics of the court.

At that Grant went silent, taking another long drag on his cigar and looking up at the star filled night with wonder. The man was clearly absorbing Jason's words, reflecting on how he might incorporate the information into his visit to best advantage.

Jason for his part sat quietly watching Grant wondering what he was thinking. It was frequently clear that Grant traveled as a private citizen despite the honors he found throughout the world since he'd left the United States. But his mind still operated as the American leader, former and perhaps future president of the United States when such information, such relationships might prove helpful one day.

By the time they pulled over to the shoreline Jason himself was ever so tired of the experience of the barges on the Peiho River. He himself had taken the trip from Tianjin to Beijing often enough but always by horse. Nevertheless, Grant's group, largely because of the presence of several women had taken the far more circuitous route by barge and then finally transferred to the sedan chairs Gong had sent for them. Somewhat to his surprise, he noticed that many among the party, even Russell Young seemed happy though with their surroundings, it was the first landscape with its vast expanses of wheat and orchards that the Americans had seen that resembled to any extent the environment of North America.

"Can't say I miss the tropics." Russell proclaimed as he pulled up alongside Jason, who astride his mount was already enormously gratified that the Prince had provided not only sedan chairs but horses for the arriving group to employ as they traveled the last miles toward the capital.

"So what did you men talk about after I turned in last night?" The journalist asked Jason, whom he'd become more open with as he became convinced Jason's journalistic interests were far from his own.

"Not a lot, he was asking me about the capital, what I knew of the leadership, which sadly is not much."

"Speaking of politics, did he say anything more about our politics...I mean American politics...you have any better sense than the rest of us about whether he is going to run next year? Had, a lot of letters, in Tianjin from friends asking."

"You had letters?" Jason perked up, "How, he had not even thought to look for letters after he left Shanghai and the newspaper offices he'd told his family and friends to use.

"Sure, plenty, the American council had a nice pile of them for me. Fact is I think he said something when I returned just before we left, something about getting letters for you forwarded from Shanghai…sorry I forgot to tell you."

"No problem, we will be back soon enough."

"But what of my question? You two seem to be getting along well, and I heard Governor Li praised you a lot, and we have all heard how the two old warriors bonded over their respective civil-war stories."

"Yes, Grant's views about China have grown immeasurably since he met Li Hongzhang. They have become fine friends; even heard Li told Grant he wanted to visit the United States one day. But about your question. I am in as much of the dark as the rest of us. The president holds his cards tight to his chest on that one. But I certainly hope he does, he'd be even better positioned to lead after this trip and all he has learned."

"Your certainly right about that," Russell said, "and you have only been with us since Hong Kong, I have been with him since we left home, through Europe, the Holy Land, the British Raj of India. Even a died in the wool Yankee like me has learned a lot."

"My friend Sam, Clemens, Twain, whatever…says, "Travel is the death of prejudice."

"That sounds like Clemens," Russell said. "Don't know the fellow well, but it certainly sounds like him."

"So, Mr. Young, Jason said glancing at the slow pace of the sedan chairs that were carrying most of Grant's traveling party, we obviously have a lot more time before we arrive at the capital. Tell me about the Holy Land, my wife insists we travel through there on our way home."

For the next hour, as the two journalists, their horses slowly walking alongside each other through what was proving a particularly warm day chatted about the president's visit to the

Ottoman realms and especially the Holy City itself. As they talked Jason tried to imagine what the city he'd heard about so often from his father, at least the ancient version of it would now look and how soon he and his family would come to know the place themselves.

# CHAPTER 73

# THE CAPITAL

Jason may have grown up in China but having been promoted in his service with the former president was giving him a very different view of China than he had ever known before. The apparently positive words Grant had heard from the great Li Hongzhang had seen Jason catapulted from his previously informal role as a guide to Chinese civilization, more often at hours either near dawn or quite late in the evening had kept him from seeing the more formal receptions China's officials had put on for America's former president. However, that had all changed. He was, now along with a small group, among them President Grant, his eldest son Colonel Grant, Jessie had been left behind, the Acting Consul Chester Holcombe plus a few others traveling through some of the capital's narrowest lanes as the summer heat passed over a hundred degrees.

"Good to have you with us." Holcombe said, my Chinese is good but with a meeting of this importance I am only too pleased to have someone who actually grew up here available."

"Thank you Mr. Holcombe, but the president asked me to observe, not serve as translator. I am sure you have been doing a fine job, indeed I have heard you have been doing splendidly."

"All very kind of you Brandt, but we both know your Chinese, even if I must say you have a bit of a southern tone at times, is far better than mine. You my good man were growing up here while I was still studying in college back in Schenectady. Did you know I went to Union College?"

"Actually I am not sure I knew that. It is near Troy is it not, where my family's taken up residence?"

"Actually, just to the west down the Mohawk river from Troy, I assume you have been to Albany?"

"Yes, in fact, my son is a student at the Albany Academy."

"Fine place, perhaps not as distinguished as the Troy Female Academy where your wife and daughter are but a fine place."

For a second Jason considered asking him a bit more about Schenectady but then the party reached the outer courtyard of the Prince's yamen. From here on, they would enter a world Jason had never seen before. He was anxious to take in every sight. Happily, as he'd mentioned to Mr. Holcombe despite his presence he had no formal duties and would be all the more able to simply take it all in.

As they entered within the walled courtyard of Prince Gong's residence the entire group, even Grant himself, not a fellow usually interested in sights that did not include technology, gaped in wonderment. Jason had never been within the walls of the imperial city but it was he imagined perhaps something like the Prince's residence if certainly larger. Indeed, for a moment Jason was reminded of his youthful experience of standing in the presence of the Heavenly King in Nanjing but the better part of discretion kept him from revealing that particular thought to any of his colleagues as they were escorted in.

As they entered, Prince Gong himself stood there to welcome them. A tall individual with a deeply serious look on his face, he beckoned his guests forward into an inner courtyard

Jason found both splendid and yet surprisingly calming. They were only a few yards away from a series of small wooden covered walkways that surrounded a beautiful inner lake perhaps thirty meters across that housed numerous fish who swam near the surface. Trees were abundant as well and helped immensely in lowering the discomfort they had experienced in Beijing's burning streets only moments before. Within minutes, the entire group, with Grant himself having been given the place of honor to the Prince's side, were seated within one of the small pavilion like rooms before a table loaded with wonderful looking delicacies.

Jason, from his perch farthest from Grant and the president watched intently, studying the man he'd heard so many speak of but had never seen. A moment later as the group made themselves comfortable the Prince speaking through Mr. Holcombe asked each of his guests about themselves, where they were from and if they had children. To the silent amusement of the Westerners, the Prince offered his condolences when Colonel Grant told his host that he had one child, a daughter. Jason, for a second thought he saw a knowing smile flash across President Grant, the young lady's grandfather's face, as he listened to Mr. Holcombe's translation.

"And you, sir," the Prince said finally turning to Jason, though he made sure Holcombe was ready for the next introductions."

"Your Excellency, your next guest needs no translator."

The Prince looked puzzled, at least for a second until Jason realized it was his turn to speak.

"Your Excellency, Jason began, nervously, suddenly conscious of Holcombe's teasing comment about the "southern tone" of his Chinese. "My name is Jason Brandt; I grew up in Hong Kong and spent most of my adult life, save a few recent years in America living in Shanghai with my family."

"You speak like a Chinese," The Prince said, staring at him with curiosity. "Are you a missionary like Mr. Holcombe, come to help us understand the Western God?"

"Thank you, Your Excellency, I know my Chinese to be very poor so your words flatter me. However, since you ask, I grew up speaking the language of the people of Guangzhou and Hong Kong and learned the more northern dialects as a young man many years ago. And no, I am not a missionary, though my father once was. I make my living writing about China and the Chinese for the Westerners."

At that, Gong turned to one of his aides and asked the man something.

"What is he saying?" Grant's son whispered in Jason's ear.

"I have no idea; they are speaking Manchu, not Chinese."

Gong then turned back toward Jason, "My aide tells me he knows something of you, that you are a friend of the Frenchman Giquel who worked with Shen Baozhen building our naval facility at Fuzhou."

"Yes, Your Excellency, I know the man and the naval facility well."

"You see, Mr. President," Gong said, turning back to his distinguished guest, "perhaps you have heard of that facility?"

Grant nodded. He had quizzed Jason at length about the project.

"That is good. There are those here who would tell you that China has no interest in such industrial development but the dockyard and other projects prove otherwise." The Prince then waited for Holcombe to translate his words.

"Yes, indeed, Your Excellency. I have heard of the great dockyard the French are helping build and of the arsenal and translation facility in Shanghai, heard about at length from both Mr. Brandt here and Governor Li in Tianjin."

The Prince nodded with a hint of pleasure. It seemed obvious to Jason that Gong was one of those men who almost always wore a frown of concern on his face but even he seemed pleased with the foreign leader's knowledge of Chinese modernization efforts.

"Indeed, Your Excellency," Grant went on. "It would give me no end of pleasure to see my own country play a role in helping China import more of the new technologies that have been developed in America to China."

"Yes, that would be good for both the people of your great nation, Mr. President, and for the subjects of the celestial kingdom, though"—he hesitated for a second—"I cannot say that everyone here is as admiring of your country's manufactures as Governor Li or myself."

"Isn't it always like that?" Grant chimed in. "Some folks like progress, some love their traditions."

"It is as you say, Mr. President, but if I may be so bold, there's another matter I wish to bring up, but wait. Holcombe, tell our guests they should eat."

"I think they are waiting for you and the president to do so, sir, just as protocol demands," Holcombe responded.

"Yes, of course," The prince leaned forward and sipped a bit of soup from a nearby bowl and gesturing with his hands encouraged the entire group to partake.

Jason knew most of them had just eaten before leaving for the Gong mansion, but they dug in with enough enthusiasm to avoid insult. And Jason even more than the rest, given that he'd used the entire trip with Grant to eat so many of the Chinese delicacies he'd missed since arriving in America so long before.

Within only a few minutes or so as most of the party quietly ate it became obvious that neither Grant nor Gong were especially interested in the food.

"Mr. President," Gong began hesitantly, signaling with his eyes toward Holcombe, who quickly put down the filled bun he was tasting.

"We would like to ask you to carry our thoughts to the Japanese emperor on a matter of importance to both communities."

"I suspect you mean those islands that Governor Li mentioned?"

"Yes, we have had little luck communicating our concern. The Japanese took the king of Ryuku islands back to Japan, the king of a community that has long recognized China as their overlord and are apparently trying to absorb them into the Japanese empire. That is something China cannot allow."

"That is certainly troubling, Your Excellency, but, of course, as you understand I travel as a private citizen, albeit one my own country, especially its navy has been very kind too, but still as a private citizen, no longer holding any rank, neither military nor governmental, in America."

The Prince stared at Grant for a long time. For a second Jason wondered if the Prince himself was about to ask Grant the same question everyone else was wondering about, would he seek to lead his country again, seek the presidency again. Whatever it was that the Prince was tempted to say he actually just nodded and then after a moment..."

"Yes, of course, we understand that your Mr. Hayes now runs America, but we would still like your help."

For the next ten minutes the Prince explained his desire that Grant, whom the prince knew had already been invited by the Japanese emperor to visit once his stay in China was complete spoke more quietly, with only Grant and Holcombe taking part about the message he hoped Grant might be willing to pass on to Tokyo.

Once that more discrete conversation was terminated the Prince stood and gesturing to the entire party outside he offered them a slow tour around the lovely pond that stood at the center of his complex. Ten minutes later Grant, Jason and the entire group found themselves back outside, now feeling the heat of Beijing's summer ever more intensely as they found their way back to the American legation complex.

# CHAPTER 74

# HEADING HOME

I t might have been true as some told him aboard ship that the voyage from China to Japan had become considerably faster over the last few years as the technology of naval steam engines advanced, he would have to ask Prosper to confirm that, but the fact was the trip seemed to be taking forever. Indeed, the last week or so had moved interminably as Grant's party had slowly made their way back to Tianjin, to allow Grant to spend a few more days with Li Hongzhang, who'd become a great friend to the former president. Indeed, Jason heard at second hand that the Chinese governor was already planning his own trip to America with Grant's help.

Once those final receptions and consultations had been complete Jason had boarded ship once again, the American naval ship that was ferrying Grant around for the voyage now headed to Yokohama. For Jason, the sense that he'd accomplished all he had hoped from the trip and his deep longing for his family made him especially anxious to leave for America. True, he would have liked a bit more time with Grant but that was rarely possible. The man was usually surrounded by others and from what Jason could tell Grant's interests were already starting to focus less on China than his upcoming trip to Japan that of course, Jason would be no help in preparing for.

But if he was somewhat disappointed, it was not a great disappointment. Jason had already learned everything he thought he needed to know about Grant and had developed an enormous confidence that the man's instincts, were he to regain the White House, would keep him from allowing the United States, to close its doors to foreigners looking to improve their lives. No indeed, the more Jason reflected on the man he'd come to know the more he was convinced that while the Republican Party might have moved past some aspects of the racial tolerance it had embodied since Lincoln sat in the White House, Grant himself, continued to carry the torch even if somewhat more quietly given the times.

No, Jason thought as he looked out over the Pacific from the steamship's railing those last few days had not gone by fast enough. Indeed, the only highlight was his discovery that there really was a pile of letters, from Giquel, from Wu and Wong, from Black Jade and the children and even a warm somewhat less businesslike than usual, letter from Russell Sage himself which had especially surprised him. The man's letters were usually so brief but this one was a bit more informal even sending his wife's regards. Still, Sage like everyone else asked the same question, did Jason have a better sense having traveled with the man whether Grant would seek to regain the White House when he returned. Hayes had made it clear he would not run again and Grant was the obvious choice in the minds of many, especially so given the time that had passed since the scandals of the Grant presidential years. Indeed, according to Sage, Russell Young's journalist letters had been widely printed and the former general and president, in the years since he left the White House, had risen considerably in the estimation of his fellow Americans. Unfortunately, as he told Sage, Wu and the others, he might have spent a good deal of time with the former president over the last few weeks and while he'd become convinced that were Grant to win the White House for another term he'd play a positive role in Chinese American relations, the man had given absolutely no clue as to his intentions.

More exciting were the letters from Troy, from Black Jade and, especially exciting, a letter from each of the children. Little Will, who had spent more time in Troy since the Albany Academy had closed for the summer spoke of his enthusiasm for some sort of new game — "baseball," he called it—that the kids were playing in the large yard in front of the church that bordered the Troy Female seminary. While little Mai-ling—he had to remind himself that she was not that little anymore— wrote about some of the new friends she'd made and something of her irritation in having to help her mother out with the Chinese language class that Black Jade had finally managed to introduce at the female seminary.

His daughter, Jason noted with amusement thought it was a waste of time and much preferred her own French classes that she insisted she was working very hard at, indeed she claimed she was getting better even than her mother whom Jason knew had been at it a lot longer than her daughter had. The mention of studying French particularly caught Jason's attention. Clearly, it seemed to suggest that Black Jade had been preparing the children for their departure, the stay in Paris and eventually her hope of introducing French at the planned school in Shanghai. Black Jade, Jason knew was convinced that being able to offer the language would help recruit the young women students, Chinese and Western her school would need.

Prosper's letter from Paris was full of news of the European student educational mission and his appreciation of Jason's comments about his short return to China. It felt odd to Jason that he was now the one reporting on developments in

China, offering gossip of their mutual friends in Shanghai whom Giquel had not seen since he'd finished his duties at the dockyard, and taken up residence in Paris directing his own educational mission. Giquel though also offered all sorts of suggestions for where the family should stay during the several months he knew Jason planned to stay in the French capital during the family's return home.

But it was his old friend Wu's letter than concerned him the most, Wu had written of his enthusiasm for France, how much he enjoyed working as Prosper's personal assistant, how he was getting used to the curious foods the French ate and even the language which he claimed he was developing a very good sense of. But it was the last sentence that especially concerned Jason.

His old friend had written: "But my friend, the many pleasures I derive from living here in Paris have not changed my basic longing for home, my sense that it is time, indeed rather late, but still time for me to return home to start a family, to open the door for the future of my line."

The latter section of the letter had been much more direct, Wu asked politely, but also with precision when Jason expected to pass through Paris on the way home. His old friend had made it clear that once Jason and family arrived Wu planned, if it would be acceptable, to join their party and return with them to Shanghai.

Under most circumstances, Jason would have been delighted. The chance to spend time with Wu, to travel with him to China, perhaps even involve him somewhat with the planned school, they would of course need extra staff, was in theory delightful. Only memory of the one especially uncomfortable conversation he had had just after boarding the ship in Shanghai for Yokohama precluded allowing him the pleasure Wu's plans might otherwise have brought.

"Mr. Brandt, I believe. May I stand alongside you?" Two days earlier, Jason had looked up from the fine spot on the railing he'd commandeered almost immediately after dropping off his bags in the sleeping space the young American seaman had shown him moments after he'd boarded the ship. Once he arrived in Yokohama of course, he expected to board a commercial vessel but for at least the short trip to Japan Jason had been invited to travel along with Grant's company. It was a beautiful afternoon and he'd wanted to enjoy the view as they approached the open sea from Tianjin's harbor. Suddenly having approached quite silently still waiting for a formal invitation was a man, almost certainly Japanese standing before him in a nicely tailored Western-style suit.

"Yes of course, please sit down. So like me you have managed to obtain passage with the American navy. There are certainly advantages to traveling with an American president, even a former one." Jason offered as he gestured for the fellow.

"Yes indeed. Let me introduce myself. My name is Mr. Kaneshiro, a member of the Japanese delegation that will be welcoming your former, maybe future"—the man's faced revealed a half smile—"president."

"I certainly don't know anything about that, but you are right. He is a very important person. The great Li Hongzhang and he became quite good friends, I am told, during Mr. Grant's stay in Tianjin."

"Yes, we have heard that," the fellow said with just a touch of irritation, at least it seemed like irritation to Jason.

"And you yourself enjoyed your short return home?" The man asking looking closely at him as each pretended to still be studying the panoramic view laid out before them.

What surprised Jason most was that the man, a fellow he did not recall seeing before, seemed very open about knowing something about him.

"Do I know you, sir?" Jason asked, turning to directly look at the man.

"I do not think so, but my government knows a lot about you." The fellow said with an irritating half smile on his face.

"And what is it you think you know about me?"

"With journalists, that is not much of a problem. You people tend to splash as I believe you say your opinions all over the papers."

"I am sorry; do you have some business with me?" Jason asked starting to feel irritated with the man.

"No, not really. My government would merely like you to know that your efforts to prejudice Mr. Grant against my people are not appreciated and could come at a price."

Studying the man even closer Jason suddenly felt he had the source of the mystery inquires and affidavit he'd received.

"What is this about...I don't know what you are talking about...those islands one hears about...I have never even discussed them with Grant, and it is none of your business if I had, and there won't be any chance to do so in the future."

For the first time, the fellow looked confused.

"You will not be traveling with Mr. Grant in Japan?"

"No, of course not, I have nothing to offer the president about your country, sir; I don't even know the place, have spent only a few days there in my entire life. No, I am merely catching a ride now with Mr. Grant's party; once we arrive in Yokohama I will be catching a commercial steamer to San Francisco."

The Japanese official looked closely at Jason and then before turning away said. "So sorry Mr. Brandt, there has been some sort of confusion. I hope you enjoy the rest of your return home." At that, he had turned quickly away and retreated down the deck. Jason never saw him again and after only a day's layover in Japan, he had managed to take passage in the next day's sailing for California.

# CHAPTER 75
# THE PRESIDENTIAL CONTEST

"I am not sure what you mean, are you ready to go back to Shanghai or not. I am confused." Jason said sitting alongside his wife. It had been their first chance to have a real conversation since he'd returned home several days before exhausted from his train trip across the country, a trip that had continued almost nonstop since he'd departed Tianjin more than a month before. Indeed, he had only stopped in San Francisco for a few days to get a sense of how much the sentiment supporting legislation against Chinese immigration had grown before he'd set off again for New York City.

He'd even managed to catch another train north to Troy before passing out from exhaustion in the empty house on First Street. His last thought before collapsing had been wishing he'd stopped to send a telegram from New York about his eminent arrival but he'd forgotten. Hours later, Black Jade, and Mei-ling had returned from the seminary to find him in a deep sleep only interrupted for a few seconds of hugs before his wife had taken her daughter and tiptoed from the room letting him sleep off the trip for the next twelve hours. Now after a hearty breakfast they'd walked Mei-ling down the street, dropped her off at school and then themselves walked back to the huge white church on Congress Street where they sat on the steps experiencing the cooling breezes that wafted in from the Hudson River a few hundred yards away.

"That is not the question my husband." Black Jade turned to look directly into his eyes from her perch on the steps. As she did so Jason was profoundly moved by how beautiful his wife, who in aging ever so slightly in the months since he'd departed for China had only become even more beautiful in his eyes. How could he, he thought to himself ever have spent so much time apart from her. In a private prayer he vowed never to take on another assignment that would keep him apart from the woman he'd loved most of his adult life.

"Then what is the question, it seems like you have accomplished your goals, the classes, become a teacher yourself, and your hope to teach French once we return to Shanghai is certainly not going to get better here. You can work on that when we get to Paris; I already have letters from Prosper on potential lodgings."

"Not that…it is more complicated. Becoming a teacher, becoming friends with Miss Wilcox, she tells me to call her Emily but I cannot, not to my former teacher who has opened my eyes to our plans."

"How so?"

Her demeanor was unusual. Black Jade almost since the moment he'd met her had usually been more certain of herself, more than the vast majority of Chinese women he'd known in his life and even more than most of the American women he'd met in the last few years.

"It was right to come to Troy. I have made friends, learned a lot more than I ever could in Rockport, Mei-ling is very happy, and Willie loves the Albany Academy, but the seminary itself is growing weaker by the day."

"The female seminary is failing?" Jason asked with astonishment. As far as he knew, the place was famous. People seemed to know all about it. Even Twain and Grant had been very aware of the seminary when the topic had come up.

"How can that be? I thought the place was still reasonably successful."

"It was, but now as a teacher, as a friend of Miss Wilcox, I have seen a different seminary than what we'd heard of or even saw when we first arrived from Shanghai. Mrs. Wilcox's great-aunt Emma Willard was famous, the driving force of the seminary, but after she died, the school, which had been weakening since the war, has really failed. They do not take in boarders anymore. The buildings are old. Ms. Wilcox is terrified the great accomplishment of Emma Willard's life will not survive much longer. Even Emma Willard's son and daughter-in-law, the Willards, have retired and speak of the same problems."

"But if we are going to go home soon, does that matter that much, I mean to our family for our plans for a school in Shanghai?"

"Yes and no, but it mostly matters because I have a much better idea of how hard starting a school will be, how great a task we have created for ourselves, learning subjects one can teach seems, not difficult compared to running the school, compared to understanding the financial part. And we will be more like Emma Willard of decades ago, simply trying to convince the Shanghai Chinese families that there is any point in educating their daughters, daughters that will go off soon enough to join someone else's family."

"But what of you my husband," are you ready to go home, did you feel what is the word...nostalgic when you first arrived in Hong Kong and moved on to Shanghai?"

"Yes, very much so, if you told me you were ready to go tomorrow, OK, maybe next week I think I would jump at the chance, except for one thing."

"What is that?"

"After the last several months I am convinced that a new chapter in American Chinese relations, between the two countries, between the people themselves is going to be determined over the next year as the American presidential race commences.

"You mean about whether Grant goes back to the White House?"

"It's more than that, the Grant I got to know a very small amount over the last several months is not the same man who served in the White House, his attitudes about people have changed, I mean even before, when he was president he tried to see that the blacks were treated more fairly in the south and now he's learned far more about the Chinese. You should have seen how well he and Governor Li Hongzhang got along."

"But how would that change things here, the sentiment against Chinese in the west is moving east, there is another important man, this time an Eastern politician named Blaine who talks all the time against the Chinese...how they will steal jobs from San Francisco to Boston. What could Grant do about that?"

"I don't really know but my feeling is Grant's gotten the idea that China could become a major market for American manufactures and would use the argument about more jobs against those like Blaine. It could work but he would need to get back into the White House to have any chance at holding off the tide of anti-Chinese sentiment.

"So you are not quite ready to go home either," she said very privately taking up his hand after glancing around to see if they were being observed.

"I'd like to see, to write about what Grant does when he gets home, he should be back within a month or so, I think he was planning to take ship right after he finished the visit to Japan.

He may not have said anything about running again in front of me but he won't be able to hide it once he lands on American soil. He'll need to arouse the interest of his supporters and the republican convention is not that long off."

"Mr. Willard told me they were meeting in Chicago for their convention."

"Then I guess I will be off to Chicago, maybe that will be my last big story from America before we leave."

"Then it's settled, we leave after the election?"

"Or before that, I don't think I will want to cover the campaign if Grant can't even win the Republican nomination."

We should walk to the station, Willie and Old Zhu should be arriving from Albany at any minute.

At that he stood up and despite his awareness of her feelings about showing him affection in public, Jason took her hand for the short walk downtown to await the arrival of his son he'd not seen in months.

# CHAPTER 76

# ROOTING FOR GRANT

"Jessie!" Grant's son, who had passed within yards of him in the incredibly crowded convention hall, had amazingly heard him. Jason could not have been more pleased. He'd spent an exhausted week trying to understand what was likely to happen at the convention, whether the republicans would nominate Grant again or not but the effort had been in large measure one frustration after another. It had been impossible to get anywhere near the former president and compared to men like Russell Young whom he'd spied from a distance from time to time he knew hardly any of those in the know well enough to give him the tidbits that any journalist needed to ply his trade.

Sure, he thought to himself, it was a lot easier than four years before, he'd learned enough covering the battle between Hayes and Tilden to avoid feeling as lost as he been during the last presidential campaign, but Jason also knew that this time was different. This time he actually cared, this time he'd convinced himself that Grant's return to the White House would be good for both his adopted country and his native land, good both for China and America though sometimes he wondered which was which.

As Jessie turned toward the sound of his voice, Jason waved his arms wildly. It was hardly that long since Jessie had seen him, indeed not that many months before near the docks in Tianjin, he and the president's youngest son had shared the heartiest of good-byes.

"Jason, Mr. Brandt, you here, yes of course, you are a journalist, sometimes I forget that, of course you are here."

"Can we talk somewhere privately?" Jason asked, looking around cautiously at the rows of reporters who sat at the tables just behind him scribbling away as the cacophony of voices, the heat of so many bodies filled the cavernous convention hall making the enormous room as uncomfortable as any space Jason ever remembered being in. He was also somewhat nervous that one of his journalist colleagues would recognize the young man as the son of the former president.

"Of course, but as a reporter or a friend the young man asked warily.

"Just a couple of old friends, frankly I don't even know how much longer I will be a journalist here…no nothing you say will pass from my lips."

"OK, old friend, let's move over there near the wall," It was obvious that if the table full of journalists had not recognized him Jessie Grant himself was very much aware of how close he was standing to the several rows of reporters.

"You know Father still talks fondly of those early morning walks we had in China, especially the one we almost ended up in a real fight in, guess he likes the idea of more straightforward fights than this sort of thing." The young man gestured back toward the center of the room, at the hundreds of male delegates who sat around the convention hall's floor and those spectators in the gallery.

"Does he want it or not?" Jason asked taking his best shot and hoping the many weeks traveling in China together with the former first family would have earned him an honest answer.

Jessie looked at him closely, clearly making some sort of decision.

"Does he want it? You know something of Father, always the soldier, less the politician—everything is about duty, honor, and dignity. I think he wants it, or at least thinks he has some sort of duty to take it on. But he won't fight for it, not as far as I can tell."

"We both know, I don't know all that much about this country, but I think I have learned enough to know that America needs your father back, needs his humanity, his sense of fair play toward blacks and Chinese." There he had said it, Jason felt he might as well have simply grabbed up a Grant sign and started parading across the floor. "Blaine is the wrong man, the wrong Republican and I shudder to think what will happen if all those southern democrats grab the White House as well."

"I know from personal experience that many agree with you, senators like Conkling certainly thinks so and plenty of others. Some say that if Father regains the White House we might be able to avoid another century of racial tensions, more suppression of the blacks and better treatment of the Chinese whom you helped Father understand so much better last year."

Jason nodded in appreciation and then asked "What does your family think?"

"This might be hard to believe, but I don't think even the family knows Father's mind much better than those here."

"You mean he does not simply say his hopes?"

"It's not that, he would certainly take the nomination if it was offered to him, and absolutely thinks he could do some good with it. That has been clear for months. You certainly know it was not by coincidence that he visited several states at critical moments over the last year when his presence, supposedly coincidental, would be helpful for his followers."

"But what is the problem then, is his family against the idea?"

"Absolutely not, indeed my mother thinks he should do it, tried to get him to come directly to the convention, no, mother is convinced it is the right thing to do but, well, maybe the best way to put is that he is willing, sees it as his duty if called, but won't fight for it." Jessie than looked across the room again and apparently spotting someone he wished to speak with turned again to Jason.

"Old friend, it was truly good to see you. I will give my regards from you to father and mother. I am sure they will be pleased. As for that other matter, I think we will know more in a few hours, I believe the first vote is scheduled about then." With that Jessie tipped his hat, gave Jason a brisk handshake and walked off into the crowded convention obviously hoping to catch up to someone Jason could not quite see. The room was far too crowded to for that.

"Are you Mr. Brandt, sir?" Jason was asked as he approached his seat again at the table that had been set up for journalists at the front of the hall.

"Yes, Jason Brandt. How can I help?" he said to the young man whom he'd seen scouring about delivering messages.

"It's not me, sir. This was just given to me by one of the other runners. Said a strange fellow..." Jason leaned in trying to hear better; the convention hall was a terrible place to try to have even the most basic of conversations.

Clearly needing to deliver more messages the fellow thrust the note in Jason's hand only staying around long enough to take the dime Jason handed him as a tip.

Sitting down, he opened the envelope,

"Don't know how long this will take to get to you. Crazy out here and this boy does not look too bright. But I suspect he will find you easily enough. Come outside at two, you won't have a problem finding me.'
Wong Chin Foo

An hour later, Jason worked his way out of the convention hall and out on to Michigan Avenue. Wong was right, the man was not hard to find. Despite the multitudes who stood outside like political barkers at a county fair, there on the street, in full mandarin garb, his queue flowing behind his back, Wu had set up a portable advertising booth proclaiming his availability as lecturer and listing his qualifications, a long list of which not surprisingly featuring his claim to be the First Confucian Missionary to America."

"So what do you think?" Wong yelled out as Jason approached him. It was clear that most of those who passed Wong's make shift booth were giving him a wide berth as they walked by.

"What do I think? I think you have not changed one bit since the last time I saw you. How did you even know I was here?"

"You're a journalist, why wouldn't you be here? Besides, I read your articles. What an adventure with Grant, have you become some sort of adviser to the man, that is quite an elevation!"

"Hardly. I barely know him." Jason liked Wong but he was too much of a loose cannon to share any private thoughts about Grant with."

"Keeping your thoughts to yourself eh…right you are!"

Standing there in the street talking to Wong, whose English was the best of any Chinese he'd ever met always amazed Jason.

Even Black Jade often said that, and listening as he stood there in his full mandarin garb occasionally handing out leaflets to those who dared pass close enough to him was, Jason thought added just another element to his sense of the crazy zoo like atmosphere that the republican convention gave off.

"So what do you think, Jason? Be honest with me," Wong said lowering his voice, they can't nominate Blaine, he's the worst racist of any of them, worse than those in the West, just using his attacks on the Chinese to win office and the scoundrel Democrats are no better."

"It is hard to argue," Jason said. "It really is discouraging."

"But what about Grant? He is better than the rest and must have learned something when he was in China, especially in the North. I accept that those damn Cantonese can give the wrong impression but Grant got past Hong Kong, met the real Chinese."

That was one of the things about Wong that made it hard for Jason to feel close to him. The man's northern Chinese prejudices were almost always up front. Indeed, too often his "friend" seemed to forget that Jason's wife, whom he claimed to admire, was also from the south.

"What of Grant? No one really knows a thing." Jason said, feeling only slightly guilty. "He has plenty of supporters but so does Blaine and the animosity against allowing more Chinese into the country is likely to grow regardless of who wins."

"So you have no hope? I know you know more than you are telling me but that is fine. I know I have a temper and can be a bit indiscreet but that is all right, I know you have done your best."

"I appreciate you're saying that."

"So when do they start voting for the nominee? I assume you can tell me that."

"Probably fairly soon, to this point they have been arguing about the voting procedures, some fashions help one candidate versus another but I think that is almost over. They should start the nominating speeches fairly soon. As I left the building I heard that Senator Conkling would be giving an official nomination speech for Grant in about two hours."

"But enough of that tell me what is happening with you. I thought you had left Chicago, that you were living in Michigan somewhere that you were going to open a tea shop or something."

"Well, that is a long story...and not for now. Some other time. You know me, got into a bit of a legal scrape."

"With the American authorities or are you fighting with your countrymen again?" Jason asked trying to suppress a laugh. It was never clear whom Wong despised more White Americans or the Cantonese. At times Jason was almost certain Wong would have joined one of the anti-Chinese organizations if it could have been made clear that it was the Cantonese that were the problem not, as he saw it the real Chinese."

"Oh you don't want to know." Wong said a little sheepishly as he made another halfhearted effort to put a flyer advertising his services as a lecturer into the hands of a sweaty but well-dressed businessman who passed them.

"Look, Wong, it is wonderful to see you but I need to get back inside. As you said, I am a journalist and need to ply my trade."

"Of course, and if Grant does win and stops the momentum against China I will know whom to credit." Wong said patting him on the back, a gesture far more American than Chinese as Jason turned to reenter the hall."

CHAPTER 77

# AND THE NEXT PRESIDENT...

I f getting out of the extraordinarily crowded, flag and banner strewn hall had been difficult, trying to fight his way
back in widely waving his journalist credentials as he did so
was exhausting. When he finally found himself inside again,
he dove for a temporarily available space near the wall to catch
his breath. But before he could, a big hand reached out to slap
his shoulder.

"Jason, Jason Brandt, Wonderful to see you. Now, young
man the tide has turned you are on my turf." Jason whirled
around to see Russell Young the journalist and his frequent
traveling companion for weeks while they both accompanied
Grant in China."

"Wonderful to see you Russell, I spotted you across the hall
a few times earlier but never caught your eye, and you are right,
in China I was the guide, but this is your world and I may know
something of China but compared to you I know nothing of
the language of American politics.

Young smiled and Jason knew he had hit exactly the right
note, Young may have tolerated China, but his real love was
American politics and Civil War folklore. Indeed, he'd barely

tolerated Grant's questions about China. Young was so anxious to get the man to share his memories of the war years that the reporter knew his readers craved.

"So are you thoroughly confused?" Young asked, relishing being in his element.

"Absolutely, still trying to figure out this unit rule, I keep hearing that is the real battle not the voting for the candidates. Is that true?"

Young looked at Jason closely, they'd developed a reasonably solid acquaintance the previous year in China but Young was after all, always the reporter, ever concerned about having the best most exclusive information. For a second Jason could see him calculating what he was willing to share or not with the younger less experienced reporter.

Obviously drawing the conclusion that Jason's question offered no special advantage Young took out his handkerchief and rubbed it. He was sweating even more than he had in Beijing and that Jason thought said something about how hot the convention hall, with all those bodies packed into it, had become over the last few hours.

"What you have heard is largely correct; the general has lots of supporters. His stalwarts are incredibly loyal but so does Senator Blaine, and even Sherman has enough to make a difference. Grant might even have the highest total right now."

"But doesn't that give him a major advantage?"

"It is not a bad thing, being ahead never hurts but the problem is that there is not a lot of room for Grant's numbers to grow. He has plenty of enemies and the third term idea makes a lot of people uncomfortable, even Washington didn't have a third term."

"And this unit rule everyone's talking about, I just read an interview with some guy named Garfield, another politician who seems to think that is especially important, important that it be beaten. Why?"

"Garfield's backing Sherman but the bigger issue is that some of Grant's supporters are trying to use a rule that says the majority in any state delegation can force everyone in that delegation to vote with the majority. If the rule stands, Grant's got it, he has that much momentum."

"You sound skeptical."

"I am. There is nothing secret about it; just an issue of numbers, Grant has the most votes but not enough to impose the unit rule that would win it for him. And his opponents, Blaine and Sherman's people have together enough votes to make sure he cannot win it that way. And they argue it is about democracy not just promoting their own man. That makes it a lot easier that way."

"But Grant is the right man, you know him better than I do. Surely you feel the same way?" Jason asked wondering if it were really true.

"What I think does not matter, what matters is who has the votes, who thinks Grant will help them, help their careers and perhaps even more who is more afraid he could pull down the party and lose in November."

"And the fact that he'd be an even better president now than before, that he now knows so much more about the world and its leaders, that does not matter?"

"Jason, now I know you spent too much of your youth in China, I may not know that much about the Middle Kingdom but you're sounding like some sort of Confucian mandarin jabbering about wise leadership. Wake up man," Young laughed, "This is America. The things you think are important mean nothing in this battle."

Turning to study the crowd it was obvious Young had spotted someone else he wanted to talk to - still he turned back to Jason for a moment.

"Jason, I know how much you've come to admire the General over the last year but don't get your hopes up."

With that, Young marched off at as quick a gate as any man could have attempted given the crowds that swirled around them.

Jason stood there stunned. The huge and incredibly boisterous crowd in front of him paled in comparison to his own inner thoughts. When he had arrived from Shanghai seven years before, he'd been full of curiosity but no real sense of attachment to America. But those years, he thought to himself, had changed him. He'd come to feel part of America come to care deeply about the country that his family had come from.

His reporting had taken him across much of it and to his surprise he'd come to care deeply about its leadership. Worse, against everything he thought he should feel about the people he reported on. Grant had become something of a hero to him, a man of tremendous experience who seemed to care about how folks treated each other. He'd done what he could to help southern blacks when the rest of his party lost interest in their fate, been interested enough in Chinese American relations to travel to China. And, Jason suddenly remembered had even been very sympathetic when, one morning in China Jason had told him about the Albany Chinese family separated by the laundry man's inability to get permission to bring his wife into the country.

No, watching the crowd, but now feeling he was looking at it through a long backward telescope he felt detached, his hopes for another Grant term fading. Shaking off his sense of loss Jason took a breath and plunged back into the crowd. As he did so he heard someone yelling to a friend that the vote on the unit rule was about to begin.

⚒ ⚒

The next few days were as exhausting as Jason ever remembered. Somewhat less to his surprise than it might have been, given his conversation with Young the unit rule went down to a sound defeat and with it the hopes of an easy Grant victory. After that, things became more of a blur as Jason tried to follow the votes one after the other while writing short pieces to be telegraphed to Sage, who'd asked him to send private reports on the convention and longer pieces for the *North China Daily News* that would not be printing anything until long after it was clear who had won the nomination.

For his Shanghai readers he'd spent extra time focusing on Blaine, the first eastern senator who'd taken up the anti-Chinese banner as an obvious stepping-stone to national office. It was after all hardly an issue East Coasters cared about and Blaine was not that many votes behind Grant as the formal voting began. As for Sherman, Jason knew far too little about the man and wished at least for a moment that he could catch Young's attention again. However, while he occasionally spotted the fellow across the auditorium it was not possible to talk further. And the other reporters around him, none of whom he even knew hardly had any incentive to tutor him. Nevertheless, if knowing less bothered him somewhat, as the votes one after another continued he found himself caring less.

After they had taken something like thirty different ballots two things were finally becoming absolutely clear not only to Jason despite his weak knowledge of America and especially Republican party politics, that the delegates were exhausted and that at least Blaine was not going to get any closer to the nomination than the former president. Indeed, Grant and Blaine had negated each other's efforts and apparently, Sherman, as he kept hearing from those around him had never had a real chance.

When he'd finally come to the conclusion that the balloting would never end, at that point all Jason wanted was to go home, indeed he found himself doodling more than writing, a rumor suddenly spread across the hall. Something had happened, the next vote he kept hearing people say would matter. Some sort of deal had been struck.

Looking across the room, Jason searched for Young but this time the man caught his eye from across the room. As their eyes crossed Young nodded slowly and decisively, "this is it," the man's face revealed and then the veteran reporter turned away.

At first, it was not clear what was going on. Grant seemed to still have a lot of support but then it became obvious that another of the potential candidates, there had initially been fourteen competing, a man named Garfield from Ohio, yes the fellow whose interview he'd read days before, seemed to be gathering more votes. Within minutes it was clear everything had changed. Blaine and Sherman had thrown their support to Garfield and between the two of them; they did have enough support to nominate their new champion.

With that, Jason realized he had lost all interest. He knew almost nothing about Garfield, but he did know enough about the momentum of American politics that only Grant had the personality and prestige to stand against the anti-Chinese drums that were building across the country. Garfield, regardless of what he might think would be unable to stand against an America closing its doors to the Chinese. And with that thought, even as Garfield's new followers were running across the room with his banners that had somehow mysteriously appeared, Jason headed for the door hoping there was still time to buy a ticket for New York. It was time to go home, home to Troy and he thought home to Shanghai. Eight years was too long to be away.

# CHAPTER 78

# HEADING HOME

To Jason's surprise, there was no one at the Troy train station to meet him as the train pulled in. Had Black Jade been there he'd of course have taken a taxi home. He always enjoyed listening to the sound of the horse hooves as they walked through Troy's magnificently fashioned downtown but lacking his usual companion, whose feet rarely allowed extended strolling he started off himself walking slowly. Happily, he was not terribly tired. The Chicago train had arrived in New York City too late to catch a train north and he had had a restful evening in a hotel catching up on the news from Chicago.

Odd, though he thought as he walked. Grant was certainly the hero of a decade or so before but few of the journalists he was now reading, he even recognized some of them as colleagues who'd worked near him in the convention, seemed at all discouraged by Grant's failure to win the nomination and potentially another term in the White House. Indeed, it almost felt as if Grant was yesterday's man.

Garfield on the other hand was all the rage with the newspapers filled with information about the "dark horse" candidate, apparently "dark horse" was the term used when someone from far behind in the pack emerged, in this case as the republican nominee for president of the United States.

As he walked further his thoughts turned to Troy itself, and after another block or so, he found himself studying the city even more closely. It had become home, a much larger community than Rockport had ever been and they'd put down roots. After another few minutes, he found himself only one street up from the Hudson River the smells and noise of the river traffic inching into his nostrils as he stood in front of the building on First Street they rented. Taking a moment to wipe the dirt from his boots he bounded up the several steps to the building's two magnificent wooden doors, iron railings on each side and entered. To his surprise, a crowd of people were standing there obviously waiting for his arrival, party streamers in the air and his wife beaming in front of him with the entire family, Old Zhu the children and several others mostly Chinese, though among them he only recognized the local Chinese laundry man.

As for his wife, Black Jade stood there smiling, though as usual she did not embrace him, there were of course too many people around for her to be comfortable doing so but still she was beaming a wonderfully large smile in his direction. Happily, he put the bag down. He was home.

⊷⊶

Weeks later, in late October as he stood in the crowd waiting for the General, the former president, the people of Hartford crowding around him seemed as usual never quite certain what to call the man, Mr. President or General. Either way, as Jason waited for Grant to be introduced by their mutual friend Sam Clemens to the crowd that had gathered for the local Garfield

Presidential Rally Jason thought a lot about that particular homecoming.

On one hand, it had been like many others, his arrival after weeks of travel gathering the news he needed to keep the family solvent, but that day had been different. There in his living room alongside his family was not only the local Cantonese laundry man and his wife but also another couple, the man's brother and sister in law, the very woman Jason had spoken to Grant about when they were in China. Somehow, Grant, in the midst of his travels in China and Japan had reached across the Pacific and smoothed the way for her to enter America to be with her husband. Everyone had treated Jason like the miracle worker, preparing a banquet like nothing he'd seen since leaving Hong Kong. Only Jason knew that he might have spoken to the former president about the problem, but it was Grant himself who had obviously taken the initiative, somehow having his agents locate the family based on Jason's story of their plight and deliver the necessary documents.

Now, ascending the podium that late October day, U.S. Grant with Samuel Clemens, Mark Twain to so many present, was preparing to give a speech supporting the man who had beaten him for the republican nomination. As Jason watched Grant, he could spy no emotion whatsoever. Indeed, as always Grant showed no emotion, no sense of any regrets, assuming he really had any...Jason had never really been clear in his own mind whether the hero of the Civil War had really wanted another term in office.

Nevertheless, Jason knew that he himself was deeply disappointed. He'd uprooted his entire family to learn more about America, become converted to the cause of both the Chinese in America and American Chinese relations and convinced himself that only U.S. Grant had the moral values, the sense of fair play and the political authority to stem the tide that was moving in America against what so many around him were calling the "Yellow Peril."

"Welcome my fellow Hartford folks, citizens of Connecticut, and a special welcome to those fellow degenerates among you who have always held a special place in my heart!" Twain yelled out as he began to introduce Grant who sat stone-faced on a chair looking the combination of authority and humility that he always exuded.

As for Sam, Jason always the fan thought him in fine form. Twain set out on a very humorous story dripping with sarcasm about how wonderfully England had treated Wellington after his defeat of Napoleon and then comparing that with America's infinitely less generous treatment of the man whom Clemens argued had accomplished so much more for his own country. It was vintage Mark Twain and under any other circumstances Jason would have been wonderfully entranced but his bitterness that Grant had been denied the opportunity to lead the nation again was too overwhelming.

For the most part Jason just stood there as the rally proceeded, hoping he might have a chance to offer his greetings to Sam and Grant before he caught the train home but even that seemed doubtful. There were simply too many people standing around hoping to catch a moment with the two celebrities and later brag about having spoken to either man for Jason to intrude. Besides, he was certain his dark mood would make even a short conversation with either man problematic. Indeed, after Clemens and Grant had stopped talking Jason simply left the rally and headed to the train station without ever making an effort to talk to either of them.

# CHAPTER 79
# DECISION TIME

Every fall since they had arrived in Troy had been a time of special pleasure for the entire family as they'd always made an effort to take a carriage up into the Adirondacks to see the fall foliage that was such a large part of what made the region's reputation for beauty so well known. But neither of them, neither Black Jade nor Jason had felt like making the effort that last week of October as they both, in their own ways, focused on the planning for their long awaited return home to Shanghai.

Black Jade for her part spent even more time with Ms. Wilcox and the Willard's trying at the last minute to gain from them the insights she was now convinced she would need to found and run a school for young woman in Shanghai. No longer was she obsessed with the skills of a teacher, studying French and English daily, doing her arithmetic sums and working on her painting. Increasingly, she saw herself as an administrator, trying to understand that role which her friends at the seminary had convinced her would be even more important than her role as a teacher.

As for Jason, he was simply waiting for the results of the election, literally, only days away so he could finish his formal reporting and settle in for a winter of writing, he had a new book in mind, before they sailed for England.

There were of course a few possible reporting trips he was considering. Yung Wing had written inviting him to visit and offering a long description of his concerns about the future viability of the Educational Mission. According to him, the Chinese government was increasingly aware of the anti-Chinese sentiment growing in the U.S. and becoming more committed to the European Educational Missions. Reading Yung Wing's letter though offered no surprises. Prosper, well settled in Paris, directing the European Educational Mission had written the same thing, and from Giquel's prospective, always the French patriot despite some assumed his pro-Chinese attitudes, Beijing's irritation with Washington could only help France.

"Have you seen this?" Black Jade, who had been sitting beside him suddenly, threw the newspaper she had been reading down on the picnic table in front of him.

"What is it?" Jason asked picking it up.

"Just read it."

It took him a moment to find the offending passage in a letter that Garfield, the Republican candidate for president was said to have written:

"Yours in relation to the Chinese problem came duly in hand. I take it that the question of employees is only a question of private and corporate economy, and individuals or companies have the right to buy labor where they can get it the cheapest.

J. A. Garfield

"What! This makes no sense. Garfield writing that he supports cheap Chinese labor, undercutting his support among American laborers…it makes no sense."

"Of course not," Black Jade said, looking at him with that look she employed when she was convinced her husband was an idiot. "It must be a fake; it is some sort of Democratic trick, to fool the voters."

She was right Jason thought; only days away from the election, someone had obviously forged a letter from Garfield to undermine his appeal to the laboring classes.

"So what happened to all men are created equal, the very words I studied so often from the Declaration of Independence?" She said bitterly. "Does no one believe them at all? At least in China, people believe in the words of the master."

"Well, Senator Sumner believed them and Twain and a lot of his friends in Hartford do as does"—he hesitated—"General Grant."

"Maybe. But all I see and I am only a humble wife from a foreign country is that this is a country that runs itself on how much hate they can generate against other people to win votes."

"What do you mean?" Jason asked. He had always known she often had more insights into the human heart than he could ever manage.

"Just think about it. Last time, 1876, was about how much the Southern whites wanted to control and exploit the blacks and in the West how much they hated and wanted to eliminate the Chinese. It is always about hate and whose hate is most useful in an election."

"And this time of course," Jason cut in, "both parties are competing for the anti-Chinese vote. Blaine made it more of a national issue than it ever was before. And Grant was the only man who might have stemmed the tide," he said wistfully.

"You have too much faith in that man. Like they say here constantly, another stupid American comment, he puts his boots on just like every other man." At that, she stood up abruptly. I am going to help Old Zhu start packing our trunks."

"So early, we are not leaving for months, not till after the winter, I thought at least that is what you wanted" Jason said as he watched her walk back toward the house.

"Maybe," she said with bitterness in her tone.

# CHAPTER 80

# STARTING FOR CHINA

"But I don't want to go back to China!" his eleven year old son blurted out with anger as the family sat at Sunday morning breakfast with Old Zhu in the background bringing one dish after the other to the large dining room table that looked out over First street.

"What do you mean you don't want to go back?" Mei-ling, his older sister, answered back sharply. Jason knew his son had become increasingly unhappy as the winter receded and their departure became imminent. Nevertheless, the vehemence of his outburst surprised him and it seemed to some extent that his wife was almost as surprised. Before either could respond, though their older daughter continued.

"Aren't you tired of being seen as different, tired of people asking if they can touch your hair, surprised that you speak English as well as they do?"

"What has that to do with me?" the little boy asked plaintively. "In China, you and Mother will fit right in and here, Father, looks like the rest of the Americans. But it is not like that for me. I will be just as different in Shanghai as here."

The boy was right. Little Willie was the only person in the family with a mixed heritage, and Jason and Black Jade both knew, had known for a long time, that it came with special complications for the only child of their union. Jason loved his daughter; indeed, he had deeply respected her now-long-dead father, but she was not his biological offspring. No Mei-ling appeared completely Chinese and given the family's efforts to keep both children's Chinese language skills current would probably fit right in when they returned to Shanghai.

"If you will be just as different there as here why does it matter then?" Mei-ling asked with the bluntness of youth.

"Because my friends are here, I don't even remember Shanghai, maybe you do, but I don't. I grew up here. I like American food, I eat it every day at the school, I don't want to go back to what you three think is home. It is not my home!"

With that, the boy threw his napkin down and ran up to his room on the upper floor. Jason started to follow him but Black Jade put out her hand and touched his arm.

"Wait a few minutes my husband, then go up. Let him calm down. He has a right to be nervous. How could he possibly remember China? He was a toddler there and he's been at the Albany Academy all this time, spending every day only with Americans."

"Mei-ling," Jason asked turning to his daughter. "You don't have any concerns about going home, about leaving Troy and the school?"

"Yes, Father, I do. I have a lot of friends, but many of them will be leaving after this term anyway, and besides, when I leave the campus, people stare at me all the time. Maybe not as much as in Rockport, but a lot. And sometimes they say unkind words and some boys yell disgusting things."

Jason glanced at his wife with surprise. She obviously had a better sense of what their daughter was experiencing.

"You know of course that in Shanghai you will still be different, you may look like everyone else there but you will still be different, different for having spent so much time in America."

"Maybe, but I will be as different as I care to be, not simply different as if I carried a bill board on my face, different, different." With that, their eldest child got up leaving the two parents sitting alone, or at least partly alone. Through the kitchen door Jason could see Old Zhu, whose English had progressed enormously well in recent years, at least her comprehension skills listening closely.

"What do you think?" Jason asked Black Jade.

"I think they are children, they will both adjust well enough as soon as we leave but for now I am less concerned about our return to Shanghai than the trip itself. Neither of us has been to Europe or the Holy Land and between the two we still can manage only the weakest French."

"True."

"But that is a problem for another day. I have just had another letter from Aouda with all sorts of ideas for our stay in London."

"And I am certain, Prosper will smooth our way in Paris as well," Jason said as his wife pulled out the map of the continent he'd seen her regularly studying over the winter. It was obvious Black Jade had had quite enough of America and was ready to move on. And if she was not quite ready to settle down in Shanghai, she was ready to begin what they expected to be a leisurely journey home through Europe and Jerusalem, the city that had caught her imagination so many years before as she sat discussing religion with the Sisters of Charity in Tianjin.

Wiping his face with his napkin after taking one more bite of the pancakes Old Zhu had finally managed to prepare at his late father's urging, Jason got up and started up the stairs to talk to his son hoping the boy had calmed a bit since he had so angrily left the table a few moments before.

⸻

The last weeks of both the Troy Female Seminary's term and then the final few days before their departure passed quickly enough. By early May, the entire family found themselves standing on the docks, the salt air of the Hudson River in their noses and the noise of both the wind and crowd all around them as they waited to board the ship. Even Willie had resigned himself to the return and Mei-ling looked especially excited as she tried her French on a little girl standing with her own parents a few feet away.

"I am so sorry that Russell could not be here, the press of business you know." Olivia was yelling above the noise of the crowd but he sends his warmest regards."

"That's quite understandable Mr. Sage is a very busy man, a busy man though with a warm heart." Black Jade smiled as she took Olivia's hand.

"Well, don't go telling people that." Olivia laughed. "He likes his reputation for caring only about business and money. But enough of that, Russell gave me this envelope, it is a small token of our faith in your effort and something of the friendship we have both felt."

"That is too kind," Jason said as she thrust the relatively large envelope into his hands.

"Not at all, Mr. Brandt, Jason. Russell has deeply appreciated your insights about America and China and expects to hear more. He has this idea that one-day China will become as enamored as America with railroads and bring a great investment opportunity for him and his colleagues." Then turning again to Black Jade, "And you my dear, Russell really did admire Emma Willard, from long before he even moved from Troy or knew me. He has a soft spot in his heart for everything Mrs. Willard accomplished for her young ladies, for their education and sees you as doing something similar for the young woman of your own country."

As she spoke, a loud whistle ran out and the crowd began to gather their bags as the ship's company, a steamer considerably larger than they'd taken across the Pacific years before began to call for the passengers to embark.

At that, Olivia gave Black Jade, Willie, Mei-ling and even Old Zhu a hug, then with a hearty handshake for Jason she marched off her own manservant following dutifully behind her.

# CHAPTER 81

# ACROSS THE ATLANTIC

"Husband, you did send the telegram before we left New York right?" Black Jade asked as they watched the coast of Britain rise in front of them from their perch on the railing. It had been an incredibly quick crossing thought Jason, who'd endured the voyage across the Pacific only a year before.

"Well, you did didn't you," she said as she pulled her bonnet tighter around her, hoping the effort would keep it more firmly planted on her head, safe from the sea winds that were buffeting them.

"What telegram was that dear?" Jason yelled over the sound of the wind.

"Dad!" Will burst out…stop that…we all know you did it."

"OK, family, the telegram was sent."

"Do you think they got it? It is hard to imagine they can run telegraph lines along the bottom of the sea." Mei-ling added.

"All I know is that it was hard but that they got it right about the time you two were born…but did the Fogg's get it? I have no clue."

"So what do we do if they are not at Dover when we land?" His wife asked. You don't know this country any better than I do?"

"No idea. But I suppose we will figure it out. Just follow the crowds to London I suppose."

Black Jade looked at him doubtfully. From almost the moment they had planned their departure from Shanghai, she'd had an idea of returning through Europe, but Jason could now see in her eyes clear trepidation. For the next months of their trip they, would truly be, as Sam liked to say, innocents abroad, with little knowledge of the lands they planned to travel through—and once they arrived in France, only the basics even of the language.

Reaching out, he took her hand and squeezed, quickly dropping it afterward. The people around him were all staring at the shoreline, but he knew she still was not comfortable with public displays of affection.

As for Jason himself, as he leaned far out over the railing to study the waters of the English Channel below him, he was feeling especially confident. The money he'd received from Sage, earned from and then invested well by Sage during their entire stay in America coupled with what he hoped to earn reporting on the European Educational Missions was making him feel reasonably confident they could make it home and reestablish their lives in Shanghai without major financial worries. And there had even been that letter from Sam who'd been quite positive about Jason's new book. Clemens was convinced that Jason's account of his discovery of his own country, they'd settled on *Home from China* as the title would sell well once the editorial, typesetting and printing was accomplished. Sam had even offered to peddle the book during his own public talks, a gesture on the part of the great writer Jason was infinitely grateful for.

"Look Father!" little Will yelled out. The boy's enthusiasm for the voyage itself had vastly reduced Jason's youngest child's grumbling about their departure from America more than a week before. Indeed, almost since they had boarded the boy had spent his time exploring almost every nook and cranny of the ship and then during meals telling everyone what he'd seen. To the family's amusement, Will had even talked Old Zhu into a visit to the engine room that had apparently fascinated the older woman who even after all the years she had worked for the Brandts continued to surprise him from time to time.

"Mother, do you think Aouda will be there to meet us at the dock?" Mei-ling asked.

"If we can trust your father and that undersea telegraph cable I assume someone at least will be there, probably Monsieur Passepartout. Aouda told me he is still with the family even after all these years. But do you even remember Aouda Mei-ling? You were so young when you saw them last."

"I remember she was a beautiful lady and seemed very different from the other ladies on the ship. Those beautiful Indian dresses she wore and she was very kind to me."

"And what of Mr. Fogg?" Jason said over the sounds of the ship's engines and the increasingly loud crowd that stood around them pointing toward the Dover pier that had become visible in the distance.

"Just the smoke of his cigar, Father, and a funny way about him."

"How so?"

"Don't remember just a funny way…that is all I remember."

Jason laughed, "Well, Mr. Phileas Fogg is certainly that, a sort of queer duck, but I think you will like him well enough."

"Look, Father, we are getting close, and there I even see people waiting to greet us."

His son was right, there was a good-sized crowd standing along the docks waiting to greet the newly arriving passenger ship.

"There, Father, that funny man!"

It took Jason a moment to locate the fellow she referred to but after a second, it was obvious. While most of the crowd was standing very quietly staring toward them across the water, one among them, a fellow considerably shorter than the average was bobbing up and down along the line trying to get a better look. At one point, he even climbed atop a bench to see better, at least until even at the several hundred yards that separated them it was obvious the looks of disapproval from those around him forced him to retreat.

Suddenly Black Jade started to laugh. She'd taken Willie's telescope, the one he'd carried with them since they had departed Shanghai and gazed through it.

"My God, it is Passepartout himself, a bit older but certainly him, she said wiping a bit of the salt water spray from her face and handing the device to her husband.

"Oh let me see!" Said Mei-ling jumping up.

For the next few minutes, until they left the railing to gather their last things and supervise the removal of their trunks the family studied the shoreline and awaited the moment of disembarkation.

# CHAPTER 82
# AN OLD FRIEND

"Monsieur Brandt, Madame Brandt, over here. *C'est moi,* Passepartout!" Fogg's French servant was yelling several rows back in the crowd of people waiting for those who'd arrived on the ship to disembark.

"Can we possibly miss him?" Black Jade said gesturing to the children to see how well the fellow was bobbing up and down and then a moment later, half way up a lamppost still trying to catch their attention.

Jason raised his hand and waved at the man to indicate they had seen him.

"I wish you had not done that, Father," Willie said.

"And why not?"

"I wanted to see what he would do next to attract our attention."

"Yes, Father," his daughter piped in as they slowly descended the gangplank, trying to keep their balance among all those who were navigating their way down the walkway. "Did you not tell us once that Passepartout had been in a circus, some sort of gymnast?"

Jason laughed, yes; I think I probably did tell you that. I'd forgotten."

"Enough for now?" Black Jade said. "Don't be distracted, one could easily fall. Just walk down and then if we get caught in the crowd walk toward that lamp Passepartout is balanced on." At that, she glanced at her husband, giving him with a look orders to grab Old Zhu's parcel who was following them down the ramp with clearly more difficulty than the younger members of the Brandt Family.

"Welcome, *bienvenue en Angleterre!*" Passepartout yelled out as the family reassembled around him and the crowd itself moved past them. "My mistress has been so anxiously awaiting your arrival. And, *mes enfants*, these cannot be your children, little Mei-ling and Willie…surely these adults are not the children I last saw in San Francisco. *Non, ce n'est pas possible!*"

Black Jade and Jason enthusiastically took up the man's hand while their children, who'd been barely out of swaddling clothing when the man had seen them last beamed with his recognition of how much they had grown in the years since he'd seen them last waving wildly as Mr. Fogg had pressed on with his bet inspired race to travel the world in eighty days.

Just thinking about Fogg amused Jason to no end. They had had plenty of time to talk, if that was what conversation with Phileas Fogg might be described as. He'd taken up some sort of wager at his gentlemen's club months before the Brandts had met him on the *Pacific Steamer* and apparently set off within minutes on a whirlwind trip around the world, dragging with him his recently employed French servant, Jean Passepartout, and eventually the Indian Princess Aouda who'd accompanied him from India on.

"Here, this way, I've taken a coach to escort everyone to the Dover *gare—excusez-moi*, the train station. Here, *mes enfant*, let me take your bags," the fellow said as he grabbed up Willie and Mei-ling's burdens and marched off.

Jason, turning to Black Jade, could see her smiling. Neither knew England, but they were already feeling welcome.

"And it looks to me like you will have plenty of time to practice your French," he whispered to his wife, who'd been convinced for years that their proposed school for the young women of Shanghai had to be able to offer the language.

"*Bien sur,*" Black Jade said, her olive eyes lighting with enthusiasm.

Within minutes, the entire family was ensconced in an enclosed railroad car compartment Passepartout arranged for as the train slowly began to pull out of the station toward London. For Jason, whose enthusiasm was as high as his children, there was a bit of regret; he'd have liked to see something of Dover before they departed, but for the moment they'd put themselves in Passepartout's, more likely Fogg's, hands, and that was not possible. Besides he reminded himself, they really needed to settle in, and Fogg certainly knew how to plan travel. Indeed, much of their conversation aboard ship as they'd traveled across the Pacific years before, when Fogg was willing to turn his thoughts away from whist his favorite game, was the best way to travel through Europe and the Orient as well, all regions Jason had never seen before.

As the train picked up speed, he watched Passepartout pointing out all the sites to the children as well as Old Zhu, who, while pretending indifference, was obviously just as interested in the views of the English countryside that were becoming more and more apparent as they sped past the city limits of Dover itself.

Nevertheless, Jason also noticed with some concern, Black Jade was not showing nearly as much interest. Something was on her mind. For the moment, he thought of asking her, but it just did not seem the right time. Rather he took her hand, squeezed it, and gestured toward one of the larger, more palatial buildings they were passing by. His wife smiled warmly and leaned a bit out of the window itself.

"It is not my beloved France, mind you," Passepartout yelled out over the sound of the engine's noisy vibrations coming from the floor and a hundred conversations seeping in under the door, "but the English can cut a fine hedge; there see that one!"

"And, Madame," Passepartout yelled even louder. "My mistress tells me you and your family will be moving on to France, on to Paris, after your visit here, *n'est pas?*"

"Yes, indeed we plan to stay there for a few months," she said, a smile rising on her face for the first time since they'd boarded the train. "I have been studying French a bit."

"A bit!" Mei-ling yelled out. "She studies French as she once studied English."

"Marvelous!" Passepartout yelled out. "We can practice together. It is, of course, the only true civilized language."

"I would like that very much," Black Jade said.

As she did so, Jason found himself studying his wife, as beautiful and yet so different from the young teenage runaway he'd met in southern China so many years before. Posed, beautiful, and expert in several Chinese dialects as well as English and now, he assumed soon-to-be-far-better in French than he would ever be. Just looking at the posed woman who sat opposite him, he found himself not just falling in love with her all over again but increasingly seeing within her not just her own strength of character but something of what he'd seen in Emma Willard, whom Black Jade now claimed as a personal hero and role model.

# CHAPTER 83

# THE FOGG FAMILY

"Oh my God!" Willie yelled out, half his body extending out the window of the carriage Passepartout had rented for their arrival at Mr. and Mrs. Fogg's residence. "Father, Mother, it is a castle!"

"*Bien sur*, my little man," Passepartout said proudly. He had asked the coachman to take a long leisurely ride through the center of London after they had departed Victoria Station with their trunks. Until that moment though, while the family had studied with a tourist's usual enthusiasm the wide and crowded streets of London, its beautifully designed stone buildings and monuments, they'd spent enough time in Boston, New York, and even Troy to have found many of the buildings relatively familiar if usually larger in scale. But here was something different.

"What is it, Father?" Mei-ling asked.

Jason, finally getting a sense of just how much he was out of his element, sighed. "No idea, my darling."

"*C'est le Tour de Londres.*"

"The Tower of London!" Black Jade cried out. "*C'est magnifique*," she said, watching for the Frenchman's approval which, in the form of a smile, was quickly shown.

"Yes, the Tower of London, been here forever, not something you Americans have many of…real castles…the price you pay for being a democracy."

"Passepartout, are there a lot of such buildings?" Willie asked enthusiastically.

"*Mon Dieu, bien entendu*, they're everywhere…here among the English and in my own country, where they are even more impressive."

"Can we see it, Father?"

"If it is possible…of course…is it, Passepartout?"

"No idea, *aucune idée*…never tried, but Mr. Fogg will know. After one sees the great chateau of France, after one has seen Versailles, there is little reason to see more," the fellow said with Gaelic satisfaction.

"Can we stop now and ask?" Willie asked with real eagerness in his voice, a tone the family had not seen much since he'd been told the family would be returning to China.

"Not now; we need to drop you and your goods at the house and release the coach, but soon enough I am sure."

"How much further is it, Passepartout?"

"The master's home is not terribly far from the city center. Mr. Fogg insisted even when the children arrived and the mistress wanted a larger house that it not be far from his club, perhaps fifteen more minutes."

"So, Passepartout, it's Jean, isn't it?" Jason asked.

"Yes, but few use my given name, indeed I frequently forget it.

"So you mention that America has few such castles, did you really see much as you raced across the country with Mr. Fogg? As I recall he was moving awfully fast to win his bet!"

"You are, of course, correct, but Passepartout saw what he could from the train and as we passed through New York, from the train station to the harbor. Indeed, Passepartout saw more than most!" he explained with a gleam in his eyes.

"And why was that?" Black Jade asked.

"Because, Madame, there are advantages to having once earned one's living as a circus gymnast, as we traveled across the country I claimed the train wagon's roof each morning and rode across that enormous country *en pleine* air!"

"Wow," Willie commented, he was already developing a bit of hero worship for the French servant and that image had clinched it.

As promised no more than fifteen minutes later, the horse taxi pulled into a quieter lane just off one of London's busiest thoroughfares and stopped about halfway up the street. As their party, descended the carriage and Jason rushed ahead of Passepartout to pay the cabbie, his entire family aligned themselves on the sidewalk just as the door of a large brick faced row house opened spilling out two young children, a boy and a girl perhaps six and four years old. Once on the street both children pulled themselves to a standstill their momentary enthusiasm being over taken by shyness.

From behind them Fogg and Aouda emerged followed themselves by a somewhat stern looking English woman whom Jason guessed might be a housekeeper or perhaps governess. Even from the top of the stairs Jason could tell the woman, with a drawn gaunt face was taking their measure.

"Exactly as I predicted, assuming an arrival on schedule from Dover, which, of course, we English do expect and then approximately a hundred minutes to traverse the distance from Victoria Station. Passepartout, you took the route I gave you?"

"*Absolument.*" The Frenchman nodded.

"Then we have it, Mrs. Fogg. Did I not predict they would arrive exactly in time for tea?"

"You did indeed Mr. Fogg" The stunning Indian princess they had come to know on the voyage across the Pacific confirmed his prediction as her husband consulted his watch. However, while Fogg checked for himself the accuracy of his timings Jason spied Aouda smiling warmly at his wife. The two women had become close on board ship and been corresponding regularly ever since.

"Well, come now let's not all dawdle on the side walk" The older woman said to no one in particular. We need to get everyone settled in, Passepartout make yourself useful for once and gather the luggage."

"Quite right Mrs. Granville, front steps are no place for a grand reunion." Fogg said putting his watch into his pocket and extending his hand to Jason."

"Welcome my esteemed journalist; I've had a cutter from the national library send me your clippings. You have certainly been busy! Now come in for a refreshment, Mrs. Granville and Mrs. Fogg have prepared not only tea but also a fine array of pastries.

"It is wonderful to see you Phileas but let me grab some of these bags."

"Nonsense Passepartout will get them. Do come in".

When in Rome. Jason thought to himself and went up the steps. Black Jade, Aouda and both sets of children had all run up ahead of him. Out of the corner of his eye, he saw Passepartout and Old Zhu starting to gather up the bags. Not surprisingly, Old Zhu was carrying even more of them than Passepartout who was chatting with amazement that now he could finally communicate with the Brandt family servant who'd not known a word of English when they had departed Shanghai so many years before.

Stopping for a second to tie his bootstrap before entering he realized Old Zhu was asking Passepartout about the Granville woman and that the Frenchman was telling her something amusing Jason could not hear.

A few moments later the entire family found themselves led to the guest quarters of the home with orders to return to the parlor in twenty-three minutes. That the timing was so precise hardly surprised either Black Jade or Jason but that the "request" had come from Mrs. Granville had somewhat surprised both of them.

Once the door was closed Black Jade leaned forward "I guess Mr. Fogg has finally found a servant especially suited for him," she whispered.

"What" Willie said looking up at his parents.

"Nothing at all...now go decide which bed you want.

"I want the one by the window!" Mei-ling cried out.

"No, I do!"

"Your mother and I want to clean up also. Just flip a coin," Jason said taking Black Jade's hand.

"Where is Old Zhu?" Jason asked as they entered the hallway.

"No idea, she went off somewhere with Grenville and Passepartout. Maybe they have special sleeping quarters for servants. We'll find out soon enough, but for now, let's hurry; I want to see Aouda."

# CHAPTER 84

# SETTLING IN WITH THE FOGG FAMILY

Within minutes, Black Jade and Jason were sitting in the extremely well ordered parlor room downstairs being served tea and small cakes by Mrs. Granville while Passepartout stood haphazardly at attention only slightly leaning against the wall to their right. Through the window they could see the quiet street they had driven up just minutes before while, just opposite them at table Aouda and Fogg sat quietly, Phileas himself carefully taking notes from a book he'd opened up alongside his pad on the table. As for Aouda, she sat beaming her deeply Indian appearance somewhat modified by the distinctly English hair and clothing she was now wearing. She was clearly delighted her long awaited guests had arrived but waiting as well for her husband to begin the formal greetings.

As for Jason himself, he reached under the table and squeezed Black Jade's hand. His Chinese wife, for the first time seemed less unique in these circumstances than usual for here in the Fogg's parlor her Chinese features certainly seemed to fit her Western clothing as much as those of the formerly Indian Princess now herself wore.

Before Jason had gotten up the courage to start a conversation Fogg looked up as if first noticing their presence."

"Ah hah…everyone's settled in. Good. Mrs. Granville, the children are down stairs in the play room?"

"That they are, sir," Mrs. Granville said, clearly as enthusiastic about a well-ordered household as her employer."

"Well, good then, I trust you had a good crossing?"

"Yes, it was excellent."

"That of course is to be expected, The English steamship lines are always the more properly run, glad you did not choose one of those French steamers."

At that Jason glanced over to Passepartout who'd taken a sudden interest in a spot of dust he'd spied on the mantel clock."

"We are so pleased you are here!" Aouda said more formally than the twinkle in her eyes revealed. Phileas and I have so looked forward to your arrival and to see how the children have grown."

"And we too, have long felt so, and to meet your children, it is a dream come true," Black Jade said almost as formally, though Jason was certain his wife was dying to grab her dear friend and run off somewhere so they could really talk.

"Excuse me" Fogg chimed in. It was clear the overabundance of small talk had displeased him.

"I have here my copy of *Murray's Handbook to London*, bit out of date…1871. Passepartout, did you manage to inform yourself about a possible newer edition?"

"Not yet, monsieur, but I will check the shops again later today."

"Yes, well, can't be helped. In any case, I have been making a list for you. Mrs. Granville, you already gave our guests the household's schedule?"

"It's in their room, sir," the older woman replied, as Jason and Black Jade gave each other quizzical looks.

"Hanging in the inside door of the clothing closet," the older woman said, clearly seeing and disapproving they had not yet studied the schedule or even apparently noticed it.

"Well, no matter," Fogg said, concerned about not letting the conversation become distracted.

"I have created a list here, one site a day, British Museum, Natural History Museum, Tower of London, recommended restaurants, best means of transport, though Passepartout will be with you most of the time anyway. Once it is complete I will have it copied at my club."

He passed over the sheet for them to study."

"This is wonderfully thoughtful of you Phileas, and my son will love this list, especially the Tower visit, perhaps we might start with that."

"Don't advise that, I have considered the ship arrivals, the number of tourists and the flow of traffic toward the sites. Try to see the Tower at the wrong moment and you will be crowded out. My suggestion—you are, of course, completely free to do as you like—is to see the Tower Tuesday next at around eleven fifteen; my expectation is that there will be the least number of tourists there…and even fewer of the foreign sort."

At that, Fogg turned back to his handbook to check an additional reference while the three seated adults all exchanged subtle smiles of amusement.

"And now you must forgive me, the Club whist game begins in twenty-seven minutes. Brandt, seem to recall you are not a fan of the game, at least not on our earlier Pacific Crossing. Can I interest you now?"

"During our visit absolutely, but right now, I think I would like to rest a bit and see to how the children are settling in."

At that Fogg appeared a bit nonplussed, the children obviously not quite as high on his list of priorities as with some others. "Well then, in any case, welcome guests. I will be taking my leave. We can talk more at the evening meal."

With that, Phileas Fogg donned his top hat, and departed. A moment later the sounds of Fogg and Passepartout's footsteps could be heard as the two descended the front steps.

"And we," Black Jade said taking Aouda's hand will be checking on the children. With that the two women both strangers from distant lands took off whispering enthusiastically with each other as Jason sat alone with Mrs. Granville standing to one side of the room.

"More tea, sir?" the woman finally asked.

"No thank you, Mrs. Granville."

"Well, then I will be taking my leave as well, lots of dinner to prepare and so many more mouths to feed."

It was obvious Jason thought the woman was not thrilled with the disruption of the household caused by the arrival of guests.

After she left Jason found himself sitting alone in the room studying the furnishings, many of which had obviously been purchased during Fogg's round the world tour, each quite small but still an indication that Fogg had occasionally noticed the countries he was traveling through despite his feverish race to win his round the world bet.

# CHAPTER 85

# REUNION

For the next hour, as he sat alone in the parlor with a calendar making notes on days when he might be able to visit the Greenwich's naval facilities. Prosper had assured him he would arrange interviews with several of the former Fuzhou Dockyard students who'd initially studied at the British naval school and more recently returned from extended voyages with the British navy. Once that was completed, he had spoken with Mrs. Granville about sending telegrams off hoping to arrange interviews.

"Don't know much about that, sir, newfangled devices those telegraphs, never had occasion to use one. Mr. Fogg will know, even think I heard Mr. Passepartout mention something about sending a telegram back to Paris once. So there must be an office around here somewhere. So, how long will you and the Mrs. be staying with us, sir?"

Jason smiled to himself, he'd only been there a few hours and was already certain Mrs. Granville, he wondered if she really were married, would not be entirely pleased if his family stayed terribly long. More significantly, he thought Fogg himself would probably enjoy a shorter visit from the guests he did not really know all that well either.

"It is not really clear yet Mrs. Granville, we really are just passing through London."

"Mr. Passepartout told me you'd be staying longer in France though, that's the main goal is it not, sir?"

"Well, as I am sure you have heard, yes we do plan to stay in Paris for a few months but we are really on our way home."

"And that is where, sir?"

"Shanghai."

"Shanghai?"

"It's in China."

"So your wife's Chinese then is she?"

"Yes."

"Oh, thought she was from someplace like the Mistress, India or something, they seem so close. Well, enjoy your stay, sir. Dinner will be in about ninety minutes."

"Thank you, Mrs. Granville."

That seemed like a successful conversation Jason thought, he might even have managed to please the older woman with his promise to move his family on to France in short order. He was sure she would not be concerned about how long they might stay among the French. As a proper English woman, he was certain she would consider that none of her concern.

His correspondence finished for the moment Jason pulled his chair away from the table and studied the room a bit more before noticing the sounds of the children, he set off looking for the room Phileas had referred to as the children's area.

Two minutes later, following the sound of laughter he found the rest of his family. Old Zhu was amusing the Fogg children with the production of another of her wondrous paper cuttings while Mei-ling was helping them to cut their own small cuttings. Willie, obviously bored with the practice he had seen almost daily since he was born was standing at one of the windows his trusty telescope in hand studying the windows across the street.

"You should come look, Father," his son called out as he entered the room. Once standing in the open room, wooden toys strewn across the room, the thought that Phileas probably rarely ventured into the room flashed across his mind before he spotted the French doors, half opened that led to an enclosed garden where Black Jade and Aouda were talking in intense and quiet whispers.

"Do look father," his son beckoned.

"You are not looking at anything you should not be are you?" Jason asked as he approached the boy.

"Well, if people leave their windows open."

"William!"

"Just some people kissing. Here, look."

Jason leaned over to glance through his son's telescope. The family had managed to obtain a tripod for it in Boston and it had become even easier to use. Glancing through the lens Jason found his son was right, just opposite them, near the window a couple were kissing, though from Jason's older vantage point it seemed more risqué than his son probably thought. The woman was clearly some sort of domestic servant and the fellow dressed in much finer clothing, probably the young man of the household.

"Yes, well, let's put this away for now," Jason said, closing up the tripod before his son had a chance to complain.

"Mr. Brandt, here outside in the patio, we have more tea, come join us" Aouda's Anglo-Indian accent, in some ways similar in some ways so different from that of his wife rang forth through the French doors.

"Come on Will you can study the buildings in the other direction. He carried out the telescope and stroked his daughter's hair as he past. Mei-ling and Old Zhu were obviously entranced by the much younger Fogg children.

"So what have you been talking about?" It was obvious that Aouda was far more relaxed than she had been upstairs. Clearly, her very English husband's exceptionally precise manner inhibited her somewhat.

"Talking about? What do you think we have been talking about - you men?" She laughed.

"It is my male prerogative to assume that!" He quipped back.

"Well, don't flatter yourself, or at least not too much. Actually just now we were talking about Mr. Fogg."

"About what exactly?"

"Aouda says she understands we'd like to see the city at our own pace and order but that Phileas really does know the best times and ways to travel about."

"I don't doubt that. I did not listen without amazement to his extraordinary knowledge of travel during our Pacific passing not to appreciate that. And it did help as we came across America on the train as well. So what does Phileas suggest? I assume we won't be seeing the Tower of London first."

"Before he left to make the copies I saw what he was writing, the first on the list was the British Museum. It truly is a wondrous place."

"Even Mrs. Willard told me I should go. She said it would be terribly helpful in my preparation for the school," Black Jade said.

"You spoke to Mrs. Willard about what we should tour in London? The woman was near death and she took time to plan out our London trip?"

"Oh, more than that." Black Jade pulled out an envelope. "I have lists for Paris and Jerusalem as well."

"Why do I think sometimes that Mrs. Willard planned out the last eight years of my life?"

"Well, she hardly planned out the entire trip, just suggestions, especially Paris and Jerusalem. And Olivia helped to."

"Mrs. Sage was in on the conspiracy from the start as well?" he said laughing reaching over to view for the first time the list Black Jade had drawn from the envelope he now realized he'd seen in her possession from time to time.

"Of course, indeed she started the list as Mrs. Willard spoke of her own travels in Europe that had so helped her in the direction of the School.

"And do tell Mr. Brandt of Phileas's other idea," Aouda said touching her friend on the arm.

"Well, Aouda has long known of my interest in seeing the Holy Land, to see the very places the Sisters spoke of with such reverence."

"Of course, we talked about that with Mrs. Stowe and many others since, to see the holy sites of Christianity." Jason responded not sure what part of that plan might be new.

"Yes, but Aouda says Phileas through his club knows an old Hebrew, a quite famous one…Montefiou…" She could not quite handle the pronunciation.

"Montefiore." Aouda stepped in to help her friend.

"Yes, Montef…" His wife closed her eyes to better concentrate. "Montefiore…who has been a great religious leader to the Jews of Jerusalem, to the Hebrews there, a man who could give us an even better insight into the place."

Jason had always known that his wife, interested as she obviously was in Christianity, especially the Catholicism of the Sisters of Charity she had known in Tianjin - indeed the only area where her feelings differed from her hero Emma Willard, was interested in the Jewish origins of Christianity. It was in fact, something of what made her interest in Christianity, as someone from outside of the West somewhat unusual. Not having been raised in the West her Christianity had not been tainted by the anti-Semitism so common in America.

"And we are to meet this person?"

"He is a man of great age, I am told almost a hundred but still vigorous, he only just recently returned from yet another trip to the Holy Land and Phileas thinks he can arrange an interview."

"Why would such a man consent to see us?" Jason asked.

"Not really us darling," Black Jade said, Aouda says she knows enough of the man that he would be fascinated meeting a Chinese woman interested in his Hebrew compatriots. Sometimes, my dear, there are advantages to being different."

# CHAPTER 86

# A CHARMING OLD GENTLEMAN

"And tell me my beautiful and charming guest from an altogether foreign land; do your countrymen really believe that the foreigners enjoy killing and drinking the blood of Chinese children?"

The question startled Jason as he studied the old man whose servant had only just welcomed them into the elderly gentleman's well-appointed but distinctively stuffy bedroom in the magnificent seaside mansion in Ramsgate they had just traveled hours by train to visit. Indeed, the smell of patent medicines, stale milk and port seemed to fill the darkened room. Happily, it was obvious that at least the windows behind the curtains were somewhat open allowing the strong sea breezes to compete with the interior smells of the room.

"You will perhaps forgive me," said the wizened old man, who appeared almost to disappear under the black velvet skullcap and blanket that covered him. "But I hope I have not been misinformed. I am told older people are deeply revered among your people, deeply respected as"—he hesitated—"as your revered teacher. Yes, Confucius taught. Is that not correct?"

"Indeed it is, sir." The elderly and scholars especially" Black Jade said flashing the sort of warm smile she and all attractive women knew men, regardless of age, always appreciated.

"Then I should be well appreciated, at least as one especially old. Did they tell you I am soon to turn ninety-nine? Of course, as a scholar I am less sure, true my people much like yours appreciate great learning, but my own accomplishments in that area are relatively modest." Moses Montefiore laughed, before he was momentarily overcome by a short coughing fit that aroused a look of concern from the older woman, obviously some sort of nurse, who sat knitting in the corner near the one open fire in the room.

Then he recovered himself, taking a small sip from the ornate port glass that stood near his bed.

"Yes, indeed, Sir Montefiore. I have heard that your own people, Hebrew people, venerate scholars as much as the Chinese...but please do not exert yourself on our account."

"Nonsense, my friend, but do forgive me. People of my age tend to live in the moment, not knowing if the next breath will come. So they told you I am nearing one hundred?" he asked, perhaps forgetting Jason thought to himself that he had just asked the same thing.

"Yes, sir, and we have heard something of your remarkable life as well," Black Jade said, glancing over at her husband, clearly somewhat uncomfortable that he had not aroused even a glimpse of interest from the oldest person either of them had ever met. For a second Jason listening to the conversation between Montefiore, the man he'd been told was easily the most influential English Jew of the century. Though for a second, he was less impressed with that than moved by a distinct sensation that felt like he was back in Emma Willard's presence almost a decade before watching the founder of the Troy Female Seminary interrogate his wife about China and her hopes for the future.

"Well, then let us return to the issue of the moment, least my heart fail before I have a chance to indulge my curiosity with such a charming guest. "So what can you tell me of the Chinese belief regarding the foreign Christians and the blood of Chinese children?'

"Well, sir, my husband, who often studies such things, can explain more of that, sir."

"Indulge me, my beautiful guest from the...the Middle Kingdom do they not call it that, a great land I am told, one that despite all my travels I have never had the chance to visit... but of my question, fear not,"

The older man had obviously noted her frequent glances toward Jason.

"I certainly have questions for your distinguished husband, whom I have heard much about...but I would like to hear this from you, a Chinese woman who speaks English, my correspondents who know your country well, tell me better than any they have ever encountered."

"Well, sir, it is true that some poorly educated people in parts of China believe that to be the case, that the Western Christians require blood for some of their rituals. It comes perhaps from some confusion regarding the communion..."

As Black Jade spoke and the older man pulled himself upright in the beautifully ornate bed he was propped up in, Jason found himself drifting off. After all, after sharing a stage with his wife for years fielding questions from Western audiences it was hardly a new topic to either of them.

Indeed, the older man's question was a common one on the lecture circuit but if the question was familiar, the surroundings could not be more unusual. In fact, so much of the last week since they had arrived in England had been a combination of the familiar and the remarkably different. England at times seemed so similar to the New England the family had come to know in recent years and yet in so many ways, entirely different. But of course, Phileas Fogg's planning, however annoying at times had, Jason was forced to admit, made the visit run as smoothly as one could possibly hope. Fogg really had planned out almost their entire trip, so much that Jason even as he glanced around the old man's bedroom he could satisfy himself that the children, Mei-ling and Will were happily exploring the Tower of London with Passepartout who was carrying with him one of the several copies Fogg had prepared on the best times not only to see the Tower but in what order. Moreover, he and Black Jade's trip to Ramsgate could not have been easier following as they did the carefully written out instructions Fogg had handed them earlier that morning.

Suddenly Jason was pulled back into the moment as a burst of merriment and then coughing burst from the blueish lips of Mr. Montefiore. Black Jade for her part looked panicked, would the old man take his last breaths after almost a hundred years in the presence of a couple of strangers from the Orient he knew she was thinking.

Finally recovering his voice, which was once again as strong as Montefiore's body was weak, the old man took another sip of the brandy, wiped his lips with a handkerchief and turned again to them.

"So my young guests, it is as I have heard, the Chinese masses have attacked Christians for using, or so they believe Chinese children's blood, for their religious rituals. That is truly rich. I love it. Life and the people who fill it are a constant source of wonderment and even amusement."

"Sir," Black Jade began hesitantly, "for many years my husband and I have earned our income in part on the lecture circuit in America and your question is a common one. Indeed, many who attend our lectures have the same question. Nevertheless, never has someone reacted with such curious amusement. There is much I don't understand of the world of the West but could you explain that to me if it is not too bold a question."

"My young dear, my own people are famous for answering all questions with a question and believing as I do in the importance of tradition let me first ask you something. Were there many of my brethren, Hebrews among your audiences in America?"

"Hebrews...Jewish people...I have no idea," she said, looking hesitantly at Jason, who shrugged his own shoulders. "In truth, Sir Monefio..." She hesitated, again having problems with the pronunciation.

"Moses—you can call me Moses, young lady. I am too old to stand on ceremony. That was probably an unfair question anyway; distinguishing one Westerner from another is no doubt accomplished with difficulty. I myself have no ability to distinguish Japanese from Chinese."

"I have heard people here think all Chinese look alike. But, sir, my question, why is that story of Chinese beliefs about the Westerners of such interest to a great man like yourself?" As she spoke, her voice became stronger, her usual confidence growing with every minute - becoming again the woman whom Jason had known for years who was rarely intimidated by anyone.

"Ah, yes...well, that amusement comes from the irony. You see what you speak of is known among my brethren as the "blood libel" an infamous slander that Christians have accused my people of for a millennium and that I have spent much of my life fighting. Now, you confirm that the blood libel in China is directed toward Christians instead of Jews. The irony is rich. However, tell me more of yourself. I am told you and your family, two fine children that remain for now in London will be traveling with you back to Shanghai via Jerusalem. That a woman like yourself is interested in seeing the Holy City is what aroused my own curiosity."

"Well, sir," Black Jade said, while leaning forward and pouring a bit more port into the old gentleman's glass, a gesture that was clearly appreciated. "As you have perhaps heard, my husband and I plan to open a school for young Chinese women upon our return."

"A school that would teach what exactly?" The old man, looking more serious than he had previously asked."

"The hope, sir, is to introduce a school for young Chinese girls and perhaps some of the daughters of Western traders, a school that would offer them modern learning of the sort I saw Emma Willard offering in America."

"To teach them to be good wives?" The older man asked with a seriousness he had not previously revealed.

"Perhaps, that might be part of it, it is often their lot in life, but the larger goal, as Mrs. Willard taught me to understand is to help them understand life beyond the small world of Chinese wives, of modern ways, of the world, of the French and English languages and something of mathematics and science."

"And of religion, I have been told you have adopted the Christian teaching."

As Jason listened, he began to wonder where this conversation was going. Montefiore's questions were getting more personal than he had expected but then he thought to himself, people the old man's age, were rarely restrained by the limits some younger people imposed upon themselves.

"Am I a Christian? Is the school to be a religious school?" Black Jade was clearly reflecting on his question, something neither she nor Jason had ever directly addressed. "Well, Christianity has played a role in my life. The Sisters of Charity taught me a lot before I ever left China…"

"And the Chinese Christians...the long-haired Taipings, I believe, as they were known among your people?"

Black Jade glanced at Jason before answering. Neither of them was comfortable openly discussing those years with strangers. They were, after all, planning to soon take up their lives in China again.

"Yes, the Taipings too had their influence. But let me say that people I have cared greatly about in my life have been Christians—even my husband's father was a missionary—and that my interest in Christianity has much to do with my interest in seeing the Holy City."

"The Christians and the Jews there? At least that is what my friends in London told me of your intentions. Is that also true?"

"Is that unusual, sir? I know very little of Christianity, but it seems to this outsider that one cannot know Christianity, the Christians without also knowing the Hebrew people. Was not the famous Jesus, not a Jew Himself as I have heard?"

Montefiore nodded and then spoke again.

"True, but not something well appreciated in the Western countries," the older man said before being overcome by another coughing fit that not only aroused the knitting nurse sitting near the fire but provoked her to direct a look of concern if not impatience toward Jason who taking this signal lightly tapped his wife's shoulder. Then speaking up.

"Sir, Moses, I really think we have taken up too much of your valuable time. We should be taking our leave shortly so you can rest."

Montefiore slowly wiped his lips with the handkerchief again and took another, this time longer draft of the glass of port.

"The mind is willing but the body fails me...and I had so looked forward to asking you about your time with President

Grant in China. That must have been fascinating. Nevertheless, you are right. I need to nap. However, there are a few more topics; I must satisfy my curiosity about. What do you know of the Chinese Jews? I have spent my life attempting to serve my own people in very distant lands but have only the vaguest idea of the community I have heard exists in a place called Kaifeng?"

Black Jade, clearly having not a clue, turned to her husband.

"Kaifeng, I know of the place, once an ancient capital found in the north along the Yellow River…"

"And of its community of Hebrews, do they really exist? What have you heard of them?

"I have never been to Kaifeng, though I know the area to the West of Beijing fairly well…a community of Hebrews…I don't think…wait, I do know something. I once heard of a community of Christian Missionaries who had an interest in obtaining copies of their sacred scrolls…yes, clearly they existed at one point, but if they are prosperous today or not is something quite different."

"Yes that is just the community of which I speak, and the interest in the Chinese Jewish scrolls is well recorded. But you have heard nothing of the present well-being of that community?"

"No I am sorry, sir, but that does not mean they are not thriving. Surely, sir, we have taken up enough of your time. We should be taking our leave." As he spoke Jason saw the nurse rising to her feet ready to send the couple off having, it was clear she felt, taken up too much of her very senior charge's time and energy. Montefiore though raised himself up in the bed and gave each of them another handshake.

"You are right my young guest, my energy is spent, but indulge one more curiosity. How do you plan to travel to the Holy City? I have been told you plan to go to Paris first and then? How will you travel to the Holy Land?"

Black Jade looked at Jason with uncertainty.

"I don't think we have even thought of that," he said.

"Then indulge an old man…and one born in Italy. You know, of course, of Marco Polo?" the old man asked Jason.

"Of course," Jason said, realizing his wife next to him had no idea who the fellow was."

"Then you must go to Venice…the city of Marco Polo. it must be part of your trip…the trip of anyone like yourselves trying to bring East and West together!" the old man was getting more and more enthusiastic, at least until a moment later another coughing fit racked his body again.

At that Black Jade and Jason looked to the attendant who herself stood again, putting down knitting but then paused as Montefiore held up his hand waving her away in a gentle but assertive fashion.

"Excuse me…I guess I really have spent my afternoon's allotment of energy but please accept my hospitality, my staff has prepared a fine midday meal downstairs where you will be able to dine while viewing a magnificent ocean view." With that, he reached out and shook both their hands a second time.


A few moments later Jason and Black Jade found themselves being seated in an open garden with a fine lunch ready for them and an extraordinary landscape to contemplate as they dined.

"Are you sure Prosper has found a pension for us to stay in Paris? Black Jade asked after taking a very small sip of the green tea she had just been served by another of Montefiore's servants.

"Well, he has not confirmed that he found a place yet but I am sure he will do so. Why are you concerned, he was never quite sure when we would arrive and we can always stay with him or at hotel if more permanent headquarters are not available. Are you anxious to move on to Paris?"

"Yes I do want to move on to Paris and of course to reduce the burden on the Fogg household. Three adults, two extra children. It is a lot to impose on people we barely know."

"Has Aouda said anything?"

"No, of course not but it is still time to plan our departure and I am anxious to begin that intensive French study program Prosper arranged for Mei-ling and myself," she said. "But enough! Eat! The food looks wonderful, and the view is magnificent, as magnificent as Phileas said it would be before we left this morning."

"Mr. and Mrs. Brandt, I trust you are enjoying your meal?" The older gentlemen, almost as old as their host, the same fellow who had originally greeted them earlier that morning upon their arrival suddenly stood alongside the small table as they sat on the estate's veranda."

"Yes indeed," Jason said jumping up to take the man's hand again. And, Sir Montefiore was incredibly gracious."

"He was himself delighted to meet both of you. And I do appreciate your recognizing his energy is limited however vital his curiosity remains."

"For a man of his age, he is truly remarkable," Black Jade said looking up at the man who stood before her. "It was an honor to meet him."

"I can assure you he felt the same, and was especially interested in your hope to establish a school for young women in Shanghai. Indeed, the delay in my arrival here was in the time it took for him to dictate a letter in support of your efforts, a small financial contribution and a list of those in Jerusalem who can help you understand the Hebrew community there.

He is anxious that your studies of Christianity appreciate the role of his own people in its growth and theology."

Handing them the envelope the fellow started to turn back toward the building and then stopped abruptly.

"Good Lord, I almost forget. Mr. Brandt, Sir Montefiore asks that you make inquiries upon your return to China about the conditions of the Jews of Kaifeng and inform him of what you discover."

"Of course, I would be delighted to do so."

"And it goes without saying that for obvious reasons sooner would be better than later. When you have finished dining, I suggest a walk around the estate, the views as you can see are magnificent and when you are ready you will find a carriage waiting to take you back to the train station." With that, the fellow tipped his hat toward the two of them and set off in the direction of the mansion again.

# CHAPTER 87

# PARIS

"Give me that book again!" William's voice, which was already just starting to take on a more adult tenor, startled Jason from the nap he'd begun.

"So, little brother, less than an hour from Paris, you have suddenly gotten interested in French?" Mei-ling said sarcastically, before jamming the grammar book into his ribs.

"Well, it did not seem very important before now. Besides I can say lots of stuff in Latin," he said sounding terribly impressed with himself. The two of them were standing just outside of the family's train compartment looking at the countryside as Jason and Black Jade observed their children. Through the window, they could see the beautiful expanse of northern France they had been studying since they had departed the Calais hotel they had taken for the night after landing from the Dover ferry the day before.

Once again, after so many years first in Massachusetts and more recently in Troy, they were on the move but this trip was different. Yes, England too had been different, but there they had been tourists for a few weeks, seeing the sites. Jason had as well been doing work related interviews but in London they'd been staying with friends, knew the language well, despite the curious accents but now they were about to establish themselves for months in a city whose language they knew infinitely less well. Indeed, Black Jade herself was becoming more and more tense as they grew closer to Paris, scribbling away in her notebook one French phrase after another and she was by far the most gifted linguist among them.

Jason himself though felt relatively calm. His relationship with Prosper Giquel was strong and Jason was quite certain that Prosper, with his usual attention to detail, would have found them just the right place to stay for the summer. Besides, unlike his wife, he had no plans to teach French at the future Shanghai Female Seminary they had spent so much time planning to establish. For Black Jade though, Paris was a central part of her entire plan, a plan Jason had come to appreciate more and more as she had finally allowed him to read the long and detailed plans Emma Willard had sketched out so long ago for their Paris stay. For a second, suddenly realizing he had no idea when Willard had herself spent time in Paris, he thought of interrupting his wife's studies and then decided against it. When Black Jade was focused, it tended to be a good idea to let her do so and besides the French countryside was beautiful.

A moment later, unexpectedly, an aroma wafted into their compartment from the dining car he knew from that morning's initial explorations was only the next one up. And the aroma, extraordinary. Not just because the food in England had been tasteless but also because it reminded them of the two meals the family had enjoyed in the Calais hotel's dining room. Food, so different from the Chinese food he had grown up with but in its own way extraordinarily aromatic and delicious, the contrast with what they had experienced for the last couple of weeks truly remarkable. Checking his watch, he reconsidered the family's decision not to take lunch on the train and wait to dine again once they arrived in Paris. Still looking at the satchel Old Zhu carried on her lap Jason wondered about the various breads and extraordinary butter containers he had seen the older woman packing up that morning. Indeed, he was just about to suggest a snack when one of the train car's passengers caught his attention.

The fellow was nothing out of the ordinary, though Jason could not tell his nationality. No, what struck him was how intensely the young man, perhaps no older than twenty was studying Mei-ling. In a rush, Jason realized the man was not looking at Mei-ling because her Asian looks stood out so much in the west, that look Jason was used to but no, he was looking at her as a man eyes a beautiful woman. When had she grown into a woman Jason thought to himself suddenly, almost embarrassed that he'd not appreciated the change. His daughter was a woman? When had that happened?

He was about to interrupt his wife with his revelation when he was startled by two young women running by, intent perhaps on returning to their own carriage yelling *"Pas Loin"* as they ran by and then a sudden stirring of people all around him, people checking bags, starting to clean up make shift picnics.

*"Pas Loin?"* Jason repeated as Black Jade looked up from her writing pad.

"Not far" now it is your turn to be at a loss my husband."

"I did OK in the restaurant last night," Jason defended himself, though the giggle from Mei-ling through the open compartment door was not encouraging. A second later Will sat down with a resigned look on his face.

"At least you know more French than I do, Father."

"We will keep you two safe," Mei-ling said, smiling at the two forlorn male members of the family as the conductor walked by announcing in a very loud voice, *"Vingt minutes à Paris!"*

"Twenty minutes to Paris?" Jason said hopefully as Black Jade smiled one of her smiles she offered when she found her husband sadly wanting. Oh well, Jason thought to himself…at least he'd be seeing Giquel and Wu soon and that was exciting enough to distract him. And the fellow was right, a few minutes later the family pulled into the *Gare de Nord* and the next several minutes were caught up in a mad scramble to gather the far too many trunks the family had been carrying since they left Boston.

Could it be possible, Jason thought to himself as he struggled to engage a train porter to help his family into the great hall of Paris's northern station, there just yards from him Prosper and Wu were approaching. Giquel himself was easy enough to spot; that enormously broad forehead had always been visible even from a distance but there walking alongside him was Wu, but not Wu. Certainly not the man they had known, not their traveling companion from years before, nor the dissipated Taiping officer they had both seen in Huzhou or even the impoverished vagabond Jason had encountered years later in the streets of Shanghai but a healthy Wu smiling as he walked toward them in the fine clothing of a European gentleman.

Reaching over to Black Jade, Jason caught her attention and directed her gaze toward the two men walking toward them.

"Oh my!" She said has he approached. "Can it really be him?"

"*Bienvenue, mes amis*! Welcome to Paris, my old friends," Wu said with accented but very clear English and French, while Jason and Black Jade just stared, and Prosper smiled clearly amused by the scene before him.

"*Mon Dieu! Mes enfants…non*, could it possibly be…Mei-ling and William, *tout à fait* completely grown up." With that, Giquel threw his arms around both of the startled children as Black Jade, Old Zhu and Jason stared dumbfounded at his companion.

"Can it really be you?" She suddenly burst out in Cantonese, the dialect of both their youths.

"Would you have me offer a few sayings from the Master?" He responded with equal fluency while Jason just stared vaguely conscious of Old Zhu to his side looking decidedly doubtful. She had never met the family's old friend but had heard enough about Wu to have an opinion, as she did of most people and especially her fellow Chinese.

"Don't be fooled, Wu hardly dresses like this normally but he insisted on an entirely new wardrobe for this occasion. Even my daughter, who inspected both of us before we left for the station, approved. But you will meet her soon enough…for the moment perhaps we should not take so much of this fellow's time and find our carriage." With that, Giquel gestured to the train porter to follow and the entire party set off through the beautiful architecture of the *Gare de Nord* at almost a run to keep up with Giquel.

# CHAPTER 88

# MANY QUESTIONS ANSWERED

The next several hours were spent enjoying an extraordinary lunch including the finest champagne Giquel had managed to order from the restaurant, a delightful place near the Luxembourg Gardens that served food of the sort neither Jason, Black Jade nor Old Zhu had ever experienced. The sauces, subtle seasonings, foul, veal, various sorts of *foie gras*, and even snails that Prosper had ordered, one dish after another after always consulting closely with the waiter with great seriousness, indeed food to make pale in comparison the meal they had enjoyed in Calais let alone what they had just suffered through in London. Finally, fully sated the small group separated, Giquel to check in on his daughter after seeing his charges to the apartments, up only one convenient flight of stairs in a district Prosper had referred to as the Marais. As for Wu, he'd stayed with his old friends, helping when necessary as Black Jade eagerly tried to communicate with the older woman, still partly brunet but with patches of gray in her hair, who managed the apartment building they planned to call home for the entire summer.

"I cannot believe you speak French so well, better than I do even after all my years of study!" Black Jade finally blurted out in Cantonese with a tone of admiration and jealousy.

"*Bien sur, Madame,* but I have had a lot more time here with real people, with Prosper himself and since we arrived in Paris helping our students from the Fuzhou Dockyard. You only just arrived and one can accomplish only so much with books. But your French is already impressive and your English, I could not believe what I heard when you were speaking with William during lunch."

Black Jade smiled one of her subtle smiles, the sort she always employed when she'd heard a compliment but refused to acknowledge it.

With that, Black Jade turned her attention to Old Zhu and the children, helping to settle them in to the adjoining rooms. Prosper had done quite well, finding them a large apartment that allowed not only each child a room of their own but even a small but comfortable servant's quarters for Old Zhu who seemed especially pleased with her new sleeping space.

"I should be leaving." Wu suddenly said standing up and adjusting the fine suit, he clearly was uncomfortable wearing.

"You are going nowhere!" Black Jade suddenly yelled from Mei-ling's room across the hall from where he and Jason sat. Both men were startled - neither had even realized she could hear them.

"You are not leaving until you tell us what happened in Huzhou after we left, and what happened to you before you approached Jason in Shanghai." She called her voice even more insistent than usual.

"It looks like you are not going anywhere." Jason laughed.

"She has not changed at all has she?"

"No" Jason said as both men sat down in the parlor again and Jason poured around for each of them from one of the several bottles of wine Giquel had already stocked the apartment with.

———※————

"It is not much of a tale, one filled with more hunger than events." He began in Cantonese as Black Jade and Jason stared expectantly at him in the small parlor of the apartment, each with a glass of wine at their side and an open window that offered a lovely view of the balconies opposite them on the street.

"Just start from the moment we headed toward the city gate with the letter of passage signed with your chop. We want to hear everything till you stopped Jason in the street in Shanghai."

Wu stared at her for a long time, perhaps remembering the moment so many years before when he and Jason had found her half dead, after a failed suicide alongside a river...how many years before had that been...and then for a second another image, Black Jade as the wife of one of the most respected Taiping leaders in those last days before the Heavenly Kingdom had fallen. He had not seen her often after her marriage in Nanjing but he had always listened carefully when either she or her husband had been mentioned.

"I will tell you the story but first I want your promise to seriously consider another matter I have to ask you about. Is that agreed?"

"Of course." Jason replied only looking to his wife somewhat guiltily afterward. "What is it?"

"Not now, later, first the story of a depressing adventure."

Jason looked back at Black Jade who was clearly very curious about Wu's question but was obviously anxious as well to hear their friend's tale.

"Agreed," she said.

———※————

After you left, I wandered a bit to try to find out what was happening, how weak the city's defenses really were, how soon the imperials would be able to breach the walls with the equipment the foreigners carried with them. Little did I know then that one of them, Prosper would eventually become my great benefactor...for a second Wu stopped to reflect while his two old friends watched him closely. Then, after a sip of wine he took up the story again. My wanderings did not last long. I had not been out for weeks, the effects of the opium and helping get you too off had exhausted me. I hardly made it back to my lodging, which in itself was a huge effort. Nevertheless, when I got there the entire compound was abandoned. My servants what few I still had, had fled, perhaps thinking I would escape with you two. I don't really know but I collapsed in my chambers taking only a few puffs on the one opium pipe that remained - expecting to be found like that when the city fell.

The next morning though I woke at dawn feeling very differently. For the first time in weeks, I realized I was not ready to die, that I wanted to live. With more energy than I had felt for months, as much as I had had for those few minutes with you, I scoured my lodgings, and to my joy found the pouch of silver Taels and coppers I had hidden months before. None of the servants had known about my secret funds and to my joy, they had not been touched.

Within minutes, I was off toward the city gates but my rank, or I suppose former rank no longer meant anything. Fortunately, the money carried a reasonable amount of influence and luckily, I passed through the walls with a bribe and the help of an officer at the gate whom I had once served with."

"Had the walls already been breached?" Jason asked.

"Not where I was but it sounded like something of that sort was happening at one of the other gates. I still don't really know what happened, my only concern was to get as far away from

Huzhou as I could possibly accomplish before my strength failed again, especially so because a renewed desire to live had also put me in terror of being caught by the imperials, being beheaded as they had done to so many others. Nevertheless, I got lucky, finding several fishermen, I convinced one of them, with a bit of encouragement from my money bag to take me down the river. My hope was to get to one of the Western Treaty Ports where I thought I might be safer.

As we traveled though my situation became worse and worse, the need for opium overwhelming and the fisherman had none to satisfy my need. I finally insisted he leave me on shore and I set out again on foot, feeling worse and worse, trying to find a place to fill my needs.

At that, Wu paused for a moment, taking another sip of wine, obviously reflecting on how to begin again his tale. "But there was nothing to be found. Every village I walked through was deserted and imperial soldiers were everywhere, looking and often finding former Taipings. Watching from paddy fields hidden among reeds, I could see that they were beheading many of those known to have been Taiping officers, men identified by the many former Taiping soldiers who had switched sides. It was obvious I had gotten off the fishing boat far too early, my need for opium was likely to kill me yet."

"So what did you do?" Black Jade asked quietly, reflecting on how narrowly she and Jason had avoided capture.

"There was nothing to do. I hid, tried to walk at night, tried to fight off the need for the opium pipe. But as I approached areas less disrupted by the fighting an idea formed in my head, that I had to find a way to stop my need for the drug and as I still had some money I approached an inn one evening and took a room, my first in weeks. The next morning after reflecting at length, mostly about my useless life, I decided to take back my fate. I arranged for the owner and his son, a very large young man to help me break my addiction." With that, Wu finished his wine and poured himself another glass.

"The son was sent off to find an opium pipe and I had one more pipe before they locked me in the vegetable cellar, where I spent the next several weeks, weeks I barely remember horribly ill, shaking, sweating, in terrible pain as my body fought the drug. Over and over I begged the innkeeper to help me, even tried to break out at least once but the son restrained me."

"It must have been terrible," Black Jade said quietly.

"And then what? I assumed it worked," Jason piped in.

"Eventually yes, but not for a long time. I did though start to feel better, began to feel less need for the pipe and after a time, felt strong enough to continue toward the treaty ports but my money was running out. It had taken most of what I had had to just leave Huzhou and after that the purse was getting smaller and smaller. So I bought what I could of more presentable clothing and set myself up as a tutor of the Confucian classics in a yet another village."

"So that is what you did until I saw you in Shanghai?"

"There is not much of a tale after that, I found it easy enough to earn a few coppers from poor families hoping for the better life a son who could pass the imperial exams would bring but it never lasted. I was an outsider and was almost always threatening some other tutor's rice bowl. After a time, rumors would be spread about me, sometimes even speculation that I might be a former rebel, which particularly frightened me. Nothing ever came of it, but always I would move on, try to find another village I could make my home in, at least until one day nearer the coast, one of the students brought me a Western newspaper. The boy's family had acquired it somehow and wanted to know if I might be able to read it."

"And you were able to?" Jason suddenly asked. "How?"

"Of course not, but I knew the alphabet, knew something of what you had taught me, and could recognize your name."

"My name?"

"Yes, it was a piece you had written, and I was able to confirm you had escaped Huzhou successfully and were living in Shanghai. It was then that I slowly formed the hope of contacting you...seeing if you could find me something in Shanghai better than that of a constantly starving tutor in the countryside. So I set off, my purse long empty to walk to Shanghai which itself took months."

"And you arrived just as I was leaving...I guess your long assumption of a bad fate was confirmed again," Jason commented.

"Perhaps, for a few seconds, as I watched you run off toward the harbor and your ship. Nevertheless, I had the letter, and after following you and watching the ship depart, I set off toward Fuzhou. Another, I must say, very long walk, as I was terrified to spend any of the cash you handed me as you ran off."

"I wish I had had more on me."

"It was enough, and Prosper did, as you know, take me in and give me employment. The rest you know."

"And your special request?" Black Jade asked, looking closely at Wu.

Wu took up the bottle, poured a bit more into his glass, and said, "I want to travel back with you to China and become a teacher again perhaps even at your new school."

# CHAPTER 89
# A CITY OF MANY PLEASURES

Jason and Black Jade both turned to each other. Neither had anticipated such a formal request. Jason's first thought was of course very positive, a chance to spend months with his old friend as they returned to China, months with an adult male rather than with his three, charming but decidedly female traveling companions. Certainly, Will was a pleasant enough and male but he was still a child and one who, unfortunately complained far too much. For the boy had after all never given up his anxiety about leaving the United States for China a land, he unlike any of his older relatives had absolutely no memory of. For a second Jason even sympathized with the boy, at Will's age he'd had no more interest in going to America than Will had in returning to a China he did not remember. Nevertheless, that was an issue for another day, Jason realized as his thoughts returned to the matter at hand and waited for Black Jade's response.

Still Jason said nothing. His old friend had asked for more than to simply travel with them home, he had asked about teaching at a school, at the school Black Jade had planned to establish for almost ten years. It was her decision and no one else's.

Looking back to Black Jade as from the corner of his eye he saw Wu eying both of them expectantly, it was obvious his wife was in deep thought.

"Of course," she began slowly, "we would love to have you travel with us. Jason has been burdened with too much women's talk for months." She added smiling at her husband, who had no idea she had understood his feelings so well.

"But why do you want to go at all? It seems you have made a life here in France, is there anything for you at home?"

"I don't know the answer, I only know that I want to try, want to have a family, open the door to the future, to honor my family and our ancestors as I have failed so often in the past. It is time, none of us is young anymore, but you two have a family, have each other..." Wu looked back at his old friend remembering how much Jason had loved Black Jade before fate had finally allowed them to be together.

"But I have nothing, had nothing in China, a good life here but a shallow one. Monsieur Giquel...Prosper has been wonderfully kind to me, offered me far more of a life than I could ever have hoped for. Nevertheless, it is not home, things here are wondrous...but it is not China that I miss every day."

But where would you live? You cannot simply show up and set up a new life? How would you live?" Black Jade asked not directly addressing his reference to the planned school itself.

"You are right, the only placed I could live, perhaps fit in, is in one of the treaty ports, Hong Kong or Shanghai, a place where one like me...one foot in each world might perhaps prosper, perhaps even seem a desirable match for the daughter of one of the compradors, one of the large merchant families, who live near the Bund alongside the river I explored after your ship departed."

"And you think teaching at our proposed school is the life you want. What would you teach?" She asked.

"I don't know, what would you need, certainly something of the classics. The families you wrote about, said you were hoping to recruit will want something of that sort. And I could teach about the West, about what I have seen here since I arrived in Paris. And it has been a lot, we have placed students from England to Germany and here in Paris and I have also taken up the study of European history, it is full of wonders I had never imagined…just a few days ago, just before you arrived I spent an entire afternoon at great museum devoted totally to…"

But as Wu started to get excited about his tale Black Jade interrupted him.

"Old Friend, friend of my husband, friend of both my husbands," she suddenly said her voice trailing off for a second. "Our school does not exist yet. We have no idea of our needs save a general idea of somehow educating young Chinese women and perhaps a few Western girls in subjects beyond what women often learn. Beyond that, we have no curriculum to hire anyone for."

Nevertheless, before Wu could say a word, though his eyes betrayed disappointment, she went on "But that conversation is for another day, let us simply agree that we will have the pleasure of your company as we return home."

At that she turned to her husband who was beaming, delighted with her reaction to Wu's proposal. It would be months before they would return home, at least six he had been guessing and the trip had become far more pleasurable as far as he was concerned.

Three days later, while Mei-ling and Black Jade were being given a tour of a French language institute Giquel had regularly placed his Fuzhou students at for advanced instruction, and as Will wandered the small park that stood just opposite the café Prosper and Jason sat sipping wine, Giquel turned to his old friend, his tone becoming more serious.

"As I said, the sisters here earn part of their keep teaching foreigners French and already have considerable experience with Chinese students. Black Jade and Mei-ling will be well served if they decide to study here. However, enough of that, we will know when their tour has finished. Now, tell me more of what you have written, more of what the papers have said here. Are the Americans really going to bar the Chinese from America? Can your countrymen be that stupid?"

Jason laughed wondering what his old friend Mark Twain would have responded if asked such a question. "Could that even be a serious question?" Jason was almost certain would be the reply though with more witticism than Jason could manage at the moment.

"When I saw you last, that last afternoon in Shanghai I could not possibly have answered that question. I might even have been offended it you were not such a fine friend...but after years in America...well, yes, indeed I am quite comfortable with the question, and yes they can easily be that stupid."

"But we are speaking of the practical fellows my own countryman De Tocqueville, whom I have often read closely, writes so enthusiastically of. You know the book of course?"

Jason nodded as Prosper went on, getting more and more agitated. "Do they not understand that China can easily become a major country again, that she really is the sleeping giant the great Napoleon spoke of and is already starting to awaken, starting in part through our own efforts, and leaders like Li Hongzhang, Shen, my own colleague at the dockyard and even your friend Wu, starting to awaken again. How can America not understand that and want to be part of it?

"There certainly are men, and women, who understand that well enough, who want to be part of China's rebirth and make those profits one can from its industrializing needs." Jason said thinking for a second of Mr. Sage and all those reports he'd written for the investor over the years.

"Then what is it…one hears from here that they might make it impossible for Chinese to go to America, that the doors will be closed. The Imperial government might be weak, but they won't let that stand…"

"You are most certainly correct…but America, as you say is quite likely to close the door to more Chinese…if perhaps President Grant had returned to the White House. But that opportunity has passed."

"But if you say—" They were momentarily interrupted both by the waiter asking if they required more wine and an especially loud team of horses that went past them at a far faster gait then one usually heard in the relatively quiet street outside the convent they had settled near while the women toured inside.

Waiting till the interruption had passed Giquel began again, "But if as you have said people of influence understand the need and opportunities available in helping China's development…how can they even talk of such an outrage?"

For the next half an hour Jason found himself, now something of an expert after almost ten years reporting from the United States, explaining to his old friend about the power of America's regionally based governing system, of the power of each state and the fear of Western states and more specifically their citizens, of whom only whites counted as voters, of cheap Chinese labor.

"So, this thing, this monstrosity could actually happen they could bar all Chinese from entering *l'Amerique*, knowing full well the Chinese would retaliate, probably end our old colleague Yung Wing's educational mission and stop any purchases of manufacturing equipment from the United States."

"I am afraid so." Jason said sadly.

"Magnificent!" Giquel suddenly burst out. "Let's drink to it. My beloved France will only benefit from America's shortsighted bigotry. *Garçon*, bring us your finest champagne!" he yelled out, while Jason sat stunned.

Thirty minutes later, Mei-ling and Black Jade, the latter looking exhausted and as usual trying to hide the pain in her feet, exited the building to find her husband and his old friend deeply inebriated, Jason looking rather perplexed, and Prosper demanding more wine, even as they called for a carriage to take everyone to their respective lodging.

# CHAPTER 90

# MORE PARISIAN STORIES

"And you saw, of course, the bones of those ancient Dragons—those dinosaurs as they call them, and have sent telegrams that traveled under the great sea...the Atlantic between the Americas and Europe?"

"Of course, I even had a chance to ride a cable drawn carriage in the streets of San Francisco. But tell me what is really on your mind?" Jason asked as they strolled the grand gallery of the Louvre. It was the first time they had spent any social time together since Jason's family had arrived and taken up their living quarters in the Marais district of Paris. Indeed, they had all been very busy, Black Jade and Mei-ling getting started with the language lessons at the Catholic institute, enrolling little Will in a sports program designed for the children of the many Americans living in Paris while Giquel and Wu introduced Jason to the equivalent of Yung Wing's educational mission, known as the European Educational Mission. In truth, few of the Chinese students were available to interview scattered as they were from England to Germany and France studying and in a few cases actually serving on English naval ships. Still, both Prosper and Wu assured their journalist friend, that site visits to each of the scattered programs could be arranged during the family's summer in Paris and more conveniently, from time to time groups of students returned for short stays at the mission's Paris headquarters.

"What is in my mind would get me beheaded at home and perhaps even give my benefactor and your friend Prosper pause for concern…but with you I can be honest. The celestial kingdom is not what it thinks it is…indeed, to use a word I learned in London it is entirely humbug!" Wu blurted out loudly enough that several of the seated young women sketching copies of the masterpieces that surrounded them looked up in surprise.

Jason smiled somewhat embarrassed and eased his friend through a great archway into another gallery where the two friends might be more welcome.

"Humbug? A curious term for the Middle Kingdom, not one many mandarins would appreciate, that is if they even understood the term. So what do you mean exactly?"

"What I mean," Wu began with a look in his eyes his friend had not seen since the failed Confucian scholar had taken up his enthusiasm for the tenets of the heretical Taiping Kingdom more than a decade before. "What I mean is that China is not even close to the great civilization we have always assumed it was. I first began to understand how much our technology lagged behind when I started working with Giquel, started to understand something of the steam engines that replace the wind and oars of their great ships. But look around you. Once in Europe with Prosper, and especially so since my language skills grew, I have spent every moment in the great museums of Europe studying its civilization, reading every book I could possibly find and master." Wu was getting more and more excited and had long before switched to Cantonese which aroused several stares from others in the gallery who watched with curiosity as Wu excitedly spoke to his Caucasian companion who clearly understood him.

"And your conclusion?" Jason finally broke in.

"My conclusion…China must itself have what they call here, a renaissance, an age of reason to bring her forward into the arena of modern civilization." Wu suddenly said switching back to English.

Jason looked at his friend more closely He was in so many ways different from the companion of his youth, the young discouraged Confucian scholar or even the enthusiastic Taiping officer become almost a European gentleman. Yet in so many ways the same romantic, still looking for a truth he could embrace which somewhat repelled Jason's cynical journalistic soul.

For a moment, Jason stopped to observe a magnificent medieval painting that hung opposite them, finally after a moment turning back to Wu.

"But isn't that what you are already accomplishing here and previously at the Fuzhou dockyard? Bringing to China the fruits of Western industrial technology?" You are already part of that are you not?"

"Technology is important, that much I have learned from Prosper and of course enjoy the advantages of every day here in Europe. But I may not be a great Confucian scholar, and you know that better than most…but I know that civilization is about what is in men's hearts and mere technology won't change that. China needs a new way of thinking, a new Confucius worthy of the nineteenth century!"

"I suppose you are right, but if that is what you are really thinking you might well get your head chopped off when we get home. Have you spoken of any of this to Prosper?"

"Absolutely not. Prosper wants his beloved France to help China industrialize and gain the profits from that growth. And he understands China well enough to know that if he aroused the antagonism of the imperial court and the mandarins with revolutionary talk all such technology transfers or Western educational missions will end forever."

"But if you really feel that way…is it advisable for you to go home, to try to make a life there?"

"*Bien sur,* Wu said enthusiastically, "Without doubt" I may not be able to find a wife at my age, might not be able to bring a new generation of sons into the world, but I want to help China itself to open the door to the future."

"And of course that is why you want to teach at our proposed female seminary?"

"Yes, to help build the future."

Jason started to ask more questions, wanting to probe further, to understand better whether Wu and Black Jade's plans for the school were even compatible, but in the distance, somehow they had circled back, he could see Mei-ling waving furiously calling them back to the spot where he could see Black Jade deep in conversation with an older man who sat nearby clutching a sketch pad.

"Husband, we have met a new benefactor," Black Jade said as he approached.

"Mr. Brandt, I am delighted to meet you. Harvey Simone at your service. Your charming wife and daughter have told me all about your family. And I am told you hail from Boston, a city, even I as a native New Yorker can appreciate." The fellow said as he stepped forward and extended a hand first to Jason and then Wu.

"Pleased to meet you, sir. But I am confused, sir, my wife talks of a new benefactor?"

"Father, Mr. Simone is a painter. He wants to paint Mother and me!" Mei-ling burst out enthusiastically.

As Jason looked confused Black Jade stood up from the seat, she had sought comfort on, her somewhat deformed feet always a consideration. "It is much more than that. Mr. Simone asked if he could paint the two of us and I agreed only if there could be an exchange, drawing lessons for myself, Mei-ling and even little Will if he is interested." As she spoke, Mr. Simone stood alongside her looking as if he were eager to begin immediately.

"And a fine bargain indeed, your family your wife and daughter sitting for a portrait would be marvelously appreciated here in Paris especially with the Louvre in the background."

"And where would that occur" Jason asked feeling protective of his woman folk.

"Nothing to be concerned about, sir, right here, we can work right here, the place is full of people sketching. Your wife tells me she is free in the early afternoons after their French lessons."

Jason looked at his wife, who was waiting for his approval, though they had been married long enough for him to know that his outspoken wife considered that no more than a mere formality. If she wanted to strike the bargain, she most certainly would unless Jason came up with reasons compelling enough to change her mind, which happened very infrequently. Besides, Mei-ling was clearly excited by the opportunity.

"Then I guess the bargain is struck, sitting for a joint portrait in exchange for drawing lessons," Jason said as he extended his hand.

"I will need to be moving on," Wu said from his side, as he waved walking off toward one of the exits.

Meanwhile Jason waited for Black Jade and Mei-ling to arrange meeting times with their new friend, the gray-haired Mr. Simone whom Jason knew to be from New York and nothing else.

"So what do you think of our Paris adventure thus far?" Jason asked his wife as they started to explore more of the Louvre.

"I love this place. I think I was Parisian in a previous life. Mrs. Willard was right." his wife said as she, attracted by another masterpiece that beckoned at a distance, walked at the fastest gait she could manage toward the enormous painting of what appeared to be tragic figures caught in a terrible storm at sea.

# CHAPTER 91

# WITH THE EUROPEAN EDUCATIONAL MISSION

"You did not need to meet me here. I could have found the Rue du Faubourg on my own," Jason said as he spied Wu standing in the street as he descended from their second floor apartment.

"I am sure you could have...but that is not why I am here. There is something we need to discuss before you arrive at the mission headquarters."

"But I have already been there, at least twice with you and Prosper...what is the big mystery?"

"Today is different, as you know a good sized group of students is returning today from the Cherbourg naval facility."

"Of course, you promised I could interview them."

"Yes, but that is not my concern, my official role as you know is merely as a Chinese assistant to Monsieur Giquel. But these students are traveling and arriving soon with Li Feng-pao, the Chinese director, a real scholar gentry mandarin of the sort you told me traveled with Yung Wing in America."

"And why is that an issue? I look forward to meeting him."

"Perhaps, but he knows very little of me, only that I assist Giquel and that somehow I know Giquel through you, information I am afraid he might use against me."

"What do you mean, surely he already knows you?"

"Not really, I have taken care for years to generally avoid those mandarins Giquel works with and he hardly needs me as a translator."

"So what does he know about you? What have you told him about yourself?"

"In truth almost nothing. What would you have me tell him? That I insulted the emperor in my essay for the Confucian civil service exams. Or maybe that I was once a fairly respected Taiping official? Now that would really impress him."

"I see your point. I shall be the soul of discretion. But I don't want to make a mistake, arouse his suspicions. What does he think he knows about you?"

"I have implied that my family was in trade in Guangzhou but well off enough to have given me something of a more formal education. Nothing more."

"O. K, that helps and don't be concerned—your secrets are safe with me. And Giquel, what specifically does Giquel know?"

"Obviously more but only in a vague way and he is discrete enough to make it clear he does not want to know more, well aware that it could only complicate his life if it were openly known that he employed someone like me. Indeed, it is a sign of his friendship that simply with that hurried note from you he hired me without asking any questions at all."

Several minutes later, as they entered the Education Mission's headquarters on the Rue du Faubourg, where apparently the student group had already arrived. Spying them Wu tapped Jason's shoulder, indicated the direction for him to continue and then himself immediately disappeared down a set of stairs. As for Jason only a few yards ahead, he entered the large drawing room he had seen during his previous visits. Only this time it was filled with young Chinese talking excitedly among themselves. And at the end of the room near the now extinguished fireplace, for June's subtle warmth had already arrived in Paris stood an older man, closer to Jason's own age whom he assumed to be the Mandarin Li Feng-pao, Giquel's co-director and apparently, he now understood, his friend Wu's primary complication.

"The famous journalist Mr. Jason Brandt I assume," the man called out from across the room. Despite his use of English and his Western clothing, the fellow had the unmistakable air of a scholar gentry of the sort Jason, over a lifetime in China had come to find so familiar.

"I do not know how famous, but I am Jason Brandt, Your Excellency."

"And I am told by your friend Wu—where did that fellow go again?—that your Chinese is excellent," Li said, switching to a northern dialect of China that Jason had mastered long before.

"I think Wu had business to attend to downstairs, Your Excellency, but I am delighted to meet you. As you may know, I have visited here several times while you were away and in America have met with your colleague who works with Yung Wing helping to direct the Sino-American Educational Mission."

At the mention of Yung Wing's mission, Jason, with years of practice interviewing people, thought he spotted a hint of irritation but the man said nothing. What could that be all about he wondered.

"Yes, I have heard a great deal about you from Giquel, and from my colleagues in Connecticut..." The man paused. "And even from that curious fellow, your friend, Monsieur Giquel employs as an assistant. However, let us leave these young men to their own devices...no doubt, once you have spoken with them to wander the streets of Paris as they do at every opportunity. For now, as they unpack, let us withdraw to the side parlor where, if the servants have been industrious, you will find tea to your liking."

"Thank you, Your Excellency. I would very much enjoy that." Jason thought surprised that Li had not, as most Chinese almost immediately did, commented on his language skills. But either he had been so well briefed that he had none of the usual surprise that a foreigner could speak as a native or there was something else on his mind, Jason speculated to himself as they entered the small but nicely furnished parlor down the hall.

"Mr. Brandt, if you will forgive me, I feel compelled to be rude, to forgo the usual pleasantries of conversation gentlemen from here to China always begin a conversation with. But this is not the moment. You do not know I presume?"

"Do not know what? Your Excellency, has something untoward happened? Wu said nothing as we walked," Jason continued, irritated with himself for even mentioning his friend, who clearly preferred to stay as far from Li's thoughts as possible.

"He would not know; word came only minutes ago. My country, the Emperor, the *Zongli Yamen*, and the grand counselors, reacting to your country's betrayal, have chosen to cancel the educational mission in America," the man finished, watching for Jason's reaction.

"What? Cancelled the educational mission? I don't understand, I know nothing of this...it is true Chinese workers are often greeted with disdain, outright hostility from those who compete with them for employment...but that is in the Western regions, and the educational mission is in the East where almost none compete with Chinese for jobs. That makes no sense. Why would your government cancel the mission?"

"Because the Americans have reneged on the agreement we negotiated - Chinese students studying in the schools and colleges in America culminating in admission to your military academies at West Point and Annapolis. An agreement that has now been broken, indeed they have long refused to honor the Burlingame Agreement...and now it has become certain that their refusal to allow Chinese students entrance into the military academies won't be reversed."

"Thus my own country's cancellation of the entire program. Word only just arrived here this morning but I am guessing my colleagues in Connecticut will already be packing for home their educational effort deeply incomplete and yet having lost the chance for a proper Confucian education as well."

Although it was obvious Li was furious, he outwardly presented a demeanor of calm and focus on Jason's reaction. Still Jason could see tension in his hands that kept flexing and unflexing an obvious sign of hidden emotion.

"I really don't know what to say, Your Excellency. I knew the situation was growing worse, at least as regards Chinese laborers but this, this is completely unexpected."

"But you cannot be all that surprised Le said studying him closely. I have had one of our students, a young man who studied English in preparation for his time in England, regularly translate your newspaper articles for me, my English skills being at a bare minimum. And Monsieur Giquel has told me what he learned from your letters."

"Of course, the general tension is building up and I had hoped until just last summer that General—*President* Grant would be returned to office. I am sure you know that he and the great governor Li Hongzhang became great friends during Grant's visit to China."

"Which you personally helped facilitate I am told."

"I had a very minor role but the honor of accompanying Grant was great indeed and his failure to win office a great tragedy for both our countries. Indeed, I am almost certain a

President Grant returned to office would have allowed the student's admission to West Point and Annapolis."

"As we too had hoped, and yet you are still surprised at the end of the American Educational Mission?"

"Only because it had so little to do with the real cause of tensions between our two countries, those white Americans, usually Irish workers who have the vote the Chinese in America lack and don't wish to compete with Chinese labor. But that has nothing to do with the educational students. Indeed, their studies, had it led to China buying more American manufactures, would have meant more jobs not less."

"And yet your politicians would allow such a thing...that is what democracy offers, bad decisions by the ignorant masses it would seem," Li said, putting his own teacup down with considerably greater energy than most mandarins with their usual concern for decorum would have done.

"I don't know what to say. Only that you are most correct. My own years, almost ten in America, you know I grew up in China of course...well, in any case, my years writing about American style democracy has made me far more cynical than most about how well it actually provides competent government rather than mere choice."

"And if I might, do you think something of that sort could also happen here, in Europe, among the English or the French? I am in truth still only learning how different they can truly be. In China, they often seemed very similar but since arriving here. I am considerably less sure."

"If you had asked me ten minutes ago, Your Excellency, I would have told you even as Chinese immigration to America was deeply at risk; I would have assured you that the educational mission which offers only advantages for America was safe from the prejudices of the streets. However, I would have been wrong. And this is a very personal issue for me. I came during my time in America to know the community Yung Wing had gathered in Hartford very well indeed."

"I too know a number of them at least their families and have even met the half American half Chinese, Yung Wing himself a few times," Li added, taking a sip more of tea.

"But, Your Excellency, I still remain fairly confident that the situation here will not follow the path of that in America for the simple reason that it is far less a political issue. Workers here do not concern themselves about competing for jobs with Chinese laborers and that makes all the difference. But what does Monsieur Giquel think of all this?"

"I am afraid we won't know for some time. He departed yesterday for another inspection tour, this time of our students in England and may not have even heard the news yet. For now, though, I have interrogated you enough. I told the students they could not start their usual Parisian wanderings until you met with them as a group and that should begin shortly. After that, I would invite you to lunch so we can have more time together to chat. Your writings have been very helpful and I would like to take advantage of your presence to learn more of your insights.

Three hours later, as Jason departed the mission headquarters, a notebook full of student observations of their studies and travels and his stomach more than pleased with the wonderful Chinese meal Le had ordered for him he was suddenly startled by Wu appearing almost without warning at his side.

"Whoa, where did you come from?"

"I left from the side door as Li was seeing you off."

"I see why he calls you that strange fellow. Do you always stay so much in the background?"

"Under the circumstances it does seem like a wise thing to do. At the dockyard, it was less of an issue. Here I have to be more careful. Did he say anything more about me?"

"No, I don't think he has any great curiosity about you…at least he did not try to learn more about you from me. But then he had other things on his mind."

"Yes, the American Educational Mission being cancelled. Do you think that will happen here? The students have worked so hard for this opportunity."

"No. probably not but Giquel, not me is in the best position to have an informed opinion. When will he be back?"

"In only a few days…normally I would have traveled with him but I made an excuse so we could talk in advance of your meeting with Li."

With that Wu turned, offered his good-bye's and started off again in the direction of the mission while Jason headed for the apartment knowing he would have several hours to work on the notes he'd just taken before Black Jade or Mei-ling returned from their morning classes at the language institute or the Louvre where they spent their afternoons painting and posing as per their agreement. Indeed, he thought to himself it would be very quiet at the apartment for hours at least until Will returned.

# CHAPTER 92

# FALLING IN LOVE
# WITH A CITY

As he walked through the Luxembourg Gardens look-ing for his wife and daughter Jason thought about how quickly the weeks in Paris had passed. I It was already late July. Where had all the time gone? Certainly he'd been busy enough traveling from time to time with Wu and Giquel to various loca-tions where students had been placed for further training. In addition, he had been able to interview with the help of a trans-lator Giquel had engaged, a number of French government of-ficials to gauge how deeply their commitment to the presence of Chinese students in France was.

Overall, what had struck him most was how much more of a sense French officials had of the advantages that would ac-crue to France over the decades if scores of potentially influ-ential young Chinese developed deep ties to France. It was not he finally concluded something those in governing circles in Washington City really appreciated.

France might be only a bit into its first decade of yet an-other effort to sustain a republic but its officials were clearly more able to take the long view then those who dominated in America. Moreover, he kept reminding himself, the lack of significant Chinese laborers competing for jobs made their friendship with China significantly easier.

There had of course been negatives, Black Jade with her usual obsessiveness, once she had taken on a task, spent almost every day either working on her French, and sketching or being sketched by Mr. Simone in the Louvre. But as her French had improved Black Jade and Mei-ling, who every day resembled her mother as much in beauty and studiousness, had begun to venture out more and more often on their own in the early evenings of the long days of Paris's summer. Of course, there had been that other nagging issue, something that he had not experienced with his wife for years that sense of jealousy that she was beyond his reach. Only now, it was not her long dead Taiping officer husband that he found himself competing with but an entire city. In short, it had become obvious that Black Jade was rapidly falling in love with Paris itself. How did a mere man compete with glorious Paris he thought as he glanced across the expanse of the great park taking in both the beauty and scores of couples walking hand in hand along the garden's many paths.

"Eventually, he did spot them, but not as he had imagined her, sitting quietly with her sketch pad alongside Mei-ling, working quietly as so many men and women did among the streets and museums of Paris. No indeed, he in fact only just spotted the two women, so surrounded were they by a crowd of at least ten young men, apparently all artists judging by their clothing, some clearly local others foreign who were all at once, it seemed competing with each other to gain the attention of the two women.

"But *Mesdames*, I am certain my purse and reputation would make me the better choice." Jason heard one fellow say loudly in English.

Even from the hundred yards that separated them, he could see Black Jade laughing and responding quietly in French as Mei-ling smiled radiantly next to her mother clearly basking in the attention of the young men.

*"Vous somme tout à fait charmant, mes amis,"* she began, her French ever so much improved since they had arrived some seven weeks before "But I am afraid my daughter and I must depart...there my husband approaches...perhaps another day we can continue our discussions of such a sitting. We are often here in the later afternoons Adieu."

With that Black Jade, now walking with the ever so fashionable walking stick she had purchased soon after their arrival gestured to their daughter and started toward Jason whose arrival had clearly disappointed the entire community of young men.

"All right *Mesdames*, we will be here again tomorrow evening to discuss further our proposal. Enjoy your evening."

"What was that all about?" Jason asked taking his wife's hands as they set off toward the street to hail a horse carriage. "And what is so funny young lady?" he asked seeing his daughter giggling uncontrollably at his side.

"We'll tell you everything in the carriage," Black Jade said smiling and in a way, she rarely did as the two women shared amused glances.

A few minutes later, after something of a struggle to hail a carriage given the number of people on the street just outside the Luxembourg Gardens trying to do the same thing as the day neared its conclusion, Jason found himself watching his daughter whose look of amusement had not abated. As he looked at her, indeed studied both his daughter and his wife he noticed almost anew how feminine they both looked. Certainly, both were attractive women but something was different.

After a moment, he realized with embarrassment what the change was. Each of them, in the weeks since their arrival had incrementally begun in their clothing choices to mirror the decisions of the Parisian women. It was not that they had spent a lot of money on clothing. No, he would have noticed that more quickly. It was more subtle, just a slight shift in how different items of clothing were chosen and worn. That subtle and yet obvious skill that Parisians, both men and women seemed to have from birth making the most of whatever clothing they could afford to look their best.

Fifteen minutes later as their carriage arrived at the apartment, Mei-ling jumped out and still giggling skipped off toward the apartment entrance while Jason struggled with the right combination of francs for the driver.

"So what was all that about at the park Jason finally asked.

"Just what you saw, all those young men offering to pay Mei-ling and me to pose for them at various Parisian locations. "

"I got that, but what is Mei-ling so amused by?"

"Oh that, some of the young gentlemen wanted us to pose nude for them."

"What!"

"Oh don't be an American prude, this is Paris," she said looking amused at her astonished husband standing dumbfounded as she followed Mei-ling up the stairs.

An hour later though she was more serious as they sat in the parlor looking out on to the street as the crowds, despite how late it was becoming, continued as if on parade down the street.

"I think you should buy the train tickets for Venice immediately?"

"Now? This soon, I thought we were staying longer, so you could practice your French more and we could all avoid the late summer heat of the Holy City. They say Jerusalem can be unbearable during the summer."

"Perhaps, but we both lived through the summer heat of southern China. We should start planning to leave as soon as possible."

"But why are you so anxious to leave Paris. I thought you loved Paris"

"That is the problem. If we don't leave soon I will never leave," she said with the tone that always meant, throughout their marriage, that the conversation was over, the decision made.

# CHAPTER 93
# TIME TO MOVE ON

"More champagne," Prosper called out as the waiter walked by them in the small *brassiere* they had gathered in for the old friends' last formal dinner in Paris, the evening before their departure for the train south toward Italy. "And another toast."

"And what, Prosper, is this one going to be for?" Jason asked while Black Jade, Wu, Old Zhu, Mei-ling, and Will watched Giquel from the other end of the long table they had commandeered at least two hours before, when their enormous and many course meal had begun.

"Why for amity, for friendship, friendship among people, among countries, and of course, between America, China, and my beloved France," the former French naval officer said loudly enough to attract the attention of several other groups also dining.

Looking a bit sheepish, Giquel took a long drag on his cigar and seemed to compose himself somewhat.

"Forgive me, my friends, but I am deeply saddened at this moment. You are among my best friends, my longest lived friends, and you are about to return to my second national home, one that I don't know when I will see again."

"But surely, Monsieur Giquel, you will through your work with the educational mission have need to return to China and of course allow us all to enjoy a wonderful reunion in Shanghai one day soon," Wu said with the tone of deference he still displayed when addressing his employer and benefactor.

"My dear friend and colleague, indeed, my"—Giquel surveyed the room for a second before continuing—"my dear former long-haired Rebel Taiping—what? You did not think I knew? No matter, Monsieur Wu. You have one of the most remarkable intellects I have encountered, but reading the tea leaves of French politics is not something you have mastered quite yet, my dear friend."

"What do you mean, Prosper?" Jason said, leaning forward, as all the adults at the table quieted, ending their own side conversations (even Old Zhu, who'd been chatting with the youngest members of the family).

"The tensions in Annam are getting worse," Giquel said in Chinese choosing his words carefully in very low tones. "I am beginning to think there could be a clash between France and China, or at least the idiots who run the government these days and China."

"That is terrible," Black Jade commented. "Prosper, you know so many people here and in China. Can you do nothing to calm the waters?"

"I will do what I can but my influence is considerably smaller than you, my longtime friends believe it to be. But enough of such concerns, I am deeply jealous of all of you, to begin the great voyage back to Shanghai and via Venice and the Holy City, two extraordinary cities I have never seen. And of course, you know about Gordon?'

"Gordon, Charles, the so called Chinese Gordon?" What about him?" Jason asked his curiosity aroused.

"Why, they say he is in the Holy City, has been there for months. You did know him in China of course."

"Not well, but I interviewed him often enough in the last year of the rebellion." Jason added this time glancing at both Black Jade and Wu who were listening even more intently.

"I have no idea what he is doing there but if he is still there when you arrive do offer him my greetings......but enough of this talk...tonight is for celebrations. *Garçon*, more champagne for my friends!"

"Marco Polo, Marco Polo!" the young Italian teenagers yelled loudly as they ran by down the narrow alley between the Rialto Bridge and San Marcos square where the Jason's party had taken quarters several days before.

"I am getting very tired of hearing that yelled out constantly," Mei-ling said with some irritation.

"They are just being children, and seeing us...how can they not think of this Marco Polo person. Everything we have learned about him makes him sound like a very interesting man...to have traveled from here to China." Black Jade offered her unhappy daughter.

"You mean everything Uncle Wu has told us." Mei-ling said suddenly looking at Wu who had been walking with at least two guidebooks and a copy of the famous Polo's history of his travels since they had arrived while constantly sharing what he'd learned with the family. Indeed, Wu had turned into the family's informal tour guide with his constant study of their surroundings since they'd set off from Paris almost two weeks before.

"Well, we have traveled a lot more than he ever did" Will said enthusiastically "someone should write about us."

"So when we get to the Plaza are we going to have to pose for those photographers again?" Mei-ling said her tone the one she often displayed just before she lost her temper.

"Mei-ling, I know you are tired, but Venice is beautiful, you have said that many times a day since we arrived and letting some of the locals photograph you is just a way to give something back."

"But they think mom and I are freaks, have they never seen Chinese faces here?"

"Mei-ling, Venice is one of the great cities of the west. You loved Paris. How is Venice so different?" Wu offered, trying to help.

"In Paris I could talk to people, use my French...have them know me as a person, not just someone to stare at...how many times a day can I say *ciao* and *grazie?*"

"OK...we are all feeling like fish lost at sea, but we have met a few people who know English and there was that waiter yesterday who spoke excellent French," her father reminded her, "and it is only for a few more days, till the ship sails for Haifa."

"All I know is that I am tired of being an outsider, Venice feels like America without the hate against Chinese. I want to be somewhere where no one notices me."

"My wonderful daughter, beautiful women are never in a place where no one notices them." Her father said gallantly though aware she was not buying his compliment. However, even as Jason spoke with Mei-ling he could see Will, remaining silent but obviously equally upset. The boy of course knew he would seem as much an outsider in Shanghai as in Troy, and perhaps more given that his English was so much better than his Chinese was.

An hour later, as the sun was setting and a bright moon partially obscured by cloud cover enveloped Venice Black Jade, Jason and Wu sat just outside yet another café drinking wine having left Old Zhu and the children back at the hotel. As usual several of the other café patrons watched them closely, their foreign appearance and Cantonese they used to converse arousing attention. Still the evening was cloudy enough that they all felt less conspicuous than usual.

"All I am saying is that it is not enough to learn western technology. China needs more of a republic, like we saw in England and France even now has had one since Napoleon III fell. And even Venice, ran itself as a republic for generations before it became part of Italy."

"So you are not as enamored of a monarchy as you were at home first of the Confucian sort and then that the Taipings created?" Jason teased.

"At home they talk all about benevolent leadership, about how only the educated sages should run society, as a father runs a household with the appropriate levels of respect and obligation."

"And you reject that now?"

"What I reject is the idea that China ever ran in such a way. The Manchus run the country. They control the Chinese and the scholar gentry. The so-called mandarin's learned advice is only lip service. It is a dictatorship like any other. Moreover, what I am tired of is China claiming to be at the center of civilization. Just look here: Venice is as sophisticated as China has ever been, and that is as true of France and England as well."

"So, my old friend, why are you really here, traveling home to a country that seems to have become such a disappointment for you?" Jason said, looking closely at Wu, whose eyes were as agitated as Jason had seen them when, as a much younger man, Wu had taken up his role with the Taipings.

"I love China. Like Mei-ling says, we are always going to be strangers here in the West. What I want is a China that embraces more of what the West has to offer, a more open government, maybe even run by Chinese, not the foreign Manchus."

"What you are saying," Black Jade suddenly interrupted, "frightens me."

"Why?" Wu asked, surprised.

"Because what we have already planned, for more than a decade, is revolutionary enough: a school for young women in China, perhaps even a school with a mixed student body of Chinese and Western young women. That in itself will arouse considerable resistance…and you talk of revolution even as you want us to employ you as a teacher." Her voice was hard, the seriousness of her tone very obvious.

Once she finished, the conversation went suddenly so quiet that those at the nearby table looked up, clearly wondering what the three strangers were discussing so seriously in their curious language.

Then Wu stood up abruptly, "Maybe we should talk more later." Wu said as he dropped a few coins on the table. "I will see at the hotel. I need to take a walk." With that, he walked off and quickly turned a corner heading down one of the innumerable and very narrow canal pathways.

"What are you thinking?" Jason asked her.

"Just what I said…he wants a democracy…if he had been with us in America he'd be less sure."

"True, but—"

"But more importantly, would his behavior jeopardize all our plans, and what if people in Shanghai learn of his role with the Taipings?"

"Well, my wife, there is plenty of time for decisions later. We won't be home for months and the school will not be ready to open for months after that. Come let's just enjoy our evening. How often have we ever been alone since we left America?"

With that, Black Jade took up her glass of wine, obviously deep in thought even as she took Jason's hand and squeezed it.

A few minutes later, as they started back from the Rialto Bridge where they had been enjoying their wine, more clouds began to darken the sky, blocking even more of the otherwise-bright light of the moon. Still even in so many more shadows, the city remained beautiful, Jason thought to himself, at least until the loud voice behind dragged him from his reflections.

"Your money...*dinero*..." The fellow with the knife stared at them as his companion smiled with a mouthful of bad teeth to his side. As he moved forward, one hand holding the knife and his other hand outstretched, Black Jade's cane shot forward, hitting the knife hand but not deflecting it, as she herself fell to the ground. Jason, momentarily in shock, dropped to his knees to help his wife.

"Give me the money," the second fellow said suddenly in relatively good English. "My friend's knife is sharper than it looks."

Jason, his hand on Black Jade, sprawled on the ground looking angrier than hurt struggled with his purse or at least tried to until the flash of a long pole suddenly appeared not only striking the man with the knife but his friend who dropped to the cobblestones, looking as if he were about to lose consciousness. A second later, Wu stepped into Jason's vision, casually bent down, pocketed the knife and then swinging what was apparently a gondola paddle stepped between his friends and the two men neither of whom looked particularly menacing any more.

"Take your friend and run," Wu said forcefully in English and then French...and seconds later throwing in a bit of Italian. Jason found himself stupidly wondering when he had learned that while he helped Black Jade to her feet.

The one, more conscious robber stared back at Wu for a second, taking perhaps the measure of the very confident Chinese standing in front of him almost magically slashing the air with the long paddle and then grabbed his half-conscious friend and ran away.

"Where did you learn to do that?" Jason asked astonished. Until that very moment, Wu in his eyes had always been the scholar, of Confucianism, of the Taiping teachings and more recently of Western studies.

"And what exactly did you think my duties were among the Taipings after they made me an officer?" Wu laughed, picking up his guidebooks he had apparently dropped as he approached.

"We should go back to the hotel right now. Black Jade, are you hurt?" Saying nothing, she stood up and took the cane Jason handed her.

"But first we need to return this paddle. The gondola I found it in is right over there." Wu said, gesturing back toward the Rialto Bridge.

For the next few minutes, they walked down the small alley that ran from San Marcos square and included their hotel.

"Chinese for any foreign young ladies we manage to recruit, and for the Chinese girls, reading and writing," Black Jade said quietly. "And no history, not of China, not of the West. Agreed?"

"Agreed," Wu said quickly as the three walked the rest of the way in silence.

# CHAPTER 94

# THE HOLY CITY

As they approached Jerusalem, his family seated as they were in the crowded carriage that had boxed them and their possessions in all morning, more steamer trunks than people, Jason felt he could not take for another moment the heat of the journey that had begun hours earlier from their hotel in Jaffa. Indeed, rather than being excited about their imminent arrival in the Holy City, Jason found himself wishing he were dead. He was completely miserable, it was still early September, far earlier than he'd hoped to arrive in the Middle East and the heat was unbearable, almost as bad as the constant shaking from the extremely rough road they were traveling over. And to make matters worse, Wu was reading aloud with considerable energy, his assumption of course that the rest of their party retained an ability to concentrate on the historical tidbits he was culling from the several guidebooks he'd been pouring over since the moment they had set off from Venice on the ship.

Indeed, Jason noticed almost jealously that both children and Old Zhu had fallen into a deep sleep, completely ignoring Wu's narrative. In fact, as he turned around to look at his wife, only Black Jade was totally awake, not though listening to Wu but staring straight ahead her eyes revealing an extraordinary level of concentration and expectation. Watching her, though she clearly did not notice his gaze, it was obvious that years of intense interest, beginning perhaps with her conversations with those long dead nuns in Tianjin and even her mentor Emma Willard had made their upcoming arrival in Jerusalem intensely personal for her.

Even Jason, half-listening to Wu while studying the rocky landscape, felt an emotion he had not expected to experience. He was, after all, he reminded himself, still the son of a missionary who had spoken of Jerusalem, the Holy Land, far more often than Hong Kong or even Boston during Jason's youth. Nevertheless, even that anticipation was not as it might have been; after all, what had he experienced so far? Barren rocky landscape baking under an intense heat unlike anything he remembered having ever previously experienced, hardly complemented the limited spiritualism he usually experienced.

But despite the discomfort and landscape, Jason reminded himself one could hardly discount the drama and spectacle of the moment. Indeed, all around the carriage were travelers of every sort imaginable. It was the greatest range of humanity Jason had ever seen, incredibly wealthy Europeans and Americans traveling in far fancier carriages then Jason's party had managed to hire, moving along among crowds of horsemen, Christians pilgrims, Catholic priests, long bearded Eastern Orthodox priests, impoverished European Jews with dark suits and hats, while among them and along the sides Arabs, Arab travelers and Arab boys begging and hawking goods were everywhere.

"Have you noticed," Will said sitting up and touching his father's shoulder. "They don't stare at us here like they did almost everywhere else?"

"Why would they, look around, almost every sort of humanity is here, our family is no different than any of the others."

"I like that." the boy said before reclining his head on his father's shoulder and drifting off again.

Jason looked over to Wu who'd put down his book. His friend was shading his eyes and then, hesitantly pointing in the distance. As he did so, Jason could feel an almost instant change in his surroundings. The people around him, those walking, those in carriages or riding horses all started to become more energized, even the horses and the few camels that had been part of their caravan seemed excited.

"*Qubbat al Sakhrah!*" he heard someone yell as several men stood up in the carriages around him. There in the distance the Holy City was coming into view, its medieval walls and turrets dominated by what Jason understood to be one of the greatest mosques in Islam its Yellow Dome itself glistening in the sun like nothing he had ever seen. Turning back to look at Black Jade he saw her staring directly ahead, a single tear running slowly down her cheek. A moment later their entire party was awake and gesturing forward, Will, Mei-ling, Old Zhu while Wu was back to his guidebook trying to identify the different buildings that were starting to become more recognizable as they approached.

An hour later they were finally resting on the roof of the Armenian hospice Sam had recommended, looking out over the Holy City. Moreover, their rooftop perch seemed perfect; just high enough to attract something of a breeze which was rolling in from what Wu insisted had to be the Mount of Olives, while low enough to have a good sense of those who walked below within the walls of the old city.

"I think this entire area is considered the Armenian quarter," Wu said, pointing downward. "And over there, below the mosque is the wall they say the Jews prayer at...hard to see but it is some sort of alley my book says - usually full of Jews."

"Father, what is an Armenian? Are they Arabs and Muslims also?" Mei-ling asked as she gazed out over the city."

"Well, actually"—Jason hesitated—"I don't have a clue. But what is the point of having a scholar with you if we don't use him. Wu?"

"I said you would all appreciate my studious nature," Wu said while tapping the pile of books he'd carried from his room below to the roof's dining area. "Armenians are neither Arabs nor Muslims, yet not the sort of Christians we knew in China either, not Catholics nor Protestants. They are from someplace to the east but not as far as China." Wu said, studying a map in one of his beloved guidebooks.

"Mr. Brandt," the fellow said rather loudly, with an American accent as he walked toward Jason's party. For a second Jason wondered how he had been recognized before realizing that a party made up mostly of ethnic Chinese would still stand out somewhat even in the extraordinary diversity of the Holy City.

"My colleague—well, perhaps not that quite—forgot to give you your letters when you arrived. These locals tend to be a bit less efficient than one might hope. So, my name's Smith, Barkley Smith. Been told you are from Boston. Mind if I sit down? Hot as hell out here as usual," he said, taking out a handkerchief and wiping his brow.

"Well, I was born in Boston…and you are obviously an American. Let me introduce my family: my wife, Black Jade, our children, Will and Mei-ling, and our dearest traveling companions, Mrs. Zhu and Mr. Wu."

Old Zhu looked at the fellow with her usual suspicion of all strangers and went back to studying the street traffic with the children. As for Wu he leaned forward and extended his hand, something Jason had rarely seen him do despite his knowledge of how curious Wu was of their years in America, a country Wu had never seen and continued to be very interested in.

"Mr. Smith, so what brings you here to Jerusalem?" Wu asked, putting aside his books and edging his chair a bit closer to the fellow.

"What brings me to the Holy Land? One could say the same thing of you, my good fellow...Lots of folks come here...from Europe, America...all over the Orient, but I can't say I have ever seen a Chinaman in these parts...and one who speaks such fine English...though I detect a bit of a French accent in there?"

"Nicely done, sir. Yes, indeed my English-language tutor was French. You have a good ear, sir, but if I might...my party, as you know, has only just arrived and, more than anything else, has been amazed at how many different sorts of people are here in the Holy City."

As Wu spoke, Jason noticed that Black Jade had turned her attention to the conversation, clearly as interested as he and Wu were to learn more about the Holy City. One could only learn so much from guidebooks.

"Well, can't speak much of the locals. Arabs, Turks, know the Armenians a bit better—folks here in the hospice who were kind enough to hire me to talk to English-speaking guests. But the Westerners, it's mostly the same, God and land. Most of us come here to walk the streets our Lord walked...to experience what he experienced, in life and His suffering on the cross. Some even cross over...decide they are Jesus themselves or, for the women, his mother, Mary. Met any of that sort yet?"

"I cannot say we have. We, as you know, only arrived a couple of hours ago. We have not even begun to explore the old city or any of the newer quarters," Jason replied, looking to his companions who nodded in agreement.

"So, there are people walking the streets convinced they are Jesus himself?" Black Jade asked with an obvious mix of fascination and revulsion.

"Absolutely, crazy as crazy can be. But you folks are Chinese, heard somewhere a while back there was some fellow in far-away China who thought he was Jesus's little brother...heard of him?"

"Yes," Wu said, adding nothing more.

"Right you are. Folks can be crazy. You will see plenty once you get out into the streets...and of course the occasional John the Baptist..."

"And most Westerners, the Europeans and Americans, are like you, sane but anxious to learn more of Jesus's life?" Black Jade asked.

"Certainly the Americans. Most of them are here for the simple reason that our Lord lived, died, and was resurrected here. The Europeans, more a mixed group, plenty of them religious enough, but there are always their rivalries. The English, the French, the Russians all want a piece of the Holy Land, want to take it from the Ottomans but pretend they're only interested in protecting Christian shrines and the like."

For the next few minutes, the conversation, mostly directed by Wu to Smith, focused on the various European rivalries that swirled around the Holy City until after a point when the conversation calmed, Black Jade asked quietly, "What of the Jews? I am told a British statesman once said one cannot know one's Christianity without knowing the Judaism of the Jews."

"Sound's, ma'am, like something that British Jew Lord, Moses Monte...something would say."

"I think it was the British statesman Disraeli," she replied.

"Same thing, couple of ambitious Hebrews...though that Disraeli, fellow I have heard tell, tries to pretend he is some sort of Christian."

"I take it you are not a fan of the Hebrew race?" Jason asked.

"Not many around here really are. Sure some of the Arabs are close to the local Jews...least as far as I can tell, both have been here forever…but the newcomers, the ones from Russia… sure you have seen them…walking around in their dark suits and black hats…mostly in tatters, hoping to die in the Holy City and expecting handouts from that rich English Jew lord…"

"Montefiore."

"Right you are, had forgotten the name…"

"But I am confused," Wu said, glancing from his books to Smith. "My reading tells me Christians like having Jews returning to Jerusalem."

"Well, that's the confounding truth, ain't it…long story. But I am afraid that is a chat for another day…got to get downstairs. Was told another group of English speakers are going to arrive shortly." At that, Smith stood up, pulled out his already-wet handkerchief and wiped his forehead. "Wait…forgot why I came up here in the first…Batch of letters been waiting for you for weeks." Then, dropping a pile of envelopes neatly tied together with string, Smith headed back down the stairway that led into the building.

"Letters!" Will shouted loudly, startling Jason, who had no idea his son was even monitoring the conversation.

"Well, let's take a look," he said, starting to take out his knife before Old Zhu carefully took the package from his hands and untied the bundle without cutting the string, which she carefully wound around her own finger before slipping it into one of her pockets.

"Is there anything for me?" Mei-ling asked, the excitement growing among the group, at least among his family. Neither Old Zhu nor Wu seemed to anticipate that the pile would include anything for them.

"Let see…" Jason said with deliberate gravity, which, as expected, was deeply irritating to his children. "We seem to have a letter from Lord Montefiore's aide. Probably those introductions he promised to send and you know that will allow us to learn more about the people here…" But the kids had had enough. Mei-ling, to her mother's delight, made a grab for the entire pile, yanking it from her laughing father's hands.

"Letters, three of them for me…from Troy!" she explained excitedly and then passed over three more to her mother. "Mom, you have letters from both Mrs. Sage and Aouda…two from Aouda."

"And don't I get anything?" Jason said, trying to mimic his youngest son's voice, who took no mind as he ripped open his own letters and began to read.

"Sure, looks like boring stuff," his daughter said, having lost interest in the game as she started to open her letters.

Jason moved slowly through the pile. There was at least one letter from Mr. Sage, an envelope with Giquel's name, and even a letter from Shanghai, from the newspaper that especially gratified him. They had started to write more often, as his return to Shanghai became imminent. That they were still interested in his writings significantly lessened Jason's anxiety about reestablishing his career as a newspaperman. He, after all, unlike Black Jade or Wu, had no interest in working at the soon-to-be-founded Shanghai Female Seminary.

One letter, though, lacked the international markings of the rest and was from a name he did not recognize. He carefully opened it, while the rest of his family read their own letters, and Wu and Black Jade chatted among themselves as they looked down into Jerusalem's streets, apparently discussing some procession that had caught their attention.

Dear Mr. Brandt:
I write as Charles Gordon's former aide to camp and current assistant.
Your letter arrived to considerable enthusiasm from Pasha Gordon. He most certainly does remember you

from his years in China that remain cherished memories. Indeed, he is not staying far from your hotel, himself a guest of a family from America, from Chicago, a city you yourself might know. If you are free, then later in the week, perhaps Friday morning, he would certainly enjoy receiving you, to share memories of China and perhaps assuming you are interested, and if you are here, that is probably a reasonable bet, a tour of his archeological work here in the Holy City.

P.S. I should probably add that the visit cannot be terribly long. Mr. Gordon has aged since you last saw him and no longer has the energy he once possessed. Thank you for keeping this in mind.

When Jason looked up again, Black Jade had a look of contentment.

"What is it?" he asked. "Good news from Olivia and Aouda?"

"Oh, I don't know yet…have not even opened their letters yet. I was reading the invitation I had hoped for, from the Sisters of Charity. As I had heard in Paris, Sister Rose, from Tianjin, is here. She was very kind to me when we were there. She invited me to visit her at their convent here in the Holy City."

"I thought," Jason asked quietly, "everyone you knew at the Tianjin orphanage was killed."

"No, not sister Rose; she was not there that day. But I have not seen her since. She left Tianjin before I even recovered. I only found out she was alive when I visited the Sisters of Charity in Paris."

"You visited them? I didn't know that."

"It was when you were on one of those long trips with Prosper and Wu. And what of your letters? Good news?"

"Yes, indeed. It is from someone who works with Gordon, inviting me to visit in a few days."

"Chinese Gordon, you are invited to meet with Gordon," Wu said, his interest aroused by mention of the English officer who'd become famous in the fight against the Taipings.

"Yes. Are you interested, both of you?"

"I have no interest," Black Jade said quietly, probably thinking of her former husband who'd died fighting against forces of the sort Gordon had led.

"Wu?"

"To meet the famous Chinese Gordon...even the thought arouses a wide range of memories..."

"Well, there is no reason to decide now. We can decide later. Come on, everyone, the afternoon's heat is lessening; now before it gets dark would be a wonderful time to start exploring the old city."

With that Jason, stood up and opened his wallet to pay their bill as the rest of his party gathered their belongings to begin what would become several days of explorations.

Over the following days, despite the very crowded streets, full of people from what seemed practically everywhere, their little group still stood out somewhat even as their faces were obscured by the bonnets and umbrellas the women adorned themselves with and the rather dashing felt hat Wu had donned to protect him from the burning sun. In so many ways, they were much like the rest of the tourists and peddlers who filled the narrow lanes of the old city, and the two Armenian guide/guards were not uncommon either; indeed many of the Western groups had hired such fellows.

Still, in the intimacy of the old city, it was hard even for the most God intoxicated—and there were certainly many—not to notice the presence of four Chinese among them. In fact, at almost every religious site, they were questioned by eager pilgrims, in every language imaginable about whether they were Christians themselves or if the great Chinese empire had embraced the teachings of Jesus. Wu, Mei-ling, and Old Zhu largely remained silent, as Black Jade had taken up the task of explaining in English or French, depending on what seemed appropriate, that they were mere travelers simply as she put it "seekers after the truth," which seemed to satisfy most of those who stopped them.

As for Jason, the lone Caucasian, he was almost completely ignored while little Will's Eurasian features, not all that different from many of those around them, seemed to attract almost as little curiosity as his father.

Though they had all found the devotion of the Jews to their prayer wall interesting, what especially fascinated everyone in Jason's party, even Old Zhu whose cynical, seen-it-all eyes rarely revealed such an emotion, were those groups of pilgrims reenacting the last steps of Christ before the crucifixion.

"Are they really whipping him, Father? And that cross, it looks so heavy," Will asked one day as they huddled against the cold stone walls of the old city to allow yet another such group to pass.

"It's not about pain or discomfort," Black Jade whispered. "It is about love and devotion."

"If you say so," her son whispered back. "Not much like the Christianity I learned about during services at the Albany Academy."

"This is not Albany," Mei-ling whispered, clearly convinced her little brother was an idiot.

"So, my old friend, you have been especially quiet lately," Jason asked, turning to Wu. "All those books you insisted on bringing with us are not offering any extra insights you want to share?"

"Father is right, Uncle Wu…You stopped offering us a steady diet of historical insights when we started walking the streets of the old city."

"I suppose you are right. It is not though that I did not study. That gate over there is David's Gate, where some say King David is buried…but since we arrived, I have found the limitations of books in a way I had not experienced before. Here one learns more from looking into the eyes of the devout who fill the streets here. There is so much to learn that the master does not speak of."

"It is fine, my old friend," Black Jade said, taking his hands. "We have all been impacted by the mysteries of Jerusalem."

"And the filth," Will piped in.

"Yes, that too," Black Jade said, stroking her youngest's hair.

"But speaking of King David…what time is it?" Jason said as he dug for his pocket watch. "It should be close to the time we are to meet with Montefiore's man. We need to get going; their offices are outside the walls to the west."

"I trust your visit to the Holy City has thus far gone well?" the fellow who had introduced himself as Elijah Solomon asked as they were served tea an hour later. Jason's small group was now reduced to himself and Black Jade, as Old Zhu, Wu, and the children had retreated to the Armenian hospice's rooftop garden to enjoy the early-afternoon breezes and the extraordinary parade of humanity that passed just below. Indeed, enjoying the lodging's rooftop setting had become something of a ritual each evening for their entire group, a ritual Jason expected to enjoy until their scheduled departure for Jaffa and then Suez a few days hence.

"Very much so. I have long wanted to see the Holy City since I made friends with the Sisters of Charity more than a decade ago in Tianjin."

Jason was quite surprised to hear his wife refer so casually to her friends from the Tianjin's orphanage who had met such a tragic fate, but the fellow obviously knew nothing of the incident that had happened so many years before in faraway China.

"I should, of course, first of all offer my condolences, Mr. Brandt. You are an American, I understand."

"Yes, at least I was born there and have lived there for the last decade...but condolences?" Jason looked at Black Jade, who clearly had no idea what Solomon was referring to.

"You have not heard? News, of course, travels faster these days, but you have been traveling. We just heard that your president, Mr. Garfield, has died of his wounds."

"Garfield's dead...We had heard he'd been shot when we were in Paris but nothing after that. Indeed, I had thought he'd begun to recover, especially as we'd heard nothing since."

"Had you ever met the man? I am told relations are very informal in your country unlike in Britain my own country."

"Well, it is a big country, but perhaps I have seen him in person; I was at the convention that nominated him in Chicago, though he was not of much importance until the very last days."

"Yes, we read about that battle even here in Jerusalem, between the former president, General Grant, and some senator, fighting over the Republican Party nomination.

"Yes, Blaine, but neither man won in the end...and Garfield, who prevailed at the last minute in Chicago and in last November's election, was of course shot...and now is dead?"

"So we have heard. And you, Mrs. Brandt, are you a follower of American or perhaps Chinese public affairs?"

"Women in China, or even America, are assumed not to be knowledgeable about such things...not about politics, nor almost anything else beyond the home."

"That would be true here as well, among almost all of the people of the Holy City, though with Jews sometimes the situation can be somewhat different."

"Why would the Jews be any different?" Black Jade asked, leaning forward somewhat.

"Among my brethren, among Hebrews, there is nothing considered more important than study. Indeed, I have heard it is somewhat like that among people in China as well. In any case, many of my people, really the men, spend their lives in study, leaving it to their womenfolk to know more of the world if only to put food on the table for their families. But I have a more immediate question."

"Ask away," Jason offered.

"You have, I am told, only recently met with Lord Montefiore himself at Ramsgate?"

"Fairly recently. It was in the late spring before we left England for the continent, but, yes, not that long ago."

"How did he, if I might ask...seem, his health, his bearing? I only ask because we in his service here in Jerusalem, who attend his flock of local Hebrews, have not seen him since his last trip quite a number of years ago."

"Well, for a man almost a century old," Black Jade began, "he is in remarkably good health. We spoke for a fairly long time. He was full of energy, at least mentally asking about America, China, telling us of his work here in the Holy Land."

"That certainly sounds like Moses, like His Lordship."

"But there is much we still don't understand about the Jews here."

"You would not be the first to come away with more confusion than understanding. But what is specifically on your mind, ma'am?"

As she leaned forward, she took a sip of tea and put down the toast she had been taking small bites of since sitting down.

"Since we arrived, we have heard many people talk of the Jews, speaking of them in both the most disparaging tones and yet the same people seem deeply pleased they are here. Some even anxious that more Jews come here to settle. How can both be true?"

"Ah, the great question, that so many ask themselves. In truth, it is less about the Jews than about Jesus, who was, I assume you understand, Himself a Jew."

"Yes, even in China we heard that, though what it meant was never clear till I arrived in America."

"Well, like it or not, Christians have come, as they have often resisted, to recognize that their Lord, that Jesus, was Himself a Jew…and their hope is that His second coming, so much a part of the teachings of Christianity, will be facilitated by the return of the Jews to Jerusalem."

"But forgive me," Jason interrupted. "My father was a missionary in China; indeed I grew up hearing of the stories of Jesus's life, and as my father spoke, he seemed to blame the Jews for Christ's death."

"And many still do, but the New Testament story of Judas's betrayal is only part of their teachings, which include a yearning, stronger in some Christian sects than others, for Christ's return and the return of His people to Zion is said to be a prerequisite for that great moment, at least as so many of our Christian brethren believe."

"But are you, through your work with Lord Montefiore, also working to accomplish that goal?" Black Jade asked.

"Well, let me put it somewhat differently. Lord Montefiore's goals here are to put in part his great wealth in service to his people, and especially here in the Holy City. And in that effort, especially in helping recent arrivals from nations of particularly great anti-Semitism, that is hatred of Jews, he is carrying out an effort that is much esteemed by Christians, but that is not his goal. His goal is a Jewish one to help his own people, to fight hatred against those who experience such hatred as we hear so often against blacks and Chinese in America as well."

"There is so much hatred in the world, and in almost every country, there is someone to hate. In England, there seemed to be as much disdain of the Irish as we saw from time to time in America."

"Precisely, and Lord Montefiore has devoted his life to fighting such sentiment. Indeed, that is why he asked me to offer what assistance I could to help you understand our little community here in the Holy Land."

"But why would that matter? His Lordship was certainly very kind to us at Ramsgate, but why does he care?" she asked.

"Because he knows of your plans to establish a school in China, and in that great land, he hopes you will offer your students an understanding of Jews and Christianity less filled with the common sort of hatred."

"But we are not planning a mission school," Jason commented.

"His Lordship understands that as well. But you're planning what could become a very influential school for young women, who can become the future mothers of a very influential new China."

"Well, I guess we should say we are flattered. And what else did Your Lordship ask of you about us?" Black Jade asked after a moment of reflection.

"Only that I offer you as good an insight as I can of our community here that I answer all your questions, even make you welcome among our community and to help you understand us better."

"That is indeed very kind…and I really do have many questions," Black Jade said as she opened her satchel and took out her ubiquitous notepad while Jason watched wondering who was the real scholar among them, Wu or his wife.

For the next hour, until just before sunset, Jason listened quietly as Black Jade asked Solomon one question after the other and arrangements were made to tour the small Hebrew colony with their larger party the next morning.

⊶⊷

"Good morning, gentlemen. Do come in. I trust you had no problem finding my modest abode. Mr. Brandt, Jason, it is indeed a delight to see you again. And your Chinese colleague."

"Wu Sek-chong," Wu offered, stepping forward and offering his hand in the English fashion. "How does one address you, sir? I have heard you called Pasha, Major General, and even Chinese Gordon."

"The world has too many titles, sir. Simply Mr. Gordon will due. But do sit down; we should take a few minutes to chat before we head out."

"Head out?" Jason asked.

"Indeed, there is much to show you and so much misinformation. I assume you have done the usual tours...with the locals, I am told those offered by the Armenian guides already."

"Yes, and yesterday among the local Jews...among the community nurtured by Lord Montefiore."

"Yes, Montefiore, fine fellow, never met him...said to be exceptional among his race...but yes...there is much to correct; the missionaries have almost nothing right. I would believe the Arabs before them, especially the Catholics who have had such an unfortunate influence on our understanding. But we can discuss that more during our walk. First, a bit of tea?"

His guests nodded while Jason studied Gordon closely, trying to understand how much the fellow had changed in the years since he'd seen him last. Never terribly military in his bearing, Gordon now seemed especially modest, both in his dress and how he presented himself.

"I am told we were both recently in China," Jason offered, hoping to get the conversation going.

"Yes, indeed, nasty business with the Russians in Central Asia, the court asked for my support…a quick visit but one that allowed me to see something of the changes since I had last been there. And you, sir, Mr. Wu…I have been told you are something of a scholar, like so many of those I have met in China?"

"I have certainly studied a great many of the works of the Sage. But in recent years, my major effort has been to understand the Western world, its technology, its languages and history."

"Fascinating stuff…would enjoy talking more…something of a modest scholar myself…mostly about Jerusalem."

"And you, Jason, Mr. Brandt, did I not hear somewhere that you had accompanied Grant to China?"

"Yes, he made an around-the-world tour after he left the White House, and I helped as an informal guide during his stay in China."

"That must have been a deep honor. My own efforts to suppress the slave trade in the Sudan and our mutual background as soldiers has always made me wish to meet him."

"I think you would have found him both formidable and deeply modest. You might have heard he and Governor Li Hongzhang became good friends while he was there."

"Indeed interesting. And he must have learned a great deal at your side. People, as Mr. Wu notes sometimes, call me Chinese Gordon, but we both know my knowledge of China and Chinese is nothing like your own."

"That is kind of you to say, but you are certainly being too modest, Mr. Gordon. And many in China remain in your debt due to your role in suppressing the rebellion," Jason said, suddenly wishing he'd not mentioned anything about the Taipings, as he noticed Wu move uncomfortably in his seat.

"But that was a long time ago. Come I see you have both finished most of your tea, and there is little time to waste. Let us take a walk...I want to show you around the sites of Jerusalem informed by a bit more science than Rome would have us use."

For the next two hours, Gordon offered a walking monologue about the religious sites of the city, their role in the last days of Jesus's life and the multitude of errors the later Romans, especially Constantine's mother Helen, had introduced into the story of Christ's presence in Palestine.

As the morning cool evolved into a more familiar and warmer Jerusalem at late morning, Gordon himself began to fade and guided his small party to a local establishment he insisted offered the best Turkish coffee available.

"But if I might ask," Wu, who had been especially quiet during the walk that had seen Gordon doing most of the talking, began to speak after the waiter, an Arab dressed in a ragged *thawb* poured the blackest coffee Jason and Wu had ever seen into three small cups.

"Ask away, my Chinese colleague."

"You seem to question almost everything we have learned about the Holy City since we arrived...even where the crucifixion itself happened. Are you yourself some sort of religious skeptic?"

"Not at all, my friend. The older and wiser I get, the more I appreciate the teachings of our Lord. The more I yearn to understand better His role in my life and His own earthly life before the Father sacrificed Him for all of us. But you are right. I have considerable skepticism about what we are shown here. Modern science, modern Protestant teachings, and my own army training, especially about the physical terrain, has helped me understand that a great many mistakes have been made by those who attempt to reveal Jesus's world in what we see today."

"So you do see yourself as devout? A committed follower of Jesus and God the Father?"

"Of course," Gordon said, looking somewhat between curious and irritated, while Jason began to wonder with some concern where Wu was planning to take the conversation.

"And in China...you favor those who wish to bring the Chinese, as with the Jews here, to Christ?"

"Well, of course," Gordon responded, flicking his fly stick at a block of insects that had alighted near his coffee.

"Then, sir, with all due respect, why did you offer your services to the Chinese emperor to help destroy the only community in China that was trying to understand and embrace Christianity?" Wu asked, without a hint of the respect he referred to.

Jason himself was shocked. Wu was normally as polite as a person could possibly be. Had he planned this verbal assault from their first arrival? Jason wondered.

"You mean the so-called long hairs? Those who followed the Taiping King at Nanjing?" Gordon asked somewhat defensively.

"That is exactly what I mean. You helped destroy the only genuinely large Chinese Christian movement my country might have ever conceived, and you did that in the service of the Chinese emperor who you would admit yourself knew nothing of Jesus or His teaching."

"But, my good man, the so-called Taipings were no more Christians than the American Mormon heretics, not true Christians."

"But, sir, are you not a Protestant, simply heir to another somewhat older heretical group condemned by the Church of Rome, whose teaching you have spent much of the morning disparaging?"

For a long moment, the man ever so often known as Chinese Gordon stared hard at Wu, without a flicker of emotion.

"Sir, you reveal yourself...and I thought that you were all dead. Well, Mr. Brandt, it was a pleasure to see you again. If in a somewhat-unexpected fashion. May the rest of your journey be safe." With that, Gordon stood up, nodded ever so subtly to Wu, and walked off.

"How long were you planning that?" Jason asked his friend with a tone of astonishment.

"Since you first got that letter inviting us to meet with him. And I must say it felt wonderful. He played a direct role in killing many of my friends...and besides, what does it matter? We leave for Jaffa and Suez tomorrow."

# CHAPTER 95

# SHANGHAI

"I cannot believe it…look there…almost everyone looks like me," Mei-ling said excitedly.

"Hardly, my beautiful daughter…they are just Chinese like you," Black Jade said, putting her arm around Mei-ling as they approached the main docking area on Shanghai's Bund. "Don't you remember anything of Shanghai? You were not that young when we left."

"What, maybe seven?" Jason's youngest daughter said.

Jason himself leaned over the railing. He had, of course, been here much more recently and yet everything seemed different, with so many new buildings along the waterfront in the few years since he'd left with the former president and his entourage.

"Well, I certainly don't remember anything," Will said. "Father, can I go back to the Albany Academy next term if I hate it?"

"You'd be a lot less nervous if you had practiced your Chinese more on the ship. We had weeks and weeks since we left Jaffa that you wasted," Mei-ling said with her usual irritation with her little brother.

"I am just saying, nothing has changed...You, Mom, Uncle Wu, and Old Zhu, even Father fits in, in Shanghai. You can see that from here, but not me. I am as much a freak here as in Troy!"

"So why are you so interested in going back then?" his sister asked.

"Because I have friends there...understand everyone a lot better than I will here...I am sure of it."

"William, you will get used to it. You already know far more Chinese than the vast majority of the whites out there," Wu said. "And we can all help you find your way here."

Jason looked closely at Black Jade, who was clearly distressed even as she looked longingly at Shanghai. She had, after all, been the person who had insisted the family relocate, and now her son wanted to leave before they'd even set foot on Shanghai's wharf.

"Be only a few minutes, folks. You will be wanting to gather your goods and prepare to debark," one of the stewards they'd become friendly with over the weeks traveling from Suez told them.

"Thank you, Marcus. We will be getting started momentarily," Jason said, looking uncertainly at his wife.

"Will, if by next summer you really want to return to the Albany Academy for the fall term, we can explore that. Nevertheless, for now, promise me you will give Shanghai a try. Is it a deal?" she asked the boy.

"OK, it's a deal. I don't want to have to run away from home like Father did."

With that, the boy turned around and started for the family's onboard cabin to gather the last of his goods, while Black Jade stared with less-than-complete satisfaction at her husband. "I always knew we should not have told him that story."

"Well, it is a good story, at least I think so. And none of us would be here if Dad had not run off, so I am not complaining." Mei-ling added, "Father, can we really move into our house today? I do remember something of it."

"That is what I was told, that the papers have already been signed and the family we bought it back from already relocated. Did not even cost that much extra to buy it back, but look, they have put out the gangplank. It is time to go. Welcome home, everyone!" And for a moment, Jason realized that with Will already back at their cabin, everyone around him really was glad to be home.

Twenty minutes later the entire group crowded into the carriage they hired to transport them through Shanghai's crowded streets, as the children marveled at the extraordinary mix of Western and Chinese elements arrayed before them. But what really struck Jason was the smile on Old Zhu's face. The woman never smiled and yet there she was with one of the biggest smiles he'd ever seen. She was, after all, Jason realized, the only one among them who really was from Shanghai.

"When we left, I never thought I would return here. I was certain that I would die in Gold Mountain," she said, noticing Jason's gaze.

"And yet here you are."

"If only my son had lived...if only he were here to greet me," she said, taking on her usual look of skeptical cynicism as she glanced around.

"But we are your family now," Black Jade said, taking the hand of her servant who'd long before become a close friend as well.

Twenty minutes later, Jason abruptly shouted for the coachman to stop.

"What is it, husband? The house is still several minutes away."

"Something I want to show you...but first let us alight for a second." A moment later their entire company was standing in front of a piece of open property that stood alongside a Protestant church, a site that included a lovely view of Shanghai's Bund behind them and even something of the river beyond that.

"This is the spot I told you about. The church folks said they were willing to rent space during the week and when we are ready...sell us this parcel of land for the school. If you like it, this could be the future home of the Shanghai Female Seminary."

At that, Black Jade took on her most serious face and walked the parcel as the entire family watched her closely. After a time, she turned back toward her group while they watched and from the seat of the carriage, the coachman looked on curiously.

"We should not even seriously consider making an offer until we are certain that it is an auspicious day," she finally said.

"And had the area's *fēng shui* studied," Wu added as Black Jade nodded.

"I thought you had dropped those sort of superstitions?" Jason asked, turning in surprise to Wu.

"That was in the West. This is China," Wu offered, laughing.

"Do you have it?" Black Jade asked, turning toward Old Zhu.

"Have what?" Jason asked, confused as he watched Old Zhu dig into her satchel.

"Yes, I moved it just this morning from the trunk," the older woman said, holding up a small red brick.

"What is that?" Will asked, as curious as his father.

"That, my son," Black Jade said, smiling down at the boy, "is a brick from the Troy Female Seminary. Mei-ling and I found it one day lying on the ground. It will be part of our new building, part of the Shanghai Female Seminary, when we have it built. But for now, everyone back to the carriage. The house is only a short distance up the road."

—✦✦—

The next few weeks were a whirlwind of activity as Jason worked to establish a renewed relationship with the newspaper, offering to write up a continuing series on the growing movement in America to end Chinese immigration. Meanwhile Black Jade planned a series of open houses at their home, energetically envisioning a far greater effort than she ever had before to become better known among both merchant communities, both Chinese and Western that were likely, as she explained, to become the future school's community base.

"But why is it so important that we build all these relationships up? We already know scores of people here, and even more know my name from my writings."

"That you are known," Black Jade explained as she helped Old Zhu bring dishes to the table, "is the only reason this is even possible. Shanghai is full of Chinese merchant families who because of their relations with the local Westerners might...and I mean might be open to educating their daughters. We will only be sure when we start advertising the school's opening."

"When do you want to start that effort? Certainly those who know us already know the plan, but we need to get the word out to far more people."

"Could you write about plans for the school in the newspaper?" Wu offered. "The Westerners all read it and I am certain many of the Chinese merchants try to follow it as well, if only for business reasons, and there are enough local Chinese who can read English to help them."

"I had not thought of that. It might be awkward for me to do it, but I could certainly try to get one of the other reporters to cover the story. When"—he turned to Black Jade—"would you want me to ask about that?"

"Not yet," she said with certainty.

"Why not, this is already October. If you want to start for the spring term, we need to get started, and we can't accomplish much without students."

"Because I am convinced that there will be resistance; educating girls is a new idea. Everyone in Troy constantly reminded me how hard it was for Mrs. Willard to get started, and we are trying here in China where families care more about the size of a girl's feet than what is in her head."

"Then how do we get started?"

"I think we should start with only a few girls, and girls from families as respected as we can possibly find."

"But what about me? I am tired of having my sister as my tutor," Will said with real emotion.

"Why is it a problem? Mei-ling tells me you are doing wonderfully with your lessons, and besides she is not your only teacher. Wu is teaching you to read Chinese."

"OK, but that is not the point. I miss my friends at the Albany Academy, and I have had no chance to make friends here since we returned."

"I suppose I'd assumed you would be a student at our new school when it opened," Jason said, embarrassed that he had not realized how unhappy his youngest remained.

"At a girls' school. You want me to be the only boy at your girls' school!"

"Well, you could continue to study here at home with the family," Black Jade offered, clearly uncomfortable.

"Why can't he just go to one of those schools the Westerners have for their children? I am almost certain I heard someone mention there is one in the French quarter."

"I suppose we could investigate it. In fact, I think one of the editors has a child there. It was mentioned when I was at the newspaper offices a few days ago."

"OK, but don't expect much," the boy said, sounding bitter.

"I thought you just said you wanted to attend a real school," Mei-ling asked, surprised.

"You still do not understand. This place is no different from America. None of you have ever understood. I am a half-breed in both places, but at least in Albany I am fluent in English and have friends."

"I really don't think you will have a problem," Jason said.

"Really? Are you *sure* they have students there who are like me—neither Western nor Chinese? That they would even be willing to admit someone like me?"

"We won't know till we try," Wu offered, while the boy's family remained silent, feeling something akin to guilt about his situation. "But even if it is not possible, this is, as you say, China, and studying with a private tutor is nothing unusual. Would you like to work more with me? Your sister would probably like more time to herself, and it allows me to earn more of my keep living here with your parents."

"Well, that might be somewhat better," Will answered, looking at his parents.

"And we will investigate the school your father mentioned as well."

"I will ask about it the next time I am in the office. Maybe we can even tour the place soon."

"OK. Thank you, I'd still rather go back to Albany. I am almost fourteen years old, and you promised I could if I wanted to."

"I said we would discuss it, but only after you gave a real effort to fitting in here in Shanghai," Black Jade said, pushing herself back from the chair and getting up. A moment later, she left the room, with Jason watching her closely. She did not show it, but he knew Black Jade was very upset.

⟞⟝ ⟝⟞

Over the following weeks, Jason's effort to document the growing effort in the United States to block any further Chinese immigration went quite well. The many friends and fellow journalists he'd cultivated in America, none of whom saw his articles, for a Shanghai-based newspaper real competition were quite willing to supply him with a steady stream of information about how the newly established president, Chester Arthur, was approaching the question. And, of course, the situation had not changed much. Those whose political livelihood was dependent on the votes of those who did not want to compete with Chinese labor, usually on the West Coast, were opposed by those whose success was often entirely dependent on those same inexpensive workers. Indeed, the story had hardly changed in the years since Jason had first arrived in America, save the aging of those older Northeastern former abolitionists who'd been among the few committed on a moral level to oppose closing the doors, for the first time in American history, to an entire category of immigrants.

But in Shanghai, most of his readers were English rather than American readers, for whom the nuances of goings-on in Washington City were considerably more mysterious, a situation that made Jason's return to full-time work as a local newspaperman significantly easier. Still, he often reminded himself, having the Americans...still a people he did not quite identify with, even after their years there, growing more antagonistic to all things Chinese, did impact positively on his efforts to re-establish his career in Shanghai. After all, many of his readers were from England, businessmen who hoped to take advantage of a backlash against the United States. On the other hand, it was not helping his wife in her long-term efforts to establish a school for young Chinese women. In that context, Jason knew her links to America and her very obviously American husband were proving significantly less helpful than they had earlier on anticipated.

Indeed, almost every evening Black Jade, Wu, and occasionally even Mei-ling returned home exhausted. Wu had taken on the task of accompanying the women on their rounds to the homes of prominent merchant families who received them well enough. Indeed they were often asked questions about commercial conditions in the west, and on occasion Black Jade, but, of course, never Wu was allowed to meet the women of the family, wives, and daughters who were always to be found sequestered away, far away from where the men of the families greeted their guests.

"Are you making any progress at all?" Jason asked one evening after the group had returned, rubbing their hands over the fire to warm them after the increasingly cold fall winds that had descended on Shanghai while Old Zhu prepared each of them cups of warm tea and then took up her usual spot, standing near the door awaiting further instructions.

Black Jade, clearly exhausted, gestured to Wu, who had quickly emerged as her primary assistant in the effort.

"Well, it depends on what you mean by progress. The church's board is still willing to rent us the temporary space and the adjourning land alongside is still available at a reasonable cost...but you already know that."

"But what of students? Are none of the local families even interested in educating their daughters?" Jason asked.

"It is not so much that; they are afraid of being the first. What we need is at least one well-known family to agree and I believe everything else will get easier."

"Is there anything I can do at this point...Should I approach a colleague about that article we spoke of?"

"No, not yet," regaining something of her strength, Black Jade suddenly said, her back still to them as she continued to warm her hands near the fire. "We need that article, when it appears to say we have registered students and give a start date."

"Well, what of trying to recruit some Western students... We always spoke of having the school open to them, especially from families expecting to have daughters marry into the China trade."

"Perhaps, but what of the American exclusionary law... Having the school overly linked to Westerners, especially Americans, at least more than it already is now, could hurt us more than help," she added, looking discouraged.

As the three of them sat there silently listening to the cold Shanghai winds rattling the building's windows, the front door suddenly opened and closed. For a second Jason spotted Old Zhu heading out into the street at a faster clip than she usually managed with her cane, one very similar to that Black Jade carried tapping against the cobblestone streets until within seconds they saw her summoning a rickshaw driver and head off.

"Where is she going?" Wu asked.

"I have no idea. I did not even notice she had left the room before I heard the door open."

"And she took a rickshaw...on her own? Has she ever done that before? Even before we left for America?"

"Almost never…maybe a few times but almost never," his wife said, looking as surprised as Jason and Wu.

Two hours later, their long and faithful friend and servant returned, but when asked about her sudden departure, the older woman merely replied, "To see an old friend."

⋯

"What can you tell me of your plans to educate our young girls from Shanghai?" Yau Xiaoping asked before taking another deep puff from the pipe Jason assumed was filled with opium. It certainly smelled of it. The request for the interview had come as something of a surprise and been quite specific; a request that he and Black Jade visit to discuss enrolling the merchant's several daughters at the proposed school.

"But what is the purpose of educating girls? They only leave the household to become part of some other family's future," he said, after letting Black Jade talk for a few minutes of her hopes to educate young women to understand the world beyond their family's compounds.

"It may not help you personally. You are right daughters leave the home. They open the door to future generations for other households. But is it not also true that you also have sons, sons that are merchants in trade with the Westerners?" she asked.

"Yes, two sons and perhaps another, wife number two, is with child. One the fortunetellers say is also likely to be a boy."

"And would they not be helped if they had wives who understood the world better, perhaps even the Western languages and some arithmetic?"

"Perhaps, but why does that matter?"

"Because if you have raised daughters who know more of the world, daughters who would be helpful wives, perhaps it would be easier to find such wives for your own sons in the future. I am not from Shanghai, but I have lived here long enough to know families often find partners for their children among those whom they have already established previous marriages."

"There is some truth to that, but my own sons are close to marriage age now. None of this will help them."

At that, Jason was almost certain the meeting was over. Indeed he looked at Black Jade, expecting her to rise, preparing to leave, but before any of that happened, Yau spoke again.

"But none of that matters. My daughters, all three of them, will be enrolling in your proposed school. Just tell me when you will be opening and I will make sure they are there at the door the first day."

"Excuse me, but I thought you had no use for educating your daughters. We are, of course, most pleased that your daughters will be attending, but why have you decided to enroll them if I might ask?" she said, very surprised.

"It was already decided before you arrived. My *nainai*, my father's mother, had a visit from your servant, Zhu, who once served her as a servant before my *nainai* left her old compound to stay with me. And once they spoke, there was nothing a lowly grandson can say. But I am sure all will be well, unless, of course, you educate them so much that I won't be able to marry them off at all!"

"We will be very careful to avoid that," Black Jade said with great seriousness. "And thank you for your trust in us."

"Don't thank me; thank your servant. My *nainai* says she was most convincing."

—⟨+ +⟩—

Despite the increasing cold in Shanghai as the winter approached, the excitement among Jason's family grew more each day as they dealt with a huge number of decisions, about the school's organization, slated to begin right after the Western New Year. And there was as well the preliminary plans for the construction of the building next door to the church even as they had already begun preparations for their temporary weekday rental.

Even more exciting was a bank draft from Olivia Sage, who'd prevailed upon her husband and his business associates to make yet another contribution to the school's founding, money that added to the substantial sum they had been building since they'd first envisioned founding such a school. More surprising was a check that arrived in early December from Lord Montefiore, who, along with the contribution, reminded Jason of his request to learn what he could of the Kaifeng Jewish community.

# CHAPTER 96
# A NEW START

"I cannot believe how nervous I am," Wu said as Jason's entire family including Wu and Old Zhu stood one cold January morning, waiting for their students to arrive. At least the fires were all burning nicely within the church, and the chairs rearranged in a classroom setting appropriate for teaching.

"Why are you nervous? We have both taught before, me in America and you as a tutor after the war," Black Jade said to her old friend, even as her eyes stayed on the road waiting for the first rickshaws to arrive with their students, fifteen of whom were expected for the spring term.

"That was for food; this is different. For the first time in my life, I feel, even more than helping Prosper with the dockyard that I am starting something I was born to do, to be part of something bigger than I have ever done, to use my love of learning to help build a new China. Something with elements of what is best here in China and what I saw in the West."

"But remember your promise. Educating young Chinese women is revolutionary enough for now. We both know"— she began to speak even more quietly—"what challenging the

Manchus meant for so many of our friends." Her voice was as stern as it was warm.

Watching the two of them, Jason could not help but remember how much both of them had changed over the decades he had known Black Jade and Wu. He'd become the scholar he was always meant to be but with a twist, as much a scholar of the West as Confucian learning while Black Jade had grown into the extraordinarily confident woman he now realized was starting to help him imagine what the young Emma Willard must have been like. However, there was no more time for such speculation, as Mei-ling suddenly pointed down the street.

"Look, a chain of rickshaws is coming. It is them. The Shanghai Female Seminary"—and then Mei-ling switched to English from the Chinese that she had increasingly been using since their arrival four months earlier—"is open for business."